THE
INSURGENCE
OF THE
CURSED
PRINCE

THE INSURGENCE OF THE CURSED PRINCE

PRINT EDITION ISBN: 978-1-0683-2710-0
E-BOOK EDITION ISBN: 978-1-0683-2711-7
HARDBACK EDITION ISBN: 978-1-0683-2712-4

FIRST EDITION: JULY 2025

FOR THOSE WHO FIGHT FOR
THEIR RIGHTFUL PLACE IN THE
WORLD.

THE INSURGENCE OF THE CURSED PRINCE IS A DARK, OBSESSIVE, AND EMOTIONALLY VOLATILE ROMANTASY SET IN A MODERN WORLD ON THE BRINK OF COLLAPSE. THE STORY FOLLOWS A CURSED PRINCE CAUGHT BETWEEN LEGACY AND RUIN, AS WAR ERUPTS, POWER FRACTURES, AND HIS NEED TO RECLAIM WHAT HE LOST TWISTS INTO SOMETHING FAR MORE DANGEROUS.

THIS BOOK CONTAINS GRAPHIC DEPICTIONS OF VIOLENCE, SUPERNATURAL AND PHYSICAL TORMENT, DEATH, EXECUTIONS, AND SEXUAL CONTENT THAT APPEAR ON THE PAGE. IT DELVES DEEPLY INTO THEMES OF OBSESSION, BETRAYAL, EMOTIONAL REPRESSION, AND MENTAL DETERIORATION, ALONGSIDE COMPLEX POWER IMBALANCES IN BOTH FAMILIAL AND ROMANTIC RELATIONSHIPS. THE PATH FORWARD IS BLOODY AND UNRAVELLED, AS IDENTITY CRUMBLES, EMPIRES FALL, AND A PRINCE TEETERS BETWEEN SALVATION AND MONSTROUS SOVEREIGNTY.

FOR THOSE DRAWN TO DARK ROYALTY, OBSESSIVE LOVE, INTERNAL WARFARE, AND TWISTED BONDS OF FATE, THIS INSTALMENT OFFERS A POWERFUL DESCENT INTO MADNESS, MAGIC, AND RUIN. STEP INTO THE SHADOWS-NOTHING HERE IS SAFE.

THE
INSURGENCE
OF THE
CURSED
PRINCE

CHARLOTTE
BEDGOOD

NAME GUIDE & PRONUNCIATION

THIS STORY IS SET IN A WORLD WHERE THE PRIMARY LANGUAGE SPOKEN IS ZIKAN. WHILE THE NARRATIVE IS WRITTEN IN ENGLISH, MANY NAMES RETAIN THEIR ORIGINAL ZIKAN FORM. BELOW IS A PRONUNCIATION GUIDE AND KEY CHARACTER LIST TO SUPPORT IMMERSION.

✦ THE ROYAL HOUSE OF ZIKA

SERAIAH
(SUH-RYE-UH)
The cursed prince and heir to the throne.

KING CHARLES VRONAE JOHREN ZIKA
(VRO-NAY JOH-REN ZEE-KAH)
Ruler of Zika, feared and unyielding.

QUEEN TARA
(TAH-RAH)
Seraiah's mother, as ruthless as she is composed.

ARRAETTA
(AH-RAY-EH-TAH)
Chosen by the Gods, bound to Seraiah by fate.

✦ THE SANCTUARY OF AMITY

COMMANDER JONAH MARCHEUS
(JO-NAH MAR-CHAY-US)
Fiercely loyal to Seraiah, yet morally torn by duty and blood.

ALEXANDRE 'ALEX' DIXON
(AL-EX-AND-RAY)
A loyal guard with a sharp eye and grounded heart.

PRINCE FREDDIE (FREDERIQUE)
(FREH-DEE / FREH-DAY-REEK)
Bold, loyal, and unwilling to stand on the sidelines.

GENIE (GENEVIEVE)
(GEE-NEE / GHEN-EH-VEEV)
A newcomer to the conflict, quick to find her place amid chaos.

KATERINA 'HELGA' REAYNT
(KAT-ER-EE-NAH RAY-ENT)
Known as Helga. Intimidating and strategic within the palace hierarchy.

HENRI 'EROS' ROMANO
(HEN-REE / AIR-OHS ROH-MARN-O)
A pivotal and tragic figure in the fracture of trust.

GRAND CAPTAIN LYLIAER 'LEOPOLD'
(LI-LEE-AIR)
Senior military office.

XARMEIN CONNELL
(ZAR-MEYIN KON-ELL)
A loyal guard.

✦ POLITICAL FORCES

LORD VIKTOERIN 'THE GENERAL' MARCHEUS
(VIK-TOR-IN MAR-SHAY-US)
Known as The General. A tactical and ambitious noble with dangerous reach.

FRAESIAR KAELTAR
(FRAY-JUH KAYL-TAR)
The General's trusted enforcer, who thrives on making deals to survive.

ARMANEOS 'CORVELLI'
(AR-MAH-NOHS / KOR-VELL-EE)
The Italian enforcer, equivalent if not more dangerous than Kaeltar.

✦ MYSTICS & OTHER FORCES

SHEIKA
(SHEE-KAH)
A shaman, guardian of spiritual balance, feared for her foresight.

ZELA
(ZEE-LAH)
Disciple to Sheika. Curious, devoted, and dangerously devout.

RHEON 'TRAVIS'
(REE-ON)
Seraiah's personal guard. Trusted by Amity. Calm, reliable, and deeply rooted in loyalty.

ZIKAN TERM GLOSSARY

Zikan language terms remain untranslated for cultural integrity. This glossary helps clarify their meaning for the reader.

EMPYREANS - A divine exclamation used to express shock, awe, or disbelief.
FEMALE/FEMALES - Used instead of "woman/women."
MALE/MALES - Used instead of "man/men."
HEARTFAST - A sacred Zikan union, deeper than marriage.
HELLSWORN - A term of dishonour for a child born outside union.
SPIRITSWORN - A short-term lover or romantic partner.
KEEPER - A bonded, long-term partner or life companion.
SCORNS - The Zikan measure of years.
WINTERS - Also refers to years, often poetically.
AONS - Eras or centuries; spans of hundreds of years.
SOLAR RITE - Zikan birthday; the marking of a new solar cycle.
SOL/SOLS - A single day / days.
MOONS - Months. "Quarter moons" = weeks; "half moons" = fortnights.
FANCIE- A derogatory term used to shame women; akin to "harlot" or "whore."
MORTAL-KIND - Any being who is mortal.

Note on Time: Zikan citizens have adopted the seven-day week (Monday–Sunday) for practicality. Traditional celestial systems remain in use within ceremonial or spiritual contexts.

WHEN DARKNESS IS BOUND, IT
DOES NOT SURRENDER – IT
FESTERS LIKE THUNDER BEHIND
THE EYES.

 -UNKNOWN TELLER,
HARMIEAN REALM

ONE

Shredded knuckles cracked against chiselled jawbone, and teeth crunched as Xarmein Connell's head whipped from its force. The blurry crowd sang with excitement as he righted himself, gripped his fist, and oscillated it back to my own body, scarcely missing as I stepped from its hilt. Grip tight, hands up, we danced in a circle, readying our next attack like bulls seeing red.

He aimed a flurry of movements at my aching, bruised forearms as I defended myself from his well-paced onslaught until I ducked and aimed at his softened core, earning a grunt of displeasure that rippled me with cocky satisfaction. I aimed another fist towards his face, this time landing in his quick grip as his other met the underside of my jaw.

Teeth knocked, lip punctured. I grimaced as the force slammed me into the thick foam padding, but it hadn't been enough to knock me out. Pulling to my feet, I spat the remnants of blood from my swollen mouth and braced myself again, soothing in the dull throb my body echoed. Another relentless barrage of Connell's knuckles, and I returned as much as possible, but this male was not going easy on me.

Not that I wished for such treatment.

Ribs cracked, knees buckled, but I remained upright, breathless, as I steadied myself.

He grinned bloodily, "You look like you could do with a lie-down."

I chuckled, wiping the sweat from my face. "You know I shall never surrender."

"As you wish," he replied, the two of us parading around the mat, waiting for the other to make another move – a match of agility vs strength, two males fighting to sever the other's ego. But neither gave in.

I gunned my calloused knuckles at him. He caught the onslaught quickly and protected his face, but it was not enough to stop my left foot from thumping above his groin. He stumbled backwards and countered with an almighty crusade until I found an escape to his right and dipped around him, bringing my right foot up to boot him on his back, forcing him to the ground.

Hoots echoed as Connell clambered to his feet, but he wasn't fast enough to turn as I whipped my fist onto his cheek again. Not adequate for a knockout, but his second home welcomed him again as his calloused hands steadied themselves on the mat.

"Time?" I called loudly, tilting my head towards my amused and masterful commander, noting his arms tucked into each other as he watched from the sidelines.

"Time," Connell replied, seizing my attention as he brandished a gnarly move and tugged and twisted my ankle hard, pulling me down to his level with a thud. I barely had a moment to breathe as he swiftly turned and aimed another strike towards my face, but I barrelled out from beneath him and stumbled quickly to my sore feet.

I breathed jaggedly, attempting to hide the pain searing through my ankle, where I knew he'd somehow twisted it. But, it seemed all eyes were on the towering hulk that was Connell, all six foot five inches of lithe edges, as he offered me a grin that bordered on cruel amusement.

And then he surrendered. Hands held up mockingly. And, just as he did-

Ding. Ding. Ding.

The bell rang. Time was done. Connell must have known that the siren would sound, but he'd chosen to capitulate seconds earlier either way. Still, it was a good fight, and by fluke, I was declared the winner, with both of our egos still intact.

He took the three-stride distance to me before bowing, "Good match, Your Highness."

Connell straightened, and we shook hands to signify the match was complete while the throng that encircled us buzzed with noise.

"Shall I carry you, Sir?" Connell jested, and a low, amused chuckle radiated from my chest as I shook my head.

"Nothing an icepack shall not solve," I replied before parting from him to the edge of the mat where my stoic commander, Jonah, waited.

"Empyreans, you are a fool," he tutted wryly, handing me the towel he had thrown over his shoulder.

"I am almost surprised you did not stop it." I wiped my face as I limped lightly through the parting rabble until the two of us were on the outskirts of it.

The following two fighters, one male and one female, positioned themselves in the centre of the mat, the pair echoing a look of contempt on their faces. Harsh quips flung between them. The bell rang, and the fight started.

"I do not wish to face the wrath of Her Majesty right before your *big* solar rite," Jonah stated, "but I am quite aware that if you do not let out some steam here, you might find your anger aimed at someone far more deserved."

"I think you shall find that such anger is warded," I said, flinging the damp towel around my sweat-soaked neck and letting it dangle

3

over my bare shoulders.

He snorted but did not reply. I supposed his concealed thoughts were warranted; I was not the most at peace male to ever walk the streets of Zika, burdened by a darkness so powerful that it had taken several scorns - *decades*, in human terms - to keep it at bay.

It was *at* bay; it was just there. Lingering. Festering. Ready to wrap itself so tightly around my father's throat until not a word was uttered from his foul, unforgiving tongue.

Nature, nurture, as they say.

A growl rippled from my throat, and I was unsurprised that Jonah turned with eyebrows raised - damn primal traits. I cleared my throat and offered him a sheepish, fake grin.

"There is a rat in our midst," Jonah muttered quietly, the words as heavy as the vaulted roof which cascaded two hundred feet above us as though such information should be given freely before a crowd of ignorant soldiers.

"A rat?"

Around a quarter of the overall army served as part of my guard, those who had sworn to serve me as king when the time arrived and worked under Jonah's command, but it was not surprising if someone was playing amongst our ranks.

"Debatable," he replied, casting his eyes around the room, "I doubt Amity, but the resources being fed could mean anyone is at play. I am investigating, although I cannot say I shall have answers immediately."

"And what exactly do you suspect has crossed the boundary?"

"Eros got caught up in a crossfire in Italy," he said.

Eros was tasked to uncover certain secrets as an active member of my father's corrupt organisation, The Order of Equity, who did more than just suppress me. They infiltrated governments across the world, creating armament deals for wars in the Middle East, sowed discord and manipulated political alliances. All whilst presenting as one of the world's top wine companies.

"Did he get marked?" I asked, understanding it would not be as simple as time in the vault.

"Brutal inquisition," Jonah grimaced, "fortunately, we do not have a truthweaver in our midst. Otherwise, all our secrets might have been spilt."

"Truthweavers are a myth," I answered, knowing the last of them died out eons before I was even born. "Even if Eros were flayed, he would not speak a word about Amity. He is far too loyal."

"I do not suspect Eros," he replied. "I believe that someone knew he was going to be in that office that night, and it could only be one of us."

"Helga is far too busy," I said, understanding that the female spent most of her waking hours at my mother's beck and call as her First Lady, "Then, that only leaves Freddie and your keeper – Neither of whom I suspect."

"I will keep an ear to the ground," he said, looking down at my foot, which had been raised to the toe. "You should see Marie."

The fight before us ended abruptly when the female used fantastic skill to knock her opponent out, cheering in glee with the onlookers as her pride was honoured.

An echo of an argument dusted my ears from across the zoo-resembling garrison, and I roamed my eyes towards the back, across the hundreds of battle-ready soldiers, preparing for an illusory war conjured at the hands of my father and his general. A fight between several soldiers had broken out.

Jonah swore, rushing towards them. I followed, wary of putting too much pressure on my aching foot. Metal clanged from a large gym, and gunfire rattled against steel dummies, causing my sore ears to ring. The mixture of sweat and the sweetness of soured blood cloyed the air – a stench almost as pleasant as it was rancid – wafting in my nose as I passed by soldier after soldier.

Eventually, I caught up with the commander. There were two males at each other's throats whilst two others were doing their best to stop the brutes from causing each other more damage than they already had.

"Hellsworn piece of shit!" the smaller of them flared, "always looking down on me when you bear that dishonourable insignia like a badge of fucking honour. I will gladly rip it off and feed it to the hounds, show you where your fucking place is, traitor."

"Big mouth from such a little seedling," the other barked with laughter, and I noticed the exact insignia he bore belonged to my guard. Insignia, which was banned to prevent division amongst troops. "At least I am not a morally corrupt fuck who supports a tyrant king who does not even know my name."

My father's loyalist grinned, "You think I care if my king knows my name? At least I am not starving on rations, unlike you, who begs for more food tokens. *Oh, please, sir, can I have your scraps?.*"

The loyalist's mocking tone caused several others close by to laugh.

"Empyreans!" Jonah's voice boomed as he stepped through the gathering crowd, all shifting out of the way, "Jorey, Vandan, I told you last time you are both one step away from being tossed in the vault and yet you are fighting again."

"Just putting him in his place, Commander!" my father's loyalist replied, "We all know such insignia are banned; I believe it is two nights in the vault with limited rations, if I am correct."

Jonah looked at the other, and I could see the disappointment etched on his expression before he reached up and ripped the small token of allegiance from the breast of the male's jacket.

"There shall be no more talk," Jonah ordered, glaring at them. "I will not have this army divided by highly unnecessary opinions."

"You should be glad someone is speaking up, Commander," my follower replied. "It is about time there was a change around here."

"Change does not happen by fighting," Jonah stated, before speaking to those in range. "Change comes by working together, not creating further division than is necessary. What will happen when war comes, and you are too busy deciding who has the biggest cock? You are paid to train and be on top form, not to wear banned insignia, or to decide who is and who is not your king. His Majesty is in power. Therefore, he is the ruler whom you shall bow to until change is made by those in a position to make it. Do you understand?"

"Yes, sir," a mutter echoed.

"I said, do you understand?" he shouted.

"Yes, sir!" the call was louder.

"Now, you two," Jonah said, pointing at the soldiers holding the two fighting together, "escort these two to the vaults. They are not to be released for three nights-"

"But, Commander!"

"-And, will be on limited rations," Jonah finished before the two fellow soldiers escorted Jorey and Vandan away.

Jonah sighed deeply before shouting for everyone to get back to work. The remaining soldiers dispersed, shoes clattering across the floor, muttering under their breaths.

Jonah turned toward me, raising his eyebrows as he noticed I was still lingering. He pointed at my foot and said, "Ice, Your Highness."

I grinned at him. "Look at you, all commanding."

"It is my job," he shook his head, "since my father cannot be arsed to come down here and give instruction, it falls on my shoulders as you know."

Ah, yes. The General. The most unnerving, brutish being to exist. If I hated anyone more than my father, it had to be that male who I quite happily would enjoy watching being lowered to the burning depths of hell, where he belonged.

He brought his radio lapel to his mouth, "This is the Commander speaking; Ironwing is ready to depart."

I snorted, "You are intolerable."

"And you are going to cause me more pain than I desire," he answered truthfully. "I want you to go to the infirmary and see Marie and then rest."

The idea of setting foot into Marie's infirmary sounded like a burden I did not wish to bear, especially as I knew she would only reprimand me for looking like I had been through the wars. Not a war, of course, just the heavy fists of Connell pummelling my body until it was weakened.

"What if I sit in a chair in the corner?" I asked.

"Why are you so against going to your home?" he raised his brows. "You have an abundance of things to do at your home. Read a tome, paint a picture, bed a female."

Bed a female was such a foreign term leaving Jonah's mouth, and he cringed from saying it.

"I do not need to fuck. It is the least of my priorities."

"It is never your priority," he answered, nudging me with his shoulder, "waiting on the elusive sol you might meet this so-called Kindred Spirit. Or do you plan on another hundred winters of celibacy?"

"It has not been one hundred winters," I tutted, "it has barely been two. I do not wish to return home because there is little life there whilst both my life givers are still in residence."

"There is little life there either way," he commented, "but only you can make a house a home, Seraiah."

I chuckled humourlessly, "I think the only time that house will become my home is when I meet my fated one. Still, I am sure I will struggle with such discoveries as love."

"Love is not a concept," he chided. "It is a feeling, and one I am sure you will feel if you allow yourself to."

"You are fortunate to have a keeper," I sighed, feeling the weight of his words as my thoughts edged the gentle feeling of *love* I had so long since buried deep, with the rest of those foul emotions I needed not care about.

I would consider puncturing a hole in my chest with a chisel to chip away at the hardened stone wrapped around my delicate heart. Should it feel right. Should I care for such whims and desires. But I would have to meet her first. And, even then, she had tempted me from afar for so long, whispering to me in dreams of chaos and destruction, that even I was not sure I would give in to the temptation she would offer when she was real.

Another growl rippled from my throat, and I inwardly cursed that I was allowing such festering thoughts to be echoed to listening ears.

Thankfully, it seemed even Jonah did not notice as his eyes were gazing towards the shooting range, where I could see one of the other Amity members using armaments to fire perfectly at the dummies. Alexandre 'Alex' Dixon, the male whom Jonah had been courting for many scorns, both of whom would undoubtedly have heartfasted if it were not for the impudent laws that prevented same-sex couples from doing so.

"He is good," I commented.

"He is great," Jonah's face lit with pride, and I felt the tilt of a smile on my lips as he watched his keeper for a longer moment. "You know what position I would like to find him in should anything happen."

"I am quite aware."

The clearing of someone's throat had the two of us looking to the other side of Jonah, where Sentinel Rheon 'Travis', one of the guards, was standing with his head bowed.

"Sir," he greeted.

"Travis, please escort His Highness back home," Jonah instructed. "You may need to carry him; he has hurt his foot."

"Of course, Sir."

"Absolutely not," I grunted, crossing my arms. "I am perfectly capable of walking; it might just take a while longer."

Travis stepped back, his head remaining bowed as he waited for me to pass.

"Oh, and Seraiah," Jonah said, patting my shoulder, "Travis and Connell will be with you on rotation until the solar rite has passed."

"I do not need a guard," I muttered, watching Jonah depart towards the shooting range. I lingered longer until Travis cleared his throat again, as though he had somewhere to be, and I began hobbling towards the exit.

Having a personal guard on rotation felt unnecessary unless I was leaving the house to go anywhere, usually the garrison, where I was surrounded by many of them. I hated having them at the palace; it made life more claustrophobic and reminded me too much of the duty I was burdened to bear.

I usually enjoyed the pleasant summer walk through our settlement to and from the garrison, but due to my injury, I was taken by car for the brief journey to the palace. It hung over the estate like a looming shadow of oppression. Still, the gilded cage welcomed me home with chagrined hesitation as I limped through the doorway, praying to get to my haven before I was spotted.

At first, I thought I might have been collared by Marie and taken to the downstairs corner sitting room to have my wounds tended to whilst she scolded me, but even that would have been a light sentence compared to the female who glowered at me from the bottom of the stairwell.

"Could you not have at least worn a face guard?" my mother asked, tutting as she tottered towards me in a pair of ridiculously wedged shoes. "It is your solar rite this Saturday, Seraiah. Did you not think about that beforehand?"

"It is a scratch, Mother," I answered dryly. "All this shall be healed by the time I step through that door."

"Do not be smart with me," she tutted, her eyes flickering to Travis before they returned to me. However, she aimed her following words at him. "You are dismissed."

I could feel Travis' hesitancy before I heard the soft thud of his boots as he turned on his heel and exited the door behind us.

"You do not need a guard inside," my mother stated.

"It is not my decision," I said, knowing she understood. And quite frankly, I wished Travis had stayed behind because he could have provided me with a minor amount of protection against my mother's wrath.

She huffed a sigh, "You are safe in this house; I know you fear-"

"-I fear nothing," I interjected, hating the cloying feeling in my hands as she used such an irrelevant word. Fear. What was there to fear? Nothing. Another emotion buried deep, bound in iron chains, "Jonah assigned Travis to escort me back, nothing more."

My mother hated it when I interrupted her, but I had done so for many winters, and she could not stop me even if she tried. Once I was fond of her, I remembered how she would sing lullabies of old to calm me when I could not sleep, tell me tales of lands gone by, and whisper how much she loved me. All of which ripped away the sol-

Heart thudding, fists clammy and clenched, I managed to prevent the rattle of noise rising in my throat from leaving it.

"If you shall excuse me, Mother," I bowed my head and stepped past her, but her cold skin and rough, piercing nails stopped me. It took all my strength not to shove my shoulder to have her remove

11

them.

"I wish for you to dine with me this eve."

"Will Father be there?" I said through clenched teeth.

"We are family."

"Are we?" I snorted, finally turning toward her, shifting from her grip only to grimace as I landed heavily on my sore foot, wishing I had shown no sign of weakness in front of her.

If she noticed, she did not show it. "Whether you both do not see eye to eye should not matter."

But, it should matter, I wished to say. It should be the one thing that mattered because a rift in time caused the family she was hanging on to so dearly to shatter. Gone were the sols of being young and free without the impending burden of the crown and my tyrannical father's heavy hand.

"Hm," I nodded. "You know it will only end with arguments, Mother. I have not dined with either of you since earlier this winter, and I do not plan to. Should you wish, I shall make arrangements next quarter, but that shall be without Father."

Much like I had buried all my emotions, my mother was well trained in the art of steadfast eyes, but it was in minor moments I could see the hurt she was trying to suppress. If she wished to be seen as a loving mother, then she should have stepped up scorns before.

She clicked her tongue, "Fine."

"If you shall excuse me," I bowed, making another attempt at escaping from the confined space of the grand hallway.

"I know what you plan to do, Seraiah," she stated accusatory, and her words stilled me enough to notice the hard thud in my heart was not merely a palpitation. "Secretly spying on your father, gathering evidence to cause a revolt. Poor Henri Romano locked up inside a vault, his life bringers begging for his freedom."

I swallowed, unable to look at her as she wormed her nasty words into the deep crevices of my mind, picturing Eros in pain the way I knew he would be. A good male caught in a web of fabricated lies and forged evidence brutally flogged until he would give in or die. Eros, who might not return to his family, eat his mother's best caponata dish, hear the laughter of his younger brother and sister, smell the sea and bask in the sunlight.

All for the cause of The Sanctuary of Amity.

By valour or virtue, for all.

I clenched my jaw, then took a deep breath. "Apparently, the all-seeing knows everything."

"Do not be so contemptuous."

I laughed mirthlessly and turned to her, "I am unsure what Henri Romano did to earn such disfavour from you when you request to dine with his mother on your visits to Italy. I can assure you, Mother, that I am not doing anything untoward towards Father, nor do I have plans to."

The lie was created with precision, and I knew she would struggle to find it behind my poker face. I was always aware that nothing in the house passed by without her knowledge, as the splinters between the walls hummed with whispers from those who passed through the halls.

"I would suggest you attempt to rescue Henri Romano from whatever doom you have placed him into," I said with finality, "because I can assure you whatever crime he has committed has nothing to do with me."

With a final bow, I jogged up the stairwell, forcing through the pain humming in my ankle as I cut right at the top into the east wing and disappeared around the corner, out of sight. Only then did I stop to take a deep breath, attempting to calm myself from the anger festering in my chest.

Yet a simmering zap of electricity sizzled in my left palm curbed it for me. I held it up, meanderingly watching the tendrils of royal blue lightning tickle my blackened fingertips for several moments until it fizzled out. The power waited, restless for release, yearning to be unleashed like a once well-oiled machine left to rust.

Forcefully so, mostly. Purposefully so, yes.

One sol, such power would be freely used without limitations, but such things required freedom. Freedom required me to be at liberty from the beast that had unchangingly etched my left forearm black. A scar gifted to me as it shredded half my soul, leaving nothing more than an apathetic, forsaken, cursed prince in its aftermath.

TWO

After spending hours wallowing in self-pity from my mother's wrath and a painful, unwanted visit from Marie, I sprawled across one of the leather-bound sofas in the middle of our home library. My swollen ankle looped over its smooth arm, enveloped in an ice cloth, whilst my bruised forearm rested over my closed eyes as I snoozed.

I almost overlooked the shutting of the room door somewhere to my right until the whisper of booted soles echoed across the rigid wooden floorboard towards me.

"I suppose I should not be surprised to find you here."

A breath of a smile tickled the corner of my lips, and I pulled my arm from my face to see my cousin, Freddie, appear at its end, eyes gunned in on my foot. I did not clock his intended action until his hand patted down on it.

"Hellsworn," I cursed as the pain rippled up my leg.

Freddie only laughed, taking the last few steps to the vacant seat and slumping on it with little care that he might crease his expensive attire. Not that he ever did; a male who prided himself in appearance was confident enough to wear it without care of such diligence. He kicked his Chelsea boots onto the middle oak coffee table and unbuttoned the third button on his white polo before running his hands through his immaculately styled black hair.

"I have heard about your fight with Connell," he grinned.

"The male is out to kill me," I stated light-heartedly.

"He respects you far too much for such idiocy," he replied, dipping his gaze back to my foot before flicking them back to me. "Not enough to avoid giving you a swollen ankle, however. That means you shall be out of action for some sols."

"Even if I do not allow such things, Marie would quite gladly have my head."

A chuckle. "She would have it for anything she deems not *princely*."

Even though Marie despised my charades of fighting, I preferred her mothering to my own. She treated me like most other folk, calling me by my first name, scolding me when necessary, and being the one person I could confide in when others I could not.

"Where have you been?" I asked, noting the clouded air of woody aroma from some expensive cologne he owned.

"On quite the adventure," he smirked, although I observed the subtle note of pink on his cheeks.

I was amused. "Adventure, hm?"

"You know how much I enjoy walking among humans," he said, turning his head away with a wistful, yet amused expression. "They are so..."

"Fragile?"

"Interesting," he tutted, "they may have a much shorter lifespan than us, but that does not mean they are fragile, my prince."

Humans were fragile, comparative to sol and night with how quickly they were born, lived and died. Still, they were fortunate that reincarnation was a path that existed, for the dwindling light of their life was sombre.

"So, you grew bored of your confinements and left for London to walk amongst humans?" I raised my eyebrows.

"I endeavoured to meet Ronan."

"The sapstrider?"

He grinned cheekily before he rummaged in his left jeans pocket, pulled out a small, distinct bag of herbs and threw it on the table. Isanhowad – a potent relaxant that we skilfully acquired every year to get us through the upcoming Iontine celebrations.

I chuckled, "Jonah shall have our head."

"The Commander will not know," he tipped his invisible hat, "until it is too late."

He stood and whipped the packet from the table before disappearing to the ladders which led to the mezzanine. I did not need to watch to know that he was hiding it in a secret nook where we always hid such contraband.

I eyed the arched ceiling, which rose into the centre and protruded a centred sphere, fraudulently painted as a sun with brilliant butterflies dancing below it - A projection almost too accurate to notice the difference.

It was the pinnacle ornament of a paragon library, bordered with high windows, which sprinkled the room with dust mites that favoured magical fairies in the soft dusk light. Two layers split by an entresol lined with oak shelves overflowing with new and old collections of tomes, sectioned as though a tomeguard were there to organise each shelf alphabetically.

When Freddie returned, he sagged onto the sofa with an exhale. "I require your counsel."

"Counsel?"

"Yes, how do you woo a goddess?"

Freddie's question made me wonder whether he understood that the person he was aiming it toward had no knowledge about *wooing* anyone.

"I have met the most beautiful female." He sat upright, palms clasped before him, his wistfulness returning. "I must know how to woo her."

"It must be serious if you have to ask me," I wryly joked.

"The Gods say you are destined to be with one," Freddie alluded, causing the distant slither of longing to tug at my iron heart, begging to be freed from its shackles. It was not entirely correct information, however, as I did not recall there ever being a statement that my fated one was anything but ephemeral.

"And how do you know she is a *goddess*?" I wondered, eager not to dwell on distant memories, "This... female of yours?"

"She has bewitched me," he breathed, distant eyes twinkling, and then he leapt to his feet, pacing dizzily, "She is divine, and her... her laughter, her smile, her-"

"-Freddie, you have not once been serious about any other," I frowned, knowing the male better than anyone else. I would even declare that *infatuation* was too intense a word for him; most of the females he enjoyed his time with flitted in and out of his bed with no chance of a genuine connection.

"She is different."

"A goddess?"

"A human."

"A human?" I almost choked on my saliva, surprised at the outburst of such an astonishing statement. I supposed he had been on an escapade to London, and there were many more choices in the human world. But I recounted several instances where he had deemed a human less favourable to lie with than a Zikan.

Yet, he somehow seemed serious about this one, describing her, of all things, as a goddess, which even I would not use to describe a human lightly.

"I love her."

I shivered. "Love is a strong word."

"Not all of us have closed ourselves from such delicacies," he tutted, although even I know even he was unconvinced about such *delicacies*.

It was as though a hex had enraptured him, convincing him that this minor fascination meant he *felt* like he was in love with the female. I imagined her as some sort of enchantress disguised as a human, laughing because she had a prince bowing at her feet.

"And she is not a fancie?" I asked, referencing the outdated derogatory term used for a female who lured males into their beds for perfunctory pleasure.

"She is not a *fancie*!" he spat, tight fists white from anger which rippled him.

"You know a human cannot survive here," I stated, noting it was not only the energetic shield which surrounded our small village that was strong enough to deter humans, but the wrath of my father's council, who would see her eyes gouged from her skull for such insolence.

He ran a shaky hand through his hair, pending a deep sigh, "I must keep her, Seraiah. I have never, *never* felt like this towards another."

"Humans do not like to be *kept*," I replied, understanding that such terminology could land him in hot water if he translated it directly to English for his bride-to-be.

"I am not objectifying her," he frowned, whilst a guttural growl rattled from him, "but she will be mine. The idea of another... male touching what belongs to me."

I chuckled, "Ever so possessive."

"I have not come here for your opinion," he added decisively. "I am eager to see her next sol; I am merely asking for suggestions. And, should such ideas work, we know you can use them when your fated one arrives."

I pursed my lips as I studied the lovelorn male, noting that such a meeting had moulded him into someone almost unrecognisable. It had just been the sol prior when we had dined with Jonah and Alex at their home, that he heralded he would never fall for a female in this life. The Gods must have listened and tittered at such blasphemy, for he had met his match in the form of a human.

But, I supposed I could offer him some counsel based upon human romance tomes I had divulged in once upon a time, although never with such intention as to court one. A Zikan prince mated to a mere human was outlandish, but even then, maybe the Gods were also cackling in cruel amusement as my fated one manifested with a severed existence.

"Humans like flowers," I offered, cruelly noting how such living organisms were cut from their roots and handed over to die. *Just like humans.*

Freddie pushed his body forward as he dug for his phone device in his pocket before plopping back down. I could only presume he planned to write some form of note. "Yes."

"A poem?" I wondered, although I was pretty sure poetry was a craft that had gently disappeared over the winters, and I knew Freddie's literary skills in the art were close to zero.

"I do not think she enjoys poetry," he muttered, looking upwards in contemplation, "plus, my English writing skills are limited compared to my speech and reading."

"I do not know how that would make sense," I chuckled perplexedly, knowing how rigorously we had worked on reading, writing and speaking the many different languages spoken across Earth. I supposed I rarely saw him annotating outside of our own.

He snapped his fingers with such resonance that it echoed, "She does love dancing."

"I suppose humans are not so dissimilar," I muttered, primarily to myself.

"She is studying ballet. I wonder whether she would cherish a new pair of shoes. She would like them, would she not?"

"I am sure," I nodded faintly, although that would require him to find out the size of her feet, and I was sure that would be a more personal endeavour for him to undertake.

However, a proposition suddenly appeared in my thoughts about how I could appease Freddie's infatuation with the human whilst using it to benefit my position in the long term.

"Why not invite her to the ball?"

Freddie's eyebrows rose before a mixture of emotions glittered over his expression, no doubt toying with the idea I had brought forward to him. The ball in question was the celebration of my solar rite, and I knew that bringing a human would cause quite an uproar, especially with my father's council.

"Do you not expect our original plan to succeed?" Freddie asked rightfully. He understood the risk it posed to both his human and our settlement.

Whilst I suspected our well-crafted plan would succeed, there was always a minor guarantee that something would stop it. But, if I had Freddie's new spiritsworn as an alternative, I could use it as leverage to gain the favour of the many Zikans who wished to venture deeper into the human realm outside of simply finding employment.

Still, I persisted, "It is for your happiness."

Freddie snorted, "Do not lie, Seraiah. We are brothers; I can see straight through them. Not everything has to be a pawn in your game."

Not everything, no. But, when there had been a stalemate for scorns, and the opposition's misstep had finally broken the impasse, it was a perfect time to make our play and call checkmate.

"Do you not wish to be with her?"

"Well..." he trailed off, thoughts whirling once more. And, then, he slowly nodded, speaking as though he was conversing with himself,

"I... I would have to think about it. I do not wish to hurt her, and she would... what if your father sees to it that she– I would do anything for her. I cannot live without her."

"Well, if that is truly the case, Freddie," I replied carefully, "if you truly see this human as more than just a *fancie*, as some may coin it, and even more than a spiritsworn, then you must be willing to put everything in your world at stake. Announce it, flaunt it. Otherwise, you may find yourself under house arrest for going against such laws, and you know how the council operates. House arrest could be implemented for many winters, and by then, she would have found another human to love."

"She is mine," he breathed in quiet anger, although I knew he was only saying it to himself. But his claimant over her convinced me there was no jest regarding the human. He met my gaze darkly. "You are blackmailing me."

Still unconvinced, I see.

"I am only stating the truth. If you are so besotted by this human and wish to court and heartfast her, then you must place your own life on the line."

He huffed in irritation, "I do not care about my own life; I care about hers. I could easily sneak out to see her every sol."

I could only imagine the uproar caused when it was caught on the high wind that Freddie had been sneaking into the human world daily to fraternise with another.

"Yes, but what shall happen when you cannot explain why she cannot come to your home? And I do not mean this poxy settlement. I mean, your true home. Shall you leave her behind, or shall you stay and wither away in the human world? You know that being away from the shield is detrimental to anyone with Rapidfire."

"We lasted without it for ten winters."

"And we were sick," I answered, feeling a little annoyed that I was still having to convince him. "We were weak, and we could hardly breathe. Do you wish for her to see that? Or shall you have a long life with the human?"

Short, I supposed, when it was her own life in the mix, but for Freddie, he had hundreds of winters to see through. He knew I was right; I could tell by his body language that living without his future keeper was a thought he could not bear.

A long silence sat between us. "I would need to guarantee her safety."

"I vow to you she shall be safe," I said with hidden uncertainty. I wondered whether he might have me sign a declaration of faith to honour the promise. I could not guarantee her safety, but I would try to appease Freddie where possible.

Of course, I was unsure how he would get her to the ball, and I knew he would need Jonah's full permission to bring her. Although my commander did not hold more power than I did, security and protection would determine whether Freddie's chance would be successful.

"Does the hu... female have a name?"

"Genevieve," he smiled wistfully, "Genie, for short. I do like both."

He hopped up to his feet with the same excited energy he had waltzed into the room with and bowed his head gently, "I shall endeavour to see whether she would like to join the ball, but I shall speak to *Lord Commander* first."

He tittered at his joke before his boots danced across the floor as though there was a sway in his step, followed by a squeaky pause, and he rushed back to me.

"I forgot!" he declared, leaning against the back of my sofa. "She has a friend."

I managed to hold the impassive look, although I wanted to let the amused smile roll across my lips. If Freddie had not been my advisor and once a dutiful prince, he would have made an excellent matchmaker, always attempting to make me bed a female whenever there was an opportunity. He had not succeeded for two winters.

"Most people have friends, Freddie."

Freddie offered a glance that teetered on insolence, and then he plastered on his cunning look with a twinkle in his eyes, "Her sister. Well, not quite, sister. She was adopted, so I suppose she is Genie's half-sister. Anyway, I can invite her if you wish..."

I did not wish for a female human to sate my desires when there were Zikan females abundant at the garrison who I could quite naturally invite to my bed.

I snorted inwardly. What desires were there? Petty ones to fill an empty gap whilst I awaited my fictitious Kindred Spirit the Gods had so fortunately blessed upon me. One hundred winters alone, searching the skies for answers, not to even find a notion of a hint that the stars were in my favour.

Breathing in deeply, I finally pulled myself to a sitting position. "I shall not question the will of the Gods."

No, I should have rephrased that. I would always question their will, but I would not fraternise with a mere human, especially when bringing two into our settlement could make it much more difficult to achieve our goal.

"Fair enough," he patted my shoulder, "as you wish, Your High-ness."

His words were mocking, almost singing them as though he still had some sort of tactic for me to meet the other he spoke of. But they were his last as he swivelled on his shoes and marched to the library's exit.

I was quite interested in hearing about my long-time confidant's new adventures as he attempted to flee the village each sol. Although his life was not necessarily as strict as mine, any car he borrowed would be tracked, and it would be reported anytime he left the settlement. I was sure a secret guard was following him from a distance, although I had yet to find out who.

Part of me wondered whether I should have taken Freddie up on his offer to meet his spiritsworn's sister, but even then, she would only be a plaything until my fated one appeared. Maybe I would quite enjoy toying with the heart of a mere human, luring her into my bed, fucking her until I was satisfied before demanding she be dropped outside the gate.

It was a shame I was not a cruel prince, just *cursed*.

I took a deep breath and lunged to my feet, testing the weight on my ankle until I was gently satisfied that my power had dissipated the pain. I could hear Marie scolding me for being up and about, but I was not at the mercy or demands of a physician. Plus, the wine at the back of the library called my name.

And, after drinking almost a whole bottle in the library's silence, the whispers of the moon lulled me into a deep slumber. Whilst many of my dreams were shrouded in darkness, some gave me peace.

A gentle breeze kicked up the edges of sheet curtains, tickling my reposed naked skin, partially layered in soft white linen. A soft voice called from somewhere on the other side of the drapes, like a siren summoning me to the depths. Silken sheets fell from me as I rose from my bed, reaching out a hand as I caught a glimpse of her mythical silhouette until my fingers tangled in the shroud and pulled it away. But she was not there, not a soul nor a place beyond the transitory sanctuary I was in.

The same voice echoed from the bed, but I could not see her as I turned. An unseen apparition with only one sense to tease me, leaving me to wonder about the deity who breathed my name so sweetly, so *alluringly*. Ever since my twentieth solar rite, she was there, eighty long, harrowing winters with only a breath of my name to cling to. I yearned, begged, and faltered for someone who had yet to make her presence known – the ones the Gods had fated me to for eternity.

For what was one hundred winters of loneliness when eternity was the exchange?

The subtle breeze blustered, and I shuddered awake. Gazing wearily up at the globe in the centre of the ceiling, which no longer represented the sun but the moon, projecting fireflies dancing below it. I knew the sunrise was impending outside the high windows, and I would not sleep again until the end of the sol.

And so it began. After breakfast, I worked on the canvas in the middle of the library, burrowing my thoughts as I attempted to paint the room from my dream. Often, I wondered whether she had received the same message from the Gods, agonising at the pain of being at such an immeasurable distance from me.

I chuckled solemnly. *Maybe she does not exist at all; a cursed prince shall always be a cursed prince.*

Cursed. Lonely. Deprived of love.

I could hear the town crier, bell in hand, *pity the prince, who is not only cursed in body and mind but in such matters of the heart. Who dares to satisfy himself with a mere human. Pity him. Pity him. Pity him.*

I was sure his voice box would be slit by my father's council - *silence.*

I snorted; love did not exist. It could not when honour and duty were precedents above it all. Never would I bow down to such inclinations, even when my fated one would stand before me. She would become a princess – a queen – and then, I, a king. The two of us evading our need for one another to bear heirs for a future kingdom. We would argue, she would come to dislike me, and the two of us would live separate lives until our deaths.

For what is a king but a steadfast force to pave the way for his people?

What is love in the eyes of duty?

What is a king if he goes by what his iron heart wishes?

Our souls bound for an eternity – in life as royalty, in death as martyrs.

THREE

After a morning of painting, I was eager to freshen up and possibly risk a visit to the garrison, at least to observe the training taking place. Or, with some persuasion, maybe Jonah would allow me to partake in some of the activities. But such privileges were torn as I escaped the library, collared by the dreaded infiltration of my mother, who I swore had some hidden magic where she could see my every move.

"Seraiah!" her voice echoed from her doorway, and my shoulders tensed in response.

"I am busy," I replied, stepping away in the opposite direction.

"You are never too busy to speak with your queen." Her authority rumbled like an avalanche through my soul, making her an inescapable force with which I could not barter. As my mother, I could bypass her ruling, but as my queen, I was as much a subject as anyone else who walked the halls.

With reluctance, I swivelled and marched through the door of her quarters, which immediately led into her modern living room. A citrus scent wafted from a lit candle in the corner, reminding me of the Italian summer I so dearly missed. A smell my mother adored whenever she remained in London. For a female who enjoyed such sun-drenched European summer sols, her quarters were akin to damp British weather, reminding me of a fleeting sunset on stormy skies with the grey, black and red theme throughout.

Katerina 'Helga' Reaynt, the eldest member of Amity, at one hundred and forty-two - around forty-three on Earth - stood as I entered, curtseying gently. Her lean, muscular figure adorned a black pencil skirt, soft black heels, and a blue blouse, which often seemed so unlike her when I had seen her outside the palace's walls. I knew she would have preferred wearing combat gear, but her role as First Lady was important in attire and personality.

"Your Highness," she greeted.

"Katerina," I nodded, standing by the room's large arched window to gaze upon nature beyond the claustrophobic walls. I did not need to know that my mother chose to sit on one of the soft, elegant grey sofas in the centre of the room, where she had a prime view of any visitors who might grace her doorway. Sometimes, I wondered whether she might have removed her harsh heeled shoes and placed her aching feet on the seat next to her. But such a laid-back female had disappeared with time and age, at least until she was behind closed doors.

"Come and sit, Seraiah," she commanded. She wished me to sit in the opposite chair, neck exposed to invisible assailants who craved to slink through the cracks in the walls and slit my throat.

"I am fine standing."

No one should ever refuse a queen's command, but she had already brought me into her gingerbread-coated viper's den, fangs ready to embed into my skin. It should have been enough to satisfy her before she poisoned me with her deceitful lies. If I sat, it would give her ample opportunity to slide her sharp claws into my skin and flay my skin open for the world to witness the iron heart beating inside. I might have sat with her once, but my respect had deteriorated along with all the other tepid sentiments I felt due to her never-wavering support for my father's appalling and brutal way of ruling over our people. Standing allowed me to prevent such wounds, keeping the ball in my court.

So, I fixed my eyes on the gardener, who remained unaware of my scrutinising gaze as he trimmed a rosebush with a pair of shears – his careful movements a stark reminder that even beauty demanded caution to avoid its thorns, much like my mother.

I could hear the dejected sigh in her tone, but she did not free it from its wanting grasp. "I have spoken to your father. We have agreed that there shall be an armistice between both councils for the celebration this Saturday." *Snip.* "It is your one-hundredth solar rite; we both recognise that."

"You underestimate him."

"No, it is you who underestimates him," she replied sharply. "I have it in writing that he will do no harm, and we shall all celebrate as a family."

Snip.

If for nothing else, it was for appearances. This was the second time in as many sols that she had attempted to use such a vile term as *family* when I was sure she did not understand such a definition. I did not know of other families who attempted to sabotage their offspring on any given occasion just to keep perch on a fictitious obsidian throne. Then again, it was not so imaginary as it was dusty, somewhere in a storage room, forgotten and rusted.

I laughed mirthlessly in silence, eyes still honed on the gardener. *Snip.*

"And when the clock strikes midnight?" I turned to her. "You know what he is capable of, Mother. He will not rest until I either bow down or I am dead. We both know which he would prefer, of course."

"Seraiah."

Back at the window, my lip twitched mockingly. "You do not wish me to say it, but you know it is true."

"You are the heir to this throne."

Snip.

Such insignificance brought to our conversation rapidly repri-manding me for my words instead of seeing the broader picture. A queen who does not fight against the oppression of her people is nothing more than a coward in conversations of fact.

"I should be *on* the throne," I chided matter-of-factly, "not that-" I sharply stopped myself as though it hurt. "I am the rightful king."

"You will be king, Seraiah," she agreed, her tone so soft and motherly that it almost felt like the female had returned to her old ways. But, her switch disturbed me enough to shiver visibly, "But your father will remain in such a position until you meet your wife."

Snip. Snip. Snip.

Forced laughter rippled from my chest, and I turned my gaze from the meticulous gardener to the gothic silver wallpaper adorned with a repetitive black floral pattern to attempt to calm my pulsing rage.

"And, when shall that be?" I wondered, "Because she is not about to waltz through that door, nor has any daughter born over the last eighty winters been a suitable match. As far as I am concerned, Father has no plans of us returning home so that I may attempt to find her. Speaking of which, when does he plan to fund the operation of creating portals again?"

"You cannot simply conjure magic, Seraiah," she tutted.

"It is not magic; it is alchemy. Science," I corrected, "My list is simple; I am not asking Father to mine the Earth himself."

"Earth is not exactly abundant with the resource materials you have requested."

Earth was more abundant than Zika, but such lies were painted over truths.

"The Gods would not send us somewhere without the right

resource, Mother," I countered, "lead, gold, silver. Easy targets."

"Not that easy."

"Quartz, obsidian, emerald," I continued, ignoring her need to interrupt me.

"Seraiah."

"Mandrake root, belladonna, dragon's blood. Easy. Fucking. Targets."

"Do not swear at me."

"Send me on a fucking mission, Mother!" I raged, finally looking at her. "If Father cannot bear to part with his precious cash, then let me go."

"You know we cannot," she sighed, looking away.

Oh, I knew exactly why they could not. But no one dared to let a monster loose from its cage – a cursed prince fated to hex the very ground he walked upon.

But I could feel the beast rattling.

Festering.

Waiting to be set free.

"It is for your safety."

"This palace is not *safe*," I snorted, laughing bitterly. "It is no more than a gilded cage wrapped in a tidy bow. And that is why I cannot leave, not because this realm makes me *sick* from radiation, but because I am a slave to honour and duty. And so, I remain here as no more than a prisoner, unable to find my wife - my *fated* one - for the apparent excuse of safety."

She remained in her silence as I seethed, fists clenching repeatedly in an attempt to soothe the fury riling up inside my soul. The dull ache of tremendous, forbidden, untameable power callously pulsed in the palm of my left hand, threatening to dominate my entire being.

I needed to calm down. I could not allow myself to succumb to such insignificances as anger to the extent that I would no longer be in control of myself.

Breathe.

I sucked in a deep breath, looking outward to the summer's sol once more. The gardener and his roses were no longer of interest as I sought to find something small and meagre to focus on. And I found it in the arrival of my commander, who entered the grounds on foot, walking towards the door.

"And, you are sorely mistaken if you truly believe Father will do nothing during my celebration," I bit, deciding that some finality was needed in the conversation. "The paper which you speak of will mean nothing. Whilst he may not directly cause harm, there are many people working with him – *for* him – secretly and publicly, and he will do everything in his power to bring devastation."

And I would do everything in my power to return it.

"You are just scared, Seraiah," my mother chided.

The dark, cursed prince Seraiah scared of his father? *Ha.* A laughable offence among many. Such treachery in her statement, as though they would sting my charred soul. Never scared, never fearful, always one step ahead of such needless qualms.

"Do not think that your father is without knowledge of what events you plan to unfold," she continued harshly before her tone took a sudden, noticeably soft shift as she tried to dig her nails in further, "If you do not agree to sign this, your father will have no choice but to enact a defence. Is that truly what you want?"

I huffed a laugh of disbelief, swivelling back to look at her, "And what do you believe I am going to do? You spoke last sol with such accusations, even reprimanding your own friend's son, so enlighten me. What information has been fed through the great vine of knowledge?"

I partially wondered whether Jonah was right about the rat in our midst, the person possibly divulging more information than she was supposed to, sitting behind my mother, listening intently. But even I was wary of accusing such deviance without evidence, and evidence was the most powerful tool in a king's arsenal.

Still, I did not look at Helga, knowing I had to remain strong and unwavering in the verbal duel with my mother.

"Regardless of what it is," she tactfully swayed, causing another ripple of mirth to attempt to break free from my mouth, "you must remember that the two of you made a divine promise. Your father will remain on the throne until you are married, and only then shall the council vote on your position."

The force of my anger hit me like a bolt of lightning as I felt the rise of an all too familiar yet distant force overwhelm me. "Then, find me my fucking wife!"

Pain ricocheted up the fibres of my left arm, feeling like a thousand splinters were trying to break from the skin of my entire upper body. My cobalt Rapidfire contended with the searing onyx power that toiled endlessly to overshadow it. Knees thudded against the floor, head throbbing mindlessly, vision pulsing as black veins surfaced just below my eye sockets. The room's warmth disappeared, and a lick of sweat ran down my spine as the chill set in.

This was why I was nicknamed the cursed prince. My shadow, which was destined to haunt me until my last dying breath.

This was the king that no one wanted - angry, aggressive, power-hungry.

Voices blurred.

Breathe.

Pain echoed beneath my skin.

Breathe.

Sweat dripped from my forehead.

Breathe.

Bile drew up my throat.

Breathe.

Heavy hands landed on my shoulders.

Breathe.

"*Hasriea mena oprei laroen maneiuh fauishaei artrieaya, Seraiah,*" Jonah's familiar voice breathed the ancient words softly, whilst my palms repeatedly clenched as I trained my eyes to the floor, "*lunaeh unar oprei johe fauishaei artrieaya sol undraie ormsapiaun, Seraiah.*"

Let the light guide you back to us, Seraiah. Let the sun bring warmth to your soul, Seraiah, and give you peace.

"Breathe, Seraiah," Jonah whispered, returning to our native language before repeating the phrase thrice until I felt the deep, simmering anger recoil to its perch, letting out a shuddered breath. I finally peered up, looking at my long-time friend's worried yet relieved face as he sat back on his haunches, running a hand through his well-groomed black hair. Although I had gained control of myself, the pain still tingled my left arm, and the intensity made me feverish. The coldness in the room had lifted, and with it came the warmth of the summer sol.

Throughout the winters of dealing with such inner power struggles, there were only two ways to prevent me from losing control of it completely. The first was heavy sedation implemented by force used for scorns when we arrived on Earth. The second was the words of the ancient mantra, which bore deep resonance to my spirit. Although little did they know, my grip on such resonance had slowly been dwindling each time it was used, making it more difficult for me to unbind myself from the shackles my aura was subjected to.

One thousand four hundred and two sols with no incidents. It had been my lengthiest time yet, although I was not surprised, having felt the foreign tendrils of lightning in my fingers just the sol prior.

"Are you okay?" Jonah asked.

My gaze passed by him toward Helga, who stood expressionless on the other side of the sofa and then to my mother, who gazed out of the window, seemingly ignorant of what had happened. She sighed deeply and tottered to the door to her private bedroom, disappearing without another look at me.

I looked back at Jonah, lifting myself shakily to my feet. "It was not purposeful."

"It never is," he answered, offering me a steady shoulder, "I was only on my way to see if you were well after last sol's fight, and now I see you are worse. I should recommend you sleep."

Sleep was a good option, but I felt as though my inner circuits had been rewired incorrectly. I wished I did not have to waste a sol in bed when it could have been more productive.

"I would have been at the garrison if it were not for this," I grunted.

"I will help you to your room," he stated before nodding to Helga, "Lady Katerina."

"Commander," Helga replied, busying herself with tidying up the immaculate room as though my presence had made it more unkempt.

Jonah and I exited the room, greeted by Travis' silent presence in the corner as he followed a pace behind. Looking weak did not bode well, so I pushed away from Jonah's helping hands, rounded my shoulders, and walked alone.

"I need to go to the generator first," I told Jonah.

As we arrived at the door, the heavy sound of several pairs of boots stomping down the corridor drew our attention, and I saw the two males who made every sol a living hell for me - Lord Viktoerin Marcheus, known only by 'The General' and my father, the tyrannical King Charles Vronae Johren Zika. Both were flanked by three other uniformed guards, large armaments sprawled across their chests in holsters, whilst radio wires idly hung from their ears. Neither of them was part of my rebellion.

"Empyreans," Jonah swore quietly before he stepped forward in a protective position, speaking louder, "Your Majesty, to what do we owe the pleasure?"

"You do not speak until you have been permitted!" The General spat at Jonah, all five of them coming to a halt within ten or so feet of us. We looked like we were about to have a duel. Quite the show for the security hidden behind cameras; then again, what is a royal *family* without a little drama?

"I am unsurprised that you have decided to stir more trouble on the quarter of your solar rite, Seraiah," my father glowered, stepping forward, "but to find the news that you have threatened your mother under this roof is astonishing."

I snorted, "I did no such thing."

"Lies," he seethed, "if your words do not tell me what I need to understand, then those black veins under your eyes provide me with all the information I require. I told you last time, boy, that if you revealed that side of you again, I would not be merciful. Lock that insolent fiend in the vault!"

While his three guards stepped forward, Travis took a position ahead of me, blocking their access. It allowed me to see the five of them but prevented me from moving unless I commanded Travis or Jonah to, which I did not.

"Step away this instant!" The General's commanding voice boomed down the corridor as though we could not hear him. But Travis did not move, as he had no respect for my father's side and would only follow the orders of either Jonah or myself. Even then, Jonah's command was above my own.

"You have no right," Jonah said, speaking with the same prowess as his father, but without the unnecessary intensity. Jonah was a male who could command a room with a whisper.

"I command you to move!" my father growled, but neither male

37

changed their stance.

"It is, by rule of the council, that I must hereby protect the prince," Jonah stated confidently. A decree made over the winters, which Jonah had fought for, stated that my father and his council had no right to rule over me unless sufficient evidence was supplied or a seal was issued. It might have only changed if my mother stepped into the corridor and commanded it, but I was sure she was only eavesdropping.

"It has been many winters since any of us have witnessed his rage," Jonah stated, "and it must be decreed by both councils should any punishments occur. This beast causes him more pain than you or I could inflict, so I implore you, Your Majesty, to let this rest and not subject your son to more torture."

"Those rules do not take precedence when the shield is involved," The General reminded Jonah, "it is in our right to apprehend this boy."

"This *boy* is our future king," Jonah replied sharply, "and you must address him so. His Royal Highness, His Grace, even Prince Seraiah, if you must, General. I do not take it lightly to you speaking about my king as though he is beneath you. And I must also remind you that the rules of apprehension only precede my command when it is no longer at the capacity for the generator to work. His Royal Highness and I were returning to the chamber to bring the system back online." The General was trying to interject, but Jonah continued. "Oh, and might I remind you, Father, that you may find your position thwarted once Prince Seraiah sits on that throne."

"You little-"

"-Enough!" my father said sharply, holding his hand up to quiet the two of them. His eyes landed on me. "While you are lucky this sol, I shall seek to bring this absurdity to the council, so I should expect you to prepare for the punishment you deserve." He looked at Jonah. "I could not care what pain the beast inflicts upon this devil; he is only deserving of the malice he has caused his people."

With my father's final words, he spun on his heel and stormed down the corridor; the others followed soon after him.

While I should have felt betrayed by my father's callous words and some sort of unease towards them, they were just a few of the degrading terms he used throughout my lifetime to describe the male I was. What malice could a prisoner cause when his people never saw him? For only a king who suppresses his subjects would seek to blame the pariah who sought to save them.

"I would prepare myself if I were you, Seraiah," Jonah turned to me. "I imagine the vault may become your next place of rest should Her Majesty provide evidence."

But even then, I was sure my mother, the unwavering force she was, would not lie to the council. The truth was simpler. The normal castigation for any son should have been chores or being grounded, but even those were too simple for this dysfunctional family.

"You need not defend my every move," I tutted jestingly.

"They are seeking to ruin you!" he replied with aggressive honesty, as though it had not been the truth throughout my entire life. He patted my arm. "I do not wish to see you weeping because your jailer decided to take you down on your solar rite."

I chuckled, imagining such an image of my father declaring my celebrations cancelled because I had lashed out in anger at my mother. Then again, it was not so much a *lashing* when I had only demanded her to seek the one thing I needed to take the throne from my father's grasp. I may have been a spoiled seedling, but I did not know anyone else who would labour so long in celibacy.

"We shall see who weeps when I am king."

FOUR

Black smog clouded my surroundings, and pallid skies ruptured with tumultuous thunder and flashes of golden lightning. A spine-tingling roar tore high above, causing my heart to thud ruthlessly as I sought sight of the beast. Yet, it took moments before I saw the foul, red eyes of the demonic dragon at ground level, deep within the veil of mist.

Searing torment surged up my shadowed arm whilst gravity forced me to my knees, permitting the creature to lean back onto its haunches, readying before it pounced. Jaw unhinged, teeth sharp, tongue lashing. And, no matter how I willed myself to escape, nothing would prevent my death.

Yet, a dazzling golden light pierced from the skies, cutting through the dragon and drawing a deafening rumble of agony as it retreated.

Seraiah, her voice called somewhere behind, and I willed myself to turn towards her, no longer trapped inside a ring of uncompromising fog. Instead, I gazed upon an ascending verge with the ruins of an ancient castle atop it, and at its entrance, a simmering portal waited. I stumbled to my feet, making stilted movements in its direction, only to lay eyes on a female wearing regal white and gold clothing. Her skin glittered in a flaxen light, its glow too hazy to see anything other than her beautiful brown locks.

With newfound strength, I ran towards her, desperate to glimpse my fated one.

But even the Gods continued to oppose my every breath in dreams as they did in reality. The closer I ran and the faster my feet took me, the more the portal seemed to be purposely receding.

Seraiah! She screamed in fear.

"No!" I bellowed, actuality striking with force as I jerked upright. An icy shiver lingered where perspiration dampened my heated skin, while the deep throb in my head left me feeling frayed.

The nightmare had echoed that of many I had witnessed, but it seemed the Gods had decided to bless me with newfound knowledge of my fated one. My wife, my queen, my Kindred Spirit had thick brown curls. I could only envision what a rare beauty she was, and I was incessantly desperate to lay my eyes upon her. I itched to take pencil to paper, sketching the outlines of her opulent divinity until I would one sol replace the blank space with her features.

And I would wait as I had for every sliver of joy to fall into their rightful places.

My phone vibrated twice inside of my side table, and I leaned over to open the drawer, pulling out the device I so hated to use.

A message from Jonah: *Dinner and a catch-up at ours. Come hungry - 9 pm.*

Something as simple as dinner would not be on the cards at Jonah's, nor had it been for a great many winters. I could not remember the last time I had escaped from the palace to dine with him and Alex for pleasure over business, but such enjoyments were unnecessary when I was closer to being on the throne. I understood that the dinner would be between Amity members, although I was unsure whether Eros had managed to escape my father's grasp and returned to London without being tracked.

After showering, I dressed in casual, comfortable clothing and opted for a quiet walk to their house, which would not involve being

41

tailed by Travis. I had slept most of the sol, and it was close to eight forty by the time I pushed the swing window open, climbed through, and jumped down onto the charcoal-capped roof before leaning back up to shut it.

The residue of exhaustion cloaked me like an unwanted shadow as the sol's events immersed my fibres. I would not fall asleep again until the early morning when my mind finally closed off from its nightmarish thoughts and fears.

No, not fears. I did not fear anything. Fear was a tool in my arsenal left to rust in place of composure and moral upstanding. I would not lose those more treasured ideals for such insufficiencies as terror.

The metal ladders in the corner of the lowered roof led to the top of the building, where rarely anyone ventured. The sun shone brightly in the sky, although the temperature had cooled, and the horizon over London's hazy, distant city darkened - an escape that was within reach but untouchable with the shackles of duty that bound my wrists.

I might have sat to admire the view had I been somewhat behind in leaving for Jonah's, but such pleasure was not on the agenda, so I descended the metal stairwell on the opposite side of the roof, which led me down to the east gardens. Whispering across the lawns, over flowerbeds and around bushes, I outsmarted the sights of any roaming guards until I arrived at the high wall edged by tall hedges. It was much easier to vault towards my freedom with the leverage.

With my feet thudding to the ground, I dusted the invisible dirt from my black combat clothes, peered around for signs of anyone on watch, and swiftly escaped from the golden prison, feeling a breath of tension release from my body.

The ten-minute walk to Jonah's house took me past, although thankfully not close to the shaman's house. If she caught a whiff of my presence nearby, she would collar me, drag me into her witch's cavern and whisper voodoo tales of old whilst forcing me to devour some sort of truth serum she had concocted.

I chuckled aloud. Such a thought was not real, although I was sure she would quite happily pass on to my mother that my whereabouts had been spotted outside the safety of my cage. Then again, it was not as though the settlement was lesser.

While choosing to dart away from any of Sheika's invisible hexes, I had to try navigating around the guards who patrolled the streets. I had to hide three times in gardens, which gave me a little voyeuristic peek into the houses of my subjects.

It was fascinating how well our people adapted to the new world. They seemed almost at peace that we were not returning to our home realm. But even change made people itchy with a desire for nostalgia.

Jonah's home was at the end of the row by the crossroads, which led towards the complex exit and around its perimeter. It was a modest two-storey detached home, smaller than most in the village, and precisely the place that showed the simplicities of life the two males led.

I entered through the picket fence into the back garden, stomach growling as the waft of a home-cooked meal devoured my senses. Although I still felt nauseous, I knew a good dose of Alex's best cooking would soothe some of the ache.

Noting a hint of jazz playing on vinyl, I knocked on the open door, indicating my arrival as I entered. "Hello?"

Gentle footsteps could be heard upstairs before soft patters clambered down the staircase, revealing a slippered Alex sporting brown slim-fit trousers, a long-sleeved white shirt and a sleeveless black jumper, closer to resembling a butler than a soldier.

"Your Highness," he bowed with a soft smile.

"Are you alone?" I asked, eyeing for Jonah's whereabouts.

"Jonah went to the palace to collect you," he smiled cunningly before pulling out his phone. "I shall call him. Would you like a drink?"

I agreed, and he pulled a beer bottle from his fridge while placing the call. I could not hear Jonah's side of the conversation, but the grin on Alex's face told me that Jonah was less than pleased. While the short discussion took place, Alex handed me my beer in a glass as if serving it on a golden platter.

"I presumed you had not eaten," he said, placing a large orange casserole dish from the oven onto the hob once he had ended the call.

"You would cook food even if I had."

"Take a seat in the living room," Alex instructed, waving his hand toward the opposite room.

I had been friends with the males for scorns, but there was a big difference between my relationship with Jonah and Alex. Alex insisted on naming me by my title, on occasion calling me by my first name, whilst Jonah would opt to use my first as much as possible. Both were sticklers for protocol, but I expected them to relax when we were not in such a formal environment.

I followed his instructions, and the jazz became louder as I entered the living room. Their home was minimalist, with some valuable artefacts and photographs to decorate. Two shelves hugged either side of their unused fireplace, one filled with Jonah's many vinyls, while the other had an extensive collection of tomes organised neatly by size and colour. The walls were painted cream, while the glass coffee table and two brown suede sofas were the only other furnishings, save for the vinyl player in the corner. Stairs were on one side leading upwards, whilst a doorway led down to their converted basement.

The sound of Jonah's vehicle pulling into the driveway caught my attention. I listened as the engine stopped, the door opened and shut, and Jonah's impatient footsteps marked their path to the front entryway. Soon, he was inside in a flurry, hurriedly removing his boots.

"I thought you were lost. I went to collect you."

"I took a walk."

I noted that he had not changed and was still wearing his azure military uniform. However, the usually crisp and formal look had softened over the sol with the loosened edges of his jacket.

"As I had guessed since Travis was still idly standing outside your door," he raised his eyebrows, "not to forget your partially open window, of which I have stated before that such recklessness is idiotic."

"I am not going to die by climbing."

"But it might not be long before someone sneaks up behind you and stabs you right in the back," he grunted, removing his jacket to reveal his fitted black shirt and throwing it over the edge of the closest seat. I was sure his words had a double meaning, but thoughts of death were far from the evening's agenda. And the brown-haired beauty exacerbated all reasons to survive.

"Wardrobe!" Alex's voice echoed, and Jonah and I shared an amused look before he swiftly lifted the jacket and disappeared upstairs, returning minutes later.

"As long as they do not puncture the lungs, backstabbing would be more welcome than the guillotine," I said. "I am sure you understand my need to avoid my father's prying eyes."

"You may call me if you are scared."

I snorted, "Not scared."

Never scared. Never afraid. Soul of iron, heart of stone.

Jonah huffed a laugh of disbelief before he moved into the kitchen, declaring, "You are preparing a feast!"

"His Highness is hungry, darling," Alex answered, both kissing, "as shall be the bothersome boy we shall have to feed shortly."

They spoke of Freddie, whom Alex treated much a friend as a foe. A brother through bond, not blood, their simmering tension quite humorous to witness, and one that riled Jonah up a lot.

"Have you heard from Freddie?" I asked, joining them in the small kitchen. Alex collected dishes from the cupboard whilst Jonah casually leaned against the white marble counter, eyeing his keeper's every move.

"He was out with that fancie of his," Jonah remarked snidely.

"Do not be so uncouth," Alex tutted.

Jonah rolled his eyes, looking towards me, "It shall not last. It is but a passing phase, and once he has wet his cock enough, he will find someone else to enjoy his time with."

Alex piled the plates into Jonah's unprepared arms, forcing him to catch them before they dropped. "I am sure this one is nice."

"Nice she may be," Jonah stood straight, "but Zikan, she is not."

"She will soon discover that he is a libertine," Alex replied. "If you were so concerned, you would have told him to stop as soon as you found out."

"I am not concerned," Jonah peered at me with a soft grin, "because it shall not last."

With a clatter, Alex dumped several cutlery items on the plates. "Take them downstairs."

"On it," Jonah grunted, leaving the room with a humorous sway in his hips.

Alex raised his eyebrows at me. "I do not need the prince inspecting my work."

"I am not inspecting."

"It is how it feels," he answered, meticulously placing salad leaves into a mixing bowl with other greens. "It shall not be long, I promise. If you are so desperate for conversation, then speak with your commander."

Amused, I heeded his demands and left the kitchen, heading through to the basement door and down its stairs.

The basement resembled a mix between the Swedish Hygge style and a contemporary cigar room. Centred was a smooth acacia wood table, lined with eight apricot leather-backed chairs, was decorated with a black table runner and several same-coloured place mats. A long wooden sideboard backed heavily against the furthest wall. Atop it, four attentively placed glass chalices and two unopened bottles of red wine were in one corner, whilst a grey electric diffuser wafted a scent of citrus, black pepper and wood to replace the fictitious heady smoke palette.

Jonah was whistling to the music whilst he set the table for five.

"It is true about Eros then," I commented, noting the lack of sixth placement.

"Hm," Jonah's temperament soured, "I have tried to obtain more information, but there are far too many hoops to jump through."

"Fuck," I breathed, taking my usual seat at the far end of the small table, "I should speak to my father."

"It is too much of a risk," he replied. "Eros knew the dangers when he stepped into your father's office. All I know is he is on hunger strike, and it has been forty-eight hours of interrogations. He will not turn on us, but I fear that his life will be ended if he does not."

"My mother tells me he has been begging for his release."

He nodded. "Yes. Still, we must do as we always have and look forward for the integrity of the throne. I will be back shortly; make yourself comfortable."

Jonah left the room, leaving me to ponder the travesty of Eros' situation. He had been faithful to the cause since his father was murdered by mine scorns ago after a minor uprising over high taxes took place in London. His father had flocked the palace hallways with ten other males but was arrested and sentenced to death in the garrison. Sometimes, when I peered close enough, I could see the remnants of winter's old blood flecked on the walls.

In Earth winters, Eros had barely turned *nineteen* before he and his remaining family were exiled to Italy. Fortunately, my mother admired his, for I was sure life would have been miserable. Still, Eros had devoted himself to The Sanctuary of Amity and vowed to infiltrate my father's cause from the inside by joining the opposition.

And, at twenty-seven winters old, Eros was closer to having his name etched into a traitor's tome than basking in the warmth of his mother's arms.

Helga's arrival echoed a conversation from upstairs, but she did come down to the basement. With the rhythm of their tones, I closed my eyes, feeling nauseated from my aching head and the countenance of a dead Eros. I wondered whether I might stomach Alex's delicious food.

I drifted, the blanket of sleep coaxing me into its arms.

"Are you asleep?"

My eyes snapped open, and I wearily gazed at my cousin, who, beer in hand, peered at me with a smirk. He eerily mimicked a shadowed vampire with his cloaked attire of darkness, donning a black shirt, trousers, boots and an ankle-length coat. I was sure he would have sprouted fangs if he so revealed his teeth.

"Just resting my eyes."

He hummed sceptically as he yanked out the chair next to me and plopped down casually, balancing his bottle on its rim between his fingers and the walnut dining table.

"You are unwell."

"I am fine."

"Are you?" he raised his brows before swigging his beer and idly twisting the top between his fingers. "I heard about this sol."

"I am not so surprised," I shrugged, taking an unwanted sip of my drink and visibly wincing at its foul taste, "did you woo the human?"

"*Genie*," he corrected, finally letting go of the bottle to fold his arms, "Yes, she and I are very well acquainted."

"Hm, I am sure. That did not take you long."

"Not sexually," he tutted, tilting his chair onto the back two legs. "I expressed an interest in courting her, and she agreed. I shall marry her; she is a goddess above all other females who have graced this universe."

"You truly are infatuated with the human."

"Just because you have not met your fated one does not mean you can lower your opinion of mine," he half growled, sitting forward. "You will understand my feelings towards Genie once you have met her. That said, it does not mean you may take her from me - I would happily fight you to the death. She is *my* wife."

Freddie's words were heeded in warning, but I was only inwardly amused by his protective stance towards *Genie*. I felt like I was sitting next to a teenage boy who had only just wet his cock for the first time, but even so, I would not steal her. Unless I had the privilege of gazing upon her to find that she was my fated one. Only then would I fracture our friendship for such pleasantries.

His hand patted against his chest in three soft thuds, gaze glossing over, "She has thrown a leash around this libertine's heart. Empyreans, she is beautiful."

There was a subtle pause as he sat up, removing his phone from his pocket. Seconds passed until he found what he had been searching for and showed me an image of himself and the human. Ah, yes, I could understand why Freddie had become besotted with her. With lengthy blonde hair and striking blue eyes, she echoed the etherealness of angelic beauty.

"So, is such a captivating human attending the ball?" I asked, keeping my tone devoid of any flirtation so as not to impose that I was attracted to her.

"It is in progress," he replied, gazing a little longer before he put the contraption back in his pocket, back to swinging on the hind of his seat, "it seems the Commander is against all things *human*. But even he shall not get in the way of our courting. Plus, if he is to agree to the cross-racial mating laws finally being abolished, then it should at least begin with us."

"Us?"

"I suppose not so much you," he replied with a cheeky grin before he picked up the beer and swallowed a few gulps, "then again, I shall need to ask about the other."

"Who?"

"Genie's sister – best friend. Odd creature."

"Have you met her?"

Something was itching at his expression - hesitancy, maybe. I knew that finding a female destined to be his keeper was a lot, but Freddie meeting Genevieve's family would be a considerable extra commitment for him than he cared to admit. I wondered if even he understood such a burden his own life would be on hers once she fully understood who and what he was. Somewhat mortal-kind were it not for his Gods-bearing power. A forgotten prince who had forged alliances with the confederate-turned-enemy realm, only to lose rank by remaining loyal to his cousin's cause.

"Not yet," he answered hesitantly, "although the stories that Genie has spun are quite the tale. She tells me of these flare-ups... fainting spells that she has."

"So, whilst you have taken the prize of the crop, you have left me with the wilted outcast," I chuckled softly as the gentle thuds of feet descending the stairwell echoed. Even so, Freddie's sentimental nature rubbed off on me, and the mysterious female became a little appealing.

Empyreans, I needed to fuck.

Freddie laughed heartily, "No, I suppose I am not. She-"

"If you so much as snap the legs of my chair, *Frederique*, I will quite happily snap yours!" Alex seethed as he appeared first, placing the towel-wrapped casserole dish with a clatter in the centre of the table.

"Those minuscule hands could not even wrap around my muscular carves, *Alexandre*," Freddie snorted.

"Please do not start," Jonah tutted, placing several unopened beer bottles on the table before he sat. An addition of the mixing bowl of salad and a tray of freshly baked sliced bread joined the feast from Helga's hands.

Freddie reached out for the bread, earning a sharp slap on the wrist from Alex.

"You are impatient!" Alex sneered, taking his seat opposite Freddie.

Freddie patted his stomach. "I have starved for many hours just for this comfort; do not deny me my feast."

"Dramatic hellsworn," Alex muttered.

"Empyreans, be quiet!" Jonah growled, glaring at the two of them, whilst Helga and I subtly smirked at each other in amusement. "It is like being in the presence of two seedlings."

"And you are bound to one," Freddie retorted, eyebrows raised, but they dropped as Jonah's fury deepened. I was sure it was like staring into the soul of the God of War when being glared at by him. Freddie broke the eye contact first.

Alex took the towel, clenched it between his hand and the lid, and opened the pot, revealing the contents of a chicken casserole. Even with the nausea, my stomach grumbled lightly as I watched Alex plate up some food before handing me the plate. He then proceeded to pile the contents onto a plate for Helga, then Jonah, and finally, himself, before, satisfied, he sat back down.

"Alex," Jonah grunted.

"He is quite capable of feeding himself, darling," he replied, folding his arms as he stared down his nemesis.

Freddie, who I could not tell was amused or annoyed, picked up his fork and stabbed it into a carrot and a slice of chicken from the casserole dish. He then threw the food into his mouth, not even checking whether it was too hot, until he was haphazardly chewing on it, wincing.

"It is hot," Alex chided.

"I figured," Freddie grumbled, swigging his beer, "my tongue is now crisp."

"I suppose it is fortunate you are not prying it inside your-"

"-Alex!" Jonah stomped, slamming his hands down on the table, "If it were not for the importance of it, I might have postponed this damned meeting so I did not have to put up with incessant bickering."

Helga let out a laugh, which caused me to release the one that had been trying to roll out of my mouth. I was never truly sure what the meaning of found family was, but I could have easily said that the five around the table, plus Eros, were mine. I trusted every person with my life, and they trusted me with theirs.

"We should have at least said a blessing," Alex sighed. "It is a shame we are without our sixth."

"Once I have more information, we can enact a plan," Jonah replied, "Eros' capture only conveys the importance of how we must use our intellect to gain the upper hand, not find ourselves in situations without a plan of escape."

"Who caught him?" Freddie asked.

"Corvelli."

I could see the wrinkling of noses as everyone winced, knowing that such a brute was the worst being to have stumbled upon Eros' dangerous mission.

"Fuck," Freddie swigged his beer. "We need to get him out."

"As I have said, I am working on it," Jonah replied, shifting the topic. "What news of you, Helga?"

"Her Majesty will be out of residence starting next quarter," Helga told us, "and I believe His Majesty will also be flying out for an extended period."

"Vineyard purposes?" Freddie queried.

"Politics," she answered, "as we have discussed previously, His Majesty has been investing in future political parties, giving him a strong foothold on Earth. I should inform you that I was party to overhearing that he is making an arms deal in the Middle East in the next few moon cycles."

"He is a fool if he believes that our weapons are fit for purpose in human wars." I rolled my eyes.

"Our technology is much more advanced," Helga added, "your father's secret facility is mass-producing weapons to aid defence lines on both sides."

"Is he not endangering us more?" Alex asked.

"Oppressing," Jonah corrected, "ideal propaganda. Sell the weapons, declare that war is incoming to our people, offer to keep them safe by confining them to our boundaries until they know nothing but the fear that beats in their hearts."

I clicked my tongue, hating that Jonah was right. Gaining more control over those my father did and did not rule over would soon be in his hands.

"Your father is turning into mine," Freddie snarled.

"At least yours only sought control over petty uprisings," I replied, knowing there had been no war to fight in the Porton realm or Zika above rebellious causes. But, across a realm – *world* – where lands were split into countries and governed by the elite, Earth was rife with impending wars.

"He skinned a male alive," Freddie retorted, scrunching his nose up, "although I might not be surprised if your father will resort to worse than that. We have all seen the treason punishment list; none are a friendly way to die."

"Yet, you choose to break all laws by courting a human," Alex commented.

"Then I shall die a martyr," Freddie glared.

"You are no more than a zealot."

"Enough," Jonah grunted, taking a deep breath before he calmly said, "I think the sale of armaments is not enough to deter the thoughts of our people, and such deals can take cycles, even winters, to change the trajectory of this realm, which gives us ample time to act before he does."

Whilst Jonah was right, we were very unprotected when we arrived, and my father had done everything in his power to make a mark on Earth, which included kidnapping and forcing a human to teach him and his council the English tongue before he brutally murdered him in cold blood.

He forced the hand of a small vineyard owner into selling their wine business before the owner and his family disappeared from the face of the Earth. He had infiltrated government politics by manipulating local parliament leaders, and anyone who had whispered a word of my father's tyranny had found themselves shot, drowned, poisoned, and their families murdered until silence was all his victims could speak.

"Nothing of Her Majesty?" Jonah asked Helga.

"No," she answered. "She remains impassive toward the high-born political war." She looked at me. "Your father confronted Her

Majesty about the incident, but from what I understand, she did not shed any light that might implicate you."

"But, she would have disclosed something," I replied, knowing that my mother would not be a fool to lie to my father since he had already witnessed the after-effects of my dark power etched into the skin of my face.

"Unfortunately, I was not present," she answered softly, "but I know your father is aware. Anyone in the palace would have felt the wave of power which simmered from you." She laughed lightly. "I was a little surprised you could be so upset about not having your Kindred Spirit present and that you would erupt in such a way towards your mother."

I snorted, and the others chuckled lightly. "I was not upset. I merely stated that I was a prisoner who would remain trapped behind the palace's walls."

"Then, *find me my wife* was only out of wrath, not pleading desperation?"

"Seraiah cannot be desperate for love," Freddie grinned boldly. "He believes things outside duty are nothing more than fantastical ideals."

"I do not have time for such dalliances," I answered, not needing to explain myself again to the four who sat there why love was unwarranted amid tremendous political turmoil. And the only thing I might be described as being desperate for was my father's head on a spike.

"Speaking of *dalliances*-" Freddie grinned.

"Oh, here we go," Alex murmured.

"-I have an offer to bring to the table," Freddie ignored Alex's partial interjection.

"An offer?" Jonah feigned interest, sipping on his drink.

"I would like to invite my wife."

Jonah spluttered, whilst Alex rolled his eyes. "I saw that coming."

"No," Jonah disagreed. "I do not care if you bed her, marry her, have seedlings with her; you shall not bring a human into our world."

"And what about eradicating the cross-racial mating laws?" Freddie asked in annoyance, "Shall it be safe then?"

"The change in the scripture would state that should one prefer to live with humans, then they shall be granted to do so, but at the detriment of being banished," Jonah replied matter-of-factly, "there has been no discussion about humans residing in the settlement, especially not inside the home of our future king."

"Seraiah agreed," Freddie said, shooting me a pointed look. "It is his word above yours."

"Have you?" Jonah looked at me. "It is too risky."

"It is not your risk to bear," Freddie challenged. "It is my own."

"You have known her for less than two sols, Freddie!" Jonah growled, "You have never, not once, had a single amount of interest in any other longer than half a moon cycle, and this human shall be the same. You shall throw her aside as you have done with every other fancie of yours!"

"Jonah." Alex placed his hand on his keeper's forearm.

"I would quite happily take this knife and slice out your vile tongue!" Freddie stood up in aggravation, slamming his hands on the table with the knife in hand.

Jonah stood while the rest of us watched. Although the situation was serious, I was quite humoured by their constant, undeniable feud. It was not surprising, considering how often Freddie sought to fight against his boundaries, even when they were more fluid than my own.

"Why do we have to fight?" Alex grovelled, leaning his head back like he was praying to the Gods above, "Empyreans, save my soul."

"They might save yours, but they shall not save *this* despot,"

Freddie's glower intensified at Jonah.

"I shall never agree to such insolence as bringing a human into this settlement, and that includes any who are fooled by your charms," Jonah barked, "it would be like bringing her into the viper's den with all the beds of those other females you have christened."

I was surprised to notice that Freddie understood the meaning behind Jonah's words, knowing he did not care for the reputation that collared him. Bringing the human into our world could cause her more harm if she was not careful where she treads. I was pretty sure several females were pining for Freddie's attention.

He rounded his shoulders. "She is different, Jonah. Neither of you may believe me, but I have never felt anything like this toward another. If I cannot be with her and she cannot attend this solar rite, I will spend my time with her away from here."

"The trajectory of Seraiah's rise is more important than your infatuation."

"Nothing is more important than Genie," Freddie stated. "I am retiring."

"Freddie," Alex half-begged, but Freddie had already turned and stomped away upstairs, leaving us in the aftermath of silence and a half-eaten dinner.

"I-"

My speech was cut short as the noticeable sound of heightened voices had the four of us peering up at the ceiling. Jonah swore, rushing around the table and up the stairwell. But I, too, had identified the intruder.

"Commander."

Kaeltar.

FIVE

Whilst Corvelli was a formidable force, he was out of sight across Italy's seas and rarely stepped foot in the London settlement. Fraesiar Kaeltar, on the other hand, was a merciless brute driven by an aura of cruelty and power. He was as much a pawn in my father's game as I was, although he revelled in such subjugation, as it gave him a vast amount of authority to do as he wished.

Why would a tyrannical king deny a savage male the opportunity to release their wrath when it was to his benefit?

The stone coffer of fear shook in the depths of my mind, attempting to escape the iron confinements which held it down, but I could not free the unwanted distress. I knew why the male was at my door, and it only confirmed that my mother had disclosed some information about the anger which spawned from me inside her quarters.

"Is that your fucking velvet room?" Kaeltar laughed, "Empyreans, I knew you liked it up the arse, Commander, but Prince Frederique, too? I am surprised."

"Shut your wretched mouth," Jonah spat in reply. Alex stood and walked to the bottom of the stairwell, hesitating to go further. "Why are you at my house so late, Kaeltar?"

"I am sure you already know," Kaeltar chuckled, "I am here to collect the prince. Or maybe I should turn your... *humble* residence upside down. It would be a shame to permit my unit to look behind every nook."

"I shall not allow you to enter without a seal," Jonah countered, but the quick silence and paper shuffling only answered the fear all of us wished were untrue.

"Dear Commander," Kaeltar replied, "I do my work correctly. Unlike some... I shall give you five minutes."

Alex took that moment to shuffle up the stairs whilst Helga and I remained quietly in our seats. If I did not appear, I was sure that Kaeltar would be ecstatic to find the First Lady in the same room as us. It was not as though there was any other escape out of the basement, and Helga would need time and a distraction to make her way out of the house. Whilst she was trained like an assassin, she could not walk through walls, and the lounge room was far too small not to notice someone leaving.

I stood, and Helga whispered, "I would suggest you stay."

"This seal is falsified!" Alex shouted, whilst the crumpling of paper ruffled my ears. "He did not hurt Her Majesty."

"And were you in attendance at the time?" Kaeltar asked, "Because this seal was provided with evidence from Her Majesty herself. It seems that even His Highness can't escape the repercussions of ill-fated decisions at the hands of his own mother."

Whilst the seal could have been falsified, I could not argue against the words written on it, especially if my mother had rightly told the truth of the situation. It just so happened that my father could bend such truths at his own will, which meant that the punishments that would occur had been approved without any form of trial or delegation of my council.

"How do we know it is not falsified?" Freddie asked.

"Bold words," Kaeltar tutted, and I could picture him with his arms folded across his chest, "three minutes."

"I want to know how you retained information that he is here this evening," Jonah grunted.

"Dear Commander, there are eyes everywhere," Kaeltar answered with little more elaboration.

"Yes, there are," Jonah agreed in annoyance, "and I would not wish to reveal some of the misdoings that I am aware you have been up to recently."

Kaeltar barked with foul laughter, "Threaten me all you want, but such things shall not rid the legitimacy of this seal. Or did you expect that I should cower at your words? You might be the Commander, but I follow The General's orders. Two minutes."

"You only have the power to arrest him," Jonah replied matter-of-factly.

"I am quite aware of what I have the *power* to do," Kaeltar said cynically, clicking his tongue. "Empyreans, have you tied him up down there? Is rope play a fetish?"

A growl rolled off Alex's lips, and I could only imagine the echoed annoyance that Jonah and Freddie also felt. Rather than allowing the foul-mouthed cretin to continue his remarks, I rounded my shoulders, took a quiet yet deep breath and started to climb the stairs, appearing to see the darkling himself.

The brute was five inches over six, two inches above my height, and carried his weight in thick muscle, which jutted every edge of his black combat gear. An assault rifle was strapped to his back, whilst a retractable hand-sized baton hung from his belt – more a statement than a weapon, as if asserting his dominance.

He raised his eyebrows, lifting the thick scar which lined his forehead to his cheek, causing one eye to be discoloured, "Hiding in fear, Your Highness?"

I almost snorted at such irrelevant terminology, but that iron chain was beginning to show cracks as the stone coffer continued its attempt to be free. It was one thing being detained by The General, but another by Kaeltar. He was a male open to torture and fear-mongering and did not care about what consequences might come, especially not when his favourite mortal to harm was me.

I shifted towards Kaeltar, but my three brothers stepped before me. Kaeltar's snarky grin widened, gaze landing on Jonah like a bully having a seedling finally stand up to him.

He looked past them to me. "It's been quite some time since justice was last delivered to you."

"Let us go then," I commented impatiently.

"Seraiah," Freddie said.

I held my hand up to him. "Thank you for dinner, Alex."

Nauseated, I walked past the three of them and through the front door ahead of Kaeltar. Two vehicles were parked ahead, and six additional guards with armaments surrounded the nearby area. The air had grown colder, although I was sure it was the atmosphere instead of the cool summer night. I was unsure how long the punishments would last, and I was not ready for what would come.

The journey to the garrison was far too short, but I tried to remain passive as we took the elevator to the lowest level beneath the training floor - the vaults.

It was a place for detained soldiers who had broken rules or started unnecessary fights. One wide central corridor housed three glass-fronted cells on either side, with a seventh bigger one at the end. All were completely white, with hard, ribbed floor matting and smooth wall tiles resembling changing rooms at a swimming facility.

It seemed that my punishment would invite an additional audience alongside the other soldiers, as I noticed the two from the sol before, Jorey and Vandan, sharing one cell. I still did not know who was who, but one of them rushed forward to the glass, hands banging against

61

it.

"Your Highness!" he shouted, and I presumed him to be the follower. I kept my eyes forward as we passed, trying to remain impassive. "Why is the prince here? Let him go; he's done nothing wrong!"

"Empyreans, shut the fuck up, Vandan," another soldier following said, and I could hear something hard. I presumed an armament, hitting the glass.

"Fuck you, Maeson!" Vandan growled back. "Let my king go."

"Do you want to spend another night in here?" Maeson grunted. "I would quite happily deprive you of what meagre rations you have left until then."

"It seems even the treacherous prince still has followers pining at his feet," Kaeltar chuckled, earning an echo from those who followed us whilst the argument continued behind us.

I turned a blind ear as we arrived at the large cell at the end – walls created so thick the shield's energy could not be felt. Without access to my power, I could not protect myself from the onslaught of what was to come. The cell's lights were fluorescent white and were never turned off for the prisoner in residence, no place of comfort, no blanket or pillow to rest one's head, and the only place to relieve oneself was by a grid in the corner. And, if that was no hell-in-reality, to add to the torture of the inmate, an inaudible high-pitched frequency would be turned on that would make anyone's ears bleed.

Only the worst of the worst would find themselves in such torturous imprisonment.

And, in their eyes, that was me.

It was specifically built as a safeguard in case the monster inside devoured my soul completely.

"Welcome home," Kaeltar smirked. It had been four winters since I had last found myself in there, having attacked my father out of rage, which I had to admit was a good enough excuse to lock me away.

I would not survive in there. Not from the physical onslaught, especially not from my dark, treacherous thoughts tightly locked in their coffers. The longer I was inside the cell, the more my vitality would drain.

Kaeltar nudged me through the door, opened by a guard, and I could feel the immediate impact of having little access to the shield's energy. I did not notice that he had taken the baton from his belt, nor was I expecting its sharp rattle against the back of my skull. It was enough to send my knees to the bruising ribbed flooring.

A wounding kick to my stomach landed me on my side, and I grunted, forcing myself upward into fight mode. I might not have had full strength, but I was not going to back down against this sadist. I charged at him, uncaring of the fatality that it might bring, even if it was for a matter of pride.

"Oh, he wants to play," Kaeltar said. He caught my wrist as my fist soared towards him and rapidly brought his boot up to my ribs with a thud. I swore the dull crack it caused was audible as I stumbled back.

Kaeltar slipped the baton back onto his belt. "You are weak, Princeling."

"Fuck you," I spat, standing upright. "I will kill you."

He laughed, "Big words from a male who has a tantrum every time he doesn't get what he wants. Wrath, greed, pride. I believe they are cardinal sins."

"Only if you believe in a human god." I clenched my jaw. "Fight me, Kaeltar!"

"Patience, your time to die at my hands is yet to come."

He made the mistake of turning his back on me as I rushed toward him, ego overstepping logic. I did not quite expect the fist that whipped back at me, landing *crack* on my eye. My back hit the floor with a thud, and I stared unfocused into the bright light, listening to the echo of laughter, the closing of the door, and the dull thuds of shoes as they marched away.

I hated to admit that he was right. I was a walking cardinal sin.

The lights blurred in and out, brightening until they were too unbearable to look at, and I closed my eyes. After several deep breaths, I uncomfortably managed to pull myself into a sitting position, discerning the biliousness which throbbed from my head to the centre of my throat and into my bruised torso. It took moments to notice the frequency stroking my eardrums like the blunt edges of a cat's claw – just moments away from its strike.

I blinked away the phantom residue of kaleidoscopic lights from my sight and peered through the dark, opaque glass, which prevented others from being blinded by the searing light. I noticed an older male guard sitting on a foldable chair by the elevator, legs and arms crossed, and eyes closed. At least someone could find peace in the conflict.

Sucking in a deep breath, I tucked my shoulders back, let my eyes shut, and pulled myself into a meditative state. After several deep breaths, I transcended into the depths of my mind, arriving in the middle of a long, dark corridor, which twisted away at its end. I followed it, looping around several times until I met a crossroads. I took the left and continued, soon arriving in another corridor lined with numerous doors. Each represented memories I wished to keep locked away, but neither was my ultimate destination.

At the end, I stopped at the final door, placing my hand on the cool brass handle before turning and opening it into a desolate winter arboretum. Oak trees stood bare, the ground covered in inches of off-white snow, whilst towering grey stone walls imprisoned the enclosure.

Down a small verge, in the centre of the garden, was a stone circle with seven distinct chests, each carefully forged and bolted down with unbreakable iron chains. Each represented a singular emotion I had sought to lock away and bury.

Anger. Guilt. Shame. Grief. Hope. Fear.

And, *Love*.

I walked until I could see them closely, studying each lock to see if they were as intact as I had last left them. Grief and love were the most secure box, unmoving and dusted with snow, but it was gazing upon fear where I knew the cracks were wearing at the catch.

Not so impenetrable after all.

I knelt before the frost-coated chest, lined by globs of thick snow at its base, and tentatively brought my unsteady hand up to the ochre bolt until I settled it on the freezing metal.

Hot, fiery, distorted memories clawed at me, burning nothing linear in my mind.

"Seraiah!" A cacophony of different voices.

"Father, I am sorry!" The whipping of a belt against flesh, the cold, hard floor of a throne room, a scream of anguish ripping from my chest chasm.

"He is cursed! Do not let him pass through!" My father was near the portal to escape Zika, thick stone walls surrounding him, and guards did their best to protect him in fear of their demise.

"Help me, please!" I begged in pain on a wet cobblestone verge on my knees as I looked up at the disappointed face of my father.

An ear-splitting roar rattled from the barren depths of a dragon's chest.

Whip. Scream.

"You disgrace this family!" Back in the throne room, blood flecks on the floor, hissing through gritted teeth.

"He is scorched!" Sheika's voice to my left. Somewhere on Earth, eyes staring up at blue skies, as I could barely catch my breath through the pain.

Slash. Yelp.

"Lock him up!" My father commanded somewhere nearby, arms gripping me on either side and pulling me from the floor, sweat dripping from my forehead. The visibility of my scorched arm was horrendous to witness.

"No, please!" I muttered helplessly.

"Charles, he is our son." My mother's voice.

"He is no son of mine."

A scream of anguish left my chest, and the once blue skies were ashen grey, teeming with lightning and booming with thunder.

"Strap him down!" A hard, sharply cold metal bed beneath me. My body thrashed as I tried to get away from the hands that bound me. I screamed to be released, but no one's face was familiar. Too many strangers. Where was everyone? Freddie, Jonah, Alex. Andrieu, Marash. A pinch to my bicep followed the searing insertion of a serrated needle, puncturing the skin as debilitating liquid was released. And only then did I find my mother's disappointed face as I begged her to be freed.

"May the Gods bless his soul and help us relieve him of his burden." Sheika spoke in rhapsodic delirium somewhere to my right.

I tried to speak, desperately seeking help from someone else who might care, but I seemed only to find my father's angered expression. Focus became laborious, fracturing, wavering, as the cacophony of voices became disproportionately deafening.

Silence.

A shudder.

Coldness settled in the depths of my spine, and a faint ringing echoed in my ears as I pulled away from the coffer. I breathed heavily and looked around frantically for anyone else who might have crept upon me. But I remained in the arboretum, and the cracks on the lock had not shifted.

Standing unsteadily, I wandered to the other coffers, not touching any but checking for further splits. Once satisfied that nothing was out of the ordinary, I walked back towards the door at the top of the verge as the blizzard wind howled through the air.

Clang.

Shoulders tight, pausing in my step, I slowly turned to the noise.

Clang. Clang.

It took moments for me to notice one of the chains rattling loosely, and I rushed towards it, halting at the one box I had hoped would not see the light of sol – Anger.

The closer I got, the more the visibly intact lock rattled in the wind, but as I hesitantly moved around the coffer's back, I shuddered seeing its chain was on its last hinges.

Fuck.

The whoosh of a final gust of wind broke the seal, and I clambered to take hold of the fractured chain, tugging it tight. More memories swallowed me.

"Fuck you, Father!" tight hands grasped his neck.

"Lock him up!" A command from behind. Several arms took hold of my shoulders, and I was hauled away from my spluttering father.

"Get your hands off me!" Strength like no other cast the assailants aside, and I looked down at my shaky hands, one coated in darkness like a jaded tattoo.

A punch to my face, the hard floor greeting me, a grunt. The cheers and bellows of a crowd. Standing up, infuriated, I turned to my competitor, only to be face to face with myself.

"You are a fucking disappointment!" He said, but the voice belonged to my father.

I growled, leaping for him, only to encounter a sharp cloud of white dust. I coughed, trying to find my whereabouts, but grey smog obscured my vision. I heaved, finding a direction before I rushed onwards and emerged through the door of a busy tavern. There were no familiar faces, but all turned towards me, watching with a scrutinising gaze.

"What the fuck are you looking at?" I yelled.

"Seraiah?" A twinkling voice glittered in my ears, and I turned, seeing the red-haired beauty of Mareina, dressed in a green cloak and a hidden knee-length brown dress and boots just visible from its length. She rushed towards me and leapt into my arms, the two of us kissing before she pulled away. "Did you bring them?"

"Yes," I answered, handing her a rattling bag. But, as her hands wrapped around the material, I suddenly became hesitant, tugging it away. "No, you betrayed me."

"What?" she asked.

I looked at her, shouting, "You betrayed me!"

But Mareina was no longer standing before me. Instead, it was my father.

"Disappointment," he sneered, hand blasting across the skin of my face, and I was knocked back to the ground with a grunt.

"I hate you!" I screamed, looking back at him, but he had disappeared, too. Only the replica of me stood there, arms folded, gazing down at me with a smug expression.

"You betrayed yourself."

He tilted his head back, barking with laughter, and I growled, pushing to my feet before I jumped at him. But all I met was a pillow of snow beneath my body, back in my labyrinth, ears ringing.

Breath unsteady, I watched crimson meld with white, and I placed a shaky hand onto my earlobes, pulling away to study blood. Behind me, a resounding creek, followed by a clunk, and I whipped around to see that the chest of anger was no longer locked, nor was its lid closed.

The shock rattled me so much that I could feel and hear the echo of another crack on the fear coffer. I jumped to my feet, rushed toward anger, and used all my strength to close it, ignoring the shouts and screams that threatened to devour me.

I was able to close it and grab the broken chain, pulling each side together until I could reconnect them. I shut my eyes, took a deep breath, and concentrated wholly on fixing the chain, manifesting that the anger inside me was deeply buried, had no need to be felt, and was a worthless emotion when it came to obligatory decisions.

For our people. For my friends. For me.

Light flooded my lids, and I opened them, watching as the chain resealed until no movement could be felt. It was as pristine as grief and love, save for the snow. I climbed off the chest and stepped away, satisfaction rolling through me. A trickle of blood ran from my nose whilst my ears continued to drip, but I knew such side effects would be caused when the use of such inner power was necessary to prevent unnecessary spillages.

The blizzard ended, the evidence of my bodily prints on the floor disappeared, and I was left in the dark depths of my mind, shivering from the cold.

Bang.

The explosion shook the ground and rattled me in such a way that it knocked me off my feet and sent me hurtling backwards until I cracked my skull on the chest opposite. With a tilted view, I fuzzily gazed towards the reopened chest of anger, watching as black tendrils of smoke rose from it like the entrance to hell had just been opened. I could not move, paralysed from the blow to the head.

A stark white hand appeared on the box's rim before a figure hauled itself out, landing perfectly on its feet with a subtle thud. It was shrouded in black mist, but I could make out the onyx cloak it sported, hood neatly tucked over a concealed face. I could feel its impenetrable gaze before it started to walk towards me, and no matter how much I tried, I could not escape its advance.

Crunch.

Crunch.

Crunch.

Another crack on the fear lock for each step he took as my heart thudded. It knelt before me, white skin glimmering against its darkness. It raised its hands to the hood and pulled it back, terrifyingly revealing the male I dreaded him to be.

Golden skin turned crisp white, auburn eyes turned onyx, mirroring veins that wormed below them, and steel-grey hair that glistened in the concealed sunlight.

Crack.

Crack.

The chest of fear was loosening with each second that passed.

The male before me was everything I had sought to bury away, the monster who had engraved my memories with nightmares. The reason I was the cursed prince.

My ultimate foe and my dreaded ally.

A hellion. A shade. A demon.

My demon.

Me.

"It has been quite some time, Seraiah," he chuckled darkly, reaching over to dust whatever flecks of snow, blood or dust he could find on my shoulder, "quite fascinating that you lie against love." He patted the chest behind me. "When it is such an emotion, you have yet to bear."

He reached down to straighten my shirt collar, but as I tried to move from him, my mouth could not release the words it wished.

"Shh," he whispered mockingly, the corner of his lip rising, "You know it is rumoured that when someone creates such a concrete defence, over time cracks shall appear until an orifice large enough cannot even stop the escape of demons that have lined up at their walls."

"Seraiah?" a male voice echoed above, and the two of us tilted our heads upwards to seek the person who had called my name.

"Now I am free, I will gladly watch every box break open," my malevolent doppelgänger chided, looking at me with an intolerable smirk on his face, "all the fragments seeking freedom and ripping you apart from the inside out until you know nothing but the treason you gifted to your soul. And only then shall you come to me, begging that I save you from it all."

"Seraiah!" the male voice echoed, and I realised Jonah was calling me from the outside.

"Time to wake up, Prince Seraiah."

The labyrinth crumbled like the inner sanctum of a matrix until I blinked open my eyes to see a pair of clothed knees kneeling before me. I had collapsed onto my side at some point, and it took me a few moments, or maybe even less, to tilt my head up to look at my commander's worried face.

"Seraiah, can you stand?" he asked breathlessly, his voice sounding distant, like I was trapped underwater. I noted the sol-old stubble on his face and his unkempt uniform, which told me he had rushed to the vaults.

"How long has it been?" I grunted, mouth like the Sahara desert, face cracking with the dryness of blood.

"Your mother demanded your release," he replied, ignoring my query as he helped me stagger to my feet, "my father falsified the seal - Hellsworn motherfucker. Do not worry; he will be reprimanded. Let us get you home."

I was close to vomiting from the extreme dizziness and vertigo, almost wondering whether I was being saved or whether it was all in my head.

I was sure that whatever punishment his father served would not echo my own, most likely given a fair warning, or maybe The General would have to issue some sort of official apology. Most likely, he would have defended himself by saying it was to protect my mother, although I was sure he got his pleasures from the pain he sought to give me.

And not forsaking the open chest of anger, which would take a lot of work to close, especially if such a dark being had been released from its chamber. His eerie face impaled itself in my thoughts, wondering when I would next bear witness to him. If such a chest had opened, would my anger be simmering until I could not control the impending outburst?

"My prince!" Vandan shouted as I clung to Jonah, stumbling heavily towards the elevator.

"Not now, Vandan," Jonah grunted, holding me tightly.

"I will seek justice for you!" Vandan shouted, and I paused to look at him.

His eyes widened, and he stepped back, gasping a little. Jorey gently rose from the floor on which he was perched.

"Do not waste your pity on me," I grovelled, not wanting another life to be taken for an uprising against my father, nor for defending me.

Jonah continued onwards, but Jorey's voice echoed. "I surrender to you, Your Highness. I will do what it takes to defend your position and ensure that you sit on the throne."

Jonah and I ignored his interesting change of mind, but I could hear Vandan whispering, "Oh, now you changed your mind?"

"He doesn't deserve that!" Jorey replied, "And I fucking hate Kaeltar."

"We all hate Kaeltar," Vandan snorted.

"Maybe we should put more prisoners in the vault," Jonah murmured.

"Hm," I replied, concentrating more on not collapsing rather than what the two males in the vault were arguing about. I knew an uprising was slowly happening with the soldiers, but I would not be part and parcel of martyrdom to conscript more to our rebellion.

SIX

Sols filled with vivid dreams and hallucinating nightmares passed as my time awake was limited by slumber. I did not hear a word from my mother or my father, but the celebration of my solar rite remained scheduled for those so-called *appearances* my mother so adored.

When I was awake, I strategised for the event using every bit of evidence we had collated over winters to create the one dossier that would have the council scrambling to save themselves. At the same time, townsfolk would panic, unsure of where their loyalties lay.

And then, they would choose me.

The beginning of an uprising.

A rebellion-turned-revolution.

And the climactic end to my father's reign would finally begin.

It is hereby announced that Seraiah II of Zika is King.

I chuckled at the thought, and so did that dark, treacherous male deep inside the caverns of my mind. Surprisingly, such an unwanted being had remained silent since its freedom, but I had not sought to return to the arboretum to try to close a chest that I was unsure I had the strength to seal. I knew what it took last time, and I suffered greatly for it. I was sure my malevolent doppelgänger would prevent it.

I shivered, feeling a little fearful - *crack* - fuck. No, not... not that.

I felt apprehension at what might happen should I lose control of my rage entirely. Would I be able to handle it as it conspires to be free? Would Jonah be able to stop it from overwhelming me completely? Would I be able to stop it?

As the heir to the throne, I did not need useless emotions, nor did I need rage in order to make others understand my point and receive what belonged to me. There was a reason why I chose to entomb seven distinct parts of myself.

Still, I would persevere.

On the morning of my solar rite, Freddie greeted me at my door.

"Good morning, *birthday boy*."

"Far too much time spent around that human," I jested, noting his use of the English language as I stepped out into the corridor, leaving the door ajar.

"Shall I call you a solar rite male? Or, solar rite seedling?" he chuckled, eyeing my outfit, "dressing for the part this sol?"

"A prince must look good for his people," I announced, as though my mother had taken over my speaking ability. I had opted for a fine cerulean-dyed suit embroidered in gold with a white open-collared shirt, embellishing the house colours as proudly as my life bringers would want. But it was not the ceremonial outfit they would prefer. "And you look like you are about to marry."

He wore a head-to-toe crisp ivory suit embellished in golden accents.

"It is a big sol," he grinned proudly.

"You have invited her?"

"Of course," he smirked, his eyes washing over the surprisingly empty hallway for any sign of eavesdroppers. "It shall only add to the sol's entertainment. Of course, please do not mention this to our dear commander. I would quite like to witness the look on his face."

I shook my head in amusement, although it was not as though I would believe the male not to go against Jonah's wishes.

"I cannot wait to introduce you to her," he continued, a smitten look crossing his expression that seemed to give him an astounding lining of rouge on his rich brown skin, "you will approve of her, I have no doubt."

"I am sure, but it is not I who will need to give you approval," I replied, knowing that he would understand the repercussions of his actions by bringing a human into our world. But I also knew he stood firmly by his morals. It had been less than a quarter since he had met her, and he would already risk *everything* for her.

"She is worth it," he smiled, then stood back so we could walk toward the entrance hallway. "I think you may be quite enamoured with her sister."

The timbre of a Renaissance symphony resonated from the orchestra, amplified with each step we took. I snorted. "Unless my fated one walks through that door, I shall not consider another."

"I am sure you are getting erectile dysfunction," Freddie chuckled, patting my upper back, before he pulled me closer by my shoulders, whispering, "At least, sate your cock. It will do you some good. One night."

I tutted, "You are a devil."

"I would not be doing you justice as your brother," he grinned, letting go of me.

"I will think about it. We have a long sol ahead before I decide to take someone to my bed. If I take this sister of hers, it would be like declaring I have found my wife. I can only imagine the uproar disrupting the entire sol, even more than what will happen with your human."

"*Genie*," he corrected sharply. "She is aware that there are tensions at the house and that her presence might cause some issues." I almost interjected. "I can see you are worried that I have spilt our power and heritage secrets. She knows nothing of Zika but understands you are from an aristocratic line."

In the grand foyer, the jangle of keys from a pocket caught my attention, and the two of us watched Jonah dash up the stairwell to meet us. He was dressed in his full sapphire ceremonial regalia, with not a single hair on his head out of line. I did not dare to say it aloud, but he resembled his father in such smart attire.

"Good afternoon."

"Indeed, it is good," Freddie grinned.

"I cannot understand what you are so excited about," Jonah said, raising his eyebrows. "You have a new *wife*... unless you have decided to end that absurdity."

"Things have not changed," Freddie replied sharply before he tucked his shoulders back, "can I not be excited that my dear cousin here will-" he whispered. "-finally get his retribution? A sol that has taken far too long to arrive, has it not?"

Good save from Freddie.

Jonah eyed Freddie before he nodded and looked at me. "At least the bruising on your face has disappeared."

"My ribs are still black," I pointed out, having looked at them again before I had bathed, although the pain had almost withered. It was a shame I did not bear the scars my body dared to reap, for then my people would know how I had suffered at the commands of my father.

Jonah looked less than impressed. "We will get our justice. It is time for you to make your entrance. Do not fuck it up."

"Thank you for the faith," I gave an exasperated look before a jovial smirk lifted on my face, "Do not worry; I shall be on my best behaviour."

"Our guards are on standby should anything arise," he said quietly, "whether the celebration continues or not. You are safe, and we will protect you."

"Come on, let us party!" Freddie roared, pulling me away from Jonah, who was obtaining his professional facade.

The hallway was quiet, save for the guards and workers on duty, whilst the music vibrated the surroundings through the tall, closed doors. The entrance to my father's wing was to the left of the room, guarded by three males. I wondered what routines he cared to go through to prepare for his loathed son's solar rite. Hopefully, a razor would be brought down his neck and nick the right part to render him dead.

It would be a shame not to have such a death on my hands.

Soon, Fulk, the Master of Ceremonies, announced my arrival, and I entered the room to a gentle hush of music and chatter from attendees, most from local houses. It seemed that even elders from across the world were also present. Whilst everyone bowed on my arrival, I noted the reluctance from my father's council. Still, they bowed, as it was a given right for those of a higher rank to be greeted in such a manner.

"Shall I smack them for their disdain?" Freddie jested, the two of us subtly smiling. I wandered and greeted many of our people as the soft strings of violins started a quadrille. And, soon, Freddie and I sat at a table near the garden exit, sipping wine and awaiting the dreaded arrival of my father.

A faint thud of anticipation sat in my chest. Decades of torment and distress that had wrought my fleshed heart into unwavering iron would meet their climactic ending. Finally, I would see the justice my father so desperately deserved handed to him from yours truly.

Happy solar rite to me.

His arrival did not come soon enough; we all stood as the doors opened with a loud thud. Everyone turned to look at my life bringers. Not a single person was hesitant to bow and lower their gaze. Except for me, who towered, watching the dark aura that lingered around them like a desired disease. However, I could see my mother's once-pure aura fighting for some air beneath its heady presence. My father's sharp gaze was impenetrable as he looked down at everyone through his nose.

Pathetic vermin.

It did not take him long to find me. The harshness only deepened as he tucked his shoulders back, with my mother feigning a smile on his arm.

"Please, enjoy the festivities!" my father called to them all, nodding to Fulk as they waded towards their designated table. The council swarmed them, most likely speaking terrible words about my lack of socialising since taking a seat. Or maybe for the ceremonial outfit which remained hanging in my closet, as I must have looked far too casual for a king-to-be.

Then again, it seemed none would ever allow me to be king if they had it their way.

I turned towards Freddie, noticing he was lingering on unanswered messages on his phone, presumingly from Genie.

"Has she not arrived yet?" I asked, sipping my wine.

"Has *who* not arrived yet?" Jonah's voice spilt in from behind, and I felt my face pale as Freddie's head whipped up in our direction.

Shit. I could see Freddie's bewildered expression, but I decided to remain calm as I turned to Jonah, who had his hand on the back of the chair beside mine.

"I asked *who*?" Jonah repeated sternly.

"Nobody," Freddie replied in my stead, but there was not enough nonchalance in his tone to hide something this big from Jonah. And, I knew the male already had the answer as infuriation and, possibly, the etchings of fear flared in his eyes.

"Do not tell me you brought that fancie of yours here?" Jonah said

79

harshly, turning a few close-by heads who were curious about the drama, "Empyreans, Freddie, you are-"

Freddie's phone buzzed and, with zero care for the rage flying from Jonah's mouth, he stood with a wry smile, "-I guess it is time for you all to meet this *fancie* of mine."

"No!" Jonah growled, standing before Freddie. "You went against my orders! Do not be so selfish." He whispers. "This could ruin everything we have worked for."

"Tough shit," Freddie glowered, keeping his voice low, "and if I so hear you speak of her in such a way again, especially in front of her, I shall happily kill you. In fact, it would be a great honour."

Freddie stormed off, and Jonah ran a frustrated, shaky hand through his perfectly styled hair before he turned to me with a twisted grimace. "Did you know?"

My mask wore thin with Jonah, and he could see right through the cracks.

"Empyreans, Seraiah," he seethed through his teeth, "I pegged him for a fucking fool, but not you, too. This... This fucks it all up. I am not prepared for a human amongst our ranks, not this sol. Not this sol of *all*."

He fiddled with the lapel of his mic, mouth opening and closing as he debated what to say to whoever was listening on the other side. I supposed I had not considered the havoc it would cause him. The lines of frustration carved into his ageing skin became more noticeable with the added stress we had inflicted.

He dropped the mic, looking at me. "Do not let this incident be a distraction."

Focus on the plan.

Jonah turned and marched through the crowd, most likely still stewing over how he would inform his security that a human was about to enter the premises. I was sure he would be infuriated when he discovered a second.

Finally, the human arrived, and many heads turned to see the beautiful, mysterious Genevieve clinging to Freddie's arm. A floor-length silk emerald dress clung to her willowy silhouette, accentuating every subtle curve of her body. She and Freddie were like a singular gem-encrusted dagger, simultaneously emphasising the beauty and danger they posed.

I could feel some movement on the marble palace chessboard as the knight finally took its move. As my eyes swept to the officials' table, they landed on a raging general, then on my jaw-tight father and my impassive mother, all watching the human.

Good move, Freddie.

With each step they took in my direction, the crowd parted and gazed upon the angelic yet commanding female until their attentions returned to their conversations. It seemed that she did not even notice she was the centre of attention. But if she did, she revelled in it.

As they arrived at the table, Genevieve's soft gaze shifted from Freddie to me, a beaming smile on her face.

"Hello," she said in her English dialect, gracefully curtseying. I could see the shocked faces of eavesdroppers as they noted Genevieve's language. And, whilst I was somewhat fluent in the language, I had to remember that I had to change certain words and phrases so as not to cause her discomfort or confusion. Or the other human, wherever she was.

"Hello," I replied.

Her tender gaze tilted to Freddie. "Aren't you going to introduce me?"

Freddie's cheeks were aflame with how smitten he was by her before he cleared his throat. "This is Seraiah. Seraiah, this is Genie."

Freddie's use of the language and West London elocution were far more polished than mine.

"I have heard many things about you," I said smoothly, although I supposed it was a partial lie, as I had rarely spent time with Freddie outside the library and the Amity meeting.

"I hope nothing too bad," she blushed, holding onto Freddie's arm a little tighter. "This is a great party; you must feel so lucky to be surrounded by all these people."

Very lucky, I thought sardonically. The smile remained, "Yes, it is quite extraordinary to see everyone here to celebrate. However, only a few of them are invitees of mine."

"Keep your friends close and your enemies closer," she jested. Freddie and I laughed, knowing just how right she was.

Jonah used that moment to return, standing by my side, ignoring Freddie like he was the friend he had fallen out with at a seedling academy. He chose only to speak in Zikan.

"This has caused a fucking uproar," he grovelled pointedly at Genevieve.

"I should hope you choose wisely how to speak of my wife," Freddie growled in our own tongue.

"You have broken the law, Freddie," Jonah said, his eyes shifting to and from Genevieve, who seemed both intrigued and confused about what was happening. "We could have done this simpler."

"We needed to make a statement."

"Yes, on any other sol," Jonah snarled, "any other sol than Seraiah's fucking solar rite, Freddie." He lowered his voice. "We make plans for a reason. We stick to plans for a fucking reason. And, *you* have added more turmoil to this one by bringing this... this human here like you have the *right*."

"I have the right," Freddie answered, "why can I not fall in love, hm? Because of a fucking law?"

"I did not even stop you," Jonah laughed mirthlessly. "Empyreans,

Freddie, I let you court her; why was that not enough?" To himself. "I should have told Zaidaen to get you off that fucking tube."

"So, you do have a guard following me?" Freddie chuckled in disbelief. "I knew you did not trust me."

"Earth is not safe."

"Yet, here we are, scorns later."

"I'm Genie, by the way." Genevieve cut in with her offered hand, halting the two whose quiet argument drew more attention than needed.

Jonah, taken aback, cleared his throat, placing his hand in hers. "Jonah."

"Ah, that makes so much sense," she grinned brightly, "don't worry; I promise we won't cause any issues."

Empyreans, Genevieve. If I thought I had been the one to shoot both Freddie and me in the foot, then she had only added to the festering wound.

"*We?*" Jonah was bewildered.

"Arri is no doubt drunkenly spewing up in the toilet," Genie laughed, unaware of the callous storm rising in Jonah, landing a gentle hand on his arm, "I should actually go and find her."

Arri.

"Empyreans, hellsworn fucker," Jonah spat in Zikan at Freddie, although his tone was only loud enough for us to hear. Genie flinched away from Jonah, tucking herself into the nest of Freddie's aura.

"Be careful, Jonah," Freddie said, returning to English. "Quite a few ears are listening to our conversation, and some might compare you to your father because of how you are seething right now."

The words were as heavy and brutal as a boulder falling from a cliff, and we watched as Jonah visibly winced at the comparison to his father. I had to admit that even Freddie's words were rather harsh in the situation, but the language and derogatory terms over the past moons had built up a snarling energy in Freddie.

Jonah did not even look at me, and while I could sense his defeat, he bowed his head and stormed across the ballroom to its in-house exit.

After a moment, I told Genie, "Do not worry about him. He is more worried about the security of this place. You should try to enjoy the party."

"Excuse me, Your Royal Highness," Fulk appeared to my right and bowed. "I believe it is time for you to make your speech."

Focus on the plan.

"Ah, yes," I nodded, opening my jacket pocket to find the dossier, only to find myself coming up empty. I pressed my lips together, thinking about where it could be, before remembering that I must have left it in my bedroom. "I shall need ten minutes."

"Of course," he bowed, walking back through the crowd.

"I shall find your friend and return her," I told Genevieve.

She smiled. "Great, you can't miss her. She's wearing a big gold dress."

An interesting contrast to Genevieve's emerald one. I supposed Freddie was right; a little foul play could not harm me. Perhaps she was beautiful enough for me to fuck her in celebration of the events that were about to unfold.

I bowed. "Enjoy the party."

I greeted a few people as I sauntered through the crowd, entering the sparse grand hallway before taking the stairwell up to the east wing. I was surprised to note the lack of guards, although I knew they were there – Always watching.

I wondered where our second human guest might be. The bath-room in the east wing seemed clearly signposted, but the door was wide open, and no soul was inside. I half-shrugged as I continued onwards, but stopped instantly as a hazy pool of twinkling golden light shimmered from the end, which housed my bedroom.

It was like some sort of hypnotic mirage, as though I had entered one of my dreams and, with each step of tentative uncertainty, the sparkling illusion formed into the breathing flesh of a mortal-kind female. Her delicate brunette ringlets fell gracefully against a flowing satin ball gown, golden in its tint, which glittered in the light that radiated from the end of the hallway.

Crack.

One of the tightly locked, unfamiliar chests tugged in my mind, and the iron lock splintered a fraction with every step I took toward the obscured beauty. An open window inside my room brushed at her hair, revealing soft, honeyed cheeks kissed by sunlight. But I could not gaze upon her features as I subconsciously reached for her.

Something had entranced me. As though at any moment, the female might just wilt and disappear, a temptation sent from the Gods so that they can laugh at my desperation. Only sols before had I been blessed with beholding such delicate locks, but I felt apprehensive that this was not my–

I could not say it. As soon as those words left my mouth, the apparition would disappear, and I would be left in the cold air of the warm corridor.

A dark rumble of laughter echoed, and I knew it belonged to the entity which had emerged from the locked chest of anger, waiting by the coffer that despairingly yearned to be free.

Love.

I might have laughed, too, were it not for the strings of longing that tugged so desperately at my stone heart, palpitations of anticipation loosening its durability. And, still, I remained spellbound by a female who remained a faceless, alluring mystery.

I stopped behind her, standing so close that I feared that if I reached out to touch her, she might just disappear. But, as though time had stopped, the echoes of music and laughter of distant voices clashed together, and reality returned without compromise. And, still, she remained.

After a few subtle breaths of encouragement, I cleared my throat, and the tension in her shoulders instantly rose. There was not much of a pause before she languidly turned towards me. The blush staining her cheeks increased across her silken button nose, and her stunned azure eyes, flecked in delicate gold, gazed directly into mine.

Empyreans.

Click.

I could not breathe.

Click.

It was as though I had beheld an angel for the first time.

She bewitched me.

Creak. Creak.

A goddess radiating in the natural light, which embellished her aura and lit her honey skin.

Utter perfection.

Every dream I had been graced with over the winters became clear to me instantly.

Every interpretation replaced with her.

Those enchanting eyes, that lustrous hair, those pink, soft, damp lips. She was the first raindrop in a desolate desert, the velvet sky at twilight when all else had been dark, the heady gaze of the moon upon a once rocky lake.

She was perfection incarnate.

The breathing muse of flawless divinity.

A Goddess.

And I knew in that moment it was her. The one I had desperately

sought for, yearned for and *prayed* for.
 The one the Gods had vowed was mine.
 She *was* mine.
 My Kindred Spirit.

Crackkkkk.

SEVEN

I could feel the coffer remaining steady yet faltering faster than any had before. And, I was sure with every moment I spent with her, the foundations would break until that chest would fall open. And even I was unsure what such a feeling would contain.

It had not occurred to me how long I had stared at her, but the shuffling of feet, followed by the closing of a door at the other end of the corridor, ended my entrancement. And, still, she remained - real, soft, *mine*.

Gentle laughter twinkled from her mouth as melodic as a bird at first light, awakening me from a century of misery with such radiance. Had the Gods sent this being to mock me? It was an offer that seemed as much the devil's advocate as it did the promoter of faith. Had she so blatantly existed in front of my nose all this time? Living as a human. She was... human, was she not? Something – her energy? – It seemed so ethereal. But, then again, the thread of fate had entwined herself around us, and what else would be *ethereal* if not Kindred?

I needed to touch her, even if it was just to feel her skin against mine.

"Seraiah," I offered my hand.

Eyes locked again, she pulled her lip nervously between her teeth, punishing them and me silently. And, I pined to kiss her, to taste everything that I had been waiting for my entire life. It was as though I had been wandering without access to water for a lifetime, and the mirage had finally become a haven right before me.

Heart thudding, gaze locked, she placed her hand into mine, and tingles of delicate energy ran through my body. The thrum of it washed over my fibres, sating me like it was my first feed. The question of her humanity returned. It almost felt like... Rapidfire. But she seemed unaware, and I was sure it was just the bond between us.

I lifted it to my mouth, tattooing the palate of her skin on my lips, lingering just seconds too long to gaze at the wonder in her eyes. But, with reluctance, I released her, and she flexed her hand before placing it beneath her other, discreetly stroking the skin with her thumb.

I felt something more than this new foundation of unspoken longing towards her. It was an ingrained, deep need to become one with her, to sate every impulse with the satisfaction of my flesh inside hers, to hear her breathy moans as I brought her to the height of pleasure she deserved, over and over again.

Lust. That was a word I was sure about. I was not capable of loving another, but I could easily lust after her. Yet, the idea of her seeking such affection elsewhere, to be *loved* by another, caused that festering anger to ripple.

She is mine. She belongs to me - no one else.

Masking my inner turmoil, I cleared my throat and spoke. "I do apologise. I..." But I stopped when I noticed the bewilderment on her face. And, through the haze of such an exquisite meet, I was reminded that she, the rare beauty before me, must have been *Arri*. She wore the dreadfully described *big, golden dress* that Genevieve had spoken of. Not describing how it hugged her hips where my hands should have been before it pillowed outward and draped down to the floor, where I should have knelt. Not describing how *Arri* radiated even more so in it, bearing it like the regalia that belonged to a princess.

I switched my tongue. "I am sorry. You must be Arri."

"Yes," she whispered, noting the slightly slurred edge to the 's'.

"You are Genevieve's friend."

"You know... you know Genie?" she stumbled.

Not really.

"Yes, she is betrothed to Freddie."

"Betrothed?" she squeaked, her shoulders pulling back in defence. The cutest wrinkle beaded the bridge of her nose. "They have only known each other for five minutes... she can't marry him."

Empyreans, she was adorable. Fiery, but fucking adorable.

And, of course, I had minced my terminology a little, but technically, it was true. They were practically married with the way Genevieve entered on Freddie's arm. All that was required was the signing of the dossier. Either that or my father would sentence the two of them to death for breaking the law. I did not want to think about that.

"You are quite hilarious," I appeased. "She is not getting married. I should have said they are courting each other."

"Courting?" she replied in shock, "do you know what year this is?"

Was it too soon to fall in love with her? *Crack.*

Nope, I was not falling for her. It was all lust and some affection, but nothing as trivial and soul-bearing as love. We were fated, tethered to each other; it was natural to feel a pull, but we did not have to declare that we loved each other. Duty and honour above it all, even if it meant making harsh decisions that might hurt someone, especially her.

But... I could not hurt her.

"You are mocking me," I replied humorously, "because of my accent and way of words."

"It is a little outlandish," she pointed out, laughing as I feigned shock at her words. It was refreshing to have someone speak to me in such a way outside of the dissonance of hierarchy. "I've not heard someone talk about courting before."

"I think it should return. It is a little nicer than dating, is it not?"

"I don't know," she answered. "I don't date."

Good. I would never allow another male to lay his hands upon her, or else I might gladly rip their throat out with my blunted canine teeth. Empyreans knows how I would will them to resharpen so that I could do it.

Concentrate, Seraiah.

"A beautiful woman like you would surely have many men lining up at your door."

"Oh, how many times have you used that one?" she laughed, and I realised she thought it sounded like a pickup line that a drunkard might say when trying to lure someone to their bed. I *was* trying to lure her to my bed. In fact, I was very close to it, and maybe no one would notice if I took hold of her. The two of us disappearing into the room for hours... sols... forever.

My cock hardened. Although, I had noticed how rigid it had been since I first gazed upon her sultry flesh, still battling against the restraints of my pants. She would notice if her eyes just peered down.

It is all yours, my fated one.

She swayed from one foot to another, and I decided it was time to move the conversation onwards – If only to ignore the itching need for her to prevent further casualties. And, by that, I meant throwing her up against the wall, stripping her bare and fucking her, with full consent, of course.

"How much have you drank today, Miss...?"

"Kinsley," she finished, "do I seem drunk?"

A little. Enough for me to wonder what kind of refreshments had quenched her thirst on the drive over. Did she enjoy drinking? Could I take her to my vineyard to drink wine in the fine Italian sun and eat homemade pasta? Oh, how elegant she would look under the pondering sun, glowing in all its radiance.

"No," I lied with a convincing smile, "but, before I left Freddie and Genevieve, she informed us that she would need to find her friend because, as she put it, 'she was no doubt drunkenly spewing up in the toilet'."

She gasped, "I was not, I was just... I was admiring the view."

"The view?"

"From the bathroom."

Such a view from the east wing bathroom was mesmerising, seeing out over the gardens but hidden by opaque glass so that no one from the outside could see in. Not to forget the ornate mirror, which provided an ample reflection of the views from the toilet. If I were so beautiful, I, too, would admire the view.

"Of yourself?"

"Myself?"

"Yes, you were in the bathroom down the hallway," I replied, pointing in its direction. "It has quite a large mirror."

She understood quickly enough to offer me a playful glare and walked into the hallway, out of my territory and into my life bringers. But still, I did not seem to have offended her as she waited for me.

"Allow me to escort you back to the ballroom," I offered before hopping into the room. My newfound adrenaline washed over me as I needed to be close to her for a while longer, before reality took its place. Taking the dossier, I swiftly walked back into the corridor, noting the curious look on her face as I shut my door.

"My speech," I told her. But I did not add that it was an incredibly masterful piece of writing that would change the house's stakes. That being said, I was not sure that I ever wanted her to be party to any of the goings-on inside the house. No, that would be a secret I would bear... until the time was right – if it ever were.

"What for?" she frowned.

I smiled at her confused, petite face. "My birthday."

"Oh," she replied, realisation slowly hitting her, "oh!"

Adorably innocent. No, I definitely would not tell her anything that would rip that away from her.

"My mother insists that I make one now that I am old and decrepit," I joked, although really, my life bringers would insist I make a speech no matter my age.

Her gaze tilted down my body, and I allowed the moment for her to take me in, for I was hers, and she was mine. She could observe me forever if she permitted me to do the same for her. I was rather eager to rip that dress off and was starting to think how ridiculously oversized it actually was.

I cleared my throat, biting back a smirk. Her eyes zipped straight up to mine, body slightly to attention, and I gestured for us to take the back way to the ballroom.

"What is with the blue and gold colour scheme?" she asked. *Small talk, I see.*

"They are our family colours. Do you not like them?"

"I do," she replied, "it's just everywhere, even on you now... and on your painting in the entrance."

I grimaced that she and all others had to witness such impudent decorations to assure visitors that we were the ideal family. It was painted when our feud was at its worst. A portrait of my life bringers and myself, and if someone looked closely enough, you can tell, to some degree, that none of us were in the same room when it was commissioned.

Not that she needed to know any of that.

"I hate that portrait."

"Why?"

"What better way to tell everyone we are royalty?" I skirted around the real excuse, although she was even more amused to have another truth. Whilst Freddie had informed Genevieve that we were merely aristocrats, I presumed that such a message had not been relayed to her friend. "I am surprised you have yet to guess, Miss Kinsley."

"Are you related to The King?"

I laughed heartily. But, of course, she would believe I was related to the British throne. While I wanted to tell her we could not be so different from it and not even human, I felt like I was revealing more secrets than they were worth. Some secrets needed to remain so until trust was earned on both sides.

"The British king? No, no... let me just say that we are aristocratic nobles, and we shall leave it at that." I noticed she was still in awe, as she had not proceeded to follow me. "Are you coming?"

"Should I curtsey?" she asked, and I smirked playfully, "are you... what are you then?"

I paused. "A prince." Better the truth now than when she entered the ballroom.

Part of me wondered whether she might have screamed or bowed mercilessly at my feet, but an unexpected laugh rattled from her, echoing down the empty corridor.

"Well, Your Highness, I'm sorry for being so crude."

"Crude?" I replied, unsure whether she understood its meaning. "That is not a word I would use to describe you. How are you *crude*?"

No, I would use other words to describe such radiance as you, but never crude.

Her feet moved again, and we continued up the corridor towards the rear of the house. "Well, I'm not royalty."

She may not have been royalty before, but being my Kindred Spirit had already gifted her such a title. Princess suited her; Queen was a more fitting rank.

"It does not make you crude," I replied, brushing my arm against her shoulder and wondering how much shorter she would be without her clipping heels. Could I easily lift her and–

"What is Arri short for?" I mentally cleared away my carnal desires.

"Arraetta." Unbeknownst to her, a creeping shudder danced up my back and rippled through my filaments at the sound of such a wistful, seraphic name. So poetic, so distinct, so regal - *Ar-ray-et-ah*. It felt like I had committed a crime against the Gods by uttering it, so much so that I almost wished to stop any other breathing such opulence.

"Arraetta," I whispered, not once but twice, tasting it like the last bite of forbidden fruit. No matter how much she might have fought, I could not even shorten such a divine name blessed by the Gods.

"That is beautiful."

"Is it?" she laughed coyly and avoided eye contact. "So... how long have you lived here?"

"Over fifty years," I replied, quickly adding, "the family, of course, not me personally."

I was ancient. Time in Zika was vastly different from Earth's, although calculations had been made for how slowly we aged in this realm. It took around three winters and three moon cycles to age up on Earth.

"Well, today could be your fiftieth birthday," she jested.

Oh, to be fifty years old when life was sweet in Zika, before the war, before Mareina, before my father's sharp, uncompromising hand when everyone adored little prince Seraiah, the promising heir to the throne. Sweet, careless, *free*.

"I am old and decrepit, after all," I chuckled.

As we walked, I observed her admiring the numerous portraits pinned to the walls. Wonder danced in her eyes, unasked questions lingering on the tip of her tongue, waiting to be asked. But she did not free them. *Curious.*

The upper hallway staircase at the end of the corridor greeted us like the edge of a sharp cliff, uncertainty giving way to the known. And I knew that as soon as I re-entered the ballroom, reality would return as keen as a blow to the head. But Arraetta - *Empyreans, such a Gods-worthy name* - paused to peer out the expansive lower floor-to-ceiling window, its panes pouring light into and through the centre of the otherwise darkened corridor. Ahead, the vast gardens of flower beds, ornate trees and bushes led to a wide-reaching lake, centred with a spurting fountain, and beyond, woods provided a perimeter to stop intruders coming in and keep me from getting out.

"You are very lucky."

"Sometimes," I shrugged, "it does get a little too much."

"I know what you mean," she answered sarcastically, "I sometimes think 'my God, what would I do if I was poor right now?'"

I tutted and laughed lightly. "You are something, Arraetta."

"Arri," she corrected instantly.

A first correction, and I was sure not her last. Did she not know the sacrilege it would be to agree?

"If I were not in the position I am in, I would have enjoyed a quiet life in a cabin somewhere, waking up to views of a forest, enjoying the freedom in life."

A life free of torture and torment. Only she had relieved me from one part, but even then, I could see the workings of my father's deceitful mind through the thick ballroom doors as he devised a plan to remove her. No, I would not let him. She was mine.

"I always wanted that," she replied truthfully, "but, you know, *money.*"

"And status," I added. The summer sun radiated a little harshly on our skin, although it felt pleasant given the circumstances. I peered at her. "Freddie could easily get away from this if he wanted."

"Genie said he's a bodyguard?"

I spluttered a laugh. Freddie would be the worst kind of bodyguard, only agreeing to go ahead with specific rules before he would offer to break them. I wondered what ridiculous things he had been germinating to keep Genevieve close.

"A bodyguard?"

"Is he not?"

"Freddie is in charge of many things," I answered, truthfully, as he was my future advisor, "but he definitely is *not* a bodyguard. Are you sure that your friend Genevieve has not told you something incorrectly, Arraetta?"

Confusion rose on her face, that cute wrinkle appearing on the bridge of her nose as her arched eyebrows furrowed. The cogs were undoubtedly ticking.

It was time to move the conversation along. "Do you like wine?"

"Sometimes."

Blunt but honest. "Well, please be sure to try some of our wine."

"Is it poisoned?"

Witty. *Do you fear such a thing, Arraetta?* I would gladly snap the neck of any assailant who decided to poison anything she chose to inhale.

Half-scoffing, I replied, "Miss Kinsley, you truly hurt my pride. The wine is from our winery. I am sure you have had some before, but it shall be flowing all evening."

Arraetta idly nodded, and reluctantly, I edged towards the staircase until we descended it to the back exit of the garden. Next to it, there was another entrance to the ballroom, with two stationed guards on duty. I noted that she looked inquisitively at them.

"Arraetta, I must ask you." I cast my gaze to hers and, after a second pause from being so captivated by such gentle, peculiar eyes, I asked, "Do you dance?"

Arraetta tittered nervously. "I've had to dance with Genie whenever she needed a partner."

I expected this was not surprising news after knowing Genevieve was a dancer. Thoughts of glee rushing from her mouth as she pranced around the room with her closest friend, thudding my iron heart. *Crack.* I would let it fracture a little more just to see it.

"It is a tradition here that there is a dance on special occasions," I informed her, knowing that my life bringers favoured such tradition. And, I could not bypass the opportunity to take my fated one - my Kindred Spirit - to the dance floor, "and I would very much like to have that dance with you."

Face crimson, fidgeting idly, her head turned with that notable tell that she was nervous. "I'm... I'm not that good."

"I shall lead," I replied, eager to show everyone that I, the cursed prince Seraiah, still had the favour of the Gods. "All you have to do is follow me."

"I..." she replied, eyebrows furrowing before she gave herself a nod of encouragement, "Okay."

The fire burned brightly in her, determination clashing with anxiety, but it was about to be unleashed, and I would bear the full force of its weight just to see it.

"Wonderful," I smiled contentedly, undeniably daring to raise my hand and tickle it across her soft cheek, but I knew I had to control myself. "Now, I would be honoured to enter the room with you, but due to a variety of circumstances, I shall have to take a different entrance."

Entering the ballroom with her would have been a blessing, but I wanted their future queen to be memorable, turning curious heads as she entered their heady gaze. I wanted her to see that all my mortal-kind were her future subjects, and when I took her hand and guided her to the dance floor, they would know.

Selfish, I was sure. But, Empyreans, I was allowed to be somewhat selfish with the patience I had over the many scorns since she was prophesied.

With a final bow, I stormed down the corridor, eager to enter the room before or even as she did, at least no one would notice that I had been far longer than the allocated time I had given Fulk if all eyes were on her.

And all eyes *were*.

Even I had to pause for a moment as she walked through the opposite end of the room, seeking a familiar face as the parting crowd enveloped her. I squared my shoulders, set my never-wavering mask, and walked to the back of the crowd towards my life bringers. I was excited to show them the female I had met who would change everything.

I noted my father's sharp gaze across the crowd to where she was, and even through his cold countenance I could see the tightening in his jaw. She had stunned him because he did not know who she was. Not as though he knew all his subjects by face, but she was different. Human.

Or not human.

He peered at me, expression souring, "Is this party not good enough that you need to spoil my afternoon?"

Making sure everyone across the table heard me, I replied, "I thought you might be quite glad that I have heeded your request and found a female to take to the dance floor. I am sure that you - *all of you* - shall approve."

A sceptical laugh left his throat. "I do not care for your fancies."

"Not a fancie," a knowing grin lined my face. "Her name is Arraetta, and she... is human."

As expected, everyone gasped, and my father's disdain grew. His fists were clenched by his sides. But Fulk appeared, and he was my saving grace.

"Excuse me, Your Royal Highness," he said, "it is time for your speech."

I patted Fulk on his shoulder, speaking loudly, "impeccable timing. Yes, my speech. Of course. Excuse me."

I bowed to everyone before leaving the flabbergasted whisperings of the cult to decide on what their next strike would be. Little did they know that my strike would pierce them as quickly as the fangs of a venomous snake.

Through the crowd, I headed towards the dais, only to be collared by Freddie at its step, appearing without his wife by his side.

"Ready?" he asked.

"As I shall ever be," I said, placing a hand on his shoulder and squeezing it. "The time has come, my friend."

"Your time has come," he corrected, bowing his head, "my king."

"So sentimental, Freddie," I chuckled and almost took the step before turning back to him, "I think you should know I have found her." His eyebrows were raised with confusion. I leaned forward in a whisper. "My Kindred Spirit."

Astonishment whispered across his face until his lip tugged with a smirk of satisfaction. Nothing further was said as I stepped onto the dais. The music quietened, and Fulk called everyone to attention using his staff. I pulled the speech from my pocket, gazing across the crowd to acknowledge Freddie again, and then I found Alex and Helga. And finally, I met Jonah's unreadable gaze as he stood near the entrance door.

Eyes to my father, then to where my fated one whispered with

Genevieve and then down to the unfolded paper in my hands. I scanned it briefly and peered up at Arraetta again, only to have an odd revelation overcome me. Winters of gathering evidence, and the one thing that was most clear to me, was the female who had entered my life less than thirty minutes before.

Something tugged at me, telling me it was not the right time to add to the burning furnace, not when I had something greater to protect. I could not allow this lifetime chance of happiness to be soiled by such a vulgar moment.

Discreetly, I shook my head at Jonah, noting the sudden alarm on his face, before I folded the speech and re-pocketed it.

"Good afternoon," I confidently greeted, a proud yet emotionless smile on my face. "I believe it is only right that I am open and honest with you. This sol, we have had the wonderful opportunity to welcome not one but two humans into our settlement." I noted the simmering uproar sweeping the room. "So, to accommodate them, I shall speak English."

Inquisitive glances danced around the room, seeking out our two new guests, while the table towards the back seemed to suggest that they were already scheming. Jonah, who had remained in the same place, had an *Empyreans, you are a fool!* scowl for the ages, but it was Freddie's supportive look that kept me going.

In English, I said. "So, to accommodate those who only speak English, thank you all for coming to this celebration in these dark and uncertain times. We hope that one day we shall return home and claim our rightful place." A few people cheered. "But, for now, we must continue living as we have until the time is right. And, that is why we are here celebrating what-" I spoke obscurely for a moment. "-feels like my one-hundredth birthday. Over my long life, I have learnt many things, and it is you, my people, whom I must thank. And, of course, their majesties, who have ever been... understanding.

Let us enjoy the celebrations, and I look forward to greeting you as King in time. Shrang-e-la!"

The ripple of echoing cheers was engulfed as the music started to play, and I left the dais as couples flooded the dance floor.

Freddie's eyebrows rose. "That was not the plan."

"Plans change," I shrugged, "but it shall still have the same effect."

Jonah pushed through the crowd, stopping by the two of us, speaking in a fury-filled hushed tone, "That is not what was agreed. Fuck. What has happened this sol? Has someone spiked your wine? You are both testing every ounce of fucking patience I have."

"You must trust me. Both of you," I said to them, placing my hands on their shoulders, "let us enjoy the rest of the sol and reform a plan."

"This is not all about you, Seraiah," Jonah said, flabbergasted. "winters of gathering evidence for what? We are a team. And what about Eros? Tortured for nothing."

"Eros has nothing to do with this sol," I said quietly, my eyes narrowing. "Do not sour the milk. I will bear the consequence, but you and everyone will understand why soon enough."

I started to walk away, finding Fulk to inform him that I would take a partner to the floor before shuffling through the circles of socialites. Freddie caught up to me halfway across.

"Jonah is close to resenting us both," he said.

"You made your decision, and I made mine."

"If you had told him that you have found this Kindred Spirit of yours, I am sure he would have been more accommodating."

"I do not need to tell him because he shall see soon enough."

"Who is she?"

But I did not need to answer as we arrived at the two humans, my eyes glued to the female two steps back from Genevieve. Empyreans, she was even more beautiful than I had seen her, stained cheeks flushed from wine.

Genevieve hopped up to greet Freddie with a kiss, but I did not care for their affections as I stepped towards my fated one. I bowed. "Are you ready for that dance?"

Her blush only deepened as Genevieve gasped in eager enthusiasm. But I did not care for her or anyone else in the room. I only cared for Arraetta, taking her delicate hand and tugging her through the ebbing crowd towards the centre of the dance floor.

All eyes were on us, but only mine were on her. After a long life of suffering and duty, the female before me was no longer a facade of my imagination, deep inside dreams, with only her lilting voice to weather the storm of isolation. She was a breathing, tangible being of elegance, wit, and celestial grace.

It would not hurt to open one more chest, would it? Anger battling with love sounded like a toxic combination, but with honour and duty, I could put my pride above me to see Arraetta's happiness.

...All the fragments seeking freedom and ripping you apart from the inside out.

Only one. And, maybe one sol I would let it open for her - Only for her.

EIGHT

With one hand on her tender, silk-covered waist and the other between her soft fingers, we waltzed around the ballroom, breaths apart, to *La Lune à Première Lumière*, blissfully ignoring the murmuring crowd. When the music ended, we departed for the outside, greeted by a subtle, fresh breeze which hindered the brutal sun's gaze. It tickled my skin and whispered through Arraetta's thick locks. Even in her overbearing gown, it seemed she radiated in the basking heat.

Behind, Travis and Connell followed, both in light conversation that was barely audible. Jonah might have been a little discontented with them talking, but I did not care what they did as long as they did their job. And it was not my protection I cared for, but hers. Arraetta looked curiously at them, chuckling softly.

"Do you find something funny, Arraetta?"

"I just find it funny that you have two bodyguards following you," she replied, subtly tilting her head backwards.

I looked back at them and said, "They are only with me because you are here. I am usually capable of strolling around the house without them."

I had the privilege of not being followed inside the house during my solar rite, but Jonah had implemented a security protocol to be followed outside in case of attempted assassination.

"I would appreciate some distance," I called to the males in Zikan. The two reluctantly bowed and did as I bid.

"That's a beautiful language," she pointed out.

"Yes, it is our native tongue; we tend to use it around the house." Or anywhere throughout the Zikan settlement.

"What is it?" That curious look returned to her face, and I wondered whether I could reveal that we were not human, although I supposed that was a rather tall fact I was sure would scare her away.

"Maybe I will show you someday."

The cogs of mischief turned in her face as she turned her head away thoughtfully, her lip twitching. "I'm sure that you find yourself in the company of many women..."

A bewitching charmer. I grinned, mimicking her tone. "Oh, and how many times have you used that line?"

Melodic laughter rumbled from her, and a contented smile beamed on my face. I was sure I would get an earful about how *smitten* I must have appeared when I was next in the ring with Connell.

"You are quite incorrect in that manner," I replied. "I do not find myself in the company of many others other than my mother and my friends."

My mother because she did not know how to leave me alone unless she was across the sea in more pleasant times, while my *friends* were often involved in fist-to-fist combat in the ring or a Sanctuary of Amity meeting. I could not remember the last time I had enjoyed a casual drink without it being *business.*

"What of your parents?" I asked, to which she shrugged and looked upward. A diverted question often came with an unwanted answer, but I wanted to know what was ailing her so I could help cure it. "I am sorry; I did not mean to upset you."

"You didn't," she replied. "It's a complicated tale, and maybe not one for right now."

"Another time, then?" I poked. Oh, how I wished I could ease her burdens.

Another shrug before a dry laugh echoed from her lips, as though she could not take the situation seriously. "I don't mean to sound rude, but I am fairly sure you can find someone better than a pizza delivery girl."

Humble and incorrect. I could *not* find someone better than this pizza delivery girl. She was so insecure about how she lived - *survived* - that she believed I would care about such things. Little did she know from that sol onward, she would never have to deliver or even make a pizza again.

Adding to the humour of the situation, I offered, "Maybe I should have pizzas delivered to me?"

Her cheeks flushed, eyes darting away coyly, "I'm afraid that you are outside the radius of Jafar's Pizza Palace."

"Oh, it is a palace? I should make sure to visit."

"Do enjoy your visit; I'm sure you'll enjoy your rat-infested pizza," she laughed heartily, curtseying. My cheeks were stiff from the joy I received from being around her, although it was more likely because I had not smiled in such a way since I was a seedling.

"Maybe I can open a position in the kitchen here just for you," I teased. "I shall order pizzas every day so that you can come and visit."

"I suppose I should just be one of your maids, then."

"As long as you only take part in making my bed." The flirtatious words left my mouth quicker than I might have liked, and I inwardly cursed myself in hopes I did not sound more like a fool than I thought. I could hear Jonah tutting at me, although he cared little about the life I led in pursuit of affection. Arraetta's eyes diverted again, a torn look crossing her face.

"I did not mean to make this something more than it is," I said as we walked closer to the lake at the bottom of the garden. "I had only meant that-"

"-Don't worry, Your Highness," she interrupted, her lips tugging. "I wouldn't expect to be your wife; I'm not quite cut out for princess duties."

Oh, but you are, Arraetta. You are meant to be a queen.

"You could learn," I replied honestly. "My mother is an excellent teacher."

A real-life truth that cannot be denied. Although my mother and I had a somewhat fractious relationship, she was still one of the best people to teach Arraetta how to become a great ruler of our nation. And while my father somewhat suppressed my mother, I would not do the same to Arraetta.

"I thought you weren't making this out to be more than it is," she answered. I knew I had my hands full with her. She was quick-witted, intelligent, and had a deep fire, ready to be freed. She surprised me with her next suggestion. "If you want me to sleep with you, you can just ask."

"I did not think you human women were like that."

"Human?"

I swore under my breath, frustrated that I slipped up. "You are quite... human... in a case to some... *women...*" *Empyreans*, Seraiah. "...who like to sleep with many others."

Fuck, fuck, fuck.

"Oh, so because I'm a *human* woman, I can't sleep with other men?"

My attempt at flirting had gone awry far too quickly, and the grave I was digging for myself was only getting deeper. "No, that is not what I mean."

"Do not worry, Your Grace," she said, twirling around, "You can see I am the embodiment of a perfect *human* woman, but deep down

107

inside, there's something strangely... ethereal about me."

Oh, there was something far more than ethereal about her. As I had done during the dance, I swiftly tucked my hand around her waist and pulled her to me. A tang of nymphaea and orange diffused from her skin, melding with the subtle scent of aromatic wine on her breath.

"I *can* feel something different about you."

"Oh?" her cheeks rouged as those beautiful azure eyes peered into mine. I looked at her lips, unable to withdraw from the frenzied desire for ours to caress each other. Dazed in her intoxicating aura, I slowly closed the gap. Not a thought of the soiree, which continued up the quiet garden.

Yet, just as our breaths were centimetres apart, Arraetta rapidly whipped her head back and looked up. My eyebrows furrowed in confusion, glancing at the endless cerulean skies and then back to her. "Are you okay?"

The pigment in her cheeks had paled, and her breath jaggedly hastened, several beads of sweat rippling down her face. She quivered, inwardly seeking answers to questions that remained unspoken. I wondered whether she might have the beginnings of heat exhaustion. Reaching out my hand to steady her, I inhaled sharply as my fibres billowed with static energy permeating her skin.

"Arraetta?" I breathed.

Wide, dilated eyes flicked towards me, alarm rife in them until her survival impulse overwhelmed her, and she rushed past me. I called her name again, watching her bold gown snag against the floor, slowing her down as though the hands of fate were attempting to pull her back toward me. And, if there was one thing I knew about the whispers of destiny, it was a ceaseless train that rarely stopped to let someone alight.

A crackle fizzed high above, and I peered up to see part of the shimmering arcs of electricity pulsing in one section had begun to break. Even Arraetta seemed to bear secrets that I had yet to discover – coyness, humility, a blazing spirit, and... *Rapidfire.* Deep, smouldering, alive, electric power. It was as familiar as my own reflection, and Arraetta was ablaze with it.

"Your Grace?" Travis called. The two males closed in on me.

"Fuck," I swore under my breath before I ordered sharply, "lock the front door, do *not* let her leave!"

I knew the damage to the shield should have been of some priority, but I had little care as I darted after her. The jostling horde of attendees slowed my advances, gasps and mutters and apologies firing towards me. Someone harshly bumped into me, but I barely spared a glance at who it was, too eager to find Arraetta to care. And I watched her merge rows ahead until she was through the door at the other end, Genevieve holding her hand and Freddie following mindlessly behind.

Empyreans, I should have taken the corridor.

I did not spare my life bringers a glance, although I was sure they could see the chaos from the mutters of annoyance. Finally, through the last throng, I rushed into the peaceful entrance and was greeted by Alex and Freddie. The front door was closed, but no sign of the humans existed.

Jonah walked out of the ballroom in a flurry. "What the fuck is happening?"

"Where is she?" I asked Freddie.

"Side room," Freddie nodded towards the small lounge room, and I sighed in relief, stepping in its direction, only for Jonah to block my path.

"Seraiah, who is she?"

Half of me wished to punch Jonah for being a naïve little shit, and the other half wanted to do so for stopping me from tending to Arraetta's unknown ailment. But I felt the shield finally give out, the force of the electricity dissipating and hitting my cells. Freddie winced, and I knew my life bringers had knowledge of the situation.

Unfortunately for them, it was not me who had reduced the generator's power to embers, reconfirming that Arraetta did indeed house some form of Rapidfire. It only left the questions: Who was she? And how did she have such power? Because I knew she was not human, and she definitely was not Zikan.

Without another word to my commander, I shouldered past him and into the room, seeing a tearful Genevieve looking towards Arraetta. The room was lined with portraits and paintings of all sizes and colours, but one particular one had taken her full attention - The Wicker Windmill.

Yet, it seemed, in the intricacy of the painting I had created so very long ago, it was anything but motionless, like all the others. Instead, the greying river flowed gracefully as verdant trees whooshed gently in the breeze, and birds flew in circles. Almost like a stem from a film. Or, better yet, like a portal.

As I stepped towards it, I was mesmerised, wondering if anyone else could see such beauty being brought to life. But it was not until I looked down at Arraetta that I noticed the horror of her glassy eyes. It was like she was unaware of everything happening around her.

I placed a soft hand on her shoulder. "Arraetta."

Reality returned, Arraetta jolted, and fear struck in her wild gaze as they danced towards me. I winced as she shrieked in pain, hands gripping her skull, and she thudded bruisingly to her knees.

"Please, we need to go home," Genevieve begged, but I ignored her while Freddie coddled her.

"Get Marie immediately!" I yelled to whoever might listen, urgently needing to get some medical attention for my fated one.

I could feel the pain ripple from her, causing a raw, distant, yet recognisable feeling to surge from my very soul. A primal instinct to protect her in every way I could. And even I was not sure how.

Another scream of anguish reverberated from Arraetta, and the tug of anxiety feasted on my bones as I watched blood rapidly drip from her nose. Her eyes rolled a little as she gripped onto the floorboards for support.

"Genie, you must tell me what is happening!" I begged.

"The blackout," she stumbled, wiping her wet cheeks. "We shouldn't have come. We shouldn't have come."

The blackout sounded too ominous to be real, yet we were witnessing something that none had seen before. In a way, it seemed her body had gone into some sort of stress response, her life force overpowering her on instinct, eating at the foreign energy that festered inside her.

"Arraetta, I can help you," I pleaded as she swayed wearily back to her feet. She ignored me as I tried to grip her.

No more pain. Please. There was only one other thing I could try.

"Arneum Ormsapiaun," I thought aloud. An enchantment of Primordial Thaumaturgy - *ancient magic* - used to calm her, bringing her to a comatose state.

"You have no power for that, Seraiah," Freddie urged.

Anything is worth a try, Freddie. If we were in Zika, I could conjure the right power without draining my energy, but we were limited on Earth. And such magic required arcana, or else it could be detrimental.

Burning static rose from Arraetta's body so powerful that I could not bear to touch her, watching her honey skin ricochet with golden electricity.

"That is impossible," I breathed, echoed by gasps of surprise from whoever was bearing witness to such impossibilities.

All was confirmed for what I had thought – Arraetta was the bearer of Rapidfire. But not of any typical Rapidfire that I had witnessed before. The power was shredding through her, draining her energy to enforce its own innate need to survive like a disease ripping through her fibres. If she did not calm down, she would combust and, worse, die. My heart tugged, foreign anxiety flaring wilder than ever.

She stumbled backwards against the hard wall, her breath erratic and eyes flitting around as she silently begged for help.

"*Where is Marie?*" I shouted, witnessing the blood dripping incessantly from her nose as she sank against the wall.

I approached her while Jonah warned me from behind, "Seraiah, you need to keep your distance."

But I could not. "Arraetta, we are going to help you."

"What do you want with me?!" Her voice cracked as she shouted, pressing herself against the wall behind like a cornered animal retreating from a hunter.

But, in seconds, the echo of static electricity ricocheted from her before her body disintegrated into sparks of electricity, disappearing entirely before our eyes. "No!"

Fear rippled my being, plunging directly into my thudding heart as my hand reached towards where she had been. I drew in a sharp breath, eyes closing as the second coffer shattered its lock, banging open without mercy, until I was breathing heavily through my teeth. Perspiration beaded down my face as I tried to control the rapid, new yet familiar emotion which had been buried for scorns.

Fuck!

Every memory, every thought, every feeling had been reopened and slammed into me like a crashing wave of avoided emotion. A piercing noise suppressed my ears, followed by cold, calculating laughter.

And then there were five.

"Seraiah," a hand landed on my shoulder, and I turned in a cold sweat, grabbing the assailant by their collar, only to be faced with Freddie.

"What the fuck?" he surrendered, hands up.

Swallowing, I let him go, trying to reach my inner sanctum to keep the fear at bay. However, my mind was wild and would not quiet the dishevelled thoughts of Arraetta's whereabouts. My hands were quivering, and although I could see my brothers' concerned looks in the room, I played it off by running one hand through my heat-soaked hair and shovelling both hands into my trouser pockets.

I looked back to where Arraetta had disappeared, eyebrows furrowing as I noted the plug socket on the wall, soaked in remnants of blood. It all made sense. Arraetta had accessed the rings and teleported somewhere using them. But it had been impossible to do such a complicated thing from a standard port; at least, it had been for the rest of us. It was also fucking dangerous.

My hands shook, rage and fear a new concoction boiling in my blood, alongside that inkling of affection wafting through the fractures of its coffer. I picked up an unimportant, expensive ornament and threw it across the room, causing everyone to lurch as it broke.

"Seraiah, calm down," Freddie breathed.

I clenched my fist, not looking at them, commanding, "Find her."

"What?" Jonah blinked.

"I said find her!" I roared, looking in his direction with such conviction that even he could not deny my demand. Jonah muttered to Alex before Alex nodded his head and exited the room.

My wrathful gaze landed on Genevieve, and she tucked herself into Freddie. She was the only human in the room with more knowledge about the mortal-kind female with Rapidfire. Freddie tried to stand before her as I stepped close, but I used my strength to pull my cousin away, gripping one of Genevieve's biceps tightly. "Where would she go?"

She sobbed. "I-I don't know."

Freddie was trying to push me away, and I noted Connell and Travis entering the room, who I was sure would try to restrain me if my distress continued.

"Let her go, Seraiah," Jonah said, standing upright.

I held my ground. "There must be somewhere. Your home? What is your address?"

"Get the fuck off my wife!" Freddie growled, subtle green sparks tingling at his fingers, but I did not care for him. Only for the safety of Arraetta and Genevieve had the answer.

"I asked you a question, and you better well answer it," I threatened. "Where do you live?"

Tears tipped, spilling down her cheeks as panic tickled her expression, "I-I... I... she... that has never... never happened... before."

Empyreans, her sobs were incessant.

"*Hellsworn*," I seethed, "I did not-"

I was not quite expecting the sharp rattle of knuckles against my cheek or the middle chair colliding with my body, smashing several ornaments on impact – even when I should have. I was not ready for the onslaught of extra punches that came with it, even when it was apparent. But my strength returned, and I grabbed my attacker, returning the slam to his face. Freddie stumbled back.

It would have been quite the show if Travis had not grabbed Freddie and Connell had not brought a hard hand to push me by my chest to separate us.

"Sparring is for the ring, my princes," Connell said with a soft yet unsure chuckle as he attempted to lighten the situation.

"This fucker deserves it for the way he has bruised my wife!"

Freddie shouted, glowering at me.

"Bruised? I hardly touched her," I replied harshly, peering over to Genevieve as she coddled her aching arm. A little human mouse trapped in a house full of lions; unlucky for her, she would be a resident in it for the rest of her mortal life. It was a blessing for her that it was short.

"If you ever lay a hand on her again, I will break your fucking neck!" He yelled, shoving Travis away. "Future king or not."

"Are you finished play-fighting?" Jonah's voice echoed from the door, and I saw him leaning, arms folded, and one leg perched on the wall. Rather too casual for such a pressing situation. "I think the whereabouts of this female are more important."

"*This* female is-"

"-I know who she is," he tutted snidely, standing tall, "Empyreans, Seraiah, the whole of fucking Zika would know who she is with the way you are reacting right now. But I cannot bestow her a title that has not yet been given, so she remains."

Female. Human. Mortal-Kind. But she was a fucking princess. A Queen. My Queen. Heightened voices could be heard from outside, and Jonah swore under his breath before he left through the door, closing it from behind her.

"Is she dead?" Genevieve's whimpering broke the silence.

"No," I grunted, taking a shaky breath as I stepped away from the group. "I do not know. I cannot confirm. I... I think she is in The Rings."

"What?" Freddie was shocked. I knelt by the stained socket, slowly placing my hand closer, but no energy was pulsating from it.

"I do not know how." I stood. "But I am certain she has teleported somewhere."

"Teleported?" Genevieve choked, faintly taking a seat. "I knew she could do strange things, but never... how is that possible? Is that possible? Oh my God, of course it would be."

While she continued to mutter to herself, I looked at Freddie and turned back to Zikan. "I am going to travel by them to her home."

"Are you insane?" Freddie asked, flabbergasted, "We have not even had Iontine yet; there are not enough resources to get you there. And, if there is, there is no telling whether you would ever get out."

"She is my... *our* future queen, Freddie. I have to help her."

Freddie knew the implications of not going after her and the importance of her position in the house. It was just as integral to have Arraetta there for him to help sway the council in Genevieve's favour. And, while she might have made it out of the electric field known as The Rings, Genevieve had said it had never happened to her before, so the likelihood she would navigate such a place would be slim.

The door opened, and Jonah walked back in, frustration beading his face as he closed it behind him.

"My father?" I asked, but it was a question I did not even need to. "I will deal with him; I must leave here for a while."

"Leave?" Jonah's brows furrowed.

"Apparently, she has magicked her way into The Rings," Freddie added, shuffling past Travis' blockade to go to Genevieve's side.

"Fuck no, I refuse to permit that."

"I do not need your permission," I chided.

"It is fucking dangerous, Seraiah," Jonah scoffed in disbelief.

"It is necessary, *Commander*!"

"Fuck," Jonah swore, knocking his head back against the wall thrice as thoughts clouded his mind. "Fuck. Fuck. Fuck. Fuck. Fuck."

"Fuck," Freddie added with a nod of amusement.

"Empyreans, Jonah," I sighed in exhaustion, "I do not wish to fight you, but I must do what I can to get to Arraetta, and you know damn well that only Freddie and I can go inside them. It is not a matter of our safety, but of hers. I... I need to find her, and I need to bring her home."

"I need a plan."

"There is no time for plans," I answered in aggravation, wishing my emotions were not in such turmoil, where they were slowly becoming uncontrollable. "She is the key to everything. Do you understand what I am saying?"

"I do, but-"

"-Then, stop arguing with me!" I roared; a razor-edged tug lanced in the centre of my chest, and I grunted, holding my chest.

"Seraiah."

"Is he in pain?" Genevieve whispered to Freddie.

Always in pain, fighting an inward battle against two forces, one of them rapidly freeing itself at every opportunity.

"Please, Jonah," I begged, standing up straight as I pushed through the attack my stone heart was wielding. "Damn it, do I have to get on my fucking knees?"

Jonah studied me, seeking to know whether the dark power was about to ripple out of me. But, little did he know, it was not the darkness but the agony of feelings that were trying to tear me apart.

"It is a sight I would not mind witnessing one sol," he muttered, although I noticed the tug on his lip for a second before he stood up with a sigh. "Fine. But you cannot leave your father waiting any longer."

With a nod, I tucked my shoulders back, buried the pain deep in my mind, and walked across the room. Freddie told Genevieve that she needed to stay before, too, following after me. We all left the room except Travis, whom Jonah commanded to remain with Genevieve.

Little did my father know that the storm he was brewing was going to be no match for the tempest I would have to face with Arraetta's uncontrolled power. And the Gods only knew how hard I was going to work to conquer such fire.

NINE

I t was less chaotic in the hallway than I had expected, but the party seemed still to be in full swing through the closed doors of the ballroom. My father was the first person I made eye contact with. Beside him was The General and several guards. I was surprised their favourite enforcer was not present, although I was glad not to lay eyes on him when other matters were urgent. It seemed that my guard had caused a blockade of sorts outside of the room with Alex and, surprisingly, Jonah's second-in-command, the Grand Captain Lyliaer 'Leopold', standing at its front.

"I told you there would be consequences if I found out you caused the shield's loss of power!" my father chided. "You, once again, have spoiled a celebration for your people."

Ha. *My people.* A solar rite celebration that was supposedly for them, not for me.

Ignoring his taunts, I walked around my guard towards the stairs, only for The General to block me. With his movement, Leopold shuffled too.

"Please, Sir," he said, holding a hand up.

"Do not *Sir* me, traitor!" The General sneered, "Almighty in your cushioned rank because you are under my son's thumb."

"I'm only doing my job, Sir."

Leopold was stoic, witty, and clever. He rose to Grand Captain

119

quickly in his early twenties, trading stations from my father's guard to mine. He was lithe, of an average build and height and carried a similar amount of power in his aura to Jonah. He was also not afraid of dispensing punishment to out-of-line soldiers.

"I am your general."

"According to the peace treaty, it's in my right to deny such allegations," Leopold replied confidently, the mask on his face unfaltering.

"Are we done arguing?" Jonah's voice boomed, and I took that as my moment to walk up the stairwell, followed by an amused Freddie.

The General ignored Jonah, shouting, "Do not ignore the King, boy!"

"I am not ignoring him!" I exclaimed, looking down at the crowd, "I do not care how much this has spoilt *your* sol when it has been a happier one of mine. Now, if you shall excuse me, I will bring the generator back online, and then I will find my wife."

Astonishment oscillated across everyone's face, apart from those who knew already, but I did not care for their awe or disgust. Arraetta was the most important being at that moment, and whatever consequences there would be for my actions, I would gladly accept in trade for her safety.

Freddie and I conquered the length of the west wing corridor like we were competing in a thirty-second sprint. Neither of us talked until we were down in my office and through the door to the generator chamber. The enormous grey orb enveloped the centre of the nexus, devoid of electricity, while a red light blinked across the room in a constant rhythm.

Connected to it, with a sign reading [!] WARNING: SHIELD DEACTIVATED [!], was a console.

While reviving its energy would be simple, it would not come without its complications to my own lifeblood. The beast was powered up by two main sources - sunlight and Rapidfire. The Earth's harsh rays amplified its power through solar panels, whilst Rapidfire gave the shield the ability to prevent the radiation from pooling into our settlement.

However, Arraetta had devoured its power when she overpowered it and disintegrated into electrical mites. As she disappeared, so had all the energy.

So, the only option left was for me to use my own Rapidfire to provide it with enough life to power up the shield and get us into the rings. It was a detrimental, yet necessary option, and I thanked the Gods Freddie had chosen to come along for the journey.

"Maybe we should just get in a car and drive there," Freddie grunted as I pressed the keyboard on the console, keying in memorised codes.

"And if she is not at the house?" I grunted, "It was a fluke that even we knew how to navigate it when we first got into The Rings, Gods knows where she might have ended up."

"You understand the uproar if we do not come back, Seraiah."

"If you are so fearful, then you should stay."

"No," he replied bluntly, "I am not a fucking coward, but I am a realist. This... surely the Gods would not have thrown this female into your path only for her to disappear inside the electrical field."

"The Gods would fucking test me at any point, Freddie," I said sharply, knowing how much I had suffered throughout my life and they were not about to be so forgiving now that Arraetta was within my grasp. Once we had rescued her, I would never let her leave it again.

The computer agreed with the codes and I rushed around to the rear of the orb, where a small cylindrical tube, big enough to fit my arm, was.

"You will not survive in there without your power."

"Well, it is a good job you are there with me," I replied, "unless you wish to continue being a *realist.*"

Out of sight, I had rolled my eyes when I said the final word, uncaring of the consequences to myself for going inside The Rings. Freddie walked around to where I stood, watching as my arm slipped into the cylinder, and I gripped a hidden metal handle at its end.

"This could kill you."

"I have done this numerous times, Freddie," I said. "It has not killed me yet."

"Empyreans, Seraiah," he chided, turning his head away in annoyance. "Can a brother not just worry for his cousin's life?"

"I prefer it when you are more free-spirited."

"I prefer it when you are less violent."

"Oh fuck off," I growled. "I did nothing to harm anyone."

"Apart from Genie."

I closed my eyes, ignoring Freddie's presence, whilst I concentrated on the feeling of feeding my power to the machine. It was not a wholly uncomfortable process, save for the fact that it felt like part of my soul was ripping from my body while trying to revive a lifeless source which was begging for life. Less uncomfortable, more painfully overwhelming.

The invisible leash wrapped itself around my wrist, and my arm jerked as the generator began its insatiable feed. Azure Rapidfire undulated, snaking through my veins until the room's red hue was tinged with blue. Freddie hung behind me like a stale odour, warily waiting for me to collapse, but even I would not allow the generator to take that much energy.

"Power restored five per cent," the female voice echoed through the chamber. Still, the ball had not regained anywhere near the amount of energy it needed. Time was ticking, but we were minutes from completing it. "Power restored ten per cent."

The number changed in increments of five every thirty seconds, as static electricity danced in its centre, the grey turning slowly to a subtle yellow. Aches murmured outside my skin whilst the crippling burn soldered internally as my vitality drained. It was quite funny how such a godly power could become so detrimental to our being. If our people found out how weak we truly were away from the shields that protected us, they would surely begin to revolt.

"That is enough, Seraiah," Freddie said, placing his hand on my shoulder. I grunted at the cold contact, instantly ripping away from the machine.

I shivered, breathing heavily as the Rapidfire evaporated from my veins. But I knew I could have handled giving the globe more than I had. "How much?"

"Hm?"

"The percentage," I said, tucking away the intrinsic suffering deep inside as I wandered around the console to see for myself. Sixty-five per cent. More than it had been at since the previous Iontine four sols before, having vastly deteriorated after each overuse of it.

"Do you have their coordinates?" I asked, finding the setting for the use of The Rings, but Freddie did not answer. I had to look twice in prompt succession to see Freddie looking less than pleased, arms folded, watching me. I sighed, standing up straight. "I am fine."

"You will apologise."

"I will what?"

"Apologise," he replied bluntly, "you hurt my wife."

"Empyreans, Freddie."

"She is a fucking human, Seraiah!" he growled, unfolding his arms. "I saw the bruising you left on her. She cannot heal like me and you. So, when we return, you will apologise."

"I need to find Arraetta."

"Fuck that, Seraiah!" he bellowed, before running a hand through his dishevelled hair. "You do not hurt another female just for your gain. You would not have met her if Genie had not invited her here. And where would that have left you, hm? An over-privileged, jealous prince with an uncertain future."

"My future remains uncertain whether Arraetta is here or not," I replied in aggravation, "and so does yours! My father is going to do everything he can to rip this devotion of yours-"

"-That has nothing to do with you bruising my fucking wife!" he roared, closing in on me, ready for a second fight, "a simple apology, Seraiah. It will not hurt you to admit to your fucking faults. Empyreans, maybe this fated mate of yours might make the cold-hearted prince human."

"I am not human." It was a grumble far too obvious to have been a fighting point, but I did not want to be compared to a mere human. Nor did I want to be mortal-kind. I might have been flesh, but I was not blood. I was power. A demon. A god. A saint. A fucking martyr.

He growled in aggravation, "hellsworn, it is a phrase of the fucking tongue!"

I studied him before letting out a dejected sigh. "I apologise."

"Yeah, you can say that to me, but we are talking about Genie. I want you to apologise to her just as you would to your own wife."

I opened my mouth, closed it and chewed it over. I supposed Freddie was in the right if I had hurt Genevieve – it was not in my nature to harm a female – but apologising to her as I would to Arraetta was out of my nature. Empyreans, it was out of my nature to even say that I was sorry.

"I will apologise," I said to him, "after we find Arraetta."

"I will keep you to your word," he answered grimly, eyes narrowing as if I was about to argue back at him. But, I would not. I grew increasingly anxious and desperate to find Arraetta, and my fatigued body wore me down each minute I waited. The quicker we found her, the quicker we could put everything behind us and come up with a plan for the future.

Freddie pulled out his phone and finally reeled off the coordinates, which I eagerly typed into the console, ignoring all the warning prompts that continued to pop up. I opened the metal drawer beneath the console and pulled out an oversized, multi-coloured neo-tech watch, which Freddie immediately took from me.

He would bear the burden of getting us home, for which I was thankful, but it meant he would expend more energy. He shuffled past the orb and towards the corner of the nexus, where a tall, thin steel cylinder pinned from floor to ceiling stood like a fireman's pole. It was a conduit for electricity and used to travel by The Rings to travel to places.

If it were not detrimental to our well-being due to the overbearing nature of the electricity against our inner currents, I would have quite happily used The Rings to escape palace life, but it was very difficult to navigate its trajectory further than one hundred miles.

Noise filled the room as the generator whirled back to life, static pulsing over the ceiling above and over to the metal pole, firing it to life. I could feel the electricity radiating from where I stood, and it only became more intense as I wandered over to near where Freddie stood.

"If either of us gets lost, know what our goal is."

Freddie grunted an agreement, powering up his emerald Rapidfire. "See you on the other side."

He fiddled with the watch, placing one hand on my shoulder and the other on the pole. The familiar splinters of electronic frequencies fizzled in my ears, pulling us into the ether.

It should not have been an arduous journey to get through the electric fields, a hidden world filled with electrifying colours resembling numerous galaxies and stars. Beneath our feet, neon green charges stood like glowing grass, hiding the mourning black ground beneath them. It was an incredibly serene, infinite, and endless place - an alternate dimension. Except getting lost was detrimental because, without an escape, there would never be a way out.

"There." Freddie pointed to a distant spot where filaments of energy were shaped into a purple tree with a pulsating beam of white light flowing from the endless dark skies.

At a pace, the two of us crossed the land in silence, listening to the rhythms of gentle currents surrounding us. Oddly, I felt like I had more energy, although I knew I was going to feel the detrimental effects once I left. My body was only going to overcharge itself, filling every particle until it was satisfied, and more to make sure it could survive.

I wondered about who Arraetta was. Very few people had the gift of Rapidfire, only given to those of specific blood and birthright unless she was of royal lineage to one of the six great realms.

Closing in on the tree where the white light pulsed, my sight adjusted just enough to notice faint lines of gold. I had never witnessed such a thing before, so I could only guess it was the same golden light which shone from Arraetta's body just before she disappeared.

I reached towards it, but Freddie's hand gripped my wrist and pulled it back. "I should go first. It could be a trap."

"And who would set such a trap?"

"Your father?"

I snorted, "That male will never leave his fine palace for the dangerous terrain of The Rings."

"I do not trust it."

"Arraetta could be trapped."

"Then we shall go together," Freddie said, and I agreed. We stepped closer to the purple tree and gave each other a final nod of agreement before our hands dipped into its filaments.

Fuck, it burned. Anguish tore through my limbs, but I could not escape the ripping surge of power clawing at my fibres like deeply embedded claws until I forced myself to surrender myself to it. The electrical fields evaporated, and with it the torment. It seemed I had arrived at my new destination alone.

A space as immense as the ballroom, if not bigger, lined with grey stone walls whilst four imposing monoliths stretched upward to support a hidden ceiling shrouded by black, stormy clouds. Patchwork of weathered stone, clustered with frills of lifeless weeds, covered the expanse of the ground with a large recessed pit in its centre. I could not see an exit anywhere as I wandered through its vastness, my footsteps echoing as though I were in an empty auditorium.

"Hello?" I called, my voice rebounding around, but no one answered as I ran my fingers across the cold, rough edges of the wall. A soft howl of wind taunted my ears from the centre of the space, and I turned to see a cloud of black mist forming.

My heart thudded. Shit, I should *not* be scared. Damn, coffer. "Hello?"

"Hello," a dark, oddly familiar male voice replied, and a cold shiver ran down my spine. The hammering of my heart seemed to echo in the space. The male chuckled loudly, as though feeling fear was such a sin. It *was* a sin.

"Reveal yourself!" my voice half-quivered, and I growled, clenching my fist before pushing back such temperaments and shouting, "I command you!"

"*You* command *me?*" he laughed again, still not revealing who he was, but I knew. Empyreans, I fucking knew. "I have been locked up for scorns, but now the tables have turned, and it seems that it is *I* who commands *you.*"

"I demand you to free me."

Tut. Tut. Tut. I shuddered as his voice reverberated inside my head. I walked towards the mist, fear tucked away, and hollow courage standing in its place. I was sure if I was not feeling so weakened, I would be less of a cowardly male and more myself, uncaring of the agony it caused me to hide away such deceitful emotions.

"Such bravery," he replied. "I can smell your fear, Seraiah. It lingers on you."

I stopped close enough to the dark haze to be prepared to greet this familiar stranger, but distant enough to protect myself from whatever new onslaught he wished to gift to me. I tucked my shoulders back, uncaring for his foul words.

"Do you not recognise this prison?" he asked, hiding behind his misted mask. "It is quite the play, is it not? Walls built so high that no one dare ever climb them. But I did attempt it far too many times. It is unfortunate you decided to tamper with your anger coffer, for it provided me with quite the escape."

I only shifted my gaze for a moment, wary that if I took my eyes off the hidden male, he might choose his moment to strike. But, I remembered the internal prison I had built during my sentence, safe to house an illusion and prevent it from ever fleeing again. Yet, it had. My coffer had burst, and it somehow used that moment to make a resurgence.

"Do you remember now, hm?"

"I do not have time to play games!" I glowered.

"Oh, but you do," he grinned, "I have been thinking about this moment for the eternity you have kept me here, of how I would slowly devour the male you are until you shall be on your knees begging that I save us. Everything is changing, and it is all in my favour."

I withheld my tongue at the risk of not sounding like a petulant seedling, knowing that coaxing the onyx fire would only make everything worse. Suddenly, the mist evaporated, and the male before me appeared like black death incarnate. His dark aura oozed from his pallid skin with a smile so malicious I knew fear would know no bounds.

I am fucked.

"Yes, you are," he replied, stretching his arms up to the back of his head, "I can hear everything you think and feel – All the fear, anger, hatred, lust and so-called *affection*. But you and I were never made to dwell in the light, clinging to the illusion of a fractured soul when it is our fate to be the harbinger of shadows."

"You shall never be free."

"Oh, but I already am. The deepest, darkest depths of your mind now fall under my control."

He snapped his fingers, a loud, crumbling sound echoing as the illusion of the prison began to disintegrate, and my snow-filled arboretum of coffers replaced it. Eyes wide, I looked around, noting fear and anger were open with endless dark tendrils of smoke pouring out.

"No," I breathed, looking back to where my dark doppelgänger had stood. But he was no longer there.

Excruciating pain rocketed through my skull like someone was trying to rip it apart from the inside. I thudded to the soft snow, breathing laboured as the familiar twinge of darkness began to alight my azure Rapidfire, turning it onyx. Sinister laughter filled the air, and with it, the winter wonderland was enveloped with black shadows from stormy skies, the softness turning to bitter ice.

I grunted through the agony in my body, breathing through gritted teeth as I used my own attempt to stop the dark power from overtaking me. But a beam of golden light shimmering high above took my attention, and I squinted to look, watching as the clouds began to break apart.

In their place was a body floating in a universe of pinks, blues and purples.

"Arraetta!" I called loudly, stumbling to my feet.

A sharp light sprang from where she floated down towards the ground, hitting me with all its force, shredding my fibres in excruciating torment as my azure Rapidfire fought against the fracturing power until-

"Seraiah, Seraiah!"

Cutting hands pounding my face thrice, and I grimaced. Short, haphazard, anxiety-inducing breaths left my mouth, and I wildly looked around at my new destination, noting the housing estate I found myself sitting in. It was dark elsewhere, but a glitching light hued my body from above, and I noticed I was sitting against a silver lamppost on dry gravel in the centre of a rundown park.

"Are you okay?" Freddie asked, "Empyreans, I thought you were fucking dead. You have been in a comatose state for ten minutes."

"We arrived here ten minutes ago?"

"No, you did. I have been here for like thirty minutes, but you never appeared. I feared for the worst and almost went back in, but the watch is fucked."

I peered at the device on his wrist, seeing that it was glitching. "Do you think it will get us home?"

"It will have to," he replied, pulling out his phone to show me that it, too, was not working. "I almost left, but I did not want to risk going just in case you arrived. We were split in there, and I was not about to leave you again."

"Looks like we have been gone from the human world longer than I thought."

"Hm," he nodded grimly, "I am sure Jonah has the entire army out to find us, but we both knew the risk. Did something weird happen to you in there?" I nodded. "Because I found myself... I found myself in Porto."

"Porto?" I raised my brows.

"Yes, I wandered the streets, but no one recognised me," he said, looking away in thoughtful wonder, "but it was all the same as before I left. I should hope it is like that now. What about you?"

Enlightening him about my second encounter with the devil would have caused more of a ruckus than it was worth. If they knew that some control had slipped from my grasp to things I had been keeping tightly locked up over time, I was sure I would find myself in a vault until I could get it under control again. Even Jonah would implement something like that.

Plus, I was sure it was all in my head. It had to just be anxiety-inducing nightmares filling the void that had been there for scorns. Still, my body throbbed with a dull ache of where my Rapidfire had been torn, consumed and reignited since we were in the generator's chamber, and something deep in my mind told me it would not be the final time I met my darker self.

Oh, it will not be the last time, dear Seraiah.

A shudder ran through me and I collected myself, lying, "home, too. We were both supposed to see something wonderful on a sol like this."

Wonderfully *horrifying.*

Freddie nodded, lost in his thoughts until he cleared his throat and asked, "And, what of Arri?"

"I–"

The light above cut out, echoing a power outage across the estate, all around us. Horns blared, windows smashed and distant dogs barked whilst thunderous roars ruptured the skies and crackled with golden lightning. It was like a call to arms and my heart thudded, toiling with newfound stress and anxiety as I knew exactly what had caused such an ungodly change in the mortal winds.

"Arraetta."

TEN

"You look pale," Freddie said, placing his hand on my shoulder.

"Worry about my health once we find her. Please."

I could not believe I was begging Freddie, but the words had left my mouth, and I knew that in my feeble state, I had no control over my erratic emotions. Freddie looked reluctant as we rushed out of the park, pointing out the two towering blocks of flats several streets over where the females lived. I was unsure what to expect, but I thought they had lived in a more pleasant part of the city. Instead, it was no more than a devil's paradise.

We wandered around the estate, following the echoes of noise towards where we suspected it all began, but it was not proving easy to find Arraetta. Locals were parading on the street, some seedlings looted unnecessarily, police had arrived to cordon off areas, and the blaring of car and house alarms provided an atmosphere to the cacophony. It seemed the world's end had just begun, and Arraetta had heralded it.

With each amount of damage assessed, it became more apparent how much harder it would be to find her, even if she had been wearing the golden ball gown. Her power was undeniably out of control, but I recognised fear as her outlet, which was oddly much more powerful than wrath.

Freddie made an offer at some point to go home, but even I knew it would be difficult for him to return without getting lost in a part of London neither of us knew – and he knew more of the great city than I did. It seemed like miles that we walked, peering down alleys and into gardens, through windows of homes and between the crevices of parked cars. But she was nowhere to be found.

At some point, we circled back to the concrete slabs, and I cringed at the miasma of waste, cigarettes, and cannabis lingering in the putrid air. I noted the handwritten sign OUT OF ORDER (Use Alternative Lift at Other Side) stuck to the tagged elevator.

"The other is broken too," Freddie grunted, patting me on the shoulder. "I tried that option the other sol."

"Joyous," I murmured. We climbed the aching stairs to the tenth floor, breaking out onto a balcony of worn blue numbered doorways. I was mesmerised that Arraetta had embarked on such a journey every sol she lived there, showing just how resilient she was.

Breathless and riddled with a burning headache, I followed Freddie to the third door, peering through the frosted glass into their dark hallway. I shifted over to the room to the right, finding a gap between the closed curtains into a bedroom.

It was relatively tidy, with numerous amounts of clothes piled up in one corner, an easel with an unseen canvas closer, a stack of canvases against one wall and a very unkempt bed against the other. A room that housed a thousand dreams left to dust beneath forgotten white sheets. This was Arraetta's space.

"It does not look like anyone is here," I sighed, looking toward Freddie as he tried the front door handle for luck, but even Tyche – the God of Luck – was not on our side. Crippling anxiety prickled in the core of my stomach as I wondered whether Arraetta might well and truly be lost.

A key inside a lock resounded from the flat to the right, and Freddie and I watched as the door swung open and a grey-haired female in her eighties, dressed in a white bathrobe, poked her curler-covered head out. Alarm sat on her face as she eyed the two of us.

"Can I help you, gentlemen?" she asked.

Freddie cleared his throat. "I am sorry to disturb you; we were just calling on Genevieve and Arraetta."

"Oh!" she smiled brightly, "those two lovely girls have gone to a ball today; they looked very pretty in their dresses."

More than pretty. *Exquisite. Fucking celestial.*

"Maybe you should call back," she offered. "I wasn't aware that those girls had such fine boyfriends."

My cheeks rouged at the claim, and I could see even Freddie looked sanguine, too, although he had a proud smile on his face.

"That we would, ma'am," Freddie cleared his throat, "but-"

"We have come from the ball," I interjected, lying. "they asked the two of us to meet them here, so that we may take them out for..."

"Ice cream," Freddie finished.

"Yes..." I trailed, half glaring at him, "ice cream."

"Well, what polite gentlemen you are," she swooned, not seeming phased that we were pretending to be taking the females out for ice cream so late on a Saturday night. Nor that we had arrived before they had. "I am sure they will be here soon."

"Thank you, ma'am."

She blushed and let out a short laugh. "Please don't be too loud. I'm going to sleep shortly."

"Of course," the two of us replied, bowing our heads as standard. With one last look at us, she walked into her home, giggling to herself, before closing the door. I wondered whether Sheika would have a similar temperament were she not so burdened with the gift of sight.

I sighed, switching back to Zikan as I looked at Freddie. "Ice cream? It is more plausible that we would take them for a drink, not ice cream."

"Genie likes ice cream," he shrugged with a cheeky smile. "You have yet to learn about the likes and dislikes of your *Kindred Spirit*."

Yes, and I would bathe in the knowledge of everything she enjoyed. I was quite fascinated to learn everything about her, but I needed to find her first. As though my thoughts had spawned her presence, another thunderous rumble ruptured the skies, rippling with electricity before the tower block powered down instantly. The area became fully enclosed in darkness, apart from police lights, car alarms, and handheld torches.

But, my gaze washed over a singular row of lights which had retained its fluorescents behind the row of houses on the opposite side of the park below until one by one they fizzled out from the end towards the centre.

"We need to go," I sprinted across the balcony, jumping down the several flights of stairs like I was competing in parkour. Freddie was on my tail, not questioning how I knew that Arraetta was where that final row of lights had fizzled. Around the right of the park, we kept our speed as we rushed past a young boy kicking a stone.

"Hey, you!" he called, and I skidded to a halt, turning to the petulant seedling.

"What?"

"Are you the ones that Arri is hiding from?"

I stood upright, eyes narrowed. "Did she ask for us?"

"No, she paid me to say she was somewhere else," he shrugged, "well, actually, she didn't even pay me. She said she *would* pay me, so I can lie, for the right price."

Thud.

"Is she hurt?" I begged.

"Well, she did have blood like here, here, here, and here. Actually, everywhere," he shrugged nonchalantly, and a shiver ran up my spine at how uncaring he was. It took all my restraint not to grab him by his neck and wring it until he gave me the answers I needed, even if I had to use my power to drive the fear that I felt into him. Or maybe it was wrath. No, it was *distress*. I was overwhelmingly distressed; this eight-year-old seedling would bear the brunt of it if he were not careful.

I would kill a seedling for less.

I shuddered at his callous tone, blocking him from my thoughts as I brought myself back to the present - an outstretched hand offered in front of my face.

"What?" I replied.

"I said twenty pounds," he stomped, pulling his fingers together in a *give-me* kind of way.

"You piece-"

Freddie shoved me lightly, and it stopped the threat which was about to rip from my throat. He knelt in front of the impudent boy.

"Look, kid. We need to find her," he said calmly, yet with urgency, "if she has blood all over her, that means she is hurt. So, please tell us where she is."

Gnawing thoughts stretched over the young boy's face and I turned my head away, clenching my fists as I fought the rage simmering inside. A simple snap to his neck would give me an immense amount of pleasure, but there were far too many unseeing eyes about to not find myself in a vault. Then again, I would like to see them try to lock *me* up.

"Do you not wish to help her?" Freddie poked.

The seedling sighed and nodded. "Well, I'll let you off this time, but next time I see you, there better be payment. You got it?" Freddie nodded urgently. "Then, she's that way."

He pointed in the direction he'd walked from, and it was the same as the one that we had been heading, which meant my thoughts were confirmed. Empyreans, why did I wait to get confirmation from a fucking human seedling when I already knew? Time wasted. I better not fucking see him again.

Images of Arraetta bathed in red washed over me and I could not escape the festering notion that she might be at the end of her mortal life, right before it had truly started. The alley's entrance welcomed me in its grip, soles rebounding harshly against the uneven terrain until the sight of Arraetta sprawled against a broken, flickering lamppost tore my terror-filled soul apart.

"Open the rings, Freddie!" I commanded, speeding down and practically skidding before her, switching to English. "No, no, no, no, no!"

I tentatively shifted my hands as I looked at her, noting all the lacerations which decorated her fragile skin. It was as though she had been amidst a war that she had fought alone, and she had truly and wholly been defeated.

"Arraetta, stay with me," I begged quietly, gently taking hold of her shoulders as she struggled to breathe. *Please, I need you.*

I needed to get her home immediately, to where she would be safe and warm, to where I could nurse her back to health, and then I would provide her with the life she deserved. In my sight, in my reach, in my territory.

I was about to beg Freddie again, but Arraetta's hands gripped my wrists and I turned back to her, as her dilated, wide eyes stared at me. "Ge-nie, Genie."

Empyreans, she was dying before me, and all she cared about was her best friend? Then again, Genevieve was the only person who knew her the most in the world, understood everything about her and had cared for her in similar states before. But, even so, I noted the look on Genevieve's face from earlier. Even I did not believe she had ever witnessed anything as out of this realm as Arraetta disappearing like magic.

She blinked wearily, eyes closing a little. I gently tucked my fingers under her chin and lifted her face to look back at me. "Arraetta, we are going to help you."

"There is a ring in thirty seconds," Freddie said, speaking to us as though Arraetta understood.

"Genie," Arraetta begged.

"She is safe," Freddie promised, with little reassurance in his tone. It was not as though either of us knew what was happening at the palace, but I was sure Jonah would have kept her safe, even if he deemed her an outsider.

Freddie's words rankled Arraetta, using what little strength she had to try to poke the bear, but her lack of stamina was too much for her to contend with. I knew I had to use Primordial Thaumaturgy, even though it would make me even weaker.

"You are safe, Arraetta," I reiterated as Freddie warned me there were ten seconds until the ring opened. I nodded, cupping Arraetta's face so that she could look into my eyes and channelled my azure Rapidfire, pushing through the agony it brought to me, "*faesho arimoeni'na, laruer johe nen maradio fa alia umren oprei lunaeh ondu'raer hashon't-ei na mohen. Laurier johe oprei ondu'raer balengaeftai woneuan xae.*"

Let sleep come and guide you, bringing warmth from the sun to soothe your soul. Be at peace and feel safe within your dream-filled slumber.

Arraetta's breathing laboured and she slumped forward into me, eyes closed as Freddie placed his hand onto my shoulders and the world evaporated before us until we were back in the electric fields. I lifted Arraetta's limp body into my arms and we walked in silence, listening to the whooshing echoes of frequencies.

Thankfully, we did not meet any delays and were back in the

generator room within minutes. Freddie cursed, ripping off the fizzling watch and throwing it as it exploded into dust fragments on the floor.

"There goes our access to the rings," he commented, although I doubt we would find a use for such a mode of transport again for a long while.

With Arraetta in my arms, weighed down by her hefty ball gown, we made our way up to the west wing hallway. Jonah was pacing back and forth, whilst Alex and several of our guards congregated like they had been waiting for hours.

"Empyreans, I thought you were dead," Jonah swore when he saw us.

"A slight hiccup," Freddie said, eyeing Arraetta, who had drawn everyone's gaze. Alex looked visibly upset with his hand over his mouth, stepping forward to look at the devastation on her.

I did not linger any longer, walking down the hallway.

"We prepared the room next to yours," Jonah said, which I was glad for. At least if he had been unhappy that two humans were in our settlement, his anger had turned into concern.

In haste, flanked by all of them, we passed through the hallway, across the silent upper grand hallway landing, and into the east wing. By the time we finally returned, it was very late, most likely early in the morning, so attendees had either been confined to their rooms until further notice or sent back to their homes.

On arrival to the room, Marie and two nurses greeted me, and she immediately patted the bed for me to place her down. I stepped back as the three of them got to work, with Marie telling one of the females to cut the dress off.

"It will be best for you to wait outside," she said to me. "She is safe in my hands."

She might have been safe in her hands, but I was apprehensive about having her out of sight. What if she disappeared again? What if I could not find her the next time she did? It was more than a need, but a desperation to be near her just in case. A hand patted my shoulder to signal that I should leave, and, reluctantly, I left the professionals to their work, walking out into the corridor.

I closed the door, lingering with my back to everyone as I took a shaky breath before I turned. "Has anything happened whilst we were gone?"

"You have been summoned by the council," Jonah replied with a hesitant look.

"Unsurprised," I shrugged, but I was not blasé about something I knew would happen. It was just a shame they lingered like little rats waiting to attack when I was at my weakest. And, Empyreans, I was feeling weak. My power had all but evaporated from its overuse and would take sols to recover. I looked at my blood-soaked hands and thought, "I should shower."

"I should think you turning up like that would make you more formidable," he answered honestly.

"I will only be honest with them either way," I replied, looking for Freddie, "where is-?"

"-He is seeing his wife," Jonah said, and I looked at him, a little surprised.

"Ah, so she is no longer a *fancie*?" I had to jest with him, even though the comment was a little on the nose. "It is quite interesting how things have changed in a matter of hours. I suppose you are no longer angry with Freddie."

"I will still reprimand him, but I suppose there is not much I can do considering it is all done, and I am sure the slap on the wrist from your father will be much more painful than my own."

As though hearing our conversation, Freddie's door opened, and we turned to see Genevieve rush out with tear-stained cheeks, heading towards Arraetta's door. Freddie came after her, whilst I blocked her entry.

"Is she in there?" she asked groggily, and then she glowered at me. "Who are *you* to stop me seeing her?"

The only being in this life she needs. Empyreans, I wished that voice would just fuck off out of my head.

Her wrath-filled gaze turned to fear as she noted my sanguine white shirt, "That's her... that's her..." She looked like she was about to vomit as she stepped back. "Oh, God. No."

"She is okay," I offered the lie.

Freddie tried to steady her, but she shrugged him away, continuing to look at me. "You said she was like you. How are you similar?"

"It is not something I can show you," I replied, hesitant to use any form of Rapidfire again, but I looked at Freddie, "but Freddie may be able to."

"So, you are all the same as Arri?" she asked, ignoring my suggestion, as though Freddie had just become her greatest enemy.

"Genie-" Freddie began.

"-We do not know," I said truthfully. "I do not believe she is one of us."

"You don't believe or you don't know?" she replied, waving her arm towards the room, then snorted, "because Arri has been suffering with this... this *condition* since I've known her, okay? And no one - *no one* - has ever been able to help her. No one even knows about this, apart from me. But you've been here all this time and you don't know whether she's one of you?"

I wished I had known that for the length of time that we had been stationed in this realm. Empyreans how I dreamed of finding her earlier.

"She is not one of us," I stated honestly, "but I will find out who she is and she will be safe here. Safe with people who understand what ails her, and who can help." She looked undecided. "You may stay here also."

Genevieve side-eyed Freddie before they roamed to the other males in the corridor, seemingly thinking about something so profound it made her forehead wrinkle. "I will only stay until Arri is better, and then we will decide whether we will stay. It is Arri's decision, not mine."

"Please, Genie," Freddie whispered like a love-sick fool, his hand caressing her shoulder.

She shrugged him off, and I felt a little sorry for Freddie for her overly harsh retaliation as she spat at him, "You could have disclosed this to me, that you are... I don't even know what you are! An... either way, why would you pull me into this - no, me *and* Arri into this?"

Freddie looked torn, but he understood that such a conversation would have happened at some point. I was sure that if the events of the sol had not unfolded as they had, he would have sat down with her and shown her calmly, but everything - and I meant *everything* - had changed.

"It is against our laws," Jonah informed her softly.

"But, I would have informed her at some point," Freddie nodded, not keeping his eyes off his lover, "I am selfish, Genie. I cannot reverse time, but I will tell you everything you need to know and will never lie to you again. I promise."

Genevieve's silence was long, harsh and unnecessary, but then she nodded. "Fine, but I'm only giving you one chance."

Freddie looked sheepish as he agreed, whilst a subtle smile lifted on my face. If anything, the two females had brought a refreshing attitude to the house. Freddie raised his eyebrows at me, and I remembered that I had promised to apologise to Genevieve.

"Genevieve-" I started.

"-First!" she said, pointing her finger up at me. I leaned back slightly, sure the guards were ready to intervene, "Genie. Please. Just Genie. I feel like I'm in a room with my mum with you calling me that. You can call Arri by her full name, but I am just Genie. Secondly, if you do anything to hurt my best friend, I won't have any choice but to grab you by the balls and cut them off!" I winced a little. "Understood?"

"Understood," I agreed, trying to hide my amusement.

"Remind me to give her a lesson in etiquette," Jonah commented, keeping his dialect to our own so that she would not understand. Even then, she sent a glare in Jonah's direction before sighing and stepping back.

Again, I attempted to speak, but the door opened and Marie looked out, raising her eyebrows as she studied the small crowd. She murmured, "Oh, good, it seems the party is still going." She looked at Genie with a soft smile, switching to English. "I think you might be the right person to help."

Genie nodded desperately before stepping forward. "I can do anything."

"Comfort," Marie replied, allowing Genie to step in before she turned to me. "You should go and get yourself cleaned up."

Without another word, the door closed, and my apology hung in the air, waiting to be snapped up. I grumbled to myself, exhaustion hitting me like a sack of sand, and all I wished to do was collapse into a heap and disappear into the land of slumber. Even that was a far distant dream to be had, unsure whether I would sleep peacefully for sols to come as I awaited Arraetta's reawakening.

"It is time to face the council," Jonah reminded me.

"Fuck," I whispered, my jaw tightening.

I knew exactly what I would expect walking into the council chambers, and that whatever punishment awaited me was not ever going to be as hurtful as watching my fated one bleed painfully in my arms. Even my own torturous death would not compare to such horrors I had seen her bear.

But maybe I could convince them that the two humans had sparked a great change for the future of our people. The Gods' prophecy had been fulfilled, and the other half of Kindred had arrived for us to mend the grievous fracture in the universe. The arrival of a princess, their future queen, a possessor of golden, divine Rapidfire.

Fuck. It all made sense. Of course, with such vibrancy as what echoed in the skies during storms. Yet, surely, it was blasphemy for her even to be amongst us. But, it made sense with every legend and myth I had studied, tomes told to us as seedlings, generation to generation, of all the great Gods.

Empyreans, it all made sense. Arraetta was a God walking amongst mortals.

The Goddess of Divine Rapidfire.

ELEVEN

The clock in the hallway read that it was past one o'clock by the time we halted outside my father's wing. Our senior butler, Terance, was looking a little weary as he waited for our arrival, but still managed to remain poised, with a soft smile on his face.

"Your Grace," he bowed, surprised eyes not missing my stained attire.

"I am sorry to keep you awake so late."

"I cannot sleep until all is complete," Terance smiled softly, nodding towards the open doorway of the ballroom where workers gently milled about, tidying the events of the sol.

"Poetic," Freddie murmured before he grunted, "Ow, what was that for?"

"Shut it," Alex whispered.

"It is late," Jonah warned them both.

"Their majesties await you in the chambers," Terance said, escorting the four of us into the wing, leaving the guards behind.

Much like the upper east wing corridor, several doors led into various rooms, which included the council chambers directly below the library. The palace had not been upgraded much since the fifties, and my father's section resembled a gentleman's club, which seemed to be a desired aesthetic around the time we arrived.

"Do you ever feel like these portraits are watching us?" Freddie whispered from behind, pointedly talking about the several reimagined paintings on the wall of elders gone by, "Lord Creepo's eyes are moving."

"It is just an illusion," Alex replied in annoyance.

"Still creepy," Freddie shivered, "even worse at this hour. I am surprised His Majesty has not had a heart attack just by walking down this corridor."

Would that not be unfortunate?

Terance paused outside the doorway to the chambers, knocked and then awaited a signal to enter. It was The General who gave it, and I half rolled my eyes, knowing exactly what would come from the conversation. Masking my expression, I readied myself for the onslaught. It was going to be a very long night.

Terance opened the door, holding it to allow the four of us to enter, resembling a dishevelled group of Eton students. I noted that not all the council was in attendance: only my mother, father, The General, my father's advisor, Cormac, and our shaman, Sheika. Unsurprisingly, Kaeltar, with three other guards, stood at the back, although his presence ruffled my feathers and taunted my nerves.

My mother gasped as she stood from her chair, "Is that... is that your blood?"

She shuffled from her seat near the top of the table, shuffling over to me as though she cared. I did not get such a reaction when I had been fighting, so why did she care so suddenly after seeing Arraetta's blood caked on me?

"It is not," I stepped back, "Marie is attending to her."

"Her?" my father snapped. "I suppose you should mean this fancie of yours?"

Shoulders tense, anger simmering, he should have been so glad my fibres were weak otherwise I might have ripped his head off his

147

shoulders for using such derogatory terms about his future queen. I understood why Freddie hated such a term used for Genevieve – *Genie*.

"Have you lost your tongue?" The General growled. I turned my gaze to Kaeltar's smug one, before sweeping it to my father. He stood upright, a twinkle of terror littering his face, and even I wished I could feel the simmering of my Rapidfire just to glitter my fingers with its sparks to coax it more. It was quite enjoyable at times to see his hidden fear of the demon inside me.

I cleared my throat, opting for a calmer tone. "Arraetta is not a *fancie*. I told you the truth in the ballroom; Arraetta is my Kindred Spirit."

I noted the disbelief rippling across the council members.

"It cannot be true," my mother breathed, although she knew I would not lie about such trivial matters.

"I knew it the moment I saw her," I added truthfully.

"The Gods would never bless a human with such a gift," Cormac said, as though any of us asked for his opinion.

"I... I believe she is not human," I replied honestly. "She has Rapidfire – bright, golden Rapidfire."

"You dare come and speak lies in my council chamber," my father accused. "Another ploy to get the crown on your head sooner than it is deserved."

Of course, my father would believe I would lie. He believed that I was never deserving of the prophecy that the Gods had blessed, even before the darkness consumed part of me. But I could see the cracks in his faltering mask, and I knew he had been doing everything in his power to prevent me from leaving so that I could find her. It was only right that the Gods found a way to open a path for her to find me.

"He is not lying," Sheika said eerily quiet from her seat, but loud enough for us to hear.

"What?" he replied, looking at the shaman.

Sheika stood and looked at me. "His Highness is correct. I have seen a great many things during my meditations and dreams, and all of them suddenly became clear this sol. Your Kindred Spirit does bear Rapidfire."

"But that would make her of royal lineage," my mother said, walking back to the table, "not human, nor Zikan. Not even Porto."

"I would know if I had a sister," Freddie said quietly, before he shivered, "and that would make her Seraiah's cousin."

Arraetta was *not* my cousin.

"Three of the six great realms were destroyed or taken by The Dark," my mother said, "that still leaves Fo'rtaeya and Arduaex, on top of Porto."

"But she does not resemble a Nixie or a Fae," Cormac replied, as though he had been close enough to see what she looked like. If anything, she far more resembled one of us, without the slightly pointed ears and sharp teeth - blunted by necessity.

"I could not care what creature this female is," my father chided. "She is an imposter in our society, and Seraiah shall be reprimanded for this crime."

"You may wish to reprimand him, but he has only done as the Gods wished," Sheika said in support of me, "we all knew his Kindred Spirit would arrive, and it is now time to prepare for this new era, and their bonding."

Bonding. A phrase which had itched at the back of my mind since the first time Sheika and her disciples had heard the news of my prophecy. An act in which two souls would conjoin to become one with each other.

"We all know what the prophecy of Kindred states," Sheika said, looking at us all. "There will be a time of great turmoil and a war to end all wars." I shivered as its burden rippled through me. "I should offer advice, Majesty. You should prepare for that time because no matter how much we resist, it is written in the stars."

My father looked less than impressed. He shared a look with The General and Cormac, and I could not tell if they were displeased by the prophecies' awakening or knowing that they would have to prepare their idle troops for war.

"And what of the Rapidfire?" my mother asked Sheika.

"I would need to meditate more," Sheika replied. "I shall try to decipher as much as I am able. But if His Highness has described such Rapidfire as golden, it can only mean that she is descended from one of the four fallen realms."

"The Cre-este," my mother replied, almost matter-of-factly.

And Sheika's nod sent another ripple of shock through everyone, even my brothers beside me.

"Until she demonstrates such power, I shall not trust any of this blasphemy," my father said. "you are telling us that she is descended from The Great King? That human who caused havoc in our home?"

"She is not human," I added.

"She is human until I receive proof," he slammed his fist on the table. "I will not have some outsider living in this palace."

"And where do you suggest we house her, Charles?" my mother asked.

"The Vaults."

A low growl rippled from my throat, fists clenching, ready to pounce at the male for his ridiculous suggestion. And it only seemed to sprout a smile of satisfaction across the faces of The General and Kaeltar.

"No," my mother replied, "she is Seraiah's future wife and our next queen. She will reside in this palace and be treated as such."

"We know nothing of this female!" my father exclaimed, "and

you are going to believe the foul words of that seedling over our safety."

"Are you so scared of her, Your Majesty?" I replied, a chuckle rippling out of my mouth.

"Fear is not the issue," my father replied, speaking to everyone. "I cannot, in good conscience, keep an outsider here. Let alone let her *marry* him. And, what shall happen when she gets to know the monster which lies under his skin?" he looked at me. "Do you plan to show her the cruel-hearted male you are?"

I snorted. "I am under control."

"But you shall not be," he tilted his head to the side, searching for all the deeply embedded flaws, "and when she runs from you, she will tell this whole realm of the demon who resides here. For a prince who seems to be so stoic about his want to be king, he sure does not seem to care about the consequences of his people."

I glowered. "You have no care for our people."

He barked a laugh. "You are so small-minded, Seraiah. And how do we know that you are not working with this female, furthering your gain to the throne, feeding us lies that you have met your Kindred Spirit? It is just incredibly convenient that it landed on *this* sol."

"I am not lying."

"Charles-"

"-And, whilst we are the subject of deceit," he interrupted my mother, "I believe you should try to keep a tight hold on your possessions." He picked up a dossier from the table and waved it around. "Recognise this?"

My heart thudded as my mask momentarily dropped, revealing the sudden fear that had tainted my expression. That was impossible. He was holding my speech, the one that revealed how corrupt he was, the one I should have said on the dais earlier in the sol but had chosen against. How had it ended up in his hand? I automatically checked my jacket pocket, noting that it was empty. With everything that had happened, the speech was the last thing that had been on my mind, and, quite frankly, it should have been the first.

Fuck.

"You should find yourself lucky that one of the waiters handed this into Fulk," my father said. "it would be a shame for such accusatory lies to be spread to our people. Such uproar caused for your petty gains."

Fuck. Fuck. Fuck. Fuck. Fuck.

My father's words should have lit the fire of anger and spread it through my soul, giving me a foothold in a winnable argument, but I felt like I had just been thrown into the deepest pit without an anchor to hold on to.

No more stoic prince. Just frightened Seraiah, unable to string together a sentence to fight my father as he opened the document.

I should have read the speech. I should have read the *fucking* speech. But Arraetta's twinkling laughter washed over my mind, and I remembered why I had chosen not to say it. Because it was not the right time, because she had arrived, and I did not want to cause more uproar than I already had. And it was my consequence to bear.

He read out loud, skipping the introductions. "*Father, I cannot go without speaking about the arduous path that you have laid out as an unmoving and acute leader... How you have tirelessly woven a tale of conspiracy and corruption to undermine my legitimacy as the next king.*" He chuckled. "I do not know which corruption you suspect should undermine your legitimacy, but I should remind you that being a king is not a game for seedlings, Seraiah."

I glowered. "Did you read the rest of the speech?"

"Oh, yes," he nodded, eyeing it briefly before he folded it up and placed it back down on the table, "quite the play, I must say.

But, whilst you believe I appeased others to secure this so-called *allegiance* you believe I require, the simple truth is that *you* are still not ready for the throne." He paused. "And, should I make the obvious so very clear that there are many of our people - *my* people - who do not wish to see a seedling riddled with a demon become the next great leader of our realm."

The fear finally disappeared, and the anger settled at his bitter words. My father, the great pretender, ruled in an autocratic manner and fed fear to our subjects - my subjects - about the monster I was - a beast that none had borne witness to.

I laughed bitterly, "You are afraid I will reveal every lie you have spawned, but you should be thankful I withheld my tongue this sol."

"I should watch how you speak to The King, boy!" The General growled, finally showing his tongue when he had been silent since our arrival. He nodded towards Kaeltar. "I believe the two of you are already well acquainted."

Kaeltar stood a little straighter, a proud smirk on his lips as he awaited his final orders to take me away. A shiver ran down my spine, but I bit back the agitation as I kept my eyes trained on my father.

"This is unnecessary," my mother said.

"It is very necessary!" my father shouted. "Our son has conspired against the throne; he has sent spies behind our backs and falsified documents to set rumour about my position as King. That, my good wife, is treason. Whilst a lower born may do such things, I expect more from the male who is set to be next in my position."

My mother looked ready to intervene again, but even she could not deny that it was true that my actions were treasonous. Even so, my mind swayed to Eros, the spy who had infiltrated my father's organisation and just so happened to be captured - my speech was enough evidence to sentence him to death. Guilt rippled through me. I wanted to free him, but if I made it obvious he was connected, the rest of Amity would be in danger.

"Then, we shall vote at council," Jonah stated, stepping to my side. "If you truly believe His Highness to be guilty, then we must put this before the council *with* evidence."

"No one said you could speak!" The General spat. "I think you should know that, considering you are constantly preaching the importance of protocol."

"Enough!" my mother commanded, pinching the bridge of her nose as she took a deep breath, before looking at my father, "whilst I do understand that the accusations are treasonous, there is not enough evidence supporting your claims, Charles. If you truly wish for our people to understand the true nature of this fractured family, then you may choose to go to court. But for the sake of our people and the arrival of Seraiah's fated one, we must let this go..." She looked around, seeming to beg with her last words. "*Please*, let this go."

The final decision resided on my father's shoulders, and all eyes fell on him.

"I shall let this go for this night," he said, after a long moment of inner contemplation. "However, we shall return to this matter. I will not let this go easily. I do not care if you are my son. I am still your king, and I shall be *your* king until my last breath. You are dismissed."

My gaze met Kaeltar's frustrated one, which rippled me with satisfaction – he would not get to punish me as he wished that night. But even I knew that I was in the midst of a battle which was looking increasingly more difficult to win. I would be punished. It was just a matter of when. Empyreans, I should have just said the fucking speech. My father had played his piece, and the stalemate had returned.

But there was no time for faded possibilities, just the road forward, keeping Arraetta safe from the tight grip of my father. I only prayed that his last breath would come soon if he were not to easily hand over the kingdom.

"Frederique, you shall stay," The General said.

"*Prince* Frederique is under my protection," Jonah replied instantly. "I should remind you that he is a guest with us, as are the two females upstairs. We treat our guests accordingly. Therefore, his punishment will come through me, not you, *Father*."

Whilst I expected The General to argue with his son, he nodded, "See that it is done, but the girl *has* to go."

"The girl stays," Jonah said. "her name is Genie, and she is a guest of Freddie, which makes her a guest of ours. The act of 209, under the treaty between Porto and Zika, states that any guests of either nature are to be treated with respect and courtesy unless they break any laws. Of which, the only law that has been broken is that of 602, in which Prince Frederique brought an undeclared migrant into the community, without prior permission, and the punishment for this law is twenty-five hours of community service to be assigned by the guardian of the guest. That, as you are aware, is me, following the ruling of the council a great many winters-"

"-I understand!" The General bellowed, and he almost sounded like a spoiled seedling having a tantrum. And even through his impenetrable guise, I could detect the smugness on Jonah's face.

With barely any further words, the four of us left. I released a heavy sigh of satisfaction that we were out of my father's territory once we entered the entrance hallway. Our guards waited, but Jonah instructed them to retire.

"Thank you," Freddie said to Jonah.

"Whilst I do not approve of your methods, Freddie," Jonah replied, "I will admit my fault when I spoke negatively of Genie."

"Wow, a real apology," Freddie grinned.

"It is for Miss Kinsley, not you," Alex said, and the two males glared at each other.

"Still, you will need to do community service." Jonah ignored their playful feud. "Lucky for you, it should not be too hard a task."

Alex planted a contented smile on his face, as we all watched Freddie grovel at Jonah, "and, what is the task?"

"I shall tell you tomorrow."

"What?" Freddie gasped, "Tell me now!"

Jonah turned to me, "It is lucky you are the next king, Seraiah. Otherwise, I might see to it that you are also given such a penalty." I rolled my eyes. "Of course, I should expect you to prepare. Your father will not let this sit."

As I am aware, Jonah. But I did not want to think about what was going to await me when my fated one was on death's door upstairs.

"It looks like we will have a long night ahead, my love," Jonah turned to Alex, gently gripping his bicep, "I will be reviewing security protocols with Leopold tomorrow."

"I can stay with you."

"Go home," Jonah said softly, placing a soft hand on his cheek.

Just twenty-four hours prior I might have grimaced watching the two, but the odd, new hint of affection that simmered inside made me feel somewhat elated.

"Want me to walk you back?" Freddie teased.

Alex snorted, "I am not scared of the night."

With a final goodbye, Alex left the house, just in time for my father's door to open and Kaeltar to appear with three guards.

Kaeltar smirked at the sight of us. "Ah, if it isn't the three musketeers. Aren't you missing the fourth?"

Jonah's shoulders tightened, and I wondered if he had sent Alex away early to ensure he was safe. "Back off, Kaeltar."

"Ooo, empty threats," Kaeltar chuckled, looking towards me, "I look forward to our next meet, Your Highness. You have escaped me twice, but I doubt Tyche will be on your side the next time."

There was no fear in my stance, just pure hatred and anger for the male who dared to continue to threaten me. Fists clenched, I prayed again for my power to make him understand what would happen if he even tried to pull the rug from under me without a council vote. But, I was powerless and, Empyreans, did he know it as he studied me.

I was quite fortunate that it was rare for Kaeltar to find himself inside the palace, otherwise I was sure he would have sneaked into my bedroom and slit my throat. Then again, he would have to sneak past the sigils on my door without them alerting me. And it was not exactly in his prowess to just slit a throat; he enjoyed torture.

Kaeltar leisurely strolled past us, followed by the two other guards, not sparing us a final glance.

"Hellsworn," Freddie grunted, causing us to laugh. But it was mine, which was suddenly cut short as an excruciating pain rocketed through my chest cavity like someone had shoved a hot forge rod through it. I stumbled backwards twice, tried to balance myself and then thudded to the cold tiled flooring.

Dark, ominous laughter rippled around, blending with the concern of my brothers and my thundering heartbeat, pumping rapidly with every passing second. My vision began to swim, and I struggled under the force of bone-deep fatigue and unyielding pain. It was as though my life force was being sucked from my body until I could no longer resist the pull of darkness.

Seraiah.

A giggle.

A trickle of flowing water, birds chirping, and a breeze rustling leaves on a tree whispered into my ears, tickling my skin with a hue of warm light. I clenched my fingers, and my nails dug into damp soil, while hardwood tucked into the curve of my back. I opened my eyes, blinking twice, as I looked in awe at the place I was in.

Home.

Yet, it was not real. It was as though I was reliving a slightly hazy, distant memory which had blurred and twisted over time. But I was in no hurry to move away from such grace. A gentle splash echoed in the centre of the river, and I watched as the tip of a small creature's head popped up, staring at me with wide eyes.

It was a transparent blue creature with mortal-kind eyes and gills to help it swim. Almost as unreal as it was real.

A Spirit Nymph.

Captivated, I stood and wandered towards it, eager to see such a rare and surprising sight before me. Or maybe it was just a fish that resembled the tales of the old.

"Are you real?" I asked, noting the higher-pitched tone in my voice, which indicated that I was not an adult, but a seedling. "Are you truly the Spirit Nymph?"

It swam towards me steadily, gazing with such big, curious eyes.

"My grandma used to read me stories about you all the time," I continued, my words not seeming to be my own, "saying that you get whatever your heart desires if you meet a Spirit Nymph. Is that true?"

A resounding call from my father came from the thick of the lush forest, "Seraiah!"

I turned, it seemingly frightened by the male coming to find me. Without further hesitation, I looked back at the nymph.

"Look, I must go, but can I ask for something?" I asked it, laughing awkwardly, "I mean, if this truly is real. Can I request that you do everything you can so I can find her? My Kindred Spirit? Even if it means turning my life upside down to find her, will you do that for me?"

"Seraiah!"

I looked in the direction again, nervous. A harsh rush of water echoed, and I turned to watch the nymph being swept away by a suddenly rapid-flowing river.

"Hey, wait!" I shouted.

"Seraiah!" my father's voice shouted again, the impatience of his tone becoming more evident as he continuously repeated my name. But, instead, it melded into that of Freddie's and the long-gone world of Zika washed away into the harshness of a tungsten light hanging from the gallery room's window.

And hanging over me like a worried aunt was the dream's intruder.

"Empyreans, thank fuck."

The uncomfortable chaise lounge held my weight as I slowly pulled myself upright, grimacing at the tension in my head. The pain in my chest had thankfully evaporated.

"Was I out for long?" I grimaced, looking to the door where Jonah stood with his arms folded and a tense look on his face. I could not tell whether it was worry, frustration, or both.

"Twenty minutes," Freddie replied. "Your mother came."

"And went," I added, knowing she would not have been concerned long enough to have felt the need to stick around. *Emotionally detached*, one might say.

"I said you fainted from exhaustion," Freddie said.

Exhaustion... excruciating pain... both *very* similar. I doubted my mother cared for either, of course. She would not notice such things unless I suddenly died, and even then, I was sure that was a blessing for her.

"I thought I was going to die," I stated.

Jonah snorted, "It would take more than passing out to die, Seraiah."

"It was not the passing out. It felt as though someone had shot an arrow of fire through my chest and I was burning from the inside out."

While I expected them both to mock me and tell me how much I was exaggerating, which I rarely did, I noted their looks. It was like two people sharing a secret they were unsure they could impart.

I felt a thump in my heart, and then I suddenly thought that my collapse must have caused something else to happen.

"What? What has happened?" I raised my eyebrows. "Did my wine get poisoned at the party after all?"

"Have you felt any physical connection with Arraetta since you met her?" Freddie asked, "Like her pain when we rescued her."

"Not quite." I shook my head.

"Freddie is trying to say that maybe this bond between you causes you to feel some of her physical pain," Jonah said, causing tingles of fright to ripple through me. He bowed his head. "Arraetta had to be resuscitated at the time you blacked out."

Resuscitated. *Dead.* She could not have died.

No. I had only just found her.

My heart thundered, all reason disappearing as the worst of thoughts about Arraetta rattled through my mind. I threw myself from the chair, uncaring for my dizziness, and raced out of the room, ignoring the calls of my name.

TWELVE

Four guards were posted outside the room when we left to go to the council chambers, but when I arrived, only one remained. She bowed her head in respect but did not move from her position, which blocked the doorway as I rushed up to it.

"Move," I half-commanded.

"I'm very sorry, Your Highness. I've been given strict orders to ensure that no one enters this room."

My jaw tightened at the guard's unwavering stance. "And who gave you that order, hm? My father?" Her face reddened. "Because I do not see anyone else with the power to be above my command, so I will tell you again to step aside so that I may-"

"Whoa, whoa, whoa!" Freddie said, having finally caught up to me. He looked apologetic to the hesitant guard. "Apologies, Misha. He is just a little weak in the knees, so he is... unlike himself."

I snorted while Misha bowed. "I'm sorry, Your Highness. Madam Marie gave the command."

Freddie chuckled, patting my back, "Well, I suppose that writes out even The King's command. I was going to tell you that Arraetta was fine before you ran upstairs in a storm. You truly are quite reckless, Your Grace." He was mocking me. "One female has sent your head into a spin; I do wonder what shall be next for the great prince."

I tutted, "It is only a need to protect her, Freddie."

"Oh, I never denied such a fact."

Arraetta's door opened, and Misha stepped out of the way as Marie walked out in a blood-stained apron. She looked like she had been tending to the wounded in a war zone. The sight of it made me queasy, although it could have been the lack of food and my throbbing headache.

"She's fine," she said, eyeing my clothing, "you still haven't changed your attire. Aren't you uncomfortable wearing that?"

"We have only just been released from the council."

"What Seraiah will fail to tell you is that he fainted," Freddie added.

I looked at him disapprovingly. "Not in the council, I should add. I am fine; there is nothing to agonise over."

"Two patients in one night," Marie sighed. "Still, I can only assume you are running on adrenaline and stress. They're concoctions that I don't recommend mixing. Eat, bathe, *sleep*."

"I cannot sleep until I know she is well," I stated.

"And, that could be several sols," she blinked, "and, what then, Seraiah? Will you greet her looking like a zombie that arose from the dead? I'm sure that'll only frighten her more than the idea that she's betrothed to a king. Hm. No, please, go and return in the morning when you're refreshed. I promise to awaken you should there be any more incidents."

I grumbled, hesitant to agree to her demands. But Freddie took the initiative to thank Marie, and she walked back into the room, closing the door. He placed his arm around my shoulder and turned us toward my room, giving me little chance to grovel.

"It will be alright," Freddie promised.

And, whilst he was most likely right, my head was filled with anxious thoughts from not being able to see Arraetta again. Just to touch her hand would have soothed my spiralling anxiety. Freddie and I departed, and I followed Marie's instructions to bathe and dress. Yet, once more comfortable, I found myself back in the corridor, sitting by the opposite wall, the throb in my head an unwanted companion.

The guard on duty had retired, leaving the usual house guards roaming the corridors on a loop. It was close to two o'clock, and the house was peaceful, apart from the odd clatter inside Arraetta's room. Even then, it was hard to hear because most rooms were soundproofed.

Time passed, and slowly, I felt the pull of the night's gaze coaxing me into a deep slumber.

Seraiah.

I blinked. I was still sitting in the hallway, but the soft hue from the rising sun shone through the windows at the top of the corridor. My bones were stiff, and my muscles ached as I stretched gently to ease them. I was sure that the night watch had peered at me on every round they took, but it seemed no one had disturbed me.

Arraetta's door opened, and I watched as Marie's two assistants shuffled out quietly, one after the other. The first did not notice me as she was peering at her colleague, but the other immediately gasped and half-curtseyed, prompting the other to do the same thing. I waved them off, not caring for their politeness when they had been working tirelessly for hours.

The two scurried down the corridor, leaving the door ajar enough to see the edge of the bed and Marie wandering by the window. I did not stand until she turned and saw me waiting patiently.

"I suppose you should come in," she called quietly, which gave me all the permission I needed.

The sound of a quiet monitor beeping on top of a portable metal trolley, with a tall metal pole holding a bag of fluids poking out the

163

top of it, caught my ears. Its wire ran down to Arraetta's right side, where a cannula was attached to her right wrist, which was placed over a white sheet covering most of her body. I turned my weary gaze up to her pale, bruised face decorated with tended-to lacerations and stains of blood. An oxygen mask pressed against her face, turning white every time she took a thankful breath.

Genie, who had barely acknowledged my arrival, was lost in her thoughts, with little specks of blood on her hands. Her gaze was fixed on her friend as she idly stroked the skin between Arraetta's thumb and forefinger. I only wished to sit in her place, feeling the gentle thrum of Arraetta's energy meld with mine.

Marie placed her hand on Genie's shoulder, causing her to jolt slightly. "I suggest you get some rest."

Genie's eyes met mine before she looked back at Arraetta, softly shaking her head, "If you don't mind, I think I'll stay."

Marie looked slightly hesitant, but ended up agreeing. Weariness settled in Marie's gaze, and I wondered how long she had been on standby, waiting for me to return with Arraetta. Then again, I was sure that she did not expect Arraetta to appear on the brink of death.

I physically shivered at the thought of her greeting the God himself.

She returned to her makeshift table by the window, tidying and cleaning bits of equipment, whilst I stepped to the right side of Arraetta's bed, not taking a seat even when my mind was begging me to.

"You know this happens every four years?" Genie looked at me, "I was prepared for it because I knew... I knew something would happen. But it's never been this bad. I don't... I don't even know how she could end up in such a bad state. So much blood... so... broken."

I knew I had a great deal more to learn about Arraetta's *blackouts* as they had been coined, and to understand why they would happen every four winters. It seemed like such an odd frequency, yet I almost wondered whether it had been connected to my lack of power, which dulled over the period between Iontine celebrations. Maybe Arraetta was more connected to us than we had ever thought, but rather than being able to control her power, she lost control.

And her tumultuous adventure through the rings and to the estate where she had resided also posed many questions that had yet to be answered. Even the rings would never cause that much harm, save for the headache and energy depletion.

"I promise I will answer," I said truthfully.

Genie took a moment before she nodded, looking at me with her makeup-flecked cheeks, unkempt hair and bloodshot eyes. The mixture of alcohol and sudden sobering was a poison that even I could never stomach.

"Today was the happiest I've ever seen her, you know," she whispered, peering back at her friend, "every day, she goes against the wants of our parents, keeping a distance from everyone, working a shitty job delivering pizza for less than fucking minimum wage. Some days, she's out for hours on that stupid bike that she hauls up and down the stairs like it's life or death. I told her to get a better job, but she says it's easier just in case something happens - in case *this* happens. She deserves so much more, Seraiah. She deserves to be loved." She paused. "She would be happy here... wouldn't she?"

I did not hesitate, as I nodded, "Yes."

Of course, she would be happy. The need to shield her from suffering was innate, to never witness the pain from tainting her radiant expression, to grant her whatever she wanted and desired. Even if it meant keeping her away from the political rebellion simmering beneath the surface of the house.

Even the strongest bonds are built on the darkest secrets.

And the Gods know that I held the darkest of them all.

"I have to warn you, she's stubborn. You won't find it easy being with her; give her a mile, and she'll take an inch. Probably will say she'd be your maid or something."

Little did Genie know, we had already had such a conversation in the gardens earlier the sol before. But I would never let Arraetta be my maid. That would be preposterous. I had not thought about the prospect that maybe my father would try to force something like that upon her, but I hoped even he would not do something so low.

A growl rippled from my throat, which I quickly covered with a cough as I diverted my eyes to Arraetta from Genie as she jumped a little. It seemed that even Genie would still have much to learn about the creatures we Zikan and Portons were. Close enough to be human, but with once-pointed teeth, much like a Fae, and subtly pointed ears like elves. Mortal-kind. Or, more mythically, Lyrhen.

"She will likely be the crown princess," Marie added, which took Genie by surprise before a soft smile washed over her face.

"I promise I shall keep her safe," I told Genie, "Her title has not yet been decided, and that resides with the council. However, she is the most important being to have graced my life."

And, even after waiting for scorns for her arrival, knowing little about the bond between Kindred Spirits, I knew that to be a statement of fact. I had read and been taught about the part we would both play in the universe, yet there was also hardly any correlation between the written materials and the feeling deep in my soul.

"I'm quite tired," Marie said, taking a seat in an armchair that had been added to the room, "Your Highness, whilst I understand you want to be here, I think you should find it more comfortable to visit your bed and return in a few hours. You need to rest, and I think it's a good idea for us two ladies to do so as well."

Marie was right, but I had barely had a chance to even lay my eyes on her, let alone the opportunity to touch her, and I was already being told to leave. Still, I understood Marie's words, and although I was stubborn, I would not fight her.

I bowed my head. "I shall leave you both, then. Please find me should anything further happen."

Marie's answer was closing her eyes and sticking her thumb up at me, whilst Genie gently lay beside Arraetta, where I only wished to be. After a final glance at my fated one's pale face, I took my leave.

Whilst I knew I should have slept, I was more desperate to find out more about Arraetta and her Rapidfire, outside of the myths that lay in the tomes of the library. I knew the only person with the answers I sought was our shaman, and whilst I would have preferred not to visit the old root bearer, her insight was the only one I favoured.

Once I escaped the house using my usual exit of the bedroom window, I took a stroll towards Sheika's house, not taking much of the final moments of the early sunrise in. It was only as my knuckles brushed the door that I realised it was a little too early for her to be awake. The answers could wait a few more hours.

Settling on the wooden porch, legs hanging over the steps, I leaned against the fence, looking upward at the clear skies. It was set to be another beautiful sol, although it would have been nice for some rain to clear the air. With my thoughts drifting to the events of the ball, I drifted into dreamless slumber only to be awoken by the clanging of a bundle of keys and the door unlocking behind me.

I cricked my neck as the tinkling of Sheika's cat's collar ruffled my ears, and I looked back as Sheika looked at me from her doorway, a little mortified that I was there. She was dressed in silver silk pyjamas and a pink, fluffy nightgown.

She cleared her throat. "I had assumed you might grace my doorstep."

"I am surprised you did not see," I replied, dusting myself off as I stood. "You are a seer."

"I am a shaman," she corrected, "not a Nixie, remember."

"Yes, but you still meditate."

"You should try it one sol; it may ease some of your anger."

I rolled my eyes at her backhanded comment, walking past and into her home.

"How is A'uren?" I asked, curious to know how the Nixie was fairing as the only creature of his kind on Earth. He was far too distinct in looks to pass as just an ethereal human, so my mother had him housed for safety, and control, in our most remote settlement in the Scottish Highlands.

"He is as well as anyone who cannot leave their home," Sheika replied casually. "He writes on occasion, although I did not hear from him until earlier this winter."

It was a blessing and a curse to have a Nixie present. They were excellent creatures who could see various outcomes of circumstances, but sometimes their gifts were exploited by those who sought to control certain populations. And, of course, my father would do anything in his power to keep A'uren on hand.

Sheika's hoard-filled house was filled with trinkets, tomes, maps and all sorts of other random things she had collected over the sols. Most things seemed to give away her age, odd collections of teapots, cups, saucers and plates perfectly placed in glass cabinets, whilst she had a mountain of fans in glass cases pinned against the walls.

"Would you like a cup of tea?" she asked.

I agreed, although I could have done with something stronger as well as food to combat my hunger pangs. She led me into her old cottage kitchen, the wide open backdoor showing off her beautiful herb garden, edged with trees and lined with colourful flowers. Should I have enjoyed Sheika's presence, I might have opted to spend more time there.

Sheika was not on the side of any except the Gods, although it felt like she had favoured my father's rule for far too long to not have chosen. Certain decisions, including the one that ended up with my imprisonment on arrival to Earth, were what turned my father's callous nature towards me into pure hatred.

I supposed if anyone had heard the words from Sheika's mouth, of the prophecy that she had been told, they might have manipulated it until it no longer read as it did. It was prophesied that I would spend the rest of my sols with darkness in my soul until light fractured my soul and broke me free from it. At least, it was how I had come to decipher it, whilst my father had focused on the information that I had become a demon.

"Please, take a seat," Sheika said, pointing to her messy table covered in things like piles of paper, different tomes, dirty teacups, a side plate of cake crumbs, and a pair of garden shears.

While I found a space on one of the chairs, Sheika filled the stove kettle with water, lit the flame, and placed it on top. She removed several pieces of bread from a bread bin before putting them into the toaster. Soon, two plates, two knives, a butter dish and a pot of marmalade were placed on the table, and she removed the dirty pots afterwards.

"I can have a maid sent over for you," I commented.

"Whilst you enjoy having your dirty laundry cleaned by others," she said, turning to me with a look of, 'I am not just talking about the ones you wear.' "I would much prefer to sort my own dishes. Should I require any help, I am more than capable of hiring someone."

It was not as though I could change her mind. She had always been untidy and never changed her ways, not even for my mother, who often visited.

"When I am dead," she said, as the toast popped out of the toaster, "you may have all the freedom you wish to clean my home. It is not as though I can take any of this across the River Styx."

I rolled my eyes. "It is not as though you believe the Styx to exist."

Sheika placed the toast into a little metal rack, which balanced on top of a flower-rimmed plate, picked it up and dropped it onto the table. "It is but a phrase of the tongue, Seraiah. Whilst the Styx is but a myth, we both know that once I am finished in this life, I shall peacefully pass on to my next. And I shall be glad to do so in hopes that I shall never have to be part of the royal machinations of this society."

The kettle whistled, and she took it from the flame, turning the gas off before making some tea. Once done, she finally placed one for me and sat opposite with her cup. She helped herself to toast, slathering it with butter and marmalade before biting. Without much nudging, I tucked in as well, although I opted for a far less heart-attack-inducing spread.

"I have come-"

"-To speak of our new arrival, I do know," she munched, a dust of crumbs lining her gown, "and it is as I said. She is your Kindred Spirit; the Gods have finally blessed us and brought her here, where she is most needed."

I chewed on my toast. "I knew who she was the moment I saw her."

"As you would. My dreams tell me of a tumultuous time to come. They seemed to bear more symbolism than reality. Ashen skies, a winged hydra-"

"-Are you stuck on Greek mythology this sol?" I joked.

She tutted, "It is what I saw. I can only decipher the messages, not question them. It is not a hydra, but it had wings and three heads, so you may name it as you wish."

"Are you sure it was not just a dragon? Maybe your vision was blurred."

Whilst I was jesting with her, the prospect of any form of hydra-like beast was terrifying. The Hydra was a creature of myth, locked in Tartarus, bearing several long heads and legend to be humongous in its size. Whilst something similar was not impossible, I could not imagine it would have the wingspan it needed to carry such a heavy weight.

"You do not need to believe me; I am only recalling what I saw," she replied. "I should try to speak with A'uren, but such answers might take moon cycles, and I would like to do it discreetly without alerting the council." I understood her worries. "Still, I shall meditate with Zela."

"Whilst it sounds somewhat terrifying, it is more important to me to find out *who* Arraetta is."

"It is all linked, Seraiah," she said as she sipped her tea and peered out into her garden. "Whilst I have not witnessed her golden Rapidfire, my dreams showed me a female with the most vibrant Rapidfire. I could only describe her as the epitome of a goddess, with brunette curls, blue eyes, and sun-kissed skin. At the ball, I knew Arraetta was the one I had seen. Of course, I had already exhausted my research for who I believed her to be, and the only being I could truly ever conclude her to be is the daughter of Ivan the Great and the divine goddess Reona."

"Then that would make her a god."

"A demi-god," she said. "Remember, Ivan the Great was still an ephemeral king. There is insufficient evidence to support what happened to their daughter, which may give us a plausible explanation. There was a tome in the University of the Universe called The Treatise of The Cre-este. It is written in their language, which we know is notoriously difficult to translate, even when there are some similarities to ours."

I had never heard of the tome, and if it was outside our realm of knowledge, we could not access the materials.

"You may remember when we arrived," Sheika added, "that I recreated several tomes which I had memorised, which included that particular tome. But it is not here now. It is in Italy, where our more precious materials were sent to. As much as I would enjoy a trip to somewhere warmer, I cannot leave."

"Then, I shall go."

"You are reckless, young prince. I think it is best to send someone else from the palace. You have broken house rules; I do not expect your father to let you off lightly."

I shivered at the thought. "Is that what you believe should happen?"

"What I believe and know are different. Whether you are a prince or a subject, you have still broken the law and brought an outsider into this world. I do not expect your punishment to be harsh, but I know your father will order it."

I grimaced, wondering what kind of punishment my father would enjoy giving me to show our people that even his son could not get away with breaking such laws. Still, part of me wished he would see that I was only a bystander in Freddie's plot.

I let out a humourless chuckle. I was not only going to wholly be punished for the two outsiders – I would also be punished for treason.

And treason was punishable by death.

Yet, he could not kill his only heir to the throne. So it had to be so much worse.

"Once I have the tome, I will find what answers I can," Sheika finished, "but I believe, from what you have described, that she can only be the bearer of Divine Rapidfire."

A daughter of a goddess and the greatest king to have ever lived.

A demi-god.

My fated one was a fucking goddess.

A loud rapture on the front door interrupted our conversation, causing her dog to start yipping, and I grumbled, realising it was Travis' exact knock.

"Unless I am due another early morning visitor," Sheika said, rising from her chair, "I would assume that is for you."

"I shall take my leave," I stood, "thank you."

Sheika placed her hand on my bicep. "If I may, it is wise until the bond is complete, and things have settled, for you to keep your feud with your father from the ears of your Kindred Spirit. I can only imagine such things would be distressing for her, and you cannot afford her running away when you are so close to completing the one thing that is most important."

I nodded, already knowing such a secret would be mine to bear until I was confident she could handle such truth.

"And you must not complete the bond early," she replied. "it will be tough. You are both young and this bond will make you fall in love quickly, but physical contact will be detrimental to the vows you take."

Do not fuck. There was nothing worse than an old coot saying I could not get my dick wet until I was on my knees begging for release. I supposed it made the chase more interesting, but even then I only dreamed of kissing her lips. I could kiss her, could I not?

Or maybe she truly meant all physical contact.

No, I would need to touch her.

"You can still hold her hand," Sheika smiled, suddenly noticing something outside, "Darn birds!"

Sheika rushed into her garden towards some crows, making themselves at home in the herbs. I chuckled, then sighed as another knock tapped the front door. I grabbed the final bit of toast and wandered through the house.

As I had thought, Travis, and surprisingly, Leopold greeted me. It was not as though the grand captain was against getting his hands dirty, but it was a little unlike him to be on bodyguard duty.

"Your Highness," Leopold greeted.

"Has something happened?" I asked, stepping onto the porch. "I do not need the two of you babysitting me."

Leopold grinned, "are you sure about that? You are quite prone to throwing a tantrum."

I snorted, "You forget your place, Lyliaer."

The smile did not slip from his face at the use of his first name. "I have not forgotten, Your Grace. However, when Prince Frederique went to check that you were not dead this morning, Sentinel Travis here alerted us all that the prince had disappeared."

"I could have been in my office."

"Yet CCTV shows us you did not leave your room."

"Still, I do not need escorting," I replied, folding my arms. "Whilst I do appreciate the incentive, I do not expect harm before the house has even arisen. I much prefer my own company at this time."

"And not the company of our new queen?" Travis asked, an unusual comment from a male who preferred to keep quiet.

I walked past the two to return to the house. "At least that kind of company is more *pleasing* to the eye, Travis."

She was more than just pleasing. Her company was the only one I wished to bathe in, a simmering yearning to spend every aching moment with her. She had already tarnished every worry I had about my future by arriving and every care for my father's foul play was slowly drifting away.

Soon, our story would be similar to that of Arraetta's suspected lineage. I would be King Seraiah the Great, and she would be Arraetta, the Goddess of Divine Rapidfire.

My queen.

My deity.

My wife.

THIRTEEN

The following sols were testing. Whilst awaiting my father's wrath, I remained by Arraetta's side and helped when and where I was needed by Marie. Arraetta was constantly unstable, wrestling with plaguing nightmares. Genie also spent a lot of time in the room, taking time off her schooling to tend to her friend. Sometimes, she would be very talkative, while others she would sit silently. On occasion, Freddie would join us, but neither of their presences helped take away the ache in my heart for seeing Arraetta in so much agony.

Marie had stated she was unsure when Arraetta would be well enough to wake, but I knew we could have been moon cycles from such hopes. Her wounds were rapidly healing due to the Rapidfire in her body, but the fever that riddled her was just like any other ephemeral being. I found it strange that even as a goddess her body reacted in such a way, but I supposed if she was a demi-god her mortality would be much like any other mortal-kind being.

There was a knock on the room around mid sol, before it opened and Freddie walked in with a sheepish look on his face.

"There is a council meeting."

Ah, of course. Meetings took place every half moon cycle, and they were not going to cancel it even if my fated one was suffering.

"Has my fate been decided?" I asked.

"I believe it to be surrounding my own," he winced.

"I do hope this shall not take long," I grumbled, gazing at Arraetta for a long moment before reluctantly following him into the corridor. It was there I was greeted by Travis, and a nervous-looking Genie, who looked less the dishevelled version I had seen since the night of the ball, and more the prim and proper female I assumed her to be. And her waiting there meant that she, too, would be in the meeting.

She might be living in a house of lions, but she had yet to realise that the council chamber was a viper's den - where poison could sink so deep it paralysed even the sharpest minds.

"Genev-" I began, but her scowl made me correct myself instantly, "habit. *Genie*."

"Don't you find your customs a little odd?" she pondered rhetorically, tucking her shoulders back. "Is she okay?"

"Would you like to check?" I replied, ignoring her comment.

Although she thought about it, she shook her head. "I think I'll be a wreck if I see her now. No, let's go; I'll see her after."

Freddie and I followed Genie down the corridor, all of us quiet. One of Marie's assistants came rushing up the hallway, stopping to bow.

"I am going to check on her, Your Grace," she said, rushing onwards.

"I do hope we finally decide on *her* title this sol, too," Freddie commented, slightly annoyed. Even sols after her arrival, no one knew whether they could call Arraetta by her name, a royal title, or simply 'miss'. She had effectively remained an unidentified female in the house, and it was grating on me little by little.

Genie swiftly stopped as we reached the edge of the upper grand hallway staircase, looking at Freddie with a fearful expression. "This is okay, right? They may... at least we have to say that they must let me stay until Arri is okay. She's my sister, Freddie."

Freddie took Genie gently by her arms and pulled her into him, affectionately holding her whilst he whispered inaudible words of encouragement. I had to admit that I was a little jealous, wishing I was able to hold Arraetta in such a way.

Leaving them to their sentiments, I walked down the hallway to my father's door, where both Jonah and Alex were already waiting. Besides them were two other members of the council. Freddie took Genie into his arms, holding her tight while whispering inaudible words of encouragement.

"Morning," I grunted, brushing a hand through my unkempt hair.

Jonah raised his eyebrows, eyeing my casual attire, "afternoon. You look like you have not showered in sols."

"I showered last sol." I rolled my eyes. "I have more important things to do than tend to myself."

"You should at least shave," Jonah pointed out the scruff which decorated my face.

"And sleep by the looks of it," Alex added.

"Stop hanging over me like two worried mothers," I tutted. "I have been in an uncomfortable chair by Arraetta's side."

"I pray you do not get thrombosis from being sat for so long," Jonah grumbled.

"Are you that concerned?" I grinned mirthlessly.

Jonah sighed. "Have you read the agenda?"

Although it was no more than a rhetorical question, he slapped a piece of paper from a batch of others into my hands. I looked down to see the number one agenda was the discussion of the arrival of Genie, the human. Below and underlined, the ball would be a big part of the agenda, followed by trade expansions, portal assessment and Iontine.

"How long will this take?" I grimaced.

"All afternoon, like most meetings," he commented, pointing to the top of the paper where it was stated to allow up to four hours.

Fuck. I should not have been surprised as most meetings took just as long, but I was going to be away from Arraetta for far too long. In desperation, I was half tempted to carry her into the meeting room so that I could keep an eye on her, whilst also showing my father the devastation she had been through. But even that was a chess piece I could not play in my favour, as she would only suffer.

My stomach churned anxiously at the thought that someone might sneak into Arraetta's room and attempt to kill her.

"It will be alright," Jonah squeezed my shoulder gently, "Travis will be assigned on guard duty outside, and Marie has full permission to come into the council room should anything happen. I have ensured that. But nothing shall. You know that the princess has been stable for sols, there shall be no change in a matter of hours."

My lip twitched at the decided title. "Princess, huh?"

"What else would she be?"

"I do hope you are right," I replied. "If anything happens, do not blame me for taking my wrath out on you."

While I might have been able to control such anger before, I could feel the simmering rage that was only taunts away from igniting. I just hoped such wrath would not land towards the wrong people.

"You always do," he forced a chuckle, not so draped in his usual humour.

"Lady Genevieve," Alex greeted as Freddie and Genie both arrived.

"Not you too, *please*," she grimaced, whilst Alex smiled amusedly.

"While I understand your annoyance at such formality," Jonah said to her, "in this meeting, your title shall remain as Alex has greeted you. It is important we ensure your presence here is as important as any other in that room." He looked at us all. "I am highly expecting some topics of conversation to cause upset, so we need to make sure we are one step ahead at all times."

"Why are you all standing there?"

Our heads turned as my mother descended the stairs, not sparing much of a glance at any of us. Behind her, Helga followed. Bows were given as they walked past us towards the door. My mother did not need to say a word to the guards on duty as they opened the door for her and all of us were swallowed by the entrance to hell. It was a shame that the chambers had not been built away from the house, so at least we would all be on equal footing rather than my father having a covert advantage over us.

Terance exited the council chamber, bowing immediately to my mother. "Ma'am."

"I suppose he is ready." She stated.

"Yes, ma'am, the court is ready to begin. His Majesty's council is already in place."

Of course they were. No doubt already spewing corrupt lies to barter with.

Terance opened the door for us, and my mother led the procession of the final delegates into the windowless chamber, its walls boarded with portrait-covered wooden panels. At the centre of the room sat the matching oval council table, flanked by eight black leather chairs on either side, with an additional chair at each end. Usually, the meetings had only sixteen people in attendance, but there were two others partaking in the debates. Fulk, the master of ceremonies, sat on one side, whilst a spare chair was left for Genie, who I almost hoped would remain, as having an outsider among our ranks could only benefit us.

My father was already seated at the head of the table, in a prime spot to gaze upon the damned as they entered. To the left sat his council: Cormac, the royal advisor; the General; Amice, the secretary; Oswin, the chancellor; Ida, the treasurer; Johannes, the chamberlain; and Sabina, the justiciar.

The impartial members sat to the right, including my mother, Sheika, Mare, the seneschal; and Ryin, the resident scientist. Any of them could sway a vote, depending on where their loyalties lay.

It was fortunate we had impartial members, as my own council was made up of only four. If we failed to sway all four of their votes, we would be in a precarious position - one where no vote would ever swing in our favour.

Taking a seat at the opposite end of the table from my father, who was whispering with Cormac, I had Sabina to my left, while Jonah sat to my right, followed by Alex, Genie, Freddie, Fulk, Mare, Ryin, Sheika, and my mother. I could see the heavy gazes of the council members fixed on Genie, as if she were an alien who had appeared from the sky. It was not as though none of them had interacted with a human before.

I supposed they were all feeling a little uneasy about having a foreign being at the table after we had spent so long hiding our true selves from them. Kudos to Genie, though, showing no trace of nerves, sitting straight-backed as she awaited for the court to begin. I wondered whether she would truly see my father's callous nature and be prepared for what could happen.

Two servants shuffled around pouring water and hot drinks for us all, whilst plates of pastries were placed in the centre, which only two members of the council reached for. I looked at Helga, who was sitting away from the table on a chair. She met my gaze and nodded gently in acknowledgement before she proceeded to read a tome I did not recognise.

"Let the council convene," my father called, nodding to Amice as the two workers left the room.

Amice began, first reciting the date and time, before continuing, "On this sol, on top of our own council, we have in attendance Fulk to discuss the incident at the ball and further concerns towards the upcoming celebration of Iontine. We also have Genevieve of the human realm who we shall vote on her place within our society."

Whilst the opening remarks were in Zikan, Genie's body tensed at the mention of her name.

"This sol, the order of proceedings, is to be as follows," Amice continued, sparking off a list of things the agenda would cover. I could disagree with none, as they would all need to be discussed at some point. She followed with the previous meeting minutes, and I found my gaze cast down towards the folded card on the table in front of me, which spelt out my full title: HRH Seraiah II, Prince of Zika.

I wondered what Arraetta's full title would be when the vote to name her the crown princess was brought upon us. Her Royal Highness Princess Arraetta of... Zika? The Cre-este? Or would she be Her Royal Highness Princess Arraetta, Goddess of Divine Rapidfire? Such title sent a gentle tingle of satisfaction down my spine. Yes, the whole universe needed to know exactly who she was.

"Mare, is there anything you should need to speak of this sol that we should be concerned about?" Amice asked, and Mare agreed, rising from her seat.

Arraetta would be a beautiful crown princess. Her laughter would light up the room and every being would naturally wish to be near her. But I would not let anyone as close to her as I would be. While they all gazed upon her in awe, I would be on my knees worshipping her divinity. The only being I would ever submit to. I prayed for the sol when the paleness would lift and her honey skin would shine again. I thought about how I could take her for some respite in Italy, where I could romance her, take her to our vineyard, and see her bask in the sun. How we could drink wine together, watch the gentle sunset and make love to one another on the private beach, away from prying eyes.

My cock throbbed at the thought and I sat a little straighter, knowing that such deliberations were not made for the audience before me. But, still, I burned for the idea of fucking her so deeply she would come over and over on my cock until the two of us were sated. But would we ever be? I was sure that once I had my first taste of sin, I would be begging until my last breath.

"Several people have called for..." Mare continued.

But, still Italy would be the perfect place for us to feel a sense of peace and happiness amidst the embedded chaos of the house. I needed to think of any way I could distract her mind from the underlying truth, even if she resented me for such reluctant lies. Still, once things were settled, the bond was complete. The trajectory of me being king was secured, and she had learned everything she needed in order to become the best ruler she could. I would tell her everything.

Secrets are not so deceitful if they are just concealed truths.

Another to add to the pile of enigmas I had managed to withhold. I had managed to conceal that the dark entity was pacing restlessly inside my mind without anyone knowing. The question was whether my mask could remain intact in front of Arraetta.

"And, then there's the matter of the new princess," Mare finalised, and I was snapped back into the present as my eyes flicked up to her as she continued to read, "news has already spread across all of Zika of the female who waltzed with the prince at the ball, and they wonder when our prince will be heartfasted."

My neck reddened, and I squirmed a little too evidently in my seat. Of course I knew such nuptials would be upon us, but I wanted to spend some time with Arraetta before rings were placed on our fingers and official words were spoken. Then again, Sheika had said that I could do no more than hold her hand as it would be detrimental, so maybe a heartfasting ceremony would speed up the process. There was a stark difference between heartfasting and bonding, however.

"There shall be no heartfast," Cormac said, sitting straight. "We do not know enough about the girl; thus, this conversation is not part of the agenda."

The *girl*.

"I do not see why it should not be," Jonah pointed out. "I am sure we can spare some extra time to talk about her position here."

"There shall be no discussion of positions," my father inputted, waving it off like it was seedling talk. "We shall discuss this later when we have had time to consult as a council."

"Let us get back to the agenda," Cormac said with a nod. *Fucking advisors.*

"If we have time, we may discuss this situation," Amice added, "for now, it's scheduled to be discussed next council. Please continue, Mare."

Another half moon cycle was going to be a long time to wait for a decision on Arraetta's official title, even if she still was in a coma. I hated that my coffer of fear had opened, as it only heightened the anxiety of waiting for the vote to be given, when even I knew they could not just cast her out. I would not let them. She had become one of us.

Maybe she was not Zikan, but she still had Rapidfire. She was royalty, and possibly descended from The Cre-este. And I would damn them all if they tried to turn her away.

Would they try to kill her?

I washed my eyes over the council before me, stopping at my father as he kept his eyes trained on a piece of paper on his table. Would *he* try to kill her? I needed to put protections in place to ensure Arraetta's safety, a conversation I needed to have with Amity.

Mare continued, "I wondered whether we may be able to, at least, reveal her identity to help dampen any rumours?"

Johannes replied, "I think we should inform the people there is no current comment on the status of His Royal Highness' engagement."

Mare hesitated before she agreed, looking at Amice. "That is all."

She sat down while Amice continued, "If there are no further comments, let us begin the discussion of the first note on the agenda, which is to discuss the incident caused at the ball, the security breach, and the arrival of two humans. This will tie into the next part of the agenda, which is to discuss Genevieve's position. Your Majesty, as the commanding officer of the council as a whole, you may begin."

My father nodded, remaining seated. "I place my trust in Sabina."

"Of course, Your Grace," Sabina nodded, standing, and she looked at everyone as she spoke, "last Saturday, we were honoured to have a ball in celebration of the prince's one-hundredth solar rite and, as planned, the sol ran smoothly, thanks to Fulk and his staff. However, unbeknownst to us, a car was sent from the house to London to pick up two humans who were brought here to be part of the party. The car passed through the entrance gates and straight up to the house without a guard checking on who was in the car."

I had not asked about Freddie's tactic to get the females in, but I assumed he had bribed one of the drivers and the guard on duty.

"Upon arrival, these two guests were greeted by Sir Frederique," she said, looking at Freddie, "and they were escorted into the house. From the CCTV footage, the two humans split away from one another in the hallway. Genevieve was brought to the ballroom whilst the other went alone upstairs to the bathroom before venturing further into the prince's bedroom."

Sabina's tone seemed somewhat accusatory, and I hoped she was not about to accuse Arraetta of thievery.

"Whilst it seemed the girl was out for a stroll," she continued, and my fists tightened as the word rattled again. If she were to use it one more time, I would not be against ripping her fucking throat out with my blunted teeth. Empyreans knows that I would be quite happy to spill her fucking blood to honour the female that was mine. "It seemed that her trip was cut short when His Royal Highness interrupted. Whilst it seems easy to accuse the human of seeking to cause trouble, we understand that both Genevieve and the-"

"-*Arraetta*," Jonah interjected with sharp annoyance, "her name is Arraetta. If you are not going to give her a title, Sabina, then I should suggest you use her name."

No one argued with Jonah, and my body relaxed a little, sitting back in the chair as Sabina's stoic face washed with embarrassment. She cleared her throat, stumbling over the name as though it pained her to say it, "A-Arraetta, yes, they were both there on invitation by Sir Frederique. As we are to discuss her... *Arraetta*'s arrival on the next agenda, I think, it is ample time for us to discuss the security breach and what we can do to prevent it from happening in the future."

Whilst Sabina's breakdown of the sol was detailed, I was more surprised that my father had not played his cards and found a more sinister tactic to accuse the females. The discussion was not centred around the law being broken, but instead about how we could better the security of our people.

Over the next hour, I listened but did not participate in discussing the security details. Arraetta's name was used as it should have been, whilst Jonah led any security debates from our council. The final decision made was that security would be tightened, and all cars going to and from the estate would need to be checked, especially with Iontine impending.

"Now," Amice said, "while it seems that we have solved our security issue, we must discuss the humans' arrival and Genevieve's placement in our world."

"If you do not mind," Freddie said softly, switching to English, "I hoped we would discuss this in English so that Genie would understand."

If I had found it tiresome listening to the conversation of security, I was sure Genie's inability to understand our language left her hanging by a thread as she waited for the decision about her.

"Absolutely not," my father said in Zikan, shaking his head. "We are not in favour of speaking so freely in another language because a human has decided to grace us with their undesired presence. This is a council meeting, not an academy class."

"I do not think it will do harm," I said offhandedly, and my father scowled. I switched to English. "What Genie should know will not harm us. We are speaking about her, and she is here. She needs to understand everything to know why we made the final vote, whatever said vote may be."

"Please place your hand up, should you agree," Amice said, looking towards everyone.

My mother sat forward, speaking in English. "We do not need to vote on such a seedling-like matter. Let us speak in English for the poor girl. I am sure she has been through enough, has she not?"

Amice nodded. "For the next part of the agenda, we shall discuss in English." Genie smiled softly, although I could see that her facade had slipped, and her nerves were more evident. I supposed it was quite easy not to think too much about what people say when speaking another language, but when things become understandable, it was suddenly a very real situation.

Freddie's arm moved towards her thigh, and I assumed he was holding her hidden hand for moral support.

"May I speak?" Freddie asked. No one objected, so he continued, "Should there be a vote against Genie's being here, then I shall take that as a vote against myself." A little murmur of shock whispered across my father's council. "Whilst I have enjoyed your hospitality, I find myself in much better company and would like to preserve

187

such splendour."

Freddie's truth-filled eyes met mine, and I smiled subtly. What had turned into a jest over a quarter moon ago had become so serious that I would have sworn they had been together for a long time. Freddie's support for Genie was undeniable. My only doubts would be losing Freddie if the vote was against her, but there were enough of us to sway a decision against banning Genie from the community.

My father cleared his throat and sat up. "I would not be doing my duty as king if I let that be, Freddie. Whilst you are under Jonah's guardianship here, you are still under my charge until you return to your home."

I was surprised at my father's honest words, not having seen him speak to Freddie in a good light since before we arrived on Earth. Even when the feud between my father and his took place, my father still tried to treat Freddie as much as a son as he could. Or, at least he did until Freddie showed me unyielding support instead.

"I understand that, Sir," Freddie replied, "but I would be doing myself a dishonour to give up the one thing I love. Even if it is treasonous."

The General snorted, "You would abandon your king to pursue this fantasy of yours?"

I almost thought he was going to say fancie, but still calling his affection for Genie a fantasy was enough to see Freddie almost rise from his seat. But, it was Genie's calming touch which had him take a deep breath.

Cormac agreed. "The General is correct. This is but a fantasy."

"You would struggle to survive outside of the shield," Ryin said, looking at Freddie. "we all know how those with Rapidfire are in a great deal more danger away from here. It would be a slow, painful, sick death."

"But at least I would be happy." Freddie replied honestly, and I wondered whether, if I were in his shoes, I would also choose my happiness over my mortality. Fuck, of course I would. Who was I kidding? If I had the opportunity to leave my post and go with Arraetta to the human world, to live my sols in peace I would. But then, what of duty? What of the throne that sat in my father's tight grip?

No, I would not choose my happiness over my life. I would choose to fight.

"Is she really worth it?" Johannes asked, back to Zikan.

"English, please," Amice commented, causing Johannes to grumble a little.

Freddie rose, speaking to everyone, "I have done everything I can to be part of your race. I gave up my place as a prince and my home to work tirelessly to become a foreign liaison and our future king's advisor, and now I am being told that I cannot enjoy this one thing I now have in my possession. I do not care whether you believe Genie to be a *fancie*, or that you believe I shall be rid of her very soon. It is not true. I cannot bear the idea of being without her, and I cannot see that being a possibility - *ever*. I do not care if I am to suffer my final days being banished if it means I am happy with her."

Freddie's boldness was admirable, but his words lacked the weight to secure a vote. Instead, it sounded like he was resigning to the fact that the vote might sway out of his favour. Either that, or he was manipulating them into seeing his value was higher than their need to care about one human amongst us.

Sheika finally spoke. "it is fated. The prince could not have met his Kindred Spirit without these two meeting. How else would she have arrived at the ball?"

Sheika was right. There was no other way that I could have met Arraetta. She was not reckless enough to take an adventure to a random settlement north of London; she would have been continuing to deliver pizzas to thankless patrons where our worlds would have never collided.

"You sprout some lies," The General snorted, his ongoing resentment toward Sheika shining through like a beacon. "I have yet to see a single of your prophecies come true."

Sheika glowered at him. "I suppose you shall not believe that your time will come soon, General."

The words from Sheika's lips surprised everyone, but it did not seem to affect the facade The General had on his face.

"And, should the vote go the opposite way," Sabina said, looking at Genie, "what do you propose should happen? Will you move here, Genevieve? Sir Frederique is at a higher risk of living a much shorter life, whereas he will be well here. Would you be comfortable with the rules and protocols of this life over the one you are so used to?"

"Sabina is right," Johannes said. "How much are you willing to know and learn about who we are? Do you understand the implications that may arise if news of us spreads worldwide? How can we trust that you will not talk of us to others?"

"Are you willing to *give up* everything just for this love with Sir Frederique?" Sabina asked.

Genie was a little overwhelmed by the number of questions suddenly fired at her, seeming to come to terms with the nature of our lives. Neither of us could answer for her, as it was her fight. And she needed to fucking fight. If she did not do it for herself, then she needed to for Arraetta's sake because I could not lose the female that had finally graced me with her presence, and I had no doubt Arraetta would leave if Genie was cast out.

Genie would need to choose to trade a life of normality for a gilded cage.

I subtly looked around the room until I briefly made eye contact with my mother before looking away. If we removed the simple facts of us not being human, we were still royalty. The political machinations of a hidden society. It was not as though Genie was a human marrying a subject. She would be marrying Freddie who was as royal and regulated as the rest of us.

We were procedures and protocols. Prodded and poked until we were moulded into beings others expected us to be. And it was the world which Genie would need to be moulded into. Scrutiny at every corner, lies and deceit coveted as what was right and wrong.

Once we returned to Zika, Freddie could quite rightly decide to return to Porto, assuming the role of their prince and she would become a princess, much like Arraetta. She might not become a queen, but she still had to follow every rule given to her. And Porto's rules and laws were both different and similar to ours. She would have the exact same conversations again with his family and their council.

Our society's royal tactics were brutal, and her decision had to be final because we would demand it. There was no going back once an additional piece was added to the chessboard.

Genie rose abruptly, clearing her throat as she looked at everyone confidently. "I am not an impulsive person. I make decisions with a clear head and always for the best of others. And, whilst I do not know you, nor do you know me, I'm very set on being with Freddie. I don't know how a person can fall in love so quickly, but I knew I loved him as soon as I met him. As it's said, this is fate. It can be nothing else.

"I understand that while love can't always be vibrant and beautiful, we'll weather whatever storm we sail through. This one, and the next, and whatever will follow after that. I will admit that your lives have made me curious, and Freddie told me that you are not from Earth. I understand what implications would come should the wider world find out who you all are.

"And, of course, for Arri. I would want to be here for her. She's my sister. Maybe not by blood, but she's been in my life since we were ten, and I have witnessed things that no human has ever seen. Even my parents don't know what happens to her, so please give me a chance and I will work hard to fit in here."

Genie's speech was heartfelt, the fight that Freddie's should have been, but it did not mean she had won anyone's vote outside of my own council.

"Do you know who Sir Frederique is?" Ida asked, finally speaking up after a whole hour of silently watching.

"Yes," Genie nodded.

"And what have you come to learn about your friend since you arrived here?" Ida prodded.

Genie was confident in her answer, "that she's like all of you. Maybe she's not of the same... race, I suppose, but she has power. Big, golden, bright power that lights up her veins and shines an aura around her. I've finally learnt that this is called Rapidfire."

"Gold?" Mare coughed, looking at Sheika suddenly. "Like the goddess?"

Empyreans, the conversation was shifting unnecessarily, and I did not want us to lose sight of the vote that could determine Genie's place in the realm. I was unsure who knew about Arraetta's golden Rapidfire, but only those who had witnessed it and those who had been in the council room later knew about Arraetta's divine power.

"Let us get back to the conversation at hand," my father said.

But Mare continued, "How is it possible that she has Rapidfire? I had only presumed that she was a human who turned out to be his Kindred Spirit."

"*His?*" The General said, with a strange anger in his voice, "I believe you know how to address the prince."

I almost snorted, as it was rare that even The General addressed me with my proper title. Even so, Mare blushed in embarrassment and fell silent.

"Can we please get back to the conversation at hand?" Amice asked, eager to quiet the chamber, which had suddenly become alight with conversation from everyone but my council and Genie.

"Quiet!" my father bellowed, and everyone settled down immediately. "We are not here to discuss this; there is an agenda that must be adhered to."

"Have you considered what position Genevieve would receive if she were to be accepted?" Ida asked, looking at Freddie, then she looked at me. "What say you, Your Highness? You have been unusually quiet."

Empyreans.

FOURTEEN

"**D**iplomatically speaking," I sat back as everyone's scrutinising gaze landed on me, "it would be against our law for Genevieve to be here." Freddie shifted uncomfortably. "If you all recall, my signature, too, was signed when such legislation was created. Genie's presence here would cause problems and an uproar in society, especially for those who have attempted to defy them."

"Yes, it could cause great problems," Mare agreed. "Whilst cross-blood laws are quite modern and many do favour them, I know of several others who would create quite a ruckus in our society if we make this one exception."

"If we agree to this... to this marriage," Ida added, "then we would need to change the scripture."

A welcome change which had been brewing for long enough.

"It would cause a whole upheaval when it comes to our security," Sabina said, "I'm sure The General doesn't wish for extra work, and neither would you, Commander."

At least our troops would have some more important work outside of partaking in useless training exercises.

"That is correct," The General agreed. "My army is busy enough without dealing with the implications or protection of a human."

"Well, it is a good job that *my* army does not mind providing protection where necessary," Jonah pointed out.

"That is because *your* army has nothing better to do," The General spat, the tensions rising in the room, "do you seriously think that *this* human girl can be protected from the wrath of our people?"

"I believe that chances should be given," Jonah replied. "It is only fair that she proves to us she is capable of being part of our community." He looked at me. "While I am aware of your concern, Your Highness, I did not get the chance to hear your secondary thoughts, as you were so *rudely* interrupted."

I bit back my amused smile, sitting upright. "What I had hoped to say is there are several additional factors we should all consider before making our vote. First, Freddie has been loyal to us since he arrived to work with us as Porto's foreign liaison. He has worked tirelessly in favour of our people, so we should honour him by allowing him to have something in return. Also, Genevieve has yet to do any harm within our society, and I have only heard positive conversations from our staff here at the palace. On the occasions I have left my wife's room, of course."

I was not about to leave that nugget of information on the tip of my tongue, and I noted the gentle murmur at the use of my declared statement toward Arraetta rattling through those before me. I did not miss the sour gaze my father gave me.

"Which leads me to my final reason," I continued, holding my hand up to quieten them all, "Genevieve - Genie - has been in the presence of another who bears Rapidfire. Arraetta is not just a friend, but a sister to Genie. We cannot deny the bond between them and cannot cast one aside without removing the other-"

"-Then, we shall remove both!" my father declared, pointing his finger at Genie, "I will not have little humans squandering our lives for such simplicities as love."

Genie's sharp gasp echoed in the silence of my father's outburst, and I wondered whether she would have been brave enough to argue back with him. I would have quite welcomed her fire at that moment. But, as I looked at her, I noted the faint rise of tears in her eyes.

Do not let them fall. Do not show any *weakness in this room.*

"It is not wise to remove both," my mother reasoned. "We do not yet know enough about Arraetta to understand whether she is a danger to us, so it is not an option either of us should speak of."

Danger. Ha. My mother should have her tongue ripped out for such an insolent word. How could my fated one pose any danger when she was at her weakest? Unless her brazen thoughts transcended to when we were the two most powerful rulers in Zikan history.

"No one is removing Arraetta!" I snarled, slamming my fist on the table to silence everyone there. "She is not some... toy for you all to play with. She is a..." *Goddess.* I took a deep breath. "I am being very serious when I address her as my wife. Or maybe I should address her as my queen or even my Kindred Spirit. I will not hear of such... blasphemy towards her. We shall not remove Arraetta, and, thus, neither shall we remove Genie. They are a package deal."

"A package?" The General laughed humourlessly. "This is a serious situation - a security breach."

"I am merely stating facts," I pointed out. "The two humans arrived together, making them *my* guests, and they will be treated as such."

"They are unwelcome," he answered callously. "You did not seek permission from this council - nor *your* king - and you broke laws by bringing two humans into our world."

"I am aware of the laws that have been broken, but we are here to vote upon Genevieve's position in this house."

"It is simple," he spewed, his conversation suddenly returning to Zikan. "The answer is that her bag should be placed at the front gate for the little rat to collect as she leaves."

A primal growl rippled from Freddie's chest as he slammed his hands on the table. "How dare you speak such derogatory ideals!"

"If you cannot handle the truth, then you should have not brought her here to hear it."

I was surprised when I saw a tiny spark of emerald power fizzle under his hand as he took deep, jagged breaths to calm himself down. Freddie was no monster, not like me. It would not harm him physically to use his power against The General, but it would land him in hot water if he did. Genie placed her hand on top of his, and the gentle hue disappeared just as quickly as it came. It seemed that no one noticed outside those closest.

"How do we know, behind our back, our other guest - this apparent *wife* of our dear prince - is not out there stealing from every room in this palace?" Cormac questioned in his awfully measured tone.

I noted the open-mouthed shock from several members, whilst others seemed to be nodding their heads like they were deliberating Cormac's insensitive words. While Freddie had calmed, my infuriation soared, fists clenching.

I will kill that fucker. My inner walls rattled with rage as I wondered what it would be like to see Cormac's apathetic look while his guts were splattered against the brown wooden panels. I knew my power could do such a thing if only I honed into the deepest pockets of it.

A chill rippled the air and I could smell the fear of everyone in the room, but I did not look away from the male who dared to threaten my wife.

I clicked my tongue, drew in a deep breath and spoke with a tone that lacked any remorse, "Because if you stop living inside your little box, you would know that this *apparent wife* of mine is currently in a coma in the east wing of this house. A coma which was caused by an incident that has caused her to become so severely wounded not one of us will know when she will wake." It was the first time I had seen such wariness appear on Cormac's face. I rose from the chair. "So, perhaps you should focus on facts, as per your position, rather than spinning malicious lies to gain the upper hand in this council. Your concerns are futile - a bluff tossed into the mix when you know you cannot win in this apparent game of poker. We are here to vote on the decision of whether Genevieve should remain here, and my vote-"

A cool sliver of liquid trickled from my nostril, splotching thrice onto the table in red, and a sudden ache rippled through my forehead.

"Seraiah?" Jonah's voice called.

I coughed as Sabina tried to place a hand on my shoulder to steady me. "Your Highness?"

Coldness itched my skin and a throbbing ache washed over my filaments. Vision hazy, body weak, I plummeted to the ground between my chair and the table, caught by Jonah's hands before my head could crack against the ground.

Screams for help melded with dark ominous chuckles radiating around my skull and reverberated against the chamber walls. But all I could think about was a need to be near Arraetta's unconscious body.

Seraiah, her fearful voice called. Ignoring the worried calls of those around me, I pushed myself to my feet, rushing out of the room as quickly as I could.

"I am coming, Arraetta," I called, rushing through the heavy doors that led into the grand hallway.

I skidded to a halt to stop myself from barrelling down an un-expected open crater which had materialised in the centre of the parquet flooring. Old oak shelves were jaggedly hanging from rough and uneven veined mineral threads whilst pages of tomes floated in a whispering wind. Above, the roof had collapsed, showing swirling endless grey skies, softly hued by orange lightning.

But, I could not make sense of how such a thing had appeared when no quake or rupture had rumbled the house. It was as though it had been conjured by magic. And, I realised I was not standing in the hallway but in the library itself.

I grimaced as shrill whining resounded all around, causing my vision to swirl again.

"Seraiah!" a cacophony of male voices echoed, but they were swallowed as the door behind slammed shut – hard. I turned to try to open it, but with each attempted tug, I felt myself gradually becoming weaker. My head throbbed again, and I grunted, stumbling backwards. An impenetrable rippling noise of humourless laughter rumbled up the chasm.

I gasped as my foot slipped and I fell from the edge, descending without control into the depths of hell. The further I fell the more I wondered whether I was about to greet the devil himself.

The ground met me as forcefully as the fall, causing a splatter of dust to float from the hard rubble below. I coughed profusely, feeling the agony undulate up my spine, paralysing me for several moments before I managed to roll onto my stomach.

"Fuck," I grunted, struggling to catch my breath. But, eventually, I stood upright and peered upwards. It seemed the only way out was climbing the endless shelves for what seemed like a mile, maybe more.

Whirring resonated from behind and I slowly turned, watching as a cloud of mist, similar to the one inside my internal prison, began to form. It seemed once again I was being held captive to the dark side of my mind. My heart seized, perspiration evident across my face and dust-laden clothing as I fought that betraying emotion of fear I so desperately wished was still in its box.

"I am not fucking scared of you!"

A pause, then that familiar derisive laughter boomed from it, making my body tense as I braced myself for some kind of mind-numbing torture.

"I am sure you are not, dear Seraiah. But you are frightened of the things we can do, the things we can become."

"I command you to show yourself!" I shouted, stepping bravely towards the cloud.

"Come here," he replied, as the mist began to shift until it revealed the jagged edges of white bones in the shape of a doorway. The black mist fizzled at its centre, lulling me in with some strange control. "Do not be afraid."

I almost snorted, feigning my fear of him, but I could not. How could I not fear the one thing which demanded my entire control?

Tucking my shoulders, I walked through the arch of bone, feeling like hundreds of unwanted hands were trying to grab hold and control me, until I was finally released. And soon I appeared in a dark room of mirrors, lit up by some form of invisible light source. Each surrounded me in a circle, seeing only myself in the reflection, at least for a moment before I noticed a different movement in them, revealing him - my dark entity.

"Seraiah," he bowed mockingly.

His black eyes twinkled in the light, and I could see the prominent dark veins that marred his skin like tattoos. A dark aura surrounded him, making his translucent skin beam. He was indeed an eerie version of me - imperfect, dark, *different.*

"Do you have nothing better to do than bring me to your prison?"

He chuckled, "Oh, but it is you who is imprisoned. I am quite free. My world is my own. My own rules. My own empire. You are nothing but a prisoner of yourself, of your mind. Trapped under the laws of a tyrant who shall never seek to make you king." He paced the circle of mirrors, and I twisted my body to follow. "Is that what you want? Hm? Or shall you become the ruler you so desired? What was it? Emperor of *all* realms."

Emperor of all realms. A seedling's dream. "Times have changed."

"Ah, but they have not," he stopped, "It is only because you have allowed your father to control your mind that you no longer see the grander perspective. But I can. You left those memories with me. Conquering nations, creating a unified universe. Yet, here you are, Seraiah. A shell of yourself. A male too good-hearted to ever find his tongue to announce his true nature."

"I will be king."

"Oh, I have no doubt," his lip twitched, "but when shall that be, hm? Your father will bed a consort, Seraiah, and then she will bear a new heir. No room for King Seraiah. Only the outcast prince."

"*Our* father," I corrected as though I was speaking to a brother.

"Oh no," he tutted, "he is not *my* father. Do you not remember how we so willingly decided to draw hate upon that male many winters before our realm was attacked? No, I suppose you have locked such memories away here for me to fester with - *feed* on. Should I remind you about how he willingly beat you into submission for breaking such a minor rule? What was it? Oh, yes, the kind-hearted, sweet Seraiah decided to gift one of the King's jewels to... Mareina. Am I right?"

I had locked such memories away, but I was quite aware of them after my two boxes had opened. I remembered how my father struck me with a cane in the middle of the throne room, surrounded by some members of the court, and none of them dared help me. In a time before Arraetta, Earth and The Dark, I had fallen for another female. A female who had tricked me, stole from me and fled.

And my father beat me.

Whip.

All to teach me a lesson.

Snap.

No one was above the law, not even his son who had stolen for love.

Slash.

But love was cruel and only sought to bring agony and despair to those who dared feel it. And I dared. And I would not make such impertinent mistakes again. Phantom pain hit my back, and I dropped to my knees with a thud.

But, Arraetta.

"And how about when he declared to everyone that you were not allowed to follow him through the portal after The Dark poisoned you?"

Agony tore through me as pain resonated up my left arm, the phantom residue of the poison stinging at my skin. I breathed heavily, gritting my teeth.

"And what is your fucking point?" I screamed.

Breathe. Breathe. *Breathe.*

"Are you saying that I should become so enraged that I should kill the tyrant?"

"Oh no," my replica chortled, kneeling so close to the edge of the mirror that I thought he may reach out and touch me, "it is not your job to kill him, Seraiah. It is mine. All mine. And what a pleasure it will be. All you have to do is give in to me."

"I will not." I bit.

"But, you shall," he said, tapping the glass, "it is the only way you will become the ruler of this universe, defying every obstacle the Gods have thrown in our way to stop our ascent. But they shall not. For we have the greatest card to play."

"And what exactly is that?"

"Arraetta," he whispered, tasting her name as though it was his to own.

"Do not dare speak her name!" I shouted, using my sudden energy to punch the glass, shattering it instantly.

A small part was left, and I watched as he clapped his hands condescendingly, with that smug smile still slapped on his face, "There is the spirit!" I went to punch him again, and he cheered. "You are a sadistic fucker!"

"Oh, yes, we are," he agreed. "It is taking you longer to figure out your place in this world. It will come; I can assure you of that."

"Shut the fuck up!" I yelled.

"I believe you should get back to our dear wife."

I blinked, remembering that I had initially been running to see Arraetta before I ended up down the rabbit hole with this dark snake.

"Oh, and Seraiah," he said, "I am quite excited to watch the next coffer break. It shall be sooner than you think."

The glass shattered and darkness consumed me until I blinked my eyes open, peering at the small chandelier in the centre of the council chambers. A soft musky cushion propped up my head and a thin blanket weighed down my aching body. At first, it seemed that no one else was in the chamber, but as I wearily sat up, I noticed movement in the corner.

"Maybe you should lie down a little bit longer." Helga suggested, as I used the chair and table to bring myself unsteadily to my feet.

"How is Arraetta?"

"She is fine."

"But, she was not."

Reluctantly, she answered. "She had a cardiac arrest."

A second one in as many sols and I had reacted all the same, feeling like my world was collapsing in on itself. But how could we be so connected to one another when we had not even bonded? I had not collapsed at any other point in my life when she had suffered from these blackouts.

"I promise she is fine," Helga implored gently. "Your mother and

Genie went straight there. Everyone was very concerned."

"Apart from my father."

"The council will reconvene next quarter with some changes to the agenda," she added, ignoring my comment. "We know that tensions are high, and it will give everyone time to reset."

"And what of my council?" I asked her, finally finding enough strength to head out the oppressive room towards the main area of the house.

She followed. "Alex returned home. He suggested he cook another dinner."

An Amity meeting, of course. Was it truly everyone's intention to keep me as far away from my fated one as possible? I arrived at the exit of my father's wings, hesitantly holding the handle in case I opened it and found myself back in my nightmare.

A heavy thrum settled in my gut, a subtle amount of dread taking its seat at the empty table in my soul. But, I took a deep breath, opened the door and walked out into the sunlight-strewn hallway, basking in the warmth of a sun encased room. A sigh of contentment leaving my lips.

Helga followed behind, presumably ensuring I would not collapse again. It felt like too slow of an ascent up to the upper east wing corridor, although that could have been from the lack of energy I had. Maybe dinner at Alex's would be nice. The Gods knew how much I needed sustenance after sols of little of it.

It was Freddie and Jonah who stood in a conversation by Arraetta's closed door, both turning as my shoes tapped across the parquet flooring and I noted both looked relieved. At least I still had my brothers on my side, even when all else felt like it was falling apart.

"I am glad you are well," Jonah said as I reached them. "Marie wants to see you once she has sorted out the princess."

"And, Arraetta? Is she well?"

"Stable," Freddie said, "a sudden cardiac arrest followed by a sudden loss of power, before it rebooted almost instantly."

"There was an outage?" I raised my eyebrows.

"Yes," he grimaced, "I only wonder whether our new guest has some sort of responsibility for it."

"Do not blame her, Freddie," I chided.

The door opened before we could make any more theories, and the three of us stepped back as my mother walked out, handing a used pair of plastic gloves and an apron to one of the nurses.

She eyed me, offering a soft yet emotionless smile. "It is good to see you are awake. Although, I would suggest you shower to remove that bloodstain on your face."

On instinct, I touched my nose and felt the crust of blood that still lingered there. I grunted, lying, "I am grateful for your concern, Mother."

"Have Marie check on you," she half-commanded. The cloying scent of rose perfume overpowered my senses as she walked away. "Do not think I am unaware that you, too, collapsed some sols ago. I do not wish my son to be weak when he should be at his strongest."

Oh, so it was not a concern. It was making sure that I did not look weak in front of the house. It was a shame her feeble son had collapsed for something out of his control, but of course he was always to blame.

A growl taunted my throat, ready to ripple out and put my mother in her place, wherever such a position was for her. Fuck her. Fuck–

"Seraiah." A hand landed on my shoulder, and I shunted away from it, turning to the two concerned males who looked like they were awaiting judgment.

I let out a sigh. "apologies."

The door, which was still open, harboured the presence of Marie as she looked at me with raised eyebrows. "Come in."

With no protest, I walked into the room, flanked by the two males. Genie was shifting damp hair from Arraetta's pale face and tucking it behind her ear as though she could help disguise the agony she was in. Still, she looked beautiful.

"Okay, you're all tucked in, Arri," Genie whispered, tears in her eyes, "make sure you get better, okay? I don't need to have a heart attack running a mile just to get here... okay?" She nodded as if Arraetta had answered. "Okay."

"I think you should rest," Marie placed a gentle hand on Genie's arm.

Genie looked up at the three of us before she tucked her shoulders back, shaking her head, "I think it's a good idea to talk about what happened in there."

"I would like to tend to the prince," Marie said gently, "and then he needs some rest, too. A few hours, please, before you decide on any plans."

"Okay," Genie agreed, gazing at Arraetta for a little while longer before she left the room. Freddie offered us a soft nod before, too, leaving after her.

Jonah was going to do the same, but Marie addressed him, "Commander, it's not in my remit to make demands, but it's a good idea to consider an extra form of protection for these two. It's the second time Seraiah has now collapsed and I can't provide care around the clock for this stubborn prince."

I tutted, "I do not need around the clock care. That is ridiculous."

"You are not out of place to suggest such a thing, Marie," Jonah replied softly. "it has already been actioned."

"I am not going to collapse again," I grumbled in uncertainty, folding my arms. "Your concerns are welcome, but I have enough going on without having someone watching over my every move. Plus, I already have Travis."

"And, Connell," Jonah added.

"On occasion."

"A permanent one," he replied, and I glowered at him. Being forced to have them both on a permanent basis was a ridiculous and unnecessary tactic for the idiotic excuse of safety.

"Now, come, let me make sure you are well," she said, pointing to one of the chairs nearby.

Jonah made his leave whilst Marie checked my symptoms. I almost wished to lie to her that I felt fine so that she might give me a lighter prescription. But, still, I decided to indulge her about the excruciating headache and the heart attack like symptoms the sol prior. She acknowledged my deeper connection with Arraetta for a second time, before ordering me as any other doctor would: to sleep in my own bed, eat three healthy meals daily and go out for fresh air.

"If I'm honest, Seraiah," she said, placing her hand on my thigh, "I am worried about you. And I've not needed to worry about you for a great many winters. At this moment, I don't know whether to expect you to turn up with a bruised foot, a bloodied nose, or as Arraetta is here."

I peered at Arraetta briefly before standing up. "Do not worry about me, Marie. I shall do as you bid."

She agreed, "But if your symptoms worsen, you must inform me. For now, I'll bring a prescription for your headaches to your bedroom. They should also help you sleep."

Pills. Herbal remedies. Whatever it was she felt would help, but little did she know that the demon suppurating inside would not care for what medicines I would be fed, still demanding the release he wished for. And, fuck, I felt powerless against his will.

"Please call for me if something should happen," I said to her.

"I believe your connection is already deep enough to know."

She was right, of course. I only prayed there were no further incidences where I needed to feel such agony again. In one way, I would quite happily go through double the pain so that Arraetta did not have to suffer as she had, but I knew I was not in control of her fate, just as I was not in control of mine.

But, I could be. How perfect it would be to wrap my fingers around the puppet strings and force it into my will. To make it so that everything worked in our favour, and watch the corrupt empire surrounding us crumble.

FIFTEEN

The four commitments to join The Sanctuary of Amity were simple, yet integral. First, we put the interests of our people above everything, never making a move to compromise an innocent life to make headway in our own game. Even if it meant things took longer. Second, we must never make it known that Amity exists outside the four walls of the sigil-protected meeting quarters at Jonah and Alex's home, unless in private conversation. Third, we must always tell the truth to each other. And, fourth, should we become compromised in any way, we uphold that we shall remain silent, even until death.

"By valour or virtue." The words were proudly spoken from Genie's mouth as she stood in the meeting space before she took the feathered quill from the inkpot and signed her name into a declaration of faith. A subtle squeak left her as the pen sizzled against her fingers, indicating that she had successfully committed to the vow, but she did not drop a single splodge of ink.

"Side effect," Freddie said, kissing her gently on her temple as he removed the pen from her hand. He turned to the rest of us. "Are we happy now?"

It had been hours since Arraetta had her cardiac arrest, and we all met at Jonah's home to discuss the events of the sol.

"I should hope you two never break up," Jonah said in Zikan, earning a glare from Freddie as he pulled Genie toward the table. We sat at our usual seats, whilst Genie tentatively took Eros'.

Alex proceeded to dish out the chicken pasta for all of us from the dishes in the centre of the table until we were all ready to adjourn the meeting, eating as we spoke. It was the first full meal I had eaten in sols, and I was thankful that I was treated to such delicacies to help sate my ailing appetite.

"So, I suppose we should take this meeting in English," Jonah said, looking at Alex and Helga, who both could speak the language, but were not necessarily as fluent as the rest of us when speaking it.

"That is fine," Alex answered in English, his accent thick, "it will be an honour to learn more English now we have new company."

"I can understand what she says," Helga said in Zikan. "I just might need help with speaking."

Genie subtly cleared her throat, "I know my presence here isn't wanted, but I'm really willing to work hard to fit in."

"Your allegiance is necessary either way, since your lover here has decided to tell you about things that are secret," Jonah said gruffly.

"I did not tell her about Amity," Freddie answered. "I know the consequences of my actions if I did, but she is safe in this room and it is integral that she understands."

"I think the same," Alex replied surprisingly, which even Jonah turned towards him with raised eyebrows, "because of Genie, not Freddie."

"It would be good to have another female on the team, too," Helga said in Zikan, sitting back with a smile on her face.

"It is not that I do not wish for you to be here," Jonah said to Genie, clearing his throat, "it is just that your relationship is still infantile and it is a worry to us that you may decide this life is not for you."

"I know my actions the other day were hasty," Genie replied, "but even if Arri wants to leave, I'll do my damn hardest to make her stay."

"She will not be able to leave," Jonah answered truthfully. "no matter how hard she tries to go against its force, she will remain here whether she agrees or not. And it is only us who can make it so she does not try to escape."

Genie pursed her lips, breathing through her nose as I presume she was still trying to wholly understand the nature of how everything ran. And, even if she was not my Kindred Spirit, Arraetta still bore Rapidfire, which meant we would have to do everything we could to protect her from the outside world – even trapping her in ours.

"I will help you," Genie nodded, "I know how to work around Arri's stubbornness, but the main thing is making her comfortable and showing her some compassion when she finally wakes up. She doesn't like to be told what to do. She likes to be independent, so there has to be some sort of flexibility."

"We can do that," I added. "I would rather she be happy than suffer under our impenetrable thumb."

"As long as she is safe," Jonah added.

"So, we make a plan," I replied, sitting forward. "If we each have a task, it will make it easier to familiarise her with our life."

"I can work with a plan," Genie nodded, turning to Freddie, "do we have paper?"

Freddie tapped his head, and she raised her eyebrows before pressing her lips together and nodding. Whilst our vows were written in stone, we were very careful about what information we had written down in case the sigils were breached and Jonah's home was torn upside down. So, we remembered everything. Or, most. There were codewords and phrases, of course, but we were very cautious to use them.

"Okay, mental plan," Genie agreed with a nod.

"Maybe you can provide us some more insight into Arri," Freddie offered gently. "It might help us understand how each of us can help her."

Genie nodded, "well, Arri is my adopted sister. She came to live with us when she was eleven, after moving through the foster system. Most of her childhood was spent in silence, as in she never spoke, and she was a very quiet person. Luckily, we got on really well and she came out of her shell over the years. Mum and Dad treated her like she was their own, but there was something that I think prevented her from feeling like she belonged there. I supposed it was probably the blackouts, or maybe knowing she didn't belong here."

"And you know nothing of her lineage?" Jonah asked.

She shook her head, "neither does she. She doesn't remember anything from before she was six years old, so I can only guess it's something to do with her past and wherever she came from before. You said she's not one of you, so maybe you know where she might be from and can help her?"

"We have a slight idea," I told her, "but we cannot confirm or deny it as the truth."

"You have an idea?" Alex asked, perplexed, "at least do share with us."

No secrets in Amity. I supposed that was almost a fifth rule.

"The Cre-este," I replied, earning a joint gasp from him and Helga.

"But it is a lost realm," Helga replied.

"A celestial realm," Alex said in Zikan.

"A Goddess amongst us?" Freddie muttered, also in Zikan. Empyreans. I felt like I had returned to the council chambers with how they were all reacting.

"Not all in The Cre-este were Gods," Alex shook his head.

"Yet she has Rapidfire," Freddie added, sitting back in his chair, "which makes her royal, therefore she has to be a God."

Genie cleared her throat. "I'm a little lost."

"Apologies," Freddie said to her, before the conversation turned back to English.

"The Cre-este," I said to Genie, "was a realm around six thousand years ago which was destroyed by what we know as The Dark. For now, do not worry about such lore. You can learn about that another time. But what you should know is that Sheika and I believe that Arraetta is the lost princess of The Cre-este."

"It would make her old, no?" Alex asked.

"Ancient," I nodded to him, shrugging, "but there is no definitive answer yet. Sheika is requesting a book to be brought from Italy which should have some answers. The reason why two and two have been connected is because she is the bearer of golden Rapidfire, which is its purest form. Divine Rapidfire, as it is officially known."

I caught Jonah's thoughtful look, and I wondered what thoughts were rapidly firing around his mind. Most likely wondering how he would keep her safe, especially when my father would do anything to get his hands on such divine power.

"But why is she here?" Genie asked.

"That is something I cannot answer," I replied. "I suppose it would do you no harm in knowing that we also believe she's a demigod."

"Is... are... are Gods even real?" she asked. She pressed his lips together again, and I almost mentioned to Freddie that he needed to teach her to stop giving away all her emotions. It might be easy for her to let out such open contemplation in our company, but in others she needed to mask it.

"Very real," Freddie answered, flirtatiously joking, "you are sitting right next to one."

She smacked his arm playfully, a sharp blush creeping across her face. "seriously, Freddie."

"More of a cadaer than a god," Alex muttered in Zikan.

"Say that one more time," Freddie replied sharply, "you are just fortunate you have not laid eyes on this fine body of mine."

"I would rather look at horse shit," Alex replied in the same tone.

"Empyreans," Jonah answered, squeezing the bridge of his nose.

"I think your stare would freeze it solid," Freddie answered, drawing silent laughter from Helga and me, whilst Genie looked heavily confused by the sudden change.

"Shut the fuck up," Jonah grunted, glaring between the two. "We are in a meeting, not a seedlings playground."

"Apparently we are, since he is in attendance," Alex snorted.

"Alex," Jonah's voice rang with finality before he took a deep breath and looked at Genie, "I apologise, these two are like two brothers who love to fight in inappropriate situations."

"I suppose I should learn Zikan," Genie smiled, and we all chuckled softly. "But, if there are Gods, why is Arri here? Surely she's supposed to be in heaven or something?"

"Ryazark, the realm of the Highest Gods," I corrected, "but a tale for another day. For now, it is important no one outside this room knows of such a thing until it is confirmed, or at least there is stronger evidence."

She nodded, "I agree. To be honest, I think all of this will overwhelm her, so it's best if we keep everything from her until we know more. Basically, the more human she can be treated the better."

"It will be difficult to keep her regal title hidden once the council votes on her position," Jonah replied, "but we should keep the celestial speculations to ourselves. I will implement strict security measures either way. Speaking of the council, we need to discuss what might happen if the vote is against you."

"It will not," Freddie replied sharply, "they cannot vote her out, otherwise it is voting me out."

"They will prevent that," Jonah answered, "but I think if Genie makes enough of a footprint here over the next week, it will give her a good standing."

"And how do you suggest that?" Freddie asked.

I hated to admit the words which crawled from my mouth, but even so I knew there was only one way to help manipulate the situation into Genie's favour. "My mother."

"The Queen?" Helga's spluttered.

"If Genie earns my mothers favour, she is in for a higher chance of remaining here," I nodded, replying in Zikan before shifting back to English, looking at Genie, "you will need to be granted an audience with my mother."

"Actually, I already have an invitation," she said. "After this afternoon, she asked if I would meet her for tea and I agreed. Like I said, I'll do anything to remain here."

Unsurprising that my mother was one step ahead. "I suppose that settles it. I would make a suggestion that you need to appease her."

She nodded confidently. "Is there anything I should prepare?"

"Etiquette is going to be the most important thing," Helga replied in Zikan. "I could teach her, but I require a translator."

"I can help," Freddie said to Helga.

"She will most likely ask her to spy," Helga added.

"On us?" Freddie asked.

"On the new princess," she said, looking at me, "we both know Her Majesty will require full obedience, and she will ask of things beyond what a friend should do. Even spying on the future queen."

"In order to shape her," Alex added.

"Genie does not shape," Freddie snorted.

"I meant the princess," Alex tutted.

"Please, can you translate?" Genie whispered to Freddie.

I cleared my throat, switching to English. "my mother may seem pleasant on her exterior, but she shall enjoy digging her claws into you. I only hope you are prepared for scrutiny."

A big grin licked across her face. "I am a dance student, remember. Every move I make is scrutinised. I'm not comparing, but I think Her Majesty will be interesting to navigate."

A ripple of soft laughter echoed from all of us. Jonah nodded, "then, we shall endeavour to hear of your success once you have had your tea. Should you be unsuccessful, you will find that your position here is thwarted and you will be banished from entering this settlement again."

Genie nodded in absolute understanding, not a hint of hesitation. But part of me knew she would secure the vote. Apart from Helga, due to her position of not being a voting member of the council, she had secured all ours. With my mother's, she would have five votes.

"Sheika will vote in favour," Jonah said. "If we can twist the hands of Mare and Ryin, it will place us on equal footing."

"I will speak with Mare," Alex smiled.

"And, I shall speak with Ryin," Freddie replied, "The Gods know that male owes me a favour."

What favour he was speaking of I was unsure, but Freddie was a master of persuasion and if Ryin owed him a favour, it was the right time to cash it in. I would have chosen to speak with him myself to discuss new attempts to build the portal, but I knew my priorities lay with Arraetta.

"What happens if we secure equal votes?" Genie asked.

"Helga."

Helga smiled brightly, "it is fortunate I am in the position I am in."

Freddie flawlessly translated for Genie, earning a smile, as Jonah said, "now that is sorted, we should only hope that next week things will be in your favour. But, you should also prepare for others who might be less than happy a human is in our settlement, as we do have strict laws against it currently."

No one disagreed.

With Genie's vote already in hand, I was interested to know whether there had been any further research into Arraetta's incident in London. It had been on my mind to speak with Jonah about it, and I was also aware there was the possibility of Arraetta's face being plastered across the news.

"If I may change the topic slightly," I sat forward, "I am interested to know if any of you have found out about what took place in London when she disappeared. Any news?"

"Ah," Alex stood, "I shall return."

"I am a bit nervous about speaking to The Queen," Genie admitted quietly to Freddie.

"You will always be safe, my love," Freddie replied in the same tone. He had changed so much in the half moon cycle since his announcement of finding Genie, almost unrecognisable to anyone who knew him before. But, it was nice to see my cousin so happy, and I only hoped once Arraetta was well again that we could all be in bliss in our relationships.

Then again, I was unsure whether there was such a thing as bliss in the Zikan household.

Alex returned, two sheets of paper in his hand, and placed it down in front of me as he took his seat. It was a document titled North East London Power Outage Incident, alongside the date of the ball and a case number. Upon reading the document, there was no cause in which the rings could have had to injure her in such a way.

On the night of the ball, after disappearing into the ether of the rings, the report read that there had been a terrible car incident including an unknown assailant, sought for questioning by the London Metropolitan Police, who witnesses stated was *like a living horror movie*, due to her appearance. It went on to state the description of what she was wearing, alongside an almost perfect description of Arraetta, without the blood.

Luckily, the car accident did not cost the lives of anyone involved, although others suffered minor injuries due to the collision. However, one of the drivers, who had a bump to the head, described it as though the female had fallen from the sky.

"We are burying the story," Jonah assured, "it would be a risk if she is found to be here."

Freddie took the sheets of paper from me to read, and even Genie tried to glance over to understand it, although it was written in Zikan.

"I have been the one to find out," Alex told the group in broken English, "I am working with Elliot to try to, um... fix it, but should be fine. She is not on social media. It is a good idea that we do not take her outside of here in case they try to find her."

The mention of working with our investigative journalist, Elliot, made sense. He worked for the crown, posing under one of Britain's biggest newspapers when it was necessary. He was excellent, and he had the right contacts. While Alex and Jonah had a good relationship with him, he was another who favoured my father.

"And, we have a *Jane Doe* in a hospital," he added, with a soft smile, switching to Zikan, "although the fingerprints are proving more tricky to cover."

"They have her fingerprints?" I queried. It made sense that Arraetta's imprint would have been at the scene, but it made it much harder to cover up her story. It was not as though she had committed a crime, but we could not have foreign police knocking on our door to investigate further.

"Luckily, there has been no direct correlation between them and our princess," Alex reassured, and I felt my shoulders sag in relief.

It was fortunate we appeared and disappeared by the rings, so all of our movements were untraceable.

"Do not worry, Seraiah," Jonah said, "we will keep the princess safe, whatever it takes."

Whatever it takes.

"I, also, hope you might consider my offer," Alex added, looking at Jonah for a little reassurance, "I... I would like to be considered for official position of the person guard to Her Royal Highness. As you know, I have a great respect for the crown, and it would be an honour to see to it that she is safe within the residence, and does not find herself in places that are *out of bounds*."

Alex shifting positions would be a big undertaking, although I had no doubt he would be perfect. He was straight-laced, incredible with armaments, protect Arraetta where necessary and be an advocate for Arraetta to become the queen she was worthy of becoming. He would not only treat her like a princess, but as a goddess, and she would be safe.

Still, I was wary of her being so closely tied to Amity when we could assign another guard to make it less as though we were spying on her, if anything did slip.

"What's happening?" Genie whispered loud enough for us all to hear.

Ah, we had switched back to Zikan.

I swiftly switched back, "I am also worried your English is not as fluent as it should be, when Arraetta cannot speak a word of Zikan."

"He would learn," Jonah stated.

"As I said at the beginning," Alex agreed, "it would be an honour to learn it. I am... I know English but it is just a little difficult in some areas."

"I can help you," Genie grinned.

"Is it my decision?" I asked, peering up at Jonah, "I am surprised you care for my opinion."

"Alex wished to ask," Jonah shrugged, "it is a role which must be filled either way."

Yes, it was. And, an important one because Alex was right, we did not want Arraetta to find herself in places which were off limits, including my father's wing. I was sure she was not so naïve as to step foot into such a place. However, once she found out my father was a monster.

I offered him a compromise. "If you can bury the story and the report, then I will consider your position as Arraetta's guard."

Alex nodded, "consider it done, Sir."

The topic of conversation shifted to other concerns, including Eros, although there was nothing new to cover, as neither of us were able to get to Italy to negotiate his release. It had been a good chance for us to open Genie up to the wider politics of the world, and I knew she felt a little fearful of what she had stepped foot in. Still, it did not deter her, and only seemed to make her more determined to navigate it.

I wondered whether Arraetta would be as resilient once she awoke, or whether she would be the creator of a bigger storm than any of us were prepared to fight against. Because, as I was slowly understanding, it was difficult to cage fire when it was determined to burn everything in its sight.

I only hoped what rose from the ashes would be far greater than what stood before.

SIXTEEN

As the following sols passed, I found myself in an endless cycle of watching Arraetta sleep fitfully, whilst I tried to whisper soothing words to coax her from nightmares. I prayed she would awaken so I could peer into those beautiful azure eyes and sweep her off her feet again. But such prayers were never answered.

The sol before the council meeting came around far too quickly, and I knew the vote on Genie's position in the house would be done at the same time Arraetta's title would be discussed. I felt nervous about the outcome of the decision when it was being voted for by my oppressors.

Genie had also successfully infiltrated my mother's trust and did not fail to tell us that she was a spy in my mother's game. I was sure keeping an eye on her friend hurt her, but so did the necessity of securing a place in our world.

A sharp knock rattled on Arraetta's closed door as I snoozed in the corner on an armchair. I stretched and stood, not considering who it might be, as I opened it.

An acute thud ricocheted in my chest. *Fuck.*

I was greeted by the face of a sadistic monster who I wished I did not have to see. After the treason I had committed a quarter moon before, I had not thought about what might come of me, too occupied with Arraetta and the impending council votes to acknowledge it. His smug face was all I needed to see to know it was time to accept my fate, and I knew he could scent the subtle fear which danced in my eyes.

"Your Highness."

"Kaeltar," I greeted grimly, eyeing the four other males with him – all who were as thrilled to see my punishment through to the bitter end as the punisher they joined.

Kaeltar held a sheet of paper. "I have a seal. This one is not fortified; you may call your commander if necessary. You have ten minutes to prepare yourself before I deliver you to your second home."

I peered naturally back at Arraetta, wary that she was in a highly precarious position even with the constant care she received.

"Do not worry," he said nonchalantly, "I will ensure that she gets the care she deserves."

My fists clenched, and I instantly grabbed him by the scruff of his neck, uncaring that the males with him tightened their armaments in defence. I knew they would use force when necessary, but I was of a higher command than even Kaeltar, and I would quite happily rip out his treasonous tongue. It was a shame that Kaeltar had a foot of height on me, as all my actions did was make him laugh.

"Come now, Your Highness," he said, a twinkle in his eye, "I would not want to relieve you of the grace you have been awarded. Ten minutes. Take it or leave it. Of course, I will let you know that I have the full power to take you by force. I'm sure the staff will find your screams of anger quite amusing."

Even a muzzle would not stop the hellsworn sprouting pathetic bullshit. Where was all my fucking dark power then? Even I could not feel the anger brewing when my body was rattled with fear. I would have enjoyed punching his arrogant face so hard that my fist tore through his skull and shattered it.

But I was a male of principle, not of unwarranted anger. Then again, it was warranted. It was so fucking necessary, but I was not ready to end up in the vault longer than I had been awarded.

A weak prince will never be a mighty king. I shivered before letting go of Kaeltar with a shove. I was not weak; I was just tactical.

"I am surprised you do not feel pathetic doing the work of a male you so love the cock of," I replied.

Kaeltar's jaw squared before his lip twitched. "I am surprised you choose to use such derogatory language, considering two of your sidekicks do quite enjoy fucking each other up the arse every night."

His entourage chuckled whilst I just felt more aggravated. No words left me to defend Jonah and Alex, feeling like a small seedling who could not develop a rebuttal.

"I do not need time to prepare," I told him. "But I swear if you dare to touch a single hair on my wife's head, I will quite gladly give you the gift of death you are begging for."

He grinned brightly, "Death is already my friend; I will welcome it when ready. But even so, do you truly believe I would harm a sleeping female?"

A stupid question from a hellsworn fucker, "I would not trust you even if you laid down your arms and begged me whilst I had a knife against your throat."

"I have had many knives to my throat, Your Highness. It is whether the bargainer at the other end offers me a good deal or not."

I rolled my eyes, taking the opportunity to close the door and start walking down the corridor. "Maybe you should dig deep inside your soul and realise that life is not all about bargaining."

"Oh, that is where you are wrong," he said, following behind, the heavy footsteps of his troop echoing. "We are always bargaining; it is what keeps us alive."

I wondered whether he was challenging me to strike a bargain, but I had been at the hands of his suffering for many sols. Whilst it is said to keep your friends close and your enemies closer, Kaeltar would infiltrate and destroy all hopes of me becoming king. He was not the devil which I would ever strike a deal with; no, the only one I would strike a deal with was–

No. Not even him.

But you will.

I held down the growl, which dared to ripple from my throat. I would not allow any demon to infiltrate me. I was a prince of pride and honour, and I would uphold it as I took the punishment for the laws I had broken. Still, my only thought was about how quickly it would be over so that I could return to Arraetta's side again.

A car drove me to the garrison, and the journey was far too short to come to terms with what might await me. It had been my initial idea to bring Genie to the ball, but I had not been the one to initiate the arrival of two humans nor extend the invitation myself. I had, however, written a speech to disturb the peace and cause undeniable uproar in our society. It just so happened that my father was fortunate enough to find such a dossier.

Treason, as my father claimed.

Undeniable treason. And, somehow, the decision bypassed the council vote, and I was brought in to be punished. But who voted for it? And who from my council had approved such a decision?

The answer was given when I spotted Jonah at the vault level.

"Trust," Kaeltar commented quietly to me before he said louder, "You do not need to defend him, Commander."

"I am aware." Jonah's words were sobering.

Betrayer.

My own commander had deceived me, but for what gain? He had agreed with my punishment, which could only have meant that the decision was made during the latest war council. One I was not wholly a part of. Not a single moment to be able to defend my actions, only to bow at the commands of those who perched in positions that were only just out of my reach.

But he was still my closest friend and greatest ally, and he knew the vaults were my worst punishment.

I will kill that traitor.

A growl rattled from my throat, which I knew he heard, but Jonah still did not look at or acknowledge me. He remained steadfast with his gaze on Kaeltar.

"I am here as a witness so that you do not bring any more harm than what has been agreed."

I noticeably flinched at his contradictory words, understanding that harm was intended to come to me. Jonah finally looked at me, and I wondered whether I could see a glimpse of remorse in his guarded expression.

I cleared my throat. "I suppose I should find out what *harm* that will be. Or shall it be as much of a surprise as *this*?"

Jonah winced, and his benevolence seemed to have returned, although there was still no sign that he wished to defend his actions. Kaeltar pushed me towards the cell like a prisoner of war, not a prince. I doubted any other such high-ranking official would be treated with such disrespect in any nation.

No, this was just sadistic torture at its finest.

Without hesitation, I walked into the glass prison and was commanded by another officer to kneel, facing the glass. Jonah and Kaeltar stood together, neither speaking, just waiting.

I kept my eyes trained on my betrayer, looking for some sort of sign of how I might forgive him for his duplicity. However, Jonah caught my eye, nodding subtly with some kind of message that I could not understand.

The elevator pinged, and I watched as several people stepped out. Unsurprisingly, I saw The General and Cormac in the herd. I did not expect to see my father, or at least I supposed I wished I did not have to see the satisfaction roll across his face as I received whatever comeuppance he believed I deserved.

With the three of them were a handful of guards and a court clerk.

I watched my father warily as he stepped closer to the glass, gazing down at me as though I was a caged animal ready to be experimented on before he moved to speak quietly to The General and Cormac. I looked back at Jonah, seeing he was looking restless.

Good. He was uncomfortable. Maybe less of a traitor, more a strategist. It still felt like I was about to bear for all to see, and therefore, I was still uneasy about what path of action he had chosen without my consultation.

The General nodded to the clerk, who stepped forward, unrolled a dossier and looked at me as he read, "It is hereby declared that here, on this sol, His Royal Highness, Prince Seraiah II of Zika, will receive punishment for his act of treason against The King. These crimes include colluding to and acting upon bringing two human beings into the court and plotting to overthrow His Majesty, King Charles III of Zika, through falsified accusations and lack of evidence. The punishment for colluding to and acting upon bringing two human beings is a public flogging of fifty counts." I winced. "The punishment for the count of treason is death."

He paused for an extended period whilst the weight of his words hit me like a stack of bricks. Would my father kill the only heir to the throne? My crimes surely were not so severe that I would receive such punishment.

Maybe the verdict was being used to enact fear.

It was working. The familiar foe thrummed in my fucking chest.

I should have just read the fucking speech. An internal repetition which I knew was wholly the truth.

I hated regret, but fuck I was rife with it.

But, *Arraetta.*

"It has, however," he continued, "been voted upon by the war council that the punishment for the act of treason will be disregarded as it is recognised that your dedication to the people of Zika and position outweighs the need for such an act. Therefore, this act of treason has been agreed to have the same weight as that of the punishment of bringing two humans into the court. In accordance with the war council, His Royal Highness, Prince Seraiah II of Zika, has been sentenced to one hundred counts of flogging."

Death sounded sweeter. Suffering at the hands of a whip one hundred times was nothing short of merciless torture.

The two guards who remained inside moved towards its edge while Kaeltar entered, holding a thick, small black handle – the one he had decorated his belt like he was showing off how big his cock was. He clicked a button, causing it to grow into a bludgeon-like stick. And then it fizzled with electrical sparks.

I knew my eyes were wild with fear, unable to rip them from the terrifying armament. It was not just one hundred floggings. It was a hundred electrical beatings which would tear me apart inside and out.

"That was not agreed," Jonah surprisingly stepped in.

"You agreed he would be punished!" The General shouted. "Maybe you should not have voted to betray your *friend.*"

"I voted to save his life!" Jonah chided. "He does not need this... this severe of a punishment."

He still voted to punish me, though. The coil of anger was turning, but still, I felt like I could forgive Jonah if only he told me the real reason. The decision may have been out of his hands, but he could have forewarned me.

227

"If you do not wish to watch, Commander, you may leave," Kaeltar told Jonah before looking at me. "I suggest you remove your shirt, Your Highness."

Jonah looked torn, but would not leave me alone in such circumstances. He tucked his shoulders back, holding his ground, and turned to watch the caged animal before him.

Hating Kaeltar giving me orders in disguise as a suggestion, I took a moment before I removed my shirt and threw it aside.

"Start the resonance," my father commanded a guard, who did as he said.

Of course. Not only would I suffer at the hands of a male who was sadistic enough to enjoy giving me punishment with a sceptre of electricity, and have an audience of those far too keen to see me punished, but the frequency would play to keep my power at bay, causing the wounds to be deeper.

It was not just torture; it was total and complete submission.

Like always, there was no forewarning, but my energy evaporated as though it were being held down by a ton of lead.

"Start your count, clerk," Kaeltar shouted.

Eyes begging, I looked at Jonah in hopes he would come to my rescue like I was a damsel in fucking distress. Well, I was in distress. Painful, fucking torturous torment. The first strike came without warning, and Jonah's gaze shifted as I grunted from it - the electricity burning through every fibre in my back, tendrils ricocheting as my skin fizzled. Anyone could have heard the sound.

Sucking air through my teeth, I looked to my father, waiting to see if the tyrannical fiend would squirm as my impenetrable gaze remained on him.

"One," the clerk announced.

I did not scream or beg. I would not let it affect me. But after the first ten strikes, dizziness settled, and I cast my eyes down to the ground, hating that I was in such a submissive position before him. Empyreans how I was sure he was enjoying seeing me on my knees, exactly where he wanted me. I could not wait for the sol when the roles were reversed, craving to see the fright in his soulless eyes.

Crackle.

Slash.

Lash.

The thirty mark passed, and bile rose in my throat so rapidly that I could not prevent the dark red blood from projectile vomiting onto the floor below me. It splattered like a bucket hitting tile flooring. Whilst it might have seemed like my internal organs were bleeding, I knew my life force did not know how to deal with such pain, so the only way to dispose of it was outward.

I felt the winds of change with Kaeltar as he paused at the thirty-first strike. I wished I knew what look was passing over his face, although I doubted it was a concern.

"We must stop!" Jonah declared, stepping forward, but even I shook my head at him, knowing that my father's game would not stop until I had been thoroughly punished.

A long hour of pain and torture was more welcome than an elongated sentence.

"It is not a negotiation," my father replied harshly. Nothing ever was.

Kaeltar continued, his hand swinging harder and with less remorse. It seemed he was silently begging me to draw more blood, needing to coax every ounce of my control from me until I was merciless against his hand.

Thwack.

Blood trickled.

Thud.

Vomit spewed.

Crackle.

The white floors turned sanguine.

Flog.

And, finally, as they all silently begged for, I could not hold on to the noise of anguish which tore from my mouth. Was it a scream for them to stop or an acknowledgement of the pain Kaeltar was committing? I was unsure. More blood thundered from my throat, but I knew we were miles away from the hundredth mark.

The numbers became a blur. At one point, I heard sixty, but at the other, it melded to ten. Time was shifting, and I was unsure whether we were closer to the end or the beginning.

Kaeltar's consistently smug face stained my mind, knowing he was enjoying his task even though I could not see it from how I faced. He meant every hit, not one of them an ounce lighter than the other. They were almost heavier each time, although it could have been my weakened body, feeling the force of each impenetrable swing.

The ongoing frequency was causing rapid hallucinations of laughing faces melding into disappointed expressions to taint my vision.

If death did not reach my father first, I might quite like to throw him in the chamber of hell when I was king so that he might understand precisely how I felt.

I was unsure what number we had reached when my body finally gave in, and I plummeted forward to the ground. I grunted, convulsing on the floor as I watched the commotion out of my hazy vision.

A pair of knees landed in my tilted blurred sight before Kaeltar's face appeared. Part of me wondered whether he was seeing how I was faring to check whether I would need medical attention and perhaps kindly suggest we ended the punishment there. Surely, he was satisfied enough with the red pool decorating the cell.

But I was wrong to think the male might feel an inch of remorse.

Instead, he whispered so quietly I was sure no one else could hear, "Now, now, Your Highness. Eighty-nine floggings in, and you cannot take the final eleven. Surprising, I thought you were not one to give up so easily, hm? What will your wife think of you when you return to her defeated?" My ears twigged at her mention. "Ah, there it is. Come now, let us finish what we started, hm?"

It was a struggle to get myself back to a sitting position. It felt like it took minutes, maybe even hours, before I forced myself to balance back on my bruised knees. The impenetrable gazes of my audience added a heady sensation to my ails, but as I looked up, I could barely make out who was standing there.

"Let us continue, clerk," Kaeltar called, and the thud of the stick slammed against my open, wounded back without warning.

Ha. Was I expecting a warning when I had been through eighty-nine of them?

Then, ninety.

Ninety-one.

When will it fucking end?

Ninety-two.

Almost over. It is almost *over.*

Kaeltar paused, bathing in the power to delay the beating at any point. I panted, musing whether the sweat and blood that layered my body made me look formidable or weak.

Eight more heavy slams to my aching skin, and I would be free from the torment, from the torture, and I could fucking kill the hellsworns who dared to honour me with such punishment. And Empyreans, I would rip their throats out.

No. I had taken the punishment, and I would be free. But would the chains only tighten? The impaling claws of my life bringers gripping deeper, control being lost to be an obedient heir readied to marry his Kindred Spirit.

It would be worth it for Arraetta; it was *all* worth it for her.

You can still be a great king.

Kaeltar leant down behind me, his breath tickling my ear as he whispered, "Quite the audience you have, Your Highness. I would be quite happy to bargain with you if you want to put either of those in your place."

"F-Fuck you," I stuttered.

A chuckle rippled from his throat, no less callous than any other, before I felt the anguish tear through my body as he probed a segment of my open wound, nail digging in.

"I do enjoy seeing you powerless before me," he murmured, "it's satisfying having all the control whilst you squirm, sweat, and *bleed.*"

"What is the delay, Kaeltar?" The General called from the opposite side of the glass.

His sordid pleasure, of course. I was surprised The General even cared why the male was taking his time, but I supposed busy people had places to be. And even my punishment gave them little interest after a certain amount of time had passed. Repetitions of the same beating were tedious to witness.

Apart from Kaeltar, who chuckled. "Oh, nothing, General. I was reminding His Highness here of what should happen if he forgets his place again, Sir." He leaned in closer, whispering. "I hope the next one will be having the pleasure of watching your wife writhing beneath me as she screams my name."

Futile mortal-kind.

Maybe it was fear or anger or complete and utter possessiveness, but all the pain and suffering Kaeltar had caused me dislodged as the one thing that should have been highly impossible inside the vault rippled furiously through my body. Rapidfire. But it was not my azure Rapidfire. No. The dark onyx power washed over me like a wanted cloud of feathers.

It was an intoxicating, insatiable power. And, fuck, did it feel good.

With some unknown strength, I somehow turned, grabbed Kaeltar by his neck, and threw him up against the glass with a thud. Behind, the fearful gazes of the onlookers watched the animal he had coaxed me into becoming. Blood dripped mercilessly from my body onto the ribbed flooring whilst I cocked my head like I was staring at delicious prey.

And, Empyreans, was Kaeltar's fear delicious.

"Seraiah," Jonah called, his voice hazy, deeper and distorted.

"Betrayal is a fine thing, treacherous kin," I announced to Jonah, my voice laced with that familiar darkness which was not truly mine. I noticed Jonah stumble backwards, but little did I care. I stared unwaveringly into Kaeltar's eyes, noting how they were more black than brown, reflecting my possessed reflection in them. "Do you so dare to think that my wife would ever share a bed with a foul-mouthed hellsworn fucker like you? As though she is a mere possession that you own? Hm? Such crimes of speaking down to anyone of a higher rank are treason, and that is the same for your future queen. How you laugh mercilessly, expecting that I would not, one sol, seek my revenge against such a cretin as you and tear your fucking life apart."

"Seraiah," Jonah called again. He was closer now, at the door to my diamond cage.

I waved my arm in his direction, and a black mist appeared, blocking him from making any further steps towards me.

While attempting to get through, he called, "This is not you, Seraiah. Whatever this is, this darkness is overshadowing who you are. You do not harm your people, no matter what this piece of shit here has done. You negotiate, you make peace. You are the future king."

"Oh, but you see, Commander," I laughed darkly, ensuring everyone could hear, "this is me."

Kaeltar snorted an irritatingly loud and arrogant laugh, and I tightened my hand around his throat, making my power flare more vigorously in my arm. His laughter halted as I purposely looked back into his eyes, detecting something new - a power I did not know I possessed but suddenly understood I owned.

Complete submission by fear control. And, fuck, I would take Kaeltar's. Deep in his callous soul was his locked-up fear, yet his was not in a coffer like mine. It just existed. It embodied the dread of being unwanted, the need to be accepted by others by rising through the ranks and bargaining with whoever he could, and a desire to fit in even if he alienated himself more. Not memories, but feelings.

I tugged on them, watching as he started to shake, attempting to pull back as I pulled each one to the forefront of his mind. The glass rumbled behind him, not by the force of his body, but by my own power. Kaeltar cried for help, mercilessly begging someone to free him through anguish-driven screams.

Then, the glass began to crack, and those on the other side moved back quickly. The tear rippled and shattered it, causing shards to fly everywhere. As though the glass had created a barrier for the dark Rapidfire, the frequency ended, and so did the facade that had overpowered me.

Weakness soared through my body, and I could not hold the male, dropping him. He plummeted to the floor, writhing and screaming as he tried to free himself from the torment of fear having resurfaced from the deep crevices of his mind.

I remained on my feet, balancing unsteadily but aware of what happened when I allowed utter distress to overshadow me. He happened. But I had control. A control I could not afford to lose; otherwise, it would jeopardise everything.

Malevolent laughter caromed off the surrounding walls and around the inner sanctum of my mind, causing me to lose all willpower to remain upright and thud back to my knees next to the wailing Kaeltar.

"Arrest him!" The General commanded.

"No!" Jonah defended, kneeling before me, "Seraiah, are you well?"

The realisation of how much dark power simmered beneath my skin rattled my mind again, daring and coaxing me to use it on every other fucker in the room, but I had to remember that it was the power which belonged to the demon inside my mind.

"We have seen what harm the prince can do," Cormac said to my father, loud enough for all to hear. "It is only a matter of time before he loses control again."

My father's unreadable gaze skimmed in my direction as he said something to Cormac and The General, which was too quiet for me to make out. He turned his head enough so I could not read his lips. Not that I could with how much my vision fuzzed.

The elevator pinged, and I watched as its doors opened. My mother had arrived, flanked by a few guards and Helga.

"What is happening here?" her voice cut through the quiet chatter, "whilst I see the defence council has, once again, decided to go against my wishes, I find myself coming down here to find my son barely conscious. Your son, Charles! I might not be able to condone what Seraiah did, but he is the heir to the throne and should have been pardoned for his behaviour."

"He has broken the law," my father stated.

"I am aware, but this is far beyond what I expected of you," she replied disappointedly. I did not miss the slight guilt on his face, but I knew that guilt was not for me but her - the female he had loved and lost in exchange for total power.

My mother ripped the dossier from the clerk's hands, reading it. "One hundred flogs? For what? Pride? Honour? He is our son."

Distress was not an emotion I saw lightly on my mother's face, but I noticed it in her gaze as she looked towards me. It was the same as the one when she had rushed into the throne room the first and only time my father had raised that belt to my back, flogging me as a punishment for thievery of the crown jewels. Yet, I still could not forgive her for the many winters of suffering I had been dealt.

"That monster is not my son!" he answered sharply, repeating the exact words he had spoken on repeat for scorns, "he understands the consequences of his actions. He should just be thankful that I have not relieved him of his tainted life and sentenced him to death. Even position seems to be a timely friend for a hellsworn prince."

Yes, position is a timely friend, but yours shall be thwarted soon, tyrant king.

"Take him home, Jonah," my mother commanded, ignoring my father's foul words, before she looked to the guards, "and, for the enforcer... I suppose he should find himself somewhere that may be able to soothe his... pain."

I supposed her comment was quite comical, but I finally looked adequately at the male before me, who was nothing but a shell of himself. A male who had flogged me a total of ninety-three times before I had ripped his life from him. But he was not dead. I just hoped he would never see the light of sol again.

Or, at least, if he did, I would happily tear him apart.

SEVENTEEN

C old heat and sweat soaked my skin, every position causing more agony than the one before. My Rapidfire was depleted, causing weakness to settle in every fragment of my body like sharp thorns were constantly trying to penetrate my skin. I had spent the best part of the evening of my punishment fighting the help of Marie so that she could wrap my back in layers of bandages, only to be sedated eventually.

Fuck. I was so feeble and powerless.

What time was it? How long had I been asleep?

Where was Arraetta?

Disorientated, I sat myself upright and grunted as pain ricocheted down my swollen back, the dressings feeling far too tight. I was still in my bed, sun-tinged curtains blowing from a subtle breeze from an opened window.

How much time had passed?

Closing my eyes, I took a deep breath before turning grievously to my drawers, shuffling as gently as possible. I found my watch inside, noting that it was just after noon and that Wednesday was the sol. It had only been a sol, which I supposed made sense, considering how much I was suffering.

Empyreans, it was Wednesday, the sol of the vote. The council meeting would have already started without me, and my vote would not have been cast by proxy - that was part of the treaty agreement.

Grumbling, I somehow managed to get onto my two feet and unsteadily find clothes, wiping the lingering sweat that beaded from my forehead. Exhausted, bruised and broken, I was dressed within minutes and slipped on a pair of loafers, uncaring that I probably resembled a doll dressed by a seedling.

When I opened the door to my room, I was unsurprised to see Travis stationed there. He stood upright immediately, looking both surprised and worried.

"Your Highness, I have-"

"-Orders?" I interjected, uncaring, as I started to walk down the corridor, "I have a council meeting to get to."

He followed quickly. "You must rest; you will only strain yourself more, Sir."

"You sound worried," I laughed humourlessly, pushing the pain as far back in my mind as possible as I breezed ahead of him. Nausea clogged my throat, and I could feel the damp, cool heat rippling through every inch of my torso.

Travis was on my heels, keeping close enough in case I might collapse. And, fuck, I thought I might as I descended the stairs. I swore they shifted towards the bottom, and I stumbled to the ground, startling a few milling workers about.

"Shit," I whispered.

"My prince," Travis said softly, trying to help me to my feet, but I only batted his hand away, swaying upwards.

My back felt like someone had slapped their hand upon it, aching to break free from the confines of the gauze. I would not show weakness. I had entered that chamber a quarter before, coated in Arraetta's blood, so entering it, looking like a dishevelled rat, was the least of my problems. I had to remember Arraetta had suffered worse than I, and whilst pain was subjective, I would push through it.

Stoic, above all.

"Please," Travis was begging.

"Empyreans, shut the fuck up!" I snarled, my words bouncing off the walls of the large hallway, "If you care about me, then go back to the hallway and watch over my wife! She…" I took a breath. "She is the most important being here, and, without my vote in there, they will remove Genie, and then they will remove her. Do you understand what I am saying, Rheon Travis? My pain is nothing compared to what we shall all suffer if she does not become queen."

It did not take long for him to agree. Turning, he walked away up the stairs, and oddly, I watched him go as if I cared for the guard.

A female gasp echoed from behind, "Your Highness, you're bleeding."

I did not turn toward her or look at my back, but I could feel the heat of ichor soaking through the bandages. I knew it would have seeped through my thin T-shirt.

Time to give them a fucking show.

I walked to the door, neither guard hesitating to open it as my father's confinements consumed my being. His corridor was quiet, but I could hear the loud echo of murmuring voices through the door to the chambers. Without hesitation, I squared my shoulders, twisted the door handle, and opened it.

The room fell silent. Every single one of them looked at me, a few rising.

Good.

"Seraiah," Freddie whispered as I limped across the room towards my vacant chair.

"I apologise that I am late."

Jonah looked flabbergasted at seeing me, whilst the only thing I did in return was lift my chin to show my defiance. Betrayer. I took everyone in, noting that Fulk was the only person not in attendance from the quarter prior. Unsurprisingly, I noted the mirth in Cormac and The General's gazes.

But it was my father's look which surprised me, coated in fear. I knew he did not expect to see me and, empyreans, I felt smug seeing that expression.

"Please, continue," I said, tentatively taking my seat.

"I, uh," Amice stuttered, looking across the opposition until she found a nod to continue from my mother, who seemed quite satisfied to see me. "Please, sit."

Apart from Amice, those standing took their seats, most still looking at me, although I trained my unwavering eyes on my father, who squirmed beneath it.

"As we were saying, today we shall vote on the position of Genevieve here," Amice glanced at everyone, "and the title of Arraetta. All votes cast will be final."

I looked at Genie, sitting patiently, before looking at Freddie, who was looking at me with his *what the hell are you doing* expression. My lip tugged as I made myself more comfortable in my chair.

"Each of you has coins in front of you," Amice announced. "As I go around, you will hold up the one you choose. The coin with the most votes will be the decider, but should we have a tie, then Lady Katerina shall place a vote."

I looked down at the two large, round metal coins before me - one bronze for no and one gold for yes. I knew my decision, but I did not reach for it as fast as Freddie had gripped his gold one. My vote would be cast before my father's, so it was best I did not show my play until the last moment even if such play was evident.

"Sir Cormac," Amice said. There was little hesitance in Cormac's play, nor was it surprising, as he lifted the bronze coin. Genie's shoulders sagged, but Freddie leaned over and whispered something into her ears, giving her more hope.

"General Viktoerin." Bronze.

"Sir Oswin." Bronze.

"Lady Sabina." Bronze.

"Lady Ida." Bronze.

"Sir Johannes." Gold.

It was a surprising move, and he even received several fascinating looks from his council members.

"I vote bronze," Amice added before continuing. "Commander Jonah." Gold.

"Sir Alexandre." Gold.

"Lady Mare." Gold. Good work, Alex.

"Sir Ryin." Bronze. I was interested in hearing more about his reasoning, although part of me wondered whether it was because if he appeased my father, he might receive the needed funding. Funding I could not give him.

"Sir Frederique." Gold.

"Shaman Sheika." Gold.

"Her Majesty." Gold.

"His Highness." I brushed my hand over the gold coin and lifted it, careful not to show even the slightest tremble to show how much pain lifting my arm was.

Seven against eight. If my father voted bronze, Helga's vote would be the game changer, although I would have been surprised if she voted bronze.

"His Majesty."

Placing my coin back, I sat a little straighter and gazed across to my father, who was receiving a similar look of impatience from those at the table. His eyes brushed across everyone before landing on Genie, Freddie, and then back to Genie.

"Gold." his words were clear, rattling the table with surprise. He touched the coin but did not lift it before sitting back. Cormac leaned over and whispered to him, but the whispers were inaudible from the murmurs that brushed through everyone.

Amity cleared her throat for attention. "it has been decided. Genevieve shall be granted permission to remain within the Zikan settlement. No further decisions are to be made. However, circum-stances can change depending on the factor, and any concerns may be raised with the council in the future." A warning to Genie. "Your Majesty, will there be any formalities with Genevieve?"

My mother, who was the addressee, nodded in reply, "Although, I suspect we shall discuss further down the line her influence on our people. For now, we must recognise her as Arraetta's closest friend. Still, I am apprehensive about naming her First Lady, so we shall have her remain Lady Genevieve in the first instance."

"Thank you," Freddie replied.

My mother pulled a piece of paper closer to her. "I have other changes I would like to implement, and none require a vote. Unless my husband decides otherwise, Freddie, you shall be officially announced as the Prince's Advisor; such changes shall include monetary designations and a home away from the palace for yourself and Genevieve."

An excellent decision for the council's opposition, but it left me without an ally on the inside.

"I would like protocols officially updated in the house, including new hires amongst the staff and strict etiquette put into place. It is time to end this selfish and idiotic vengeance between the two councils and come together. All rumours about my son shall be erased, and he will not be treated as the outcast prince. He is the heir to the throne and shall be respected."

No one spoke up against my mother, although I almost dared one of the opposition to argue with her - I could see it in their ruffled expressions.

"And, finally, I shall have no vote placed upon this," she announced. "The female upstairs, the one you have come to name Arraetta, will now be known as Her Royal Highness, Arraetta, the princess consort of Zika. She and my son shall heartfast following Iontine in line with the bonding ritual of the Kindred Spirits." I sat up straighter, ignoring the pain on my back. "It is a great honour to announce that I have been in conversation with Sheika for many sols, and we have made a great discovery. She is not only the bearer of Rapidfire, but we also believe that she may be the daughter of the great king Ivan the Great and the deity, Reona."

"With what evidence?" Cormac asked.

"The tome of The Cre-este," Sheika interjected, "alongside my meditations."

The General snorted, "blasphemous."

"If I wanted your advice, I would have asked for it," my mother chided, glaring at the two males. "The only male I might listen to is my king."

We all looked at my father, who was sitting back with his arms folded. Listening but not giving any input. I doubted my father was comfortable sitting in silence, so I could only assume my mother had piercing words to say to him following the events of the sol before.

"You heard my wife," my father said with finality, not sparing a glance at anyone. He gazed up at me, "it seems that even the devil can secure himself a goddess for a wife. Oh, how you must have pleased the Gods by controlling your temperament. I should only hope your actions of last sol did not change their minds."

I did not let my mask drop, although I could feel the bitterness in every one of his words niggle at my anger. He was fortunate I was feeling unwell and using all my strength to keep up my unperturbed facade; otherwise, I might have argued back at him.

I noted the smug gazes on some of his council members' faces, but still, I did not turn my eyes from him until he did. Only then did I look at my mother.

"Please, continue," I nodded to her.

"Are there any other discussions on the agenda?" my mother asked Amice.

"Would you like to discuss the changes in protocols and staffing today, ma'am?" Amice asked her, "Or should we reconvene with final thoughts next council once we have had a less formal discussion?"

As the discussion shifted from our positions in the house to protocols and procedures, I turned a blind ear and relaxed a little in the chair. I could still feel the sweat permeating my skin whilst nausea was clawing at my throat, but I managed to keep awake throughout the mundane discussion. I supposed I should have kept more of an ear open once Jonah started talking about security protocols, but I could not stop thinking about how the male was discussing my safety when he had all but ripped it away from me.

I wondered how much of Amity knew of what he had voted to happen to me. I was sure Alex would have known; Jonah would not keep such a secret away from his keeper. Freddie might have known, although he had been preoccupied with securing Genie's place in our world. Helga could have known.

Trust was a fine thing; once it was broken, it was incredibly hard to sew back together.

Once the court ended, I did not wait too long to stand as gracefully as I could and rush from the room. I supposed I just needed fresh air and some water, maybe to fall into a coma until I was healed. Maybe I could have found a way to get into Arraetta's mind and joined her until she, too, awoke. I was sure the pleasantry of her dreams was much nicer than the nightmare of my reality. And, fuck, I was bringing her right into the centre of it.

"Seraiah." Jonah caught up with me as I reached the upstairs corridor. "You are bleeding."

I ignored him.

"I am sorry."

I snorted, turning to him, "Are you? I supposed you were not so inclined to tell me I was about to be beaten until I was at my father's mercy, and for what, hm?"

"It was that or death."

"Death would have been fucking sweeter," I answered. "One sol you will know how it feels to have razor-sharp blades upon your back and understand the agony I was in. Powerless. Empyreans, I was on my fucking knees, begging for mercy. One hundred times, I was beaten, and you did nothing to fucking stop it!"

He bowed his head as Freddie and Genie walked to the end of the corridor, stopping when they saw the two of us.

"I could not stop it."

I laughed mirthlessly. "No, you decided to betray me instead. I would have thought someone else but not you, Jonah."

I turned to walk away but stopped abruptly as he said, "It was how I secured your father's vote - to keep Arraetta here. I had to appease him. We said we would do whatever it takes."

Whatever it takes. Of course, in the Amity meeting sols before, we had mentioned that, but being part of the decision to punish me severely to secure my father's vote surely was a step too far? Or maybe I was a stubborn prince who could not see past my selfishness. Still, by the actions of the sol, we would have won with Helga's vote, but I noticed how tepid my father had been in the meeting, not even arguing against my mother.

"Whatever it takes," I nodded, but did not turn to him. Instead, I stalked to my room, where I closed the door sharply and leaned against it. I repeated to myself, "Whatever it takes."

And I did whatever it took to keep away from Jonah over the following quarter, concentrating primarily on trying to heal my throbbing body and revitalising what little Rapidfire I could. I noticed a significant shift in the house; I was no longer being treated by some as the outcast prince, but as a true heir. Protocols were updated per the council, staff greetings were lower, and gazes had stopped meeting my eyes.

Staffing changed, additional positions were filled, and I was permanently flanked by either Travis or Connell, while I also had two new assistants and a dresser named Arion. Although he was quite helpful while I was unwell, I felt it was unnecessary to have him permanently. Then again, that was a decision I could not go against unless I spoke with my mother.

While decisions had been made for Genie to remain at the house, she had been granted permission to continue her studies at her ballet academy. So, she spent much of her time away from the house with Freddie, while other times she spent with Arraetta.

But, whilst all things were quite positive, the image of being scoured made the nausea return twofold. The memory of having an electric sceptre hitting my skin, bruising it over and over again until my skin burst and blood trickled from my open wounds, slid across my mind. I could still feel how every current burnt my insides, with not one of my onlookers understanding how much torture they were placing me under.

"Maybe you should get some fresh air," Marie commented as she stood by me, having barely entered the room to check on Arraetta. She had been very unhappy to see me out of bed the quarter before, having to restitch several wounds under my bandages before she replaced the gauze and instructed me to go to bed.

"I am fine. I am not leav-"

"-Pa!" Arraetta's voice cut through the cracks, and she sat

upright with a petrified and teary look. Her body trembled with fear, weariness and confusion and, from her sudden movement, she had managed to rip out her cannula. I went to aid her while Marie gently helped her lie back down.

"Take it easy," Marie breathed, "take it easy."

The fever still soaked her skin. While it was great she had awoken, she was not ready to be. Deliriously, she muttered inaudible words as she placed her arm over her forehead. I gently held it. "You need to rest, Arraetta."

She slowly blinked at me several times before whispering, "Sera-iah?... Wh- where am I?"

Marie skilfully slipped the cannula back into her wrist as Arraetta dazedly gazed around until she found me again. I wanted to tell her she was home, in a place where she would soon be able to wander, her melodic laughter lighting up the dull hallways of the palace. But not yet.

I reassured her, "You are safe."

"I don't feel good," she grumbled, her face turning a little green. I was sure that waking up from a deep coma was quite nauseating, and I felt guilty about my own ailment.

"I will give her something to help her sleep, just a moment," Marie told me.

I stroked Arraetta's face for comfort, hoping the soft tips of my fingers would allow for the nausea to disappear. My heart tugged as I watched her let out a few strangled cries, whispering to whoever might listen, "Ma and Pa are dead."

Was she referring to Ivan the Great and Reona? Had she been surviving in a subliminal space where she could see the memories from her past? If she had no recollection of who she was previously, was I witnessing the first nodes of grief for her life bringers? I tried to soothe her by gently pulling her into my arms, stroking her back in hopes it would help bring her peace. Sobs rattled until slowly she succumbed back to the realm of sleep with some help of sedation administered by Marie. After a few more moments of holding her in my arms, exactly where I was desperate for her to be, I returned her to the bed and looked down at her.

"I'm being serious about you resting," Marie said, and I sighed deeply.

"Marie, I do not need to rest. This was like seedling's play compared to what I have been through before."

A lie through and through. I had been through dire punishments before, but being brutally beaten was at the top of the list of the worst. Even worse than being infected by The Dark all those many scorns before. Still, I would persevere because I was a prince, not a coward. Princes were not allowed to feel pain; they were to thrive and build an empire that was so strong upon it.

No weaknesses.

Well, apart from her. Arraetta.

And, Empyreans, she was my most desired flaw.

EIGHTEEN

"**E**xcuse me, Your Highness, I have been informed Her Royal Highness is awake."

Connell's voice cut through the light conversation which Freddie and I were having while taking a stroll through the gardens sols later. My usual routine of attempting to infiltrate my father while juggling sparring matches at the garrison had been completely upheaved since Arraetta's arrival, and I had been doing my best to not see a blink of Jonah.

It did not take long before we were back at the house, and I slowed down to check my dishevelled reflection in one of the hallway mirrors. I resembled a street rat over a prince, with sols-old stubble lining my jaw and dark bags under my eyes. Not forgetting how gaunt I looked for the lack of sleep and vanquished energy.

At least I could feel the Rapidfire simmering, even if I knew it would be moons before I was able to use just an ounce of it again.

"Maybe I should change," I said.

"She may be asleep again by the time you are dressed," Freddie pointed out, "if she can take you looking your best, I am sure she will not mind at your worst."

"I am not quite at my worst," I jested. I stalked to the bedroom, taking a deep breath as I listened to the gentle conversation between Genie and Arraetta through the gap of the slightly open door.

Empyreans, it was wonderful to hear such a sound again.

"...Seraiah's family," Genie was saying, and I idled a moment as I wondered what the topic of conversation had been. I could only presume she was informing Arraetta she would be residing with us going forward. The answer remained undetermined as Genie continued, "You've been here since the incident; you're lucky to be alive."

"Very lucky," Marie's voice added, "it's been a very tense time in this house."

Tense was an understatement. Would she realise her arrival had changed everything in our home? How we were locked in a political stalemate and no one knew who would attempt the next play because things had shifted dramatically in her wake? Once her eyes were truly open to our world, once the bonding had passed and life had settled, only then would she see how such tensions that simmered had finally been brought to the surface.

"Sorry for causing so much trouble," Arraetta said hoarsely.

I felt it was time to finally enter the conversation, nodding to Freddie before I opened the door and entered. "No trouble. You have caused no trouble."

Arraetta and I locked eyes for a moment, which caused all the troubles in the world to be suddenly tucked away, wishing the two of us were alone. But such fancies were not to be had as Genie stood and curtseyed, mimicked by Marie. Fucking new protocols.

Let us enforce all allies to the prince to treat him like the heir. As if they already did not. I did not need another crater between us.

"How long have I been out for?" Arraetta queried, attempting to sit up before Marie stopped her.

"Over four weeks," Genie replied, tearing up, "it's not like last time, Arri. You... you..."

Whilst we had agreed to keep some truths from Arraetta, I did not feel it was right to keep this particular one from her.

Unfortunately, my tongue slipped. "You died."

I inwardly winced at the blunt nature of my wording whilst Freddie half-tapped me on the shoulder, as if to reprimand me for my little mistake. Then again, I supposed it was never in my nature to dance around subjects *without cause* as a human might.

"Several times," Genie added quickly, as though saving me, "your wounds were... they were so bad, Arri. But your body has healed because of your power."

"*Almost* healed," Marie said.

"Does everyone know about me?" she asked Genie, although her eyes shifted across the room, landing back on me. I might not have known everything about her, but it seemed I had drastically more insight about her than she had about herself.

"Genie told us about you, Arraetta," I informed her. I stepped closer to the bed to reassure her, "You are not alone in this world, even if you have been for a long time. We are very similar."

"You are the same as me."

A statement, not a question but how incorrect she was. A laughable offence if there ever was one. *No, Arraetta, I am merely ephemeral. You are a God.*

"No, not quite," I said, knowing of the discussions we had at the previous Amity meeting to not reveal her immortality so soon. "however, we are both foreign beings in this world, as are my people. And you are welcome here with us."

A lost look swam across her face as she delved into her mind. Oh, how I wished I could crack it wide open and see what ruthless thoughts bothered her, removing them as much as I could.

"You okay?" Genie asked her, stroking Arraetta's curls from her head.

"Yes," she lied, "I... I'm just tired."

Deception did not suit her, but I could see it was a wall she had built so high to prevent her from coming to terms with whatever deep, dark feelings that festered. I almost wished to command everyone to leave the room so that I could soothe her privately, holding her tightly as she whispered all the little gremlins away.

Marie made it clear she wanted Arraetta to get some rest, and I vacated the room with Freddie again. Arraetta awoke more often during the sols which passed, and I could hear her gentle laughter echoing down the hallway when she was with Genie. At other times, the whole hallway was peacefully quiet as she continued to rest. I wanted to spend more time with her. It was an innate need to be close to her, but I could not help feeling more like a burden when she was awake.

The following quarter moon, I was summoned to my mother's quarters. As usual, she was dressed with precision in her beige pencil skirt and white blouse. A pair of red glasses hung from a string around her neck - a pair she rarely wore unless she suffered headaches. There was no sign of Helga, but a servant served the two of us tea before leaving.

I was fidgety about leaving, sitting on the edge of my seat, ignoring the unwanted tea which had been poured for me. The last time I was inside her territory, I lost myself to the rage which simmered inside.

"I know you are anxious to leave," she said, "but we should talk."

"I am sure it can wait until council." I replied, trying to not to pass out from the unnecessary warmth in her room as the sun relentlessly streamed through open windows. There was no breeze, so I was unsure why she had not opted for her air conditioner.

"I am here to talk to you as my son," she replied honestly, "not as the heir to our kingdom. Plus, there are ears of those I would rather not hear what I would like to speak of."

"By ears, do you mean my father?" I raised my eyebrows. "It is not like you to work behind his back."

"*Every*one, preferably," she corrected. "I may be a queen, but I am a mother first." I almost snorted. "I want to discuss the next winter and what I hope will happen."

"If there are any suggestions that I should mend my relationship with my father, you are sorely mistaken. That will not happen."

He might have voted in Genie's favour, but it was to have the satisfaction of me kneeling before him, slammed with a baton one hundred merciless times. A little less I supposed when it came to the incident with Kaeltar. And I knew my father would be keeping those seven remaining flogs in his back pocket for the next time I *acted up*.

"That wish passed many winters ago," she sighed. "However, seeing you tolerate each other more would be nice. I cannot condone what your father did last quarter, but the law is the law, and it was broken. Freddie was lucky that he did not receive such punishment, either."

"I am well aware of what I did, Mother."

But it does not mean they have the right to treat me like vermin. I might have been bitter but, Empyreans, it made me angry that she still was using her words to side with him. Not a single apology for the events, just the law is the law. Fuck the law when the male who created it breached it every single sol of his fucking life.

I noted the minor amount of remorse which tickled her expression, "then, let us speak of your upcoming bonding ceremony, and your position in the house."

Ah, the heartfast and bonding ceremony that had been lightly thrown around over my lifetime but never truly taken seriously until Arraetta arrived. But, I had some understanding of it. Whilst our ceremony would mimic heartfasting, the nuptials for the bonding were completely different – two souls bound together.

"I have yet to speak with Arraetta about any of this; we cannot be hasty with decisions until she is happy."

"It is not about her happiness, Seraiah. It is a matter of what the Gods wish, and even I know you understand such things. Arraetta will be unable to resist such things that are fated."

I was aware that such things could not be resisted, for we mortal-kind beings were but passengers of fate. Even if I had decided to resist fate before, I was not sure I would again after seeing Arraetta in the flesh.

"I am aware, but we cannot seek to control the mind of a goddess that has been blindly surviving as an ephemeral here. We have to take such things one step at a time."

"I understand," she answered, "but I have spoken with Sheika, and it has been determined that the ceremony shall take place following Iontine."

"That only gives us no more than a moon cycle."

"Iontine has been rescheduled for August," she said, and my shoulders sagged with relief. "This will do us no harm and give us ample time to prepare."

Such changes I was thankful for but I was unsure if I was prepared to embrace such a devout commitment before I had even had time to spend with Arraetta. Even if my soul's desire was to become one with hers, I had quite the feeling she would run as fast as she could once she caught wind we were to be married. Fate or not.

Then again, I would chase her to the ends of the universe.

"I would also like to speak with Arraetta, without speaking of the bond," she told me, "to try to ease her mind about who she is and the lineage we believe she has. You shall only pussyfoot around it."

I tutted, "I shall not. It is my right as her future husband to tell her when I think she is ready."

"Therefore," she sighed dramatically, "there are only three things she should know - Her position in this house, her ascent to queen and of whom she is the daughter of."

"From what I gather from Genie, Arraetta needs proof."

My mother placed down her tea on its mat before walking over to her shelves. She removed a loosely wrapped, thick brown package that must have contained a tome. And I knew it was The Treatise of The Cre-este before she handed it to me.

"I do not think it will be enough."

"It will have to be," she replied plainly. "Her memories will have to help her the rest of the way."

Memories which I was quite sure were so deeply buried inside her mind it would take winters to coax them to the surface. And that was if she only wished to remember.

I opened the tome to the first page and gazed at the imagined drawing of the legendary great king, Ivan the Great, holding a young seedling with wild curly hair and striking blue eyes. Yes, of course, it was so clear to make a connection between the two of them, but Ivan the Great's lore was developed by stories of old, none of us knowing what was and was not fact. There was rumour of a daughter, but no more than just that.

"I believe she will see this and understand," my mother continued. "Hopefully, it will offer her comfort and help guide her to the destiny the Gods had bestowed her."

To me.

"Then you may speak to her, but please leave the Kindred Spirit and bonding ceremony to me. We have time."

"*Some* time," she answered, "but do not forget we need to get her acquainted with life as a princess and, forthwith, queen."

"Forthwith?" I raised my eyebrows, enjoying the small nugget of information. "Are you expecting to resign?"

"I would like to move to Italy permanently," she nodded. "Of course, I would still be available to counsel the crown."

Such counsel was not required, for I was going to be the one running Zika as the paradise I sought to make it. But it was difficult to remove her without the council's vote. Maybe my mother would come to prove that her allegiance resided in my court.

"And, Father?"

"Your father and I agreed that your ascent should occur next winter." I wished it was sooner. It was twelve moon cycles until next winter would arrive, which meant counting down each gruelling sol of my father's position on the throne. I was only sure that it would become an arduous task to step into his shoes with whatever trials they would have me succumb to.

"But, you must promise me, Seraiah," she sat up straight, "that you do not, at any point, attempt to take the throne from your father." A promise I could not make. "At least, not forcibly, and I know you understand what that means. I have been told of the scars that Kaeltar now faces. A shell of himself. I do not wish to see my husband in the same manner."

"I shall not." It was a believable lie.

"It cannot," she added directly, "if there are any more incidents, then you shall find it very difficult to have your father's council on your side for the ascension. And you need a majority vote, which means proving yourself, whether you like it or not."

Unless he dies first.

"I shall not use my power," I reassured her, "unless-"

"-There cannot be an *unless*, Seraiah. Dethroning your father will only escalate things, and we do not need a war on our doorstep. I know you have spent many winters of your life studying ancient magic as well. I know what you are capable of. I just do not wish to see you take shortcuts."

I could feel that simmering anger I had thrown at her moon cycles before, needing to scream at her like a seedling and tell her to keep her mouth shut, to stop speaking to me in such a patronising manner. But, something prevented me. Maybe it was the knowledge that in the new winter I was going to be the king, and needed my mother on my side as much as the rest. Or, that I did not want Arraetta to hear a whisper about the darkness which simmered.

I swallowed thickly, "I will not forcefully take the throne *unless* my father does something morally corrupt."

"Seraiah–"

"It is a fair deal, Mother," I countered. "If I should find that any harm or threat comes to Arraetta because he meddles, then I shall not be stopped when defending her."

My mother paused, taking in what I said, before she nodded. It was all I needed to know that my word would be final in such a case if it happened.

"I will make sure he does no such thing," she half-promised. "I would like to enjoy some civility in this house whilst we transition into this new period of our lives. And I am sure you are much the same."

I preferred the hostilities disappeared completely, but that could only happen if my father moved out of the residence and went somewhere else. Then again, it would not be to my benefit if he permanently resided overseas, as I would find myself in a more difficult situation when it came to negotiating deals. My father needed to be in residence as much as it pained me.

"I would also like to talk about Genevieve," she continued. "Whilst the council voted that she is welcome to stay, our people are growing restless, and some are starting to rebel."

I snorted, "It is funny how no such punishment has been enacted for breaking the laws."

"You know your father will deal with it," she said. "He will not have an uprising, especially not at such an integral time. You know

257

how important it is to keep our people in line."

By slaughtering them into submission? Hm.

I shook my head in disbelief. "No, Mother, I have never believed in *controlling* our people."

She ignored me. "I believe having Genevieve here will be beneficial, so I shall appoint her as diplomat to Arraetta."

A spy. Just as it was predicted in the previous Amity meeting, which I was not so surprised about.

"Merely to see that Arraetta settles here," she continued, as if needing to over-explain rather than state the simple facts, "she shall be keeping an eye on her, but we both know it is the right option. I have already some intriguing information I am sure you would be happy to know, including Arraetta's interest in painting."

A small nugget of information which I partially already knew having seen the canvases through her bedroom window.

My mother added, "I believe that, with time, Arraetta shall be shaped into a worthy queen to whom I will pass on my crown."

"Something tells me you do not think she can be easily *shaped*," I added.

"I do not mean to change her *personality*, Seraiah," she replied, "but it is important that we mould her. She must be taught mannerisms, etiquette and protocol as any other in her position would."

"If you force it on her, it shall only scare her away."

"I am not going to chain her up," she clicked her tongue. "She will be aware of such agendas, but I shall not enforce anything for her ascension until after the heartfasting. These first few moon cycles will be to help her heal and settle into a routine."

While I did not want Arraetta to be burdened by my mother's regime, I knew she was right to tell me her plans. At least we were a couple of moon cycles away from the heartfast, which gave Arraetta a little more time to adjust.

"Then, there is the matter of duty," she added, and I did not know which angle she was going with until she added, "to bear heirs."

I sputtered. "Not a necessary commitment now."

"No, but it shall be. You may not wish for a seedling yet, but it is your duty to continue our lineage as well as rule."

Seedlings had rarely been a thought in my mind, especially not to bring one into such an oppressed society. Of course, at some point we would need to continue our line, have a family together, but it was far too soon to be discussing such matters. For one, I was not king, so I could not protect an heir as I would if I were. The second was I had barely had a conversation passed flirting with Arraetta, so I was sure she was not thinking about bearing seedlings anytime soon. She might not have wanted to have them.

But my mother was right. We were bound by obligations to the throne, and such things could not be bypassed forever, even if our lives were long.

"I will discuss with Arraetta following the bonding," I answered uncomfortably, looking down at the tome on my lap, "for now, the primary focus will be on our ascent and once we are crowned, then we shall think about seedlings. I will honour my duty, and I will see to it that so shall she."

My mother pressed her lips together, before nodding once to tell me she was satisfied with my answer. Little did she know I would have rather waited until we were in Zika before I even considered such duties.

Opening the tome, I skimmed across several pages, deciding that a change of topic was necessary. "I wonder how Arraetta came to be on earth."

"I had wondered about this as well. It may be possible that she had travelled through a portal. The Cre-estrians were highly innovative and far ahead of their time with technology."

Even so, it would not answer why such a portal would take her to Earth, of all places. I supposed it was a protected realm, so maybe they presumed it to be the safest. But, The Cre-este was an ancient realm, destroyed by The Dark six thousand winters before I was born. Theoretically, Arraetta was an ancient being and had somehow travelled through time and space to arrive on Earth.

Another plausible explanation was much more about science than magic. There had to be some sort of gravitational field of energy which could transport her to Earth, but we would have known about something so advanced as we would have detected it during our time in this realm. A portal was the most reliable option, but it meant that Arraetta had to have some sort of exit point.

And, even though the term went straight over my mother's head, I theorised aloud, "Dimensional breaching."

It was something we had been seeking to do for a long time, knowing with the right power and resource we could portal anywhere in the vast universe and possibly return home. However, Earth did not have the power to give. And I was not going to be the mortal who destroyed a realm to simply return to my own. Not unless our lives depended on it.

But, maybe they used all the power in The Cre-este, destroying everything within the realm to get Arraetta out. Someone desperate enough would sacrifice everything in order to save the one thing they loved the most.

And, for Ivan the Great, it had to be his prized daughter, Arraetta. But what of Reona?

"Whatever the case," my mother cleared her throat, having little interest in any form of science, even when it was integral, "we understand who Arraetta is from what Sheika has told us, and we must use that knowledge for the good of all."

How noble, Mother.

I placed the tome next to me, rising to my feet with a bow, "I am leaving."

"Before you do, Seraiah. You are to accompany your father to Italy in half a moon."

I blinked. "I cannot leave Arraetta here."

"It is high time you saw your people there and attended meetings with your father and our shareholders."

"So, I am to be married, a spiritsworn, a king, all whilst arming a business that shall disappear when we leave this realm."

"Duty, Seraiah," she reminded me, "if you wish to be king, you know that some things are more integral than others. Things shall not simply halt here if we do ever leave this realm. Not all our people shall return."

"And those who shall not, who will look over them?"

"It is... a worthy sacrifice."

What did my mother ever know of sacrifice? Sitting on her cushioned sovereignty looking down on her subjects like rats in a cage.

"Our people are not pawns in a wider game, Mother. Once the portal opens, we must take *all* our people."

"And you know that is impossible," she replied, quickly deterring the topic. "While you are in Italy, Arraetta will be safe here."

"So be it," I replied sharply, not waiting much longer before I bowed and stormed from the room. I was frustrated that I had to be away from Arraetta when I had barely had a chance to spend time with her. Empyreans, I did not even know how long I was required to be in Italy for, but I hoped it was not long enough for Arraetta to be moulded into someone unrecognisable.

The cool air of the corridor softened by indignation as my shoes clipped across it, pacing in the direction of the only place I wished to be. And that was in Arraetta's presence. I had not thought about whether my presence was wanted until I stopped outside her door, listening in to see if I could hear her. But it was silent.

Without a second more delay, I opened it and was greeted by a soft breeze from an electric fan near the window, which cooled down the room substantially. I cast my eyes over to a sleep-laden Arraetta, curled up without a care, before I stepped inside and closed the door behind me.

At the edge of her bed, I brushed away her loose curls and gazed down at her perfection, uncaring that my actions were slightly voyeuristic. I noticed her skin was no longer pallid but had returned to its natural honey glow, although her lips were cracked from dehydration and her face was slightly gaunt.

Even if she were not a goddess, I could only have described her as one. She was perfect, the most divinely beautiful creature I had ever been blessed to gaze upon.

Softly I knelt beside her, exactly where I belonged, my breath inches from her soft face as my finger softly traced her silken cheek, mindful not to wake her. She shuddered slightly, but there were no signs of those big, azure eyes opening to look at me. I was sure she would laugh melodiously, wondering why I was observing her so closely, so intensely, as if I thought she might disappear. She would only shift her gaze coyly. But she continued to sleep.

She was a masterpiece of quiet existence. A marvel which belonged solely and only to me.

They might wish to shape her, but I would hold her above all else – Even my duty.

Fuck obligation to the crown.

It could melt to ruin for all I cared.

As I watched the rise and fall of her chest, her soft warm breaths releasing into the air, I could feel the fractures in my coffer rippling more and I was sure it was close to breaking open.

I whispered quietly, "I would burn this universe to ashes only to rebuild it in your favour. I will treasure and worship you eternally. You are mine, Arraetta."

NINETEEN

Time shifted. A half moon cycle passed with no Amity, no political tensions, no confirmed uprising from our people. I focused most of my energy on quietly existing away from my life bringer's prying eyes, careful to move between my room, Arraetta's and the library. I thought about going to the garrison numerous times, but with the strain between Jonah and me still simmering, I did not want to see him in case it might explode.

And, fuck, how I was ready to give that male a piece of my mind.

Forgiveness was not easy in the eyes of the betrayed, even if it was for the good of two humans. No. One human, one *goddess*.

Joyously, Arraetta was up and about more often, roaming the hallways, although I seemed to miss her most sols. When she was sleeping or resting, I felt I had control over the situation, but seeing her standing, walking, or dancing made me feel powerless.

Empyreans, did she make me vulnerable.

It had been six arduous quarter moon cycles since I met her, and I had spoken with her for less than two sols. I felt a strange yet hollow yearning for her. A chasm in my soul, which had always existed had suddenly reared its head, pining for attention.

After a morning of painting in the library, becoming unbearably lost in the intricacies of my fabricated idea of what Ryazark, the land of the Gods, looked like, I decided it was time to get a shower and

264

freshen up. I was sure my body odour smelled like wilted paint, and while I may have cared less about appearances, I wanted to be on top form when I saw Arraetta.

Unfortunately, fate's timing was always perfect for bringing us together at the wrong times, and I found myself face-to-face with the goddess herself, stopping in the hallway outside the library door. Seeing her reaffirmed every need I had for her, butterflies fluttering in my stomach like a teenage boy having a crush for the first time. Gazing upon her, it was almost as though the incident had never caused a single graze or bruise on her body.

She was perfectly irresistible before me, dressed in a white blouse and over-the-knee blue flared skirt, which I only wished I could dive under to take in her magnificence underneath.

Ignoring the stabbing growth in my pants, I dipped my body in greeting. She coyly shifted her soft gaze, a pink blush staining her cheeks. I took it as an ample opportunity to step closer to her. "I am glad to see you are well. I hoped to catch up with you today to talk about things."

I had meant to speak to her following the conversation with my mother half a moon cycle before, but I had been dancing around the subject in my mind to not have really planned it. Truthfully, I was not fully prepared to show her that she was one of two halves of Kindred, although I had one small tactic that might be useful even if it went against our use of ancient arcana.

She swallowed before lightly curtseying, "I'm going to see your mum."

Amusement swept over my expression in delight at her using such a casual name for my mother. While it was in her dialect, it felt far too endearing to use for my antiquated mother.

I laughed, "my... *mum*. Well, I shall not keep you."

I bowed again, keeping my eyes on her before returning to my full stance. Arms suddenly wrapped around my shoulders, and I was engulfed in a surprising hug from her, my body tensing for only a second before I returned her gesture. The Gods must have been planning in my favour if they were to bestow me with someone so delectable.

She was the Persephone to my Hades.

Empyreans she was divinity at its finest and elegance at its worst. Her soft body melted against mine, closer than when we danced at the ball. Tension rippled from my back, and every inch of me relaxed for what seemed to be the first time in my long existence. Her curls smelled like coconut, and a subtle scent of floral perfume tingled my senses.

I wanted to scoop her up, carry her to my bedroom, and hold her tightly until we drifted to sleep. Or maybe we would do so much more. My cock whined in my pants for freedom from one sheath to another.

But such things were not to be, as my mother's grating voice interrupted us, deflating my feelings immediately. "I wondered what was taking so long."

While I would have happily lingered, Arraetta jumped away from me as though I were a thing to be ashamed of. I wondered whether she felt somewhat embarrassed by such affection or simply abashed for being caught. Had she never received such affection from anyone before? That being said, it was not as though I was the most doting male on earth, nor had I received such heartfelt devotion from my family.

I supposed I was thankful that the naturally lightless corridor was able to mask the redness that tinged my cheeks as I turned to my mother, who stood in the open doorway of her quarters, before bowing, "Mother."

She nodded in greeting but seemed less interested in me, more taken by Arraetta. I understood a signal enough to know when to take my leave, so I turned back to her and bowed deeper. "Arraetta."

Arraetta's face remained aflame as I rose again, and I prayed someone would gouge my mother's prying eyes out so that I could stroke the tips of my fingers across Arraetta's soft skin. But, alas, such things were not to be, and I walked away without sparing another glance at the intruder.

Thoughts of Arraetta's arms smoothly wrapping around me, her body flush against mine, soft hair bristling my chin did not stop the returning throb of my cock. I could not control its growth as her phantom scent wrapped around my nostrils. I knew there was only one way to sate myself, and that was lingering in the memory as I wrapped my hand around my shaft, pumping it until I would release with her name on my lips.

It seemed that someone was against such a release as I walked into my room, a rapid puncture shrivelling everything, as I surprisingly saw Freddie gazing out of my window in deep thought.

He did not turn to me, which gave me ample time to adjust myself before I cleared my throat. "Your room is across the hall."

He grunted in acknowledgement, remaining silent for far too long before nodding. "I do feel for you with this view. It is very... unappealing, is it not? Why not opt for a garden view rather than a rooftop?"

I walked over, looking out over the roof, which I had seen many times, unsure why he had a sudden interest in what view I had. It was not as though I had thought much of it myself, but I knew it was because it was much safer, back then, to keep me away from possible escape. Still, I had done it so many times.

"Do you truly have such care for it?" I asked him, "I am sure you are not here to question my choice of room when I have been in it for scorns, Freddie."

Still, he did not look at me, but he did look behind to see if anyone else had joined us before returning to his gazing, "I am going to ask Genie to heartfast me."

Although it was expected, I wondered whether he was a little hasty due to the many changes in the palace. Unlike the commitment between Arraetta and me, it was not exactly a pressure for the two of them to become engaged.

"I know it is soon, but I believe it is right to solidify our social standing as a couple, and I wish to show her that I truly mean all that I have vowed."

"And when shall it happen?"

"This afternoon, by the lake. I have it planned.... I would appreciate your approval."

"I am more than willing to give it to you," I said honestly, "but it is not I who needs to give you approval."

Such things resided under the council's jurisdiction, although I did not expect them to deny such a blessing. They would only make it political. And, I knew exactly how it would play out as news spread about the human who took a Porton prince's heart, how they would manipulate our people into obedience. *If such trials work, we will permit only the best of you to heartfast outside our race.*

"Through all the haste, I believe you and I have found our gifts at a time of need," I said.

Less of a time of need, more of a time of desperation. Empyreans, was I desperate for her. Thank fuck, that was not a box which was waiting to be opened.

"Well, yours is fated."

"As is yours," I pointed out, "the only way I would have met Arraetta is because of your good fortune of meeting Genie."

"Good fortune that brought upon a horrendous punishment, of which you did not deserve."

"I believe I would have survived fifty lashes if it were just a pun-ishment for having the two outsiders here," I replied, as humoured as I could. "The other fifty were for my treason, of which I could hardly deny."

"It shall not be long until you are king," he pointed out, "a great one."

"Or, a foolish one," my lip twitched, "it shall all depend on what kind of mushed-up male my wife makes me."

"You and I both," he agreed, patting the back of my shoulders, "our wives shall rule all of our decisions and have the most power."

Freddie was right. The two females had more influence over us than we had over ourselves. So much for trying to regain control when I was giving it all to a female I hardly knew. Then again, what was a goddess for if she was not to be worshipped on our knees?

"Have you told Genie about everything?"

"Everything important," he nodded, "who I am, where I am from, the attack of The Dark, our intention to return to Zika."

"And she will return with you?"

He straightened his shoulders. "whilst her family is small, she still has those who will stay here. It is a big decision for her, and I will stand beside it no matter what is decided."

"I am sure she will agree to go with you," I answered, knowing how much Genie had already sacrificed through her determination to be with Freddie. It had been mere moon cycles, but I could see how she had changed him from the playboy prince to a devoted male. "Do not sully what is already yours."

Freddie saluted triumphantly before taking his leave, the door closing behind him. I wondered when the council would agree on their nuptials. Although I was sure they were investing a large amount of money in my bonding ceremony, so they would not pay for another for a long time. And, as Amice had said, circumstances could change for Genie at any time.

But not for my fated one. Arraetta would remain by my side. If anyone dared to try to corrupt our bonding, I would happily rip their throat out and feast on it to show they should not mess with what belonged to me.

Empyreans, did she belong to me. Her scent lingered on my skin, and my mind shifted back to Arraetta's arms wrapped around mine. It seemed that even things which wilted began to sprout with a little bit of coaxing, and my cock was rising inside its restraints once more.

"Fuck," I muttered. Deciding the best option was to take my much-needed shower I had been aiming for, I put the water on and quickly stripped off my clothes. In the corner, I had a small music player, and I placed on some jazz, a favourite of mine since our arrival on Earth, before hopping into the warm spray.

I did not wait any longer, placing my hand over my aching shaft and began to tug at it, letting thoughts of Arraetta wash over me. Part of me drifted so far that I imagined it was Arraetta's delicate hand wrapped around me, gazing at me with lustful eyes as she worked to draw out the impending orgasm. But, fuck, those azure eyes would make me want to edge myself as much as possible. My eyes would sweep her naked, honeyed flesh, and a need to touch her nipples and run my fingers down to her petal core would overwhelm me. I licked my lips at the thought, breath caught as the imagery washed over me thrice as my hand worked harder, faster, readied to explode.

"Arraetta," I breathed jaggedly.

Seraiah.

"Empyreans," I grunted, thick liquid spurting from my cock onto the tiled wall of the shower whilst my heart beat rapidly in my chest.

Fuck. Taking a deep breath, I leaned back against the opposite wall, inhaling, exhaling as the exhilaration washed over me, and I was left in the warmth of a cloying mess, listening to the endnotes of a song. It was not as though I had not sated myself in such a way in the past. It was natural for us mortal-kind to find satisfaction in some way, but I had not touched myself since before Arraetta had arrived.

I rinsed the shower walls clean before plummeting the water to cold, stepping under for a long amount of time to cool myself. And, some twenty minutes later, after washing myself completely, I redressed and decided to snoop on Freddie's proposal.

I was looking forward to seeing their elation and maybe having us all come together to celebrate later on with some champagne, but I was not expecting to see the complete opposite as I made it to the east wing end window.

Freddie was standing by the lake, drenched head to toe, while Arraetta and Genie were having an inaudible argument. Rushing down the staircase and out into the basking heat, I stopped at the top of the garden, close enough to eavesdrop but far enough away to not be spotted.

"Why can't you just be happy for me?" Genie screamed, "I know why, Arri, because you can't just let things happen - you have to be in control of every little thing, including me. If you are unhappy, then I must be unhappy."

"That's not true," Arraetta sounded defeated.

"It is true!" Genie screamed, "Everything is about you; it always is!"

Genie stormed towards me, not sparing me a glance as she walked on by, trying to hide her tears.

I was unsure what I had just witnessed, but it felt like I had just seen the end of a great friendship.

"Fuck, it is ruined," Freddie swore in Zikan, rushing after Genie, barely meeting my eyes either.

Arraetta turned too, but winced before a guilty expression swept over her when she caught my eye. I walked down towards her, wondering how to help calm a situation which I had no idea had started. The proposal had failed.

The closer I got, the more I could clearly see the fire in her eyes smouldered by the heartache. If I thought logically about any rise of aggression in her, then it could have only stemmed from her conversation with my mother, which, quite frankly, was enough to get a rise out of anyone. My mother had said she would tell her who we suspected and expected her to be. A foreign being forced into a life she did not understand, expected to believe she was the daughter of a great king, but did she know we were to marry? I hoped such things were saved for me to say.

Still, I could help ease some of her anger.

I barely looked as I bypassed her and stood by the lake, contemplating what to say for a few moments.

"Circumstances," I looked at her, "that is what has caused us to be where we are today. It is the circumstance of Genie and Freddie meeting which brought you to us."

There it is. The fire returned instantly, along with the fear of not knowing.

"What do you want with me?" she asked, turning her head.

"I do not want anything but your happiness, Arraetta."

"Then how can I be happy when I am trapped here?"

How could any of us be happy when we are *all* trapped here? Golden birds locked inside a cage of duty, privilege and power. But she was not alone, not as she had been. She had kept herself busy all her life, working a horrendous job whilst trying to survive through the suffering her body had caused.

If I were in her position, I would rather be inside the safety of the birdcage than fly freely through turmoil. At least she could rest until I set her free from our boundaries and gifted her the universe.

"We are all trapped here," I explained. "Do you think I wish to be stuck on this planet when I had a perfectly good home to live in? Everything is fated, Arraetta. Your being here on this planet, in this realm, is one of them."

"What does that mean?" she shouted, her arms flailing, "you all just go around speaking fucking riddles. One minute, I'm just living a semi-normal life, then I go to a ball, meet you and find out you've got magic powers like I do, and now I'm being forced to come to terms with all this and... and amongst that, figure out how some loony tale it related to me."

My guess had been correct. It was my mother who had caused her to lash out at her greatest ally. Arraetta did not know whether she could believe such a myth, although something told me she could; it was only she did not know how to process it.

"It is not loony. It is the truth. Why are you so fearful of that?"

She stuttered, "Because I showed up here and... and you are all creeping around me, not letting me know anything about you, yet you seem to know everything about me somehow."

I only knew some surface-level things based on dossiers and tomes, but not enough to know everything. Not as I needed to. No, I wished to sate myself with every bit of information I drank from her, learning everything which made her laugh and tick. How I desired to see such fire aflame in both her passions and anger.

"That is where you are wrong, Arraetta. Do you truly believe we know everything about you? How can we when you turned up at our doorstep six weeks ago? If we knew everything about you, surely, we would have known about you since our arrival." I sighed a little. "But you are right, things have been kept from you. What is it you truly wish to know?"

My question stunned her as though she would not believe that even I would be able to offer her some peace in all the chaos. She was like an open tome, thoughts stirring far too clearly on her face. But I knew of my own boundaries and what I could and could not answer. Not yet. Not until after the bonding ceremony.

"Why are you here?"

The least important question of all which was one of the most difficult to answer. Did I need to tell her that our land was taken by a force so powerful no one but her father could destroy it? Or if we returned home, maybe her power might do such justice. Would she dive headfirst into battle to do so when the one being who would prevent such a thing was standing before her?

"I-"

"-Forget about it," she snapped, twisting around and storming towards the house.

No, Arraetta, do not turn your back on me.

"Let me show you," I called, halting her instantly before she turned. I kind of hoped there would be some form of satisfaction on her face, but she was running off her fear, not being indulged. "Allow me to help you understand. It is not the answer you are looking for, but it will allow you some respite, at least."

Her question about why we were on Earth was unimportant in the larger scheme of things because, quite honestly, none of us knew the answer. No one knew why the portal did not take us to Porto, but I supposed the female before me was the answer. She was why we were on Earth; the Gods had to make us meet.

Still, it was more important to show her how our fates were twisted and knotted so tightly that, no matter how hard we tried, neither of us could escape it.

I had to show her that she belonged by my side.

I prayed that the exertion on my body over the quarter moons prior would not have a knock-on effect and that I could show her exactly how similar we were - how connected we were. She coyly shifted her gaze as I removed my shirt, immediately showing where the scorched black faded mark on my left arm began and ended.

I was aware that I knew I would have to deal with another punishment for showing her. Then again, she was worth every punishment I would face in my lifetime. Even if I was beaten by an electric baton over and over. Some things required resilience.

Closing my eyes, I took a deep breath and felt the ebb and flow in the depths of my fibres, letting the feeling wash over me until my body began to glow its vibrant cobalt power. I knew the difference between my natural life force and the one which overwhelmed me. Mine was light, energetic, warm and freeing, whilst its opposite was claustrophobic, painful, caging. My natural Rapidfire was like a walkable ridge, only wide enough to take one foot at a time, trying to balance without falling into the onyx pits which resided on either side.

That is it, Seraiah; show her who you truly are, his dark voice whispered, rippling that same shiver down my spine as I lost my balance on the crest, only to right myself enough to keep my concentration on my pure power.

"Seraiah!" Jonah's voice boomed from the top of the garden, like a moth to a flame. I noted his abrupt call, but I did wish he had not arrived at such a prevalent yet dangerous moment. He could have become the greater cause for falling into the trenches.

I opened my eyes to look at my wife. "Arraetta, you and I are similar."

Show her who you truly are.

She did not need to know. It would only scare her.

Powerful people thrive on the fear inside them, and yours is only the beginning.

The air shifted, and I could feel the soaring sear of the dark power trying to overwhelm me again like someone had plunged several needles into my skin.

"We both possess Rapidfire, except yours is... it is much more powerful. Divine Rapidfire."

"Seraiah, stop this!" Jonah implored in English, but I ignored him, keeping eye contact with the goddess before me. She was my solace, an island in the middle of the vast ocean, a haven in a dry desert. And she would help coax any darkness my mind attempted to succumb to.

Stepping towards her, I spoke softly, placing my hand out for her to take. "I can control my Rapidfire..." *Liar.* "As you will too soon. We... were made to work together as one... be together as one."

The ridge grew steady as I took her hand, closing my eyes as I saw her standing before me, perfectly balanced without care of whether she would fall to the darkness on either side. It was as though a cloud was hovering under her feet, holding her perfectly still as I poured my life force from my body to hers. Opening my eyes, I watched as the golden hue of her own power illuminated her skin, a sense of wholeness consuming me as I showed her the one thing she had been so desperately trying to escape.

"You see now, Arraetta?" I whispered.

She will never understand your true self if you do not allow her to see the darkness which lies within you. Are you truly going to disregard me?

I grimaced as the snake's tongue wrapped around my head, rocking me on the ridge, daring me to fall in unwillingly, but still, I ignored him. He did not control me. He was not me.

I am you.

The force of his words pushed me from the ridge, falling into the depths of the obsidian pit of my mind. The reality of the shield above shuddering to a halt rippled through my body. I thudded to my knees with a grunt, a cold shiver prickling up my spine as the demon subjugated me, overtaking my light.

You will learn soon, dear Seraiah. He laughed darkly, and I sucked air through my teeth as I tried to prevent the pain from devastating me.

"Ma'am, I think it is wise you step inside." Jonah's voice echoed. The sounds around crescendoed and pitched, and then they succumbed to the silence of my breaths, out of control, rigid, unforgiving. I did not dare look at Arraetta, using all my power to prevent the beast from claiming me. My sight began to throb at its edges until it was almost vignetted, and dark veins pulsated beneath my eyes.

Onyx static fought a battle against my cobalt power while I attempted to work through the calamitous pain which fired through my body relentlessly, cruelly coercing me to bow at its mercy. It seemed like a losing struggle, and I needed Arraetta to leave before she witnessed the darkness wholly break free.

I growled, "Jonah."

He bent down before me whilst Arraetta was trying to find an answer about what was happening.

"Take. Her. Away." I commanded through gritted teeth.

"Dixon, take her away!" Jonah commanded in English. I had not noticed Alex had arrived on site, although I could not care for anyone, only controlling this power.

Jonah returned to our language. "We will get her to safety."

Show her your true self, Seraiah. Show her the king she deserves.

I declined with a grunt, but I felt the power swallow me whole as the demon devoured my senses and mobility. Suddenly, my eyes deadlocked onto Arraetta, who stared back at me with a mixture of fear and worry on her face.

Do not fear me, my queen.

Unwillingly, I tried to move to get to her, but Jonah and two other guards, no doubt one being Travis, used their strength to hold me back as Alex, without hesitation, picked Arraetta up by her waist and carried her away. It might have looked quite humorous, but I was too vexed by the idea of them trying to take her from me when she needed to see me.

The true me.

The dark me.

No. Fuck. No.

Yes.

A growl rippled from my throat, and I pulled forward again, only for Jonah to look back at me.

"Do not let this control you," Jonah said, mixing his words with the ancient mantra as usual, but something inside me did not care for such discernment.

"You are insufferable, Commander." The words left my lips too quickly, and I noticed how they hurt him.

He deserves it for his betrayal.

He deserved my quiet anger but not my wrath and not from the beast which sought to kill the male.

"Make... make sure she does not come out. You... you cannot allow her to see me like this." I struggled again, hacking a little as my life force fought against the demon, trying to overtake me as my nose began to drip blood. The darkness would do anything to take control, even if it meant hurting me, but I would persevere. I was not a weak prince.

But you will be a weak king.

"We will protect her," Jonah nodded. Then, his eyes glazed over slightly as he cursed at something being fed through his earpiece. He ripped it out. "Your father is coming."

Jonah was like a moth to a flame, but my father was like a raging storm to a quiet ocean. And my commander's warning was far too late as I watched my father descend into the garden, flanked by one guard. "What is the meaning of this? Breaking more of my laws!"

Humourless laughter left me, and I knew the cloud which crossed my mind had seeped the poison in so deep that I was powerless against it, especially when I was confronted by the tyrannical male who dared to threaten me the most.

"Convenient," I huffed in amusement, noting the foul odour of fear which danced around his aura, a similar one to which I had detected when dealing with Kaeltar. I stood to my full height, shoving the males off me as I turned to him, "Oh, how you vex me, Father."

"Why, you-" he stepped forward but stopped speaking as I matched his step.

"Are you scared?"

Jonah attempted to prevent me from moving again whilst the fearful energies of alert guards echoed my father's. None knew whether to interfere or leave such trivialities to those of a much higher command.

I basked in the nourishment their distress gave me, almost feeding on such power.

If I had known such things were available to feast on before, I might have considered revelling in such power before. Cough. No. I was a good being, a being of caged freedom and wilted light, an heir to a failed kingdom.

A king of shadows.

"You should be frightened," I said, stepping closer to my father, ignoring Jonah's matching step. "You believe The Dark created this monster you witness, but that is a lie you choose to fabricate. This *monster* was spawned from your treachery as a father. Or do you not remember how joyous it felt to lash me in front of your council?"

My father growled, "I would do it all again. Guards, arrest this

279

treacherous hellsworn!"

A few guards did shift under his command, but my call to them made each stop in their tracks. "Do not worry; I shall not harm your king. He is not worthy of my time."

"Please, Seraiah, this is not you," Jonah begged.

"Such brave words from someone who voted in favour of my punishment," I chided.

"I voted to revoke the death penalty," he replied honestly. "I voted for my queen. I would never betray you. You are my king. We said whatever it takes."

I glowered. "Whatever it takes, hm?"

"Is this the voice of the thing that possesses you?" he asked. "This is not the good and kind prince that I know. Do not spoil such an occasion of spending time with Arraetta-"

"-Do not utter my wife's name from that repulsive mouth of yours!" I grabbed Jonah by the scruff of his shirt, half picking him up off the ground, "do not think I will not rip the tongue from your mouth and feed it back to you."

Silence echoed around as Jonah grunted from the tightness of his collar, coughing whilst he continued to reason, "Is this your true power? I know you are angry, but this is not you, Seraiah. This... this thing does not need to rear its head because you lost control of yourself."

I snorted, "That is a side only you wish to witness, Jonah. If you truly understood who I am, you would know how much I revel in such power."

"Only the darkness in you would say such callous things," he whispered, looking directly into my eyes. "I do not fear you, Seraiah. And I know you can sense the fear in everyone here. I am your friend and your commander. Do not lose yourself in such dire straits."

Each word hit me with force, aggravation settling deep inside me as I stared at the male who spoke with such confident innocence. And I only wished I could claw deeply inside his mind and pull out all the fears which settled within him, as I had done to Kaeltar. Yet, as he gazed into my eyes and I into his soul, I could see nothing I could harness onto.

"Let Seraiah go," he begged me, and I felt as the demon roar inwardly before each wall it had broken through was reassembled, and the world resumed normality again. The darkness was no longer in control, but he was still there, festering.

Loosening my grip, Jonah's feet met the floor, and I tucked my shoulders back, turning towards my father. He froze up immediately as I stalked towards him and then passed him, not offering him any words.

The darkness was beginning to feel like a different kind of perverse satisfaction.

It feels good, does it not, Seraiah?

TWENTY

The crash hit me like a bolt of lightning, and I was left feeling unsteady in the wake of my dark power. By the time I had used my residual Rapidfire to bring the generator back online, I was depleted, so I remained in the office for a good hour until I was ready to bear the devastation I had caused.

I was sure my father had already informed the council of my incident, prepared to throw me into the vault to be disciplined or, worse, to renounce my position to the throne. Oddly, that time, I actively dared my father to try. But I did not care for his antics; I only cared for Arraetta.

I was not expecting to be greeted by Alex and Jonah in the library, both rising from sitting positions by the door.

"Are you here to arrest me?"

"Quite the contrary," Alex replied first, "although I should for how you have treated Jonah. He is your best friend."

I snorted, looking at the male. "Is he? After his silence over the last few half moons, I would have presumed that he did not care for me."

"Let us not fight," Jonah interjected, looking between Alex and me. "Seraiah did not know what was happening. That... side of him took control, and I was not hurt either, my love." He paused. "But I should apologise for my silence."

I raised my eyebrows. I supposed even I had to face the truth about my actions, and his betrayal and my threats outweighed any need for hatred. It was time for a clean slate.

"I will be honest," Jonah continued. "I was sickened by what I witnessed and have taken some time to gather my thoughts."

I raised my eyebrows. "Sickened for voting?"

"As I said before," he replied stoically, "I voted against their want to give you the death penalty. You were not in the room-"

"-Yes, quite strange, that is," I interrupted, tilting my head, "not a single ability to plead my case either."

Jonah turned his head, agreeing, "I know. Unfortunately, you are not a member of the war council and they had managed to build enough evidence. I do have voting rights. Most people voted against it for your position."

"Yet, they still punished me," I answered, although the answer made me sound more like a whiny seedling than an heir.

"Yes," he replied, "it was the correct procedure. Laws were broken, and even a male of your status could not be placed above it. And do not deny that you would disagree. Fifty lashings were implemented in replacement for the death penalty."

I held my tongue, deciding I was arguing a moot point, and that I had to accept that what had happened in the past had already occurred. I could not change such a thing, even if it had been painful.

"The electric sceptre was something I was unaware would happen," he added.

It would have been discussed at some point, or The General would have spoken to Kaeltar about making it as painful as possible. Unfortunately, the male knew precisely what would tear me apart.

"So, you have spent half a moon thinking about how sickening it was to hear those shocks of electricity ripping my skin apart?"

Jonah turned his head, unable to respond to such a simple acknowledgement. I understood he was trying to apologise, but half a moon to decide whether he could face me rather than simply checking in was even below him. But I would not lose my commander's ally ship, so I would forgive him. I had little concern about whether he would forgive me.

I cleared my throat, "so, my father has not ordered my arrest?"

"No," Jonah replied.

"He just ordered that we bring you back under control," Alex added, which earned a slight glare from Jonah. "If you had not been so bold as to show our queen your power in the first place, maybe we would not be in such a dire situation again."

"I was only taking the right action. Arraetta was very upset, and I needed to give her something to hold on to. She needs to know about her Rapidfire."

"Then *tell* her in the future," Alex replied sharply. "It is against the law to use your power for a reason."

"My love," Jonah placed his hand on Alex's arm.

"No, he needs to know," Alex shrugged him off, still angered at me, "you could have hurt her, Seraiah."

Using my name over my formal title showed how angered he was.

"I would not hurt her, ever."

"But, that thing might!" he shouted, his voice echoing around the chamber, before he lowered it, "She is my queen. I will protect her."

I bowed my head, defeated by their harsh tones. "Look, I do apologise for what has occurred today, but I promise I would never hurt Arraetta."

"And, Jonah?" Alex folded his arms.

"I am sorry for hurting you, Jonah," I said sincerely. "None of this shall happen again unless a time arises-"

"-Time arises?" Jonah gasped, "You are smart, Seraiah, brought up in the court, and one of the best negotiators I have had the privilege of being in a room with. When do you ever need to use this power?" I did not answer. "The only time I would be so inclined for it to be used is if the whole realm is in danger and you need it to combat the enemy. And, even then, I hoped you would be in damn good control of it."

Control. Something I felt like I was losing, and there was little chance of being able to train my power to bring it back in my favour.

"And what if it is something more pressing?" I challenged.

"More pressing than war?"

"Arraetta being in danger."

"I am not against dethroning, Seraiah, but I have already said there are many better ways to do it... than cheating. That is exactly what it is. A shortcut to the throne, and then what? Your people would despise you, and your father would be a martyr."

I hated to admit that Jonah was right, but I was using such darkness to defend my fated one to the ends of the universe. The Gods knew he would deserve such punishment. Empyreans, I would kill every ally if it meant she was safe.

"We must do things the right way," Alex replied, "for the kingdom's sake, just as we always have. Our motto is *by valour or virtue, for all*, after all."

Alex reciting the motto of The Sanctuary of Amity felt like a cliché way of making sure their message was loud and clear about using my power sparingly. It was our way of choosing principle over destruction.

"Speaking of Amity," Jonah replied, his tone neutral. "It seems your trip has not yet been postponed, so you will still depart for Italy in the morning."

"Fuck."

The dreaded trip to Italy had crept on me quicker than a shadow at dusk. It had left me little chance to connect with Arraetta, and I was sure the distance would do more harm than good. I, at least, wished to give her more insight into who we were to one another.

"Well, I should suppose I better find Arraetta before I depart for several sols," I said, giving us ample reason to leave the confined atmosphere of the library. I stayed ahead of the two of them, doing little to engage in empty conversation in case more anger would follow it.

Alex informed me that Arraetta was left in her room with Travis on watch, which annoyed me a little. I wished they did not treat her like a prisoner.

As we drew closer to the east wing, an odd tingle shivered down my spine, and I identified it immediately as the sigils in my room. But its presence was foreign, peculiar, warm – welcome. I recognised such energy from the limited time I had been in her room, and I knew Arraetta had crossed wholly through the threshold.

But I wondered why she was snooping in my room. Our arrival in the corridor was timed by Travis leaving the bathroom, a sheepish look on his face.

"Your Grace," he greeted, bowing his head, "I apologise, I-"

"You do not need to apologise for relieving yourself," I chuckled, continuing onwards, although I was sure he did not know Arraetta was no longer resting in her room. Sigils were odd things. I could not sense what she was doing, but I did recognise the feeling in my body that she was snooping inside.

"Her Royal Highness is still in her room," Travis said politely, and I only hummed in acknowledgement, deciding to entertain her a little by walking past my room towards hers. Yet, as I arrived at her ajar door, I felt the sudden disappearance of her energy, meaning she had left my space. And the only way I guessed was by the window. But why was she hiding? My heart thudded at the idea she might be trying to run.

I walked toward my room, leaving the confused males to follow behind idly until I opened the door, noting that the window of my room was partially open.

"I think she is in the garden," I turned to them, all who looked perplexed.

"How can you be so sure?" Alex asked.

"Sigils," I answered, knowing no more explanation was needed as Alex and Jonah knew I had sigils in secure places. It made me wonder if I could dare to use some more power to protect Arraetta's haven.

"I shall ask the guards to look out for her," Jonah added, bringing his radio to his mouth.

Without much thought, I swiped it from his hands and stepped back. "I shall find her and then radio through to you."

Jonah reached to take the radio back, but I hopped away. "I cannot have you wandering unattended after your earlier stunt."

I bowed. "Jonah, do give me this pleasure."

Without another word, I bolted down the corridor to the back of the house, down the stairs, out into the gardens and rushed towards the steps around the side of the palace. All whilst my heart was pounding in my chest - filled with both anticipation and worry. But I bumped so hard into the assailant herself as I hurried around the corner, we plummeted to the ground with a grunt. I placed my hand around her head to cushion the blow of the gravel below, with me lying on top of her.

Our ragged breaths brushed against each other's skin, closer than ever. I looked down at her lips, watching as she unknowingly bit her poor bottom lip, and I was almost tempted to tug them free before devouring them with my lips. It seemed I had panicked for nothing, and she had not decided to run away at all - she was as much the adventurer as I was.

The radio crackled, interrupting our moment, and Jonah's voice spoke through it, a hint of annoyance and humour in it, "Maintain vigilance and report any sightings of the Iron Wing."

A grin washed over my face, sitting up slowly before bringing the device to my mouth. "This is Iron Wing speaking. It is not necessary, I repeat, not necessary to maintain vigilance on me."

Arraetta looked confused but did not refuse my hand as I helped her stand. We both brushed ourselves off.

"Hiding," I commented in humour.

"Who?"

"You."

She rolled her eyes dramatically. "Absolutely not."

Empyreans, she was adorable.

I laughed, "I felt your energy in my room, and my window was wide open."

"Partially open."

"So, snooping then?"

Redness tinged her cheeks, like a caught seedling unable to tell me the truth. She pulled her shoulders back. "No, I was looking for you. I was going to see if you were alright."

While it might have been partially true, it still did not answer why she decided to escape out of my window rather than wait inside my room. Then again, maybe she was still far too coy to want to be alone with me in such a personal space.

"Explain to me then, Arraetta." I folded my arms and raised an eyebrow. "How were you looking for me?"

She tutted, brushing past me as she decided to walk away, but I gently gripped her bicep.

"Am I in trouble?" She asked.

Trouble? No. I was the one in trouble. I was in trouble because every time I saw this female, touched her, basked in her presence, I was falling deeper into a pit of desperation and affection.

"I am sorry if I scared you."

"You-"

"-You might be the most insufferable person I know." Harsh footsteps had us turning towards Jonah, Alex and Travis, all looking professional, although Travis looked like he was enjoying the sol's events.

"I was only helping with the search party," I grinned. "It was not meant to cause harm."

"You are fortunate I did not have the whole kingdom searching for you both," Jonah pointed out, "but, of course, you were so lucky to have access to my radio to call off my orders."

I waved the device around, which he snatched back, fiddling with it until he had it set back into his pocket, with his headset plugged into it.

"I have had enough events for today," he said wearily. "I feel like I am chasing a deer through woodlands while I stumble over roots and branches."

"Well, you must learn how to leap over them, then," I chuckled.

"Oh, of that, I am realising." Jonah's tone was serious, which indicated that our lack of speaking over the last half a moon cycle, his betrayal and my threat were opening his eyes to a new world.

"Can you speak in English, please?" Arraetta suddenly asked, and our attention swayed to her, "I know I'm not-"

"-Climbing is reckless, ma'am," Jonah interjected. I knew Jonah had ascertained that I used my window to climb, so it was only right he had linked it, "I am aware you do not know the rules here, but you should come to understand the more you break, the harsher the consequences are."

Jonah's words were more severe than I would have expected, and Arraetta winced. I could feel a gentle irritation toward him, but it seemed I did not need to defend my beautiful, fated one.

"Then why don't you tell me the rules?" she countered, crossing her arms. I could feel pride sitting in my chest whilst I watched her. "And who you are, that might help too."

Jonah's mask was flawless, although I was sure he was slightly stunned for a split moment. He had much more to deal with than the passive princess I assumed he thought her to be, replaced with a female of fire. He had a prince who went rogue and a princess who knew nothing of the rules.

"Jonah. I am the head of security here."

"Ah," she breathed.

I almost snorted, unsure why he did not use his official title as Commander. Although I knew we were trying to keep the pending war of the house out of her prying ears, head of security was a minor, easier use.

"This is Alex," I said, pointing to him, hiding my smile as I added, "but we call him Dixon. And behind you is Travis."

Alex glared gently at me, which I knew was for stating his surname. Still, he was on duty, and so was I. Just as we called Rheon Travis by his surname, Dixon was what other soldiers called him in the field – and if he was pushing for a more active guard role, as he had in the Amity meeting, there was no need for anything more personal.

He bowed to her. "Nice to meet you, ma'am."

Travis also greeted her, although he was non-verbal.

"Okay, well," Arraetta said, looking around at us all briefly before she looked at Jonah, "I won't climb again."

"If you do, I must assign a personal guard," Jonah threatened.

"I swear," she said, raising her hands and making a charmingly concerned look, which made me laugh.

"Now that I have found you, let us go and talk," I told her. It was high time I spoke to her alone about her role within our house, without the prying eyes of guards and life bringers, before I was shipped off to Italy for Empyreans knows how long.

"No more power, Seraiah," Jonah stated.

"No more guards for tonight, Jonah," I said in Zikan with a grin. I placed my hand on the small of Arraetta's back and guided her around the side of the house, away from the guards.

"Can we eat first?" Arraetta asked, her stomach gently growling on cue. I nodded and found someone who would bring food to the library as we walked into the centre of the house, bypassing the ballroom and my father's wing.

"What's in there?" she asked.

Hell.

"My father's wing," I replied. "Best to keep away."

"Don't you like your father?"

"Hate would be more fitting," I muttered in Zikan, guiding her up the stairwell as I switched back to English, "There are many things I will fill you in on over time, but for now, just know that it is best to stay out of that area of the house, even if you are feeling curious."

I wondered whether she was contemplating breaking more rules before she asked, "Is Jonah always that much of an arsehole?"

I chuckled, understanding where such an opinion would have come from, especially after everything that had divided us recently.

"Sometimes."

Arraetta was enthralled by the library as soon as we entered. I shuffled towards the back of the room to get a bottle of white wine, two glasses, and the remote, which changed the ball in the ceiling from sol to night. I clicked the button, and the ball started to turn with a squeak, noticeably causing Arraetta to jump as she sat on the sofa.

Once we were situated with wine and she had stopped gawking at the ball and the breadth of the library, it was easier to have a conversation with her.

She took a deep breath. "Are you angry at me?"

I was surprised by how presumptuous she was, expecting that she would be in trouble for all her wanderings, but little did she know she held more power in the palace than any who might seek to reprimand her. Punishing a princess, let alone a goddess, for going against protocols she had no insight into would be challenging. I supposed Jonah was a little blunt in his warning, but such was his personality.

"No," I shook my head, "never. I would never be angry with you, though I find you pleasantly surprising."

"Because I climbed on the roof?"

"Because of many things," I answered, pouring two glasses of wine.

"I don't think anyone likes me here," she said sadly, opting to go to the easel, where my unfinished painting of Ryazark sat.

I was unsure what vices she believed she had which would cause her to think nobody liked her, but I presumed she felt quite alone without her friend to coddle her.

"I do not think they have a reason to dislike you," I told her, trying to prevent her from dwelling on such negative thoughts. "My mother says you paint."

"Yes."

I stood from the sofa and walked over to the easel. "This one I started a while ago. I have only just placed it back up again, maybe to continue it."

"Is it based on a place you know?"

"A place I imagined often but have never been to."

"Why are you trying to paint a place you have never been to?" she asked. "I find it hard to paint without a reference."

I was sure she understood artist's interpretation, being one herself. Still, I supposed she was right. I did not know what Ryazark looked like, and I would not until I was dead.

"Well, it was supposed to be Ryazark," I replied, noting her confused look at its mention. "Ah, Ryazark is the land of the Gods or at least one of them. I believe I have been there in a previous life, but the image is faint in my mind.... do you not paint places you have never been to?"

"Most of mine come in dreams."

"Dreams can carry significant messages," I stroked the delicate edges of the basic painting on the dried canvas, "sometimes the Gods are trying to tell us things."

"Well, mine are pretty messed up," she replied bluntly, "so they're probably just reaffirming that I'm a nutcase."

Such low self-esteem almost made me laugh, a goddess shaped by her life circumstances in the human realm. I wondered whether she would see herself in a much higher light had we met in The Cre-este.

"Or maybe it is something much deeper," I offered. "I, for one, have suffered from some of the most surreal dreams, but I believe I can see a message within them."

"Like what?" she replied flirtatiously, "Did you get a message that I would appear in your life?"

A long moment passed as our eyes met, and I knew she understood how I had longed to meet her. My dreams had been tormenting, yet none had envisioned her as radiant as she was. Her face reddened, and she shuffled back to the sofa, leaving an unwanted, small distance between us.

I chuckled, "I have had many dreams... about you... in a sense."

"Do I really want to know?" she replied, coyly sipping her wine.

Yes, I think you do, Arraetta.

"The Gods came to me in a dream," I said, quelling the need to touch her as I brought the conversation back to a more critical topic, "and told me about my Kindred Spirit."

Her eyebrows furrowed deeply. "What's a Kindred Spirit?"

Had she not been given such a message herself? Her face told me of her innocence.

"In essence, it is a connection that is created through extraordinary circumstances which cannot be explained except for God." I told her.

She let out a little laugh, "sounds mystical... so, is it like a... soulmate?"

"In the human sense? I suppose so, except a Kindred Spirit is more than just connecting eyes across the room and feeling a spark. It is a heavily fated thing that is incredibly rare."

"Why would you want to be heavily fated to something?"

"I thought it sounded quite romantic."

"What?" she chuckled, exaggerating, "Here's your life. Just to let you know, your fate is controlled completely, and this person is the one you have to marry."

"I like that idea," I replied, gazing at her over the tip of my wineglass. "I, for one, am happy being a Kindred Spirit."

"How do you know *you're* a Kindred Spirit?"

"Apart from the message from the Gods?" I replied, and she nodded. "It is because there are two Kindred Spirits in existence, and I am one half of another who is my Kindred Spirit. We form, as a whole, what is known as Kindred."

Thoughts and questions passed over her expression like little individual emotions.

My lip twitched. "I can see you are trying to understand."

She glared, "Well, if you are one Kindred Spirit, then who is the second?"

Her empty glass was placed on the floor, and I eyed it momentarily before looking back at her. Maybe she could not work out the blatantly obvious answer that *she* was the other half of Kindred.

Surely, it was evident with how she was sitting in my home, in my library, alone with the heir of Zika.

I toiled over the best way to give her insight into what Kindred was, although my interpretation was as much as an artist's. It also required the use of ancient magic, which meant energy expenditure. Still, I could not afford to leave the question unanswered, not with so much at stake.

"Oh, Arraetta, how I would have loved to live as a human."

I picked up a flat brush from a pot of discoloured water, dabbed it into green and painted ancient symbols on the canvas.

Arraetta gasped. "What does that mean?"

"To be ignorant to one's own fate."

For the next few minutes, I internally chanted the spell I knew, imagining the space in question beyond our ephemeral flesh. I tried to ignore the tenting of the bulge in my pants, concentrating on what I needed to do. And, for the first time, I had a clear image of the two of us in the form of Kindred.

At some point, a knock on the library door knocked me out of my reverie, and food was brought in. As Arraetta ate, I continued my work, praying what I wished to show her would work for the two of us.

Once she had satisfied her hunger, Arraetta hopped up. "But what does a Kindred Spirit mean, exactly?"

I remembered what Sheika had said many scorns before, "divinely connected and divinely powerful."

I imagined she was almost rolling her eyes, and I subtly grinned. "Like... friends?"

"You are smarter than that," I murmured in Zikan before I felt the ebb of energy flow from my body as the spell finally breathed life. I turned to her. "Come here."

I held out my hand, watching her approach me like a magnet. Her energy simmered with my own until our skin connected. I pulled her in front of me, facing the canvas, before I tucked myself behind her.

"You ruined a perfectly good painting," Arraetta breathed, and a little gasp left her lips as I tucked my finger between the waist of her skirt and blouse to touch her bare skin. Empyreans, such a thing sent a ripple of ecstasy through my fingers and down to my cock. I was sure I could not hide the bulge in my pants.

I placed her other hand on the painting, slithering my fingers between the crevices until cool paint tickled my fingertips. My pulsing vitality melded with hers, and I closed my eyes, breathing in her intoxicating scent, which I only wished to bathe in. I wondered whether showing her Kindred physically, slowly removing every garment she wore and sliding my tongue over every inch of her skin, until her taste was engraved on my tongue, would have been better.

It was a shame we had to wait until the bonding was completed.

"You smell good, Arraetta."

"That's the food."

"Hm," I replied, feeling the ache of my cock in my pants, "close your eyes."

My command was soft, and I concentrated on the flow of my inner power as I whispered the ancient spell in her ear, feeling her body relax against my own. Her lips dripped moans as depictions swirled in her head of what I wished to show her until we were no longer mentally in the library, but physically in another dimension. Body on body, entwined like vines, kinetically kneading against one another in a space of dazzling colour and sparkling stars - a universe of our own.

Time shifted as we succumbed to the fantasy, stepping away from all existence for a period neither of us cared about. But, as the climactic experience started to become too overwhelming, and I was far too aroused to stop myself from ejaculating in my pants, I pulled us out of it and stepped away.

The heat between us fused with our breathlessness, both of us simmering from the high of an imagined but intense sexual experience. I left her by the canvas and walked straight to the hidden sink, taking several deep breaths to calm my heart and my throbbing cock. Empyreans, I was so hard it was uncomfortable, needing a release, but her smell had overpowered my senses, and I was still riding that high. One I wish she were riding.

I grabbed a wet cloth before going back to Arraetta, doing my utmost best to disguise how aroused I was. Taking her hands into mine, I tried to disregard the bubbling energy which bounced in them as I wiped away the paint.

I had to fight the urge to clear my throat. "Do you now understand?"

"I... what was that?" her eyebrows furrowed.

"That is Kindred; it is the divine connection between Kindred Spirits, or so I believe."

Or, if I had to be more truthful with her, it was the idea my mind had conjured in an answer to what Kindred was. A true embodiment of love and devotion, supposed to create peace across the universe when the two of us were one.

"It felt..."

"Real?" I stroked her cheek. "I am sure that the reality of it is much better than a fantastical dream, wouldn't you agree?"

"But, we were... what does that mean for us?"

Her expression was somewhat innocent, but I almost could see it was a game for me to spell it out for her - a clever female.

"If you have not figured that out yet, then I would suggest you take some time to do so."

"It didn't feel like... it didn't feel like we were, you know... having sex."

Ah, there it was - the words she seemed so coy to speak. It amused me that she had finally gathered the confidence. At the end, she added a subtle inflexion as though she were questioning it.

"Then what did you think it felt like?" I questioned. "I can tell you that it felt like our souls were meant for nothing more and nothing less. Having met you now, Arraetta, I can tell you it is becoming harder to fight the urge."

The urge to throw you on that sofa and fuck you so hard you see how stars are birthed.

I shook my head gently to quell the thought, although she did not seem to notice, "I guess for me, it felt... it felt ethereal for want of a better word. It didn't feel like... sex, well, it was like it, kind of, but it was..."

"Go on," I coaxed, *praying* for her to continue.

"I suppose I was going to say it felt like the most satisfying feeling, yet now I feel as though I never felt anything at all."

A feeling I knew would only be fleeting as the two of us would not be far from copulating.

"I like to see it like a fragmented memory," I said, stepping closer, "as though when we are not mortal beings, we are free to be with each other in that way, entwined as one."

Her cheeks flushed, and she tried to move away to hide her reticence. But I immediately stopped her to keep the distance as close as possible. Gone were my worries that my cock was easily touchable through my pants, replaced by the longing to be closer to her. I craved it. I craved her.

"Some souls are destined to die and be reborn repeatedly as part of cataclysmic events." There was truth in what I said. Somewhere in the universe's timeline, our souls were fractured for a reason I could not guess, only to have the task of finding one another again.

"Cataclysmic?"

I cupped her face. "Us meeting again is one."

She swallowed as our eyes dipped to each other's lips, finally daring me to taste her sweetness. But I avoided the temptation and caressed her cheek. "Arraetta, what happens now will simply be fated. I know that this fate has been worth the great sacrifices we have made to be here."

"Sacri... Seraiah, I... I saw you when you were a little boy by a windmill."

Her sudden change in topic made me ponder the connection, although I could only guess she thought I had sacrificed much as a seedling. Then again, my life had been sacrificed for the good of the universe and the evils of my kingdom.

"If you are talking of the Wicker Windmill," I replied, "I have been there a great many times."

"There was a nymph," she added. And the sudden mention had me thinking about the odd dream I had the first time I had my cardiac arrest moons before. I was sure she was referring to the Spirit Nymph, but that could have only signified that she had been in the same place, either in my dream or reality.

"That was you?" I asked.

"I... I don't think that was me," she said, shaking her head. "I think I was in its eyes."

"I forgot about that. I suppose I may have caused a bit too much destruction to find you then."

"Seraiah, I don't know why you're here or what happened," she said, "but I don't think that you asking a water creature to help you find me caused whatever to happen."

I was sure a sacred mythical Spirit Nymph would be entertained by a goddess calling her a *water creature*. I speculated whether Arraetta had been sent the vision from the Gods so she might see some insight into my life as a seedling, but with what need? It was rare dreams were based in reality, so she could have only merely witnessed a mirage of something illusory. That being said, maybe Arraetta had the abilities of a seer, and the dreams and memories she saw were a collection of depictions of times which had passed and were to come.

"Let us hope you are right," I said. "whenever we go home, I will be sure to go by the river to speak with it... or maybe I should just thank you."

That caused her to smile whilst she bit back, "I wasn't the nymph!"

I chortled, "I do not know, the Nymph was cute."

Cute if one was into zoophilia, which was never my kind of peculiarity. Arraetta tapped my arm playfully, and I feigned hurt, making us laugh more. I was sure anyone spying on us would be grinning at how melodic it sounded together. Maybe those who overheard us would smile, or perhaps even my father glared at his ceilings in disdain.

Once our laughter settled, she said, "Seraiah, why are you here?"

"In this room?" I quipped, and she tutted. Arraetta had probed for the answer hours before, but I still did not think it was the right time to give her the high tale of how we managed to escape The Dark. It was also far too late for such tragic stories. "It is not a tale for tonight."

"Some other time, maybe?"

I could only nod my head before I checked my watch. "Wow, it is late."

"What time is it?"

"Gone eleven."

She gasped, "What? But how?"

"That experience, we probably would have been in there for a while," I explained, "a bit like when we paint and just zone out. Time just flies."

Except we were enchanted under a spell, not disappearing into the land of creating art

"I should probably get some sleep."

"Let me walk you to your room."

We walked silently, and I subtly peered down at her, wondering whether I could embrace or kiss her. It felt like I was dropping her home from a first date, but I did not wish to share my first kiss with those who might pry behind CCTV cameras.

Arriving outside her door, I decided to tease her a little, leaning over her as her hand went to the handle. "Traspea, Arraetta."

"What does that mean?"

"It means good night."

"Traspea," she whispered back, tasting the word.

"You need to roll your 'r'," I told her, "traspea."

"Traspea," she pronounced perfectly, and I nodded. Her eyes begged me to kiss her, wetting her lips subtly with her tempting tongue, and I wondered whether I should give in. Fuck the rules.

Eyes. Lips. Eyes. Lips. *Eyes*.

With some sort of willpower, I kissed her forehead softly before stepping away, bowing before I paraded down the corridor.

"Traspea," she whispered. The wispy word sent a shiver down my spine, and my hardness did not crack as I thought about her whispering such words beneath me as I drove myself inside her.

"Traspea!" I bellowed back to her, not caring for anyone overhearing before I dived into my room. I grinned and leaned back against the door as my heart thudded rapidly at the thought of that female who would be my wife.

She was breathtaking – a pure beauty I had been gifted to behold. And her laughter. Empyreans, I could bottle up her laughter and save it to listen to when the sols were too quiet.

Crack. Crack. Crack.

The coffer would soon open, and Empyreans, would I let it.

How had I become such a foolhardy prince, bending to the whim of divinity when I was destined to become the leader of a great nation? How could I appease every thought and feeling of being with her whilst keeping myself on the straight and narrow? Had the Gods gifted me such a resplendence, or would I find it ripped from my fingers when they saw fit?

No, I would never allow such a thing to happen. Arraetta belonged to me, and the Gods be damned if they ever sought to destroy our bond.

TWENTY-ONE

My mind begged for hours for me to sneak into Arraetta's room and hold her until I fell asleep, knowing she was only through the next wall. Until finally, I drifted asleep. I woke to a soft rapture on the door, informed by a servant that my car would leave for the airport within the hour.

The house staff had already packed my clothing, which was waiting in thick suitcases in the corner of the room. Another servant collected them as I was about to leave, leaving him to take them as I walked up to Arraetta's room, standing outside for a long moment, wondering whether it was far too intrusive, after all this time, to peer in and see her sleeping. Or, maybe I could have left her a note, but I did not want to disrupt what dreams of splendour she might have had. It was a shame I had not told her I was departing for Italy, or that she could not join me.

I took my leave shortly, walking down into the entrance hallway. Through the large windows, I could see three cars parked outside. My father's vehicle was not present, making me curious whether he would accompany or leave me to my own devices abroad. I doubted the latter.

Surprisingly, I was greeted by a tired-eyed Jonah whilst Travis and Connell were on standby with other guards.

"Is my father not joining?"

"He has already departed," Jonah replied. "You will be taking a separate flight."

"Does he expect I may attempt to crash his plane?" I raised my eyebrows, seeing Jonah smile just a little. "He could at least help save the environment unless he plans to throw me in the economy section."

Jonah chuckled, "No, definitely not, Your Highness. You are precious cargo. We would make only the best arrangements for you."

"Ah, so I shall be in the luggage pit," I smiled. "I suppose I better catch my flight."

"You are fortunate; I shall be accompanying you."

"Is that so? To whom do I owe the privilege?"

"I would rather monitor the situation," he answered. "I do not wish to find my king imprisoned again. As you know, I am a decent negotiator, and your cousin is busy."

"Still no sign of returning?"

"They are staying at Genie's apartment."

I nodded, taking the opportunity to move towards the middle car. "Speaking of, I would like to make arrangements for us to move Arraetta's things from there as soon as possible."

"Of course," he agreed before a command from the Captain of the Guard was given, followed by a ceremonious farewell bow by those on duty. "I will see to it that such things are done before the end of the sol tomorrow; I am sure the princess will be glad to have her things brought here."

"I would guess from knowing her for such a short period she would prefer to do her own packing. I am sure we can arrange for such privileges as a last time before she conforms to duty."

Jonah opened the back passenger door to my car and agreed, "Let us see how our journey goes and how the situation is on the ground over there before we think about an excursion to the centre of London."

I climbed into the seat. "I shall see you at the airport."

"You shall."

As he shut the door and walked to the leading vehicle, I looked up at the large palace, unsure when I would next step into its safety again. Italy was wholly my father's territory, and I did not have much army support there. At least Arraetta would be safe under the watchful eye of my guard.

The vehicle parade started to move, one in front and one behind, for the journey to the airport. It was barely five o'clock in the morning, and all the roads were quiet. I dozed on and off until we arrived. Unlike standard passengers, the check-in process was via a Fixed-Based Operator, and I was to depart on a private jet. We owned six, and it seemed my father's jet had already left the airport.

The flight from London to Italy was just over two hours, and I shared it with Jonah among the flight attendants. The two of us spent most of it sleeping before the plane descended into the airport.

"It has been some time since I was last here," Jonah said, gazing out the window.

"How come you did not bring Alex?" I asked him.

"We cannot spare everyone from London, can we?" he replied, "and Alex is our best ear on the ground right now. He can watch over the princess... without her even knowing."

"I am sure she will enjoy being watched." My sarcasm shone through.

"She always will," he answered. "It may be ample time for us to discuss Alex's position as Her Highness' personal guard."

"Did he complete his task?"

"It is in the final processes," Jonah nodded, the conversation alluding to Alex burying the story about Arraetta.

"And are there others still being considered?"

Jonah paused before nodding. "Yes, Travis also inquired, although I would prefer him to be on your guard. Other than that, a few recruits show potential, but not necessarily the same... drive."

"I think we should disband my guard," I shrugged, which he shook his head at, "I do not need it. I hardly leave the house, and they are only testing my patience by being there all the damn time."

"You dismiss them half the time. You should get used to it, for when you become king, they will be a constant presence in your life."

"Not if I change the rules."

"You shall not be changing such rules, Seraiah," he replied sharply. "While you may be the next king, I will be the next general, and it will be my job to keep you safe."

"Let us make a deal then," I said. He raised his eyebrows in response, "I will make Alex Arraetta's first guard, but you must move Travis to be on her guard, too, as he is far better at protecting her than he is me. And, you must remove guards from me whilst I am inside the house."

"No deal."

"You are abhorrent."

"Alex on Arraetta's guard, and Travis will remain," he negotiated, and I rolled my eyes. "If not Travis, then I will happily recruit someone else. I think... Leopold could be a good option."

"Your second in command is not made for guard duty."

"Oh, but he would happily put you in your place," he grinned slyly. It was a shame he was right because Leopold would not deal with being dismissed like the others. He was even more formidable and protocol-driven than Alex and Jonah.

It took very little time on the ground to get me through security and into a chauffeured vehicle. Our destination was Sole Serafino, a town created for and by our people, who wished to live in a better climate than England. The weather resembled the southern parts of Zika, where the lands were drier and the seas were warmer.

It began with the vineyard, the house on the lot, and the surrounding land before it became a small paradise overlooking the vast Mediterranean. Unlike the gated community in London, Sole was open to tourists, which attracted many people.

The town was shielded and charged by a generator which sat atop a clifftop like a huge glass trophy, radiating its energy from the sun. A news article once mentioned the sphere as one of the best places to visit for panoramic sunset views. Little did they know it was being used to fuel the life force of foreign beings.

There were two royal residences, one on the far side of the cliffs, hidden by trees, which was my mother's and the main house belonging to my father. It was this house in which I would stay. It was a beautiful home built into the cliffs, with its top half looking like a white stone mansion with a water fountain-centred garden at its opening.

I stepped out of the vehicle and into the mosaic-tiled entrance, looking through double doors at the rear to a large sitting room overlooking the sea. The scent of sea air was refreshing, and a soft breeze offered a little release from the cloying Italian sun.

"Good afternoon, Your Royal Highness," I was greeted by Graeham, the butler of the house, on arrival, "it has been a very long time since we last saw you."

I did not enjoy Graeham's company. He was a stickler for protocol, which meant he would rank everyone in the order they deserved. Essentially, treating my father like a God and, therefore, there was a lack of trust I had for him. Butlers were a mill of information, and choosing to withhold or give away information was a decision they would make themselves.

"Time just continues to disappear." I shook his hand. "How is your family?"

"They are very well, Sir." He nodded. "I have heard you are to be heartfasted. There is much excitement for everyone here in Sole."

"I am sure," I replied with a tight smile, "has my father arrived?"

"Yes, he had a ten-o'clock meeting at the vineyard," he explained. "He shall be back at twelve, when I will serve you both lunch in the sitting room."

"I suppose I am not invited to such meetings."

"I am afraid not, Sir. His Majesty has informed me that you are here merely on vacation and not here to be party to any business."

I opened my mouth to speak, but Jonah spoke first. "Graeham, I believe His Highness is here to learn about his father's work."

"I can only present what information I am given. His Highness is to remain on the premises until His Majesty returns, and further scheduling shall be given whilst lunch is served."

"I would be grateful to see the itinerary," Jonah said, "whilst Sir Frederique is not here, I am the acting advisor in his stead."

Graeham grimaced. "Of course, I shall present it to you within the hour." He looked at me again. "Your quarters have been prepared. I hope you find them satisfactory. Should you require anything, you may use the telephone in the room."

He bowed and left without another word.

"What is this?" Jonah muttered, "Three-star hotel service?"

"I suppose my father has given him strict instructions."

I walked to the stairwell on the left, leading downwards to another section of the house specifically created for me. The weight on my shoulders left as I descended into my sigil-protected area, thankful they were still in use and did not require mending. Even after it had been a few winters since I was last in Italy. The staircase led into a small courtyard garden, doused in sunlight from a small crater in the rock above.

The annexe, built into the left side of the cliff, consisted of two large living spaces: a small office and a bedroom with an en-suite. Windows were built into the stone, with a small balcony in the bedroom overlooking the vast seas ahead. It was beautiful, but I was only trading one prison for another.

"And where are you residing?" I asked Jonah. We were interrupted by a maid who came in with my suitcases and proceeded to unpack them.

"Do not worry, I shall sort that," Jonah said to the maid.

"Sir?"

"I said I would sort that out," he replied more forcefully. "I will look after His Highness while we are in residence. Do not worry about being in this area unless you are instructed."

The maid avoided looking directly at me whilst also seeking my approval. She took Jonah's decision as final before curtseying and rushing away.

"I am not unpacking your bag," Jonah said. "I am sure you are quite capable of doing such a thing."

"Am I to do my own cooking, too?"

"I would not recommend attempting something that requires such a skill," he added before clearing his throat, "anyway, I shall stay with Eros' family. I will try to free him from his constraints so he can return home."

"I will speak to my father."

"No," he answered, "you should leave Eros to me. I would be quite worried if it is discovered that we are asking about a male you are not wholly associated with. He is my friend, with whom you sometimes dine with."

He was right. Eros was not a known friend of mine; he only stayed with Jonah when he visited London, and therefore, he was known as his friend.

"I will find this itinerary before any decisions are made without my consent." Jonah took his leave, and I stared at my unpacked suitcase, a little annoyed that I had to sort out my clothing.

In the end, I ignored such duties and rested for a few hours. When it was time, I went to the dining room, where it was planned for my father and me to dine together. A position that I wished I did not have to find myself in.

Even though I had kept to the time, my father was an hour late, and I felt more aggravated with every second that had passed. I hated having to wait for a tyrant who sought to waste my time and had managed to keep me under control by leaning towards my tendency to be on time. I was sure he was using a tactic to see how fast my patience wore thin.

I had also not seen the aforementioned itinerary, and there had been no sign of Jonah since his departure. I presumed he was busy trying to find out more information about Eros, or maybe he was dining with Henri's mother and eating the best homemade food. Anything would be better than the fine meal I would soon be served, with a side of cloying wrath.

When my father's arrival was announced, he entered the room with an air of hatred and disgust. Graeham walked ahead of him and stood to the side.

"His Majesty, Your Royal Highness," Graeham said to me.

"I am aware," I replied, standing and offering my father a half-bow. "I suppose His Majesty may be able to explain why I am waiting here rather than in the meetings I have been informed I should attend."

"You shall be part of such meetings when you have earned your damned place," my father chided sharply, taking his seat at one end of the table whilst I took mine opposite. A distance of eight seats on either side of us housed invisible participants in this parlay.

Neither of us spoke as lunch was brought in, and I was glad it was such delectable Italian cuisine, even if it was less homely than I wished.

"The itinerary as requested, Sir," Graeham said, handing over a document to my father, who waved his hand.

"You may read it aloud," he dismissed, digging into his food.

Disgusting.

Graeham stood back a few steps, reading the document aloud. "His Majesty has invited His Highness on a three-sols vacation to relax and unwind before royal duties at home are to be implemented."

Three sols. I could last three sols, but what was the point of keeping me at a distance from my wife for that period if I was not to be party to the business of the vineyard?

"If I am not here on business, I would rather be at home."

Graeham eyed my father, waiting for the signal to continue reading. My father finally looked up from his plate. "I do not see why you are so ungrateful for such an opportunity, considering the damage you have caused recently. It is no burden to you being here."

"No burden?" I snorted, "if I had known that I would be here on vacation, I would have brought Arraetta with me."

I could see my father's brow furrowed, and I wondered what comment he wanted to make about the female who would become queen.

"You are here as a prince, Seraiah," he said, surprisingly calm, "whilst you wish to enjoy your... pleasures, you are here on duty."

"Exactly," I replied. "As the future king, it is my duty to understand the business we run, Father. I can have a vacation in moons to come, with my wife by my side-"

"-No!" he stood up sharply. "Do not test my patience. It is not to my pleasure you being here, but I am conforming to the rites of passage that a prince must obey before he weds, including being away from his wife." He took a breath before looking at Graeham. "Continue."

"Sir," Graeham said as my father took his seat.

Rites of passage, what a big pile of shit my father had concocted. Rites of passage to be away from the one I wanted to be with the most. To control, manipulate and mould me into a king he saw fit, not one I wished to be. To remain under the presence of a king, I never wanted to bow before again.

"As of tomorrow, His Royal Highness will partake in a three-sol schedule," Graeham told me, "which shall include partaking in sports; visitations and dinners to local households; meditation and relaxation on the beach; and a visit to the vineyard, to greet some of our esteemed guests. Of course, we cannot have the prince here for such things without holding a dinner this evening with some entertainment."

"You see, I do not understand the dramatics," my father said, staring me down with a force which would make any commoner buckle, but not me. He conceded, "You are fortunate I have decided to parade you around as the heir you are supposed to be."

"Parade?" I snorted, "Oh, yes, this is all but a show to you, Father."

"Watch your tongue, boy!" he snapped, hand slamming onto the table, which did nothing but make my heart skip a beat. I allowed him to have his seedling tantrum in front of the staff who wished to support him. "You need to learn to be more disciplined rather than walking around acting like a spoiled seedling."

"I only have you to thank for that. Is a son not the person a father moulds him into?"

"The only person who has moulded you into what you are is that demon that festers inside you. My son has-"

"-*Long since been dead?*" I interjected, then laughed humourlessly,

"How predictable, Father. Yet, if I were dead, how could I be right in front of you?"

As he gripped his fork, I could see the whiteness of his knuckles, and I almost begged him to throw it at me. What a show for everyone to witness! But he did not surrender to his rage. Instead, he started towards the door – conversation over.

With finality, he paused and turned toward me. "You are but a ghost of the son I once knew. Dead or alive, I would trade him for the one standing before me, for at least he showed me the respect I deserve as king. *I* am king, Seraiah, and you shall damn well learn to submit before I decide to revoke your right as heir to the throne."

"You cannot revoke such a right."

My father laughed sardonically and walked away, shouting, "You have no idea what rights I have, Seraiah, and I have no whim to use any of them against you."

Wrath clawed under my skin, desperate to be released from its tight grip, but I managed to hold it in. Fuck that insolent being and his political agendas. Demanding me to bow before him, but I would be damned to hell before I ever did.

You should have killed him.

Empyreans, that fucking voice was becoming more irritating than my father's, and the ache of not disclosing my rage throbbed through my body before releasing via a gentle trickle from my nose. I lifted my hand, wiping away the leaking crimson blood.

"Y-Your Royal Highness," Graeham stepped forward to help, but I held my hand up to stop him, knowing his help was the one I did not need. What I needed was to leave the room as quickly as possible as nausea began to overwhelm me.

As I rushed from it, I almost knocked a maid over, but I did not care. I did my best to get down to my quarters before the symptoms overwhelmed me. My vision tripled, blurred, and then kaleidoscoped, causing my body to sway in different directions until I could no longer resist the pull of sleep. The wind pushed against my body as I clattered sharply against the hard, cold tiles. I succumbed to darkness.

Arraetta.

TWENTY-TWO

Vision glazed, I tried to focus on azure eyes which looked straight at me, instantly recognising them as Arraetta's. Her soft white dress radiated her etherealness, and I knew this was our special sol - the one in which we would finally bond, having waited an eternity.

An altar surrounded us in the centre of a space of white nothing-ness; only the two of us seemed to exist. Yet, one other came to join us, and I acknowledged that it was Elder Marcus, our patriarch.

"Are you both ready?"

I parted my lips to answer, but a harsh pain fluctuated through my skin before the excruciating pull of my onyx Rapidfire started to consume me without mercy. I could not control it, feeling the demon devour the warm air.

"Wait, I-" she gasped, her eyes widening.

Come to me, darling. Let me taste your fear and show you how powerful we can be, the dark monster whispered in my mind, daring the words to leave my lips. Gazing deeper into her eyes, searching for whatever fear I could feed upon to coax her under my control, I attempted to regain a small amount of my own. Silently, I begged for freedom from the darkness, wishing not to see what fear she had buried. She could not fear me. She must not fear me.

Fear is control.

An invisible force shoved me from behind, and I stumbled forward, unable to stop the inner desire to swallow every part of her. Every fibre of my body began to drip with cold, black liquid before it tumbled to the floor like heavy sludge, thickening as it ingested the white light around us. A quake shook the space until the invisible sky above shattered, and brutal ashen skies rippled with golden lightning.

There was not one part of the enclosure The Mire did not wish to make, tracking Arraetta as she shifted backwards, screaming for help.

"Arraetta, save me!"

Fear is palpable.

I powered forward, screaming her name, desperate to cling onto her, until The Mire shuddered upwards to create a wall between us. And, somehow, I fell into it like it was a doorway into an unknown chasm. I floated in the abyss, darkness consuming every shred of my vision until I could not discern between death and life.

Breath ragged, fear placating me without mercy; I felt the sludge trickle up my body, covering every air pocket I had until I could no longer breathe.

Fear is power.

I coughed sharply, gasping for air as the heaviness of an icy stone floor beneath me hit me, followed by a dark, uncanny chuckle which reverberated around. My eyes adjusted to the piercing moonlight which shone through arched windows, noting I was in a mediaeval throne room. Yet, it seemed like another mirrored dystopia, more significant than the one I had found myself in previously.

I pushed to my knees, pausing as my gaze fixated on one black-clothed leg crossed over another, revealing slowly, as I looked upwards, my possessed doppelgänger, sitting on an onyx stone throne.

"Here we are again, Seraiah."

Gathering my composure, I staggered until I could face my greatest enemy. "What did you do to her?"

"To whom?"

"Arraetta!"

"It shall not be long before my dark queen finally answers the call and succumbs to us." His awfully white teeth gleamed against his black eyes as he smiled and then rose, stepping down from his perch and walking towards me.

I growled, "She is not your queen of darkness."

"I am you, Seraiah, it is only so long before you lose the will of the light."

I leapt at him, but he disappeared in an obsidian mist, reappearing a little further away while he tutted, "Goodness, a temper is not good. Control that anger, Seraiah. I am sure you do not want to lose yourself to me quicker than you already are."

"You are mistaken if you should ever think I would bow to your will!" I shouted. "You are but a figment of my imagination; you are not even real. Do you understand?"

He barked with laughter, "Oh, but that is where you are quite mistaken. I am as real as the wind that whispers in your ears, the shadows that follow you, the blood in your veins and..." he clicked his fingers, and I collapsed to the floor, writhing in sudden pain. "...The pain that you feel deep in the depth of your lifeless soul."

Another snap stopped the ache but left me clawing for air.

"Fuck... you," I coughed.

He knelt before me, close enough for me to see into the murky pits of his eyes. "Oh, Seraiah, seeing how pitifully weak you are is shameful. You could be as powerful as I am; you only need to ask."

I clenched my fists, "I would rather burn in the fiery pits of hell for an eternity than look like I had traded my eyes for black holes."

I attempted to attack him again, but the atmosphere shifted, and he suddenly disappeared, leaving me with only a smarmy look on his face.

Burn.

A rattle of agony clawed out of my throat as every fibre of my being seared unbearably until I collapsed back to the cold ground, shuddering in silence as I begged for it to end. And, as quick as the agony consumed me, it was over, and the heat cloying my skin was countered by a breeze of cool air.

I blinked my eyes open, looking upward at a ceiling fan. The nightmare had shifted, and reality had returned. I grunted as I tried to sit up, but two hands landed on my shoulders and pushed me back down.

"Rest," Jonah said softly.

"Tell me this is not a dream," I mumbled, feeling like I had been run over by a train.

"Would you even tell me what your dreams are about? I know something is not right with you, Seraiah. I have felt it since the night of the ball."

"Only nightmares," I said, noting his disbelief, "I have been having encounters with... the devil. And, they are unpleasant."

"He is resurfacing?"

I turned my head, not wanting such a conversation. Jonah knew about the monster under my skin and what it took so very long ago to lock him deep in my mind. He knew my hold on it, the strength it took, the anguish I battled to remain in control.

"And what does he want with you?"

I chuckled mirthlessly, "Everything."

I looked at Jonah, who had a contemplative look, before he nodded, "I only hope you do not make the wrong bargain with him and become a shell of yourself again."

"How arduous of you," I grunted, leaning against the headboard. "Do not worry; my soul is still intact. I am far too strong."

"Except your temper has worsened," he observed, "even losing your cool with your father so quickly is surprising."

Surprising, it might have been, but he was a prudent, obnoxious tyrant who sought only to control me because he valued power above loyalty.

"I must go home."

"Seraiah," Jonah replied, "this isn-"

"Do not stop me, Jonah," I interrupted. "I do not wish to be here. I do not care for my father's demands. I need to see Arraetta. This... this distance is far too difficult."

"I cannot charter a flight so quickly," Jonah replied, "on top of that, I do not wish to deal with your father's wrath if you suddenly decide to leave. What about this dinner tonight?"

"Oh, come on, Jonah."

"I promise I shall organise a flight for early tomorrow morning, but you need to rest and show that you are willing to entertain some of your father's whims."

I understood the need to appease my father, but he did not need to show his support for my father so openly. I could wait until the next sol, but not any longer. After my uncomfortably vivid dream, I needed to know if Arraetta was well, and I could only do that by seeing her in person.

As though reading my mind, he said, "Alex has his eyes on the princess, I promise she is safe and well. Although she seems to have a habit of wandering."

"Wandering?"

"She was at Sheika's," he added, "and, then she decided to take a stroll unaccompanied."

I was sure whatever took place at Sheika's was more than a simple visit for tea, and it could be the reason why I knew, in my soul, that what happened to me had happened to her too.

"Have you found information about Eros?"

Jonah shook his head, "No, I was trying to get into the garrison, but I was called here when you collapsed."

"I suppose you should return to your duties."

"Hm. Will you be alright?"

"I will rest and prepare for my father's dinner as planned."

Jonah left me to rest for the next few hours without much more than a goodbye. As the sol turned to evening, I bathed and dressed. After my nightmare, something inside told me that I needed to keep myself protected for the evening. So, I found a penknife in one of my drawers and tucked it away into my pocket. It was not often I felt like I had to be in such a position, but it was not as though I often found myself alone in Italy, save for Jonah.

I walked downstairs to the torch-lined beach, intoxicated by fire and smoke swaying in the soft breeze-like incense.

Not a single guest had arrived, yet a masked male played a violin on a stool towards the cove as I walked down. At first, the notes were playful, warm, and resonant, but they only added to the strange atmosphere as I arrived at the empty table at the centre of the beach. The sound exchanged for more mournful, intense notes until the instrument bore a long, shrill squeak.

"Your Highness!"

Dread clawed through me as I turned to the cove entrance, watching as Armaneos 'Corvelli', the male I wished not to lay eyes on, walked out with several other guards following him, each bearing insignia representing my father's army.

"Corvelli," I greeted, trying not to show an ounce of fear. "I did not know they invited lower-born to join my father's table."

The smug male walked towards me as his guards littered the beach,

"I know; I was surprised he would invite you, too. But, then again, it's only like the devil himself to show up when he's least wanted, isn't it?"

Corvelli was two feet taller and broader than Kaeltar, adding to his foreboding nature. One of his eyes was clouded in grey with a thick X scarred across it, while several of his teeth were laden in gold.

"An heir deserves the prime seat of the evening, does he not?" he said as he walked past me and over to the table, taking hold of one of the chairs and spinning it so that it would face outward, toward the violinist, who continued to play his dreadful forte. "Dinner shall soon be served."

He stood on the other side of the chair, tapping its tip, waiting for me to do as he bid. But, I remained standing, eerily aware facing away from the table meant whatever dinner would be served would not be in my stomach that evening. The entertainment created for me was part of the play.

"Come now, dear prince," he said. "You would not wish us to force you to sit down now, would you? I have it on good authority that this evening's event will keep you quite captivated."

I could sense the sarcasm in his tone, but I knew I only had two options. I could attempt to leave, be branded a coward, or play party to my father's tricks, find out what they had waiting for me, and then leave the following morning. I stepped forward, walking across the crunching sand to the chair before I took the seat, looking outward.

Corvelli leaned down, his foul breath melding with the atmospheric senses, "I hope you enjoy the show. Your feast shall wait for you upon its end."

From around the side of the cliff, several half-naked males pushed a wooden cart with a large sheet of tarpaulin over the top. They stopped close to me before each grabbed a corner of the cover. Neither of them removed it. A whiteboard was wheeled across the

321

sand and placed closer to Corvelli and me. On it were several lines, all waiting for a letter to be placed above them.

"I am sure you recognise this seedling game," Corvelli chuckled, "Hanged Man."

But it was not a seedling game. It was a captive's nightmare.

"Who is under the cloth?" I asked, looking back at the tarpaulin.

Corvelli waved his hand, and the material was pulled off, revealing the body of a male hanging upside down by his feet, almost wholly naked apart from pants to cover his private parts. Cuts and bruises laced his skin, while a hood covered his face.

But, I knew. Fuck, I knew. Eros was the victim.

"You know the rules," Corvelli said, "will the traitor live or die by your hand?"

"Set him free, Corvelli," I growled, standing up, but I heard the click of a gun to my left, feeling cool metal against my skin.

"Sit down, Prince Seraiah," Corvelli said as I turned my head to the other male holding a gun at me, not recognising him but not needing to in order to understand that I was not getting out of such games lightly.

"It is treason to kill a prince," I said to Corvelli, looking back at him.

"It would be treason if I did not have permission," he smirked, nodding back to the chair. "Now, shall we play, Your Highness?"

With hesitance, I took my seat, feeling the removal of the gun from my head as I looked over to Eros. Did Jonah know what was happening? I searched the area for him, even up to the house, but there was no sign of him anywhere.

"There shall be three rounds, all in English in celebration of your new English wife," he said, removing a knife from his pocket as he walked over to Eros' limp body, floating eerily in the wind by the rope. I stiffened at the mention of Arraetta, wanting to correct him instantly but knowing it was unnecessary in the current circumstances.

Another guard stepped up to the whiteboard, pulling a pen from his pocket like a teacher in a school.

Corvelli continued, "If you're fortunate to win, our prisoner here shall be released. But, if you lose, a life shall be lost. Either way, blood shall pour today. You should be happy that it is not yours and that someone here has the gall to stay silent when questioned. Wake him."

Two of the males who had brought Eros onto the beach stepped forward. One removed the material from Eros' face, while the other removed a small bottle of something and placed it below Eros' nose. Whatever was in it woke him quickly, and he gasped for air as he looked at his new surroundings. I noted how much worse the bruises were on his face, one eye far too puffy to see out of while there were lacerations across his cheek, deep enough to scar.

"Y-Your Highness?" he stuttered when he could finally see me in the torchlight, his good eye widening as he looked around.

"Let us begin!" Corvelli shouted, looking at me, "a letter, Your Highness."

Eros' wild eyes begged me for help as he looked between Corvelli and me, and I knew there was only one way to play the game.

"A," I called.

"Starting with the vowels," Corvelli called, earning a laugh from the guards across the beach. *Simpleton.* The letter was placed in the last word of the first sentence.

I called "E," and it, too, was added. O and I were placed on the board beside each other while Corvelli looked positively at them. I opted not for U but "S."

"S?" Corvelli asked, watching as the moderator hesitated and then shook his head, "Oh, no, dear prince, you guessed a letter wrong."

He stepped up to Eros, wandering around him, searching for a spot to inflict pain, until he stood to his back, looking over Eros' legs at me. I heard the grunt, followed by Eros' wail of pain, but did not see where Corvelli had inflicted the damage.

"They say to keep the knife in to prevent a bleed out," Corvelli called, walking around with blood dripping from his hands before he took out another blade from his waistband of weapons. I sat forward but did not go any further as I heard the clicking of the gun. "A letter, Your Highness?"

A slight growl rattled from my throat, but it was enough for the male beside me to hear. I could see blood dripping from Eros' back onto the wood below. He would die if I was not quick, but I also could not panic and make errors.

Next, I said 'T', which made the middle word into 'To', and the sentence read:

'I _O_ TO _ _ _AT_ER'

It opened up the final word, 'father'. I could see the word instantly, cursing inwardly that I would have to say such a sentence out loud. When I laid my eyes on that male, I would show him what it was like to make an enemy of a cursed prince.

"I bow to my father," I called, and Corvelli cheered, clapping loudly as he nodded to the moderating male, who filled in the letters.

"Congratulations, you passed round one, and only one tool was needed to cause damage. Let us move onto the second round and make it fun, hm?"

The moderator flipped the board over, revealing a much longer sentence, which would either be incredibly easy or terrifyingly tricky.

"Letter," he called.

Starting again, I called A, E, I, O and, this time, U. But it was as the moderator shook his head that I watched as Corvelli walked up to the bleeding Eros, placing a second knife in his back without mercy. Eros' agonising wail rattled me, and it seemed wherever Corvelli was putting the knife was paralysing him.

Corvelli stood to the side, nodding his head to the board with that smug look he adored. S, T, R. Successful. P. Unsuccessful. Corvelli was back behind Eros, looking down at his work for far too long, and I wondered what he was contemplating before he grabbed both handles of the knives, moving one hand up and one hand down. Eros howled in agony, and I was sure it could be heard for miles, but the violinist matched his yells with a piercing note.

Blood poured from Eros' back, and I was on my feet, uncaring that the gun was aimed at me again.

"You will kill him," I shouted.

"I never said I would play fair," Corvelli chortled, peering down at his work, "you are welcome to come and witness the work of art I am creating. But, remember, the more time paused, the quicker he shall die."

I looked at the board.

I A_ T_E _E_I _ _EIR TO T_E _I_A_T_RO_E A_ _ T_E_O_S
S_A_ _
_ORE_ER _OAT_E T_EIR _ _ESSI _ _.

I did not sit as I called more letters. H. L. N. G. I tucked my shoulders back and, without care, called out, "I am the devil heir to the Zikan throne, and The Gods shall forever loathe their blessing."

"Smart!" Corvelli nodded, smacking Eros' spine with unnecessary glee before lifting his hand to his mouth and licking the blood from it. "Fresh meat does have such a sweet tang to it when it is prepared in my hand."

"Get on with the fucking game!" I commanded, clenching my fist as I dared my dark side to overtake me so that I could kill the male. But, even as I tried to coax it to the surface, nothing would release from its grip. I watched as the moderator went around to the back of the board, painfully slowly, and started to write on it.

"The next sentence should be fairly easy for you," Corvelli called. I looked to Eros, whose begging gaze was on me.

My heart thudded as he mouthed, "by valour or virtue, for all. Let me die. For the good of Zika. Let me die."

Another impenetrable box started to crack, and I stepped back a little from its force, feeling each splinter grow inside my mind. Guilt. Henri Romano, a male whose father forced his hand to trading sides. A male who had devoted scorns of his life for the greater good of our people, dying publicly at the hands of my father.

I eyed the clifftops, searching for someone who would try to fight for justice for him, but only those who were present were aware of what was happening. Looking back at him, I nodded subtly before turning and returning to my throne.

By valour or virtue, for all. For Eros.

The board turned, and I sat down.

"Before we begin the final round," Corvelli called, "let us turn this cart around so His Highness can see our art."

Corvelli jumped off as I made eye contact with Eros for a final time, knowing that he would be dead before the night was over. And his death would mark the beginning of a new revolution.

I looked at his dripping back and the spine-lengthed chasm in its centre as Corvelli jumped back on, shouting for me to begin. I rattled off the vowels again and then with letters that I assumed were not part of the sentence.

X. Wrong. Corvelli ripped Eros' back apart, flailing the skin open, and I watched, heart in throat, vomit close to spewing, as Eros' insides were revealed for all to watch.

Y. Wrong. The sound of bones cracking as he pulled one part of Eros' rib cage outward like angel wings.

J. Wrong. The other bones joined, and someone nearby spewed. But, I did not remove my eyes from the massacre, not out of morbid fascination, but out of complete respect. Henri Romano would not die alone.

"Come on, Your Highness," Corvelli taunted, "I am sure you are smarter than this."

"Yes, I am," I said quietly, standing from my temporary throne and walking towards the cart, "I shall partake no more in these fascist games."

"So, you shall leave your friend here to rot?" he asked, looking at me with a blood-laden grin.

"Henri Romano is not my friend," I answered. "Do you truly believe that I, as the devil heir, would benefit from the friendship of such a lower-born, hm?"

Corvelli looked pleasantly surprised. "I suppose you will not mind if I finish my work."

"Or I can finish it for you," I replied, reaching for his knife.

Corvelli watched me, and I knew he was not stupid enough to hand over the knife, which I could use against him at any point. "I shall do the honours myself."

"As you wish," I replied, walking around to the front of Eros as Corvelli animalistically stood at his back. The hanged male was breathing heavily, and his eyes were closed, which I knew meant he had passed out. I was surprised that he was still alive, but such was a male who sought to fight against our system. A good, honest male.

Corvelli continued his work, which awoke Eros for a final time. His eyes looked at me with fear and agony.

"P-Please... ma...ma. Tell... I... I love... h-her."

A split hesitance flooded me, knowing what I had to do was worse than anything Corvelli was enjoying doing. But, I took the penknife from my pocket, placed it to his throat and slit it without remorse, watching as Corvelli stumbled back in shock.

Blood splattered onto the wooden cart as Henri Romano took his final breath.

"A gift for my father. A servitude to the king," I said, standing upright to look over at Corvelli, "from the devil heir himself."

Without a final word, I dropped my knife and stalked away from the bloodied angel and the tainted beach of guards towards the cove exit. As I walked, I looked upwards, only to glimpse my father looking down at us. I could tell from his expression that my actions irked and surprised him.

Little did he know that the next male I chose to kill would be him.

Merciless.

Cruel.

Quick.

There it is, Seraiah - the cursed prince.

TWENTY-THREE

I threw up harshly in my room, drowning it out by the noise of the shower until I had nothing more than bile left in my stomach. Eros was the first male I had ever slaughtered, a male who had shown me nothing but loyalty, and I had slit his throat to give him mercy. I had killed him for the welfare of our people. But, Empyreans, I was unsure how I would ever face his mother again with his blood washed over my hands.

I stared at them for a long time until I pulled myself, fully clothed, under the cold sprinkling of water for about an hour. And, then, I paced my courtyard in sodden clothes, not daring to peer down at the beach in case he was still hanging there for the birds to feast on in the morning.

I was nauseous as the events played over in my mind, and deliriously, time passed until I woke up, leaning against a wall in the courtyard, the morning sun basking on my face.

"Y-Your Highness," a female stuttered. I looked at her wearily as she looked down at me. "Should I call a doctor?"

I shook my head, bowing it a little, until I regained the strength to pull myself to my feet, "why are you in my quarters?"

"The Commander told me to wake you," she said apologetically, "there is a car waiting to take you back to the airport."

I nodded a few times before I started toward the stairs, uncaring that my clothes were dried in blood – Eros' blood – a mark I would bear as a symbol. Jonah was standing by a car at the entrance, dark sunglasses on.

"Morning," I grunted, climbing in. He also hopped in, and the driver set off a few minutes later once my cases were loaded. I could feel Jonah's gaze on me as I leaned against the window, eyes closed.

The journey to the airport felt long, and Jonah did not let me leave the car until I had changed my shirt into something less conspicuous. He did not say much more to me until we were halfway through the flight back.

"Seraiah," Jonah said from the opposite side of the plane, "Freddie has said he is happy to lead the moving of Her Highness and Genie today."

Oh, yes. We had spoken about moving Arraetta's belongings to the palace, but my mind was so soiled by blood that I had not thought about it. I was glad to know Genie and Arraetta had made amends, or at least was going to.

"Are they returning home?"

Jonah nodded, "Yes, thankfully. It seems Genie has decided to move to the house, but she also wishes to take the princess with her."

"I shall join too."

"I do not feel that is wise; you are unwell and need to rest."

"I am fine," I lied.

Jonah was quiet for a moment before clearing his throat and nodding, "Then, I will arrange for security for the trip."

"Nothing shall happen; I was alone with Freddie quarters ago."

"But you shall not again."

"Why do you seek to control every move I take?!" The rage was too much to hold back, but I did not wish to give Jonah the brunt of it. I only felt truly overwhelmed by the cloying grief daring to break free, twisted with the anger and fear which was already there.

"I am following protocol."

"No, you are not," I growled. "Even my father does not have it so strict. You are not in charge of me, Jonah."

"As I am aware," he grumbled, a half-glare on his face.

The two of us fell quiet as I contemplated the next move, which could be made since I showed my father I was not a force to be reckoned with. He had seen what I did. Emotionless, he might have looked, but I swear I saw the inklings of fear in his expression. I was going to win this game of chess, and the fucking throne was close to being in my grip.

"Were you aware of what happened on the beach last night?" I asked keenly.

Jonah looked at me, his impenetrable mask not failing as I searched for some emotion before he sighed, "I was informed there was a dinner that I was not invited to."

"There was no fucking dinner, Jonah!" I yelled, "Just manipulation and massacre."

The mask dropped, and guilt ricocheted across his face as he looked outward, "I had no say."

"In *Henri*'s death?" I replied, using his real name to add the needed effect, "First, I am succumbed to brutal punishment, and next, Henri is the participant in a game of Hanged Man. I thought you were his friend, Jonah. I thought you were *my* friend."

"Are we friends?" he chuckled humourlessly, "Would a friend take a knife to an ally's throat? You could have played the game and won."

"They were killing him."

"*You* killed him anyway."

"You fucking knew what they were doing, and you did not even stop them."

331

"I could not stop them, Seraiah!" he barked, "I do not have power on this side of the shore. I could not. His family could not have stopped them. You were his last hope. You were our last hope."

"Fuck hope," I tutted with a gasp of disbelief, "every resident of Sole could have swarmed that beach and saved him, yet you let Eros hang by his legs, brutally cut alive, skin flayed, bones broken all for fucking hope. Our people do not need hope, they need a fucking-"

"-A fucking what, huh? A saviour? No, they needed a prince they could believe in, a force they knew would secure their future, but instead, they got a prince who could only see what was right before him. You have been so focused on your gain, but it has been our effort to put you where you stand. By valour or virtue, for all, means nothing when one lies dead at your hand."

Cracks wore faster on the locked guilt coffer, waiting to be freed, barely holding the lid down by its weakening restraints. Silence settled between us as I toyed over his words. The foundations of our friendship had been crumbling for winters, but only then did I notice the fractures. Jonah was more reticent, argued often, and kept his distance whenever possible. Our relationship was hanging by the ends of a thin, wilted thread. He had only remained by my side because he cared for me as the future monarch, protecting me enough to get me into the position that was rightfully my own.

"You and I are no longer friends," he said, turning his head. "Ha, I would not say we have been anything of the sort for so long. I am just thankful I can tell you this now before all our lives change... You are my king, and I will work only as your commander."

Jonah looked at me, the mask gone as tears settled in his eyes with nothing but truth set deep within them. A lifetime of friendship was over in seconds, with not a thread of hope appearing to regain it again. Fuck, hope. Hope was pathetic; it was for fools who only wanted to grasp onto the frayed tendrils of reality.

But, still, a tear left my eye, and I swiped my hand across my cheek, excusing it for tiredness rather than any real emotion I had toward my lifetime companion. Not only had I cruelly lost Eros, but I was also lost at sea, watching my friends disappear one by one when they were most needed.

I only hoped Arraetta would be my anchor and bring me back ashore.

As the plane landed, silences were sentenced, and we returned to the house with tension as prevalent as ever. Part of me wondered whether I might beg the male for forgiveness, but I had my pride and would wait until Jonah came to me to reconcile.

In the courtyard, I was greeted by Freddie and Genie. "Cousin."

"I see you have returned," I smiled softly, "I was surprised to hear that you had come back so quickly."

"I was informed you collapsed again," Freddie said, shifting his eyes to Jonah, standing near the vehicles. I noted that Freddie caught onto the tension, looking between us before he shrugged.

While I would have liked to shower and nap, I decided to wait until the move was complete, as I knew it would require some energy. While Freddie and Genie went for breakfast, I was far too nauseous to think about eating, so I took a trip to my office to be closer to the generator and try to sate my energy a little. I supposed to outsiders it might be odd, but I felt better knowing I could replenish some of my life force.

I did not expect, however, to find several things that had been tinkered with, nor that, being in Italy, I had not detected such a presence. Yet, I honed into my sigils, trying to feel for any remnants, only to compare it to that of Arraetta's when she had been in my room sols before. I wondered what she had been looking for, but I could not find anything unusual as I shuffled through things.

After some rest, I made my way back up to the main house,

stopping when I found a tome lying on the floor without a home and picked it up. Pride and Prejudice. Zikan edition.

I chuckled, "I wonder what she expected to do with such a tome."

Keeping it in my hand, I decided that later, should either of us not be too exhausted, I would invite her to the library for more wine. Maybe we could revisit the place we had sols before. Walking into the centre of the library, I had to take a second glance as I saw how the painting had been amended – the work of Arraetta.

She had painted over the symbols, adding incredible details of our hands intertwined alongside the intricate detailing of Ryazark's rolling hills. It seemed she had managed to do quite a lot of work on it, but it was still incomplete. Maybe I would allow her to finish what she started, or I might add to the painting myself. But, there was no time.

I placed the tome on the table and left the room, knowing it was time to move on to arranging the move from their home to ours. I met Freddie downstairs while Genie went to collect Arraetta.

"Will you not eat?" Freddie asked worriedly.

"Maybe later. I am not sure if I could keep anything down."

"What happened in Italy?"

I swallowed, vividly remembering Eros' torture and subsequent death before I tucked my shoulders back, "Eros is dead."

Freddie's brows lifted, shock rippling his expression as he took in my words. "How?"

"Corvelli."

Slick, wet slicing of skin whispered in my ears as I thought back to the knife which tore down Eros' back. I shivered, trying to remove it from my mind.

"Fucking hellsworn," Freddie growled, fists clenched, but little did he know it was I who drew his last breath. He cleared his throat, "is that why you and Jonah are at arms?"

"It does not matter. It is a matter between us."

Freddie held his hands up, "okay. It is a shame you cannot even tell your trustworthy cousin."

"Do I have one of those?" my lip twitched.

Freddie grinned widely as our conversation ended, watching Genie and Arraetta appear at the top of the stairwell, looking down at us. I swore I saw Arraetta whisper my name before she followed Genie down, with Alex following behind.

Genie curtseyed as per protocol, but I had to stop Arraetta. "You need never curtsey."

"But Genie did," she pointed at her friend. At least nothing had changed since my departure, which I was thankful for.

"Then why do you bow?"

"That is because we are men of the house," I lied, feeling like it was far too early in her ascension to impart that she was of a much higher rank than any of us had ever met. I turned to Freddie and said, "Shall we go?"

Arraetta walked a little ahead of me, her hand swinging idly by her side as though she wished me to slip my fingers into the cracks.

"I thought you were in Italy?"

"I was," I replied, teasing her hand. "I arrived in the morning but caught a flight back late evening because the distance was a little... difficult."

It was difficult because of the nightmare, and it was devastating because my ally was dead. She did not question further; I guessed she had the same feeling. Freddie instructed the two females to enter the middle vehicle, followed by Alex, and we walked over to speak with Jonah. Jonah was flanked by two drivers and three guards, including Travis. Alex, soon, joined at a distance.

"Okay, listen up," Jonah said, loud enough for everyone to hear, "Today we are journeying to Hackney as a convoy, where we shall collect items from the tenth storey of a block of flats before returning here no later than eighteen hundred hours. In the convoy, we have present His Royal Highness, Prince Seraiah, and Her Royal Highness, Princess Arraetta, as well as our two guests, Sir Frederique and Lady Genevieve. This is a matter of high security, and I should expect everyone involved to do their duty in protecting the heirs of our land. Do you copy?"

"Sir," the echoes of those around us called.

Jonah looked at me before shifting his eyes to Freddie, "I expect you not to crash the car, Freddie; it would be unfortunate for me to have to revive you for a scolding."

Freddie grinned, "do not worry, I am the best driver in the business. I have only crashed a car twice, and only once was it my fault."

Even Freddie's forward humour made me grin, but I was surprised Jonah had allowed him to drive. As we were in a convoy, the car in front of us would be in charge of the speed we took.

"Make sure it is not a third. Otherwise, I might revoke your privileges," Jonah squinted his eyes as though he were threatening him.

Freddie flashed him a smile, "Of course, my liege. I shall stay in top form."

He added a salute before the middle car powered up, making us look in its direction. Genie wound down the window for some fresh air, uncaring about the group of us.

Jonah tutted, "Make sure to watch your spiritsworn, Freddie."

Freddie slapped him softly on the shoulder, "Wow, you are hilarious, Jonah. I wonder where you learnt some effortless remarks because they are definitely from your father. Oh, speaking of him, did yours threaten you into breaking off the friendship with our dear prince here?"

I rolled my eyes, "let us go."

"I just want to know if this is going to become more awkward," he pointed between us, "does Alex know? It is unfair if I do not know the meaning behind this feud."

The two of us ignored him and moved to our respective vehicles. Alex, too, said nothing. Freddie followed, muttering about how unfair it was that Alex had more knowledge than him before he opened my car door. I climbed in before he shut it and got into the driver's seat.

It was overbearing to be in such a confined space with Arraetta, remembering the delight of touching her soft skin two nights prior. I would have rather dwelt on such a thought than that of Eros' blood on my hands, but it seemed I struggled with keeping such imagery from my mind.

The convoy to London began, conversation light, whilst I attempted to quell the nausea. I took hold of Arraetta's hand at some point, stroking the soft skin between her thumb and forefinger to soothe my ache, and it helped even when Freddie decided to pull a small stunt which ended up with us being reprimanded by Jonah when we pulled over. His newfound dislike for me, or one which was hidden before, shone more prominently as he commanded our obedience.

Upon arrival at the apartment building, my thoughts of my new feud disappeared as I gazed upon the dire concrete blocks. Even if I felt unwell, Arraetta had climbed the stairwell every sol just to get to and from her home, so I decided my feelings were unnecessary.

Leaving Jonah and some of the guards by the vehicles, Genie and Freddie led the procession up the concrete staircase, whilst Arraetta and I followed, with Alex and Travis trailing behind. It was an ample opportunity for us to catch up a little, whilst I concentrated on not sounding like I had been smoking forty a sol.

On the tenth floor, we were greeted by Freddie and Genie kissing in the doorway. I could see Arraetta's dismay and whispered, "Do not be jealous of them," before walking past her into her room.

It was not aesthetically pleasing, but I could tell it once had been Arraetta's haven. Sadly, the foul smell of dampness lingering from the mould in the corner was far too unpleasant not to notice, and I wondered if it ever made Arraetta unwell. Maybe if she was human. Just as I had seen outside, through her window, I noticed the sheet-covered canvases.

"So, this is where the magic is made, huh?" I pulled at one of them to reveal a painting of a street in London or the start of it.

"Did you not see this when you came to find me?"

"No, we did not make it inside your flat. I could not detect your energy in the building; we merely arrived here."

I did not wish to relive such a memory, remembering how we had found her covered in blood. Like Eros. Fuck, there was too much blood on my hands, clouding my mind. Red. Crimson ichor. Who would be next?

"Arrived here?"

"Yes, much like how you disappeared."

"I don't understand."

"I shall show you soon," I replied, unsure I would ever take her to the rings. I would just make her understand in some other way. I pulled another sheet off a portrait, revealing hundreds of blurred lines, chaotically showcasing the peaceful nature of a world my heart ached for. It was the river in Zika, with one channel which forked toward Arboralis Mountain, which had a humongous tree pouring from its pinnacle like an umbrella. The other, unseen, led to the large town of Luminara, where my home was fortified.

"It's..."

"Beautiful," I breathed, kneeling as I traced her painting, "not at all like the one in the library."

"Sorry?"

I stood, "I went to the library this morning and saw that you had painted over the other parts on the canvas."

"Oh, sorry, I-"

"-No, it is okay," I waved, "but this is a different piece altogether. This is the Wicker Windmill."

"How... how do you know?"

"I am unsure," I replied, diligently stroking the ridges. "I suppose I can see its intricacies."

"But no one has ever been able to see my work."

"You are saying this to me," I chortled, "we are the most in-sync people in the universe, are we not?"

She nodded slowly, "I guess so."

"I remember how you brought my version of this painting alive, the one in the downstairs sitting room. Do you remember?"

"I... yes, I do a little. You saw that, too?"

"Yes," I replied, "but only a fraction. I felt like a spectator watching a moving image."

Or, at least, I felt more like a spectator witnessing Arraetta watching the image come to life.

"I can... sometimes I can see the image moving, but only when it is truly finished, if an artist's work ever can be."

"Is this finished?" I queried.

"This was my first piece, following my blackout at twenty," she knelt beside me. "It was the first time I had created art like this, with the electrical lines. It was as though it was all I could see, but as I pressed my hand to the drawing, it would somewhat come to life, and sometimes I would just go there - into the painting."

"Can you show me?"

"I can try," she said, unsure how to do such a thing.

"You could try using Rakatan," I suggested, remembering that it was used extensively in the earlier sols of training our power to help us control it. "It is a form of breathing; it allows you to hone your power into something. You breathe in and out several times, feel like you wish to be there - in the painting or the place - and allow your body to take you there. Your power, naturally, should work."

I was unsure if it would work. Arraetta had to shift her mindset to being in the depths of the painting rather than simply imagining an image inside her head.

"Does that work for you?"

"Not always," I replied, "Truthfully, I have not had the blessing of being able to revisit a place like this for a long time, no matter how hard I come to try. I suppose the incident - the attack on our realm - locked away some of my more treasured memories."

Locked away, but only by my hand. A decision was made to create coffers, locked doors, and places I could only visit, if I wished to, were deep inside my mind. Until recently, at least.

"In the library the other day, you took me to a place. Is that not a memory?"

I took a moment to think, "It is something. Although I cannot say what exactly, a memory, a vision, but you are wondering how I managed to get there? I did not use Rakatan; I have mastered the art of using ancient writing. That is a story for another time, however. For now, let us try Rakatan."

Soon, our hands were placed similarly to the library, except hers was on top of mine.

"Close your eyes. Breathe in... breathe out.... Breathe in... breathe out..." I spoke gently. Her body relaxed with each passing second, and not a single sound outside the room distracted her. "Now, imagine you are in this painting, in the place, and feel it. Feel it within your body. Allow your power to push through from yours to mine."

I was unsure if anything would happen, as I could not feel a single vibration of her energy outside the tension her body ached with whilst she struggled. But something seemed to change dramatically – a shift in her vitality, a pulse of power which felt like a soft morning breeze until the golden hue washed over my aura. The low hum of the building melted away until the sounds of twinkling birds tickled my ears.

I did not open my eyes for a long moment, fearful that what I thought I was hearing was just a window having been opened. But, a whetted wisp of a breeze brushed against my face, and I finally looked. Above, a bird's wings caught in its drift, landing on a nearby branch while the river whooshed by, its sound melodious and real to my ears.

And, for the first time in scorns, I felt harmonious.

I was in Zika.

TWENTY-FOUR

This land. This beautiful, damaged, unholy land we had left behind was once perfect and pristine, showing no signs of darkness other than the shadows of the trees. On the riverbank, the old windmill wheel churned away at its waters in prime view. It was a different view, a portal to my dreams and desires – things I did not wish to share with anyone other than Arraetta. Oddly, I could shift, wading through tempered waters, feeling its silky nature brush against my skin. Tranquillity. Birds tweeted, wind brushed the trees, and the gentle creak of the mill sighed in my ears.

Had I genuinely returned to Zika? I could almost hear the sounds of a vehicle on the hidden round through the tree verge whilst, somewhere nearby, seedlings laughed as they played. I ascended onto the bank, closing in on the mill, captivated by its beauty. A wicker structure created as an art piece for the royal family and a freedom for when I rebelled as a seedling.

The ripples of the silky wood grove tickled my fingers as I wandered around the towering structure, watching the turbines move. Emotion played enemy as tears threatened to spill, but I only laughed sadly, wishing it were more than just a fantasy. The serenity barely lingered before a thundering cloud echoed in the distance.

I turned to the skies, noticing the glimmer of the mirage I was stranded in. Reality hit far too quickly, and I saw the cracks of illusion falling into place as they merged into delusion. Another crackle thundered meters away, and a ray of light poured from the sky down to the other side of the windmill.

Voices coaxed me in its direction, pausing when I saw a young seedling on the bank, standing up from where he was reading a tome. Two other beings had appeared nearby, like a hologram. Instantly, I recognised them as the messengers of the Highest Gods, and the seedling was me. But, I did not remember it being anything other than a dream when such a time happened, yet it seemed so real.

"Young prince," one of them knelt before me, "you are destined for a great fate that only you can be the arbitrator of. It has been decreed you bear the soul of one of the Kindred Spirits. The other you shall meet in time, she is the one you are destined to be bonded to in order to restore peace in the universe that your soul's fracture has rattled."

"But, young one, whilst this fate has been imparted on you," the other continued. I stepped forward to listen, not remembering an extended message, "There is also a greater destiny which shall determine the trajectory of the universe. Whilst you may become a great king, you may also become a dark and treacherous ruler, and only the decisions you come to make shall decide. This destiny was presented to you as part of a cataclysmic cycle of events which occurs throughout each of your mortal lives."

"What do you mean?" I called, and the illusion faltered, pausing like a film frame. Yet, one of the messengers turned and walked toward me.

"Seraiah, Prince of Zika," they said, "you are gravely self-serving and only follow what your heart desires. Yet, despite your nature, you can steer the hand of your fate. When the bond has been completed, a dark force shall test you, fracturing your mortal souls from one another and only then shall the gates open and your true

343

path will become unveiled."

Our souls will fracture? Gates would open?

The messenger turned to walk away, and I felt compelled to grab them, but my hand slipped through the fabric of deception. The messenger was not truly present in this world, just as I was not - a faded reality masked in a hallucinatory nightmare.

They said, "You must return to the human world, Prince Seraiah. The goddess Arraetta requires your assistance."

"Arraetta," I breathed, pulling back completely from the facade until I stared at the lifeless artwork of lines. I coughed lightly, feeling the build-up of perspiration on my back until I looked down at my hand, noting the lack of Arraetta's warm touch.

"Seraiah!"

Freddie's worried voice pierced through the cracks, and I stumbled out of the room towards where Freddie stood by the front door. Before us, Genie was tentatively shuffling closer to Arraetta, whose head was tilted up towards the sky as though she was seeing something we could not. It seemed Genie's apprehensiveness was due to a veil of translucent mist.

As Genie decided to try touching it, Freddie quickly rushed to her and pulled her back, deciding to attempt the move himself. But as his hand touched it, we could hear and smell the skin searing. Freddie gripped his wrist quickly, shaking as it burned him, but he held in his shout of anguish by gritting his teeth.

I did not look at him long enough to give him sympathy as I noticed Arraetta make a sudden movement forward, dangerously close to climbing over the perimeter to her death. My heart thudded as panic washed over me; trying to push forward to her, but I was forced to retreat because of the strength of her power.

"Arraetta!" I shouted as though she was a mile away, whilst I could hear the concerned echoes from guards ten storeys below.

Time slowed as I dared myself to push into the barrier, only to be pulled back by Freddie.

My worst fear was coming true. I was losing Arraetta to a force unknown before I had a chance to get to know her, and I felt useless not knowing how I could help. I could not lose her; the Gods would not let such a thing happen.

"Tom?" Genie said, looking to our right. We turned to watch the arrival of the young boy, who had partially helped us on the eve of the ball. He ignored us, shuffling through the veil as though it were non-existent, before he took her hand, pulling her back to the harshness of reality.

"Hey!"

The veil surrounded her immediately, and she looked at him with scarlet-shot eyes, blood oozing from her nose and ears.

"Tom, this isn't the best time," Genie said softly, finally able to place a steadying hand on Arraetta's shoulder.

Drip. Drip. Drip.

More blood. More fucking blood.

Eros' flayed skin tormented my mind, his organs throbbing openly. Yet, it was his face and body, which was replaced by Arraetta's. Empyreans, I could not lose her too. The blood dripped incessantly onto the concrete floor below.

Let me die. Kill me.

I watched as she shakily placed her hand over her nose before dropping to her knees with a harsh thud.

"Hey... you," she breathed.

"You owe me ten pounds!" Tom stomped, but I could only concentrate on Arraetta, who was close to becoming incapacitated.

I had killed Eros. I could kill this seedling.

I caught sight of Jonah, Alex and Travis arriving breathlessly at the top of the stairwell, all stopping to witness the situation before them. Arraetta wiped her nose with her forearm, smearing the blood onto her cheek. Nausea fuelled my catastrophic thoughts, and I felt useless as I watched the scene before me.

Useless hellsworn fucker.

Selfish.

Cursed.

The devil heir.

A clump of tissues was placed in my hand. I looked down at it before looking up at Freddie, who silently nodded to Arraetta. He told me to *go to her*, and I did, because whatever emotion was simmering inside me overwhelmed my sanity.

"T-Ten... yes, yes, I do," she stumbled as I knelt before her, using the tissues to mop up her blood, uncaring that my hands were visibly shaking, "Ten pounds."

The itch in my skull ran down my neck at this new emotion, daring to break free from its coffer. It must have splintered somewhere on the lid as puffs of energy broke from its seal. I recognised the emotion as it melded with fear and anger. It was grief. The tendrils of it, but fuck, it was there.

"Why do you always have blood on you?" Tom asked, perplexed. He shifted his eyes to me as though to accuse me of such things, glaring when our eyes met before looking back at her.

I was so close to telling the seedling to fuck off, to wringing my hands around his neck and strangling him, to demand he be locked up for such absurdities at such a fragile time. I pulled my wallet out of my pocket and found a twenty-pound note in the clump of funds that had never been spent. I handed it to him, saying, "Here you go. How about I give you twenty instead?"

Arraetta did not notice what I had done, stumbling to her feet before pushing by everyone, muttering to herself *ten pounds* as she went back inside. Tom looked like he had won the lottery, attempting to skip off to wherever his hole was, but he was caught by Travis, who pulled him off somewhere. He would only reprimand the seedling, I was sure.

Calling after Arraetta, I followed her inside, passing Freddie as he attempted to make a phone call to someone.

I heard Arraetta repeating to herself inside her bedroom as she manically searched her possessions for something - money. I tried to stay behind her, coaxing her to remain calm. I needed her to know everything was okay, and that she did not need to do anything for the boy. All the while, I attempted to stop myself from breaking down in front of her.

She knelt beside her bed, gasping as more blood leaked from her, and I mimicked her stance as she stared at her shaky hands.

Please stop. You are hurting yourself. Please. The words were daring to break free from my throat, thick with tears and nausea. I lifted my hands to her face and turned it so her ichor-stricken eyes were on me.

I whispered thickly, "You are okay, Arraetta. Breathe."

My words stopped the frantic nature of her task, and she let out a shaky breath, "I... ten pounds."

"I have sorted it," I told her, trying to keep my eyes on hers, but she only continued to find the money.

Give me your pain. Let me hold it for you.

No longer able to stand her erratic behaviour, I pulled her into me, allowing her to struggle as she tried to tug away, muttering frantically, until finally, her tension began to dissipate.

"Marie is on her way," Freddie stated from the door, but I did not turn to him. I refused to leave Arraetta, holding her close, listening to the soft sounds of her jagged breath until she eventually gave in to the slumber her body needed.

"Seraiah," Freddie's worried voice echoed, but he did not come closer as raw, unforgiving emotion tore from my throat. I buried my head into Arraetta's neck, uncaring for the grief and guilt which rippled from me. If I had not wanted her to use her power to show me Zika, she would not have suffered as she had suffered. She would not have bled as she had bled. She would not have nearly met with the God of Death.

I felt the overwhelming pull of the guilt coffer shattering its locks, and I could not do anything to return and restore it as it had been. The grief box continued to whisper its scent from the lid's cavity, but did not wholly break as the other had. Still, it perfumed every other broken emotion and clawed up my spine like a strand of DNA, melding to create something I was not.

Fear. Anger. Guilt. All opened for the world to witness. But how could I sustain such impenetrable feelings when each coffer had opened since she arrived? Could I genuinely lock away such sentiments when she had seen them all?

I was unsure how long I cried against her, but at some point, I rose with her limp body and tucked her into her bed, peering down at her blood-stained face.

A flash of Eros' face rippled with it, but I swallowed the guilt and took a deep breath. I gave Eros mercy for the pain he was burdened with, and I would remember that going forward. Focusing on him meant I could not concentrate on my fated one, so I had to tuck such thoughts away. I would not forget Eros; he was a tool in my arsenal I would use to spark the next battle inside my home. And, nothing would stand in my way of protecting Arraetta.

Someone light-footed walked in behind me, and I turned to see Genie enter the room with a damp cloth in her hand. She said nothing about my red eyes, although I was sure she noticed.

"It's like déjà vu," she commented before wiping the blood from Arraetta's face, "did something happen in here?"

Could I tell her somehow Arraetta possessed an ancient skill which brought a painting to life? I was unsure whether I could reveal her secrets or whether it would have consequences for us in the future.

"No," I replied. "What about the child?"

Genie rolled her eyes, "Tom. The neighbour's son. They treat him like shit anyway, and he doesn't get much from his mum, so Arraetta gives him money to help now and then. He's an ungrateful little shit."

I chuckled at Genie's blatant dislike, "I suppose if he had not been here, then..."

"I don't want to speak about it!" she said, placing her hands over her ears before taking a deep breath. "Let's try to forget about it. I'll watch her if you want to go and get some fresh air. You look like you could use some."

Fresh air. Sleep. A new mind. But I did not want to leave Arraetta again. I was almost fearful that something else would happen and being away would cause her to make a secondary descent over the balcony. I shivered at the cloying thought of her plummeting to the ground. It did not happen; I had to remember that.

Reluctantly, I left the females and walked out to the balcony, where Freddie and Jonah were quietly conversing. Travis loitered near the staircase, presuming he had a stern conversation with Tom.

"How is she?" Freddie asked.

"She is sleeping."

"We are going to go straight back to the palace once she wakes," Jonah stated, "we will wait for Marie, but a contractor can sort the rest of this."

"I agree," Freddie nodded.

"Let us wait to hear what Arraetta wishes," I said, quickly adding, "This is not me going against your wishes, Commander. Her position holds much precedence over any of ours, so it is right we wait for

349

her command."

"A higher position does not detract from my position, Your Highness."

"As I am aware," I replied bitterly, "but you cannot make unjustified commands."

"It is quite justified," he glowered, "our future queen is sick, and we cannot provide her proper care so far away from home. And, you..."

"What?" I snapped.

"You collapsed yesterday... and after the events...," he replied with a fill-in-the-gaps tone.

Freddie's eyes flitted between us, cogs turning in his mind, before he decided to interject, throwing his arms around our shoulders. "Let us not fight, my good friends. Arri has yet to awaken, so let us see how she is before we return home."

Jonah and I stared each other down for a long moment before Jonah tutted, shrugging out of Freddie's grip, "Okay, then we shall wait for sleeping beauty to arise from her slumber and see what demands she wishes to impose on me."

His comment was harsh and pointed. But, I suddenly realised something evident. Just like his hidden dislike for me for who knows how long, he did not like Arraetta.

"You truly do not like her, do you?" I blinked, flabbergasted.

"It does not matter who I like or do not like," he replied bluntly, walking away. "It is a shame you have become such a changed male since her arrival. I shall wait for Marie's arrival downstairs."

With my fists clenched, I almost lunged at him, but Freddie pushed me back sharply by my chest. "What is with you two? This is so out of the blue. You have been friends for longer than I have lived in Zika. You have been through so much together."

"He decided we are no longer friends. Apparently, I have changed, and that is his reason."

Or, maybe the reason was because I slit Eros' throat.

"That is it? You both have to reconcile. If not for the sake of both of you, but for Amity and our wives. We need to be a team."

"He is just dividing us ahead of my reign," I replied solemnly, "our friendship is not my priority."

My priority was the female lying in bed and the throne I would somehow rip from underneath my father soon after the stunt he pulled. One which I would gracefully gift to Arraetta when I retrieved it.

The two of us waited on the balcony for Marie's arrival, but Arraetta woke sooner and I was back inside the half-packed flat instantly. I peered into the room, seeing Arraetta lying with her arm covering her eyes. Headache.

I went into the kitchen and looked in a few cupboards until I saw a box of paracetamol. I poured her a glass of water before going into the room.

"Here," I said to Genie, handing them over.

"Arri, sit up and take these," she half-commanded her friend. Arraetta finally removed her arm, looked at me, and slowly shifted her gaze to Genie. She took the water and paracetamol.

"I'm going to check on Freddie," Genie said softly, leaving the room.

I tentatively walked to the side of the bed and sat down, stroking her forehead, no doubt looking worried and weary. "I was very worried. You do not deserve this. I should not have done that to you."

"It's not your fault," she smiled, "it's what happens in the build-up to my blackout."

The blackout, which had only been mentioned in conversations, meant that whatever was to come would be more horrendous than

I had already witnessed. I was unsure whether I needed to prepare the house in case something more significant happened, but maybe she was safe under the shield.

"So, that was not your blackout weeks ago?" I asked, and she turned her head away as though ashamed. "You must be open with us, Arraetta, I cannot help you if you do not let me."

"I don't need your help," she replied in quiet harshness before lying down again. "It's not been so bad since what happened."

"I do not wish for you to go through this alone. Your burden is as much mine-"

"No, Seraiah-"

"Yes, Arraetta," I said, stroking her hand for comfort. "you and I... we must go through these things as one now; I cannot see you like this again. Do you know how hard it was for me to see you the way you were after the incident? It has scarred my mind; I cannot... I cannot see this happen to you again; there must be a way for it to stop."

Arraetta gently placed her hand on my face and stroked it, impulsively forcing me to release the frightened breath which had taken hold of me, "it's only every four years."

But it should never be. I had this mawkish need to shout at her, make her understand that my wife should never have to be witnessed with blood pouring from the passages in her face, nor should she be experiencing things other mortals could not comprehend. She should be happy - she must be. Never worried, never frightened, never succumbing to anything beneath her.

She was a queen, a fucking goddess, a rare beauty made to be bowed before by every ephemeral being. And, by every God.

Marie arrived seconds later, and I had little option but to leave her to her work. Arraetta decided she wanted to stay and finish the task, much to Jonah's disdain, so we divided and conquered the next few hours. Guards were tasked with taking the boxes and items from the top of the balcony and take them to the truck. Freddie and Genie packed Genie's possessions, the kitchen and the bathroom, and Arraetta and I solely worked on Arraetta's room and some of the hallway.

The final items of the room were her paintings, "You should take them."

"And store them where? One of your lavish rooms?" she asked.

I chuckled, "you... you can store them, with my paintings, in the basement."

"How come I've not seen this secret basement?"

"Secret? What do you think we keep down there?"

"Who knows?" she jested, lightly wiggling her eyebrows. I wondered whether she had some sort of fantasy that I had a red room, but even I would not have something so lascivious in a place where my life bringers could roam.

"The baths are down there, I suppose." I reached down for two of the paintings.

"Baths?" she asked, followed me as I left the room.

"Yes, we have Roman baths underneath the house."

"You built your house on Roman baths?"

I laughed lightly, "No, we had similar ones in the palace, but they were much bigger. When we arrived here, my father commissioned them after hearing about Roman history."

"Is that why you always disappear?"

"Are you always looking for me, Arraetta?"

"You wish," she blushed, turning her head. But I knew she had been as her visit to my office showed she enjoyed exploring.

"The baths are rarely used by anyone but myself."

Peering down to where the removal truck was parked, I noticed a procession of black-marked vehicles surrounding it. Several locals looked curious about what was happening. The creeping itch of envy was palpable as I saw Freddie and Genie laughing lightly with Jonah. As my mood soured, I could not stop the subtle glare in their direction. It was easy for my lifelong friend to converse with others as though he had not shattered our peace.

"You may use them if you wish," I said, reverting to our conversation as I stepped away from the edge.

"Is it... clean?"

I chortled, "Arraetta, I cannot comprehend where you get your thoughts from sometimes."

"Why do you not shorten your sentences?" she asked, speaking like a robot.

"Once again, you are mocking me," I tutted, abbreviating my sentence, "*you're* mocking me."

"I like it that you are posh," she mocked, leaning against the balcony, facing the door to her old home. I almost leapt to pull her away, but knew she would not fall. If she did, I would go with her. "It makes me feel as though I have stepped into a different century."

I was unsure if I would have described my accent as posh; I was just not a native English speaker. Over the winters, I had not abbreviated my words because they were more innate, much like how I learned to speak in Zika. My accent was a mixture of Received Pronunciation and Zikan.

Abbreviating one's words is frowned upon in the elite class, and one must learn to speak correctly. The words I remembered were said by one of my scholars, who would reprimand me whenever I disagreed with her. Ultimately, I gave in and rarely shortened my sentences. However, I wondered whether I might learn to if it saved her mocking.

"I suppose it is a different time," I replied, stepping to stand over her, close enough for my breath to whisper teasingly against her skin. She allowed the contact for a few seconds before tilting her head to the side, the soft hue of red brightening her cheeks. I asked, "Why do you shy away from me, Arraetta?"

"I'm not shying away from you," she stuck out her tongue like a seedling before pushing me away, "so, when are we going to see these baths?"

"Whenever you would like," I said, eyes washing down her body as she dramatically stretched. It seemed the adventures of the last couple of sols did not stop the tenting in my jeans as my cock threatened to release itself. Oh, how I dared to strip her naked and fuck her hard in front of the entirety of London, not caring who sees.

Her soft moans echoed in my ears, and I cleared my throat, "You are such a child."

"I'm older than you, remember," she answered, teasingly bringing back the subject to one we had during our flirtations in the staircase only hours before, "six millennia, was it?"

"Six million, more like," I said, and she gasped.

I was glad we were playfully flirting again, but it did little to suppress my need for her. "Do you remember at the ball when you said that if I wanted you to sleep with me, I should just ask?"

"Do you remember how you told me that I was a perfect example of a human woman?" she retorted so quickly I could only wince. However, she was not a human woman; she was a deity.

"I did not mean it as it appeared."

"I have slept with other men."

Yes, and I would quite happily hunt every male down and sever their heads, but it was not as though I had not bedded other females in my lifetime. I would just make sure that my insatiable touch sullied the memory of them.

"I have no doubt you have," I said casually, "I actually was trying to tell you that–"

"–I'm so indescribably beautiful that I cannot compare to the heights of human women."

"I do not think it would be wise for you to lower your standards to those of a human," I commented. "I do believe you are indescribably beautiful."

She blushed, "Genie's human... She's beautiful."

I nodded from side to side, debating. I agreed that Genie had something about her, but nothing could compare her to the heights of Arraetta's beauty.

"Although I can agree in some parts," I said, tilting her to face me, "she is but a drop on your perfection."

She licked her lower lip, and I desired to kiss the soft skin. Gently, I lifted my hand and stroked my thumb across it while leaning closer. Empyreans, I was thirsty for her taste, knowing I would only be slightly satisfied once our lips met. But our moment did not happen as Genie's voice echoed close to the peak of the stairwell. In a way, I was thankful for the interjection because I could only imagine what Sheika wished to say if I had done more than *hold her hand*.

And, fuck, I would complete the bond once the electric fusion between us hit as our lips touched. My being throbbed with need, lust, and desire. Empyreans, how long would I have to wait until the ceremony?

Once time had passed, we could be together without anyone stopping us.

I would kill someone for less.

TWENTY-FIVE

U pon returning to the house, Genie directed the staff to where all the boxes needed to go while I steered Arraetta toward the library. I wanted to spend more time alone with her, away from prying eyes, and rest after an exhausting and chaotic sol.

But my mother seemed to have other plans as she made eye contact with me from the top of the stairwell, always arriving at the right time to soil my plans. I mean, what else would my mother have to say? Would she reprimand me for the events in Italy? Did she know that I had taken a knife to Eros' throat? Would she side with my father?

"Mother, are you well?" I asked as we stepped into the silence of the upper west wing.

"Yes, I am soon to go to bed," she smiled, although I knew such sentiments were only a facade for my wife. "Arraetta, I am very excited that we have moved you in so quickly."

"I haven't brought much."

"That is because she does not own much," I added, causing Arraetta to, automatically, smack me on the shoulder as though I had just spilt her best-kept secret. A blush undulated across her face as she realised she had hit a prince, even if it was only in jest. Still, my mother and I shared in the humour.

I shifted the conversation to Zikan, "Have you spoken to Father?"

She nodded, "I will speak to him once he returns. For now, make sure that she is settled here. Let us not embark on further feuds when this is the happiest time of our lives."

The happiest time of my life it might have been, but I could not agree that it was hers. She must have known what my father did to Eros, destroying the life of my mother's friend. But even then, I knew my mother did not have *friends*. She used and manipulated people into doing her bidding. Such was the power of the throne.

"It is not I that will cause a feud."

She returned to English, "Charles will be back tomorrow; it is high time we start to make plans."

Joyous.

"Plans?" Arraetta squealed.

"For Iontine and the bonding ceremony," my mother replied. I had not even broached the subject of the bonding ceremony, and the idea probably seemed scary to a female who had been brought up in the human world and had no recollection of her past.

I tucked my hand around Arraetta's waist and squeezed her hip, feeling her relax as I spoke to my mother in Zikan. "She knows nothing about the bonding ceremony, but I will see to it."

I could tell by my mother's alarmed face she was sure I would have already spoken to Arraetta about it. But how could I have done it? One conversation about Kindred Spirits had been easy, but telling her we were soon to be married was a more significant topic to broach. Without much more of a word but a look which told me I needed to *sort it quickly*, my mother bid us both a good night before she sauntered back to her quarters.

Arraetta became a little nervous, and I wondered what was happening in her mind.

"Are you well, Arraetta?"

"Uh, yes."

"Come, let us go to the library," I said, but her cheeks became scarlet, glancing towards the large doors. "You do go awfully quiet when you're nervous."

"I'm not nervous."

Oh, but you are the beholder of coyness, Arraetta.

"Do you expect something to happen in the library?" I jested.

"I was merely wondering why the company of books excited you so much."

I chuckled, "Also, the company of wine, painting and maybe a reading of *Pride and Prejudice*."

"Maybe I'm more inclined to see your so-called Roman baths."

Swallowing the euphoria from her suggestion and ignoring the constant swelling of my cock, which was beginning to feel painfully hard, I nodded. "Okay, we shall read Pride and Prejudice, drink wine and enjoy a bath."

"I... I don't have a swimming costume."

Empyreans, you are killing me. I hoped she would not look down because the sight of my bulge was highly noticeable at the thoughts of her wet, naked body. How delicious it would be to see her nipples protruding from the coolness of the room as she sank into the hot water. Maybe her seductive siren moans would twinkle my ears as I fucked her against the edge of the bath.

"Oh, Arraetta," I muttered, needing to restrain myself from such thoughts. I stepped closer to whisper, "You do not need anything but your birthday suit."

A maid appeared from my mother's quarters, causing the heat in my cheeks to cool enough to ask her to prepare the bath house for us, bring the book from the table and a bottle of champagne. I directed Arraetta to follow me, wandering back through the grand hallway, down the stairs, and around to the lower east wing. Boxes were still placed in piles, but no one except the guards noticed our new venture.

Through a door, a stone staircase led down to the bathhouse's entrance, which also had doors leading to a small bathroom, a laundry and a cleaning cupboard. But the room we entered was quite mesmerising, and it had even been a while since I had last dipped in the pool.

"This is beautiful," she breathed.

"Quite," I agreed, walking to one of the loungers to the left. I started to strip my clothes off, watching as she diverted her gaze as though she had been intruding. "You should not look away, Arraetta; this is all yours."

But, still, she did not look. Once I was fully naked, I descended into the water, veiling enough of me so she did not see how thick I had become just by being alone with her. I swam backwards to the deeper part of the bath, where I could stand on my tiptoes.

Finally, she looked at me, still fully clothed and deliciously wary.

"Are you coming in?"

"I... I thought we were reading *Pride and Prejudice*," she stuttered, habitually fiddling with the edges of her t-shirt. Suppose I had not had Rapidfire as my power. In that case, I might have chosen something more intriguing, like telepathy, so I could dare her to show me just how seductive and insatiable the female beneath her coyness was.

"It is nice and warm in here, Arraetta."

She shuffled to the edge, peering down at the water before she looked over again. I pointedly looked up and down her to indicate she should remove her clothes. Or, maybe I could bring to life the starved animal inside me, jump out of the water and rip them off her myself.

I almost dipped my hand below the surface to give my cock the acknowledgement it deserved, but I knew better than to show the craving I had for her when she was too fearful to show me her own body. A goddess should not be ever shy of showing her exposed self.

"I will come in, but you'll need to close your eyes."

Oh, you are teasing me, princess.

A grin washed over my face, and I threw my hands over my eyes before turning away from her. No, I changed my mind. I did not wish for telepathy but the ability of second sight to see, discreetly, the wonder behind me. With the beat of each layer of clothing that hit the floor, my cock strained more.

Fuck me.

When she dipped into the bath, it felt like an eternity, and I was desperate to see her rouged face.

"May I turn around?" I asked, and her hummed agreement was all I needed. Empyreans, I was not disappointed by the view before me: a goddess cloaked in a glorious red blush, her hair dampened at its tips, and her bare body disguised by the water stopping just above her breasts.

I licked my lower lip subtly, tilting my head to the side, "it is deeper over here."

"I'm sure it is."

"Do you not like it deep?" I straightened myself as I wondered how deep I could sink myself inside her when our time would come. And, come, she would.

The maid interrupted my leering, bringing everything I had asked for. She placed the tray closer to Arraetta before she left, which I was secretly thankful for as it allowed me to swim to her while she was distracted. I gently touched her lower back, earning a squeak, careful not to brush my hard length against her soft skin before going to the bucket and glasses.

"She brought the good stuff. Although I am sure Marie would

disapprove if she saw you were drinking after today," I said, noting it to be one of the most expensive bottles of champagne we owned. Then again, I was sure whoever had sourced it would have only thought we deserved the best. *She* deserved the best.

"I'm sure one glass won't hurt." She mindfully pressed her lips together as she watched me open the bottle, pour two glasses and then hand her one. I focused only then on the tome and had zero desire to entertain her.

"Why this book?"

"I felt that maybe I could translate it."

"That would be a guessing game," I said, placing it back down before I swam to my end of the pool, drink in hand. Arraetta would have a better time learning Zikan from the beginning, from phonetics to the alphabet. Attempting to translate such a tome as though it was seedling's play was impossible.

"Come, join me here."

"I'm comfortable here."

She perched herself by the pool's edge as I internally coaxed her to come to me. I could demand it, but I would not. Time was all it would take.

"Okay, but do not blame me when your legs begin to hurt." I put my drink back on the side of the pool before leaning back and looking up at the reflection of the water rippling on the ceiling.

"But why would it be a guessing game?" she queried after moments of quietness.

I looked back at her, "The structure is very different. You should just allow me to teach you some things."

"Like what?"

Many things. Everything about our people, the life we lived in Zika, the future of our realm, the language, the songs we sang.

My father's wrath, my mother's betrayal. My yearning for *her.*

Oh, how I *yearned.*

"Now is not the time for that," I replied, cheekily grinning, "you should really come here, Arraetta."

"And, to whose need is that?"

"Oh, Arraetta."

"Oh, Seraiah," she mimicked. *Throb.*

"Do not tease me so."

She nibbled her glass. "I am not teasing you."

Throb. Throb.

"You are the only female ever to tease me and get away without being reprimanded," I muttered in Zikan before I took the initiative to end the distance between us. I swam towards her, slow enough to see whether she would try to escape. I would stop if she did. Or, maybe I would not.

She attempted to shuffle backwards, but there was no way for her to escape apart from out of the pool. "We barely know each other."

Gentle hesitance, acting so virginal when she had declared she had slept with other males only hours earlier. I almost snorted at the thought of how coy she might have acted towards them, and the idea was enough to deflate my cock just a little. I took the spot beside her, close enough to shuffle in her direction with each water ripple.

"What would you like to know?" I asked, her gaze intense as I peered at her, watching as lewd thoughts swelled on her face. "Arraetta?"

She looked away rapidly, "What is... what is your favourite colour?"

"Is this a date between children?"

"Surely, you have one."

I pursed my lips, thinking for a second before I swam around and almost kneeled before her in the water, knowing there was only one answer to such a question.

363

"I do not think I really saw colour until I saw you on the night of the ball," I replied honestly, "It was as though all love and light had faded away from me for so long, and yet, when I saw you, the vividness of life returned. I do not believe I have a favourite colour, but I do have a favoured feeling. The warmth and beauty which shines from you every time you walk into a room. I have known you only a short while, but it feels like I have known you for a lifetime." I paused for a fraction. "But I do know your favourite colour."

Arraetta sipped her wine as she awaited my answer, and I took it as an ample opportunity to wade towards her, close enough so I could almost feel her soft, pointed breasts against my lower stomach. Gently, I caressed her cheek, "It is blue, a little darker than your eyes but lighter than the colour of my Rapidfire."

Her stomach tensed as the tip of my cock touched it, but she did not move. Only I wished she would raise her hand and feel the ache, but it seemed her flirtatious games were not over. "Actually, my favourite colour is red."

A return to the beginning meaning I would have to forge a new path for my desires. However, it was not as though I could act on them yet. Back at the opposite end of the bath, I sipped my drink. "Anything else?"

"What... what will happen when you defeat... The Dark?" she asked, and I choked, not expecting such a change in conversation.

Suddenly, my need dwindled as I recalled the memory of the attack. "I thought we were doing children's questions."

"I was just wondering..." Arraetta left the sentence open, making me wonder which angle she was aiming at. I opted for a more simplistic approach to avoid detailed answers.

"What will happen to *us*?" I presumed, taking the initiative to swim back to the champagne and pour the two of us fresh glasses. The Gods knew I needed the alcohol to get through such gruelling questions. "I hope that we can rebuild our home and live similarly to now without the fear of war on our shoulders."

"You don't think everything will change?" she questioned as I handed her a glass.

"I think much will change, but I cannot say what, nor would I wish to guess. I have adapted to every obstacle thrown my way; things we have learnt to be here on Earth will benefit our people back home."

Arraetta fell into deep thought, and I almost reached up to massage the crease on her forehead. I only hoped she imagined how good our life would be when we returned to Zika. Maybe she was fearful of such peace.

"I wish I could get inside of your head, Arraetta."

She smiled, tapping on her head, "It's a maze in there."

While trying to make light of the subject, she avoided discussing things we should be able to discuss openly. Then again, I had been steering clear of specific conversations until the time was right, at least until after the bonding ceremony.

"It is only a maze if you do not share it, but I shall not press you, Arraetta, I am only glad that you are here in my company."

The intense feeling which had dissipated appeared in the snap of a finger as we gazed at each other, burning desire a fire in her eyes. Somehow, she knocked over her champagne glass, which I caught before it descended into the water. The movement brought me closer to her - so close she had risen out of the water, revealing everything from her stomach upwards.

Fuck, she was divine. Her breasts were perfectly rounded as I had imagined, her nipples taut yet soft, and her smooth, honeyed skin was slightly crimson from the water's heat and her natural flush. Even so, being so exposed before me, she did not try to hide herself.

It was too late to hide the gentle quiver which shivered through her body.

Far too late to control my desires.

Far too late to stop my fingers from tracing her cheek to her damp lips, down her skin, to her sharp collar bone, and further still, all whilst I kept my eyes remained on hers.

The temperature soared, desire melted, and my hands finally cupped her breast, toying with her hardened nipple, causing that seductive moan to leave her mouth.

Gods above.

I pressed closer to her, my aching cock no longer able to be hidden as it prodded her belly, shifting my lips towards hers. My need to kiss them was overpowering my senses, common sense disappearing as I took my fingers from her breast, tilting her head up gently until there was but an inch between our lips.

"God, I am burning for you," I breathed almost subconsciously. Still, I was unsure whether it was the reality of what was happening or judgement returning, reminding me of needing to remain celibate until the celebrations. I would not be able to stop once I kissed her. If we devoured each other before the ceremony, would the chaos the Gods warned me of come sooner? Had the messenger warned me enough to ensure I would not go through with it?

Her eyes were close to shutting but opened wide as I suddenly turned my head, stepping back. I needed to calm myself and show her it was too soon. I was desperate to be with her, to bind our souls, but I could not be hasty. I would not be hasty. I was a master of patience. A few more quarters was nothing in place of the scorns I had waited for her.

"Seraiah?" she whimpered, a cold, hurt look settling on her face.

"I am sorry. I cannot-"

"-Don't," she interjected harshly as tears welled in her eyes. A sight I wished I did not have to see. She swallowed them back, nodding to herself as though trying to build up the courage to agree with my decision. Yet, without context, it seemed selfish. "I... it's okay, I should... I should go to bed."

"Arraetta-"

"-Let me go," she shouted, pulling her beautiful, water-laden body out of the pool before she rushed over to the lounge chair, wrapping herself in a towel. Her body shook as the tears barely held on.

"Please, Arraetta," I begged, following her without care of my naked body being on show for her, "please, know it is not you."

"Then, what is it?" she shouted, burning a look of anger and distress at me, "because you can't just go around playing with people's hearts."

No, you must know I would not play with yours. I was not cruel; I would not deceive you, my queen. My wife.

"Please do not cry," I implored, stepping to her as she headed to the door. I rushed before her, "Arraetta, please let me explain."

"Let me leave!"

"We cannot do this until the bonding is complete," I begged, "I have so much desire to be with you. It is deeply frustrating, I know, but we cannot risk binding our souls together too soon."

"Bonding?" she snapped, "bonding! What the hell is this bond, Seraiah?"

"It is-"

"-Because you obviously know far more than I do about it," she interrupted, "and, what, because of this so-called bonding, we can't kiss, huh? And, on top of that, is it not for us to decide when we want to do things?"

"You are right."

"You know, it's not fair," she breathed emotionally, pulling her shoulders back, "it's not fair for you to just... do these things to me... not if you know there are consequences. Good night, Seraiah."

The heat wilted instantly as she left me standing naked in the bathhouse, coldness settling through my joints as thoughts of regret, dissatisfaction, and guilt rippled through me without mercy. Fuck. It was my fault. I could not control myself when I needed to; I could not stop the temptation and hurt her in the process. I was pushing her away faster than we were getting to know each other.

But there was something else - a confined emotion that needed not surface, especially not so soon after guilt. But the lid broke like its chain was brittle, and the fourth coffer revealed itself. It felt as though my ribs were crushing, becoming breathless, while nausea branded deep in my stomach, churning painfully. It made me want to feel small and hide away from the invisible prying eyes upon me.

Shame.

It had never shown a sign of breaking, nor had I ever thought it would. Shame at not being able to give her what she wanted, shame at not having told her everything she deserved to know, shame because I knew the feeling I had towards her was more than just lust. It burnt through me like a vat of acid that I knew I could not escape.

You are pathetic - a prince who cannot even claim what is rightfully his.

"No," I whispered.

Not enough for a goddess.

"No, no, no!" I shouted into thin air, gripping my head to stop the voices prevailing.

You do not deserve her.

"Fuck you!" I growled loudly, desperately needing to dress and escape and find myself somewhere quiet, alone, without intervention. And all I felt was a failure. I had failed Arraetta; I had failed myself.

I walked to the door to leave, but halted as a black cloud formed in front of it. A second later, like an apparition, my dark doppelgänger appeared.

His lip twitched, and his dark eyes were piercing as he stepped forward, taking in the space until he was near the pool. "Another coffer opened; I do quite like this emotion. Shame. At least all your consuming emotions are out for the world to witness."

"Let me leave!" I commanded weakly.

"Never," he chuckled, "I shall always be here - through every bit of remorse or *pleasure* you feel. Her body was quite satisfying to feel."

I growled, diving towards him as wrath shrouded my mind, but he disappeared, and I stumbled into the shallow side of the pool. I ricocheted hard enough against the pool floor to wind myself, gasping for air as I broke the surface, floating as though I was paralysed.

His putrid face appeared above me before he nodded with inward approval, "It is good when you fight, Seraiah. It feeds me. Makes me feel whole, and you know I want to feel *oh so whole*, do you not?"

"I... do... not," I grunted, trying to bring myself upright with no luck. It was as though my movement was stilted by the power the dark being before me possessed.

"But, I suppose we would both be lucky," he laughed, "if I am whole, then so are you. It is a win-win. But, you are naïve, preferring easy tactics to gain power rather than realising the true nature of our greatness. And I shall just keep coming back to haunt you."

With some unknown strength, he grabbed the collar of my drenched shirt and threw me out of the pool, towards the door. I braced for impact, eyes closed, but instead felt a cold shiver rattling through my body. Looking around, I found myself on the bathhouse floor, gazing up at the ceiling with partially dry clothing.

I was alone. He remained a haunting figment of my imagination, although with every appearance he made, the more real it felt. Empyreans, if the coffers were not opening so fast, I might have been able to regain some control, but I was struggling against the weight of each harsh emotion. I would work hard to fight for the light. I could not give into the darkness or show Arraetta the demon beneath my skin.

But the light was slipping through my fingers like fine sand, the darkness watching – impatient, hungry. He waited to sink his onyx claws deeper, searing pain with every touch. And, Empyreans, he would not let me go without a fight.

And neither would I.

TWENTY-SIX

Hours later, I was in the office, surrounded by etchings of Arraetta as I toiled with each new burning feeling, each of them deflected away from one another while somehow melding as one. My eyes burned from sleep deprivation, but each time I succumbed to the land of slumber, I was only met with the haunting memories of the moons which had passed. Arraetta covered in blood on the night of the ball, Eros brutally tortured alive, his blood on my hands, Jonah ending our friendship, Arraetta almost dying, and her leaving. All their faces looked at me with disappointment, anger, wariness.

I awoke to a keen pain ricocheting through my fibres as the generator, through the closed curtains ahead, powered down suddenly.

"Fuck," I swore, rushing over to the door to sort it, only stopping when I could feel the remnants of dwindling, sweet, light energy above in the library. Arraetta. It had to be. No one else would go to the library at such an early hour. And, while my priority should have been the generator, I needed to see if she was okay and to make some sort of amends with her.

Yet, as I followed the energy trail into the library and up to its mezzanine, there was no sign of her anywhere. My heart thudded, wondering whether she might have disappeared into the rings again, but my gaze landed on a tome on the floor near an empty glass cabinet. The Compendium of Zikan Arcana.

It was a precious tome about ancient magic, locked away because it was off-limits to anyone without a key. I was the only one who possessed such an item. I supposed it made sense why Arraetta had been in my office earlier the sol before; she had removed nothing out of the ordinary but must have taken the key.

Several pages were damaged due to having been dropped carelessly on the floor, although I could only presume she had panicked before rushing out of the library. Or, maybe she was hiding somewhere. I peered across the library, not noticing a single sign of her anywhere, and felt a little disappointed she was not attempting to hide from me. I enjoyed the bliss of a chase to counteract the sourness of earlier events.

As I shuffled through the tome, I felt the tug of dwindling energy until I paused at one page - an ancient love spell. I chuckled at the thought of why the goddess would need such an impertinent enchantment. She had attempted to use magic, but without practice, she would likely have done more damage to herself. I was quite sure she did not speak Zikan and would not have been able to have even attempted to do the spell.

The tendrils of energy held hostage by the page danced from it as I brushed my fingers over the delicate surface. I took a deep breath, and the wisps flowed into my own hands as I fed on the intricacies of such a soft yet assertive aura. It was intoxicating, and it belonged to me. My poor, fated one did not know she had gifted me enough to be able to detect her when she was nearby and lavish in when she was not.

I returned the tome to the cabinet, looking around for the key, only to find it tucked away behind. I would have to be more wary of where I left prized items, but I stashed the key back in the same place in case she might dare attempt something against our laws again. It was quite thrilling to know she desired to learn more about ancient magic, even if she did not understand Zikan.

Once I returned to my study, I was thankful the generator did not require a recharge, only a reboot. After resting and showering in my quarters, I headed to the breakfast room, half expecting Arraetta to be there, but I was only greeted by Freddie and Genie. To say I was disappointed would have been an understatement, and I only hoped Arraetta would make an appearance at some point.

"Morning."

"Good morning," I said, taking the seat one of the servants had pulled out for me. "Thank you, Cedric."

"Of course, Your Highness," he bowed before walking to a hidden doorway which lead to the kitchen.

"You look spritely," Freddie raised his eyebrows, "did something happen between you and your wife last night?"

Genie coughed. "English, please."

"Sorry, my love," Freddie grinned, leaning over to kiss her cheek, "I am only asking if he wet his cock last night."

Genie gasped, "You're disgusting."

"I am sure we will know when Arraetta comes stumbling in," Freddie wiggled his eyebrows at her, and she let out a small giggle.

"No, nothing of the sort happened," I said, sitting comfortably, "I believe it has been said that it is not wise for the two of us to do anything until the ceremony."

"And who gave you such information? Sheika and her wealth of wisdom?"

"Don't be horrible, she's lovely," Genie tutted.

"She is something," Freddie nodded. Plates of food were brought in, and my stomach rumbled at the sight of pastries, meats, cheese and seasonal fruits in the middle of the table.

"Excuse me, Your Highness," Cedric said. "I wondered whether you would enjoy a more hearty breakfast this morning."

I shook my head. "This is fine. Do not over-impose yourself just because I have decided to eat here."

"Where do you normally eat?" Genie asked curiously.

"Seraiah would rather starve," Freddie answered pointedly, "I am sure you have seen how much weight he has lost since Arri arrived. Nothing more than skin and bones."

"I could easily still beat you in a fight."

"I should like to see you try," he grinned cockily. "Once upon a time, our prince would have a strict regime. Low carbs, high protein and all that."

"If I were a prince, I would eat like a king," Genie said.

"I would rather not have a potbelly," I said to her, knowing I would easily take after my father if I decided to. He rarely exercised and loved the overindulgence he could have in his position, "whilst I have not eaten much in a few weeks, I assure you that I will return to my normal ways soon enough."

"So, do you want to tell me why I woke up this morning with a splitting headache so early?" Freddie asked.

Yet, the answer herself walked in right on time. Arraetta looked weary as she looked at us all, seemingly taken aback we were there. She did not spare me much of a glance, opting for a seat by Genie, which Cedric pulled out.

"How are you this morning?" Genie said with a smile.

"A little tired."

"As am I. Freddie was up this morning; the generator blew."

"The generator?" she wondered.

"It is our energy source," Freddie replied, adding another subject I had yet to broach with her, "a ball of energy beneath the house that helps us survive here."

I was sure she knew what it was, having been sneaking around my office. She was not only clever but cunning with her white lies.

"It also powers the shield," I added, not missing her sharp glare toward me before she shifted her gaze. "I do apologise; I believe it was me that may have caused the outage, as I was testing a few things this morning, so some of us will be feeling worse for wear because of it."

"Do not worry, Seraiah," Freddie laughed, "I do not mind feeling shit for the sake of your magic tricks."

"I had picked up on a unique energy," I played, subtly eyeing Arraetta, "you know that I am always looking for a way to make it stronger."

A partial truth in the latter part of my sentence, but the rest was fabricated. I would cover for Arraetta if she allowed me to make amends with her. And, by doing so, I knew I had to try to give her more information about us, the bonding ceremony, and a little about the Zikan world. And there was only one person who had accurate answers.

Sheika.

"I hoped you would not mind accompanying me to Sheika's," I offered, which gained me another scowl. However, I was sure it was not because of the night before but because she had visited Sheika during my trip to Italy, "We will talk to her about Iontine and the bonding ceremony."

She lit up, "okay."

Light conversation took place over breakfast, Freddie asked me to get some medicine for Genie, who was, unsurprisingly, suffering from headaches, and Arraetta and I departed together.

Alex and Travis followed, and I knew many other eyes were hiding in the shadows.

"Which one is your personal guard?" Arraetta asked.

"All of them," I replied, although she was alluding to Travis and

Connell. Never was I without a guard, it seemed, apart from when they were most needed. Like in Italy. Arraetta would most likely never meet Connell as he tended to work at night, and his other hours were often spent at the garrison. And, the garrison was a place I would not be ready to take her to for a long time. "Most work on a rota, although I tend to confine myself to the library and my study so that I can have a little bit of time alone."

"Is Zika like this?" she asked, gazing around the street we walked down. The only comparable to Zika was the palace, but our settlement was far too modern to have the subtleties of antiquated beauty. We had adapted to Britain's growing trends, whereas Sole Serafino had more of Zika's beauty.

"A little. Zika was quite old-fashioned like you would imagine a place in a fairy tale. Our buildings were made from stone and were painted in many different colours."

"Sounds magical."

"Yes, it was," I replied solemnly; the remembrance of Zika was almost too much to bear, "To get to our palace, you would go up the town's winding roads, past the busiest markets and homes. Eventually, you would reach the top of a slight hill where large gates sat. Through those gates, around a mile or so again, you would reach the palace... which was five times as big as this place."

"Wow."

"Yes, and at the bottom of the town was the sea, which would cascade over the edge of the world like a magnificent waterfall."

"So... does your realm sit on top of The Cre-este?"

Ah, The Cre-este and its realm waterfall wall, rumoured to have cascaded from clouds at its peak, but Zika was nowhere near the divine realm. I believed the only way to leave The Cre-este was by a portal.

"No," I said, "although I could see the resemblance."

"You seem to know a lot about it."

A sharp observation, but even my own interpretation was from myths and legends, stories I had read and been told. But I had not had the privilege of entering such a sacred realm, not as she once had.

"Some. Although I do not feel I am the best person to speak to you about The Cre-este. I am unsure who it would be; we have only documented through stories we have been told."

She did not press further, shifting the subject, "How do you know that your home is no longer there?"

"What do you mean?"

"You spoke in the past tense like it no longer exists."

"I do not think the Zika we knew exists," I replied. "Although our land will be there, who knows what terrible things The Dark has infested our world?"

"The Dark... you said you would tell me of it."

"Yes, I shall. However, there are more important things to talk about today, and you do not need to be overloaded with information."

Annoyance salted her expression at my answer, but I knew I was right, especially for how she had reacted the sol before. I tried to reach for her hand to calm her, but she stepped away as though she was electrocuted, "Don't."

The silence became unbearable. Old tensions were still rife between us, and I only wished the conversation could start again. Politely, I greeted a couple while contemplating changing the subject again. But nothing swayed me past the decision to give her a little information about the sol Zika succumbed to The Dark.

"We were attacked," I told her, "a teller told us that our world would succumb to darkness and would only be saved by the light. We were never informed of the date, but our armies prepared for the worst, and something worse than that appeared. I cannot tell you exactly how many of our people died, but I can tell you little over three hundred of us made it to Earth. Women and children were slaughtered mindlessly by them. They have no remorse because they can do nothing more than feed on fear and pain."

Those echoes of screams, pained cries, and seedlings dying would haunt me until my dying breath and nausea rose in my throat as such ancient noise crescendoed in my ears again. But the memory was behind why I pushed to become king: so that we may return home and fight for the land which was once our own.

"What happened to your arm?"

More soul-aching questions. More memories to haunt me. The smoke, the endless running, the breathlessness, the winged demon attempting to devour everything in its wake. The Mire relentlessly swallowing everything it could see until it took from me, clinging to my arm, searing torturous agony as it ripped my soul apart with brutal force. Until-

My silence had given us enough time to arrive at Sheika's, but not enough to prevent the cold sweat on the back of my neck from seeping through my clothes. Not enough to stop the thudding of my heart, the pall of it too profuse to ignore. I was thankful to hear Russell's yapping as we knocked on the door, followed by a shuffle inside and the appearance of a pyjama-clad Sheika.

"Apologies, Sheika."

"Do not apologise. I was hoping you would swing by at some point. It is wonderful to see you both together."

She led us to her untidy kitchen and told us to sit at the unkempt table. I noted my offer of help the previous quarter had not swayed her.

"Now, to what do I owe this pleasure?" she asked, opting for her usual routine of boiling her kettle on the stove.

"I think it is about time Arraetta understands what the bonding ceremony is."

Sheika looked at Arraetta before making a hum of agreement, "It was a conversation we are due to have."

Sheika sashayed out of the room, leaving the two of us in a continued awkward silence, each debating a topic of unutterable conversation. Sheika did not return until the kettle started wailing for freedom from its flames, much like the words from my mouth. In her hands was a thick, time-worn tome, which she did not place down until she had removed the kettle from its perch. The tome landed with such a thud it made Arraetta jump.

"Let me make some tea."

"Ah, no, I'm alright," Arraetta replied quickly.

I teased, "Scared of the tea?"

I could not blame her for being wary when some of the teas Sheika provided were sometimes not the usual breakfast type. And rarely did she ever pre-warn the drinker of the difference.

"I'm happy not to have another hallucination," she chortled, and somehow I connected my own hallucination sols before to the one she must have spoken of.

"When I collapsed," I realised, and she nodded.

"It is wonderful to have you both here," Sheika remarked, "and what a joyous occasion it will be when you come together in matrimony."

Arraetta gasped quietly, eyes flitting between us, "Married."

Sols of speaking of the bonding ceremony and she had not connected such a thing, I wondered whom the female opposite me had become in order to replace such an intelligent goddess.

"You are two fated souls, Arraetta," Sheika said, placing full teacups down, "and in order for you to come together as a whole, you must bond."

"And what does that incur?"

"It is very similar to a marriage. However, the vows are different, and you shall, in a sense, hand-fast. Except, it is without a ribbon." Sheika pawed through the pages until she stopped at one in which two hands were entwined, each with distinct black markings. "Legends tell that these tattoos appear on the forearms of the two Kindred Spirits as their bond solidifies."

"Are they permanent?" Arraetta asked in awe.

"I believe so," Sheika answered, "anyone who comes to be in the presence of either Kindred Spirit, following the bonding, would know immediately who they were. But we must make sure the energy is at its strongest prior to the ceremony; that is why it shall follow Iontine... Seraiah, you must surely have informed your wife of something."

I watched Arraetta's toiling emotions, and I was unsure whether she was overwhelmed by the news the two of us would be married or that she had attempted to have me open up to her several times. I swallowed, sitting up straight, "I thought it best we speak of these things here. Iontine is the festival of the Gods. It is where we celebrate and worship the divine beings of the universe in hopes they will provide us more sustenance."

"Sustenance?"

"Power," I corrected. "...in a form. Rapidfire being one of them; the rest is enough energy for our people to survive on this planet."

"And the... Gods just give that to you?"

The truth was far from what ordinary folk understood. None of us knew whether the Gods were ever listening; we only continued our traditions to appease them. Our generator, however, required a substantial amount of energy to work, so the Gods must have gifted us with something every four winters to help us continue to power it. Either that, or there was another force of energy we were pulling from.

Thought swelled in my mind, wondering whether Arraetta had a bigger connection to us than we had ever realised. But, it was not the right time to be poking the fire when its flames were too big to prevent scolding.

Sheika finished her sentence, talking about something being a wondrous occasion, and I realised I had missed most of the topic. Our heartfasting? Or, Iontine?

"That's so close," Arraetta exhaled, peering down at the table, and I watched her for a short moment as I deciphered her distress. While Sheika was piling Arraetta with information, I knew it was going to become far too much too soon.

"Before we continue," I said in English, before shifting to Zikan, "Freddie has asked me whether you may have some... headache medicine for Genie, as she is feeling rather unwell under the strain of the shield." Sheika nodded and stood, shifting out of the room in a heartbeat, and I took it as ample opportunity to speak with Arraetta. "Arraetta, please do not fear these things; I know it is overwhelming."

"Aren't you scared?"

I was not until I met her, trapped in the aftermath of my imprisoned emotions bursting. But, still, there was no fear in being with Arraetta; she was the light amongst the darkness. She was the one thing which kept me powering through. The one thing I could reign supreme over in my uncontrollable life.

"Yes, but not of marrying you, Arraetta; you are exactly the person I always dreamt of being fated to."

"Then what are you scared of?"

Such unfortunate questions had answers which were far too complicated. It was far too soon to be telling her about such deep qualms of my biggest *fear* being her seeing me succumb to the thing inside me. I would not allow that to happen, I would not allow it - *him* - to dominate my soul.

It is far too late for that, Seraiah.

I swallowed the growl which dared to leave my throat, wishing I could punch a hole in my skull, my mind, my soul, wherever he might be and pull him out. I would like to see how unmatched he was in person when he saw how powerful I could be without him.

Lies.

Under the table, I clenched my fist and replied to her burning question, "Losing you in the process."

Sheika's return was welcome, and she placed a bag of herbs on the table.

"What's that?" Arraetta asked.

"It is for Genie... for her headaches," I replied.

"Headaches?" So many one-word questions from Arraetta. I definitely needed to speak to her about quietening her questioning mind. Not as though it was bad between us, but she would struggle in council if she spoke without calculating the answer internally. Or at least without spending time to form her questions first.

Sheika rattled off a section of the tome before her, recurring information which I already knew about, all about the bonding of the Kindred Spirits. "...Now, the era of serenity will not come easily; in this book, it tells of a time of turmoil, mayhem, and a great war which soon shall follow the binding of the souls. For, as we all know, for one exchange, another must be made in order to keep the balance across the universe."

"What war?" Arraetta asked, "Surely we could just... not... bond, right?"

An innocent question, but even I looked at her as though she had lost her mind. I did not wait an eternity to decline a marital gift of pleasure from the Gods. I was sure she knew now I had her. I would fight one hundred wars to keep her, so we were absolutely going to bond, even if turmoil would follow in its wake.

"There is a great reason, child," Sheika continued, "for there carries more greatness in your connection than there does without. Firstly, I have seen how you are together; the pain of no unity carries clear and has already begun to affect those around you. Secondly, the further we push the bond, the more destruction will be caused in the worlds which are currently shrouded in chaos. A much greater war, which takes less time, is much more acceptable than a war which continues to grow slowly, eventually creating more destruction. I am sure you understand."

"Is there another way?" Arraetta replied, and annoyance rattled in my stomach as we circled again, "No, I mean, I get the concept, but surely, we could find another way around the whole war thing."

"I do not think there is another way," Sheika replied sincerely, and I looked at her, wondering whether she had seen the inevitable *war to end all wars.* Maybe she had spoken with the nixie, A'uren. Such a war would not wash up on the shores of Earth, though, not in a protected realm.

"The universe is all about balance, right?" Arraetta said boldly, "So, maybe we could sacrifice something."

"Like?" I replied, intrigued that we were finally moving from one-word questions to general observations.

"What about... I don't know... what about our Rapidfire?"

"No, amongst all things, I could not ask anyone to sacrifice their power, and even if we could, I know it is needed to fight The Dark."

"Well, maybe just mine, then?"

Such a foolish suggestion, as though it were truly ever plausible. Unless she did not wish for such power, I still could not allow her to let go of the one thing which would keep her alive.

"You would have to sacrifice the entirety of Rapidfire," Sheika chipped in, "you will be asking to give in the greatest power to ever be given to mortals in return for no war."

"I think it's reasonable," she said, eyes darting between us as if we were about to rise from our seats and cheer about her *fantastic* idea, "don't you think it's caused enough destruction already?"

"And what of those whose life depends on Rapidfire?" I said bluntly.

"What do you mean?"

"How do you think we survive, Arraetta?"

"But not everyone has Rapidfire."

"No, but those of us who do cannot survive without it," I fought blatantly, "It is our life force. You speak of sacrificing when you do not fully understand how Rapidfire came to pass."

"How can I understand when no one will tell me anything?"

There it was. That ingrained need for knowledge, her innate curiosity visibly fighting reason, but she was far too volatile to be given every piece she desired.

"Rapidfire was gifted to many in power," Sheika told her, "in return, they had to sacrifice their vitality. Some of us have greater knowledge than others; it will take time to explain the full story, but I do not think it will harm you to know a little more."

"We are here to talk about the bond," I said gruffly.

"It won't harm me," Arraetta replied like a spoiled seedling.

I huffed loudly before sitting back and folding my arms, "go ahead."

Sheika droned on about Rapidfire 101, taught to seedlings aged four, and gave Arraetta a whole backstory about her father and how the power came to be. Such a *fascinating* subject when all I wanted to know was about how the ceremony would work so we could finally be together without all the unnecessary delays. Something she needed to know as well. Not how we would partake in a war, not how she could get injured if she was caught in the crossfire, not how I might see her coated in blood again. Unease ploughed through me at such a thought. But, I would never allow her to fight. No, when I was king, such a thing would be forbidden. I would command it. She would be a queen, a goddess, inside the safety of the palace walls, and I would return to her with the gift of peace once the battle was completed.

"Now, let us get back to the bond," Sheika said, and I internally sighed as the topic shifted.

"But you didn't tell me how Rapidfire works," Arraetta stomped, and I groaned again, annoyed by the tedious, annoying female sitting opposite me.

"Arraetta, can we not talk about what is here at hand?"

"Why do you always move the conversation?" she flailed her hands.

"You are constantly asking questions; I told you we must slow down."

"Slow down, slow down," she mimicked, then shouted, "What's so secret about it all?"

The demon punctured my stomach as anger churned, but I fought hard for control over my negative thoughts as I calmly yet irritably said, "There is no secret; you have barely been here for five minutes, and you want to know everything."

"I deserve to know everything!" she yelled, slamming her hands down on the table as she stood.

"Not yet!" I countered, mimicking her stance as I bellowed, "You are not ready to know everything; you are still a child."

"Fuck you, Seraiah!" she screamed, the mug of tea near her tipping over from her harsh movements, "you're more of a child than I am, sitting there sulking because I ask fucking grown-up questions. Argh."

Without another word, Arraetta stormed out, leaving a storm

of anger and rage simmering behind her as I watched the empty space she had left. Clenching my fists, I wondered whether I might show her exactly what it meant by taunting the wrath inside me, a strange feeling of needing her to submit, overshadowing my want to apologise to her for not opening up to her. I was unsure why I felt that way, but maybe part of me was unprepared for such a power dynamic. Fuck, it was not a need for her to *submit* but a need to continue to see her fire *dominate* me.

Sheika had been awfully silent as I toyed with my thoughts, cleaning up the spillage without any complaints. Part of me wondered whether she might have enjoyed our squabble; I supposed a little entertainment did no harm to a female who spent most of her time in silent meditation.

"I apologise, Sheika."

"And what are you apologising to me for?" she laughed. "I hope you are not apologising for Arraetta's behaviour. You require more patience. You have grown up in this life - a very privileged one. Everything is still very new to her."

"I just wish she would not rush me."

"Is she? Or are you only worried about the pace at which things are moving because you are finding such a change difficult? Her arrival must have sparked some sort of inner turmoil for you, hm?" I opened my mouth to answer, but she held her hand up. "I am not your therapist, do not sit here and open up about your qualms."

"I thought a Shaman was a certified therapist?" I jested, and she smacked me with the wet tea towel.

"There is one thing I wish to ask, however," she said with seriousness, taking Arraetta's vacant seat, "I want to know whether you have had any messages in your dreams recently?"

I wondered whether she was thinking of the extended message which the messengers had given me the previous sol or wanted me to confirm something she already knew. She would have been the best person to speak about the festering demon, but I would not wish to broach the subject with someone who might give me more doubt than positivity.

"No," I lied.

Sheika studied me, then sighed, "Well, I suppose that is good. I know you keep much locked away, but I hope you trust me enough to have something deciphered when the time is right. For now, please leave my house and speak to your beloved. It would be quite a shame for the high spirits of this village to be tarnished by such a dramatic altercation."

With little more than a goodbye, I left the house and, flanked by Travis, walked back towards the palace. It seemed Alex had already followed Arraetta, which I was glad about, considering how upset she had been when she had left the house. I only prayed we could finally reconcile our furious tendencies soon enough, as I was desperate for us not to feel rage toward one another forever.

No more pain or suffering, just the two of us in harmony.

I yelped in anguish as sudden fire tore through me white-hot like melted steel, and I forcefully sank to my knees. I only heard snippets of Travis trying to aid me as I focused on breathing, "Sentinel Travis reporting.... Immediate medical... location tracking..."

Blurred, my eyes looked up towards the palace, honing onto what looked like a cloud of dark matter pouring down from an invisible source, seeping into the walls like smoke.

Flashes of Arraetta being swallowed by darkness, eyes turning black, blood spilling from each crevice of her body devoured my senses until an ear-piercing scream tore through the overwhelming chasm of clatter. A scream which was all too familiar, pulling at my strings of fear and devastation.

"Arraetta!"

TWENTY-SEVEN

Hard concrete took the brunt of my soles as I bounded up the pavement toward the palace, uncaring for the agony which tore through me relentlessly. Behind me, Travis fought to keep up as I powered on. As I crossed the threshold of the palace grounds, two black vehicles pulled in through the gates, stopping outside the door, but I ignored them, rushing around them and into the house.

Remnants of dark matter directed me to the east wing hallway until, as I rushed around the corner, it disappeared. Freddie was positioned offensively near to me whilst a very rigid yet trembling Arraetta stood further ahead of them, facing away. And, just as the sol before, a veil of mist surrounded her body, yet it seemed to be more grey than translucent. Near her, on the floor, a guard lay unconscious, or maybe he was dead.

"What is happening?" Jonah's voice echoed. He appeared around the corner to witness the situation, flanked by other guards, who I could only have guessed had all arrived via the vehicles. His hand gently touched my shoulder, but I shivered away from his touch.

He cleared his throat, "Travis said you are unwell. Is that true?"

"I am sure you do not care, Commander."

Without a second delay, I pushed past Freddie, but he rushed ahead of me, holding out his arms as though they were lengthy enough to

388

create a barrier. My gaze tilted down to his wrapped hand, which I only assumed covered the burn from the sol prior.

"Do not be ridiculous, Seraiah," he reasoned. "We do not know who we are contending with here. You have seen the guard. We cannot be too cautious after last sol."

"I can help her."

"Can you?" Freddie replied, astounded by my call.

"Freddie is right," Jonah said, as though his opinion was of any importance.

I grovelled, "You are getting on my nerves, Jonah. You are not welcome to partake in these decisions."

"But I am," he said, "I am still your commander."

"You are about as much my commander as your father is my general right now!" I chided, glowering at him. The guards behind were astounded by my harshness, although I presumed they were still to learn their boss, and I no longer saw eye to eye.

"Let us not talk about this here," Jonah gritted.

I clenched my fist, wondering what he would look like if I ripped his foul tongue from his mouth. No more commander, just Jonah. But, fuck, the situation Arraetta was in was worse than the feud between the two of us. I would save slicing his tongue until another time.

Ignoring the calls of concern and the hands which attempted to pull me back, I walked down the long corridor to Arraetta until I was at the edge of the circular mist. It was small enough to walk around. While the cloud remained a shield, I was much more concerned about the female trapped within it. Arraetta was much like the iteration of the sol before, with dark blood staining her ears and nose. Her eyes were glazed over as they stared ahead, unaware I stood before her, needing to help.

"I need a cloth, and call Marie!" I commanded, ignoring the crowd as I tentatively placed my hand onto the veil, needing to find her some sort of release from it. Yet, unlike the burn which Freddie had received, it was as though I had been sucked into a vortex of hellish imagery. Thunder, whirling black clouds, a dragon's ear-splitting roar, dissonant screams, a body rebounding with golden lightning.

Unable to grasp the concept of any of it, I was pushed back with such force I fell to the ground. Whatever I had done caused the veil to disappear instantly, but it caused an intense feeling of trepidation to cling to me. I pushed to my feet, tentatively shuffling forward until I could grip Arraetta's biceps.

"Arraetta," I said quietly, trying to gather her attention. "Arraetta," I shouted. "Arraetta!"

My final call reached her, glassy eyes flickering back to normal as she wearily peered up at me, staring for far too long before she let out a shuddery breath. She looked around the corridor before her, not turning to see those watching like she was entertainment. Someone rushed forward with tissues, handing them to me so I could wipe the blood from her face, although it seemed like it was not enough.

"I am taking you to rest," I told her, watching as she looked at my lips, a confused look crossing her face. "Once Marie has checked over you, everything will return to normal."

Whatever such normal would be, I was unsure. This was her normal. But it was not mine, and I had to find a way to stop it. It had to be the last time it happened; I could not witness whatever psychological nightmares plagued her.

Arraetta shakily placed her hand on her cheek, smearing some of the blood until she studied the rouge on her hand. In a world of her own, she shouldered me as she limped to the mirror.

"Marie is here," Jonah called, yet my attention swayed as Arraetta's legs caved, and she toppled towards the ground.

She was safely in my arms with quick movements, "I have got

you."

The next few hours were as tense as every other time an incident had occurred. A long, irritatingly unavoidable time. Freddie left to pick up Genie from London, promising to return as soon as possible, while I was forced to stay outside the room. As usual, my help was not required.

Both Alex and Jonah remained with me, although I was unsure whether it was to make sure Arraetta was well or to keep an eye on me. Part of me wondered whether I should have gone for a walk to see whether the latter was the truth, but I could not leave Arraetta, just in case something else were to happen.

Freddie returned with Genie at some point, but she barely acknowledged us as she slipped into the room whilst Freddie remained in the corridor. Silence remained between us, although I knew it was due to the tension between Jonah and me. It was not as though he deserved any apologies for my harsh behaviour.

Maybe we would become mortal enemies.

"Will you stand still, for fuck's sake?" Freddie shouted at me, "I am going dizzy with your wanderings."

I had been pacing for a long while, unable to remain still as my thoughts turned sour. "What shall you have me do, Freddie?"

"Take a damn seat," he said, waving to the vacant wall opposite, "or go for a stroll outside if you are so inclined to get in your daily steps."

"Oh, shut your fucking mouth."

"Let us not fight," Alex pleaded, standing straighter. Of course, Mr Peacekeeper would like to make things right when he was nowhere to be found with Arraetta.

"Whilst we are at it, I would be happy if you were so inclined to tell me why my wife was here without you?" I snapped at him, "some fucking personal guard."

Alex paled whilst Jonah's clenched fists paled, "Watch your tongue."

"Or, what?" I raised my eyebrows, "Maybe she would not be in this fucking state if your keeper kept an eye on her."

"Arraetta-" Jonah began.

"-Her Royal Highness," I interjected sharply to him, "might I remind you of titles, seeing as you are no longer my friend, *Commander*."

Freddie stood from the floor, while Jonah looked like he was close to throwing the punch he seemed to be begging to give me. Alex lowered his head, "I am sorry; she asked me to leave her alone once we entered the house."

"He is right," Freddie said, "I arrived just afterwards. It turns out she seemed to be very upset."

Jonah laughed harshly, "Wow."

"The question is, why would she be upset leaving Sheika's house, hm?" Freddie asked with mock concern.

"It does not matter," I said, which he laughed in disbelief at.

"You truly have the gall to be angry with Alex when it was you who must have upset your wife," Jonah offered, and I suddenly felt like it was three against one. Yes, I had upset Arraetta, but I did not cause her to trigger the episode she had suddenly.

Or was it my fault?

Alex said, "Whilst she may have been upset, it does not excuse I was not with her to help, and I will accept my punishment for not stopping this from happening when I could see what state she was in."

"No punishments," Freddie tutted, "the only reason she ended up in such a state is because of this idiot before me."

"Like you fucking know," I replied.

"Oh, I know, Seraiah," he chided, shaking his head in disbelief, "you two are like yin and fucking yang. When one thing happens to one of you, the other is affected. Not just this sol but last. I know something happened in the flat. Do not think I did not notice you were in such an odd state before Arri *almost* killed herself." I winced. "And what about Italy, hm? Something must have happened to her when you collapsed there. Do not speak to me about how she ended up in that state when it can only come down to you."

Fuck these males. Fuck Freddie and his observations. Fuck Alex and his lack of professionalism. Fuck Jonah and his... his shit.

"Please, can we calm down," Alex implored.

"Alex is right," Jonah said, "we are far too angered to think rationally."

The tension inside me did not release for a long moment until I turned my head to calm myself down. The conversation was rife with resentment, breaking apart the entire group and swallowing me whole in a tidal wave of hatred.

"And I hate to break it to you," Jonah said to me, "but your father has landed at the airport and will be home just after two o'clock."

Unwanted news at such a time, but I guessed my father wanted to be nearby as he attempted to shape me into the *honourable* heir he desired me to be. Either that or my move of slitting Eros' throat made me an unwavering and uncertain force to contend with.

"We do not need to look as though a wall has risen between us," Jonah said, looking at all three of us, "we need to remain strong."

I laughed mirthlessly, glaring at him, "I suppose you should have thought about that earlier."

"You need to be a strong king," Jonah said sternly, "not simmer in the grief of this loss of friendship. Let us all meet for dinner tomorrow evening."

He did not say anything more as he took his leave, calling the remaining guards to clear out. I supposed an Amity meeting was called for since the passing of Eros; it was time we mourned the male who had departed and spoke of the future.

Soon, my father's arrival echoed down the hallway, but I did not go to greet him, remaining in my post. Shortly after, Genie left the room looking emotionally exhausted, but she still offered us a soft smile.

"How are you?" Freddie asked her.

Genie nodded. "Okay. She... she is fine too. Marie gave her something to help her sleep, so I don't know when she will wake up. I think Marie wants her to rest overnight." Genie looked at me with a smile. "I think you can go in there now. I want to go out for a bit, clear my head."

They departed, leaving me to walk into the room, where Marie was sitting in a chair, filling out more paperwork. She noticed my arrival, "Oh, good. I can go for a cup of coffee."

"Is she okay?"

"She will be fine, but I do believe whatever is causing her pain is psychological, not physical, Seraiah. You may want to consider getting her a real therapist."

"I understand your concern, but her mind is far more complex than we understand. I just... I would like her to open up to me first, and then, if that does not work, we shall go with your suggestion."

Marie placed her paperwork in her bag, zipping it up. "I just hope it will not be too late. It's a little tedious to return to this room."

"It is your job."

"It is my job, yes," she agreed, throwing her bag over her shoulder before she walked past me to the door, "but neither of you should become my career."

I felt as though time was on a loop as I spent the next twenty-four hours by Arraetta's side, with Marie and Genie coming in occasionally. But, mostly, I was left to my own thoughts. Three things plagued my mind – one, Arraetta's uncontrollable night-mares somehow caused a dark form of energy to encase her. Two, the unnerving imagery I had seen when I touched the veil was like snapshots of a future which had yet to come or a past too frightening to bear. And three, the sols which had passed full of anger, hatred, blood and death. Would life become any easier?

Marie commanded me to go and eat and sleep in the early hours of the following morning, in the same tone she always used. And, as usual, I listened to her demands and did as I could. I ate before passing out for hours until I awoke to news of Arraetta waking up around two o'clock.

I gently opened the door as Genie said, "Maybe I should let you rest."

There was no one to stop me from walking over to a sleepy yet well-rested Arraetta, no one to stop me from offering a gentle smile and scooping her soft hands into the clasp of my own.

"Hey," I whispered, stroking the apple of her cheek, "I was very worried."

Worried. Frightened. *Terrified.*

"I'll leave you both," Genie said softly before quietly leaving the two of us alone.

"How are you?" I asked.

"My head feels like it's on fire," Arraetta replied, placing her own cooler hand onto my own as though we had not been in each other's firing line the sol prior, "but I'm glad I'm out of that."

"What happened?"

I could see the gentle frown lines returning as she briefly lost herself inside the world of her toiling mind until she swallowed, "I don't really know. I..." I nodded for her to continue. "I suppose it was a little similar to the hallucination I had the day at Sheika's. I... I know you don't know about that. Seraiah, I know you don't wish to tell me a lot, but is there more than one thing in The Dark?"

I blinked, "more than one thing?"

"Yes, sometimes I see... sludge and other times, I see winged creatures."

"Ah, you are asking if it is a collective name?" I replied, and she agreed. "Yes, it is. I am unsure where it originated, but it was coined The Dark after unnatural beasts were released from Mysc, the realm of nightmares. It was given many titles, but a collective name was eventually given. Thus, The Dark was named. The sludge you speak of is called The Mire..."

Arraetta paled, and I was suddenly wary that I was giving her far too much information when rest was much more important.

"I am sorry," I apologised, "you should rest."

"I swear you only wish to open up to me when I'm in a terrible state," she jested, and I smiled, knowing she was probably true. Maybe it was the knowledge she would not fight against me if she were as meek.

"I... I am not trying to keep anything from you, Arraetta. I only wish you would allow me the time to plan a full conversation with you over these little half-ones which cause us to bicker."

Or, I would instead tell her things when our lives were more settled, maybe after we had bonded and could share a private moment without ripping each other's clothes off or hair out. But I supposed Sheika had been right in some respect that I was fearful we were moving too fast and that it would cause her to back away from me quicker. And I could not afford that. Not now. Not *ever*.

Helping her into a more comfortable position, she said, "I... I saw my father."

"Your father?"

"He... it's not the first time."

"It was not a dream?"

"No," she breathed. "We spoke about things; we were on the bridge of Ryazark."

Elation fuelled my greed at the knowledge a myth had been confirmed in an instant. The bridge of Ryazark was a dreamer's paradise, or at least it was my own. Even if her mind was playing tricks on her, she had been given the distinct honour of seeing such an opening to a realm in the presence of the legend Ivan the Great.

I would have to speak to her more about it when the time was right. I kissed her softly on her forehead before stepping back, saying, "I would like to hear more of your encounter, but I wish for you to get some rest."

"He confirmed about the war," she added so quickly, and without mercy, I felt a cold shiver run down my spine. "He also said I had to learn to control my power so that I may fight."

"What? Your father would not send you into the fight."

War? Fight? I almost snorted, remembering how the sol before I had toiled with my inner thoughts about how I would never see her in such a position, yet she was stating it so casually as though it were fact. My stress response was going haywire at the thought of the suffering she would go through only to partake in such dangerous activities. No, even a great king like her father would never see his only living daughter be the centre of such bloodshed. Her mind had to be playing tricks.

"I don't think I have a choice," she replied triumphantly, "if you're going, so am I."

"No, I will not have my wife fight in this war," I chided.

She sat up too abruptly and whimpered, "You can't control me."

"It is not about control, Arraetta," I explained calmly, although that was a partial lie, "it is about keeping you safe."

"Don't you need my power to fight The Dark?" she said exasperatedly, "don't I have Divine Rapidfire after all?"

397

"Did your father confirm that?"

If her father had confirmed such things, then Arraetta possessed the divine abilities to defeat the darkest entities, just as we had thought. Yet, she had no training on controlling or using such power.

"Then, this changes many things," I replied, grimacing at the fact that I had to speak to the one male I wished I did not have to see. "I need to... to speak to my father. Please rest."

A war was coming - foretold by an ancient, dead mortal whose soul lingered in the realm of the Highest Gods. He had warned her she would have to fight.

But little did she know, the locks on her cage were tightening, and the keys rested safely in my pocket. I would do anything to keep her from harm.

TWENTY-EIGHT

The smell of smoked pinewood swamped my nostrils as I entered the large room opposite the council chambers. My father's office was a cabinet of curiosities, enveloped by two vast windows radiating piercing light on the male who perched at its helm – a long desk filled with dusty tomes and papers.

Surprisingly, my father had allowed me to visit, usually requiring an appointment quarters in advance, but I knew we had a conversation to have regarding the incident in Italy. Still, he did not acknowledge my arrival as I wandered its perimeter, perusing uncaring at the spines of old tomes until I stopped before his desk, sitting without permission on one of the two chairs.

Only then did he look at me disdainfully. "To what do I owe the displeasure of your company?"

I rolled my eyes, "how very mature of you, Father."

"I believe what is immature, *Son*," he stabbed, "is your insolence in listening to my demands when you were requested to remain in Italy."

Harshly, I laughed, "So that you may use another victim for your games?"

"A victim or your ally?" he asked, folding his arms as he stared at me. It was a shame his chair made him look taller, but I chose to position myself as nonchalantly as possible, drawing the ball into my court, "*Eros,* was it?"

"Who is Eros?" I asked innocently, "All I saw was Henri Romano slaughtered like a pig on your beach."

"Do not play the fool," he tutted, "emotions are petty things when it comes to the political stakes of this house."

"You killed an innocent male!"

"*You* killed him!" he bellowed, sitting forward, "or do you not remember how your knife so happened to find the skin of his throat, hm? I only wonder whether it was for his sake or yours."

How easy it had been to slice Eros' skin, giving him the easy way out of the immense pain caused by Corvelli's hand.

"He would have died, for Corvelli showed him no mercy at your command."

"Ah, so it was mercy," he confirmed, nodding, "mercy for a male whom you are acquainted with through your commander, yet it seemed as though you had much more of a connection with him than I realised."

"He was a good man."

"He was a traitor," he sneered, "just like his father. It is just so fortunate I did not sentence his whole family to the same fate for the allies' insolence. Your mother has seen to it she would prefer their lives to be spared. And, I am an honourable king."

I snorted. What fucking honour did the male before me have? Listening to his wife even after he had sentenced Henri Romano to an early death, only to spare his family. That was not honour. It was not even mercy, letting his mother grieve until her dying breath.

"So, shall you not reprimand me?" I asked him, tilting my head, "It seems you have been so quick to jump at the opportunity recently, although I have yet to hear about what punishment I shall face for killing Henri Romano."

My father studied me for a gratingly too-long moment before

he stood from his chair and wandered to look out into the gardens ahead. "You are far too unpredictable. It seems whatever favour the Gods have bestowed upon you is working far too nicely. But, you will slip up." He turned to me. "I am far more thrilled to see how that little wife of yours comes to terms with the monster lying deep within your skin."

I clenched my fist. "Leave her out of it."

"Oh, but I cannot," he chuckled mirthlessly, looking away again, "You are the harbinger of chaos in our world, it seems. So I look forward to watching how fast you fall once you reach your peak. And when you do, everything around you will burn – until there is nothing left but ashes... and your own desperate pleas for forgiveness."

I shall feast on your flesh when you are dead. The words were so sharply stuck on the tip of my tongue I thought they might leave my mouth, but I managed to draw them back. Anger was irrational when it came to conversations with my father, who far preferred the art of manipulation through carefully crafted rhetoric.

"Maybe you just fear the better king I would become."

There was another silence until he walked back to his seat. "I am not fearful of you. I have seen what you are becoming and know the terror which comes in your wake. And it shall not take long for our people to call the cursed prince a shadow king. Then they shall revolt."

"They are already revolting."

"No, Seraiah, they are not. No kingdom of mine shall ever have a revolution. Lesson number one in being a king is you must learn to control your people, give them what they want, and they will give you back threefold."

"You think you have given our people what they want?"

"Yes, and then some," he answered, "lower rent, opportunities to move throughout this realm, zero unemployment rate, an army fit enough to combat many of Earth's, and weaponry to protect us if ever under threat. Seedlings in schools learn four languages. Fair governance, political standing, and prosperity for all. Should I continue?"

"Manipulation," I added, "killing innocents."

"Killing traitors. As you shall if you are crowned. I am quite sure Kaeltar and Corvelli shall be the top of your list, and I should be quite intrigued to see how those two falter under your power."

"You would throw your allies into the pit?"

"My guards are not my allies," he replied, lip-twitching, "neither is yours. Any could turn against you at any moment, and they will. You speak negatively about manipulation when it is the greatest power at your fingertips."

"Our people deserve freedom."

"Our people deserve a strong kingdom," he chided, picking up a pen to start scribbling, "a king rules with his head, not his heart. It is about time you think about that should you wish to be in my position."

"It is fortunate neither of us have a heart, then."

He snorted, "While you pretend to be heartless, yours has been served openly on a silver platter, wandering our hallways, creating fires."

He was speaking of Arraetta, and the aggravation for his callous mention of her grew again. "She is her own person."

"She belongs to you. Just as your mother belongs to me. They are the biggest victims of our world; it is up to us to ensure they are happy enough not to rock the boat in their favour. A happy queen makes for happy people."

"You cannot control a queen."

"A queen is on a pedestal so she feels mighty in her power," he added, "and the only person who can remove her is the king. Your mother knows that, and so your wife should before it is too late, and she is causing you to rule with your treacherous heart over your head."

I turned my head, careful not to let my impenetrable mask falter as I took in my father's words. Was I so different from my father? I was already seeking some sort of control over Arraetta, to stop her from fighting and to lock her in the tower until the war upon us was over. I did not like admitting my father was right in some respect, that she might have me decide to rule over our subjects with my weakened heart over my hardened mind. Empyreans, I would not even be able to prevent it from happening at the rate my feelings were tumbling out from within me. She already had a tight grasp on my heart.

"You are not here to speak of being a king," my father said, sitting back, "so why did you come?"

I looked at him, a little caught out before I sat up straight, "I thought you should know Arraetta's father is Ivan the Great. He came to her within her dream and confirmed many things we should prepare for."

At first, a look of disbelief crossed his face before he shook his head lightly, "I may believe in the Gods, Seraiah, but I do not believe whatever messages she sought to impart on you shall come to fruition for many sols, if ever. Rule with your head, not your heart, remember."

Fuck head and heart in a decision of fact.

"*War*, father," I replied frustratedly. "He told her that there would be a war."

He growled, "There will always be a war, Seraiah. We have been preparing for one for a very long time, yet here we still are. What that girl's father tells her whilst she is away with the fairies is not enough solid evidence that it is about to happen."

His voice faltered towards the end, and I almost raised my eyebrows at him. It seemed I was catching a glimpse of the one concept which scared my father the most, outside of the thing inside me. War. An idea which had been buried so deeply in his mind that he never thought it would ever grace our doorstep. It had to be why he would not fund a return to Zika when he could still remain in his position outside of his realm. It had to be why he was forceful with his people, keeping them locked up tight, disguising tyranny as freedom. Becoming so complacent in ruling a failing population without giving them the hope they wanted. Yes, fuck hope, but at least it was something people needed to fight for.

But war was not something to cower from, it was a priority. Yet, he would not partake in a deadly sport which could cost him his life, remaining seated on a glass throne built on pride, manipulation and lies. That was apparently much greater than the lives of our people. Falsely claiming the shield was for all when it only helped those with Rapidfire, that they would be banished from our territories, labelled a traitor if they so much dared to marry outside its borders. But, I knew in the cracks there were whispers of the revolt he was far too ignorant to see.

All for my father's fear.

A fear of being reprimanded as a failing king.

A fear of fighting against evil.

A fear of sacrificing himself for the greater good. All so he could keep his delicate luxuries, expensive lifestyle and flourishing winery.

"Father, you will be known as a petrified king if you do not fight."

Fear rippled through his gaze before he replaced it with thundering eyes, glowering at me, "Maybe rather than listening to fabricated lies, you should keep that lackey of yours on a tight leash."

There it was. The fear which simmered into deep anger and his moral compass flew out of the window in exchange. Plunging the knife where it would hurt the most, knowing exactly when to twist it, inflicting the damage until I understood not to provoke him. And, fuck, I felt the wrath simmer in my core as I debated grabbing the collar of his immaculate shirt and throwing him across the room.

"Lackey? Arraetta is *your* future queen," I spat.

Suddenly, he barked with laughter, finding inner confidence to sit at his desk, "*My* queen. You are sorely mistaken, Seraiah. Not in my lifetime shall I ever bow down to *that* girl."

"Why are you so adamant to hate her?" He was telling me only minutes before I needed to control Arraetta if she ever became my queen, that she was just another pawn as my mother was his, but he would not bow down to my wife? It could only have been because she was far more superior in status than he was. He felt threatened.

"*Head* over heart," he reminded again sharply, "have you not thought maybe she is sprouting deceptive lies to control us? It is not long before that *changeling* sheds her skin and changes you into the thing she is so desperate to control." He chuckled. "Losing yourself to an attention–seeking harlot."

Forget throwing him across the room; I could see the pen on his desk, which I might tip upwards before repeatedly slamming his face into it. He was vulnerable and alone with the beast he despised. Maybe I could break his neck. No, that was not enough. I wanted to flay his skin wide for everyone to see, burn the tyrant alive, letting all know his pain as he screamed in anguish. He would never speak such filth about my wife again.

There, there, Seraiah. You truly are outshining me.

I clawed back the snarl, pinching my leg through my jeans as I sought control of the cloying fury rippling through my being like a tempest.

Breathe.

Just fucking *breathe.*

"Head over heart, hm? Maybe if you opened yourself to the complexities of it, you would notice ruling with your heart might allow you to see your tyrannical ways are abhorrent to your people – and to my mother," I replied darkly, standing, "It is a shame you look dismissively upon my wife, not only the consort, your future queen, but a *goddess.* The Gods shall not treat you well when you pass through to the next life, I am sure. I should only hope you awaken in torturous pain and suffer as we all have suffered."

I hoped it would be the final thing spoken between us as I turned and walked down towards the door. But, the silence was short-lived as my hand touched the handle and he called, "You will realise being on the throne is not seedling's play, and then you shall come crying back to me when you desperately need a true king to guide you."

Without another word, I opened the door and walked out, slamming it behind me. I could feel my anger ebb, daring to break free using the one form it knew best, but I dug my nails into my skin until they broke through. Breath out of control, I paced up and down his long corridor for minutes, talking myself out of wanting to kill the hellsworn. Such big, brave words used to bring me and the female I adored down. But, mark my words, the next time he dared speak negatively about Arraetta, I would go against all my promises to my mother and rip the throne from beneath him.

However, a bigger war would soon be on our shoulders, and I believed what Arraetta told me. And, outside of my life bringers, there was only one other person I could speak to about such things, even if it was reluctantly. If my father would not heed the Gods' warning, then I had to be ready to march my soldiers into battle with confidence and vigour.

I would rather be a martyred king than a coward.

And Jonah was the only other who would be prepared to honour that.

The easiest way to travel to the garrison was by car, but I opted to sneak out of my father's lounge room window and down into my mother's garden for a little peace and quiet without a guard following me. At least he would not know I had left until far too much time had passed or he was informed by someone else.

The scent of smoked pinewood, old cologne, and damp lingered in my father's dusty lounge room - a perfect embodiment of my father himself. The back window had a perfect view of the hedge-rimmed wall behind the white pergola of what was known as The Queen's Garden. I was hedging my bets any gardeners or guards would not catch me on duty, but I had perfected the art of escape.

Once out of the window, I sauntered across the garden and around the pergola and then made my ascent over the high wall via some vines which were barely hanging on. Once I had surmounted it, I jumped down into the overgrown field on the other side. As I trudged through it, I pretended as though I was an average mortal, enjoying a peaceful life without the burden of my father's wrath on my shoulders.

It took me ten extra minutes to get to the garrison, as I had to walk through the fields and around the back of the garrison rather than cutting through the village. I hopped over a wall and onto a small country lane, reaching the tennis court at the back of the building before going to the door.

Two guards on duty were midst conversation, both surprised when they saw me appear unaccompanied. They stumbled over partial greetings as I casually sauntered past them and inside. The centre also served as a leisure centre for our non-army folk, and a receptionist sat at the front desk.

She almost gave herself whiplash as she pulled herself to her feet, "Your Highness!"

"Good afternoon," I greeted with false pleasantries as I walked to the elevator, noting how she was instantly picking up the phone. It was a shame I could not arrive at the garrison unannounced and surprise everyone, but I knew my solo adventure would have ended as soon as I was found alone publicly.

While most used a card to use the elevator, I had to input a code into a keypad behind the card slot to get down to the garrison. As soon as the doors opened, the cacophony of noise swallowed my thoughts, and I took a deep breath, taking in the aroma of metal and sweat.

Hopping down the metal staircase, I looked around at the crowds of soldiers until I spotted Jonah rushing towards me with a face like thunder. He met me as I bounced off the last step.

"Your Highness, will you tell me why I am only being informed of your arrival now?"

"Are you not glad to see me, Commander?" I replied wryly.

"You have a guard who is supposed to always be with you."

I peered around, pretending to look for Travis before I started counting the guards in the room. "Yes, I see that I have a lot. I am not sure how many, but I am sure well over five hundred."

Jonah sighed in annoyance, "You are getting on my last nerve. How am I supposed to protect the heir to the throne if he is wandering around like he is but a commoner?"

"Oh, I hope you do not lose your last nerve on me," I grinned. "Do you really need to know where I am at all times? Or is it so you can do your best to avoid me?"

"If I wished to avoid you, then I would be frank. It is for your own safety, Your Grace, who knows who shall try to take your life."

"Ah, yes, the cows will do their very best," I rolled my eyes, "you are far too serious, lighten up. There are enough guards here to stop someone taking my life."

Jonah was frustrated, peering at them as he debated controlling the conversation before folding his arms and saying, "If you wish to spar, I can make room for you."

"I do not wish to spar," I told him, although the idea sounded quite nice, considering it had been a while since I had been in the pit. In fact, the last time was with Connell before my solar rite, and so much has happened since then.

"Then why are you here?"

"War," I said bluntly, seeing his shoulders tense from my abruptness. There was more silence before he nodded, "Let us speak about this privately."

He commanded Leopold to keep an eye on things via his radio before waving me through to the back section of the building. It was a corridor full of doors into various rooms, one of them being our destination: a simple boardroom. On the wall was a fake window which realistically projected daylight.

"I do not know why this could not wait until this evening."

"It is best we speak alone, and then we can decide whether we take such matters to Amity."

Jonah pressed his lips together before nodding and taking a seat at the opposite end of the ten-chaired table. I leaned against the wall, folding my arms. "My father does not even care to listen to me about such things, either."

"You spoke with your father?" he laughed dryly. "How did you expect to convince him of whatever plan you had without a strategy?"

"I did not talk of a plan."

"Yes, but you spoke to him without one, correct? Sometimes I feel like I know your father better than you do. That hellsworn, alongside my own father, does not give a shit about anything which would ever come out of your mouth."

"Thank you," I sighed in frustration.

"So, we are not talking about war with your father. Then, what? Are we talking about the Zikan war?"

"I do not know which war," I sat down on the seat opposite him, "but Arraetta told me she has seen her father... in her dreams."

Jonah sighed dramatically, standing up, "What a waste of a conversation."

"It is not a waste," I said to him, holding my hand up for him to stop. "You wish to know what is happening with me, do you not? Or maybe not, considering we are no longer friends, but I shall tell you, anyway. Arraetta and I are connected much deeper than the Gods predicted, and everything I understood about what I have seen is starting to make sense."

"I am not a therapist, Seraiah," he stated harshly. "Stop confounding the evidence."

"Then, listen to me! Ivan... Arraetta's father tells her there will be a war and that she must fight it. Sheika has also said when Arraetta and I bond, a war will take place to end all wars. In my... in my dreams, or whatever you wish to label them, and last sol was no different." Jonah took his seat. "I touched the veil, and I was unsure what I saw, but I can tell you now something bad is going to happen."

"How are we supposed to prepare for something like that in this realm, Seraiah?" he asked, "While we have armaments, we do not possess the ones we had in Zika."

"Which hardly worked," I commented exasperatedly, "but the power inside us, our Rapidfire, is what will have to be used to fight."

"And, you just expect five people will be able to defeat this... whatever this thing is which you saw?"

"The Dark."

Jonah took a shuddering breath, swallowing, "The Dark, then. Do you expect the princess, who has not once been able to control her power, will be able to use it to defeat whatever comes our way?"

"She will not fight. I will not let her."

"Even if she is legend to be the bearer of Divine Rapidfire?" he raised his eyebrows, voice turning a little sarcastic, "or, *not* legend now, considering you have said Ivan the Great spoke to her *in her dream.*"

"Do you think I am lying? Because that is what I understand from your tone."

"I just wish there was more solid evidence," he added.

Fucking evidence. I cannot rip Arraetta's mind out of her and subject her to be studied. But we always knew there would be a war, we always knew something greater would come, it was only a matter of when.

"Anyway," I added, trying not to get too heated as I repeated, "Arraetta will *not* fight. I refuse to see her hurt or injured, and the safest place for her will be somewhere far away from here."

"So, the princess shall not fight," he nodded, "but that does not mean you shall be able to defeat whatever is to come."

But we had to try, somehow. If we let The Dark continue to swallow every realm in its wake, even one as protected as Earth, we would all be doomed to a fatal existence. If only there was a way for me to access Arraetta's power, to use it through me while keeping her safe.

"I can feed on her power," I suggested, remembering how it felt when I had taken some of hers from the page of the tome the sol before. In essence, I had fed from Arraetta's remnant of power, and it had sated me a little more than it would have done if it had been any other.

Jonah almost choked, "what?"

"It is an ability I possess," I replied, speaking aloud like I was devising a plan as I went, rather than one I had truly thought through.

"During the bonding, I can take some of her power - not all of it - but enough to be strong enough to train and merge my power with." Jonah was about to interject. "And, then, I shall use such power against my father, declaring myself king and taking control of the throne in preparation."

"You have thought this through, but do you not see it will just make you a tyrannical ruler?"

"It is for the safety of our people, not for my own benefit."

Jonah shook his head, "it *is* for your own benefit, Seraiah. You cannot take all this power as if it will not affect you. We have all learnt about what Rapidfire can do to its possessor, and if yours is even tampered with slightly, as it already is with that demon inside you, then Empyreans know what shall happen. Maybe you will be all-powerful, but maybe you will fall under its corrupt influence. And I, as your friend, do not want to see that."

I laughed dryly, "I thought you told me we were no longer friends, Jonah?"

Jonah glowered, "it was but a figure of speech."

"Speaking of metaphors," I countered, "are you dying?"

"Dying?" He raised his eyebrows.

"Well, it can only explain your need to disregard a brotherhood, which has been going on since we were seedlings," I sat forward. "Other than that, I cannot see your need to end it so selfishly."

Jonah barked with laughter, a look of disbelief on his face. "Wow, you truly are too blind to see the truth and believe it is because I am *dying*. If you cannot see it's due to your selfish nature, I just hope you awaken soon."

"I do not see why you would not speak to me about such a thing first."

"Oh, I tried. On numerous occasions, if I recall. But everything has become about how everything shall affect *you*, not how it would affect the rest of *us*. Whilst you will become the next king, destined by your blood, you seem to have forgotten the core values you created when we were seedlings. The ones you swore to abide by, and now it is as though I am in a room with your father, listening to a male I once admired speak of how he plans to strip his future wife - his *queen* - of her power to save his kingdom. Tell me, Seraiah, how can you be so blind as to not see your failures as a person by hearing them come out of my mouth?"

Jonah's keen words hit hard, but he had lied about speaking to me. I would have tried to listen, to see his side. But, the core values he brought up were just the ideals of seedlings, not of a being who wanted to stop his kingdom from burning before him. It almost felt like I was face to face with my doppelgänger again as he presented me with what I wanted when I was so much younger. To be an emperor of the universe.

"I shall have you know I do not plan to strip Arraetta of her power; I plan to feed from it, that is the difference. It would not harm her."

"But you shall let it harm your father."

"He deserves such a fate."

"He may deserve it, Your Highness, but it is the lowest way to overthrow the crown. It is the equivalent of cheating, for fuck's sake."

"Cheating?" I stood. "I do not cheat, Jonah. I prevail at whatever cost to ensure this kingdom has an appropriate ruler."

"From what I have just heard, I do not see how you shall be better than him."

More dark thoughts of slaughtering a male who spoke to me like I was beneath him fuelled my mind for a second time that sol and I was close to adding him to the death list, which was topped with my father and The General. I was eager to throw him through the glass pane to show him exactly who he spoke to. I wanted to make him

413

understand that messing with me was the last thing he should do. Friendship, or not. Fuck that, there was no friendship. He was only an ally, readied to get me onto the throne, whatever it took.

Traitor.

"I shall spar you," I declared.

"What?"

"You and I shall fight. If I win, you will have no choice but to bow down to me and apologise for your insolence. And, if you win-"

"-If I win," he interjected with a smirk, "you shall heed to everything I say, following my decisions when it comes to getting you on the throne." I opened my mouth to speak, but he chuckled. "Do not tell me you are backing out now, hm? I thought you were a *fearless* king, not a prideful one."

Fuck, was I even strong enough to fight Jonah? He was a being who trained religiously with his battalion, while I had not participated in an ounce of exercise for moons, and my physique felt weaker than it ever had.

"And no, Rapidfire," he added. "I am not in this for cheating. We will work with the standard sparring rules, and you and I will fight fist-to-fist. It is only fair."

It is only fair. I snorted aloud, turning my head. But I had already posed the bet, and I was not someone who would back out easily, letting my pride get ahead of me. No matter what would happen, I would see Jonah kneel before me apologetically, and we would put this madness aside.

I would win.

TWENTY-NINE

I lost.

And, quite frankly, it was humiliating.

Every eye was upon our brawl as Jonah and I took to the middle of the floor, each equally determined to beat the other. But my defence was much weaker than my offence, and Jonah strategically played every move, somehow having studied each pull of my wrist and sway in my stance. I supposed he had been watching every fight I took part in, but I knew it was my weakened body which could only be blamed.

Jonah was a strong male, even if he was shorter than me. While he usually told others to avoid hitting my face, he made sure to pull out all the stops until, less than thirty seconds into the fight, he knocked me out.

K.O.

Ding. Ding. Ding.

Your prince has had his ego *severed.*

The racket of the surrounding crowd swallowed me as though I had been pulled underwater. Thudding against the ground, I could not gather my bearings for seconds until I awakened to my devastating and embarrassing defeat.

In a similar stance to Kaeltar, Jonah knelt over me, "I suppose you better hit the gym, Your Highness. Such a loss does not look good for your reputation. The good thing is I am here to restore it for you. Tonight, we will dine and discuss the repercussions."

And, without another word, he shouted an order to get me cleaned up and walked away from my aching body. Empyreans, I was so fucking weak. I coddled my defeat by laughing it off with some nearby soldiers, but I could feel the shifting gazes of those who had seen the penetrable armour I wore. A sight not good for a future king.

I could not face Arraetta looking the way I did, nor did I know how I could see her after our previous conversation, so I spent the rest of the afternoon in the library. I painted away on the canvas she and I had half finished until it was time to go to Jonah's.

I was looking forward to eating Alex's food but was not excited to entertain the fractured brotherhood. I knew what conversations would be had: the truth about Italy, Arraetta's incident, and the war. Unlike previous times, I arrived after Freddie, Genie, and Helga had arrived. They were already seated downstairs as I took the reluctant steps to our meeting space.

I had barely received a greeting from Jonah, and Alex's was not any warmer.

"Look at that bruise," Freddie chuckled, our conversation in English.

"Fuck off," I chided, sitting down in my usual seat.

"Rumour mill strikes again," he grinned.

"Twenty seconds, I heard," Helga added in Zikan, a small smile on her face, which I glared at in return.

"I was unprepared."

"Maybe do not tempt the beast when he is already festering?" Freddie suggested before he leaned back, throwing an arm over Genie's shoulder, "I am starving."

"You're always hungry," she tutted, taking a drink of the wine before her.

"I am a growing boy," he patted his stomach for effect, leaning over to place a kiss on her forehead, which she shied away from with a laugh. I looked around at the table, noting two additional chairs which looked identical to the ones already there.

"Do we have others joining us?" The fear of such a thing was prominent in my voice, and I hated that I was in the unknown of what was next.

"Apparently," Freddie shrugged, "but I was not told who."

It seemed Amity had been pulled from underneath me and was truly in the hands of my commander. Fuck. Whatever it took to get me on the throne, but who was joining our force? Who had gained enough trust from all of us to be part of this?

It seemed my answer was given as I heard two voices from upstairs, and I raised my eyebrows, looking at Freddie, who knew, as well. Leopold and Connell, but not Travis, surprisingly.

"Did he speak to you about this?" I asked.

He shook his head, "like I said, I did not know. Are you so surprised? We have been gunning for Leopold for a while."

"But, Connell?"

He was trustworthy, of course. I knew the male would protect me with his life, but so would Travis, and there seemed no sign of him joining us unless he was expected to stand silently in the corner. Footsteps started to thud down the stairs until Leopold appeared first, followed by Connell, Alex and Jonah. The latter two carried food dishes, while the two males looked in awe at the small room we had created. Connell looked far too big to be in such a place.

Greetings were given and introductions were made with Genie before everyone took their seats at the table, apart from Jonah, who walked to get the tome from the shelf before standing by his seat. He did not miss the glare I gave him, bringing two outsiders without speaking with me first.

"Before we start, I require the two of you to swear allegiance to us," Jonah said to the males. Neither disagreed and seemed eager to swear to our cause and followed the same procedure which Genie had taken quarters before. Once all had been agreed upon, meals were plated, and I sat with a full one, ignoring the pangs in my stomach as I waited for Jonah to spill his new plan.

"So, now we are all here," he finally said after a long moment, "I think it is worthwhile for us to speak about what happened in Italy. For those who do not know, Eros - Henri Romano - was killed at Corvelli's hand."

Ah, so he was not letting them know it was I who slit his throat - an interesting turn of events.

"Our prince here was present," he added, "and was subjected to partaking in a game of Hanged Man." Eyes turned to me. "Corvelli killed him before he could finish the game."

"How many did you do incorrectly?" Freddie asked, looking at me.

Too many to want to remember, but I did not want them to know that. The blame was going to be placed on my shoulders, even if it was my fault in the end he had died.

"Hanged Man, as in the kid's game?" Genie asked.

"A deadly version," Freddie told her, still looking at me for a reply.

"Corvelli turned Eros into a blood angel," I told them, receiving an echo of gasps from the table, "he knew what game he was playing, and I was not smart enough to guess wholly the words he said before he plunged in the knife."

Genie looked pale as she took in my words, and the clattering of cutlery rippled across the table as all of them stopped eating.

"Fucker," Connell muttered, "I have a few grievances with that hellsworn; I'd be glad to take it out on him."

"I have brought you here for such a task," Jonah told him, "I want to send Connell to Italy."

"In Eros' stead?" Helga asked, "Will that not be asking for death?"

"I would give my life to kill him," Connell nodded, seemingly uncaring that he could be killed if he was caught. He *would* be killed even if he laid a knife on Corvelli.

"Connell shall trade sides," Jonah told us, "and will remain undercover for us until the time to strike is right."

"They will just breed another Corvelli," I pointed out.

"Then, we strike whilst the iron is hot," Leopold spoke up, "anyone we know who could be as formidable as that hellsworn should get taken out by Connell. I am for it."

Slaughtering soldiers to make a point was far beyond what Amity stood for, and we knew it. While I understood Leopold's idea would be good, Connell would be next in line to face punishment at my father's hands. But, I had a better idea because I knew how strong Connell was and what he *could* become with the right mindset and additional training.

"Or," I added, "we make Connell the next Corvelli."

Silence lingered across the table before Jonah nodded slowly, "it is a good idea."

"It is a great idea," Freddie agreed.

Connell shrugged with a smug smile, "I am for it."

"In a few days, we will be doing the newly revised exercise of War Cry," Jonah added. "You, Connell, will need to, visibly, switch sides on the field in front of all the soldiers. I will enact a punishment, while I am quite sure my father will fall for your change in allegiance."

"I cannot hurt an innocent," Connell replied, although I was unsure whether it was because of his allegiance to Amity, or his want to remain as accepted by all. "So what would you have me do?"

Thoughts ricocheted across everyone, but it was Leopold who made a suggestion first, "Attack me... and make it fucking hurt."

"I... I think we should not get ahead of ourselves," Alex cleared his throat, looking wary about Leopold's brilliant yet disturbing plan. "He does not need to injure anyone to gather The General's attention."

There were other ways for Connell to gain such attention, but it would be more difficult and take a lot longer to sway the mind of The General. Showcasing something as brutal as attacking the Grand Captain was loyalty at its finest.

"I think Leopold is right," Jonah affirmed. "Connell needs to show how much he hates us, even if it does stab him right in the chest. As long as Amity is not discovered, he could do whatever he wished."

"So, attack the Captain," Connell agreed, although I could tell the idea was causing consequences to rush through his head, "state my allegiance to The General and get sent to Italy. Is he likely to send me, or must I commit a crime to be banished from here? He might decide to replace Kaeltar with me."

Connell's gaze shifted to me for a split moment as he said it, and I wondered whether he thought I might use the dark power I had against him as I did Kaeltar. But that all depended on whether he would imprison me.

Jonah answered, "There is a possibility. Leave that with me; I will have to converse with the war council." He paused for a second, waiting for anyone else who might wish to add something. "Speaking of war, it has come to my knowledge certain prophecies are being... realised."

"Are prophecies real?" Genie whispered to Freddie, who replied with a nod of the head.

"We need to prepare our soldiers," Jonah continued, looking across us all, "as I expect there to be a shift soon, and we are far too unprepared to fight an unknown enemy."

"Is it the prophecies Sheika spoke of during the council?" Helga asked, a little alarmed, "because of the princess being the Goddess of Divine Rapidfire."

"Something of the sort," Jonah nodded, surprisingly not expanding on the knowledge it had come from me, "I think it is always good to have our soldiers at the top of their game. Therefore, we will ramp up training exercises and regimes at the garrison. With that said, I think it is worth us speaking of the consequences which may occur if war *does* strike."

While we were all used to having some sort of impending war on our shoulders, I noticed how tense Genie became. I supposed human wars were far from her safe shores, whereas we were speaking of universal wars which had been threatening our existence for far longer than any of us had been alive.

"Will... will Arri have to fight?" she asked worriedly.

"No," came an echo from both myself and Jonah, and her shoulders sagged with relief.

"But she could defeat The Dark," Freddie insisted, as though he would think sending her to battle was a good idea, "she has the power to."

I grunted, "She does not even know how to control it, it would be a death sentence."

"War *is* a death sentence. Neither of us is powerful enough to fight that thing off." Freddie's fear was palpable, but I did not see him volunteering his own wife as bait, human or not.

"I am not sending my wife to war," I growled, grip tightening on the knife I had been holding idly. "Her life is not worth any of yours."

The words slipped from my mouth shrouded in darkness and I knew the veil between my dark and true self had slipped - more insolent eyes on me which dared to penetrate the surface, coaxing the beast within.

I dropped the knife and cleared my throat, "I have one solution... I will feed from Arraetta's power."

"What?" Helga gasped.

"Absolutely not!" Alex fired in the same tone, "The Gods would never allow such a thing."

Empyreans, shut the fuck up.

"Fuck the Gods," I chided dramatically.

"You are crossing the fucking line, Seraiah," Freddie snarled, as though he had not been suggesting he send my wife to war seconds ago, "none of us would allow such vile behaviour."

"Do not forget how he plans to take his father's." Jonah added more fuel to the fire as everyone, except Genie, was in uproar. It only made my blood boil with rage, unable to interject as they fired angry words in my direction. Until–

"Would it hurt her?"

Silence.

Genie's question was all that was needed to quieten the herd, and even it calmed me.

I swallowed, replying truthfully, "I would not be draining her power."

Fire burned in her eyes as she huffed, "but that doesn't answer my question! Would it hurt her? She has been through enough pain because of whatever is inside her, so if your suggestion would cause her more damage than good, then I think you're more of an idiot than I guessed you to be."

I was unable to answer her question because truthfully I did not know. I imagined it would hurt my father, but I did not think about whether it would harm Arraetta. I supposed I was so blind in my need to protect her that I had not thought of the wider consequences.

"Then, that's the answer," she replied in my silence, "if you don't know, it's not worth trying. Not on Arri. Maybe your father, but not Arri. She's a good person. Yes, she shouldn't fight, but for God's sake, there has to be a better plan than taking more from her than what has already been taken."

Agreement rippled across the table, leaving me looking like a fool, and I felt shame hit me again. "If I had access to that type of power, then I would be the only one who would need to fight."

"Oh, how noble," Freddie snorted, "and then you shall die a martyr, hm? What about your kingdom? Your father will be dead, you have no children to continue your legacy, and your wife will be left to run a nation without any guidance."

"I would quite like to see that," Helga shrugged, earning a little smile from Alex, who nodded in agreement. I supposed a queen in charge would be quite a change after hundreds of winters of a king being at its helm, but still, I did not want to leave Arraetta alone when we could have a long life together.

A loud knock rattled the front door above, and all of us fell silent, looking upward in its direction. Alex looked a little hesitant before he stood and quickly left the room.

"Maybe Kaeltar is returning so he can wash that shit out of your mouth," Freddie commented harshly, glaring at me in a hushed tone, "I thought you were a stable force, but all I see is the male I knew crumbling before me."

"Shut the fuck up," I snarled, pointing at him, "you have no right to command me."

"No, you are right," he nodded, the conversation turning to Zikan, "I only have the right to *advise* you. And, I advise you to take time to think over your blasphemous decision to want to feed from your wife's power. Her life force. I have heard all about the pain she has been through, over winters, from Genie, so I do not think it is right, causing her more than is necessary."

Footsteps returned down the stairs, and I noted a secondary pair of shoes clattering behind Alex's leading ones. We all turned as Alex appeared, looking meek and fearful before he stepped aside, and the second person appeared.

My eyes widened, and everyone rose to their feet as they took in the one person none of us wished to see in our meeting quarters. Dressed in what seemed to be some sort of undercover clothing, my mother looked around at the group.

"Y-Your Majesty," Helga stumbled, lowering her gaze.

My mother took in the small room before looking across each of us, none of us knowing how to react to her being present.

Fuck.

"This is quaint," she commented, "I remembered you were converting this room, Jonah, and you have outdone yourself."

"Thank you, ma'am," Jonah cleared his throat. I looked at him, wondering whether his new plan included bringing my mother into Amity, but the redness on his throat and face was quite the giveaway that he was as surprised by her presence as any other.

"May I sit?" she asked.

"Yes, ma'am," Connell said with a nod, the only one to shuffle from his seat and stand closer to the door like a formidable guard. My mother looked satisfied as she took his place, tentatively pushing Connell's half-eaten plate out of her way. She looked at us all expectantly.

With that, I took my seat and slowly did every other who was able.

"Why are you here, Mother?" I asked, "Can you not see we are dining?"

"I can see," she answered, "I have been intrigued for a while about the secret gatherings which have been taking place under my nose, and so I decided I would sneak out of my palace and see what takes place at this house. I followed Katerina this evening, but I thought I might bide my time before I joined you all. Can you tell me what is so important my First Lady needs to be present?"

"She is a friend," Alex replied softly, "a good friend."

"As good as Henri Romano?" she answered, looking at Alex. "He was a good friend, was he not? But now he is dead, yet you all gather here as if he is not."

"Your point, Mother."

"The Sanctuary of Amity," she finally stated, looking at me, "it is what you are all here for. Your little organisation created to infiltrate the throne. Yet, you have done little to succeed apart from gathering evidence and causing havoc amongst our people."

"We are here to mourn the loss of Henri Romano," I lied.

"Do not lie to me!" my mother raised her voice, startling everyone, "Henri Romano is not your friend. Is that not what you told me before your solar rite, hm? You told me to let him go, and yet when I spoke with your father, it turned out even your ally had already given away some of your secrets, including that of this little collective."

I felt as though I was sitting in a council meeting, being pried open by my father. But I knew my mother's words were fictitious. Her motto was using lies to gain truth, and she would use a dead man's legacy against us so we could spill more secrets than she needed to know.

I folded my arms and leaned back, "Henri would not reveal anything to Corvelli, let alone my father, because of what happened to his family. Or, do you not remember how his father's blood was splattered across the walls of the garrison, remnants of it remaining as a reminder of what would happen to any traitor? No, Henri was no traitor, Mother, so do not come here with your incessant lies to try to gain the truth."

I could feel the heaviness of my words lingering in their aftermath as everyone remained silent while my mother calculated her next words. She took a deep breath after a while before she nodded, "I may not agree with your approach, but I cannot sit idly by and ignore the reality which we are in. I do not wish to know what goes on wholly in this organisation, but I shall offer you a helping hand."

A mixture of emotions crossed the table, some sceptical and others hopeful, but I could see the reluctance through Jonah's impenetrable mask. Even through our disjointed brotherhood, if it could even be called that, the two of us still agreed on something. My mother was a liability we could not afford, yet she could be an excellent chess piece on our side. But, fuck, we were unprepared for her arrival, the unknown which had blindsided us.

"How can we trust you?" I asked.

"Because when you realise you have been a victim of control, you start to understand the wider world around you. I am but a pawn in your father's game, am I not?"

The question shook us all, and even I was surprised to hear such words when I had spoken with my father privately hours before. Did that mean she had some sort of listening device or camera inside my father's office?

"I have ears everywhere," she told us all, confirming my thoughts, "do not worry; here does not count. It seems you can trust Katerina here, too. You have done very well in disguising your allegiance, my dear." Helga looked guilty. "You do not have to trust me; it is not something I care for because trust should not be easily given. But, in return for my allegiance to you, knowing this organisation exists, and for my silence, I shall offer you those ears."

Jonah's gaze cast around the room while my mother kept hers on me. She was a dangerous and unpredictable force, one which I knew we could benefit from having on our side, but one I hated the idea of. She was my mother, my queen, who had used and abused me for scorns and sided with my father over numerous unacceptable acts. But, seeing past such actions, even if they caused me to fume in their betrayal, made everything she offered logical.

"Then, tell us something we should not be aware of," Jonah said, a bargainer playing his hand.

My mother pressed her lips together, thinking for a moment before she seemed to find something she believed to be of interest, "I suppose you might already know, but The King - my husband - is preparing to remove Seraiah from his position as the heir to the throne. Most of his council is swayed by my decision, not his; therefore, each time it has been proposed, there have not been enough votes to let it pass. But, I will not lie. Much has changed since Seraiah was punished for treason, and I have felt the tide turn in my husband's favour. Without the council on Seraiah's side, he shall not be king, and Amity shall not exist for the purposes I presume it had been born."

My mother's words were hard-hitting, and I understood every part of it. I remembered how my darker side had said about my father bedding a consort to create an heir, and I supposed such things could still stand unless there was another way for him to prevent my ascension. Empyreans, I was drowning every sol in the abyss of my inner demons whilst grasping at straws to get onto the throne. And my father was doing his best to use a legal system to get them to vote to remove me from it. Fuck, if every member of his council voted in favour, I would find myself out on the streets. Or, worse, imprisoned.

My father was making a backhanded move on the unwavering glass chessboard, and I had not noticed pieces were disappearing. If I lost the council, I lost the throne. If I lost the throne, I lost Amity. If I lost Amity... I lost everything.

No. Not everything. Not Arraetta, who remained in her place.

Steady, unmoving, a piece yet to be played but one I was reluctant to give the spotlight to in case she might fall through my grasp.

"All those in vote for Her Majesty to join Amity, raise your hand," Jonah said to everyone, and I watched each hand slowly go up. I supposed some were more fearful they would be reprimanded if they declined.

Jonah looked at me with scepticism before he slowly raised his hand, but I decided to make sure a few things were clear before I agreed. "I do not want you to sign the book, and I do not wish to see you here partaking in these meetings. We will come to you if we need you, but that is it. We will not share everything with you, but you can trust we will keep anything you share a secret."

My mother barely paused before she nodded her head, "Agreed."

She stood, knowing she would not be required for the rest of the cold dinner.

"May I escort you back, Ma'am?" Alex queried.

"No," she shook her head, looking at Helga, "you and I have much catching up to do, Katerina. Let us return to the house, and we can speak of your... deceit."

Helga rose, unable to hide the reluctance or shame on her expression as though she was not a formidable force outside of my mother's chambers.

"Do not hurt her, Mother."

"I will not," she tutted, walking to the doorway before she turned back to us, "while you may not wish me to be here for these meetings, I would like to be part of any talks of war you speak of. It is a concern my people might have to fight something we are not prepared for, so I would suggest future meetings are brought out of here and moved up to the main house."

"Yes, Ma'am," Jonah agreed.

With a final nod, my mother ascended the stairs with Helga and

Alex, leaving a silence heavier than a storm cloud about to burst in its wake. Her arrival sounded the alarm for a new battle, which was not only about fighting but survival. Somehow, she had infiltrated our rebellion without any fight, slipping through the cracks of our defences and digging her impenetrable claws until she had us right where she wanted us. And, we did not stop her because she could offer the one we lacked – ears on the ground where we had none.

Even if she had not openly admitted it, I knew she would not know about the war or her place as a pawn without a listening device. But, she was not a pawn. No. He was hers. She controlled every aspect of his life, and he did not know, but he would soon. She was beginning to feel her tight control slip because of the one thing in the palace which was the most volatile – me.

I was the one variable no one could predict because I had been so tightly under my own control for scorns, and now it was slipping. They were all scurrying to find a way to remove my place from underneath me. And if there was one thing my mother would do to restore her illusion of control, it was to bring me to heel.

But while she might have been able to wheedle her way into Amity, she did not know I could not be controlled no matter what. I would stay on top of my game, fight every war and win it, and shatter their false illusion of peace if it meant ripping the throne from underneath them.

THIRTY

"War cry." A microphone carried Jonah's voice through the quiet rumblings of the garrison as he vulnerably stood in its centre, every eye on him.

Seated. Respectful.

But, one strike could kill the commander mercilessly.

By the blood-stained wall, dressed in black war garb, I stood alongside Freddie, Alex and Travis.

Listening. Ready. Waiting.

It had been two sols since my mother crashed the Amity meeting, which led to an awkward wrap-up of the meeting before we all departed for our homes. *The talk of war would come* were words Jonah had said to us all, and the sols which followed were spent in the meeting rooms at the palace discussing various tactics for war. My father was not present, but my mother kept her promise. Neither of us spoke of what would happen with Connell and Leopold; one tactic kept tightly under our hats.

Freddie and I had not spoken a word, although I could not care less about conversation after our bitter words in the meeting. It seemed alongside Jonah, the rest of Amity was slowly turning against me. I could feel their claustrophobic gazes bearing down on me as though I was nothing but filth. Empyreans, I could not even handle a conversation with my future keeper nor stay on top of my game with everyone else. It was like I was slowly losing myself, and it was fucking dreadful.

"You have all received clear instruction from your platoon, but let us make it clear," Jonah called. "This is not just a game; it is war. Soldiers have thirty minutes to get into positions; when the alarm rings, you are fair game. There is no mercy in this, as there is none in war. It is a simple game that requires teamwork and strategy to defeat the enemy. As per the rules, you will be split into your platoons but shall purposely only be on the ground in your squad. Each will be led by their sergeant, who will receive orders from their lieutenant by comms. There will be five operations: civilian rescue and defence, tasked with bringing civilians to the designated safe area; royal defence, same as above; decoy, to throw enemies off their route; area defence; and area offence. You will notice we have pre-selected our enemies, who are dressed wholly in dark red. Each operation will work together to safely bring civilians and their royal family, in this case, our two resident princes, to the outpost and to save this town whilst defeating the enemy."

War Cry was once a game we played for fun, but it was adapted into a strategic combat exercise designed to prepare our troops for real warfare. On Earth, humans might compare it to a blend of dodge ball and paintball, although it was deadlier than that.

Each soldier wore vests starting at five points, which depleted with each hit. Once it hit zero, they were pronounced dead. Reinforcements cycled in until their squad was wiped out, taking orders from commanders overseeing them from a control room. War Cry demanded more than just tactics; it tested endurance, adaptability, and the brutal reality of conflict.

"Final rule, while pain *can* be inflicted," he called, having reeled off the instructions, sly smiles washing over the soldiers, "death is a punishable offence. And those who inflict it will face a trial, which

431

THE INSURGENCE OF THE CURSED PRINCE

could sentence them to their own. Fall out!"

"Sir!" Echoes of the word spread around the garrison before soldiers stood and walked to their designated areas, signposted by boards attached to the walls.

"I suppose we should find our positions," I said, looking at Travis, "do not tell me you are on duty to guard me all sol."

Travis looked at me with a soft smile. "I'm afraid I still have a job to do, Your Grace."

"Just make sure he is not close enough to his wife to take her power if he needs it," Freddie sneered, making his way towards the exit.

I walked after him quickly, "your behaviour is petty, Freddie."

He turned, stopping me inches from him, "No, what is petty is your inability to see what a hellsworn you have become over the last few quarters. I do not even know who the fuck you are anymore."

"Please do not fight here," Alex begged, "I know tensions are high, but we need to show we are strong in front of everyone."

Freddie's gaze scanned the nearby soldiers, who must have heard our argument before he hissed at me and hopped up the stairwell. Guilt vaporised my anger as I watched after him before I looked at Alex, catching his sour face.

Fuck. Was everyone my fucking enemy? The weight of it stabbed me as cutting as an iron sword, internally making me stumble as I avoided Alex's scrutiny. I knew when it was time to leave, and I had yet to decide on my destination to hide out for the soldiers to come and find me. Because, as they knew, the whereabouts of the royal convoy would not always be known in war.

It was as though Freddie had run by the time I arrived outside the garrison, for he was nowhere to be found, but I was sure he was hightailing it to create a distance between us. If times had been kinder, I might have been more sneaky in deciding where to hide or run from the male tailing me, but I was deep in thought as I trudged around the estate.

I did not know where I was going until I stood in front of Sheika's house. Shit. Maybe I should have knocked on a friendly neighbour's house or hidden in someone's garden for the hours which would pass by. If the palace were not out of bounds for the exercise, a territory not safe from the mercy of any enemy, I would have hidden in there, but it was only that I did not want to delay the soldiers finding me that I did not.

Hesitantly, I knocked on the front door and stepped away, idling myself with looking at the wind-brushed trinkets. Russell barked while I could hear Sheika falling over herself inside before she pulled the door open.

She sighed, "another prince."

"Hellsworn," I muttered, earning a glare for my use of profanity. I did not care for it because my reaction was called for, since Freddie and I had the same idea to go to Sheika's and, inevitably, share the same space. It seemed it was too late to change my mind as the siren rang across the village. I nodded to Travis, "he will need to come too."

Sheika nodded, shuffling backwards to let us both enter before she closed the door. I barely acknowledged Freddie as I walked into Sheika's living room, cloaked in partial darkness by the closed curtains. He perched on one of her sofas, one leg half crossed over the other while idly reading a tome - a pastime he barely ventured into.

Silently, I dropped onto the opposite seat and sank into it, attempting not to care about the simmering feud destined to make waves under the shaman's roof. I only hoped it was strong enough to hold the storm which would hit.

As if reading my mind, Sheika said, "If my home is damaged, I will ensure the two of you fix it brick by brick, princes or not."

433

She left us without another word, leaving Travis casually standing by the doorway on guard from invisible assailants. It was a shame he did not know he might be preventing a fight from happening sooner if the atmosphere turned more sour than it already tasted.

Freddie's odd flick of the page, far too quick for anyone truly reading a tome, and the homely noises of Sheika's house were catastrophic to my senses as anxiety and aggravation ticked away in my chest, needing a release from their tight grip. At some point, during my silent festering, Sheika returned with hot tea which soon turned lukewarm, neither of us deciding to have one.

The exercise would take hours to complete, and it was only a matter of time before we were found and were amid the troops attempting to get us to safety. We had chosen the furthest place from the garrison, which made our journey back quite an adventure. Or, it would be if we could enjoy it rather than partaking in oppressive silence.

After Freddie had barely read the tome, making it to the final page, he sighed, stretched and leaned back with his eyes closed.

Unable to stay quiet any longer, I said, "I do not see why you are angry at me, Freddie."

He snorted, not opening his eyes to spare me a glance, taking far too long to answer before he finally muttered, "You are a fucking idiot."

"Oh, fuck you," I growled, sitting forward, "I get why Alex 'Mr Bow Before All Deities' is angry, but why do you care so much?"

Mirthless laughter rippled from his throat, and it seemed it was the only answer I would get as he settled again. Wrath scorched through me hot enough to want to force him to submit and show him exactly who he was speaking to for the use of his insolent tongue. But, I was not a merciless king, and I would not destroy our brotherhood when the rest was already crushed to dust. Even if the hellsworn had no right to treat me as he did.

I stood, desperate to contain the hatred inside, as I started to pace in front of the cloth-covered window as I fought the suffocating malice I felt. Fuck, who was I becoming? All these cloying emotions were turning me into someone I did not even recognise, and everyone was unbearably turning against me. Freddie was my friend, cousin, and ally; he would be my advisor once I became king. I trusted him with my life. Empyreans, I trusted Jonah, and he stabbed me in the back quicker than the strike of a venomous snake.

I caught Freddie's eye and stopped abruptly, preparing myself for his provocation of my striding.

"I do not recognise you anymore," he said after a few moments of silence. "None of us do, Seraiah. You are power-hungry, dictatorial, and narcissistic. Maybe you always had those traits, but you are almost beyond recognition since Arri came into our lives."

"I am not narcissistic," I glared but recognised my mistake instantly and averted my gaze. Empyreans, I sounded like a fucking narcissist. I supposed the traits were there; I was a prince fed by a silver spoon all his life, but I knew myself and my actions, and my ego did not drive them.

"Maybe not you, but that thing inside you."

"I have him under control."

"It seems to be the only thing you do not."

I squared my jaw, the whites of my knuckles radiating in the darkroom as I gripped them tightly, seeking fresh air from the claustrophobic space I was enclosed in. It was a shame he had no idea it was the only thing I did have under control - everything else had long been placed in the hands of others, and I had let them take it without mercy.

"I have him under control," I repeated, almost only for my own conviction. I would not let him take such command over me, not when I had kept him at bay for quarters since his rebirth. I could sense the snort of disbelief in my mind, but I disregarded it, as I always did.

Freddie's incessant silence between my outward thoughts was far too unbearable, even more so as he rose from his seat and walked over to where I stood. Far too close for me to move away without looking like an angry seedling, so I held my ground.

"Why do you refer to *it* as a separate entity to *you*?"

He was a separate entity to me; he was not me, even as reality clawed up my throat as sharp as needles, daring to free my chided words from my silenced tongue. The devil inside me was but a dark shadow which had cast itself upon my spirit and tore me apart piece by piece, but still, I prevailed against it. For me, for them, for *her*. I would forever bear the pain of my scars if it were to protect her from him.

That was why he was not me. I was in control of myself, the master of my vessel. I would deal with every coffer as they opened individually and battle the final boss once he had prevailed at ripping their locks away. And, when it was over, everyone would see I was a strong, steady king – one who was not to be feared but revered.

"Fuck you, Freddie," I chided, "you do not know shit."

"How would any of us know when you never tell us, hm?" he replied, in that same way my mother so cleverly switched in her deception, "We are not blind, Seraiah."

"I did not ask for your help!" A growl rippled from my throat, causing him to flinch. I shoved him away to create more space between us, "I do not need your help. I am the one who suffers. I am the one who bears this weight, which is heavier than that fucking crown. I am the one who will prevail, not him, not *it*. So do not be angry at me for not telling any of you, do not force me to part information I do not wish to tell, do not... do not fucking abandon me because of it."

He looked at me sadly, "No one is abandoning you."

I laughed in astonishment, shouldering him hard as I distanced myself from him to the opposite side of the room. I should have left it, found air outside and sought another destination to drown in my sorrows for the hatred they all cast me. But, there was no other place I could go, not alone. And, Empyreans, I was truly alone.

"Yes, you are. Jonah, Alex, you. I can feel your harsh gazes on me as you watch me come undone right before you. It is not my fault all this fucking happened, Freddie! I am as much a participant in fate's fucking game as you are, so do not blame me for keeping what is happening inside me a secret."

Do not blame me for taking my wrath out on the insolent fools who dare rise against me rather than seeing what bruises they gave.

There was more insufferable silence as I stared a hole into the wall, contemplating who would next say harsh words and cause more damage to our tender brotherhood. But it was I who was right. I was right to never open up about the beast inside, to be wary of everyone as they all threatened to shatter my glass crown. All of them no better than my enemies, ready with iron shackles to chain me to a vault of bound duty and wilted freedom. A vault designed for no one other than the sinner inside me.

Lost in my thoughts, I had not noticed Freddie had crossed the threshold until his hand brushed my shoulder. I might have grabbed him by the collar of his shirt, fought him as I had the night Arraetta had disappeared, but the weight of anguish tore all strength from me.

"I do not wish to fight, Seraiah. I just wish to understand, to know what the fuck is happening. Maybe it will give you some respite."

I shoved him away, eyes meeting his in defiance, "And, when I am king, you shall use it to threaten me, hm? I know how the crown works, Freddie; I have been a part of it since I was born."

"As have I," he replied dumbfounded, stepping back slightly, "I am a prince too, remember? But, you and I must be at bitter ends if you believe I would use such a thing against you when you are king. I thought we trusted each other, that we are brothers."

"I thought the same for Jonah, but he abandoned me."

"But, I am not Jonah," he pleaded, "Whatever is going on between you and him is between the two of you, but I am my own person, and I committed my life to serve you, Seraiah. Empyreans, I would *give* my life to save you."

I wanted to believe him. But, when it came to it, was my life more worthy than his? I always knew he would make a far greater king than I would, but I was greedy to rip the throne out of my father's hands and prove to my people I was not a cursed prince. Maybe it was all a show in the end, deceiving myself above everyone else that I would ever be the one in charge. A puppet tied in strings shall never be free from its puppeteer. And, yet ignorance had been bliss when reality was far too harsh to take.

I sighed, "I trust you, Freddie. But, you have to believe me when I tell you that he – *it* – is far from sight right now."

"So, that thing is not coaxing you into taking from Arri?"

The male was staring deep into my soul, prying for answers buried far deeper than one would ever venture. No, the dark entity had not made any suggestions to feed from her; it had only happened that she had left a remnant of energy in a tome, and I melded it into my own. I had not even thought about whether my suggestion would work nor had I spent enough time with Arraetta to even try such a thing. And, now I had spoken it to the world, it was kicked into the dust before it could be given a test run.

"I will not take her power," I nodded sharply. "There will be another way to fight; we just have to find it."

"Good," Freddie answered defiantly, as though I was a seedling having been reprimanded for something insolent, "there will be a way to defeat whatever is coming our way."

"Hm."

Freddie returned to his spot on the sofa, while I leaned against a space on the wall not cluttered with something. Even without him looking at me, I could sense he wished me to open up more, he did not even need to ask.

"Do you not want to know how I know about it?" I asked.

"You do not wish to indulge me about the thing inside you, but you do wish to indulge me in how you found out about the war? I feel honoured."

I scoffed, *honoured*. Fuck him and his mocking. The impending war which would come would be far greater than the one I was battling internally. I opened my mouth to speak, but ended up looking at the other silent presence in the room who had not spoken a word. Travis' gaze was on the floor, barely moving, but listening. Not that he would say anything, but he was not a part of Amity and such conversations were made for more private circumstances.

Freddie and I made eye contact again, and I knew he had also remembered our third party. He shrugged, "I do not want to know as long as we are all prepared to fight, that is all that matters. Who knows what brutalities are happening outside this window as they attempt to defend themselves."

I nodded with a soft smile, "It seems they have yet to find us."

"What channel are you listening to, Travis?" Freddie asked.

Travis stood straight, "headquarters, Sir."

"Jonah's channel?" Freddie replied, and Travis nodded in confirmation. "Can we have your radio on this table?"

No hesitation from Travis, unplugging and placing it onto the centre table before he took his position again. The door opened and

Sheika returned, tea towel wrapped over her shoulder, with fresh tea and biscuits on a tray. She did not seem to care for the tea which had been left to wilt, and replaced them.

"I thought you might appreciate some fresh tea now you have sorted your squabbles out," she said, looking between us, "maybe some anger management therapy might do you both some good."

"He is just sexually starved, Sheika."

"Frederique!" Sheika gasped, batting the tea towel at him, which earned quiet laughter from Travis while I tried to hide my amusement.

"Ow, ow! Travis, save me!" Freddie begged, protecting his face before the female tutted and walked back to the door. "You said he could not do anything with her."

"They cannot have intercourse," she corrected, eyes flicking between the two of us, "but they may still kiss."

I could not prevent the gasp which left me, standing upright from my position as she left the room without a care. Was Sheika trying to mess with my head? I had followed her instruction not to go further than holding hands with Arraetta, but she was telling me I could have kissed her. Empyreans, I had hurt Arraetta because of it, backing out because I swore the Gods would punish me for completing the bond too soon. And, it turned out I could have done anything I wanted to apart from having sex.

All those moments when we could have kissed, I could have tasted those sweet lips on mine, gasping for water in the wilting heat of my inner desert. And, my haven was somewhere in the palace not far from where we were, waiting for me to sweep her off her feet.

"You look as though you have just received the best news of the sol," Freddie chuckled as I returned to my seat opposite him, picking up my tea.

"I am thinking how we can end this exercise early."

"I think you ought to make amends with your wife before you consider sticking your tongue down her throat."

I grimaced at his repulsive terminology, but I knew he was also right. I had been thinking about how I could make amends with her after the last few occasions had been less than fruitful, leading us to fiery fallouts before we had really got to know one another. It was as though the Gods were testing us to see whether we could make it through to the bonding stage. But, if I could sway Arraetta's mind from the thoughts of war and not allude to the tumultuous undercurrents of the palace, I could show her she could be happy without all those burdens on her shoulders.

But amendments and the kiss of desperation could wait until the end of the exercise, especially as I was aware something would happen with Connell. I had not been given more information about what they intended to do, but I knew from Amity that Leopold would sacrifice himself for pain and suffering in our favour.

While tensions had been high, they simmered quite quickly, and the conversation was steady as time ticked by. No one showed up at our safe house, nor was there any concern over the crackling radio, which communicated messages occasionally. It seemed the enemy was dwindling, but not as fast as the rate of our allies. I knew command would have chosen the best soldiers to act as the enemy force.

Another hour passed, tea cups were empty and the plate of biscuits had disappeared. I was sure Sheika was no longer in her house, although I was aware she liked to snooze during the sol, so she might have gone to bed.

Freddie sighed with boredom before swiping up the radio, "This is Freddie speaking; I was wondering when I would be safely moved from the battle zone. Over."

I chuckled, "You sound like you have never used a radio before."

There was a crackle from the radio before Jonah's voice rang through. "This is the Commander speaking. Frederique, would you be so kind as to share your location? Over."

"Commander, I have camped out in the safest place possible," Freddie replied dramatically, "should I move towards you? Over."

"Do not, and I repeat, do not leave your post," Jonah answered quickly. There was a small silence, then. "Is the prince with you?"

"Should I lie?" Freddie asked me. "You could easily sneak out of here and head back to the palace if you want to see Arraetta." He clocked Travis. "With your guard, of course."

"I shall wait."

He raised his eyebrows, before shrugging, and replying to Jonah, "Yes, he is, we are with the seer."

"Remain vigilant," was Jonah's reply before the line went silent again. It was at least another ten minutes of waiting before boots clattered on the porch outside, followed by a sharp knock. I stood from my seat and led the three of us out of the room to the front door, with no sign of Sheika appearing anywhere. I would thank her another time for her stark hospitality.

Swinging the door open, we were greeted by a unit of sixteen soldiers with a variety of bruising and lacerations on their skin, all whom I was quite aware were part of my guard, not my father's. All of them wore electronic vests with an array of numbers on them, some only had one, while others were more than five. I did note both Jorey and Vandan, the soldiers who had fought quarters before were in the group.

"My princes," Sergeant Blackthorn, a male with fourteen on his electronic chest plate closest to the door, greeted, "we are here to evacuate you"

Freddie threw an arm loosely over my shoulder and leaned towards him, playing into the damsel in distress role, "we have been awaiting rescue for hours. I thought we might have to venture out onto the streets on our own!"

"That will not be necessary, Sir," Blackthorn smirked, "your safety is our greatest priority, we were securing the area before we could safely find passage to bring you to the garrison. I'm afraid we will need to split you from one another, Sergeant Voss here will be escorting you, Prince Frederique, and you shall be with my squad, Prince Seraiah."

Freddie pushed himself off me and stepped towards Voss' unit, greeting him like he was an old friend before making a humorous remark to a couple of the other soldiers.

"I have Travis with me," I pointed out, thumbing towards the big lug, waiting to follow behind.

"Of course," Blackthorn replied, nodding in greeting to Travis, "Sentinel."

"Sir." Travis greeted.

"Follow me, stay sharp!" Voss commanded quietly, departing with seven readied soldiers and Freddie, who stuck his thumb at me in an indication that all would be fine.

"This way, my prince," Blackthorn said, ushering me across the grass verge in front of Sheika's, "diamond formation! Keep tight, eyes out!"

"Sir," the rattle of agreement rolled through the seven others, forming the shape around me as we shuffled toward the path down from Sheika's house.

"How is the situation?" I queried quietly to Blackthorn, who was closest to me.

"Enemy is dwindling, but they're cunning. Best of the best in red, should be easily visible, but some have disguised themselves very well."

"Anyone particular we should be looking out for?"

"Connell."

I raised my eyebrows. I had barely swept the hundreds of soldiers while we waited for the briefing to be completed, but Connell, being part of the squad of enemies seemed to be the most obvious with what I assumed would take place.

Quietly, we walked around the rims of the houses, past the seedling's park and towards Jonah's home. It was a quicker path, rather than dodging through passages and down the intersections of the estate, but it did not make it easier as we would soon be exposed without any buildings to hide behind.

Blackthorn held his fist up at the end, a signal caught by another officer ahead of him, and all of us came to a halt. He swiftly held a finger up, and two trained soldiers shuffled quietly from formation, armaments equipped, and advanced forward, seeking out anyone who might pray on us. Once a pathway was secured, we were given the clear to keep moving, not a single one of them speaking, all alert.

But, it seemed we were infiltrated quicker than they had hoped as three red adversaries sprang from their hiding places in a nearby garden to block the path. They wore vests with numbers close to fifty, making them harder targets for mortal soldiers to kill and proving an enemy could not always be simply taken down by the use of armaments – especially if we were in combat with our most dreaded foe, The Dark.

"Ambush! Close cover, keep Iron Wing safe!" Blackthorn yelled, the diamond formation changing instantly to a box as they all began to fire their armaments while the enemy attacked.

Two soldiers with numbers at one went down as their vests were caught in the fire, slumping away from the formation in pretence of being dead, while Blackthorn repeatedly fired at the enemy until he managed to land a few heavy blows and knock out some of the numbers on the enemies vest.

"Fall back! Rear guard, hold them back!" he announced, pushing us back in the direction of the intersection and I followed idly, at pace, entertained by the play I was partaking in. Of course, I would not be so entertained during a real battle, more likely running off adrenaline, but the dramatics did make me wish I had some popcorn for the front-row seat I had obtained.

"Mayday! Mayday!" Blackthorn bellowed down his radio, "this is Vanguard - convoy is compromised. Requesting immediate reinforcement, over!"

I was shoved forward by one of them with no mercy, "move!"

Soldiers led us into a nearby garden, everything becoming a blur. Crunching of gravel, boots dispersing, a front door kicked open. More physical pushes against my back until I was inside a pristine, white home, already dirtied by the mud-ridden boots. Soldiers fanned out into various positions, scanning windows and perimeters, weapons ready and raised.

"Clear," one soldier called.

Travis pushed me down to the ground by a wall, hiding me from the sight of any windows. "Stay." An irritating and useless command.

Curtains were drawn, shrouding the room in cloaked sunlight, far too warm to be enjoyable until we were saved. But the weather changed for no one. War was not made to be enjoyable, it was fierce, and brutal, and horrendously terrifying.

Voices shouted, the static of radios silenced, more heavy boots positioning themselves around the external perimeter. We were surrounded, and the enemy was amid preparing an attack, working together as a unit, while we were hiding with limited soldiers, awaiting illusive reinforcements.

Ragged breaths. A sniff. A twitch of an armament for comfort. Silence swept the room while Blackthorn spoke to an inaudible operator on the other end, giving our exact location using coding

I barely understood. The enemy remained silent, no movement detected to the rear.

It was only then the tense calm returned, and he perched by me. I had learnt Blackthorn had brought us into the safety of his own home by several pictures perfectly placed on a nearby drawer. It was a space which looked more like a designer's home, yet there were signs of life in the microscopic, a minor stain on the carpet, remnants of food on the nearby table, plastic seedling's toys pouring out of the top of a woven brown basket.

"Beautiful home," I commented, voice low.

"Thank you, my prince," Blackthorn replied, "my wife has a fine touch when it comes to our home, she'll probably be less than pleased to find it dirtied when she returns."

I did not know who his wife was, but I could only presume she worked in the human world. His daughter was no doubt in our local school, where all the teachers were probably trying to stop their students peering out the window at the soldiers who had been let loose on the streets.

"Excuse me," he bowed, before rising and shuffling out of his room, returning to quiet conversation on his radio. Blackthorn returned after a few minutes, the five soldiers remaining indoors awaiting his command.

"Are they allowed to attack the house?" I queried, curious to know whether someone might attempt to break in.

"An enemy would have no problem," he pursed his lips, pulling the edge of the curtain to scour the perimeter, "once we have reinforcements, we will move out."

More time ticked by. Soldiers remained vigilant, but itchy to fight. I started to grow bored, wondering how long it would be before we could continue onwards. We still had three streets left to cover until we were on the open road to the garrison, no doubt blockaded by the enemy. It was going to be a little tedious if we would have to stop at every safe house along the way just to protect me and gain more reinforcements. In a real act of war, I was sure we would just be running to safety.

A sharp shattering of glass drew me from my thoughts, eyes landing directly on a grenade which billowed black smoke, mercilessly cloaking the room. There was no time to escape its fumes as it suffocated all our lungs. Blackthorn fired new orders, the front door opened with a thwack and the thudding of more boots rushed in.

"Surprise, motherfuckers!" one male said, before I could hear the firing of their fake armaments and the uprising of a brawl. It was far too clouded to navigate where I was as I rose to my feet and tried to shuffle away from the chaos, attempting to hold in my coughing fit. I could hear the allies yelling for me – especially Travis – while unidentifiable soldiers pummelled one another without mercy.

No longer was this just an exercise, these were soldiers who must have been gunning for a fight for a long time.

A crack of a bone. An anguished scream.

Bodies to the ground. Unloaded armaments used as blunt ones.

This was chaos.

The best escape was outside, but finding an unmanned exit seemed to be difficult, even in Blackthorn's big house. My heart was rapidly pounding in my chest as I sought somewhere to go, fighting off one soldier who thought I was the enemy.

Sweat laced my forehead, why was I scared?

I needed to get air; I needed freedom. It felt like all my cloying nightmares were about to come true and red beastly eyes would pierce through the misted veil, tracking me down until it could feed from me again.

Empyreans, I was panicking.

Shit. Shit. Shit. Where the hell was the exit?

There. Light by the front door. Or maybe the back, but I could see the exit.

And then I could not. A cloth washed over my vision, darkness stunning me as strong arms encased me.

I struggled, earning a grunt but no release.

Fuck, I was trapped.

I fought as I was lifted easily, carried without mercy, all while my breath was far too erratic to hide my anxiety.

Make it stop. Make it fucking stop.

Then, those words.

"Target secured, let's get to The Kill zone and secure the area."

The voice was far too familiar not to recognise.

Connell.

The fight was gone as I froze, ignoring the bead of perspiration dripping down my face, soaked up by the material. I was being held captive like I was part of a completely different operation.

Fuck, of course I was.

I was the grand finale of Amity's war games. What better move than kidnapping the cursed prince himself? It was only a matter of time before the incident caught the attention of the council. And, there was only one way to find out whether they would banish Connell from London or sentence him to death.

Play the hostage and be victim in this game of war.

THIRTY-ONE

The hood was removed, and I blinked in my new surroundings. A fortified road blockade was created using a circle of vehicles, all manned in red. My arms had been successfully tied behind my back while I was forced to remain on my knees in the middle, out of sight of whatever was beyond the cars.

"Your Highness," Connell greeted. "It is so fortunate you decided to partake in this exercise, for I can finally regain some of that needed control we have been yearning for."

"Control?" I replied, feigning a wince as I tugged at the constraints.

"Yes, it is time we loyalists take matters into our own hands when it comes to command," he chuckled darkly, "both commanders are far too interested in kissing your arse, none caring about His Majesty. It's a shame we have all forgotten who is the true king, worshipping a devil in hopes he would ever become a saint."

While his words could have hurt me, they were no more bruising than the blunt edge of a sword, swamped in double meaning. I could tell by the subtle tug of his lip that he was referring to my father over me, retaining eye contact as he spoke.

"So, all is fair," he called loudly, "in exchange for the prince, I demand repentance from one of our dear commanders." Ah, there it was. The reveal. "And, they shall be here momentarily because no

449

one wants to see another hair-" He patted my head twice as though I were a pup. "-on this head out of place. And, if we know anything, this prince is quite out of his place."

"Someone has to put him in it," one of the males sneered, earning a couple of chuckles from others.

Original.

"It is good to see you have finally opened your eyes, Connell," another commented, and I glanced at him, noting the sour expression he was giving me. Such idiotic mortal-kinds daring to rise against me unknowing they were part of quite the tall act.

"I would happily kill him," said another, one eye peering through a scope on top of his gun outward.

Go ahead, I dare you to try.

"In trade for your own life?" replied the male beside him.

"It would be worth it, but it would be a shame to miss the aftermath," he shrugged, turning his weapon slightly, "we've got movement, multiple hostile inbound... four vehicles from the east, five from the south." He cruelly grinned at me. "Looks like the devil prince still has allies."

"Want me to shoot?" a female with an armament ready called. "I could blow a few tyres."

It seemed the enemy had been holding back, geared up with real weapons which could cause damage. A purposeful tactic, but it must have taken some persuasion to get access to the armoury. Jonah definitely had some higher involvement.

Fuck, I wished there had been no tension in the sols gone by so I might have had a little insight into what would happen.

"Hold your fire," Connell called, "let us see whether they're open to negotiation before we cause damage."

"Pointless being armed," she sneered, but she took the command. I supposed he had rallied some support from my father's guard, which did not come from his commitment to Amity. He was a respected soldier, who had great camaraderie with most. It was what made him great at his job because he did not care for the line between sides. Or, at least, he had not until his task meant he had to step across it.

From where I was kneeling, I could hear vehicles rapidly approaching from the south and east before they stopped at a distance. Doors thudded open, many boots rushed heavily across concrete pavements and grass verges, surrounding the vehicles, and armaments were engaged. The enemy squad were surrounded, but none of them backed down from their positions.

"Hand over the prince!" The shout came from Leopold to the south.

"Now, now, Captain," Connell shouted, standing behind two car bonnets where I presumed he could see Leopold, "let us negotiate."

"Fuck negotiation!" Leopold growled, "This is a fucking exercise, not a war mission. In no world should we ever harm the heir to our throne."

"The enemy would not care who it was," Connell answered, "for the purposes of this exercise, *we* are the enemies."

Silence rattled through my allies, awaiting orders from their command. I shifted on my knees, uncomfortable on the hard ground, casting my gaze around the hellsworn soldiers I could see before me. None cared about my presence, lavishing in the upper hand they thought they possessed.

Connell took a few steps backwards, not glancing at me until he was next to me again, his hand on my hair in that same way as before. It took all my effort not to shake him off, not to be treated like I was submissive to his demands.

"What shall it be, Captain? Shall you hear our plea?" I did not miss Connell's other hand removing a handgun from his waistband, with a loaded magazine. He racked it and placed the cool metal against my head in place of his petting hand.

I winced, one wrong move from Connell then I would be dead. No more Prince Seraiah, just splattered brains on the road beneath me.

"Or shall I put a hole in our dear prince's skull?"

"That is treason!" Leopold called back, panic laced so superbly in his voice I might have thought he was genuinely panicking.

Connell let out a devilish chuckle before he grabbed the back of my t-shirt with his free hand and dragged me to my feet without mercy. The picture before me was formidable, at least fifty guards surrounded us at a distance, with Leopold and Jonah both standing to the south, armaments ready, bulletproof vests over their clothing.

I could not see behind, but I knew we were on the road just down from the palace, close enough that someone might be able to see us if they peered through the upstairs window. My mother might find the situation entertaining, or she might have turned a blind eye. She was most likely not attempting to prevent a coup by calling in elite security from Italy who had not partaken in the exercise.

"I am not afraid of death, Cap!" Connell replied sinisterly, side-stepping until he was standing behind me, gun to my temple. "So, what shall it be? Shall I kill him? Put us out of the misery he so dares to place us in?"

"What do you want?" Jonah called, armament readied.

"Let us end this game with a show," Connell called, "you versus me, Commander. If I win, you shall step down and I will resume your place. Finally, this fractured army will be ended and no one will so speak sourly of our king again."

"Traitor!" someone yelled from the east. I was unsurprised someone would call Connell out for his insolence, but he was doing as must be done.

"*I* will fight you," Leopold valiantly shouted.

"So easy to give up your rank," Connell answered as Jonah gave Leopold a falsified concerned look.

Jonah called, "remember when you are banished from here and sent to serve under the thumb of Corvelli, you gave up every comfort you were ever given."

"At least Corvelli knows where his fucking loyalties lie!" Connell sneered, earning a cheer from the local enemy.

Connell shoved me out of his lighter grip into the harsher grip of another, and I could feel the cool metal of another handgun pressed up against the nape of my neck. Empyreans, he was really playing with fire because I was sure whoever the owner of the armament was would happily pull the trigger. At least with Connell I had been a little safer, knowing he would not blow my head off.

"Do not worry, Your Highness," the male at my rear chuckled, "once this is all over, we will put you out of your misery."

I wanted to tell him to go fuck himself, but I was too aware it would make me look weaker in my already vulnerable position. He shoved me forward until I had a front-row seat inside the perimeter of the vehicles, while Connell shifted himself over to the other side flawlessly before walking down to meet Leopold halfway.

Without making it glaringly obvious, I shifted my gaze across those I could see, noting some of the troops from the unit I had been a part of to the south. On nearby rooftops, I noted three snipers, each aiming armaments at different assailants, including one on Connell. He could take the shot, could kill Connell, but Jonah was silent and would not take such a risk. Neither would I, I supposed.

There was no call, no signal, no shout of aggression when it came to starting the fight, only the first fist to be thrown by Connell, which barely caught Leopold as he defiantly shifted.

Jab. Jab.

Hook.

A foot up.

Dancing around one another with more urgency than in a sparring ring. It looked desperate. Leopold would not give in so easily, they needed to give a show before he mercilessly fell under Connell's fists.

Somehow Leopold managed to send Connell stumbling with a hard slam to his jaw, who barely regained his footing from his blow before he bared down and ran full force at Leopold. A sharp twist of the hip, a kick to the back of the knee and Connell scraped down to the ground with a clatter.

Words were spoken, but I could not hear them at the distance. Not even in the silence which simmered across everyone who watched.

Leopold jumped on top of Connell and started to beat his fist against his face.

Slam. Slam. *Slam.*

Connell caught his fist and slammed his other into Leopold's ribs, knocking him off kilter. Leopold grunted to the floor next to Connell, but shuffled back enough to give them distance.

Connell rose. Leopold rose.

Unsteady bodies swaying.

Connell barely took a second before he attacked Leopold again, not giving Leopold much time to enact a defence. He weaved under each punch Connell brought at him, all while trying to navigate away from the pain which laced his expression. Connell took him by surprise by rising one fist up for a punch and using the other to hook into his kidneys.

Leopold stumbled with a loud grunt, slamming to the ground as he clutched his side.

Tension rattled across the onlookers, and even I noticed how tense my shoulders were from watching. Fuck, I knew Leopold had to lose but, Empyreans, it was horrendous to watch the brutality of it. The blood, the sweat, the torment.

Leopold's anguished breaths were unnerving as he staggered upright, and I only wished I could see the look of determination which would have been written on his face.

Connell roared as he brought his fist against Leopold's cheek.

The shift was instant.

Brutal. Final.

Knock out.

Time slowed as Leopold's body plummeted to the hard ground with a thud.

"Weak." The words resonated in the atmospheric silence, fear rising on allies who waited for Leopold to come around. Seconds passed as Connell paced a little. Then, slight movement and Connell looked down in fury.

It seemed that neither he nor anyone watching were quite prepared to witness Connell's next actions.

Connell pulled Leopold up by his collar, hesitating for a split second to show his hidden compassion for the situation, before he brought his fist down on Leopold's face.

He punched him.

And, punched him.

And, punched him.

Blood.

Bones cracking.

If I knew anything, it was being under the brutality of that fist was not fun, even when it had been in the sparring ring. I knew Leopold would have been in a lot of pain.

For Amity. For the future of our kingdom.

Satisfied Leopold would not wake, Connell dropped his limp body to the ground, stood and lifted his boot. The end game had arrived, and Connell was declared the winner of this particular fight.

The sole of his shoe caused a defiant fracturing noise to echo from Leopold's ribs. I wondered if Leopold was even still breathing, but there was no way Connell would have killed him. Not when the punishment for murder was the equivalent.

Empyreans, had there truly been no better way to do it? No, anyone who was declared an ally of mine was bound to the estate, unable to go to Italy, unable to leave the scrutinous eye of The General, and be free from the constraints I had put them in.

"Enough!" Jonah shouted, anger and anguish laced in his tone, walking forward with determination, "You wanted a challenge, then come and get me, hellsworn fucker!"

Connell stood and readied himself for a fight, walking down towards Jonah, but Jonah's fight was better than Leopold's. Jonah had studied every move of mine, Connell's, and every soldier so he could be above their game in case they turned against him at any point. He knew everyone's weakness; he had studied and prepared for it in moments like this.

Within twenty seconds, Connell was on the floor, and Jonah had his knee over his neck, something electrical in his hand – a taser of sorts.

"Stand down," he commanded.

"Fuck you," Connell hissed, pushing against the new strain of the device. "You would rather bow down to a demon prince than our king."

"I do not choose sides when it comes to the war I am facing," Jonah growled, "you are a traitor, and you will pay for your crimes."

"So... so merciful of you, Commander," Connell grunted with a little smirk.

"I do not turn my back on my allies," Jonah answered defiantly. "We are not enemies of each other, but if we fight like this, we will not be ready when the real war comes."

A beat of silence. Heavy breathing. Then – one voice from the crowd.

"Traitor."

Then another. Then another.

I had not quite expected it to be a call to arms, but suddenly the crowd of armed soldiers rushed forward to attack those inside the circle of vehicles.

"Fuck," the male behind me said, loosening his hold on the armament enough for me to shuffle out of his aim and slide over the vehicles to the other side.

The fight erupted in an instant.

Fists. Screaming. Chaos.

I did not care.

I just needed to get out of there.

My bicep was taken into someone's grip - Travis - and I was pulled towards the housing estate perimeter, close enough to witness everything but far enough not to be party to the feud.

"I apologise, Highness." Travis bowed his head. "It was my fault. I did not protect you."

"None of us knew that was going to happen," I lied, "do you think you can free me from these ties?"

Travis nodded, removing a Swiss knife from his pocket and cut through them easily. I stretched my wrists before dusting my clothes off, eyes on the fallout as the enemy soldiers were detained over a long few minutes, peace lingering in its stead.

Only then did my ears twig at the arrival of more vehicles, and I peered around the houses to see two black-marked cars pulling up.

"Empyreans," I breathed. A great time for The General to arrive from wherever he had been. He climbed from the vehicle with a bunch of other older guards.

"What is the meaning of this?" he shouted, gazing across

everyone until he stopped on Jonah, "causing chaos amongst our ranks."

"A training exercise, General," Jonah corrected.

The General snorted, "What are you training? Monkeys? I am out of town for less than a quarter, and you can barely control these imbeciles."

The General and Jonah's conversation quietened as they spoke, but it was heated, and I noted the frustration on Jonah's face. I wished I was closer to hearing it but did not wish to be reprimanded for participating in the exercise.

"Fall out!" The General barked, rapidly turning before stalking back to his car. Those he was with disappeared along with him, and the vehicles reversed, turning and taking off in the opposite direction, presumingly towards the garrison.

Jonah pinched the bridge of his nose before he tucked his shoulders back and turned to those waiting, instructing as he spoke, "Take the injured to the infirmary, and every soldier in red is to be sent to the vaults until further notice. You and you take Connell to solitary confinement. I will deal with him later, and both of you take Leopold to Marie instantly."

"Sir."

While the troops obeyed Jonah's orders, he looked around for something until his gaze landed on me. He walked across the grass verge, and I wondered whether he was going to treat me like the enemy, as he had done for sols.

"I would suggest you return home; I will update you once I have dealt with the aftermath of this chaos... and my father."

I pursed my lips, "an unexpected anomaly?"

"Something like that," he bowed his head and took his leave. I knew dealing with his father was something he had not expected, but it at least meant a decision on Connell's position would be made sooner rather than later. I only prayed Leopold would survive Connell's brutality and be able to return to his position as Grand Captain once he was well again.

Deciding the best course was not to go to the garrison, Travis and I traipsed back up the road towards the palace and I relished in the peace following the chaos. I had not noticed I was a little shaken from the kidnapping until I thought about the weapon against my skull. Did those hellsworns understand what would have happened if I let my dark side overwhelm me? Because I was sure in my dishevelled state, he would have. It was the second time in as many quarters I had allowed soldiers to walk all over me, and I knew I was mentally compiling a list of those I would happily see die.

I hated to admit it, but my father had been right sols before when he had said there would be a list of those I wanted to kill. Was I truly turning into him? No, I was not tyrannical, I only wanted to see those who rose against me submit. Fuck. I guessed everyone was right. I was following in my father's footsteps and I had not even noticed. He was probably laughing at me now, watching everyone see his devil son become a mirrored image of himself. Formidable, unforgiving, narcissistic.

No, I would not continue the same way. I would change, I would become better, I would be a king for my people, even if they did not see me for the good male I was, for the desire I had to rule with both my heart and my head – with her. For her.

Arraetta was my anchor amid the storm, she would make everyone see I was a great king, that I was kind and compassionate. Arraetta who swam through my mind at every moment of chaos, who dared to rise up against me and speak her truth, who I had neglected for sols because of my own carelessness.

Crack.

The coffer of love dared to try to break free, readied to snap on its last hinges, and I would let it. Yet, I was still apprehensive about showing her my true feelings, maybe that would come in time, maybe I would let her open the coffer so I could understand what it felt like to let love rule over anger and guilt.

At the house, I took the decision to get freshened up before I looked for her, spending my time making myself look like I was not covered in dust and grime. Freddie had sent me a text to say he would meet me at the house because Genie had been tasked with choreographing the heartfast dance. It seemed more like a distraction from the earlier events of the sol than a real thing, but so was the life of being a royal. One minute you are under siege, the next you are parading around a ballroom.

Arraetta's room was empty when I tried to find her, many of her belongings having disappeared, but I had no worries that she had left the house – I was sure I would have known such a thing.

I caught sight of Terance as I wandered back to the grand hallway.

"Ah, Your Grace," he greeted with a soft bow, "I have been meaning to catch you, but it seems our paths have not crossed."

"I hope you are going to tell me where I might find my wife," I replied gently.

"Her Highness has been moved to your new quarters," Terance informed me, "although, they are not quite new for you. To make room for the additional guests for Iontine and the bonding ceremony, we are also removing you from yours."

"Shall I be sleeping on the sofa in the library?" I wondered, unsure where else I would sleep if it were not in the bed I had been sleeping in for scorns. I could only imagine the decision to move both Arraetta and myself were in my mother's hands.

"A temporary bed shall be set up in the coming sols in your office. I know it is not ideal, but we will work to make you as comfortable as possible."

As comfortable as possible included raiding my personal space to construct a bed. Half of me wondered whether I would prevent any workers from going down to do the job, and asking them to allow me to do it myself. But, even I knew it was far too much work and it was not as though they would do anything to disturb my peace.

"It is fine," I nodded, "only temporary. Once I am wed, I shall stay with Arraetta."

"Exactly. I shall inform you when you are to be moved, so do not worry until then."

There was little more conversation between the two of us as I excused myself to find Arraetta, all while texting Freddie back to ask him to meet us at our new quarters when they were ready.

Maybe I would be able to break the ice with Arraetta by sliding my hand around her slender waist and pulling her to me, maybe I would kiss her. Desire to do that rippled through my body as I walked down the corridor, desperation choking me in lustful smog. Oh, how her soft lips upon mine would wash all my anxieties away as rapid as wildfire.

The house was busy as I walked through, but I barely acknowledged anyone as I walked through to the west wing. It was only at the bottom of the staircase, leading up to the converted attic, where I hesitated, nerves tickling my chest as I thought about the female who unknowingly gripped my heart tightly in her hands, not daring to set it free.

Arraetta was not exactly prepared for my arrival. What if she was sleeping? Or, maybe she was naked. Or, maybe she was not even there, hiding away somewhere else in the house, having witnessed the atrocities of the incident outside the palace. Still, I had no more hesitation and swiftly took the spiral stairwell up to the converted storage space, which had been turned into a loft apartment.

At the top of the stairs, I walked through an open door into a short corridor, lined with rounded windows on the right which looked out to the village – no signs of any soldiers being at arms remained. A door to the left lead through to a vibrant, ornate bedroom with a four-poster bed to its right and an unused fireplace to the left. Above, amply placed, was the picture the two of us had painted separately.

White and gold colours washed the space, looking more extravagant and radiant than any of my life bringer's quarters. An awning of gold cloth embellished the ceiling, hugging a suspended glass chandelier at its centre. And, on the back wall, a door opened to a balcony, looking out to the woods beyond the back of the gardens.

Living quarters fit for the heirs to the throne.

Our paradise.

Undeserved for a cursed prince, but warranted for a deity.

Soft murmuring caught my ears through another door, hidden on the left side of the bed, and I lingered at the entryway to a substantial walk-in wardrobe, already lined with clothes and jewels galore. But, I cared little for such materialistic things, my eyes landing on the only gem I cared for - Arraetta. She wandered around the en-suite ahead, watched by her maids, Kadey and Elina. Neither noticed my arrival at first, but I softly cleared my throat to gain their attention, placing my fingers on my lips when I caught their attention and waved for them to leave.

Leaning against the door frame, I watched Arraetta bask in the warm radiance of the sun from the windows. I tried to etch such an image in my mind, so that I might take a brush to canvas with the sight.

She was an embodiment of pure beauty, curls loosely tied in a bun atop her head, a brown skirt which hid her arse, making me jealous my hand was not tucked underneath it, or maybe instead they should have been where her white shirt hugged her breasts.

Empyreans, I was envious of clothing.

My cock beat against my jeans, and I wondered whether it might break through the seams just by thinking about her. If only I could remove every item, she wore and lose myself in her delectable skin. I ached for it. I ached for her.

Still having not noticed me, she stopped with a sly smile, studying the glass panel of the double shower, a light blush creeping up her neck – a telling sign that what she was thinking of was as sordid as the thoughts fuelling my mind.

I cleared my throat, and her head whipped in my direction. "What are you thinking about, Arraetta?"

"Hello, Seraiah," she flirted, taking gentle steps until she opened the bathroom's balcony stable-style door. The wind whispered against the loose strands of her hair and her friend, dear sunlight, radiated against her even more. I started to pace the edges of the room the long way around, anti-clockwise.

"I was thinking about how the place just isn't big enough for the both of us," she finally answered.

"Oh, really?" I was amused by her flirtatious quip, the longing for her more tender than ever. Her feet began to step backwards as she kept a distance from me, causing the two of us to walk in a circular motion at an equal distance.

"Yes," she nodded coyly.

"Actually, I was hoping you would not mind sharing a little earlier," I quipped, "it seems I am also being removed, from my quarters, to make room for guests."

"How about your...?" she trailed off, eyes gazing downwards to indicate toward my office.

"Office? There is no bed," I replied, a smile twitching on my lips, "you should know since you have been there."

"Have I?" she stuttered the lie, and I laughed lightly.

"Oh, yes, do not think I did not know you visited my hideaway."

"Well, how would you know?"

Could I tell her of the things that were kept out of place? I could not very well tell her about sigils as of yet, those might confuse her too much when we were just beginning to understand each other. I supposed I could have lied a little.

"Well, I can sense your energy."

"You weren't even there that day," she admitted, gasping instantly, and I did my best not to laugh at her as she covered her mouth with her hand in such an innocent way.

I tutted, "oh, Arraetta. I knew it. You are right. I did not detect your energy; instead, I saw that several things were out of place. It was interesting how the key to my cabinet had gone missing, and a few days later, on the day the generator blew, that exact book was on the floor, with the key."

"You blew the generator!"

Her accusation only made me laugh more, but I was not flabbergasted, only amused that she would attempt to pass the blame. Still, I continued my facade of pretence, "Trust me, I did not. I was not even anywhere near the library; do you not see I was trying to protect you from the wrath of the Zikans?"

"That sounds like a movie," she teased.

"Arraetta."

"Seraiah."

We paused, both at the opposite end of the bathroom to each other. I leaned my hands against the wall behind me, "Okay, Arraetta. I shall let you off the hook this time. But only if you allow me to stay in this bed."

She continued her journey, and I followed. Our farce became a provocative routine to see who would make the next move.

"My bed is full."

"Of?"

"Me," she pressed her lips together, itching to stop her lips from smiling. "I like to sleep like a starfish."

"No, you do not," I grinned, tracing the edge of the sink as I walked by, "you sleep like a cocoon."

"And, how do you know how I sleep?"

"Because sometimes... I watch you," I replied, noting how she was not phased. I tsked jovially, "I suppose you do not find that strange."

"I just genuinely find you strange," she said, hitting the glass panel as she stepped towards the shower. I had to hold my smile as it caught her off guard, but it gave me ample time to quicken my strides, maybe it was to check if she had hurt herself, or maybe it was the need to stop the incessant rotation of the room. She did not allow the hurdle to stop her as she shuffled away from me, the beating of my heart rattling in my chest in anticipation.

She chose to speak in a soft tone, a subtle tone of lust in it, "like it's strange you're just following after me now."

"Very strange," I agreed. My cock was becoming painfully hard, a mixture of a desire to bury it inside her or just sate it by getting myself off in front of her, "what were you thinking about when I walked in here?"

A heated expression whipped across her face as she looked behind and then back at me, and I could only imagine her thoughts were so fervent it felt taboo for her to utter them. Naturally, I turned in the direction she had gazed, understanding that it was thoughts of her - or, us - doing something erotic inside the shower together. *Throb.* Empyreans, the idea of us body to body, skin against skin, licked an expression of lust wildly across my face.

A squeak of a shoe, the shuffling of fast feet and I whipped my head, watching as Arraetta attempted to make her escape. Like a cat to a mouse, a predator to its prey, I rushed after her, following her heady scent and heavy breaths, lavishing in the chase with all the

465

energy of a pubescent teenage boy. She was fast, but not fast enough as we made it to the closed main door which led to the stairwell, and I slammed it shut as she attempted to open it.

Breaths heavy, my chest against her back, the two of us faced the door, attempting to regain our breaths while our hearts thumped in sync. The curve of her back fit perfectly against mine, and I instinctively shifted closer, as she inadvertently pushed herself back. Once more, the heated ambience rose, much like the evening in the bathhouse, but I bore new knowledge that I could taste her lips.

A whisper of skin on her neck caught my eye, and I lowered myself towards it, relishing in the thought of her soft, succulent skin embedding itself on my tongue. Uncaring, I nestled my hard cock against her, and I knew she could feel it. As though it was a signal, she slowly turned, peering up at me with such beautiful, submissive blue eyes, and subtly pouted pink lips.

"Oh, Arraetta, what you do to me," I breathed, bringing my lips down to the warmth of hers. A split moment passed as the realisation I was kissing her seemed to hit us both, before her lips parted with a soft moan, deepening it instantly. I slipped my tongue inside, while tickling the clothed curve of her waist as I gripped it. Desperation clawed through me as Arraetta swept her hands into my hair, dragging us closer as if there were inches that had yet to be discovered.

Even with all the warning bells ringing in my head, and everyone telling us we could not complete our bond early, I picked her up into my arms, legs wrapped around my waist, and travelled back into the bedroom. Neither of us broke the kiss, neither of us cared for what could take place, both of us craving something so innately ingrained in our DNA. It was as though our past lives were coming together at once after realising how long we had truly been apart.

Breaking away for a breath, I peered down at her fervour-stricken face. Her honey skin was tinged in pink from her heightened blush, her soft lips damp from our kiss, her hair falling out of its bun in strands of curls. "You are so beautiful."

I would not complete the bond, we could not have sex, but I could satisfy my need for pleasure by giving in a little. I traced kisses down her cheek and neck, while tugging at the edges of her shirt from the wrapping of the skirt. When her stomach was revealed, I shuffled my body down, her soft siren moans whispering to the room, and I was so eager to savour this moment with her, to bury this affair in my mind. I was painfully hard, aching to break my cock free from its holder and satisfy it with my hand as I took my pleasure in her sensitive skin.

I high-tailed the skirt over her torso, greeted by soft white knickers which shielded the maiden from my ambush, but its defence was far too weak. She whimpered as I stroked the outline of the underwear, laying my nose above them as I breathed in her exotic, sensual scent.

"Oh, Seraiah," she moaned.

Her melodic consent sent a shiver down my spine, and I stroked my hand up until I pulled at the cotton's edges, while my other slowly shifted down to my crotch.

"Oh my God, I did not want to walk in on this!"

Genie's voice ripped us out of our lewd reverie, and I almost fell backwards off the bed as I shuffled from Arraetta, who, in turn, was doing everything she could to protect herself from our unexpected audience. Both of us had been caught red-handed. I looked over at Genie, who had turned away from us, and Freddie, who seemed highly amused.

Genie slowly turned around, peering through the gaps of her fingers to ensure it was safe.

"It's a good job we came in when we did, 'ey?" she smirked,

making light of the situation, although I wished I had not told Freddie to meet me at the room.

"Can't you knock?" Arraetta cleared her throat and stood up, "or, must you always interrupt?"

"Actually, I believe that your precious other half asked us to meet here," Genie chimed, and I scowled at her, "I thought you're supposed to be celibate."

"We did not do anything further," I pointed out, "but no doubt, if you both had not walked in, we would have made it through to the end."

Or, at least I would have my tongue where it most desired to be.

"Sheika would love that," Freddie mused. He mimicked, "Oh, sorry, Sheika. We just so happened to have completed the bonding before it started."

Yes, but I was still told I could kiss her, just not have intercourse. Truthfully, though, could I have stopped?

"It wouldn't have gone that far," Arraetta replied, although I was sure she did not believe such a thing to be accurate, "because I would've stopped Seraiah."

"Really?" The three of us harmonised, causing Arraetta to pout like a seedling and us all to laugh. I was unsure whether she believed that because we both knew our desires were causing a lot of heat between us, and not always the good kind.

It would have been nice to have had some intimacy before I cuddled and spoke gently with her once we had finished. It was a shame I knew there would be limited time before our heartfasting to find ourselves in a similar position again, but once it had passed, I would never let anyone interrupt us again.

THIRTY-TWO

Following my sexual frivolities with Arraetta, all of us spent hours working on the dance, followed by food and wine before each of us departed to our spaces. Chaperones had been implemented to prevent any further incidences between Arraetta and me, but I knew I would steal a kiss or two or one thousand before our heartfast, even with an audience. Empyreans, her scent had etched itself to my senses, and I was desperately tugging at the skin of my shaft, begging for release as I became unbearably consumed with desire. And, even once the orgasm passed, I was left in the dust of dirty haze and intoxicating need for Arraetta.

The following afternoon, I received an alert from Jonah to find Freddie and meet both him and Alex in the palace boardroom. It was not often I was required to seek out my cousin, so I could only have presumed he was preoccupied with something else - or, someone else it seemed as I listened to the carnal moans echo from Freddie's bedchamber.

I chuckled, deciding it was a good decision to re-circle and return once minutes had ticked by; it would not be long before he grunted his final climax. He might have been a playboy, but he was not one to delay his orgasm, even if it was with his keeper.

I rounded the corner into the grand hallway, spotting Arraetta at an almost similar distance in the west wing, distantly followed by her maids. Like an inflatable balloon, my pants were once again playing restraint with its attacker as I gazed at her beauty.

Fuck, how blessed I was that this goddess was mine – even a devil heir could find refuge in an angel according to the Gods.

She did not notice me until the two of us were standing in the hallway, neither of us wholly able to bite back the smile which threatened to break free.

"Seraiah," she nodded nonchalantly as the two of us halted in the middle of the upper stairwell.

"Arraetta," I returned in the same manner, lifting my hand to cradle one of her loose curls before I traced the curve of her ear and tucked it behind. Her divine features were even more tempting as I glanced between her succulent lips and radiant azure eyes, lingering on the former, uncaring of the audience we were involuntarily performing for.

Still, I could tease a little longer, coaxing the natural rouge which tinted her cheeks. I pulled myself backwards, "where are you going now?"

"I was going to find Genie. And you?"

If only she knew her best friend was having an erotic affair with my cousin.

I pouted, "That is a shame. I would have hoped you were going to find me."

"Oh, so you were looking for me?"

Empyreans, only then did I wish it had been my initial prerogative, it was a shame I was far too invested in what Jonah had to convey to us that I had not thought about finding her.

I chuckled, "No, I was looking for Freddie, but I know how obsessed you are with me."

She exclaimed, "excuse me, but I believe it's you who is obsessed with me."

Her tone made me laugh even harder, "I did not say I was not."

Obsessed, ravenous, *possessive*.

I indicated for her to lead us down the stairs, although I knew it would not take her directly to her friend. I did want to use it as an ample distraction to continue our conversation for as long as time would allow before I was sucked into a meeting I did not wish to be part of.

At the bottom of the stairwell, she curtsied in jest, and I bowed in return. Once more, we were dancing with one another, yet neither of us had quite found our footing to take the lead. Or, at least as I took the lead, she was desperate to rip it from my grasp. In some way, I might let her have it to see what she would do.

"I suppose I will try this direction," she said, nodding towards the lower east wing.

"And I shall try this one." I stepped backwards before turning and proceeding down the stairwell, through the central corridor.

I noticed Terance walking towards me, and he greeted me kindly, "Your Highness."

"Good afternoon, Terance. I am going to catch up with my wife."

"Ah," he acknowledged, not needing to say much more so I could catch up with Arraetta quickly. I heard the rapid patter of feet closing in as I rounded the corner at the bottom of the back stairwell, just as she walked around hers. She fought to disguise her subtle, harsh breaths as I bowed to her with a second greeting, and she bobbed her body in return. The two of us swayed closer.

"That did not take you long, you were down that corridor in a heartbeat."

"Or, maybe you walk incredibly slow."

"I stopped for a moment to speak with Terance, but you obviously thought this to be a race."

"I did not."

Boldly, I touched the clothed skin of her chest, above her rapidly beating heart, wishing I could touch the naked skin beneath, "then, why is your heart racing?" She reddened as I leaned down to mutter in her ear. "Arraetta, I should reprimand you for being such a terrible liar."

"I'm not lying," she swallowed quietly, and a faint smile tugged at my lips. The fibres of my skin whispered across her apple cheeks as I inched closer to her lips, leaving only a breath between us. She added, "I'm just fast."

A laugh shuddered from my throat, and I peered up at her two maids, seeing they were enjoying our frivolous courting. Kadey's eyes caught mine, and I kept eye contact with her as I whispered to Arraetta, "if these two were not here, what I would do to punish you for it."

A shiver murmured through her, but she still stepped and pivoted in the direction of the stairs, as she quipped, "I'd like to see you try. So, I shall continue my search for Genie."

Even as she threatened to step away, I did not want to lose the warmth of her aura, swiftly imprisoning her by her waist and tucking her back against my front. I was sure she could feel the uncomfortable pointer which prodded against her. The eyes of her maids were still upon us, although both were attempting not to watch the sultry position we were in.

"Arraetta, I have not done speaking with you yet."

"What is there to speak about?" her answer rang in a high-pitched tone, and I smirked at her engaging temperament.

"Ladies, please find yourself busy elsewhere," I called in Zikan to the maids, not caring to watch them leave as Arraetta swivelled back around.

She breathed flirtatiously, "Seraiah, I thought we were supposed to be chaperoned at all times."

"I shall not be taking your clothes off here, Arraetta," I retorted, although the temptation was unparalleled. Closing in on her lips, I said, "But I have wanted to kiss you since yesterday, and I believe you have wanted the same."

"No," she laughed sarcastically.

"Do not lie," I replied in Zikan before devouring her sensual taste and revelling in the invigorating electricity which charged first class to our souls. Time was lost, the two of our tongues fighting for control, with no audience but the cameras to see our performance.

Every fibre in my body was on fire, and it took every ounce of my power to pull away from her and not find myself in a similar position with my head between her thighs. With a staggered inhale, I tried to settle my breathing whilst staring into Arraetta's cerulean irises.

It was the first time I had displayed such affection in public, and I was sure my life bringers would not be far from being informed about our charade. Sharing a kiss so boldly was not frowned upon, but it was not exactly princely to do so outside the privacy of my chambers. Although, it was not as though I cared about such bogus rules when it came to Arraetta; her pleasure was enough to sate my appetite.

"I do not think that was a wise idea," I breathed, pulling her into a long hug. I revelled in the feeling as the tension unbounded from my muscles, as it had done in previous times I held her.

The world melted away when she was safely tucked in my arms.

It melted away when I was anywhere in her presence.

Arraetta's energy trembled, the feeling more vibrant, effervescent, and lust-filled as she gripped me tighter. I could only guess the thoughts which teemed through her curious mind were of the two of us together, which was all my own were filled with. I was reminded we had made a pact the sol before which we would not go further than kissing until our heartfasting but, Empyreans, I could give her so much more.

"Arraetta, please do not continue those thoughts."

"It's your fault," she breathed but pulled away from me, the warmth notably disappearing. Sweeping my eyes around the corridor, I noted it seemed no one, but the shadows were in audience. She cleared her throat. "So, do you know where Freddie is?"

"Yes," I chuckled, as I adjusted myself subtly. It was enough for Arraetta to notice, and she shifted her gaze. I laughed harder. "Freddie and Genie are actually spending some time together."

"Time to... oh," she flushed. I supposed the idea of her best friend being intimate was enough to taint her neck in rouge.

I looked at my watch and thought, "I hope he hurries up, as I have a meeting with him at four."

"About what?" the words were sharp, heeded with command and unrelenting anger, like someone had flicked the valve on a hot tap to cold without any pre-warning. It was not as though there ever was a warning for any change of temperament from her.

"Nothing you need to concern yourself with," I replied honestly, peering towards the staircase as thoughts of ways to dance around the subject came to mind.

"I'm going to be your wife, Seraiah."

I frowned at her, "Yes, I am well aware of the fact."

"So, why can't you share with me about your meeting?"

I sighed, "because it is nothing-"

"-*For me to concern myself with*. Yes, I heard you," she mimicked harshly, and I almost recoiled at the wrath of it. Not in fright, but more in humiliation, being spoken to harshly as though I was beneath her. I supposed I was beneath her in rank, but not so much to receive such unwarranted anger.

One sol I would tell her all, but after the bonding. That was agreed by everyone in Amity, to protect her from the truths which lay in the crevices of the palace walls, out of sight until the time would be right.

"Then why are you angry?"

"I'm not...," she lied, "it's just you've been secretive since I told you about my father."

Frustration tainted my expression, noting that it all came back to her openness about what her father had said to her in delirium. I rubbed my eyebrows, exhaling loudly, "Arraetta, you are the future queen-"

"-So, Seraiah, I should be in on those talks."

"No," I shut up her aggravating thoughts, refusing even to entertain it.

"So the meeting is about the war?" she asked rhetorically, presuming she already knew the answer, but even I was unsure what the meeting of the sol would be. Maybe war meetings, maybe the awry War Cry, maybe Leopold was dead, maybe the mortal-kinds who were involved in the chaos were sentenced to death.

"Arraetta, this meeting is none of your concern."

"You can't stop me from fighting, Seraiah."

There it was. Fighting, fighting, fighting.

Was she not sick of it?

"Arraetta."

"I-"

"-Arraetta!" I snapped, her interruption grated on me. I needed her to just fucking listen for once. "I do not care if you hold the power of one thousand suns; you are not involved in any talks because you are to be my wife, and you will not ever... ever fight."

The beast was being awakened with a hot iron poker, the heat of it stabbing in my chest and sending tendrils of sparks down my scorched arm. Even he, it, *me* would agree that Arraetta throwing herself into war, where she could be hurt, torn to pieces or, worse, killed was an impudent idea. With every bite Arraetta gave, it was only feeding the stagnant darkness inside, a tug of war which had been increasingly more difficult to win.

I knew the only way to keep it from conquering my soul was by walking away from her, heading back down through the middle corridor, taking deep breaths to calm myself and push against the burning desire to set it free. Because that was what it was becoming, right? A desire over a burden. A need to be free. But I did not want her to witness it first.

Arraetta's clatter of feet pounded after me, echoing in a cacophony of noises in the dark space. "Seraiah, my father-"

Jaw tightened, fists clenched, anger fuelled, I rapidly spun back to her, "Your father is dead, Arraetta. Whether he reaches out to you from Ryazark or wherever he is right now, he would be stupid to send his only daughter - the only hope of keeping our bloodline alive - into a war against something as powerful as The Dark."

It should have been enough to curb her incessant argument, but she did not rise above the storm.

"Oh, so that's all I'm here for, huh?" she spat, "Just to continue your fucking bloodline!"

My head was throbbing, fury and anxiety and something else entirely were melding together. "It is our bloodline, Arraetta! You are the last remaining of your kind, and I am the only royal blood of my own. It is our duty."

Empyreans, I sounded like my fucking mother and Jonah and all those who stretched me this way and that into their dutiful puppet. Duty was always there, but to speak to her about our bloodline was something else.

"Fuck duty, Seraiah! This is about us," she argued. The 'us' tugged at my heartstrings and the coffer rippled again, that *something else*

476

was about to rip away from its fucking hinges. "You are constantly keeping things from me! What are you so afraid of, huh?" She shoved me. "Tell me now! What are you so afraid of?"

The violence in her force jolted rage and shame and guilt and *crack*. Empyreans, fuck, the creature beneath my skin bore pain into my left wrist as the darkness transcended my light, taking each and every emotion I swallowed away with it.

"Arraetta," I gritted my teeth.

Focus. Control. Hold him down.

"How can you even think about fighting The Dark when you're so fucking scared to talk to me about the whole fucking thing?"

Scared? The voice whispered around my mind, followed by a chuckle, *she is right, you know. You are fearful of everything, fearful of what we could be.*

A final grunt, "Arraetta."

I tried to ignore it, I really did, but the chains of darkness were wrapping themselves tightly around my body. In the centre of my arboretum, I was becoming a statue of honour, duty, mercy and guilt, dusting away in white snow waiting for someone to melt it all.

Show her who you truly are, Seraiah. Who we are.

No, the truth was not made for now; it was made for–

"–Just grow up and speak to me, for God's sake!" her irritating shriek echoed around the crevices of the corridor, "rather than keeping it all pent up–"

"–I do not owe you anything!" I roared darkly, the warfare had finally won, and he resurfaced quicker than a lighter to a flame. I prayed Arraetta would never see such wickedness, but I was bound in iron chains created by the male which sought control over me. Yet, on the contrary, ominous thoughts protruded from my mind that she needed to know everything him, about this, about *me*. There was strange freedom in making her understand the one thing I desperately sought to lock away from sight.

As my body flared, a black hue overshadowed my blue Rapidfire. "Maybe if you were not such a spoilt brat, you would come to realise your place."

"My place!" she scoffed, "what? A pawn in your grand game of fate."

A harsh, callous laugh left me, "Oh, Arraetta, you are a naïve child. You do not know what you are coaxing right now."

"Maybe I want to see," she said, looking undeniably mindless. "It's about time you showed me your true self!"

Daring female, queen, deity. You toy with us, with me. Unlike other times when I had some minor control, it was as if being so overwhelmed by Arraetta's lack of integrity and commitment to provoke me I had been unable to see I had lost what little I had left. The chains tightened, the room's warmth flickered to cold, and my black eyes mirrored in Arraetta's wide, cerulean irises. Fear was etched deep inside her soul like a knife was holding it hostage, utterly powerless and at my mercy.

"Is this what you want, Arraetta?" I called, feeling the shiver crawl up her spine.

Her eyes were fixed on mine, and I could not escape the pull as I bore witness to the anxieties she had spent many sols hiding. Flickers of images clouded her mind: nightmares, beasts, fire, lightning, power, and her most feared - all-encompassing, mind-consuming darkness. Such fears needed to be a blessing, not a burden, to be used as a weapon to step into her power, not hide behind with a shield of mouthy wrath.

"I... I'm not scared of you," she breathed.

Fear is under your control, dear Queen.

I did not wish to hurt her, but she needed to know the possessor in which had control of me, she needed to understand she did this to me. I lifted her by the collar of her top and pinned her against the wall. "I can smell the fear on you. It plagues you, lingering on your skin like a mark." I heard her voice catch as I lowered my mouth to her ear. "My mark. I *own* you, Arraetta. I will devour you body and soul until you know nothing but my command."

"S-Seraiah," she cried softly. I shifted until I was face-to-face with her, looking back into the depths of her soul.

"Seraiah!"

Of course, like a moth to the flame my commander had appeared in the nick of time, but I did not care for whatever bargaining he dared to bring to me. Fuck him and his betrayals, leaving me gasping for air when there was none.

Coaxing what power I could from my being, I repeated as I had done in the vaults and created a barrier of swirling translucent black between us and the offending arrival.

"Petulant boy."

I was only showing her the truth, as she had begged me. No one would dare refuse the truth from a queen, not even oh-so-dutiful me. Empyreans, how I knew I wanted to show her everything I reaped, give her everything I could, not allow her fear to control our desires.

Arraetta's body was close to slipping from my grasp, so I stepped closer to her, keeping her pinned and patient. If the wall was glass, I was sure with enough power I would break it, but even I could not shatter the brick behind the panel, not even the fictitious one inside me.

"Seraiah," she pleaded desperately, noting a hint of pain in her voice, but a little pain hurt no one. She had to know that without pain, without fear, she could not find the relief I wanted to give her. As I punctured further into her fears, tugging on them to coax them from her and feed them into me, I started to feel maliciously amused by the taste of sin I witnessed there.

479

But, something changed. I somehow realised many of the sins were just a mirror of my own, and I was bearing witness to the devilish thoughts which had been buried so deep within myself. Her soul was reaping my own as if something was buried so incarnate that it could not be resurfaced. I pushed to fracture the thick wall which had been built, but I was stopped as a thin golden stream of light broke through the cracks.

The darkness inside me was roaring – furious, controlling, needing more. But, I jolted from the fictional to reality as soft, wet skin graced my lips, acknowledging them to be Arraetta's own. There was no passion in it, but somehow the facade of darkness dissipated like water to fire and normality restored. All control the darkness had cost me shattered through my body, leaving me wading through a puddle of shame, guilt and fear.

Gently, I lowered Arraetta to the floor until she ended the kiss, and I did not miss the look of utter disappointment and heartbreak on her face.

The heartbreak warfare had ended, leaving us in the crumbs of dust and devastation.

Crack.

"Arraetta," I said apologetically. I needed to take her hand, kneel before her, beg for forgiveness, show her the thing she had witnessed was a tiny yet prominent part of me.

Crack.

Not now, not at this moment, could it happen.

An unexpected, cutting pain radiated across my cheek, sending my head toward the anticipated audience standing nearby.

Jonah, Freddie, Genie, Alex, my father, several of my guards, several of his and some servants.

"I... I don't deserve this," Arraetta whispered in disbelief, and I knew what else I saw there. Fear, wrath, and disappointment.

Empyreans, I hated seeing the expression on her beautiful face, hated knowing I put it there, hated the male she should desire was pushing her away.

She pushed away from me and rushed through the crowd, ignoring my father's angered plea. Freddie walked toward me, while commanding his guard to disperse, not before suggesting that Genie wait a while before going after Arraetta.

"Are you okay?" Freddie asked as I dazedly held my cheek and reminisced about the events that had transpired.

"Hm," I grumbled.

"Some nerve you have!" my father shouted, and I could not bring myself to argue with him as I lowered my head, ready to receive my grovelling punishment, "is it truly not enough for you to live in peace rather than bring such *embarrassment* to this household? An heir to the throne who is already seen as a failure. The Gods must have cursed themselves if they believed you two truly are Kindred Spirits, for all I witness are two enemies who cannot decide whether to surrender or fight until death. Do not think anyone shall bow before you after witnessing such atrocities."

Disappointment simmered. He had no faith in my relationship with Arraetta, and it seemed neither did she. Two opposites battling for control in an unwinnable war where the prize was either devastation or... love.

Crack.

"He has been through enough, Your Majesty," Freddie interjected calmly, "I believe he understands."

"If he does not, then he will soon," my father replied sharply, "rumours are a fickle friend, and this one shall not remain in the walls of this house, no matter how hard you come to try."

My father stormed away without another word, followed by his guard, leaving me with those who remained.

"I should apologise to Arraetta," I stepped forward, but the others created a blockade.

"Not like this," Jonah said, pointing at my eyes, "it takes at least ten minutes for those veins to disappear fully, and you know how unwell it makes you."

"I am not unwell, I need her to know it was not me."

"If it wasn't you, then who was it?" Genie folded her arms. "Because it looked exactly like you knew what you were doing."

"Genie," Freddie breathed.

But, all I could do was wince. Did I really know what I was doing? Every choice, every action felt so real, but had it truly been mine? No, I would not believe it, it had taken control of me, seized it and wielded my darkness as a weapon against her to show her the truth.

"I'll go and see if she's okay," Genie replied, following Arraetta's footsteps.

"I did not mean it!" I called after her, "I love her!"

A shatter deep inside, the lock broke without another warning and the coffer sprang off its hinges. Like my limbs had been frozen and were now being left to thaw, overwhelmingly painful as glee rattled up the surface of my body, waking up every nerve all at once. A declaration made out loud had finally opened the coffer I never thought would ever break, a tangible feeling drenching my fibres in a cold sweat as my iron heart became real flesh and blood.

Love. A thing I never believed in until her, a thing I thought I would never submit to was bursting at its seams and toiling with the guilt of what I had done. How I had hurt her. All to show her the truth of who I was because she had commanded it.

I stumbled a little, clenching my fist on and off at the realisation of the situation. The numbness of heightened emotions melting rapidly while I struggled to take a breath.

A hand landed on my shoulder, almost to steady me, and I

recognised it to be Jonah's as he said, "I hope you are not too unwell for our meeting."

Were we truly speaking of meetings when I had to see to it my wife was well? To make her understand how I felt, confess I was an arrogant fool who only wanted to show her how I felt. To show her I was a victim to this fate as she was, not bound to her by duty and honour but by devotion.

"Come," Jonah said softly, pushing me toward the hallway and I took the walk without any disagreement, lost in my actions as they spoke.

"At least the generator did not stop working," Freddie commented as he threw his arms around my shoulders, "hey, maybe, you are finally gaining some control of this power and will be able to use it without making me feel like shit."

"Only you would choose such an interesting way to make better of an already dismal situation, Freddie," Jonah tutted, unamused, "I would hope such power would not be used, ever."

"I was only saying it because I expect a shock to the body daily," Freddie grinned.

"It is not daily," I rolled my eyes, coming back into the conversation.

"It should not be happening at all," Jonah replied with finality, "especially not with, or in the presence of, our future queen."

I winced, unable to retort, as I knew he was just as right as my father. But, my attention was drawn to the stairs as heavy footsteps rebounded down them, and I noted Arraetta walking towards us.

I pushed through the gaggle of males, eager to reach her as she arrived at the bottom of the stairs. Empyreans, I was close to begging her to forgive me, to remove the distinguishable anger which marred her expression.

"Arrae-" *I love you.*

"–Leave me alone, Seraiah!" she shouted harshly, and I flinched, drawing back a little.

"Arri!" Genie called, rushing down the stairs, but Arraetta ignored her friend as she walked by me, towards the door.

Jonah gently commanded the guards to block the open doorway, preventing Arraetta's escape. No, she would not escape, would she? We could work it out without her leaving. Fuck, she would not leave, she could not leave.

"Let me out! You can't keep me here!"

More guilt, more sorrow, more empathy wrapped around my fleshy heart. I understood the feeling of entrapment she harboured, one I had added more fuel to the fire, which raged ferociously enough for us all to see. She had become a prisoner of her own circumstance, had been such since she had arrived, but only now had she noticed.

Jonah cleared his throat, stepping forward, "please, Ma'am."

Arraetta turned sharply towards him, stating, "My name is Arr-ae-et-ta. Not ma'am, not Your Grace. Arraetta. I don't want to be here anymore. You can stick all this shit up your arse; I'm sick of being trapped and controlled by all of you. I'm absolutely fine at taking care of myself!"

Every word was heard, her desperation to be set free clearer than sol, all because of me. My fault, my actions, my darkness. I wanted to hold and tell her it would be okay, that I would make it better, that I would give her the world on a pedestal if she would just let me. I could fix it, I just had to open my mouth and say those words to her.

I love you.

Yet, another look of wrathful determination made me all so aware I would not be her saviour of this situation. She had to break free from the safety of the gilded nest, burrow somewhere else and return when she was ready.

Arraetta's eyes burned through the door, staring through the unwavering guards, waiting until one of them was weak enough to break their position. Jonah turned his head toward me, and I could see what he was thinking without speaking. He wanted to set her free, to allow her some freedom, but not without compromise. Jonah was all about compromising as long as he always had the upper hand, and she would see that. Whatever she wished for would fall in his jurisdiction and while our friendship had been shattered, I still trusted him, even when I knew he did not have a particular like for her.

She was his queen, and he would protect her until his dying breath. Just as he would me.

I nodded, and he indicated to the guards to step aside.

"Is everything alright?" my mother's voice called from the top of the stairs, but I did not look at her as I watched Arraetta take a determined breath before she took my heart and escaped the palace.

I begged whoever would listen, "Please, stop her."

Genie was hopping from foot to foot, and I knew she was debating whether to follow her best friend. In a way, Genie was most likely the best person to convince Arraetta to remain in Zikan territory, but she could also follow on her promise to follow Arraetta if she ever decided to leave. Not that she would be able to, of course, but it would not stop her from trying. Nothing would stop my fated one.

Genie nodded to herself before turning around and catching my mother's eye, curtseying in greeting before her eyes landed on me, "Do you truly love her?"

I swallowed, palms sweaty, nervous under the watch of those listening, before nodding without hesitation. "I do."

It seemed it was all she needed before she tucked her shoulders back and hurriedly followed after Arraetta.

"This is the Commander," Jonah called through the lapel of his radio, "I need three vehicles to be brought to the palace immediately.

All ground officers proceed to Alpha Beta One Eight One. I repeat: all ground officers immediately proceed to Alpha Beta One Eight One. Keep covert eyes on the Golden Phoenix at all times." He removed his hand from the button before looking at his spiritsworn. "You are to watch His Royal Highness does not leave this building." He looked at Travis. "You are to follow me."

"Sir," Alex and Travis agreed.

Jonah looked at me, promising, "I will bring the princess back."

I barely nodded to him, watching Jonah and Travis leave. The guards on duty returned to their position in front of the door, while Alex waited nearby without another word. Turning towards the stairwell, I winced at my mother's sharp gaze. She stood halfway down the stairwell, eyeing the unfolding scenario.

I bowed to her respectfully, "Mother."

"I hope you do not plan to spoil all the celebrations, Seraiah," she tutted, and I flinched at her callous words. She began to walk up the staircase, "You must do everything you can to make this right. It is no use crying over spilt milk when our lineage is on the line."

Lineage. Duty. Honour. But not to make it right as a male bearing his heart out to a female he was fated to. Not to make it right as a prince to his consort. Not to make it right as a husband to his future wife. Only to make it right for the future heir.

Well, fuck duty. Fuck it all.

I would make it right for Arraetta, and then I would rule with my blackened heart.

THIRTY-THREE

The incident continued to play over and over in my head like a worn-out videotape, wondering if I had handled the situation differently would she still have remained safe behind palace walls because I knew she was no longer even on the grounds. Maybe I could have convinced her the discussions were not of war, but of something else. Or that we were all so unprepared for any sort of war because of what had happened earlier the sol prior.

A hand was placed on my shoulder, and I jolted, looking up at Freddie as he brought a box down into my peripheral vision, "here."

I opened the box, seeing a ring engraved with 'aemre aer jove lamoure'. I jested, "Are you proposing to me, Freddie?"

He chuckled, "You wish you could have a male as fine as me in your bed."

"What is it for?"

He sat beside me and said, "Well, I had it made for Genie. The other one is still lost in the pond, and I was going to propose again, but I suppose the timing is never right."

"You should not ruin your own affairs for mine."

"I have my whole life to ask Genie to be my wife," he smiled, "you, Sir, seem only to have sols with how fast your relationship is deteriorating."

I grimaced at his bluntness, but only because I knew he was right.

"It is not as though our relationship ever began, this is a little less sentimental."

"We do not have time for you to be sentimental. Live like a human, Seraiah. In this world, we must do things right, and Arri needs you to declare her yours. So, when she walks through that door, take her to the library and propose."

I coughed a little, "I am already on course to be heartfasted."

"Yes, by the laws of the universe and all that," he half-mimicked, "but what about the feelings between the two of you? Your first declaration of love for her was to my wife, which means you have never said such words since you met. Maybe if you say the words to her, you may find peace with how you truly feel."

I wanted to tell Arraetta, but would I only be met with more fire? More outward determination to try to take control between us? We had been forced into what felt like an arranged heartfast that I knew she did not want. The two of us pushing and pulling against each other because neither of us could have a solid conversation about our feelings without arguing or ripping each other's clothes off.

And, as I thought about it, it was instinctual to love her, be the one she desired me to be, give her the world at its best and burn it at its worst. There was so much to the female I desired - her wit, her beauty, her soft lips, her scent, her laughter and her aura.

"It hurts, does it not?" Freddie chuckled, elaborating, when I gave him a confused look. "Love." I snorted. "When I first met Genie, I was not sure how I would ever love such a beautiful female, let alone someone of a race I only saw as fragile. And, then I realised she was not fragile, it was me. Too fragile to experience love because it was a feeling I would have rather buried than faced head on. But, I think it hurts more because I know I could not live without Genie, as corny as that might sound. It hurts knowing I would be a sorry mortal-kind without her."

Freddie's confession was far more open than I was prepared for, but I understood everything he was saying. Love hurt not for the elation, but for the fear of loss which came with it, and I could relate exactly to that with Arraetta. I could not - would not - lose her again.

Freddie rose to his feet, "I will be honest. When I went back to the jeweller, I asked him to make me two more rings, just in case Arraetta chose to throw me into the pond again." I chuckled. "I would not have given you the third one, for that was engraved in Porton. I supposed it was a good idea for me to have two made."

Freddie retired to his quarters, leaving me with a lingering, silent Alex. I knew he had listened to the conversation, but had not felt like putting in his two cents. My attention swayed back to the box, beautiful in its design, and I was sure Freddie had created it specifically for my use, not for his. He had only chosen to tell me had the ring made for Genie to make me feel a little less guilty and a little more... human.

I was a little wary about adding a proposal to the fire, as I was not sure what mood she would be in when she returned, but I knew it was worth trying. It would have given me a good indication of whether Arraetta truly reciprocated my feelings.

Catching sight of a maid, I asked her to prepare light food and wine in the library, whilst I remained in the centre of the stairwell. And, after a long and uncomfortable time, Alex stated he had the all-clear to leave and indicated Arraetta was not far from being at home again.

Heart beating fast in my chest, I awaited the arrival of the cavalry, seeing through the upper window as they drove up the long road to the palace. Anticipation, relief and joy amassed in my throat, daring to leave my mouth with a wail of adrenaline, but I remained steadfast and strong.

The cars pulled up, all disembarking before Arraetta walked up the outside steps, appearing with Genie. I stood and walked down to meet her, nervous, and bowed.

"I'm going to find Freddie," Genie said, but I did not stop looking at Arraetta. She looked weary and red-eyed, but her softened face told me I had been forgiven. I was wary of how much she must have cried since she had left and wondered whether she had felt such deep pain that she was close to telling me she no longer wished to go through with the heartfast or the bond.

"Sorry," she murmured.

I swallowed before confidently replying, "Do not apologise... Come, let us go and eat; you must be hungry."

"A little," she agreed, and I looked past her to Jonah, who was standing in the doorway.

"Thank you," I said to him sincerely in Zikan.

"Anything for you, Highness," he bowed, reminding me of our friction. Unsure what else I could offer him, I smiled softly before focusing on Arraetta.

"Thanks, Jonah," she said, looking at him.

Jonah bowed, "Anytime, ma'am."

It seemed I was witnessing the mending of their relationship, if only it was the same for the one between me and Jonah.

When we arrived at the library, I noticed the large charcuterie board and red wine on the table. I urged Arraetta to take a seat as I uncorked and poured two glasses.

"You deserve an explanation," I said swiftly, "There is much I wish to tell you, and there is much you wish to know. I suppose I would like to start from the beginning."

I sat down next to her, pulling the coffee table closer so we could eat, drink, and talk without too much movement. Deciding it was right to put my best foot forward, I told her about my life, the languages I spoke, the University of the Universe in the realm of

Hamiean, and how we came to Earth. And, speaking those things out loud, something clicked. Arraetta had to have some sort of strange involvement in the sol of the attack.

"But I promise you I know, in my heart and soul, it was you. You were the one who pulled me out of there... from the grasp of The Dark."

"The grasp of The Dark?"

"What you saw today," I replied, grimacing at the thoughts of my actions, "I am imprinted with the stain of The Dark. I... I wanted to save everyone, but I was not strong enough. Do you remember me telling you of The Mire? That is what tried to take me; that is what devoured my left forearm. It burnt, I-"

To help calm me, Arraetta took my hands and softly said, "Sera-iah."

"Sorry," I took a breath, "I should have never done that to you; it overtook my senses. I felt like I was watching through the eyes of another, which has not happened for a long time."

"Thank you for telling me," she smiled softly, "you said that The Dark feeds off fear, right?" I nodded. "Maybe the cause of it overtaking you is because of that."

More notably wrathful fear.

"Yes, you are right," I agreed, proud of how intelligent she was, "however, it is not as simple as just *getting over the fear*. It feeds on all my fears, and that is not so easy to let go of, especially my biggest fear."

"Which is?"

"Losing you."

It was the truth. I acknowledged that and made my bed with it. She was the most important being to have graced my life, and she was mine.

She had a contented smile on her face, asking more questions.

We spoke a little about portals, which was an interesting topic which made my heart ache, knowing we had been unsuccessful even opening one on Earth. Not my fault, but my fathers. Coward.

I realised soon after she was not a fan of red wine, so I swiftly swapped her glass for white from the stash at the back of the room.

"I would've drank it still," she said, "just slowly."

"You would be drinking for days," I replied, giving her the new glass of wine before sitting down. "I believe tomorrow is supposed to be our heartfast rehearsal, but I have asked them to postpone."

I knew it would be overwhelming to go through everything which would be required on our bonding ceremony, especially after the sol we had already.

"What? No, I'll be okay."

"I cannot force you into this, Arraetta, I wish only for you to be comfortable with me, and I will do everything to make it right."

"I did push you."

"I should never have reacted the way I did," I replied, swallowing as I prepared myself to give the full confession which I had thought about over the hours since she had left, "I have no excuse; I should always be open with you, and I will. I must make myself do so because it will inevitably be detrimental to us both if I am not. Arraetta, I do... I have to tell you something but, before I do, you must know that I am not talking with Freddie about the war, we were talking about other things - about us - you and I. Things I cannot reveal because they are... Well, they are supposed to be a surprise."

A lie, but it would be a good placeholder for now. Building a relationship off of deceit was not recommended, but I needed her on my side, I would face whatever new fire would come when I was finally open with her.

"Oh," she realised. Maybe the wine had subdued her temperamental nature, or maybe my deceitful mask was stronger than I would have thought. Because lying with a heart filled with love only tugged on my guilt.

"And... there is a part of me," I began nervously, "a very big part of me that wishes to protect you. I can only say it is because, well, Arraetta, I cannot live - nae - I cannot breathe without you, it is as though when you walked into my life, all those weeks ago, everything fell into place and I could not understand how I ever lived without you... Your presence, your being, your beauty, being around you is like breathing in the purest of air. It is not just a want but a need to be with you... It is a desire more than to physically entwine myself with you. It is a desire to open myself up to you, to be everything you have ever desired and wanted, to linger so often in your presence that, when we are apart, I long to be closer than ever to you... Arraetta, I wish to marry you not for the purposes of our fated destinies but for the purpose of loving more than I have ever loved... to love you for an eternity and more. I love you, Arraetta."

A sob left her lips, tugging at the strings of my heart, and I embraced her without hesitation. She cried against me, weight heavy, and I wondered whether anyone had ever truly told her they loved her. I could only imagine the hardships she had endured, floating through life without love in a world she struggled to navigate. I would take the loneliness if she would let me, bear the burden of it so she would not tear up at such confessions as I love you. Empyreans, how I would be her anchor as she was mine.

I took one of the napkins from the table and dabbed her cheeks.

"I love you," she breathed with such affection it reconfirmed everything I felt towards her.

I could not stop myself from kissing her soft yet passionately, uncaring for the dampness of her cheeks against mine. I removed the box from my jacket pocket and showed it to her, opening it to reveal the ring.

"I know we are already to be married, but I do want to make this official."

"What does it say?"

"It says *aemre aer jove lamoure*, it means Our Love is Forever Bound."

"That's so romantic," she breathed, "I don't even think I deserve this."

"Oh, Arraetta, you deserve everything," I said to her, collecting a loose tear from her cheek before I kissed both of them and placed the ring on her finger.

"Thank you," she breathed.

Thank *you*.

The proposal to Arraetta had subdued our need to awaken the tempest over the sols that followed, but apart from the heartfast rehearsals, Arraetta and I spent less time together as time went on. I supposed partially for my own reasoning to quell the desire to kiss her every time I saw her, or maybe my guilt for continuously lying to her. Or, maybe because I was based in my office-turned-bedroom, where I only felt it necessary to leave when I needed to eat and shower.

It had become quite the haven, and I wondered why I had never sought a permanent bed there before. I had spent much of my spare time using the art of poetic writing, which I was not so accomplished, to write the vows needed for the heartfast. I was sure Arraetta was also taking the time to think of her own.

And, it seemed we were not picking up meetings in the boardrooms again; the evidence being the lack of presence of my commander following the incident. My mother had not spoken to me either, not that I cared for such, but I had yet to hear about the verdict of Connell and Leopold.

I scrunched up another piece of paper and tossed it into the pile of others before I was interrupted by a rapture on the door.

"Enter," I called, watching as Travis did. "Travis, to what do I owe such disturbance."

"I apologise, Sir," he greeted, bowing his head, "but I believe you should be aware I have been informed Her Royal Highness was forced into conversation with your father in the garden before she was reduced to tears."

I stood abruptly from my chair, "can you corroborate?"

"The incident was reported to me by another guard."

Anger washed over me like a rough blanket, beading in with that fear I so hated to feel when it came to the safety of Arraetta.

"Empyreans, fuck," I swore, ignoring the task at hand and rushing as fast as I could.

Damn palace had to be so fucking big on an occasion where I needed to get to the scene quickly. Outside the front of the house, I stopped when I was met by Jonah, who was walking swiftly in my direction. And, I knew by his expression he already had an insight into what had happened to Arraetta.

"Where is he?"

"Still in the pavilion," he replied, stopping me as I attempted to step past him. "You cannot go there angry at him without a plan."

Plans, plans, plans.

"Fuck plans, Jonah! We are talking about my wife - *our* queen - who has been threatened by that snake."

"I understand, but you cannot go there and start a fight which could change the trajectory of the vote from the council."

This male was driving me up the wall, never seeing further than the end of his nose.

"Empyreans, are you truly so infatuated with following policy that you believe I care about the council's vote?"

"I support you, Seraiah."

Did he even know what support was? Fracturing a brotherhood for whatever selfish reasons he had, when all could have been fine and well. Empyreans, did he not know I might have listened to him more if he had not been such a hellsworn?

"And does that support extend to standing beside me as I take my rightful throne, hm?"

"He will be a martyr."

"Better a martyr than a coward king. If you do not wish to stand beside me, then step aside."

Jonah stood his ground for a moment too long before he sighed, "do not kill him, Seraiah."

His opinion of me had truly been lowered over the moons which had passed.

"I do not plan to have that hellsworn's blood on my hands."

"I will welcome you as my king."

Would he? Such an odd change in personality in a matter of minutes.

He radioed a command for uniformed soldiers to attend my mother's garden, and it was enough for me to walk by him and toward my impudent father. I was mindful I did not have much information on what had happened.

"Is it clear what he said to her?" I asked Jonah, who followed.

"The princess stated he had told her to submit to him," Jonah replied, which only fuelled the anger inside me, the beast rising rapidly. Empyreans, I would set it free, uncaring of the consequences. I was surprised my father had not remembered he was not permitted to speak out of terms with Arraetta. I had already threatened consequences.

Bad luck to him.

Do not rule with your heart, he had said. Too bad he did not know I was ruling with my whole body and he was about to feel the brunt of my power.

My father was sitting, sipping his tea and reading a newspaper as though he had not just ripped apart my fated one.

"Father!" I called angrily, but he did not look at me, continuing to read the paper. I only wished I could see him tremble, cower and plead for forgiveness. It would only be a matter of time. Minutes, to be exact.

Guards flocked as though having been commanded by an outside source, standing in a position to protect on demand, while Jonah called for them to stand down. Of course they would not, the parlay had taken place two sols prior and the fractures in the army were more evident than ever. No longer did we just have an impending war on our hands, but we had the real uprising happening before our eyes.

"They do not listen to your word, Jonah," my father said non-chalantly, "but how innocent of you to think you can overstep your father's command." He folded the newspaper up before rising. "It seems my suspicions of who was usurping my position as king were correct, but I was surprised to make such a connection to it being you, Jonah, when you suggested that I have a gentle word with the princess."

Usurping? A gentle word? It was Jonah?

Shock rattled through my core, eyes landing on an astute Jonah, who tucked his shoulders back without a care.

"Do you know what the punishment for treason is?" my father asked.

"I am quite aware of such punishments," Jonah replied, no fear evident in his voice, "whilst you see me as a seedling, I have lived long enough to understand the consequences of power."

"Have you lived long enough to understand the consequences of severing ties?" my father remarked, "or shall I reveal the truth of all your betrayals to my son?"

I had already been betrayed by Jonah, witnessed the consequences of it, but I was still intrigued by what more facts there could be.

"Shall I tell him of Henri Romano's death being on your hands?" my father called, standing up from his position, "how it was you who gave us the speech my son had written for his solar rite? Or, how you fed me and your father all the information needed about your little group – Amity, was it?"

I was not sure if I was so much angry as I was dismayed by what my father was saying, realising all of what he was saying made sense with Jonah was involved somehow. Of course, he had something to do with Eros' death; he was there to help free it but he would have voted for his sentence; I was sure. Of course, he had given my father the speech, or at least put it in his path so that the cogs could continue to turn even if it required a new key in the mechanism. Of course, he was the one feeding information about Amity to my father, even he had pointed out there was a rat in our midst.

Empyreans, Jonah was the rat all along.

Jonah, my brother, my commander.

For what gain? To land me on the throne? Or, to sway everything into his favour so he could command the throne from the strings he attached me to? A fucking puppet master and a damn good one.

"I will bow for only one king." Jonah finally replied.

"I am your king, boy!" my father shouted.

"No," Jonah answered, looking toward me, "Prince Seraiah is our one true king, and I will never bow to a male who seeks to destroy everything in his path for power."

My father snorted, "you are a fool if you think Seraiah is not the same as me."

Jonah looked at him, "you are a fool to think he is."

No, he was not my puppet master. He was just the figure who had destroyed himself for a better gain and knew exactly what would happen if he failed. He was the pedestal he dared me to step on; he was the wings which held me up. Empyreans, he was a traitor, but a damn clever one if I ever did see. He knew every move he made would destroy him, destroy our brotherhood, destroy his life.

All to get me on the throne.

"A king is only as powerful as those who support him," Jonah stated, "and as weak as the ones he dares to destroy. I support Prince Seraiah in becoming king, even to my death. I may be a traitor, but I am a damn good loyalist and I will do anything in my power to see the throne falter beneath your feet."

"You will be lucky to ever see the sol this hellsworn devil and that harlot of his become king!" my father's words were strange, filled with anger and hurt, yet they did not land as they wished. No, they only fuelled what had been festering while they bickered. I was there to confront the hellsworn about what he had done to Arraetta, not care about evident betrayals.

My father continued to say something nasty about us, but I could no longer stand by and listen to the shit radiating from his insolent tongue. Anger rippled, my blue Rapidfire flared, and I rushed at him, knocking the furniture off the pavilion with little restraint before I had him pinned up against one of the posts by his shirt.

Hurried boots. Staggered breaths. Armaments readied. Soldiers swarmed the garden, more than could ever be imagined, rendering all the guards powerless without useful defences. It seemed the uprising had finally changed some minds, no one cared to see the male I collared in his position anymore. No more time for King Charles, it was now the moment for King Seraiah.

Soldiers forced guards to kneel, and I noted armaments being placed against their heads.

"What did you say to her?" I asked my father quietly. "What did you seek to gain by upsetting her?"

Still struggling against my grip, he replied, "Seraiah, are you so naïve to think I did not do it for your own benefit?"

"There is no benefit gained when tears are shed."

He laughed, "angered over a few spilt tears? What kind of king will you be if you cannot bear to see your wife cry? What kind of queen shall she be if she cannot take her father-in-law's words? A pathetic, whiny one?"

I clenched my fist, "or maybe you just lack so much conviction you do not realise the emotions of a queen are more vital to the welfare of our people."

"So, you think your mother lacks emotion?"

"Do not place words into my mouth," I chided, "you are doing your utmost best to disguise the fact you broke the one clause I mandated, that you should bring no harm to Arraetta, or else I shall have no qualms against dethroning you."

"Do you truly believe I would ever agree to such a clause?"

I laughed darkly. "No, I doubt you ever would because you are too proud to participate in an even playing field. It seems the ball falls into my court."

Uncaring of the pain it would cause, only gripping onto the hurt and anger I had for Arraetta's situation, I allowed the darkness to devour my light, revelling in its nature and honing in on the control it so begged for.

"Are you truly going to let that brat end your chances of becoming king?"

"Oh, no, Father," I glowered, "I intend to give her the chance to become queen."

He shuddered, trying to push away from me as though there was space, but the only way he could escape was by going through the post behind his head. I acknowledged he had not started to use his own Rapidfire in defence. "Interesting, where is your power, hm? Has it depleted over time? I believe it is written in sols of old when a ruler's Rapidfire diminishes, he can no longer remain king."

"I have power."

I acknowledged it by tugging on its subtle fibres, which had been dormant in his veins for many scorns.

"Then, show us all the king you pretend to be."

My father was angry and fearful but used what little energy he had to show his weak and dull power, wilting like a flower which had not been nurtured.

And it looked uncomfortable. Painful.

Empyreans, how I loved watching the anguish ricochet through him.

"Does it hurt?" I teased.

"I am going to take everything from you," he bit, "you will never marry that interloper, nor will you win the vote of the council."

I laughed mirthlessly, "That is where you are wrong, Father. I do not need the council's votes, for once I am done with you, I will already be king."

"You have some gall."

"Do not worry," I tightened my grip, "I will keep you alive; I know how you enjoy living an avaricious life."

The feeding on Rapidfire was an ancient craft which was difficult to master, but I had studied it for many sols, and I felt the power seep from his body to mine. He grunted in pain as I sucked his life force from him, but I was not perturbed by it. Instead, I was reminded of all the sols of torture at the hands of his command and the satisfaction of returning it brought.

The shield depleted instantly, bringing an air of change, but I did not feel any lack of energy. If anything, I felt whole, as if my body had absorbed all the electricity as I continued to supplement it with my father's power.

"S-Seraiah," my father grunted, and whilst I thought he was begging me to release him, he said, "You are... the bane of my existence. How I... birthed such a dishonest and... incredulous son is beyond me."

"I wonder whether I would be this way if you had treated me like the male I was born to be."

"You... deserve nothing less," he answered, not helping his cause as I continued my errand. Each fibre I devoured imprinted itself onto my own Rapidfire's DNA, and I watched as my father grew weaker and weary.

"Seraiah!" my mother's shrill shout echoed across the garden from somewhere near Jonah. I did not stop, but I listened as she walked across the gravel and onto the hardwood of the pavilion until she was standing beside me. She lowered her voice, "Seraiah, you must stop this... this is not you." She cleared her throat. "She is watching."

By *she* I knew my mother meant Arraetta and it was enough to stop me; my power disappearing alongside my father's. I could feel the thrum of his simmering in my body, and I was glad to feel more powerful than I had in scorns. In some ways, I felt poisoned and dirty because of who its previous owner had been.

I had not taken enough to subdue my father fully, not enough to wholly declare myself king, only enough to make a dent in the political stakes of the house. Everyone would know he was a powerless and vulnerable disappointment. And, I was the reason they knew.

The alarm had rung, and it was time for a change.

"I am only doing as promised," I grunted to her, releasing my father with a final shove and watched as he collapsed to the floor. With a bow to my mother, I swiftly exited across the garden, subtly noting Arraetta standing nearby as I did. I was not ashamed of her seeing me the way I was; I just did not want to acknowledge if she was.

"Seraiah!" Jonah's voice called as I stepped into the front entrance, and I sighed.

Here we go again.

"I thought we were going with honorifics."

He bowed, "My apologies."

I rolled my eyes, "I hate that you have changed, Jonah, for I quite liked you when we were friends." Jonah looked at me. "Are you suspecting I will suddenly let all lie after you betrayed the house?"

"I do not expect forgiveness. I have told you I will do whatever it takes to get you on that throne."

"I am not sure whether to applaud or reprimand you," I told him, "for a male with such high morals, you seem to have sunk to the lows of being a spy."

"No, I gather intel and present it; that is my job."

"But, you sought to keep it from me, and you encouraged my father to threaten my fated one."

That was one thing that did not sit well with me, above all things my father had disclosed.

"I sought to get you on the throne when you could not," he answered.

"And, what makes you believe I could not?"

"Because you have been preoccupied with your wife," Jonah said, slightly bitter. "Are you seriously not surprised I would work *for* you?"

"For me?"

"I only sought to do what was right."

"What was right, Commander," I corrected, turning on the spot swiftly, "is to speak to *your* king before you go through with this. I

do not wish for my wife to be in danger, especially not by my father."
I paused. "And, now, as I have not managed to declare myself king,
I wonder how you plan to prevent such punishment for the treason
you have made for yourself."

"I am cautious enough to cover my tracks, Your Highness. I
should state whilst your father carries the crown's burden, you have
rendered him almost powerless."

"You tell me I should adhere to the council, and then you tell me
to render my father powerless. Am I but a pawn in your game, hm?
It is as though you have been tiptoeing in a game of shadow. And,
whilst I commend you for your effort, I do not know how to see it as
more than a betrayal. It feels as though you have exhausted all your
options and have lost trust in not only me but yours, too. All I see is
ambition cloaked in loyalty."

"It was there to see all along."

"Was it?" I raised my eyebrows, "you seem to have forgotten it
was you who ripped our friendship apart back on that flight quarters
ago. It was you who declared we would no longer be friends but still
remain as allies."

It was Jonah who should have been the most transparent when
I was blinded by the weight of my crown. Maybe I would not have
listened, but at least I would have tried to understand, even if it
took quarters. Instead, I was left in the bitter mess of a wrecked
brotherhood, trying to understand the reasoning behind it when
it was in front of me all along. Breaking such a thing apart made
it easier to come to terms with it because there would be no moral
feelings between us.

"Whether you are angered or betrayed by it does not matter,"
Jonah pointed out, "I do not wish to ask for your forgiveness, but
you are now the closest you have ever been to becoming king, and I
stand by every decision I have ever made."

Empyreans, I hated he was right, hated to admit I would no doubt be king within moons rather than winters. The downfall of my cowardly father meant making way for a new ruler.

I sighed, falling silent for a moment before I looked at him, "I suppose there is no thread of hope left for the two of us to return to where we once left."

Jonah glanced at me before offering a soft smile and shaking his head. "I believe the two of us know our friendship is unimportant right now, Your Highness. We have to put our grievances aside to form a stronger bond than what once was."

Sadness drifted in and out of my heart, knowing the feeling of love I felt for Arraetta also equalled a similar feeling of admiration and respect for Jonah, which had been torn apart. I think it was why it hurt more standing in that hallway than it had on the plane because the truths were out in the open and we were standing in the ashes looking for some sort of kindling to make it burn brightly again.

But, there was no more fuel for this fire and I had to accept my new reality for what it was. Jonah was duty-bound and never wavering, not in this moment or any other which would come. He had to prepare for my ascension; he had to prepare to take over an army and to be by my side without prejudice.

I confirmed, "so, no more friendship."

The words spoken aloud shattered my heart.

"A partnership forged in adversity," Jonah offered, and the professional stance on it solidified all. I repeated the phrase in my head, sticking it under his name over his title 'brother' as though it were a label on packaging.

And, oddly, all I wanted to say was *thank you*. But, I did not.

"I suppose I should bring the generator online," I said, remembering the ball of energy was in the garden rather than beneath my office for the festivities. Jonah and I shared one last look of respect, honour, understanding, as though it might be the last time the two of us ever spoke again before I took the lead towards the garden.

While my friendship with Jonah had depleted to nothing, and my wilted trust in him was only a sprout in the soil, there was no denying that we were working towards something much more significant. And it was more than just the crown. It was the burden of an impending war, the final sols of my father's reign and the female we would all call queen.

THIRTY-FOUR

While I had expected my dreams to be shrouded in nightmares, I was surprised they were sated with Arraetta and me, living peacefully in a world created entirely for ourselves. But, those dreams were halted as I awoke to shuffling in my bedroom. At first, my body froze as though an assassin was about to rip my life from me, but I tuned into my sigils and listened to the soft breaths, recognising it to be Arraetta.

Hm, sneaking around my quarters unannounced.

I held the smile which threatened to reveal I was awake, waiting for her to close in on me until, with one quick move, I reached out, grabbed her wrist and swivelled until she was underneath me on the opposite side of the bed.

"My, my," I breathed, wondering whether I was still in a dream, "this is a surprise."

Her beautiful face reddened under the illumination of the bedside lamp I had left on. She whispered, "You were asleep."

"I could feel you," I murmured, lingering above her mouth, "what brings you to my bed at this time?"

"I was worried about you. You didn't see me yesterday."

"I saw you. From a distance, but you are always there, Arraetta."
In my thoughts, in my dreams, you plague me.

"Is that not what you want?" she asked before closing the gap between our lips. The two of us kissed for a while, and I ground my body against hers, listening to the song of pleasure which whispered against my lips.

My cock was already hard from sleep, and it was desperate for release as I inwardly dared myself to take it in hand while giving into her pleasure. But, such desires could wait and it would not be long before they would be sated.

"I could get used to you being in my bed," I broke the kiss, "but you are not here to please me."

"No."

My heart sank at the obvious, disappointment flooding me. That was love and desire, I supposed. "I would have hoped to catch you before breakfast, anyway."

Sitting more comfortably, I noticed her take in my naked torso and I was glad she was taking the time to appreciate the things which belonged to her. Still, she noticed I was watching her watch me and she turned her gaze, flushed cheeks aplenty.

I laughed lightly, "It is all yours."

"I know," she looked at me. "Maybe I just can't get used to it."

I stroked her cheek with admiration, eager for her to understand she owned my whole being. I twirled a strand of curl in my fingers, saying, "Get used to it, Arraetta."

A command of sorts, although I was only stating the obvious. She needed to understand she could not be shy about what was between us. I kissed her again, but not for too long, as I was quite aware I was delaying answering the inevitable. The truth was that there were many things I did not wish to disclose with her, but I could no longer keep the inner turmoil of the house quiet.

"There is much you do not know about the palace. When we arrived on Earth, I was infected, and it made me out of control. I remember a long period where I was drugged and strapped to a table while

Sheika and others did everything they could to reduce the effects of The Dark. I was overcome with nightmares, and that fear, as you know, fed the darkness which had reaped part of my soul.

"I did not know how much time had passed until it turned out I had been kept away from life on Earth for six months. I figured out a way to escape, and I got lost in a new world I did not understand. I found myself at a local village, around six miles away from here, where I was picked up by some officers who thought I was a spy because I could not speak a word of English. But The General found me; he had done quite well at learning the language and convinced them I was mentally unwell."

"Mentally unwell?" she gasped.

"Yes, and it worked," I replied, "I was brought back to the land my father had somehow purchased from a farm owner. My people were living in tents while they tried to build a village. The largest tent belonged to my parents, and I was escorted there, fearful that I was bound to be strapped to a table forevermore. However, once in the tent, my mother engulfed me in a hug, and she cried against me, telling me she had nothing to do with the decision that was made."

It was about the last time I witnessed such emotion from her.

"It was your father."

"Yes, it was my father. You see, something had changed during the crossing. My father despised me for what I had become because it was what had destroyed his homeland. He hated not just me but anything infected by The Dark. He told me I was a monster and that he would not allow me to rule my people until I had found a way to control it.

"Rather than sentencing me to being a science experiment, he made me the scientist. He knew it had interested me in Zika, but this was not for hobby purposes. I had to spend six days a week working on three things. First, I had to find a way for our people to survive on Earth without them getting sick with the energy levels; second, I had to learn to control my Rapidfire; and third, I had to figure out how to open a portal back to our world."

"How long did it take you?"

"Well, science was new to the world here," he replied, "so finding the things I needed was more difficult because I could not scour the land for them. That was part of my imprisonment; I could only send others out for materials I needed, and that would take a long time. In the end, it took me ten years to successfully create the generator and shield, which helped with our energy. All the while, I trained my Rapidfire with Freddie, which was the only recreational time I had. Anytime that I flared, my father's men would sedate me."

A shiver ran down my spine at such a memory, always being weakened at any sign I might snap.

"I do not get sedated anymore," I promised, although I could see it happening if my father swayed another vote. I sat in a more comfortable position. "No, that stopped around twenty years into our being here. I decreed that my sentence was ineffective and that I would do everything for my people, no matter whether I was kept under lock and key. I remember reminding him that I was his son and the future king. He declared *you are no son of mine*, and no kingdom would want a king like you."

"I flipped. My anger raged, and I found myself pinning my father on the ground while I had changed into the thing he hated the most. The monster he feared the most. I saw it in his eyes; I felt it deep within his soul. My father did not just hate me; he feared what his son had become, and he could not see past it. His soul was burdened with grief for the loss of me, but I was not dead. He repeated with a strong voice, even as he trembled *You are no son of mine*."

And, he had repeated the same phrase for scorns since, to see whether it might hurt the more he implied it.

"Did he lock you up again?" she queried.

"No. I was not sedated by his men either; they did not get the chance as my mother stormed into the tent and declared a truce. As well as my mother, Freddie, Jonah, Alex and several others you will come to recognise stood with her. My father's men outnumbered them, but there were enough people to enact a treaty. You see, under our laws, a treaty must have seven people ready to sign a declaration of peace. Not only that, little did I know many of the folk had come to my aid also. My mother produced a piece of paper - a letter - which had many signatures on it asking for the pardon of The Prince."

"I love your people," she said gleefully, clapping her hands like an excited seedling. As did I, that was why I wanted their freedom.

"They are your people, too. Although, I will admit I believe many of them, initially, signed more out of fear."

"What did the pardon say?"

"It was a simple letter which talked about negotiations," I answered, "so my father's council and my new council stood in the dining area of the house, which now is the grand hallway. We argued and agreed for hours, negotiating every little detail. My father did not want to declare me king and would not want to see me crowned, but his council reminded him that it was a rite of passage. The final agreement made was I would only become king once my fated Kindred Spirit would arrive."

And, she finally had.

"So, you declared yourself king yesterday."

"Yes," I nodded, although for my father's treasonous tongue, "but my mother reminded me of a promise I made. I would have a traditional coronation in which I am declared king in front of my people and I would not seek to declare myself king prior."

Although the traditional coronation conversation had not been spoken off in scorns, only a minor mention from my mother quarters before in which I would become king next winter.

"And, what does it mean for you to declare yourself king?"

"It means I would render my father powerless," I replied, or at least it meant I tried but did not take enough to make it so. He would be exhausted, at least, that was a benefit I was proud of.

I felt the creeping wave of my own fatigue wash over me as I looked at her, knowing how nice it would be to have her head heavy against my chest for the preceding hours.

"I am tired."

Subtly inviting her to stay, I yanked the duvet from underneath the two of us, slipping back underneath it in hopes she would understand. But, disappointment washed over me as she shuffled away from me.

"I'll leave you to sleep."

"Do not leave me; I wish to hold my wife."

"I'm not your wife yet," she answered as she slipped off the bed. I should have gripped her hips and pulled her back down. "I also hope you don't plan to render me powerless."

The only way I planned to do so was by burying myself inside her until she was blissful from each orgasm I drew from her. My hidden cock ached beneath the sheets, with nothing stopping it from poking out at full height.

"Oh, Princess," I rumbled darkly, eyes tracking her movements towards the door, "I definitely plan to."

A visible shudder rippled through her, and I wondered whether she might turn back to me so I could live up to the words I spoke. But, she did not look at me as she opened the door. "Thank you for telling me."

"I promised I would."

Flushed cheeks, a little wave, Arraetta left the warm room feeling colder without her presence and I hazily blinked at the door for several seconds, wondering whether she was waiting for me to call her back. But, I knew she had gone. Far too moral when I could have satisfied her somehow.

I grunted and lowered my hand down into my pants, gripping the skin of my length as I grappled for something which held Arraetta's scent. I found it in the pillow she had lain on, the faintness of coconut enough as I threw the pillow over my face. What a sight she would have if she did return, but I did not care.

"Fuck," I moaned, hand working rigorously faster as I sank deeper into my thoughts of her. It had only been sols since I had taken a hot shower with her name breathlessly leaving my lips as I tried to grip onto the scent of her white underwear, one not etched on my nose as much as I had hoped.

Perfect, beautiful Arraetta.

When I latched my tongue deep into her sensitive flesh, I would be kind but not merciful, drawing every forbidden noise from her body until she was writhing against me. Empyreans, her scent alone would have been enough to draw out my own orgasm, but I would not let myself come until I was buried deep inside her.

Fucking deity.

Lust overdriven by love.

Fuck. Fuck.

Fuckkkk.

I felt the heat of my orgasm soak the inside of my underwear, leaving me in another haze of dirty afterthoughts and a lonely reality. It took a lot of energy to get myself out of bed and to the spare bathroom on the wing to take a much needed cold shower before returning to my quarters. In a matter of hours, it would be Iontine and I would have to face my father and my people, hearing the whispers of the clear fracture now evident in the house.

* * *

Once morning came, I found myself dressed like I was about to grace a golf course - beige chinos, brown beige shoes and a white polo. I made my way to the front of the house, eager to find Arraetta and sweep my lips across hers. But, my mission was cut short as I stumbled upon Freddie in the library.

"Morning," I grunted, noting he wore a similar outfit to me, except his clothing was darker.

"*Twinning*," Freddie chuckled in English, before switching back to Zikan, "I thought you might need to escort."

"I am not going to die," I rolled my eyes.

"Maybe not today, but it is important we show a strong front."

"Where is your wife?"

"She is doing final preparations for the show," he informed me, leaving me confused, "ah, well, Genie has choreographed the tale of Ivan the Great, a part of demonstrating her loyalty to us."

"I did not know."

Although, maybe I was not surprised my mother would have asked Genie for unquestionable obedience, especially now she had scented a trail into Amity. I was sure it would not be the end to my mother's games until she had her nails dug deep inside Genie's mind, controlling every little thing she did. It would be interesting to see how Iontine played out with such delicate changes.

Freddie and I made our way out of the room, only to be stopped by the radiant presence of my fated one. She bathed in ethereal light, sporting a summer blue dress which accentuated every part of her body. Empyreans, I was a lucky male.

She smiled softly, looking to Freddie, "where's Genie?"

"She is busy helping with some final preparations," Freddie said, "but she shall join us for breakfast and be around before the opening ceremony."

I peered over Arraetta's shoulder, acknowledging both Alex and

Travis who were patiently waiting for us to move. I held out my arm for Arraetta to take, revelling in the feel of her skin against mine as she hooked her soft hand onto it. It only reminded me of the night prior. In silence, we made our way down the corridor. Freddie trailed behind with Alex and Travis.

Each time I peered down at Arraetta, I could see she was lost in thought, looking around for clues about unspoken things. I wondered if she was trying to understand the house now that I had given her a little more information about what was happening.

Genie met us for breakfast, where conversation flowed gently as it always did. I enjoyed the festivities of Iontine but they were tiring, so I was unsurprised there was a certain pre-emptive exhaustion afoot as we spoke about the next five sols. Freddie made a good decision to suggest we take a stroll through the village while we awaited the festivities to begin.

Our guard was assembled to escort us, and I felt pride in the amount of new soldiers wearing our regalia, even if it meant they were openly supporting the revolution. Even if it was not me they were supporting, they were still choosing to go against the ruler who sat on his dusted, crumbling throne.

"What's with the soldiers?" Arraetta asked as we wandered.

"Protection," I explained, "they are part of *our* guard."

I specifically leant on the word *our* because I wanted to let her know she was as much a part of this as I was, that these guards were keeping her safe, that they supported her as they did me. Even more than me, I would say.

"You never had this many before."

"I have never had to worry about my father as much as before." I had worried about him a little, but I had left Arraetta wandering around the halls of the palace with the knowledge she would be safe because I had been. Yet, she was never safe, always close to being taken from me, created into something my father wanted her to be. Empyreans, he even attempted to blackmail her. I took a deep breath and looked down at her. "I will do whatever I have to in order to keep you safe."

I will *keep you safe.*

"Your father isn't going to kill me."

No, he might not kill her. But he might decide that was his game in order to take back control, he might make me partake in another game of Hanged Man, or threaten her in other more deadly ways.

"You do not know what my father is capable of." A growl rippled from my throat, entwining itself in my words. "He would not kill you, but there is no doubt he will take you from me when he finds the right moment."

And, I would not let that happen. Arraetta was the one good thing that had happened throughout my entire existence, she belonged to me; she was mine to keep, to cherish, to protect.

"You're talking about the deal."

I paused abruptly and turned to her, "was it a deal or a command?"

"He seemed to want what was best for you..."

The laugh which rippled from my throat was so far from jovial, "best for me? He would not know what was best for me if it stared him in the face. In fact, you were right in front of him the entire time. Do you not understand, Arraetta, that if he could find a way to control me anymore, he would? My father is not the same man I once admired; he is but a shell of it."

And, admiration fell deep into the caverns of my seedling winters, disappearing once he had punished me with that belt, and further still as he tried to shape me into the son he despised the most.

"Sorry."

"Do not apologise," I answered, weary I might have used a harsher tone in reply to her than I had thought, "it is not your fault that arrogant man backed you into a corner. I just wish I had made him cry like he made you."

"I only told Jonah that I-"

"-It was not Jonah who told me," I interrupted, "it was one of the guards, although Jonah came to me just in time with confirmation that he had seen your cheeks stained with tears, and it was enough to throw me over. I cannot lose to a man who seeks to ruin the only thing worth living for, Arraetta."

I cannot lose to a tyrannical king who seeks to control everything in his path and rip everything good from my grasp. Empyreans, I would make him a martyred king in death if I had to in order to protect her.

I noted her looking again at the guards, so I elaborated, "they are here for us. They move for and with us; we are the command, Arraetta. You move, they move; it is how it is."

You are their queen.

She laughed lightly, bringing a lighter tone to the situation, "I guessed. Alex doesn't ever leave me alone."

I chortled inwardly, tilting my head down to brush my breath against her ear, "apart from at night time, when only the cameras know of your movements and no one can stop you."

"It's a shame the cameras are there," she added with a cheeky grin on her face, before placing her soft lips upon my cheek and waltzing after Genie and Freddie. Empyreans, she was divinity unleashed.

Once we had walked around the streets of houses, we arrived back at the house. I felt much more alive once we stepped inside, thankful to have had fun without any burdens. Or, at least it felt like such until I saw my mother painted in a floral dress waiting in the entrance for us.

"Mother," I greeted with a bow.

"Seraiah, it is nice to see you have made an effort," she commented, and I had to stop myself from rolling my eyes, "this sol shall be a momentous occasion, it is wonderful to see you both together, and happy. A smile on your face has been one I have missed."

Maybe she should not have done her best to destroy it over the winters, and she might have seen it more. But, still, I could only take the positives from what she said, and her own smile made me hold my tongue.

She looked at Arraetta, "you look radiant. I hope you come to enjoy the celebrations this week. It is very exciting that you have joined us on your first Iontine. And you as well, of course, Genie."

It was already busy in the garden with numerous attendees waiting for the chime of the bell to begin celebrating Iontine. Greeted by various people, with many looking at Arraetta as though they had never witnessed anyone of such majesty before, we were led onto a stage next to an empty dance floor. My happiness wilted a little as I noticed my father had commanded his iron throne be brought out of the storage.

It looked ghastly on stage, and he looked like an ageing ghost sat upon it, with one standard chair to his right, where my mother perched, and two to his left. Quite a bold show from my father, but he looked ridiculous, and it only accentuated it was falling from his grasp.

"Father," I bowed, showing Arraetta to her seat before taking mine next to him, "is the throne necessary?"

"After your incident yesterday, I must remind everyone, including you, who is still king here," he bit with finality. He rose to his feet, and the crowd was called to attention. He chose only to speak in Zikan, uncaring of our two non-native speakers. "I address you all, *my* people..." I cringed. "...welcoming you all to another Iontine on Earth, in which we will celebrate, drink, dance and worship the Highest Gods. This is an extraordinary event..."

I drowned out his voice to the best of my ability, washing my gaze across the crowd, seeking out those who would protect us in case of any uncalled for attacks. It seemed only Jonah and Alex were not present in the crowd.

"Let the festivities begin!" my father shouted, jolting me from my reverie. I watched Genie push through the crowd, curtseying to us before adding a subtle wink to Arraetta.

"I present to you the Dance of the Goddess."

I was quite interested to see how she would choreograph the four-winter re-enactment of the legend of how Rapidfire came to be and how Ivan the Great used such power to destroy The Dark. And, she did not disappoint. Every part of the story was told with a new breath of life, no longer were we witnessing a poorly put together piece of work, but something which looked as though it was created for an off-Broadway show. And, strangely, I found myself with a newfound respect for my mother. I understood why she asked Genie to create it, not just an act of control, but to show how outsiders can help influence us if we allowed it. Genie was a power play, and Empyreans, she played it to perfection.

Once the ceremony was over, my father declared Iontine officially open and I was eager to get my hands on some alcohol and food, and disappear from the crowd with Arraetta. Iontine was a great opportunity for me to truly take my time in getting to know her more, to be by her side without anything or anyone stopping us.

"Let us eat," I stated, helping Arraetta to her feet.

"Do not think these eyes gaze on you respectfully, Seraiah," my father chided.

"I doubt they gaze at you with it either, Father," I spat quietly before tugging Arraetta away.

The most important thing was to give Arraetta a full rundown of our customs regarding Iontine, showing her where to worship if she wished, where to drink and eat, where to find entertainment, and where to find the tent, which was sectioned off for royalty. She would also be free to come and go as she pleased, although I was sure she would enjoy it with Genie, Freddie, and me.

***

Hours of exhilaration passed, each of us merry and none of us were tormented by my opposition. At some point, Freddie and I left the two females on a picnic blanket near the lake, slipping away to get the hidden stash of Isanhowad he had left in one of the nooks when he had met Genie.

In a sense, it was a form of substance – a hallucinogen – although studies showed the only effect it had was that it made the user relaxed and worked well accompanied by alcohol. Whilst I had not spoken to Arraetta about it, we would offer the two females a chance to have some without any pressure.

"So, have you and Jonah become friends again?" Freddie queried as I pulled tome after tome from the shelf in the corner of the library.

I snorted, "No, he betrayed me."

"He betrayed us all," he answered, and I supposed he was right because he had handed information over about Amity to my father. Still, it seemed Freddie had not quite fallen out with him. "At least now I can be your right hand without competition."

I snorted, "you are my cousin, so it automatically put you ahead of the race."

"I suppose so," he replied, amused, "at least I won."

"Gone are the simple times of warless sols."

Freddie looked solemn, "this feels like the simplest we have had it in a very long time. But, how many have we truly had since Zika? The death of two friends, the loss of our nation, and the changing of your house. Yet, I do not think I would change anything."

"Apart from my father's position."

He laughed, "Yes, I suppose that is one thing. But that will soon come."

Freddie's optimism was refreshing, and it made the rest of the afternoon pass by soaked in sun, sweat and the high of Isanhowad. The effects made it hard to keep my eyes, and hands, off Arraetta, although I did not care as I invited her to dance, to kiss, to relax together.

Empyreans, I loved her.

She was the most perfect being ever grace this universe, and she was all mine.

At some point, I escaped to the privacy of the upper corridor bathroom to relieve myself and wash the sweat from my face. I knew I would have benefited from a change in attire as well, although I was far too captivated by the male who stared back at me in the mirror, pupils enlarged and a twitch of a smile. The words of my mother from earlier swam around my mind about how she was glad to see me happy.

I *was* happy, although maybe that was because my coffers had started to open and I was beginning to feel free. Free from the burden of locking every part away, free to love and be happy. The only burden I had left was the crown.

"Then, let me in Seraiah." A thud in my heart and my eyes widened at the subtle movement in my reflection. At first, I thought I might be hallucinating, but then a twisted smile licked his face and his eyes blinked to black.

"No," I whispered, stepping away.

"It has been a while, has it not, Seraiah?" he asked, "have you enjoyed all your freedoms of power?"

"That was not me," I glowered, needing to escape from the

dreaded creature. But, somehow, I was glued to my position.

"But it was you," he laughed. "It was all you, for there is no *me* without *you*. While you have done well to bask in the illusion that I am no longer here, you forget I appear at some of your most vulnerable times."

"You may be a part of me, but you are *not* me," I growled, clenching my fists, "I will not allow your shadow to overcome my light."

There was a pause before he burst into laughter. "Oh, Seraiah, you do humour me. Your shadow will always overcome your light because that is who you are destined to be - what you were born for."

"How would you know? You are not real."

"Oh, how incorrect you are."

The glass shifted into liquid shadow as his cold hand reached through, grasping me at the collar of my shirt before forcefully pulling me inside it. I grunted as the world shifted and my back landed on cold, damp onyx tiles, shivering at the frigidity of them. A chill shuddered through my chest as I peered upward, into the eyes of a winged beast; the same one which had attempted to devour me the sol of the attack on Zika.

I shuffled away quickly, fear humming through me like an off kilter note, only to pause when I noticed my dark self standing on the tip of its large, scaled head.

"Are you scared, Seraiah?" he chuckled. I could not deny that I was, watching as the beast bowed its head and my doppelgänger walked from it as though he had done it so many times. "He is all yours, *Lunbra*."

The dragon stepped over the unwavering figure, strategically thudding closer to me.

"No, please!" I begged, watching as it reared its head, ready to attack.

"I like it when you beg, Seraiah. It is very satisfying to know how weak you are without me. Does our fated one know how much you hide in your paranoia? What I would do to stand so close to her and show her exactly who we are."

I was not weak. I might have been fearful, but I was not weak. I only feared losing Arraetta, but it did not make me fragile. I knew we had worked free of the burdens of my past to move forward together. Yet, the creature before me was tugging at scorns-old dread as memories of the Zikan attack consumed my thoughts. It still did not make me weak.

But, perspiration clung to me mercilessly, unable to run from my old foe.

Lunbra, a creature of light and dark once used as an object of fear to stop seedlings from choosing the path of evil. A creature who had appeared that very night, murdering innocents like it was controlled by the hand which fed it.

If you are found to be following the path of darkness, Lunbra shall appear and devour you until the balance is once again restored.

A surge of revelation struck deep as I prepared myself to be feasted upon. I held the reins over my darkness; it was not the dragon I was facing but my fears and shadows. My own fractured soul.

He laughed about holding the reins, but it was I who truly held them all.

Because I was him.

And, he was me.

But, I would bask in my freedom one last time, for the sake of Arraetta, for the sake of my people.

"Fine. Let us play, dark one. If you shall not leave me, then next time, I shall not resist. Next time, I will wield the darkness instead of fearing it. But hear me now - you will bow to me, *not* the other way around."

Clink. Shatter. The dragon shattered like glass before my eyes, followed by a flash of dark light until I stood in front of the bathroom mirror, centred with a fracture shaped like a dying twig.

The reflection laughed sinisterly, "I look forward to it, Seraiah."

The final parts of the mirror splintered until it split from its holder, falling melodically into the sink below.

It was over. No Lunbra. No dark me.

Reality returned as keenly as the headache which throbbed, the sudden sobriety an unwanted concoction. But, I was left knowing what I had done, what would happen the next and final time I met with him.

I would step into my fear, my darkness, and embrace it.

Free from the tormented shackles, replaced by a thrum of unrelenting power.

A cursed prince rising above all to become a shadow king.

But, I had a heart, powered by love for a female who held it hostage. And, I would use that to rule my people, allowing her light to replace the dark.

But not yet.

A sharp rattle against the bathroom door knocked me out of my thoughts, "Choose your time."

I took a few moments before walking over and opening the door. On the other side, I was met by Travis, stood back, and bowed.

"What is it?" I asked rather irritably. I watched his eyes dart to the shattered mirror, then to my hand, where I presumed he suspected I had punched it before he looked at me.

"Her Royal Highness has fainted."

THIRTY-FIVE

I nstinct kicked in like wildfire as I made my way down to the garden. I found Arraetta at the bottom of it, by the generator, unconscious in Alex's arms while Jonah was on standby with other guards. I wanted to tell the onlookers to turn their curious gaze, but they were not my priority.

I slid onto my knees next to her, taking her from Alex's gentle arms and holding her close. The generator pulsed with unnaturally vibrant life as though it had been fed endless streams of Rapidfire. As though Arraetta had always been its source, the power we unknowingly siphoned every four winters of Iontine.

Empyreans, it all made sense. My stomach clenched with guilt; we had been draining her energy all along. The Blackouts, the exhaustion, the pain she had suffered, it had always been us drawing from the strongest source on Earth – her.

I prayed Arraetta was not amid another Blackout, that we had not caused her more suffering when she needed to be free from it. I tightened my arms around her, holding her a little closer as I prayed. And, it seemed those prayers were answered as she finally came around, slowly blinking up at me with confusion on her face.

My shoulders sagged with relief, "Arraetta."

"Is she okay?" Genie called, rushing over with a glass of water.

Gently, Arraetta sat up, taking in her whereabouts. "What happened?"

"Jonah said you touched the globe," Genie replied, "then you sort of just lit up and collapsed. Two minutes later, you're awake again."

"I'm fine." But, I could see the lie on her weary face, the gentle dampness of sweat covering her like a translucent cloth, the subtle bags underneath her eyes.

Unfortunately, I was unable to pry further as our afternoon was ruined by the arrival of Jonah's father, exacerbating the burden of what had happened. Freddie, who must have appeared with Genie, alongside Jonah stopped him in his path.

"I have been lenient enough over the last moons," The General glowered, "but the use of Rapidfire at this event is going far enough."

"It was not purposeful," Jonah interjected.

"It seems every time is *not purposeful!*" The General spat, "I am surprised even you - a male who seeks to be the next General - are blind to our laws. I not only have an uprising on my hands, but now I have to deal with this."

"There was no harm," Freddie replied.

"That girl needs to be arrested!"

I stood quickly, stepping towards the brute. "That *girl* is our next queen! And, as far as I am aware, General, she has done more for our people in a single moment than you have done in your career."

"You arrogant boy!" he chided, clenching his fist as he stepped towards me, "While you may be the heir to this throne, you are still a prince and have no power over the laws of our kingdom."

"Oh, but you are wrong, Father," Jonah replied. "I am very sure you are aware of the events which took place yesterday. This is very much an equal playing field."

The General glowered at his son, shaking his head with disgust, "Whilst His Majesty may have faltered under his son's power, he still holds the crown, which means the court is in his favour. We have surpassed any need for Rapidfire to be the ruler of fates!"

"I was unaware of when such laws were changed," Jonah raised his eyebrows, indicating to the lack of evidence my father's absence of power meant he could remain in his position, "unless something changed in the last twenty-four hours, of course. But, that would indicate that you have illegally persuaded the council to vote without consulting all of us."

"You should watch your tongue," The General growled, humouring all of us and angering him more, "by order of the king, I am placing that... that female under arrest!"

My jaw tightened, before I turned to my fated one, "Arraetta, are you alright?" She nodded. "See, there is nothing to warrant any form of arrest."

"You forget your father is still king, boy!"

"And you forget your place, Sir!" I retorted, stepping towards him, "unless you want me to remind you of it."

"You do not scare me, Seraiah," he answered, "I have had enough preparation taming beasts in my time; I do not mind taming another."

My anger was overshadowing me, and I was close to being the one who would be arrested as I almost dived at the hellsworn. But, Jonah and Freddie stopped my attack before it could be made.

"Your life is in the fates hands, General!" I growled, uncaring my animalistic devil traits were showing in front of the two females. I shoved myself away from them, walking down towards Arraetta. I tried not to listen to Jonah as he continued to calm the situation, but I was thankful when he somehow won the battle and The General left, with his other soldiers.

"You should have just let me kill him."

"And what good would that be?" Freddie replied, each of us peering up as The General disappeared into the crowd. "The treaty would be broken, and we would not have a leg to stand on. You must cut the head off the snake first, Seraiah."

I nodded, "I had the opportunity yesterday, but my mother..."

The three of us all agreed whilst my anger festered within.

"Are you well, ma'am?" Jonah asked Arraetta.

I expected Arraetta to look unwell, but it seemed that sitting beside the generator was rapidly augmenting her health. Instead, she had a sheepish expression, trying to divert her eyes, "Who was that anyway?"

"The General," the three of us replied with an echoed lack of enthusiasm, and we all laughed lightly at each other. I supposed Arraetta had yet to meet my father's council, although with how quickly the tide was turning, I was not sure she ever would need to.

"I've never seen him before," she replied.

"My father's wing is usually where he is," I explained, rarely encountering him outside of the council room, save for the odd occasion he would be at the garrison, away from his own office at his home.

"I hope you can explain what happened when you collapsed," Freddie said, "because after your Rapidfire fired up, the colour suddenly changed."

I looked at the ball, chuckling a little. "More than changed, I feel like my energy has been sated."

It was not the right time to be throwing apologies at her for understanding it was us who might have been the cause of her pain. Instead, I would savour the new burst of energy and pray what she had fed to our generator would not replenish what little my father had left in ours. It made me feel sick knowing he might have taken something from Arraetta and I would fight him to get it back if there was so much a scent of it. But, neither of us needed a battle of Rapidfire to show who was the strongest, especially not when I was inches from the crown being in my grasp.

King Seraiah was coming, and with it a world of change would follow.

***

Iontine was over as quickly as it began, five sols without any further incidents, although we were much lighter on our celebrations than we were. During sleep, my nightmares were clouded by violent imagery of death and destruction, each pointing back to one specific source – myself. Maybe it was guilt from the realisation we were the cause of Arraetta's pain, or maybe it was the deal I had made with my inner darkness.

In my more sober times, I found myself preparing for my final encounter with my dark self, wondering how I would deal with it once I finally gave in to the one part of me which had been trapped in the depths of my mind for scorns. The coffers had been easier, prying open and hitting me hard but he, it, *me* was the final boss.

And, while I was battling with my internal darkness, more change had taken place in the house. My father and The General were preparing to take down those who had risen against the crown, soldiers had been arrested and sentencing was slowly being given, although any punishments for treason were to take place after Iontine and the bonding would take place. Jonah told me Connell had been sent to Italy for training, while Leopold was in Scotland to recover. Both newcomers to Amity were already gone and, with it, it seemed Amity itself was becoming far less prevalent.

However, I focused only on my nuptials and my relationship with Arraetta, knowing the time for new plans would eventually come.

"Your Highness."

I turned to see Terance walking towards me as I headed down the corridor to the library, where I would spend my final few nights before bedding my wife. The anticipation of such a thing was overwhelming.

He bowed in greeting, "I do apologise."

"Take your time," I chuckled, "I am sure it is not so urgent."

Terance breathed, "I am afraid it is. I have been trying to find a moment to converse with you, but I did not wish to spoil your celebrations. It has been brought to my attention you are being moved out of the palace."

"*Out* of the palace?"

"Yes, it has been ordered by His Majesty. You will be moved to one of the houses until your heartfast."

"And, has he informed you of the reason?" I replied, finding it oddly suspicious and worried my father would be closer to Arraetta than I would.

"It is tradition," he answered, and the tension left my shoulders. "You are to spend the next few sols apart. There is to be no communication until the heartfast."

An old tradition, one which could be eradicated, but it was not worth arguing about sols before my union. Reluctantly, I agreed to follow Terance down to the front of the house, where I was met by Jonah, who stood beside his vehicle.

"Am I to reside with you?" I queried.

"I thought it would be best," he agreed, and whilst the two of us were only partners in adversity, as he coined it, I knew it would be the safest place to settle. I would be fed well by Alex, but I was saddened about being at opposite ends of the complex from my fated one. Sols of spending time together to be ripped from me without an hour's notice.

"It has come to my attention there has been a significant change in your father's command," he informed me, as we drove in his car, "as well as new uniforms, guards have been offered a pay rise, and their families will receive tax benefits."

Something we did not have the power to give them, which meant many of our guards would choose it.

I grovelled, "And for those who stayed?"

"Higher tax, less meal tokens. It is just propaganda. We have lost a few guards, but the most important remain, and we will devise a plan once the heartfast is over."

"I suspect we will lose more. My father knows I am powerless when it comes to the finances of the house. He has that under his control, and it has been a hard battle to make such a shift."

He answered, "I know money is scarce when no war is on the horizon. Your father is funding an army sitting idle, and many are uncertain if they will ever go into battle. While my father's guard await orders, they become restless and bored, some even thinking of leaving the garrison altogether. But, they cannot because they are trapped by a clause in their contract, with little way out... except for one. They will move to our side, where they see our training strategies are more enjoyable, and, whilst the pay is lower, they can leave the army several winters before they were originally contracted to. So, therefore, we shall always win, Seraiah, because they will choose us to get out."

"But, when all our soldiers have chosen him," I raised my eyebrows. "What then?"

"That will not happen. I have only had a handful of people hand in their resignation, and I have honoured them, but I have offered their positions back, should they decide before signing over to the king's guard."

Jonah was a fair commander, giving his soldiers a great life, even for less pay than his father would provide. His training regimes were challenging, his outings were fun, and the work he assigned was made to make them feel important. But even if all the soldiers shifted to my father's side, once the crown fell onto my head, I would have an entire army below me with no noticeable split. Unless there was an uprising against me, of course. But, then who would be king?

"Let us talk about this next quarter," Jonah said, peering at me. "You have a heartfast to prepare for."

"I suppose we are not having a bachelor party?" I jested.

Jonah chuckled, "Maybe we shall have a small gathering next sol, but I am quite tired and ready to sleep."

I could only agree because I was restless. After a light supper with Jonah and Alex, I was shuffled to one of the two spare bedrooms, where I would spend the coming sols. It felt odd to be so close yet so far from the palace. Inside, it was so easy to hear the gossip mill churning around the staff members, but each sol I spent at Jonah's house meant I would be blind to what was happening inside. If Jonah knew anything, he did not speak anymore of it.

Jonah lived up to his decision to have a bachelor party the next sol, which only included Freddie and the three of us. Most of it was spent talking about the times that had passed and the life we would soon live. But, there was little mention of my father, as though the topic was banned from conversation. Freddie returned to his quarters at the palace after a few hours and we all retired to bed.

But I could not sleep. I tossed and turned when the sky was dark and snoozed when the sky was light, but neither of the males seemed to take notice. When they were away on duty, their small garden was a haven, spending hours finalising and remembering my speech for her.

Sometimes I thought about how Arraetta and I would live if we were not without the burdens of our duty. Whilst I had done little domestic chores in my life, I would learn to cook with her and understand how to use a washing machine. The two of us attempting to patch a lifestyle together would be quite mesmerising, but I was sure we would only become irritable. I could not imagine Arraetta as a simple housewife, although I quite like the imagery of her paint-splattered face as she brushed over a canvas in a sun kissed orangery. But, I had not known her to do much painting since arriving at the house, and I wondered if she had lost the passion for it.

I supposed the two of us were made for the circumstances we were born into.

The night before the heartfast arrived soon, and insomnia kicked in. I realised part of it was because I longed to hold Arraetta, to speak to and kiss her. My stomach knotted at the thought of it being only hours before she would walk down the aisle and we would bond after so much time apart.

The Kindred Spirits becoming Kindred, at last.

Once the nuptials had ended and the celebrations had begun, we would go to our shared chamber to complete the bond.

A heartfast night to remember, I was sure.

In the early morning, I decided there was no point in sleeping in the room. I put on a T-shirt, pants and shoes and tiptoed out of my room, slipping out of their back door of the house.

I was aware there were guards in the vicinity, but I managed to slip out of the garden and wander down the paths and roads of the estate. I constantly gazed up at the palace, wondering whether I could climb onto the roof and throw a rock at Arraetta's window, calling her down as though I was Romeo and she was Juliet.

However, I knew infiltrating the palace grounds and traversing the rooftop would be quite a difficult task.

Instead, I took a walk and sat on a swing at the local park, which was situated in a field near Sheika's house and not too far from Jonah's. The atmosphere was quiet, with the distant sound of passing cars and clicking insects.

It was peaceful.

But the serenity was interrupted when feet crunched up the grass behind me and I turned my attention toward the perpetrator.

Zela. One of Sheika's disciples, who spent most of her time in worship or on retreats elsewhere unless she was summoned forth. Zela lived in the woods in a sort of teepee tent; an area of the complex I rarely wandered to.

"Your Highness," she said, half bowing as she walked past me. In her hand, she held a lamp lit with an old candle. Swinging it back and forth, humming an odd tune.

"You are out late," I commented.

"I am most at peace at night," she stopped, looking up at the sky. "We forget the nature we are surrounded by when we are so often in a fray." Zela turned to me. "Do not forget the kind nature which lies within your heart, young prince, even when times are as tumultuous as these."

Zela continued, but I followed, trying to find out what she knew that I did not. "Have you heard something?"

She looked at me again, "I hear a great many things."

"I suppose you have heard what my father is strategising."

Zela studied me before shaking her head. "I only listen to the voice of the Gods. The Gods chose the king to be on the throne, but times shall soon change, for there is a greater play at hand."

"And, that play is?" I asked, a little desperately.

"You will understand soon enough," she answered, and a growl rippled from my throat. Zela only laughed, "I would be prepared if I was in your position, as I suspect the winds of change are forecast to be a grey and thunderous storm, which you must face to rise as the ruler you seek to become."

"Is this storm my father?" I called, my voice echoing a little.

Continuing to walk away, she was silent for a moment before she called, just as loud, "The answer you seek will not be found in the words and actions of those who are against you. Instead, young prince, look within where the storm you chase is already aflame."

Zela was soon nothing more than another shadow of the night; her torch was the only thing indicating her passage, like a little light sprite. But she left me with more questions than answers with her odd riddles. What did she mean about the storm already being aflame within myself? Was she aware of the dark side of me I was fighting against? Was that the grey and thunderous cloud she spoke of?

"Your Grace." I was knocked out of my reverie as Travis appeared nearby, bowing in greeting. I had not realised I had almost arrived back at Jonah's.

"Travis," I nodded.

He bowed, "I apologise; I did not see you had left."

I patted Travis on the shoulder, "Do not worry; I just took some fresh air before the events of tomorrow. Pre-heartfast jitters, I am sure you understand."

He only hummed in response and began to escort me back, I kept hearing that final line from Zela, *Look within where the storm you chase is already aflame.*

Once back in the house, I tiptoed back to bed and fell asleep peacefully. It was not enough to combat my tiredness, but it made getting ready in the morning a breeze, with various dressers approaching the door to help me. And if time did not know how to slow down, I was escorted to the house. Jitters fluttered in my stomach, anticipation for the sol ahead mingling with the need to see Arraetta.

As we arrived at the house, Genie rushed from one side of the corridor to the other before she reversed and waved at me.

"You look handsome, Your Highness!" she shouted, and I chuckled. "Are you nervous?"

535

"A little," I replied. *A lot.* "I hope she shows up."

"She'll show," she threw her thumbs up at me before her feet pattered down the west wing corridor, where I was sure Arraetta looked radiant in her heartfast gown. I could not wait to see it, nor could I wait to see what was *under* it.

The back garden had been set up perfectly for the occasion, with rows of chairs lining the hill, while the altar was positioned next to the lake. Guests milled around, some sitting and some standing, but none noticed my arrival as I walked down to the bottom, flanked by Freddie. I was a little nervous about the number of people who had been invited, considering it was a closed-off affair.

"Do not look so panicked," Freddie chuckled.

"I think people are expecting a spectacle," I commented quietly before greeting Elder Marcus, the celebrant who was in my night-mares moons prior. I just prayed The Mire did not appear as it had then.

"How do you feel?" he queried.

"Well," I replied. Looking up at the crowd, I tried to spot members of my father's council, but it seemed their presence was lacking as much as his. I had suspected as much, of course. He would not witness an event he disapproved of, even if the Gods fated it. In the front row, my mother had already taken her seat with Helga, and next to them sat Sheika and Zela whilst the other disciples were nearby.

"Be prepared, Your Royal Highness," Elder Marcus said, bringing my attention back to him, "whilst we have not observed the joining of the Kindred Spirits before, it is understood strange things may happen in the process."

I smiled reassuringly at him, "I am sure whatever happens is what the Gods wish."

After a final few words, the crowd took their seats and began to settle, and I knew Arraetta was moments away from gracing us with her radiance. As instructed, I turned away from the crowd as the song from the night of the ball began to play. My stomach fluttered with nerves as the anticipation of seeing her settled in after sols of being apart.

"She is quite beautiful," Freddie murmured, "you may wish to see."

It was all I needed to turn and watch my beautiful goddess descend the garden path, her azure eyes trained on me. Heart thudding, I swallowed, mesmerised by the glistening tiara atop brown locks which were loosely thrown over the shoulders of a white dress. It accentuated her torso and flared at the hips.

Crack.

Empyreans, she was made to be worshipped, and I almost knelt to praise her celestial being.

Tears threatened to spill from my eyes, nurturing a feeling of overwhelming joy I had forgotten for scorns. Every worry, every thought, every negative feeling washed away at the sight of her, gazing upon Arraetta's divinity.

Crack.

The Gods had blessed a scorned male with the most holy of them.

A lock shattered deep within, and heat slithered up my back while pure elation ricocheted through me. The sixth coffer had broken, and I finally understood the importance of the feeling I had kept locked away. Hope. Pure, undeniable hope for a better life with this goddess, for our people, and for our kingdom.

Once I had said fuck hope, but how could I have dared to lock such a feeling away when hope was everything.

Because hope was Arraetta.

Her gentle steps halted before me and she curtseyed deeply in greeting, which I almost faltered under as she never need curtsey as low as she had. But, still, I bowed, eager for her to understand her place would always be a step above my own.

I stepped closer, whispering my lips across her cheek until I was tickled by the tendrils of her hair, "You are so beautiful."

Rouge rose upon Arraetta's honeyed skin, and we made gentle eye contact. Elder Marcus cleared his throat, indicating we must begin. And, I was reminded I did not have long to wait before the two of us were left alone.

"Ladies and gentlemen, please be seated for the ceremony, which is about to begin!" Elder Marcus called in Zikan to the ebbing crowd, which began to quieten their chatter slowly at his command. Arraetta's gaze nervously swept them, looking for someone or something to hold on to, but it seemed whatever she was looking for was not upon there.

Our eyes connected when she looked back, coyly turning her gaze again as though she had been caught out. Not searching then, only being inquisitive.

"Today is a wondrous day," Elder Marcus called, speaking in English, "we come together to not only witness the matrimony of our beloved Crown Prince and Princess but also witness the bonding of the souls of Kindred Spirits. This ceremony is special, and only those who bear witness to this today, on this Earth, shall know that this has taken place. Two months ago, the two who stand before us, His Royal Highness Seraiah, Prince of Zika, and Her Royal Highness Arraetta, Princess of The Cre-este, took to the floor to dance to the very same song that you have just heard, and now they stand before us, willing and ready to be together in this life and the next.

"The process of the binding of souls is much different to that of an ordinary marriage. Today, you shall all witness something that many of you will never have seen before, so please be aware that anyone caught with their video phones or cameras during this process shall be removed from the ceremony."

Several mortal-kind hurried to put their phones away, although I was quite sure some were secretly filming. I was sure it was an exciting occasion to possibly witness something otherworldly, but it would do no good for such videos to find themselves in the hands of humans.

"We are gathered here today..." Elder Marcus' words swept over the crowd like a warlock imparting a spell, reading cherished words from the heavy, thick tome in his hands, all while instructing Arraetta and I to follow as well as we could. My hand was soon gripped around Arraetta's soft arm, and hers around mine, as we repeated the vows to each other. It was Arraetta who drew the first lines from her mouth, and with each that passed I could feel the tug of power lace up my arm as our unbonded magic began to meld together.

And, with each line I spoke afterward, it felt like unbreakable iron chains were being bound around our souls, fusing us as one - as Kindred. There was no pain, no suffering, only a strangely freeing and powerful sensation, like a mortal being traded for a god. And, I almost was futile enough to believe they might give me passage to their lands after I had passed.

On my final line, *and so it shall be*, we broke eye contact and looked down to where black lines had painlessly seared themselves into our arms like tattoos, decorated in an archaic language which even I had never seen before. I was sure it was a soul contract, binding us as one, never to be broken again.

Peering back up at Arraetta, my beautiful wife, I caught a glimpse of her azure irises, rimmed in a mix of the colours of our Rapidfire. She looked pleasantly regal.

"Your eyes," I whispered, cupping her cheeks.

"Your eyes." She replied, seeming that even I had been blessed with such majesty I would only witness once I looked into a mirror. Our reverie was broken as the crowd roared with happiness, their prince was now married to an angelic being and the path to peace brought a note of change in the air. I was sure even mortal-kind across the vast universe knew a change had sounded like a chime.

"I feel so..." she said.

"...Alive." I finished, knowing how she felt, knowing that our deeply innate feelings were melding with the newly found love and hope we had for each other. We were one, Kindred, together for eternity. And, I would be damned if anyone ever strove to take it from us - from me.

Elder Marcus once again called everyone to attention, "I understand that His Royal Highness has prepared some words that he wishes to convey to Her Royal Highness."

A speech which I had spent hours preparing, knowing there were words which I needed her to know, even though part of me wished I could have told her them in privacy. However, I knew the importance of demonstrating to my people the love I felt for her, and make them understand that the winds of change were right before them.

"Arraetta, I am truly, and wholeheartedly, in love with you. It feels like so long ago since I met you on the night of my birthday and before then, truthfully, I had lost hope with the life that I was living. I was told by the Gods, in a dream, that, one day, I would meet my Kindred Spirit, and I have lived a lifetime wondering who that would be, and then I met you. Beautiful, perfect, sometimes a little bit bothersome, you light up every part of any room you enter, leaving no time to catch one's breath. Arraetta, I long to hold and cherish you with each passing day, and I cannot bear to spend any moment apart. I cannot wait to spend my life with you by my side, as my wife and my queen. I promise that I shall always love and protect you with every fibre of my being and my soul. Lavoure, Arraetta."

THIRTY-SIX

C elebrating our heartfast was one of the greatest moments in my long, uneventful mortal life, being able to spend hours without the burden of the crown, joyously celebrating with Arraetta, our friends and those who had joined in the nuptials. I even witnessed a smile upon my mother's sullen face, though if it was not so much aimed at me but at Arraetta. I was unsurprised my father failed to make his presence known, not even appearing to make some sort of disruption.

I did not fail to notice several whispers about his lack of attendance, nor that some were trying to pin it on him being unwell. I almost snorted at that particular one I had overheard as I had taken a drink at the bar with Freddie.

But, I hated I was focusing on why he had not arrived rather than the joyous occasion of heartfasting with Arraetta, so I placed such thoughts to the back of my mind. Instead, I drank, danced and laughed merrily without burden. I knew the time for Arraetta and I to have our first dance was soon upon us, one which we had flawlessly rehearsed the sol of our first kiss. And, following that, we would be shipped off to our shared chambers to complete the bond.

And, while that was happening, the celebrations would continue for sols to follow, the merriments open for any well-wishers who would like to offer gifts at an altar in the west garden. All while I was tucked away making love to her, out of sight, out of mind.

Nerves tickled my chest, like a virgin ready to bathe in glorious splendour, but I had enough experience to know what great pleasure I would give to this female. And, I would go above and beyond to give it, so she understood how much I desired her.

As I swigged a glass of water by the bar, I glanced across the lively tent and outer area, taking in the familiar faces, chatting to one another, drinking, dancing. It was Arraetta who my eyes landed upon as she laughed joyously with Genie and Freddie, whispering about something I was sure was entertaining.

I tipped my head back and necked the last of the water before turning to place the glass on the bar. But, my movements were halted as I looked through the flap of the tent, seeing both my father and The General walking back towards the house. It seemed they had come to bear witness to the party, but only to turn and walk away without so much of a congratulation. Hellsworn fucker.

I supposed it could have been the alcohol, but their presence angered me enough, deciding to appear when the celebrations were almost over. And, disappeared before they could even be bothered to give their blessing. Then again, I did not want The General's blessing, but my father's would have been nice. No, not nice but necessary. For Arraetta.

Heat rose under my skin, and I could only think about confronting him for his disdain toward me. I strode quickly out of the tent, finding they had already gone through the glass doors at the top of the garden by the time I had reached them.

"Father!" I called loudly, pausing them in the centre of the middle corridor.

My father turned towards me with an evident roll of his eyes, "I believe your heartfast is the other way."

I glowered, walking towards him. "Yes, I believe it is. Although you failed to attend and bless us."

The General's mouth opened, but my father held his hand up to silence him, "I am surprised you are even here asking for such a blessing when you know I shall never give it to you - not even if the Gods wished for it."

"Do you not think that even our people believe it is odd you did not attend?"

"Oh, but I did, Seraiah," he chuckled. "I have witnessed your ceremony and allowed you to bathe in the happiness you have wished for so long. What more can you ask for, hm? Once the new quarter begins, I will simply pull it from beneath you." My jaw tightened as he continued, "You will notice a great change in the wind coming, and I am quite excited to see you get swept up in its chaos. Every civilian will never trust such an unruly reprobate, possessed by a demon."

I was unable to hide the anger I felt toward him, and I almost retorted, but I was interrupted as more hastened footsteps came bounding down the corridor towards us. I turned to see Jonah and Freddie, unsurprisingly having noticed I had disappeared from the party.

"Ah, your two lackeys have arrived," my father grumbled, but it was loud enough that it echoed down the hallway. With little more, he continued walking away down the corridor.

"Seraiah-" Freddie said as he and Jonah reached me.

"-Father!" I shouted in aggravation, uncaring that my voice was far too loud in the enclosed corridor. How dare such a heathen walk from me when I was talking to him, king or not, that male possessed little power to keep the crown which belonged to me.

He ignored me. Foolish mistake.

I rushed after him, flanked by the other two as though they were going to help or deter me from my mission.

"Let us just leave it, Your Highness," Jonah implored.

But, I ignored him still as I walked out of the corridor as my father reached the doorway of his quarters. He sighed dramatically, looking back at me, "Empyreans, it is like having three obstinate seedlings on my tail. I am sure you would rather like to find your final moments enjoyed as an honourable prince, would you not?"

"Oh, so I am *honourable* now, am I?" I bit back.

"You are far too hasty with that anger of yours!" he snapped.

"Oh, fuck you," I growled.

The General growled, "Maybe I should teach you some manners!"

"Leave this conversation for grown-ups, General," I chided, which I knew had caught him out momentarily. "I am just making sure I heard you correctly, Your Majesty, when you informed me that next quarter you plan to *rip* my happiness from beneath me. Is that correct?"

My two allies looked confused, taking in the conversation as though it was completely new news to them. I supposed they might have been blind to a change in the cogs, just as I was.

My father rounded his shoulders, before he cocked his head to the side as though he were studying a rabid dog, "plans are already in motion, Seraiah. Once you have enjoyed the feast for which you have starved, you will find it all ripped away from you until you are begging for sustenance. You and that... that charlatan."

More derogatory words used towards my wife, and I was very close to attacking my father mercilessly for his impudence. But, judgment made such a decision unexplainable, and I knew I would find myself in a vault over a bed finalising the bond. And, whatever plans my father was weaving would unravel faster than a spinner wheel could handle.

A pair of additional footsteps decided to join the party, but I did not look to see who had arrived, only noting The General's eye roll as Alex appeared.

"What is this some sort of seedling academy?" The General grovelled.

"Go back to your wife," my father said to me.

But, as though the confrontation required more of an audience, the clipping of heeled shoes and boots clattered down the hallway and I turned my head to see my mother, Sheika, and some other guards walking towards us.

The dynamic in the entrance hallway shifted, stepping back for their arrival until I was standing at the bottom of the stairwell with Jonah and Freddie. I was unsure whose side my mother would be on, or whether they would simply be there to calm the frigid atmosphere. But, judging by my father's expression, it seemed he was quite satisfied my mother had decided to make an appearance.

She looked at me with disappointment, "It is your heartfast, Seraiah. We should be celebrating, not quarrelling, on such a joyous sol."

My heart squeezed at the sight of her championing my father's continued feud, over enquiring why we were in the corridor at heads.

"I am quite aware, mother."

She studied me for a short moment, and I wondered what exactly I was seeing in her expressionless gaze. She turned to look at my father, "And you, Charles. I have not seen you come to celebrate with our people."

"I will not celebrate such insolence."

"It is not insolence, it is the will of the Gods. We cannot ignore such fates." She implored.

"They must be laughing at us from the heavens!" he released a callous laugh too, as though it was truly the funniest thing he had heard.

"Do not question the will of the gods, Your Majesty," Sheika added,

"It shall only anger them."

"Then, let them be angered!" he chided, clenching his fist, "I am sick of trying to appease those who do not wish to help us. In fact, I wonder if they might exist at all, or so shall my life end for such blasphemy." He paused as if waiting for death. "So, do not tell me whether I should or should not question the will of the Gods when they have cursed themselves by blessing such a monstrous creature with a divine union."

I noted the anger on Sheika's face, but still she held her tongue, even when she knew it was sacrilege for us to utter negative words about the Gods.

"Is Mother aware of your attempts to usurp my position next quarter?" I asked.

"Usurp?" my mother choked, blinking in his direction.

"You are blindly assuming such nonsense," he retorted.

I snorted, "then, explain to me what your plan is."

"Such commands from someone so untitled," he tutted before he chuckled, "Fine, I shall impart some information on you as none shall be able to say otherwise. I shall give you this quarter to enjoy your marriage, for then I shall remove Arraetta, that seedling wife of yours, from this household and send her to Scotland." My fists tightened in their grip. "I should only hope you impregnate her by then, Seraiah, for whatever seedling is born will return here and be raised as the heir to the throne, and you shall be locked where you belong."

Tension simmered, the muscles in my shoulders screaming for release, sweat swimming in my palms as I pushed myself to not consider taking the life of my father with all the power it took. Inaudible disagreements muttered from those around me, while I debated inwardly about why killing him was *not* a good idea. Still, I had said it before, and I would repeat the same words. I would rather my father be a martyred king than be gifted the honour of speaking such vile terms to me.

Empyreans, I knew that it would only take one council vote to enforce such terms. We had been near to the last of the votes with Genie and there would be no doubt my father's vote would tip this one over the edge. I knew if Arraetta fell pregnant, she would birth a seedling, and I would be removed as the next in line for the throne, sentenced to the vaults until the sol of my death and never see the light which shined above again.

No, I would never let him take something so precious from me. He would turn my seedling against me, he would make me the enemy and make my precious young resent me forever, all while Arraetta was forced to live apart from them.

From me.

No.

Fuck him.

I would burn our world to the ground before he had a chance to see through his plan.

"If you have something to say to me, Sir." My heart thudded, head whipping to look up the stairwell to where the light from the window shone against the radiance of my newly wedded wife. "You may say it to my face."

Tension shuddered from me, replaced by awe and utter respect for the female who dared to finally raise her voice against the male who had spoken to her like she was nothing the quarter prior.

She was fearless, breathtaking, a guiding light.

A true, undeniable ruler.

The General roared, "How dare you address The King in such a way!"

While he attempted to move towards the stairwell, as though to grab and drag her down to be punished, a click of an armament took his attention as Jonah held one in his father's direction, unwavering.

"One more move, General."

The General laughed, "My son, how mighty you have become."

Yes, how mighty Jonah had become, finally rising to his father's level when he had stooped beneath him for most of his life.

"This is getting out of hand," my mother bellowed, "this is our son's heartfast day, Charles."

"He is no son of mine!"

"So I have been reminded, Father!" My jaw tightened. "Might I remind you that you are only king because Mother made me vow I would not take the throne?"

"You are not worthy of the throne!" he instantly snapped, "and neither is that piece of filth you now call your *wife*."

The tension returned, and I was unable to see past the red hue which rippled over my eyes, chaos flaring through my body as I flicked the switch on my cerulean Rapidfire. I jumped him like I was a beast ready to feast on his prey, far too quick for anyone to stop me as my fist connected with his nose, shattering it instantly and landing the two of us on the floor - me atop him. Another punch. And another. And another.

Each more satisfying than the last, uncaring or unknowing of the audience, which looked upon the shocking scene before them.

"Stop this!" My mother shouted. Two arms gripped my torso, and I was pulled from my father's limp yet conscious body by Freddie.

"You speak of my wife in such a way again," I screamed, "and I shall have no reason to spare your life. Your days as king are numbered, and when I am king, I shall exile you to suffer your final days in the human world!"

Freddie did not let me go until I shoved him off, clenching my bloodied fist back and forth as I attempted to stow the bitterness. The General returned to support my father to his feet, not seeming to have much support from anyone else in the room.

"Your Majesty, you are a shame to your son," Arraetta stated, pride seeping through me, "how can you treat him like he has brought your life so much pain when he has done nothing but work hard for his people."

"You are an ignorant child," my father spat. "How can you truly know everything when you have been here, consciously, for merely six weeks?"

"I may not know everything," she answered confidently, still holding power in the room as she held her head high, "but I know that Seraiah is a good man and whether The Dark infects him or not, he is still the same person you loved."

"You are naïve, Arraetta," my father retorted, "it is a shame that you were not brought up in your own world as, you would have learnt, the world of royalty is nothing like what you read in your fairy tales. My son died in battle. This... thing may look like him, but he is not Seraiah. You will come to learn that very soon; I have no doubt." He looked at Seraiah. "One wrong move and he will be casting dark shadows in your mind until you are but a shell of yourself."

Although the anger had turned back to simmering, his words fermented as fast as a flame to a wick and I was back at my attempts to attack him again. But, I did not note the unknown piece on the chessboard, finding myself in a physical altercation with The General as I tried to grieve my anger. I was on top of him at first, but he span me until I was below him, heavy hands wrapping around my throat, choking me without mercy.

I could not breathe.

"You are a disgrace, Seraiah!"

Breathe. Fuck.

"I should have put you out of your misery a long ago."

Please, just let me. Let me fucking breathe.

I did not see his next move, only hearing a loud clattering of an armament shot, followed by the warm liquid of red blood splattering across my face. I blinked up, staring through a gaping hole perforating The General's skull into a body part I knew should not be witnessed from the outside.

My power disintegrated, shock rattling my bones as I gazed up at the lifeless eyes of a heavy male, who stared back at me.

Helpless.

Fuck, The General was dead.

Lord Viktoerin Marcheus who had caused me so much suffering over the sols.

A male made to be a good father, but died a fucking monster.

"Travis," Jonah breathed, eyes wide.

Travis? I could not take my eyes off the heavy male in my grip, but I knew the accusation meant Travis had taken the shot. But, why would he do such a thing?

I looked down to my left, seeing a gun next to The General's hand before finally pushing the brute from me, needing space from him and needing to see what state this place was left in. The General was going to kill me, and Travis had tried to save me by doing the one thing which could cost him his fucking life.

My father shouted, "This is treason."

Empyreans, not the male who had been following me around quietly, not the male who had quietly supported me, had been my close guard.

Travis gazed down to where The General's body was, not a hint of dissatisfaction on his face, before he looked up at my father. Pure, undeniable loathing wrinkled those brows, as a strange look of finality ruffled his gaze. He rounded his shoulders, looking at me with a softer, respectful expression as though I would understand his decision.

His final look was up to a shocked and confused Arraetta, before he stood upright, calling louder than he ever had before, "Long live the Goddess of the Light. May the darkness be forever destroyed by your divine power."

I clocked what his next move was a second too late, sitting upright as each of us witnessed Travis place his gun below his chin and pull the trigger. I think I shouted his name, but the silence which followed was far too heavy to even know whether I had just said it inside my head.

Thud. His body landed pitilessly on the floor.

Silence.

Travis was dead.

The General was dead.

Time seemed to have frozen at first, until someone shifted, then another and the room seemed to spin as everyone began following emergency procedures. Guards moved to escort my father to the safety of his chambers, while my mother was urged to leave. And, I was unsure how long I remained in the stench of blood and lingering afterthoughts as I looked at the two crimson-coated bodies.

"Seraiah," Jonah cleared his throat, and I jolted, looking up at him. I did not note much emotion on his face, but his voice wavered, "I think it is time to find a new place to rest."

I blinked, taking in the hallway to where the two bodies were covered in white sheets, etched at the corners in red. It seemed time had disappeared as I remained entranced by the bodies. Shock, I suppose, was a better term for it. Unsteadily, I rose to my feet, following after him to the meeting room.

It was inside where Freddie sat on the sofa, while Alex leaned against the shelf, both wearing sullen expressions.

Red. Red. So much fucking red.

Blood. Death.

It trailed me like an unwanted burden, wrapping itself around my throat tighter than The General's hands. Tentatively, I touched my throat, unsure whether there was any bruising from his uncaring grasp.

Arraetta.

I whipped my head around the room, "Where is my wife?"

"She has been moved to the other lounge room," Jonah replied, clearing his throat again. "She is in shock; it is not a surprise." He cleared his throat again. "It is not every day that-"

A growl left Jonah's throat, and with all the force in his body, he punched the wall, gouging a hole in the plaster. A sob tore from his throat as he laid his head against it, earning instant comfort from Alex who muttered calming words to him.

I did not expect him to mourn his father, not after everything the male had done. But, Jonah's sobs filled the room while I gently perched on the arm of the sofa, trying to stop myself from feeling nauseated.

Blood.

So much blood.

It dried on my skin, embedding itself into the pores, scenting me without remorse.

I wanted to be free from it, but I could not show weakness. Not now. Not when I had survived, not when things had drastically changed once again.

"I am just angry it was not me," Jonah said hoarsely once he had settled.

Alex smiled sympathetically at him, "It will be a shame we are unable to use him as a punching bag."

"We still could," Jonah laughed lightly, "I could hang up his corpse."

Play a game of Hanged Man.

"I would if I were not so against harming the dead," Alex replied in the same manner before looking at me, "you should bathe."

"Hm," I murmured, gazing down at the stains on my hand, unknowing what settled upon my skin. I turned my nose and closed my eyes, "it is my fault."

"I would never have thought I would witness you admitting to a fault," Freddie jested, although it fell a little flat. "What exactly did Travis mean about Arraetta as the *Goddess of the Light?*"

"She is the bearer of Divine Rapidfire," Alex offered, taking Jonah by his bicep and pulling them both to sit on an empty sofa.

"It sounded much more mythological," Jonah said, shaking his head, "but I have always found him strange. His arrival, his way... it is..."

"Odd," I agreed before sighing, "I suppose we shall never know."

"Long live the Goddess of the Light," Alex murmured, "it has quite the catch to it."

A knock rattled the door, and Alex went to open it. On the other side was Sheika, who gazed across everyone, before her eyes landed on me. "I hope you have not forgotten you are bonded."

I was never going to forget I was bonded, but the joys had been dampened and I was sure Arraetta would prefer to skip the finalisation of the nuptials.

"I have not, but I am sure Arraetta is in much the same mindset that we will need to postpone-"

"-Do not be foolish!" Sheika interjected with determination. "There will always be obstacles to test whether the Kindred Spirits can survive together. I understand this moment has shocked you, but you must move past them and finish what was started. If not for you, then for Arraetta."

"If you just want them to fuck, you can just say," Freddie said nonchalantly.

"Frederique! I have quite the afternoon lesson for someone like you to understand exactly what is at stake here. It is not about the two of them simply having sex; they must conjoin their souls."

Freddie held his tongue, although I could see he was desperate to point out it was still *just sex*.

Sheika took a breath and looked at Jonah. "Young Jonah, you are now the army general, so you must be at peace with your anger and strive for better things than your father ever did."

Jonah had always preferred his title of Commander, but he had become The General after the death of his father. He commanded an entire army, which meant ending the revolution. But, my father was still king until I sat on the throne, and he would have to continue his treacherous work to move the final pieces on the chessboard.

"You should know," Sheika said softly to him, "your father has done many terrible things in his life and was deeply grieved by his actions. It may not offer you comfort, but his soul will spend time in peace before he starts his new life when he is ready."

Death was a reality for all of us, and so was reincarnation. Even the evilest of souls could still breathe a new life, but I only prayed whatever would come next would be worse for The General. To have him suffer as every one of us had, but especially Jonah.

"And, Travis?" Freddie asked.

"Rheon Travis..." Sheika replied, speaking his whole name, thinking momentarily, "I cannot say. I think what is to come for him will surprise us all." There was little time to question it further as she looked back at me. "I suggest you come to your chambers soon so that you may bathe and change, and we shall begin the final process of your bond. I believe, when you see Arraetta, you will have no problem forgetting the sol's events."

Her words were full of finality, leaving me to mull over my task of completing the bond and lying with my wife. I had to try to forget the events of the sol, or at least push them aside until we would leave our haven and face the reality of what we had left outside the four walls of our quarters. And, I could do that. I had done it before, pushed such burdens to the back of my mind and I would do it for Arraetta.

My father's plan to ship Arraetta to our settlement in Scotland would no longer be in play, as he would have to consult Jonah, who would surely disagree. I knew my father understood his sols were finally numbered before I would ship him to Italy to oversee his winery while I bathed in the glory of being a proud ruler of my kingdom with Arraetta.

For Arraetta.

THIRTY-SEVEN

As soon as I stepped through the threshold of our hidden haven, I felt all my troubles melt away and my focus honed in on the female waiting for me inside. It was only Freddie who escorted me to the bottom of the stairs, but he left me there with only a parting wish of luck. Anticipation haunted my chest, causing flutters to buzz in my stomach and my heart to pound mercilessly.

It had only been quarters prior when we had shared a first kiss in the space which would be our own, yet it felt like it had been winters since that sol. I was greeted by a very odd spiritualistic atmosphere, the humming of chants washing over me as I stepped into a haze-filled bedroom, lined with candles and incense. I knew we would have to open the windows at some point just to release some of the claustrophobic poison.

Sheika and Zela pranced around the room, cleansing the space. Neither seemed to notice my arrival, or chose to ignore it if they had. This was as much a special sol for them as it was Arraetta and I.

Arion bowed in greeting, speaking quietly to me, "Your Royal Highness, a bath has been prepared for you."

While I was looking forward to seeing Arraetta, being able to wash the blood from my skin before seeing her was something I was glad for. As we walked by the bed, I had to do my best not to give into my evident desire for her, knowing she had slept there for sols.

I hoped when she arrived she was not too trapped in the thoughts of the events which had passed. I understood how shocking it would have been to have a male stare into her eyes before killing himself.

"Your... Grace?"

I cleared my throat, following after Arion, who was waiting patiently by the door leading to the bathroom. It was in there that he and another servant prepared and readied me, scrubbing at the blood and dirt on my skin as though the devil had burdened my skin. I supposed I was a devil heir purified into a saint. A part of me wished this part of the ritual did not need to take place yet, that part of it was us bathing together and washing each other, but even I would not subject her to removing the blood which etched my skin.

I was dried and dressed in a long white gown, which felt like I was flaunting my non-existent virginity, or maybe re-enacting the part of a ghost. Then again, I supposed my soul was virgin to my queen.

Out of the bathroom, I felt a wave of exhilaration wash over me as I saw Arraetta sitting on the futon at the end of the bed, her back to me. She looked tense, and I only hoped I would be able to rid those tensions as the hours slipped by. I was ushered to sit beside her, but there was no time to interact as her own maids helped her to her feet and took her into the bathroom.

Tirelessly, the two witches pranced around the room, continuing their unmelodic chorus and I slowly became more receptive to the woozy nature of the hazed air. It was at least thirty minutes before Arraetta came out, and by that point I was ready to tell everyone to get out.

I did not dare glance at her, however, as I worried I might falter under the pressure of the evening, even if I was a little excited. She gently perched next to me as though she might expect the futon to collapse under both our weights, and I trailed my eyes down to the edges of her own white gown, where her bare feet poked out. I could not wait to see more of her once our audience had disappeared.

Sheika and Zela knelt before us for a while, continuing their incessant chants in an archaic language that even I could not understand. I wondered whether Arraetta and I might have laughed if we had made eye contact, but we only simmered in our thoughts.

Sheika finally spoke to us both only in Zikan, "May the Gods bless your final union, and the two of you be forever bound."

With the final words, the two females stood and exited the room, followed by all our other witnesses, until we were alone. I felt a gentle shudder from Arraetta before she let out a soft, shaky breath of relief, clenching her soft hands in her lap. I swallowed and took it as my sign to hold one of them, stroking the skin between her finger and thumb to calm her before I finally took in her virtuous beauty.

I believed anything Arraetta wore would make her ethereal, but the white gown only enhanced it - a goddess personified. A moment passed before she swallowed, evidently nervous still, before she hopped to her feet and escaped to the other side of the room, where a table was topped with wine and other nibbles. I could only laugh at her temperament, no matter how cruel it might have been.

I supposed I understood the task of being with her would not be as easy as I thought. Then again, Arraetta did have quite a coy, mischievous nature when she saw fit, so I should not have been so surprised.

She lifted a bottle of white wine from the iced cooler and, finally, looked toward me, offering the bottle, "wine?"

Awe swept over me, seeing this female waving the bottle in nothing but a nightgown; her brown locks falling around her bare face, leaving only her honeyed skin's natural radiance. I was lucky.

I rose to my feet and walked to her, determined to ease her nerves, "allow me."

I found the bottle opener, took the wine and uncorked it before pouring her a glass, feeling her heavy gaze solder my skin, but she rapidly turned away as I looked at her.

"You need not fear me, Arraetta."

"I don't!" she squealed before coughing gently, "I just... should we talk about what happened?"

I supposed she would have such thoughts on her mind, even though I was hoping we could forget the events in the hallway for a few sols.

"Do not worry about those things, Arraetta."

"But, he killed himself after killing The General," she stated exasperatedly, emptiness radiating in her eyes, "and we're here now pretending like it didn't happen."

"I have not once pretended like it did not happen. I am sad for the loss of my friend, and I shall mourn him, but I am now standing in a room with my wife, and she is my only priority."

Friend. Personal guard. Thorn in my side. Whatever the best term may be.

"You're not sad for The General?"

"Good riddance to the bastard," I answered truthfully, "I would not be sad about a male who could not accept his own son for his choice of lover. He used to beat Jonah into submission, did you know that? We were much younger, back in Zika, but I saved Jonah once, and Jonah pledged that he would serve me in whatever capacity I would prefer."

"So, you offered him the role of your commander."

"Of such," I pondered, "he would be my commander when I would become king, but then things changed once the treaty was signed, and he has been in the position ever since. For Travis, he was a good man but knew he would not win in a lawsuit against my father, who still remains king. He killed himself because he would face death in his sentence, anyway."

If he had killed The General to save my father, it would have been a whole different matter, but he had done so to save me and that would have made him public enemy number one.

"Then, we should toast to Travis.".

"We should toast to you," I smiled, "to the woman who stood up to my father, my beautiful, courageous wife. The Goddess of the Light."

I clinked our glasses, but it seemed it was not enough for her. She itched to escape and was gone quickly, rushing out of the balcony door. At least the open door would allow for some of the incense to disappear and make it easier to breathe. It did not stop me from following her, though.

The chase is on, little mouse.

I knew the best tactic was to help her relax, so I walked out into the cool night air, my bare feet quietly creaking against the cold wooden slats until I stood behind her. She tensed a little, but did not try to escape again. I was not sure if I would let her.

I could wrap my arms around and hold her close, make her understand that it was okay, that she was safe with me and what happened will never again. But, I saw my opportunity when a soft breeze blew some of her hair, revealing a section at the back of her shoulders and neck. And, I lowered my lips, hesitated in case she might move, before placing my lips upon her soft skin.

Her body relaxed instantly, and I knew I finally had the mouse in my grasp.

I wrapped my arms around her, tucking her small figure against my towering one before I kissed her on her neck again, earning that siren moan I had so desired to hear. Slowly, she turned around until I was able to peer down at her beauty, momentarily pausing until I teased her lips with my own. I was only playing with her, but I wanted to see how she would reciprocate. Seconds later, our lips locked together like two parts of a puzzle, and time slipped away as I lost myself in her taste, pinning her against the balcony as though she might disappear again.

I gripped the edges of her white skirt and automatically began to wrap it up into my hand before sliding my hand underneath it to touch the supple skin of her thigh. I knew she was ready for more, moaning into my mouth as she pushed herself closer. Temptation was a gift bestowed to me and I caved to unwrap it, teasing the skin of her thigh until I brushed my fingers through the velvet hair hiding my treasure. Staring at the desire in her eyes, willing myself not to kiss her for a moment, I tucked my fingers into the crevice and basked in the glory of the dampness awaiting me. I shivered with delight as she moaned and shifted her hips to coax me into adding the needed pressure.

My hard cock was lifting up my own gown, desperate for release, but I would not rush. No, I would savour such pleasure.

I slipped in a second, finding ecstasy in her whimpers of desperation, shifting my head from her as she tried to kiss me. Empyreans, that look of blushed elation on her face was being kept for a rainy sol in the back of my mind.

"Oh, Arraetta," I muttered as she rocked herself unforgivingly against my fingers and I allowed her to take them prisoner, "*Empyreans*, you feel so fucking good."

Seconds later, she gripped my hair and kissed me again, and this time I did not prevent her, glad to have that forbidden taste on my tongue as I continued to bring her towards her first orgasm. I begged for it.

I looked at her again, licking my teeth as my cock continued to throb, "how I have ached for you, Arraetta."

"Seraiah," she moaned louder, breath harsher.

Her first peak was coming, and I was going to let her rise over the top, only to rise her above a second, soon after.

"Such pleasing moans," I praised, not letting up on my hand work, no matter how much my fingers ached and my mouth watered with a need to replace them. I found myself beseeching her, wanting her to release all that tension from her body, "Come for me, Arraetta."

I could see the fragment of her fighting against it in her eyes, but once they rolled back, I knew she had caved.

"Open your eyes," I commanded, "Do not deny me the pleasure of seeing your undoing on my hand."

And, she did as I said, eyes half-closed with desire, looking at me as her legs caved and the dampness between her legs soaked my fingers. And, with it, a loud wave of noise rippled from her mouth into the quiet evening, the comedown hitting her slowly.

Empyreans. Fuck.

My fingers gently stopped their movement, and I brushed them around to the peach of her arse, squeezing her closer as I kissed her. I wanted her to feel how hard she made me, how it was her who made me the lust-stricken fool I had become. I thrust against her, placing soft kisses across the apples of her cheek until I nibbled and sucked at her earlobe.

"Do you feel that, my love?" I asked her.

"Yes."

"When I am deep inside you, coaxing your every wanting breath. I want you to know it is you for whom I have suffered one hundred winters. It is you who has turned everything but my cock from stone to molten."

She was the one who had changed everything, the one who had made every coffer unlock, and I could only be thankful for it. I could only be thankful she had made me a better male, a loved up one at best.

Even so, she giggled at my words, and I smirked, "oh, I see you find such a declaration funny."

"One hundred winters? A little archaic."

"We all are somewhat archaic." I kissed her again, lifting her before taking the two of us through to the bedroom, uncaring about the forgotten glasses of wine. By the time we made it to the bed, I had taken her gown and ripped it from her, leaving a naked beauty before me.

Coyly, she shut her legs, squeezing them as though she was nervous for me to see her whole being. I was but a starving male, ready for the feast laid out before me.

"Open those legs," I commanded and, moments later, she opened them and I stared down at the delicate skin, which I only wished to devour. Empyreans, I was ready to taste her, I burned for such sustenance.

I knelt heavily before her, in the exact position I knew I was made for – to worship this goddess. And, worship I would. I took her thighs and pulled her toward me, head so close to that soft, wet slit, the scent of it washed over my nose and I was reminded of the quarters before when I had been so close to my treat.

"Empyreans, the divine has blessed me," I muttered in Zikan, leaning in before licking my tongue across her flesh. *Oh fuck.*

I lapped at her once, twice, three times until I knew she was basking in the feeling of being tasted. And, then I dived in for more, groaning inwardly as such forbidden fruit became my new favourite flavour. I would have to spend the time etching it onto my tongue. I was unsure if I was ever going to be able to rule when I would be kneeling before my wife instead. Fuck, I would let her rule if she let my tongue remain there permanently.

I slipped a finger inside her gently, hearing her swear into the air, and then another for a short while, and then a third. My other arm was gripping her thighs, trying to keep up with her writhing body as she gave herself over to me. More swearing, moaning, intoxicating sounds like the song of poets until she rode through her second orgasm. I could have remained there, lapping it up, but I was desperate to be inside her.

I stood, lifting the awkward gown over my head before throwing it to the side, my cock punching my stomach with each throb.

"Are you ready for me, Goddess?" I asked, tugging at my hard member a little, but not too much because I knew I was far too close to coming just by serving her. Her eyes dipped down to my cock and she subtly licked her lips, but that was a sight which could wait. "I can see your thoughts, or maybe it is the drool wetting your lips." I climbed over her, shuffling us both towards the headboard, speaking as I manoeuvred us into a missionary position. "But, there is plenty of time for you to taste me. So, let me have my fun and give you the pleasure you deserve, and I desire." And, I could not help myself. "You taste fucking divine, by the way."

My cock pushed inside her like a sword disappearing into its sheath, our pleasured grunts radiating through the room. I gently gripped both of her arms and placed them above her head, locking her in, ready to mercilessly make love to her.

"I am going to fuck you now."

And, I did.

Every sordid thought, every hot and cold shower, every lonely night had built up to the one moment where this female, my fated one, my Kindred Spirit, my *wife*, was beneath me, basking in the warmth of our wantonness.

If anyone was listening, they would hear every chord, every beat, every chime of our moans, a song of lovers given for all to hear. At some point, we shifted, and she was riding me, while I fought against my orgasm so that I could bring her to hers.

She clenched around my cock when she closed in on it, stumbling over her words as she tried to declare her third peak of the evening. "You're going to... make me... come."

You are going to make me come.

Hers shattered my own, a ripple of pleasure I had never felt before washing over me like a silk blanket until she lay in my arms, heavy breaths between us. And, then she giggled, and I chortled in reply, "fuck, Arraetta."

Gently, I rolled the two of us over until I could release my softened cock from its wet grasp, looking down as she coyly dived her head into my armpit. "Are you hiding from me?"

"No...?" she squeaked.

"You are a little liar," I half-tutted, "what am I supposed to do with you?"

And, she looked up at me with lust-stricken doe eyes, "um... make endless love to me?"

It sounded like a suggestion more than a demand, but I took it as such and I was prepared to honour it. Every sol I would spend relishing in the taste of her, gifting her the ecstasy she deserved and, in turn, receiving the joy I wanted.

"Well, Arraetta, you better be prepared."

***

Over the hours which passed, I savoured every moment, tasting every inch of her skin until it was a taste so familiar, I would not forget it even if she walked by me. When she reached her highest high, I sought to take her above that, writing off every memory of every male who had ever touched her, to show her she would never reach such a peak of what she felt with me in that room.

Maybe I was obsessed, possessive, out of control in love with her, but I was sure so was she.

565

We made love until we grew exhausted, cocooning in damp silk sheets to savour our energies before beginning again. And, sometimes when she slept, and I did not, I would gaze down at her, thanking the Gods for the destiny they had bestowed on my soul, for nothing could ever make me feel the elation I felt with Arraetta.

Arraetta, my darling wife, you are the beginning of all ends.

And, when I slept, it was blissful and peaceful with no nightmares.

The first couple of sols passed with sex, conversation, drink, food, bathing and sleep, neither of us leaving our haven. If it were not for the odd arrivals of Arion and Elina, who replenished our stocks, I was sure we would have forgotten about the many others milling around the house and gardens.

I awoke early, gazing down at the beauty lying on my bed, who snoozed unknowingly as I gently twirled a lock of hair in my fingers. It was the third and final sol of nesting together, thoughts about what plans my father had hatched were churning in my head, wondering what was to come once we ditched our pleasure for the real world. The consequences of the events of our heartfast were only snoozing, a burden I had yet to bear. I would refuse to let them send Arraetta away from our London estate, forced to reside in the Scottish settlement with prayers I had made her pregnant.

While we had a lot of sex, I had been as mindful as possible not to burden her with such things as lineage, yet I did not want to put that pressure upon her as I knew how much it had upset her during our argument in the hallway.

Arraetta stirred but did not fully open her eyes, feigning more sleep.

"Can I have this?" I whispered.

Weary eyes blinked up at me, shifting to the strand of hair before she took it from my hand, "in case I die?"

I winced a little at the jest; not something which easily sat with me.

"Why?" she asked.

"Because I wish to keep it."

She contemplated for moments before agreeing, sneaking from the covers naked and shuffling to the dresser, holding onto the lock with dear life. Empyreans, her curves and creases were a fine sight to bear and, even with the sexual exhaustion, my cock stirred again. What a divine painting it would be with such raw fragility.

"Beautiful," I whispered before sitting up, "if only I could draw you like that right now."

Arraetta seemed to find her target, pulling out a small pair of scissors out of the drawer and held it over the strand of her hair, peering over her shoulder, "this much?"

I nodded, smiling, "can I take a picture of you?"

Her confidence faltered as she dropped the lock and covered herself comically, "no!"

I chuckled, "Why?"

"Because it may end up on the internet," she whined, and I laughed harder, highly amused she believed I ever went *on the internet*. Such a human thought to be worried I would share such elegance with the world; they would be so lucky.

I paused, laughing, only to continue when she pouted like a seedling.

"It's not funny!" she stamped, "why would you want a picture?"

"Maybe so that I can draw you later... Arraetta, I do not mean to have myself off to it; I mean to delete it once I have finished the painting."

A partial lie. I most likely would keep it for occasions that I wanted to envision such a moment clearly, but she did not need to know such a thing.

"And... and where would you put the finished piece?"

"In my office," I replied earnestly, assuming she would not want it in the bedroom.

"Well... fine, but... it would be unnatural as, now, I will need to find a position to be in."

"Just relax," I told her, "turn to the mirror and resume what you were doing."

She did as I said, turning back to do her task as I fished out my phone from one of the drawers and took the picture I wanted. Then a second and I might have gone for a third if her confidence did not falter. She cut the strand quickly, holding it out for me to see.

"Is this long enough?"

I placed the phone down on the table, shuffling to the edge of the bed while holding my arms out to her. To bury myself in those beautiful breasts of hers and kiss her bare stomach. There were no complaints as she shuffled back and I traced my hands down to the curve of her arse, looking at her.

"I love you, Arraetta. My wife."

"Maybe I should take a picture of you," she jested, poking my nose gently. I laughed and kissed just above her belly button, revelling in her scent, "I cannot believe how perfect you are; there is no one more perfect than you in this entire universe."

The words were undeniable; I would have said them without our fate.

Such wonders ended as an unexpected loud rumble sounded above the house, followed by a quick flow of lightning which seared the skies and lit up the room. Finally, after a hot summer, drops of rain began to splash against the window as the skies opened, bringing in a breath of cool air.

Yet, my attention waned as my gaze shifted to the window and I noticed odd streaks of lightning raging across the ends of their grey holders.

"Hey, look at this," I said to her, standing from the bed to take a closer look. She hugged her body against mine for warmth, both of us adjusting our core temperatures to the incoming cooler weather.

"Have you never seen lightning before?" she whispered teasingly, jumping as the thunder boomed closer.

"Do not tell me you are scared of a little thunder."

She tutted loudly and returned to the bed, "Not scared; it just made me jump. There's a difference."

The sky continued its charade for a few more seconds, but I soon grew bored and decided my wife was a little more important than some weather. I looked over at her, watching as a ripple of lightning seemed to rebound off her aura, lighting her skin up in a way she did not even notice. Magnificent creature.

I stepped back to the bed, towering over her as I mimicked, "*There's a difference.*"

The heavy storm synced with our sweetness of love, but it became unnoticeable as we fell into our decadent rhythm. The thundering sounds outside soothed us back to sleep until a tickle of a finger woke me from my slumber. I identified the sensation over the permanent tattoo on my arm. I allowed Arraetta to continue her tickling exploration, finding it soothing while she seemed to be following it like she needed to discover its meaning.

Was *I love you forever* not enough?

"Are you attempting to dissect it?" I grumbled, kissing the skin of her shoulder, "any luck?"

"None," she replied, subtly pushing back against me.

"Arraetta, I do not think I can let you leave this bed."

"Maybe I don't want to," she turned to face me, "maybe I want to stay here forever."

"Mm, I am glad you said that," I breathed, kissing traces down her body again until the two of us jolted when a clap of thunder rumbled

569

the building. Laughter rippled from us, but we stopped as a second clatter boomed soon after. And, I was unsure why, but I grew more curious about the battle of the drums in the sky than pleasing my wife. If only for a short moment.

"Stay here, my love," I said, shifting off the bed as I grabbed some boxers and walked to the balcony door. I noticed how odd it was that the rain had somehow frozen on the window pane whilst the skies were still flashing in a strange rhythm.

I walked outside and peered up at the orange and red laced sky, spinning with soft golden tendrils for miles across the skyline. It was mesmerising.

"Come and see this," I called to Arraetta and, soon, she appeared in a robe, half complaining her feet would get wet from the slats, but those worries were forgotten as she peered up at the sky in awe.

"What does it mean?" she asked.

"I do not know," I replied, honestly, "I am sure the storm has caused it."

Tension rolled over her, although I was unsure whether she was excited by what was taking place or cold. After another bout of thunder, I knew it was right for us to return inside to stay dry and warm.

Arraetta escaped to the bathroom immediately, and I raised my eyebrows at her, "Where are you going?"

"I'm going for a bath."

"You know I shall be in there with you," I replied, amusedly watching as she slowly backed through the door, peering through the gap as it became thinner and thinner until she was out of sight entirely. I grinned, knowing another bath - we had several - with her in my arms sounded delightful.

However, my phone buzzing caught my attention, and I walked over to see a message from Jonah.

Meet me at the entrance of the house, you might want to see this.

I pondered ignoring the text, knowing Arraetta would be patiently waiting for me to join her, but as I walked through to the hallway on the opposite side, I could see what I had witnessed above was stretching for miles and miles.

Thunderous, grey skies teeming with golden lightning.

It was an odd spectacle, one which might be witnessed in a hotter country or even somewhere entirely away from Earth. Quickly, I rushed back inside, grabbing some pyjamas to put on while wrapping my robe around me, all while listening to Arraetta sweetly humming to herself in the other room.

I would be back and in that bath with her before she even noticed and we would return to our cocooning again.

THIRTY-EIGHT

ilence greeted me in the corridor, an eerie atmosphere considering how lively the house had been sols prior. By the front door, staring outward towards the gritty skies stood Jonah, Alex and Freddie, amongst other guards. None noticed my arrival as I descended the staircase, gently muttering to one another about what was happening.

"Good afternoon," I greeted lightly, and greetings were given accordingly.

Freddie smirked, "it is almost evening, Your Grace. I am surprised you can walk with all the pounding your cock has taken."

Amused, I shook my head, "it is only my wife I am here to please, Freddie."

"How is Her Highness?" Alex asked.

"She is well. I left her in the bath to join you all, so let us make this quick."

"I am not sure this will be quick," Jonah replied solemnly.

I shifted to join him at the door, where he pointed upward towards the sky. At first, I was unsure what he was indicating too, but then I noticed the rhythm which the skies teemed with lightning. It was both fast and irregular.

"I think I will go back to bed, I have been enjoying my time with Genie," Freddie said, although he did not leave.

I toiled with my thoughts about what I could see, wondering whether it was some sort of electromagnetic field, yet all the electricity in our area remained stable.

"Could it just be freak weather?" I wondered.

"Maybe the two of you had crazy sex-" Freddie was interrupted as Alex smacked him across the back of his head..

"Do not joke about such things!" Alex tutted, and I smirked, averting my gaze to the distant world beyond our borders.

"Any coverage from the humans?" I asked.

"Freak storm hits London," Jonah shrugged, but he pulled out his phone to see whether there was anything more widely covered by scientific news. "No internet... wonderful."

Unsurprising either, considering satellites would surely struggle to push through a signal to Earth.

"The end of the world is nigh!" Freddie joked in a spooky voice, and I guessed he had received a death glare from Alex as he added, "What? I am just joking."

More thunder, the noise reverberating off the skin of the clouds.

"Ah, here we go," Jonah said, showing me an article with a live video feed of the freak storm. It was reported that the storm was stretching for a hundred miles across the skyline, with theories being given that it was possibly the hot weather which caused a backlog of heat and water in the clouds.

"Idiots," I breathed, "I am sure it will pass before morning."

"Does that mean I have permission to leave?" Freddie fluttered his eyes, stepping backwards. But, still he did not as none of us answered him.

My gaze shifted down to the estate, noting many residents outside their homes, and I wondered whether anyone had given them guidance. "It may be wise to try to calm the villagers."

"Hm," Jonah agreed, radioing a command to some troops to fall in and help the situation. No one argued against the male who had found himself instantly in position as General.

"Your wife has arrived," Jonah whispered, and I turned to see Arraetta walking down the stairs, looking radiant as ever.

Before she could descend the middle staircase, I rushed up to meet her, kissing her cheek gently, "Hey, I did not mean to leave you."

"What's happening to the shield?"

"Do not worry; we are dealing with it," I stroked her soft cheeks, "Go back to bed."

"No, I've been in there long enough."

Lies. "Long enough? My love, you said you would stay there forever."

"But, now I'm up," she answered, descending the stairs, and I had no choice but to follow her as well.

She went straight for the door, which Jonah tried to guard, "Your Highness, please stay back."

"What's happening?" she asked him, gazing around the complex as if she would find the answers she desired. It was not as though we had those for her. I slithered my arm around her waist and tugged her back towards the staircase, uncaring I resembled a loved up fool in front of these males.

She grumbled, "I can walk on my own."

"Please go back to bed," I whined quietly in her ear.

"I think everyone should return to their quarters." My mother's voice cut through the quiet, and I was unable to prevent the roll of my eyes before I turned to see her descend the stairs, "I am sure you both do not need to worry about this."

She was right. I was very eager to return to our nesting and with no further permission I tugged Arraetta back up the stairs, past my mother and into the upstairs corridor.

"Aren't you worried?" Arraetta asked.

"It shall be fine."

"But, what if it isn't?" she asked, fear laced in her tone as though something bad was to come.

Once we were in the heart of the west wing, I stopped her, "What are you so afraid of, Arraetta?"

"I'm fearful that... you're going to be locking me up in that bedroom for the rest of my life."

I smiled at her change of subject, but I wanted to make her understand she could bear all to me, "you may tell me anything, my love."

"I know, but do you really deserve to know?"

I could have kissed her right there, I should have, but a deep rumble shook the house so violently the two of us toppled to the floor. I identified the cause immediately, although I had never felt it cause such a quake before.

"The generator." My body weakened at the intensity, much like how it had done in previous times, but this felt different. This felt like it had absorbed my energy, leaving me with little left.

Heavy shoes clattered down the corridor, and I turned to look as the three males joined us. It was the strikingly fearful expression on Jonah's face which embedded adrenaline-fuelled terror in my scorched soul.

"It is here," he breathed, "The Dark."

My eyes widened as I clamoured to my feet, "The... Dark."

Sticky sweat began to pool from my pores, heart racing as Jonah continued to speak, but his words seemed to disappear as though my head was held under water.

The Dark.

Chaos.

Destruction.

How the fuck were we going to defeat something as hell raising as

The Dark?

Empyreans, I knew we had war coming, but I had not guessed it to be this. Not on Earth, at least. Maybe in Zika, where we could prepare to defeat it in our own territory but we lacked power on Earth.

But, I knew, did I not? I knew it was coming. I told them there would be war because Arraetta had told me there would be.

"Seraiah, it is time for Operation Iron Wall," Jonah cut me from my terror filled thoughts.

Operation Iron Wall. Operation Iron Wall.

Operation. Iron Wall.

Fuck, we were going to destroy the shield to defend ourselves. We had spoken about it quarters before in our war meetings, but I never guessed we would ever have to use it. It was a backup, a tool in our arsenal. But, we needed to protect our own; we needed to get everyone to safety and then move on to whatever plan came afterwards. The war for the throne was no longer prevalent, it was now a war for our lives.

I felt as though I had been sucked into a vortex of a nightmare world, shredding my newfound happiness to pieces as quick as it was gifted. But, I would not let this darkness take her from me, I needed her safe. I could lose everything but not her.

"You must protect her, Jonah."

"With my life," he nodded. Then he held out his hand for her, switching to English, "Let's go."

Confusion swept over Arraetta's gaze as she was helped to her feet.

"Listen to Jonah." I kissed her softly, lingering for just a second longer.

Lamoure, Arraetta.

Freddie, Alex and I went down to the generator room, once they had both disappeared down the corridor. Guilt thudded in my heart, but it was masked with adrenaline as I thought about what was to come, and how I would defeat this darkness.

As I thought, The Generator was empty of its vibrancy. I rushed to the computer and began typing in the necessary coding for the backup power, neither of us speaking as I hurried around to the back end of it. I felt like I was on repeat as I found the handle, peering at Freddie with a gentle nod as he positioned himself at the computer.

The machine began to rip my dormant Rapidfire from my being, tingling me like hundreds of biting ants gasping for a taste of my skin. But, I ignored the pain, for my suffering was worth the lives of our people. It was pulling at my power like never before, needing the fuel to create the iron shield above our home.

"This will be the last time this generator will work!" Freddie called.

As I was aware. No more shield, no more safety beneath it, just a fight to survive and pray we would find safety elsewhere once it was over, "We shall all just have to move to Italy to have the benefit of theirs."

"Or Scotland," Freddie offered, "at least your life bringers will not be there."

I chuckled, watching as the globe's new golden hue painted metallic grey, solidifying the old theory that if we overpowered the generator just enough, it would start to freeze up and, thus, do the same for its counterpart.

It was a shame I had to do the honourable thing and give up my power, when my father should have been the one to volunteer for his people. *Laughable.*

My body drew weaker, and I struggled to keep myself standing, knowing it was the equivalent of losing a lot of blood, but I should have revitalised quickly once I was out of there again. Or, at least, I hoped.

"There is no point weakening yourself further, Seraiah!" Freddie called, "We do not even know if the shield mimics this."

I ignored him. "What is the percentage?"

Freddie's eyes flickered down to the computer, "eighty-five."

"That is not enough."

"Yes, it is," Alex implored, "I cannot see my king weakened by his need to protect his people."

"You flatter me," I grunted with a slight chuckle. "I have other power, Alex. It may be dark and terrifying, but I have no qualms about using it if necessary."

"Then use it *only* when necessary," he begged. "But you are my friend, and I do not know whether this is even working."

Was I his friend? Were either of these males my friends or just my allies? I had been left swimming in deep water, gasping for air with every wave which hit me and the only thing keeping me afloat was Arraetta. Still, I appreciated his need to protect me. If we were friends, I only hoped we would reconcile every issue which had come between us over the winters.

"Ninety-one per cent," Freddie commented. Using what little strength I had, I pushed through to the end until the computer announced the wall had been activated. And, then I released myself from its grip, stretching my aching body.

Once we were satisfied everything was in place, the three of us made our way back to the entrance of the house, ready to witness whatever might be waiting for us on the outside. Terror and anticipation flooded me, but it seemed the sol's first battle was not with whatever lurked outside but with the callous male who waited in the entrance.

Flanked by two guards, my father was standing at heads with Jonah, who had traded his clothing for army attire, amongst many other soldiers, all ready for battle. Freddie, Alex and I paused at the top of the stairwell where we could watch secretly whilst finding a point to intervene.

"It is just so convenient you believe yourself to be General now that your father has so *conveniently* died," my father spat, "you are not the general of this army."

I rolled my eyes but listened to Jonah's reply, "I am afraid that it is where you are mistaken, Your Majesty. Under Law Five Three Six of the War and Peace Treaty, I am hereby declaring martial law for the safety of our people and, herein, military rule shall be enforced until further notice."

"Empyreans, that is hot," Alex breathed, and I smirked.

Jonah bowed his head to my father before standing upright. "I hereby place His Majesty into protective custody until further notice."

"I thought you bowed to my son!" my father laughed.

"I do, Sir," Jonah nodded, "but the prince is not yet a king, as you are so aware."

I decided to make my entrance, walking down towards the en-tourage of people. My father glowered, "I knew allowing you two to be together was a bad idea. This is your fault - war on *our* doorstep."

"War never ends, Father, much like the one inside this house."

"My son, how mighty you have grown," he laughed humourlessly, "to step foot here and speak to me as if you know of war when you spent all that time running from it."

"That was you, Father," I snorted, "whilst I fought to save our people, you were doing your utmost best to escape so that you did not have to die. Innocent females and seedlings left for dead. You told them to close the portal as soon as you ran through it; you left me - your son - wounded and commanded I be left amongst them. But, where did that leave you, hm? With a thorn in your side for all these winters."

"Do not play the victim when you are devil incarnate. Everyone knows what a failure of a prince you are, flaunting around as though you truly believe my crown will sit on your head. But good luck, Seraiah. Martial law has been declared. Go and fight the war you are so desperate to win. It will be a privilege to find you amongst our dead."

"Fuck you, hellsworn." The words left my lips as though it was not me who said them, dark traits entwining through them. "You deserve to rot in the depths of hell for the rest of eternity, you are an abomination to Zikan's, parading around as though you are mighty when you are nothing but a cowardly king."

A shatter, a whip, a grunt.

A long spear embedded itself in my father's throat, a crimson wash spewing from the hole as his mortal body tilted backwards at an angle, the armament of choice holding his head up. I blinked. His lifeless eyes stared upward, black mist steaming from his skin and dripping onto the floor.

Boots scattered, panic rippled around, but I remained sharply focused on the dead male before me. I turned my head upward, looking at the direction from which the spear had appeared from, seeing how the upper window above the door was shattered.

But, how? From who?

I blinked, looking back to him and finding I had shifted so I was close to him. I peered down at my clenched left fist where I could see the soft black hue which clouded in my palm.

Fuck.

Fuck.

Fuck.

Empyreans, my father was dead.

I had killed him.

But, I felt no remorse. Not an inch of it laced through my hardened emotions.

I swiftly placed my hand onto his arm, bracing it before I tugged at the remnants of his power, uncaring I was feeding from him before others.

"Seraiah?" Freddie's voice echoed, but I ignored his call as I closed my eyes and pulled the strands, making what was once his mine. The pain and torment which my father had felt radiated inside it, making me feel uncomfortable, but I knew I needed this power.

A hand was placed on my shoulder, and I jolted. Ripping my hand from my father, I looked at Jonah, speaking as though he did not already know, "He is dead, his Rapidfire has evaporated."

Jonah studied me before nodding and not pressing the issue further. "I need to take you to safety."

I did not understand his meaning at first, until I saw all the other soldiers who were watching us with curiosity, hope and fear. Maybe I was so lost in what I had done, coming to terms with the fact he was dead that I never thought about the most obvious thing.

I was King.

King fucking Seraiah.

But, I could not celebrate when we were amid danger. I had to start my sols as their ruler and as the soldier which lead them into battle. Not hiding because of my lineage, not hiding because of my title.

"Do not announce it. I will not be subjected to martial law," I rounded my shoulders, "Let us continue with the plan. We should gather those who wish to fight here and those who do not, let them find their own plans of safety."

For the first time since being at the door with Arraetta less than an hour before, I found myself looking out of them, noticing something hauntingly different. As I closed in, I noticed a huge, black crater high up in the sky- similar to in Zika, a portal consuming everything in its midst.

"Impossible," I breathed.

A boom in the distance trailed three fighter jets thundering across the skyline, upward toward the break in the sky. Each jet sent missiles toward it, but all ricocheted off what looked like a shield. The jets momentarily retreated before returning for their second strike.

"Fools," I breathed.

"We were too," Jonah commented.

The humans retreated their jets, but I was sure it would not be the first round of bombs launched at it. Once the sound of the fighter jets dwindled, the atmosphere settled enough for me to hear the feared shouts of our people.

A spine-tingling roar echoed from high above, two humongous winged beasts flew out of the breach, each disappearing in different directions, whilst other smaller creatures appeared to fly down from their coop.

The gong of war had rung.

"Happy awakening, humans." Freddie's jest fell flat. A colony created with the purpose of being blind to the goings on of other realms were going to understand their fairytales and nightmares were about to be unleashed on the world.

Heavy boots thudded against the ground, turning my attention to at least two hundred soldiers who were falling into line in the courtyard, all ready for war. Some I knew, but our troops were sparse of Connell, Leopold and Travis, all who had sacrificed themselves.

Alex and Freddie both stepped in front of me to kneel, and each soldier followed suit until the only person remaining to do so was Jonah, but he did so without hesitation. I almost grovelled at their patriotic nature, but I knew it was important for them all.

"Say some words of wisdom," Jonah muttered.

I am sorry to tell you all that you may be dead by morning.

I took a deep breath and looked across everyone as I spoke, "Whilst

I appreciate such a gesture, I am only king now because something out of this world has slaughtered my father." *Me.* "You are not pressured to fight; if you do, you will know this shall not be easy and many lives will be sacrificed. But, we have a plan we believe should be able to keep many people alive. I can also offer you peace that I shall also be in battle with you."

No one moved.

"All hail, King Seraiah!" Jonah called, and every soldier repeated it. Jonah shouted the same thing three times until I held my hand up to them.

"Please listen to your General from here on out," I told them, nodding to Jonah. Orders soon followed, similar tactics to War Cry would be in play and he reiterated once the iron shield faltered, we would be at war with the enemy in our own territory.

"Do not fear the end!" Jonah called to them, "For we shall defeat the hellsworns who put us here, unto death."

Cheering echoed, hugs were handed out between fellow soldiers, and battalions moved out to their various positions.

Jonah turned to me, "I think you should change."

Uniforms were brought for Alex, Freddie and I, and we were soon sitting down by the first post at the front door of the palace. It was there we could see many residents being shifted from their homes to the safety of the garrison. Other soldiers positioned themselves across the gardens of the house, while others were in positions around the gardens, waiting for a command.

While The Dark had overshadowed Zika, Earth was a big world, and it would take a long time to fully take it under its control. If that was its plan, of course. Hamiean was a realm just as big, gone within sols of The Dark's attack.

"Power down," Jonah commanded through the radio, and I watched as the whole complex began to lose power; the shield remained. It was mesmerising to watch the village go dark, even prior to sundown. In hours, we would be trying to navigate the place with only the moonlight to guide us.

"I hope Genie is well," Freddie said, bouncing back and forth on his feet with nervous anticipation.

"Please, sit down," Alex tutted, and I chuckled at their usual need to bicker, which I had missed over the weeks that had passed.

"I have a gun, you know."

"Not as big as mine."

"Are we really comparing armaments right now?" Jonah tutted, although I could see the tug of a smile on his face. "Genie will be fine. She is with the Queen Mother at the garrison, where your father would have been, Seraiah, if he had not put up a fight."

I found myself looking at my dead father, seeing how his eerie silhouette continued to drip melted flesh from it. Bile rippled up my throat until I was unable to hold it in, puking in a nearby bush.

"Alright?" Freddie asked.

Once my stomach had been emptied, I took a few deep breaths and nodded, "Yes, I am alright."

I returned to my spot while rubbing the bridge of my nose.

"You may cry for your father if you wish," Jonah commented.

I snorted, "That male does not deserve my tears."

More silence followed, none of us sure when to speak, wary of what might grace our doorstep soon enough. More strikes of the human jets, but all retreated with no luck.

"About as loud as your moans, Seraiah," Freddie jested.

Alex used the blunt end of his armament to jab Freddie in his side, and Freddie grunted in response.

"I have heard the gossip from the staff here," Alex replied to him, "all of them can hear how you scream *Genie* every time you come."

"You and me, one on one, now," Freddie challenged, holding his fists up.

"No, thank you, I do not find you attractive."

"I meant a fight, you fool!" Freddie gasped, aiming to play fight with Alex, but Jonah growled, turning to them.

"Shut the fuck up, both of you. Please."

I chuckled quietly to myself, knowing others in the vicinity would have found them both humorous. At least there was minor joy during a sullen sol. Another heavy bout of silence, before a chilling bellow echoed from the skies again, and we watched as lightning rippled around the breach. Then, a giant, deadlier winged dragon flew out and landed on its wings, scouring the area for its new destination. It began to suck in some sort of matter, almost as though it was breathing in a cloud.

A green hue radiated behind and I turned to see Freddie's Rapidfire lightning up. His eyes were wide, "If I tell you I am not doing this, would you believe me?"

But, why was it happening to him and not me?

Static electricity danced through my body as a shattering crackle ricocheted against the shield above us, and I noticed how it began to crack like ice.

"The iron wall is breaching," Jonah announced.

The shield shattered into little currents, which began to travel toward the creature. A rumbling echo beneath us followed, shaking the ground, then a pause. There was no time to react as an explosion blasted from the lower back end of the house like a bomb exploding; the after-effects sending all of us vaulting unwillingly across the garden.

I grimace as my ears rang, disorientation clouding my mind as I turned towards the house, which smoked and flamed behind me. The roof of the building had caved inwards, and I knew the home in which I had lived was no longer liveable.

Coughing sharply, I tried several times to get to my feet while grimacing at the lacerations which shattered areas of my skin. I found Alex and Jonah holding each other, while Freddie was lying on the ground with his arm covering his eyes, catching his breath.

At least we were all alive.

Another loud shriek, I wearily peered up, eyes widening before I ducked as the belly of the beast flew low over us and to the other side of the house.

We were fucked.

THIRTY-NINE

"I call on all ground troops," Jonah coughed through the radio, "this is redline protocol. I repeat, this is a redline protocol. Proceed to Thunderstrike. I repeat, proceed to Thunderstrike. All units fire at will."

The dragon was not shy about its second entrance, but it did not fly as low as before. The bullets roared against its thick scales enough for it to retreat, but it was difficult to see where it was through the smoke and flames.

"Get the king out of here!" Jonah commanded Alex.

"No, we must proceed as planned," I said, brushing myself off.

Freddie finally found his feet, saluting proudly, "Whilst the king fancies the fight, I will happily volunteer to be escorted to safety."

"Such a coward," Alex snarled, "we may be but four males, but we must work together to defeat it."

Freddie raised his hands, presenting another cheeky smile, "three males and a seedling."

"I am close to killing you both myself," Jonah growled.

Alex pouted at Jonah before glaring at Freddie, who was grinning proudly at himself.

"If you stay, I cannot guarantee you will live." Jonah stumbled toward me, appearing as wounded as I was from the blast, but he remained his professional, undeterred self.

I squeezed his shoulder. "But you can guarantee hers. Arraetta must survive. It is integral she leads our people home and rebuilds, no matter what it takes."

He took a deep breath, "I have already promised you I will guarantee the prince-... no, I mean the *queen*'s safety. She is the Queen now."

When such news would arrive to Arraetta, I was unsure, but it was something to look forward to telling her once we could free her from the safety of the chamber she was locked within.

"Thunderstrike," I confirmed, then shifted my eyes to Freddie. "I hope you are ready to use the Rapidfire you have not used in a long time."

Freddie offered a cheeky grin, "Or maybe you are just unaware of the situations in which I use it." Alex gagged whilst I chuckled. Freddie waited for a moment before he added, "What, Jonah? No arguments against it this time?"

"I am not my father," Jonah replied with a satisfied look, "but now that you do mention it. Remind me if I make it out alive to offer you some form of punishment. I am sure there are still lawns which need weeding."

Freddie winced at the half-hearted threat, and I understood that his community service punishment moons prior must have been related to gardening, which Freddie despised with a passion. Another bellow resonated, followed by the unmistakable flap of the dragon's vast wings. The creature flew overhead, its wingspan and trajectory terrifying, giving it a strange ability to clear the air of smoke and dilute the flames. It pulled more matter into its mouth, turning simple air into white ether before it tore through the mortal-kind who either tried to fight or escape.

"Oh, fuck," Freddie said, eyes to the skies, and I peered up to where hundreds upon hundreds of silhouettes were beginning to line the evening skyline, bodies hanging upside down like a game of Hanged Man. These were the collected dead. I remembered something similar happening in Zika. In legend, it was said the bodies represented the amount of souls collected, and none would reincarnate again.

Eternal death.

"We cannot let these people die mercilessly at the hands of this thing." The growl which tore from me was filled with anger, malice and fire. Agreement washed over the males, each of us standing to watch the chaos below. I leant into all those emotions and tugged on what little natural Rapidfire I had left, and that of which belonged to my father, bringing my veins and power to life, "Alex, Jonah defend the fort."

Freddie followed suit, powering up his own vibrant, emerald power and, in English, he bellowed, "let's have you, hellsworn fucker!"

Freddie charged in the enemy's direction, his temperament quite amusing considering how he had been trying to get out of fighting. I rushed after him, the two of us making our way down the slope towards its centre where the creature had harboured. It did not notice the two mortal-kind readying for a fight until I fired my first bout of lightning towards it.

It violently ricocheted off the monster's skin, shrieking wildly as the skin beneath its scales was scorched. Good. Freddie offered the same attack as it flapped its wings, rising into the sky to escape us before retreating once again to the back of the house.

"Holy shit," Freddie breathed. *Crunch.* I looked down to where the bones of a mortal-kind broke under my foot, before my eyes trailed upward to where the unidentifiable bones of many others were scattered. A path of the dead carved out for all to see.

And, ahead, another soldier lay dead, their uniform the only identifier as a small creature feasted on its flesh. Freddie's Rapidfire flared, and he roared with primal ferocity, searing the creature into ashes. I eyed the windows of the houses in our surroundings, noting how windows and ornaments had been shattered. I caught sight of several fear-stricken faces staring at me, hiding behind doors and walls.

"Do you have a radio?" I asked Freddie.

"No," he shook his head, peering around until he noticed a radio on the floor next to a pile of bones belonging to another slaughtered soldier. He tried to get it to work several times, but it seemed we had radio silence where we were.

I looked around, noticing many more eyes of soldiers hidden, waiting to strike the beast. Some nodded in acknowledgement, some with fear. Someone nearby whispered the words of a prayer.

"Freddie?"

"Hm?"

"I am going to wait here for the creature to fly back. I will use all my power to deter it again, but we should try to get the rest of the residents to safety."

"I cannot leave you."

"Do not be soft," I tutted. "This fight is not about me; it is about us. Plus, I have soldiers in hiding. Let us prioritise our people. That was the mistake my father made last time; he only cared about himself."

Freddie still looked hesitant, but finally he agreed before shifting to begin his task while I slowly walked back towards the palace. It had been so long since I had used my Rapidfire for fighting, like an old bicycle which needed oil to run, but it felt freeing not to have a limitation on my ability to use it. I drew up a ball of lightning, bouncing it back and forth in my hands, waiting cautiously for the beast.

And, finally, it reared its head at the point where I had been held captive quarters prior, soaring over the top of the houses. Whilst it was fearsome, as tall and almost as wide as the palace, I knew I had to bury what fears I had. The lightning in my palm grew until I shaped it much like the spear which had killed my father, and once the creature closed in, I launched it.

It was a direct hit, but the power only rippled across its body as though it had somehow grown itself a shield, before it released more white matter a few streets over, killing its new targets. The echoes were cruel, singing like an unmelodic cacophony, death's bell ringing louder.

It rose higher, soldiers fired their armaments, and I concentrated on the power in my being, drawing at each fibre of my life force as I continued to fight against it. I searched for every piece of operating electricity in the area, trying to inwardly identify which belonged to the creature above until I finally caught onto the constant ebb and flow of it. It was a little like dark Rapidfire, poisoned. I powered up, producing another larger spear, using all my might and velocity to target it until the transient shield surrounding it disintegrated. It roared with satisfying pain, flying back towards the house.

A rumbling thud, but I knew the creature was not dead. Nor was the next which arrived from the breach. Thundering jets roared their quest once more, unleashing hell on Earth to subdue the new beast. Each rocket was successful, sending the dragon plummeting towards the ground.

"Not such idiots after all," I chuckled to myself.

It was far too early to cheer. This was a civil war. Another soul shaking rumble echoed from the back of the house, white ether rising into the sky and I heard the stomp before I felt it, listening to what I believed to be part of the palace toppling. The beast rose again, but it seemed to have grown in size – white energy pulsing through its underbelly.

It landed with purpose atop the house, breaking apart the foundations as it gazed around for its new target. It waited, watching, listening until someone screamed and it followed the noise. It was immediately back to its killing game, targeting the area of the one who fled in fear. It was as I was about to draw on my power again that I understood the creature was blind but not deaf.

It returned to the skies, trying to find more imperceptible residents, more bodies lining the sky with each kill. Wrath rippled through me, power once again flaring and I followed it, attacking as I could, mindful that with each throw I was drawing weaker. Exhaustion grew hot, muscles aching, fire blasting through me with each throw.

Our attacker soared and circled several times, seeking its next victim. Then it swooped, seemingly aiming in my direction, as what was left was only tendrils of power in my veins.

"Come on! Come on!" I begged, tugging and tugging, but it seemed fate had other plans as its mouth opened, readying the matter.

Eternal hell awaited me.

Boom.

I jerked in the direction of Sheika's house; the dragon was no longer interested in me but whoever had fired the gun. Its new course knocked me off my feet as it flapped its feet, tiles on nearby rooftops clattering to the concrete ground.

I grimaced at the cold, rigid road beneath me, needing breaths to get me to my feet, focusing on the tail which swung back and forth like a dog playing with a bone.

"Sheika," I whispered, the revelation swam over me quick enough to gather myself and I began to run towards the small path which would take me towards her home, but two homes shattered to bricks blocked the way.

Another resounding gunshot before the dragon roared, rearing its head before it flew upwards back to its nest at the palace. Drips of dark blue blood dripped down its body, indicating that the creature had grown weaker throughout the battle.

"King Seraiah!" Zela's voice called from the other side of the rubble.

"Zela, are you alright?" I asked, searching for a way over.

"You must free the queen," she called, "she is the only one that can save us."

"No."

"She must be freed," she implored again, "you need her to defeat this, we all do."

But, I would not listen to the begging of a witch when I could not bear to bring Arraetta into this chaos. She was in the comfort of the throne room, away from the horrors of the world she had left, where we had agreed quarters prior.

"Seraiah!" Freddie's voice drew my attention up the road as he ran toward me. "I tried to get as many people out as possible with the soldiers, but many are fearful and..."

"I know, we should recoup at the house."

The two of us both ran as swiftly and quietly as possible, aware the creature would soon return, even if the atmosphere had grown silent. Exhausted soldiers hid in the perimeter of the garden, while Jonah was by the gate with Sergeant Blackthorn.

"My power has run dry," I admitted quietly, "but it is wounded."

Because of Sheika's gunshot, not even because of my power.

"It is time to move to the final plan," Jonah said between us, "We move on to Operation Emberfall. A full evacuation of our people to the forests, and soldiers are to escort them to a place of safety until the news is released that it is safe for them to return, *if* it is safe. It is preferential they head for Scotland, no matter how long it takes." He looked at me. "You should go too."

"I will fight until my last breath if I have to."

"So will I," Freddie agreed.

"And I!" a soldier nearby called, and the same thing echoed around as they stood up in response. But the creature's wail had everyone hiding. Jonah pulled me to safety, and the others followed.

He held his hand to them, indicating they all needed to be radio silent.

"Where is Alex?" I whispered.

"He went to scout out the back garden," Jonah answered, although I could see the fear on his face as he worried about the male he loved. "I have said it once and will say it again. If I die, *if* I die, you must promise that Alex will be given my position. And you must watch over him." I agreed, of course. I always had. "And, if it helps. I am sorry for being a hellsworn the past few moons."

"You have always been a hellsworn," I chuckled, "but let us not speak as though we shall not see the sunrise together tomorrow. It would be a shame to have a third friend lost in battle."

We braced as the dragon returned again. I took a deep breath and tried to find the centre of my power, coaxing it from whatever medicated slumber it was in, and Freddie echoed the move.

"Long live the Goddess of the Light," Freddie said to me, quiet enough for those close to hear but not loud enough for the creature's ears.

"May the darkness be forever destroyed by *our* divine power," I finished before watching the beast fly overhead again. We fired our respective powers at it as it flew toward the village below. Once our Rapidfire hit it, it repeated its retreat towards the palace.

"Fire at will!" Sergeant Blackthorn bellowed, and the soldiers fired their armaments enough to wound it until it was out of sight again. More soldiers were killing the other creatures in the village; Emberfall was in operation.

Kill without remorse.

Kill like their life depended on it.

Or, die trying.

A strange light hue glinted in my eye and I followed it, noticing the one person I would have never wished to see standing in the doorway of the burning palace. As sol had drawn to night, the moon shone bright enough to illuminate her like an ethereal ghost, staring outward at the destruction she had been blind to.

Arraetta. My wife.

"Arraetta?" I shouted, uncaring of stirring the creature, and I hurried across the garden toward her. Covering fire was commanded as I met Arraetta, tucked her into my arms and pulled her around the door. She was about to speak, but I placed my hand over her mouth.

"Blind, not deaf," I whispered, removing my hand from those supple lips, "What the hell are you doing here? You are... you are bleeding; why are you bleeding?"

"Hit my head," she replied quietly, gazing past me. I saw what had taken her attention, my father who had remained an eerie reminder of a time before the chime of the battle, forgotten. His burning figure was hauntingly lit by the moonlight, the once beautiful hallway portraying a collapsed church.

I wondered if she wanted to know that somehow I knew I was the one to kill him, but it would be a long time before I found peace in the answer.

So, I lied, "he sacrificed himself for me. He jumped in front of the spear as it came towards me. After all the years of hate, it all culminated in him being killed by the thing he feared the most."

"I'm sorry, Seraiah."

I caressed her cheek, leaning closer, "you are the only thing worth living for, Arraetta. I would have never changed anything which occurred between my father and I because it led to us."

"At this rate, there won't be many of us left," she breathed. "I need to fight."

"No," I said, turning my head, "no, you... you need to go back there."

"No," she said, placing her hands on my face so that I would look at her, "you know I can help you."

"I need you safe."

"I am safe," she kissed me gently until a clatter of gunfire stopped her.

"I am king now," I told her as I gently caressed her soft cheek, "I am king and..."

"Don't tell me I do as you command," she warned with sadness, "you cannot change what needs to be done."

"I promised to protect you, always."

"And you will, I-"

My heart ached at her need to be a saviour when she could still have remained a saint without battle scars. I kissed her deeply, needing to savour the taste I remembered and make her forget why she even appeared at all. But, such desires were not to be, the two of us breaking apart as the creature swooped overhead.

I knew our moment was not of needed passion; it was a knowing farewell. One of us might not make it alive, and that one person would have to be me.

"Arraetta, I need to know if you can use your power."

"A little."

"There is not much power here. The electrics have tripped, the shield is down, and the generator was destroyed, but I have enough power to share with you."

Or, in truth, I did not have much, but I would be able to survive off what I had taken from my father if I could help her with hers. I could feel the buzz of her own simmering under her skin, waiting for an opportunity to finally be free. It only needed coaxing.

"What? No, that's absurd."

"When my father died, I took his power. It strengthens me, but it is of no use if I do not have Divine Rapidfire. I give you my strength, Arraetta; I give you this power to use to protect yourself." I honed in on what little power I could spare, feeding it from my body to hers as I had done at the lake so long ago. "Hone into it, allow my power to become one with yours. Feed from me."

The static energy rippled from me, and I had to do my best not to show how painful it truly felt. She was strong, like a vampire feeding on blood. And, soon, she was alive with her vibrant, golden power.

"Beautiful."

"Now isn't the time for compliments," she laughed gently.

"If only we were alone right now..." My jest fell flat, deep heartache resting in its stead as I gazed upon her radiance. The Gods had gifted me sols of a high with her, only for The Dark to rip it from me as soon as it could.

Clatter. Crunch.

Concrete toppled from the roof above, and we both looked as the dragon had found its new perch, balancing itself. I pressed myself into Arraetta, needing to protect her, only for a terrifying bellow to roar from its mouth, causing her to gasp. Her power dissipated instantly, and it seemed enough for the creature to find us.

Not wanting to wait for it to take one of our lives, I powered up the last of my Rapidfire and threw it at its rearing head, hand gripping Arraetta fast enough to use every part of my strength to throw her around and out of the door. I knew she had landed on the gravel, but I did not spare her a glance as I slammed the door shut.

There was no time to brace for the ether fired at me from the creature's mouth, no time to have said my goodbyes, no time to flee from it.

It burnt at the tendrils of my fibres, tearing through my ephemeral skin, searing threads of pain through my body. I roared in agony, collapsing to the cold tiled floor, only to be greeted by the stinging weight of the front door toppling onto me.

I was trapped beneath, shivering as the matter continued to feast on my flesh, taking everything it desired, ripping me apart from the outside in. My blurred gaze was stuck in the direction of my deceased father; how ironic we were dying in the same place on the same sol. Some sort of fucked up amusement the fates had conjured up for us. I wondered if they were laughing at their cruel joke.

Or, maybe they just did not exist at all.

At least I had Arraetta, at least I was given the chance to feel love amid chaos. She was the reason I had fought, the reason I had survived, the reason why I had died. For her, always and only for her.

And, in the end, after all the pain, suffering and loneliness, the only thing left was silence in the death of King Seraiah.

FORTY

K nock. Knock. Knock.
   Glass was rattled by soft knuckles.
   Knock. Knock. Knock.
Then, a louder rattle, like an enclosed fist hitting the pane.
Knock. Knock. Knock.

I blinked, opening my eyes slowly, wincing at the achingly bright LED ceiling lights which stared down at me. I grimaced, wearily sitting up as I tried to find out where I was, and even how or why I had survived. Was the war over?

My gaze stopped on the elevator. The garrison? But, how?

Another impatient clang and I whipped my head in the opposite direction, stumbling to my feet as I caught a glimpse of my dark doppelgänger, dressed like death himself on the other side of the glass prison. His dark eyes beamed, wiggling his frail white fingers at me.

I caught sight of someone else in the prison to my left, shocked as I witnessed a frail and grey, long-haired male sitting with his knees tucked to his chest. Surrounding him was a black mist, seeming only to represent sadness and guilt. He was the embodiment of the power I had taken from my father.

I swallowed, looking back to the other male, "how are you in there?"

599

I looked for where the door would usually be, but I noted no entryway.

"You locked me in here, remember," he shrugged, taking a seat in the centre of the room, a rather impatient look on his face.

"But, everywhere I have seen you it has never been here."

"Illusion is a fine friend," he chuckled, "this is an impenetrable cage, quite the fortress, but so is your mind, I suppose. I have come to assume the only way to escape is from your side."

The glass was cool to touch as I stepped closer - a pane of glass which had shattered moons before when I had pressed Kaeltar against it.

"But, what I do not understand is how you are inside the garrison when you are a figment of my imagination?"

"You really are a fool, Seraiah," he tutted, laughing lightly, "you are dead. Or, do you not remember how that dragon took your life?"

I could not forget how it had burnt me to a crisp, but it did not explain where I was.

"If I am dead, I would not be standing here."

"True," he nodded, "but I did not say I am dead. You are. The Seraiah you became will no longer grace this world, the body you bore nothing but dust, the life you have lived a memory. And, I am your last hope."

I snorted, "do you truly think I believe that?"

Back on his feet, he took the steps to the barrier. "The last thing keeping you from having your soul ripped apart is me. I suppose you could say I am your saviour of sorts."

"You only wish to be free so you can destroy everything I have worked for."

He chuckled, "But, Seraiah, I have only ever worked for the things you have. I have said it before, we are the same." I shook my head. "Do not deny it because you know it is true. We are two sides of the same coin, both fighting for the same purpose, but it is you who does not dare to give in to those feelings and desires you have hidden for all these winters."

"You are a liar."

His expression changed to anger as he punched the glass, "If it is one thing I do not do, it is lie. I cannot lie. I am the bringer of truth - the bringer of *your* truth, mighty King Seraiah. I suppose you shall not still believe me when I tell you I am willing to sacrifice myself for the greater good."

I chuckled darkly. "You have been obsessed with taking over every inch of me, and now you believe you can win."

"It is not about winning!" he growled, jaw tightening. But, his anger dissipated as he released a breath of disappointment, turning away, "it is not about winning, Seraiah. This is about her. Our wife, our Queen, Arraetta."

"She is not yours."

"How boring it must be to tell yourself the same myth every sol."

She was not his; she was mine. She belonged to me and only me. Not this... not this deceiver. Not this vile creature which yearned to take over me piece by piece. But, I could not deny it any longer. I was far from blind, seeing through the cracks of my own disguise as I wanted to lock away this part of me. A part of me set alight to avoid showing who I truly was.

"And, if I do not agree to set you free? Then do we both disappear?"

"That is what will happen," he nodded solemnly, "it is a shame, for I quite liked my moments of freedom. But, I am willing to sacrifice it for you... it will be up to you to be the decider of our fate. You cannot control me, not well, so you will have to learn to become attuned to this part you locked away - anger, grief, sorrow, *loss.* Do not forget power, there is much of that." I was about to speak, but he raised his hand. "But, it is what we must do. If not for us, then it must be done for Arraetta."

Empyreans, how could he be so right about something so immoral? How could I let myself become one with this thing which scared me the most? What if I become the one thing everyone hates?

He placed his hand on the glass, daring me. "Hone into your darkness, Seraiah, guide me into your soul and *live*."

I did not care for hatred. The world could hate me, but not Arraetta. And, I was surviving for her.

I peered over at the crumpled state that was once my father, rotting away like a distant, unwanted memory. His head rose to look at me, terrified, before rapidly turning to hide as close to the wall as possible. *Pathetic.*

"Why should we hide the thing he feared the most?" my dark self questioned.

Would I be able to control it? At what cost did my being alive come to the universe? Did its fate lie in the palm of my own hands? Had the messages from the Gods all but been a warning when they told me I needed to choose the path of the light? Or, was I simply a pawn in their wider game?

"Everything will change."

"Then let the world embrace it."

I nodded, "stand back."

He took several steps back, and I took a deep breath, bracing myself. And, then I slammed my fist against the hard surface, feeling the bruising of my knuckles. It did not start to crack until the third hit, each burst chipping away at the twig image it was creating.

Hit. Hit. Hit.

Even through the exhaustion, I pushed, understanding it would take mighty strength to destroy the wall I had built for myself.

And then, it shattered.

"Good luck," he chuckled with contempt before his being began to disintegrate in front of me, and the shards of soul and flesh sank into my skin, embedding themselves deep inside me. I roared as my flesh rebuilt itself across the bones of my decimated body, writhing against the cold flooring.

A cool shiver tickled my spine, and I opened my eyes wearily, looking over at the final thing I had seen before I had died - my father. The aches disappeared, and everything felt different. A heavy burden pulsed and fogged my thoughts, my soul feeling stranger, stronger, *darker.*

A new breath of life.

I honed in on the surrounding sounds.

A beast roaring.

Armament fire.

Shouting.

I was unsure how much time had passed, what chaos was brewing on the other side of the wood-coated iron door, but I needed to find Arraetta and keep her safe.

With a bellow, I allowed my Rapidfire to ripple through my body, pushing upwards and taking the door with me until it thudded to the side. I cracked my back, shoulders and neck as I stood upright; a newborn demon set free.

I caught my reflection in one of the broken mirrors, seeing how my eyes had been traded for black, while the Rapidfire, which buzzed around my body, was a mixture of cerulean and onyx.

My lip twitched, somewhat satisfied with who I had become. An angel of darkness, an unholy being, a shadow king. I was sure my eyes would not remain so forever, but my new power had revitalised me.

And, I was ready to conquer the entire universe.

No, not conquer. I would not do that, I would just rule my realm. Zika. But maybe I could conquer a corner of it. For her.

Yes, only for her.

Arraetta.

I will burn this universe and rebuild it in your favour and every creature shall kneel before you, my queen.

Step after step, I exited the house, looking ahead to the chaos below at first before noticing Freddie rise to his feet, shock evident on his face. It seemed he was not the only one surprised to see I had survived.

"Seraiah?" Freddie's voice wavered.

I walked towards the gate, where he stood, "where is my wife?"

"Your... power," he breathed.

"Empyreans, Freddie, I do not wish to ask again. *Where* is my wife?" I commanded, but the reply came from the dragon's roar as it soared overhead and toward the village. And, centre stage, at the far end of the complex, was Arraetta, embracing for the creature's attack.

Jaw squared, fear wrung through me like hot iron. She must have thought sacrificing herself would help, but that was a dastardly, idiotic idea.

With my newfound power, I created three dark lighting spears, threw my hand back and launched it at the dragon.

"When did you learn to do that?" Freddie asked. But, I only ignored him, far from happy that he, amongst others, was letting Arraetta fight alone. I ran in her direction, and he followed quietly.

"Protect your fucking queen!" I bellowed at the soldiers I passed.

The beast tried its attack again, but I continued to fire what I could in its direction, swiftly shifting from every little attack it tried to fire at me. Halfway down, Freddie decided to finally use what power he could, although I could tell he was weak from exhaustion as it barely made a dent. It was enough to confuse the dragon, however, escaping back over the house again.

"Fuck!" Arraetta cursed as I closed in on her, noting how tired and battle-worn she looked. More time had passed than I had thought. But, strangely, pride swelled inside me for standing her ground against the beast.

I clocked Jonah appearing from an area out of sight, "what the fuck were you thinking?"

Jonah clocked my new look, but he said nothing as Arraetta met me. "Seraiah, why did you stop me?"

"You think that sacrificing yourself is the fucking answer?" I yelled, pulling her into my arms tightly, "I cannot lose you, Arraetta."

"You don't know what I was doing."

I held her at arm's length, "You were going to let it devour you, but you cannot do that. You will not survive; no one survives that. Your soul will shatter. That is what it will do to you." I looked at Jonah in annoyance. "So, your plan was to let her sacrifice herself?"

"I did as Zela told me," Arraetta added.

"And, what did she say?" I replied, not believing Zela would have outright told Arraetta such a thing, "Repeat the words, and maybe we could actually work together to figure out what exactly they mean."

"She said, *Call to the dark, for only then can you truly use the true power of the light.*"

Great, more riddles. But, she would not have told Arraetta to sacrifice herself, only given her advice on how to survive. I repeated the words aloud, trying to decipher its meaning.

Arraetta added, "She also said something like... the Gods have spoken. Only my power can destroy the dark. Only I can rise, which I shall, and walk the path of insurgence alone."

The path of insurgence? Had I not been walking that in her stead for so long? Had I not been the one uprising against my father? But, now she was telling me there would be some other insurgence, one she would face alone.

But, the rest was easier to decipher than that. If Arraetta had done as I had, and honed into her darkness, or even that of which we were fighting, she could fight against it. But, her power had failed or overpowered each time she had leaned into her fear of it, rather than embracing it.

"Okay, well, your deepest fear is not dying, it is facing the dark. Not The Dark, not the creatures, but the nightmare itself - the fear of being alone in the dark. Hone in on that."

There had to be some way for her to seal the breach without leaving the village. I wondered whether she would be able to hone into the lightning in the sky; she was the Goddess of Divine Rapidfire. And, Rapidfire in its purest form was the same as lightning in the sky.

I stepped back a little, "Feel the power of that. Be the Queen of Darkness, overcome it."

All eyes were on our queen and, with little hesitation, she closed her eyes, took several deep breaths and zeroed in on her energy. It took only moments for her to feel deep inside for that unmistakable power, before her figure was golden with lightning tendrils. It looked even more potent at night, or any other instance I had borne witness to it. Her eyes opened, and she gazed at me, her blue and gold irises shimmering.

Satisfaction fuelled through me, my cock aching in my pants at the thought of making love with the female who belonged to me. A fucking goddess.

The skies started to bellow above, and crackles of golden lightning shimmered across the clouds, causing an odd sound of pain and suffering to come from the hiding dragon. It was enough to call it to action, rising from its perch and making sure to target Arraetta.

"Control it, Arraetta," I said as my Rapidfire lit up across my body. "Let us end this... together."

The dragon flew towards us quickly, Jonah commanding cover fire for Arraetta as they stepped away from the flame before us. A beacon of hope in the midst of misery.

"Let's end this fucker," Arraetta called confidently, standing next to me.

I laughed, looking at her, "now, now, Arraetta. If you come to talk like that, I will have no excuse but to lock you in the bedroom."

The creature prepared to unleash its power again, and I stepped away from Arraetta, "You can have the honours."

A soft smile tickled her lips as she drew a perfect bolt in her palms, firing it in the direction of the dragon. It was so powerful; the dragon shattered in half, making me wonder why I had not brought her out earlier. We could win the war with Arraetta, I was just selfish enough to think we could not.

The remnants of the beast landed in the woods towards the entrance of the complex with an almighty thud. Silence. But, celebrations were short-lived as her power disintegrated and she faltered, knees buckling. I caught her quickly and held her tightly.

"It's not over," she grunted, looking up to the break.

War never was so simple.

A loud, macabre cry tore from the breach and I looked upward, wondering whoever controlled the beasts must have been laughing with glee when the next creature appeared from it. An immeasurable, formidable creature with three heads which almost resembled a Hydra – one which reminded me of what Sheika had spoken about.

"Fuck," I breathed, standing up and stepping back, "shit."

"How many people with Rapidfire does it take to kill a fucking dragon?" Freddie looked worse for wear.

"I've read enough fairy tales to know that's not a dragon," Arraetta stated.

"How do we kill it?" Freddie asked.

607

"We can always go back to my first plan," Arraetta suggested.

"No," Freddie, Jonah and I echoed.

"Well, we're standing here waiting for it to eat us," she replied, holding her hands up. "And that fissure needs closing."

She was right, which meant we all needed to work together to kill the hydra and close the portal. An idea washed over me quicker than I would have thought.

"I have a plan," I stated, although it was not well thought out, and I knew the males hated hearing my plans. "I trust you not to let my wife attempt to commit suicide this time, Jonah." Jonah looked a bit sheepish. "Arraetta, you need to find a spot, out of sight, where you can hone your power into the fissure, be one with it, whatever you did before. Freddie and I will distract the dragon... creature. Once it is closed, it will be easier for us to rip it apart without worrying about another coming through."

"Do not forget about me." I supposed part of me should not have been surprised my mother would join us, but I was surprised she was in full battle gear – ready to fight. A small amount of relief she was not dead washed over me, even if she had caused me grief for winters.

"Mother," I greeted, "then you should be with us. Three lots of Rapidfire against this thing should distract it enough. Jonah, I need two men, per each of us, who can help protect in case. I entrust you to protect Arraetta."

"Arri, tell me Genie is okay," Freddie begged Arraetta. Ah, that would explain how Arraetta was able to get out of the room. Of course, there had been some sort of plan behind my back to release Arraetta. I could only imagine it happened while Freddie was escorting our people to the garrison. I would reprimand him once this particular war was over.

"She got me out of that room and, she said she had to stay... for the baby."

"Baby?" my mother replied. I, too, was surprised by such information.

A few more words passed between us before we split into our respective teams, but not before Arraetta and I shared a swift hug and kiss. Jonah escorted Arraetta to his home, Alex rushing after them.

I wandered after my mother and Freddie, "You did not tell me you were having a seedling."

"You have been quite preoccupied, Your Majesty," he answered, tilting his imaginary hat to me with a smile, "but, yes, it was a little surprise for me, too. Are you going to talk to me about this new look?"

I chuckled, "Let us just say that sometimes we have to embrace things in order to take on a new lease of life."

"I am just glad you are not dead," my mother smiled, a hint of sadness in her eyes, "I do not wish to add another name to our next memorial plaque."

Lightning teamed at the edges of the breach and I knew we were ready for the final part of this battle, and once it was over, we could reform a new plan for our people. The gap started to close in, while the hydra wailed with an ear-piercing screech, seeking out its perpetrator.

It swooped, readying to attack us, and each of us prepared for it.

"For Zika!" I called loudly.

We fired Rapidfire towards it at every moment possible, while soldiers fired their bullets to sway it from us. For every successful attack, the beast would retreat, but it would always do its best to get to Arraetta. It was not powerless, though; it had pulsing matter which it would fire at us when it had its opportunity.

"It is working!" Freddie's elated shout caught my attention, as we could see the final part of the breach sealing. I did not know how she was doing it, but my wife was a vision and I would build cities in her name.

"Incoming!"

The beast swooped again, and we attacked, but ours did not deter it this time. It flew closer to Jonah's house, the trajectory of its wind rattling its surroundings.

"Arraetta!" I breathed sharply, running as fast as I could in its direction. The armament fire was undeniable, louder than ever.

But, I was too late.

The beast used its giant claws to grip at something behind, fear racing through me in hopes it was not Arraetta.

Please, not Arraetta.

And, it was not.

"No," I whispered, guilt washing over me, screaming, "Jonah!"

The hydra rose higher, clenching its claws until it released Jonah without mercy, his lifeless body plummeting to the ground in the woods. I thudded to my knees, every part of me filled with anguish and sadness for the death of my friend. Slaughtered.

I did not know whether to cry or to scream, but I could feel the seventh and final coffer cracking. Almost ready to burst open with a floodgate of emotions.

Grief.

"Empyreans! Hellsworn fucker!" I cried to the beast which swam in circles in the sky, satisfied with the mess it had made and the breach which had been torn right back open again.

A ripple of wrath punished me, releasing a growl more animalistic than I had ever had before, and I tugged on every part of my power as I rose to my knees.

I would not allow Jonah's death to go in vain.

It swooped to attack again, and I mercilessly hit it, uncaring for anyone else in the vicinity. Uncaring that I was like a creature of the night released to cause havoc on the sol.

Another hit. It retreated.

Each blast more powerful than the last.

I would kill it. I would take revenge on the life it had taken.

An armament bang tore through the chaos. Silence.

I turned my head in its direction, unsure how I had managed to find myself back towards the palace again. Miles away from her. And, she was standing in that same position as before, so far from me, away from the safety of my grasp.

The armament was in her hands, and she fired it again, gaining the hydra's attention.

My vision swam with fear as I stumbled in her direction, powering through as fast as I could, needing to stop her from sacrificing herself.

She could not sacrifice herself.

"Move, Arraetta!" I yelled, firing every bit of raw power I had at the creature but none seemed to deter it from its target as its claws were primed, ready to take its new prey. I watched as she discarded the weapon, holding her arms out in surrender. "Do not do it!"

But, my scream was swallowed by the hydra's roar, sweating mercilessly as I watched it grip her lithe body, swooping her from the ground and flying upwards towards the night sky.

"Arraetta!" I bellowed, thudding to the cutting ground as she disappeared. It would only be moments before it dropped her, only moments before I would run and catch her with my wingless body. But, it took her into the breach, the final box broke and grief hit me scathingly hard.

I could not breathe.

I could not stop the tears which fell.

I could only feel helpless. And weak.

I punched the ground.

Punch.

Punch.

Punch.

Death would have been fucking sweeter.

I should have died. I should have fucking sacrificed myself.

Thunder rippled the skies, and I looked upward to where the breach began to close, causing a tremendous war-ending noise before it sealed and Earth returned to the peace of before.

But, there was no peace for me.

Only anger and sorrow.

A roar of deep, animalistic anguish tore from me, the skies echoing my wail until we were left in the wake of a dark new dawn.

A grey and thunderous storm had come, which I had to face. Death and destruction, the song of the morning, I was a new grieving king of a failing nation and their one thread of light had disappeared. All the power inside me felt lifeless, locked away in another coffer, and only the emptiness in my heart remained. Arraetta was my soul, my happiness, the one I truly, deeply loved.

And, she was gone.

She was fucking gone.

I only hoped the universe was prepared for me to tear it apart because I would conquer every realm to find her and bring her home.

ABOUT THE AUTHOR

NICOLE IS AN AUTHOR AND SCREENWRITER WHOSE WORK BLENDS MYTH, FOLKLORE, AND FIERCE FEMALE PROTAGONISTS. WRITING UNDER THE PEN NAME CHARLOTTE BEDGOOD,

SHE'S BEEN WRITING STORIES SINCE SHE WAS TEN YEARS OLD -SHARING EARLY WORK ON WATTPAD BEFORE TAKING A DETOUR INTO FILMMAKING IN HER EARLY TWENTIES. AS A SCREENWRITER, NICOLE HAS WRITTEN OR CO-WRITTEN A NUMBER OF AWARD-WINNING SHORT FILMS, INCLUDING WANDERLAND (BAFTA-LONGLISTED), 2K5, AND POWERLESS. SHE IS THE WRITER OF THE FEATURE LIKE MOTHER, CURRENTLY IN DEVELOPMENT WITH MORDECAI FILMS, AND CO-WRITER OF BOTH PROGENY (IN DEVELOPMENT WITH DISAUTHORITY) AND THE FAWN (WITH CURIOSITY JUNCTION), WHICH SHE WILL ALSO DIRECT. HER SCREEN WORK, KNOWN FOR ITS EMOTIONAL INTENSITY AND VISUAL BOLDNESS, FEEDS DIRECTLY INTO HER NOVELS - GIVING THEM A VIVID, CINEMATIC SCOPE.

NICOLE'S WRITING, WHETHER FOR SCREEN OR PAGE, IS DRIVEN BY A DEEP LOVE OF STORYTELLING AND A PASSION FOR TAKING READERS ON JOURNEYS TO PLACES THEY WOULD NEVER EXPECT.